THE **DARK HEART** OF **REDEMPTION**

A CHRONICLES OF ACTAEON STORY

DARRAN M HANDSHAW

THE **DARK HEART** OF **REDEMPTION**
A CHRONICLES OF ACTAEON STORY

FOREWORD

CORWIN, THIS BOOK IS FOR you.

As Actaeon once said: 'It will be a difficult and perilous journey, but all things worthwhile are.'

Thank you for making life worthwhile, my wonderful son. Never stop dreaming and exploring!

TABLE OF CONTENTS

Foreword 3

Map 7

Dramatis Personae 9

Conspectus 15

Prologue: The Blade that Falls 19

Act One: Invasion 23

Act Two: Ultimatum 247

Act Three: Calamity 411

Epilogue: Starsphere 623

Afterword 629

A Brief History of Redemption 631

About the Author 636

Also by the Author 637

Redemption

Redemption
Key:
Raedelle
Shield
Ajman
Thyr
Niwian
Czeryn
Keeper
Arbiter
Loresworn
The Iron Mountains
Suntower
Kendra
Holdfast
Amphis' Ledge
Lazi's Tomb
Fallen Towers
Ridge
Stormstair
Bridge
Sea Caves
Craters
Mechanical Man?
Rust
Felmere
Boneyards
Redoubt
Temple
Ardianteki
Blacksands Beach
Pyramid
Marketplace
The Underforest
Ruinic Tribal Domain
Refugee Camp
The End
Arena
Workshop
Avenue of Glass
Glass Spire
Flamewoods
Stone Gardens
Windmoor
Adhikara
Canal Keep
Pools of Light
Great Sea
Sunken City
Memory Keep
Glorious Redemption
Aqueduct Keep
Pillar Artifact
The Wall
Incline
Blackstone Fortress
Travail
Shore
River of Arches
The Colonies
Caliburn Castle
Lakehold
Lake Wither
Wither
Tribune Lake Tribes

DRAMATIS PERSONAE

RAEDELLE DOMINION
THE ROYAL FAMILY

Eisandre Rellios Caliburn: newly anointed Princess of Raedelle, former Knight Arbiter

Actaeon Rellios Caliburn: Prince Engineer, husband of Eisandre

Aedwyn Caliburn: Eisandre's older brother, former Prince of Raedelle, lost to the pillar artifact, presumed dead

Eshelle Caliburn: Eisandre's older sister, lost on The Wall, presumed dead

Gwendolyn Caliburn: Dowager Duchess of Raedelle, Eisandre's mother

Ambrosius the Wise: Elder Advisor to the Caliburn family

WARRIORS OF RAEDELLE

Itarik Faris: First Companion of Raedelle, bodyguard of the Princess

Wayd Arbrigel: Companion of Raedelle, Goader, Caliburn family friend, bodyguard of the Princess

Brigert: Companion of Raedelle, bodyguard of the Prince Engineer

Yanelle: Companion of Raedelle, bodyguard of the Prince Engineer

Geodric Caider: former Companion of Raedelle, leader of the Fist of Arandel warband

Gorgrian Keric: traitor, former Companion of Raedelle

Tarcy Hael: Warbander of Lakehold, Steward of Saint Torin's Hold

Guybon Hael: Tarcy's younger brother, attendant to the Princess.

Drystan Beiloff: Warchief of Shore

Varisk Conmara: Warband Captain of Incline (Eisandre's Wall Breakers)

Jezail Vren: Warbander of Incline, archer, bard

Oragnar: Warband Captain of Southward

Areyna Ackart: Warbander from Southward

Cafry: young Warbander from Southward

Torg: Cafry's twin, young Warbander from Southward

Mirvea: Warband Captain of Eastern Rim

Hargum: Warband Lieutenant of Eastern Rim

Jey Vellit: Warband Captain of Western Rim

Brewer: Warbander from Western Rim

Hake Rim: Warbander from Western Rim

Phalto: Warbander from Western Rim

Phelto: Warbander from Western Rim, Phalto's twin sister

Tacia Fleg: Warbander from Western Rim

Varse Perialt: Warbander from Western Rim

LORDS AND LADIES OF THE CONCLAVE

Hamnin Dafryl: Lord of Lakeguard in Lakehold

Tridarch Hael: Lord of Bastion in Lakehold

Neryl Vanora: Lady of Whiterose in Lakehold

Jad Perth: Lord of Lakefeed in Lakehold

Aethelred Ackart: Lord of Southward in Lakehold

Gunther Arcady: the Lord Shore, Lord of Blackstone, seated at Blackstone Fortress

Cathaoir Conmara: Lord of Incline in Shore

Julip Tanderly: Lady of Highwater in Shore

Delle Fletcher: Lady of the Western Rim in Shore

Cadmere Blarth: Lord of the Eastern Rim in Shore

OTHERS

Ithelie Faris: a Voice, one of the religious leaders of Raedelle

Lauryn: Woodcarver, Actaeon's associate, Engineer-in-training

Grameera: Balin the Blacksmith's widow

SHIELD DOMINION

Indros Immerai Zar: Prince General of Shield

Endira Zar: Indros' daughter and oldest child, the Lady of Amphis' Ledge

Enrion Zar: Indros' son

Pierxon Hyk: A farmer in Lazi's Tomb

Kiroko Xan: Lady of Rusthaven, benefactor of Lazi's Tomb

AJMAN DOMINION

Nadiya Ajman: Raja & High Priestess of the Ajman Dominion

Calisse T'ra Coletka: Warrioress of Ajman, sworn to protect Nadiya

Gaemri Ip Monjata: the Raja's Portent

Viyudun sil'Mujarba al-Arshad: the previous Raj' nephew

Cafu Ilugamesh: General of the Armies

Maerdia Bazardjan: an Artist

Selnij sil'Mujarba Tri'akala: Grandson of the former Raj's brother.

NIWIAN DOMINION

Thernaxis: Lord Protector of Memory Keep

Faschin vor Steubick: a Niwian Lord

Torot vor Steubick: his son

Wronka: Captain of the Niwian Reds

THYR DOMINION

Amodeus Jarval: Supreme Captain of Thyr

Harvand Xula: Captain of the *Glorious Redemption*

Lucerd Cominga: Bosun of the *Glorious Redemption*

Vash Nellko: Helmsman of the *Glorious Redemption*

Ainhara Craft: Major in the Flashbolt Marines

THE FALLEN CZERYNIAN DOMINION

Berk: Warlord of a band of surviving Czerynians

Dek: Shield Warden

Strog: Shield Warden

THE ARBITERS

Cignith sof Iarnus: Paladin Arbiter

Phragus sof Luep: Sentinel Arbiter

Mitrius sof Cignith: Sentinel Arbiter

Garth sof Belidur: Knight Arbiter, former partner of Eisandre

Trello sof Allyk: a Knight Arbiter

Kylor sof Haringar: Knight Arbiter

Corvin sof Haringar: Knight Arbiter & artifact expert

Delus sof Comitis: Knight Arbiter

THE ALTHEANS

Seraeta: Healer

Phyvia: Healer

Fallis: Shieldian Attaché

Cortecha: Apprentice Healer

Largrival: Czerynian Attaché

Shard: Herbalist

THE LORESWORN

Sollemnis the Gray: an elder Loresworn

Kryo: a Loresworn leader

Inditrovalis Jem: an Adept Loresworn

Quronos: a guardian of Travail

THE KEEPERS

Fatuan Molvich: Elocutor of the Allfather

Atreena Covellet: Keeper Knight Captain

KAINAI, THE CHILDREN OF THE UNDERFOREST

Saundrak: Litomar of the Kainai

Heimgar: Interglot

OTHERS

Trench: Actaeon's associate & bodyguard

Wave: Actaeon's associate & bodyguard

Phyrius Ricter: First of the First of the Waiting Ones

Oril: Owner of The End

Vez: an old Carter

Markor: unsavory character from the Warrens, a servant of the Veiled One

Lady Ruinic: a Ruinic tribal warrior

The Veiled One: Leader of the cross-faced raiders

Rin: an artifact dealer

Garrag: a carpenter

Milopitas: a Witherian tribal warrior

CONSPECTUS

WHEN LAST WE VISITED REDEMPTION, the Engineer Actaeon and the former Knight Arbiter Eisandre had just finished battling across the ruins of the Wall to reach their homeland of Raedelle. With support of the mercenaries Trench and Wave, wood carver Lauryn, Eisandre's childhood friend Wayd, and the unflappable Companion Itarik, they managed to free the legendary sword Caliburn from the pillar artifact which had caused Eisandre's brother, the Prince Aedwyn, to mysteriously disappear.

When tribal attackers tried to interfere, Captain Varisk and Jezail of the Incline warband along with the Voice Ithelie helped them fight their way through. Ironically, the Incline warband had been sent by the Lord Shore to arrest Actaeon and Eisandre, but Varisk and Jezail were friends from Actaeon's past and decided to support him after hearing his side of the story.

With Caliburn in hand, Eisandre marched her much-dwindled force into the meeting of the Raedellean Conclave. Her timely arrival foiled the plans of her uncle Gunther Arcady, the Lord Shore, who had expected to be anointed as the next Prince. Instead, the Conclave selected Eisandre to succeed her brother as Princess of Raedelle.

This should have been impossible. For one, Eisandre was the youngest of six Caliburn siblings. Even more importantly, she was born Lost – one of an outcast minority born with a shattered mind, prone to delusions and madness. Prudently, her family had secretly removed her from the line of succession when she was still young and sent her off to the strict Order of Arbiters, the neutral defenders of the Pyramid and one of the few factions that accepted Lost recruits. But, when Eisandre arrived at the Conclave with Caliburn in hand and so many allies behind her, the Conclave chose her to lead Raedelle.

The new Princess promptly surprised everyone by taking the Engineer from Incline, Actaeon, as her husband, by Raedellean tradition. This was not a future either of them had thought possible. As a Knight Arbiter, Eisandre had not been permitted to marry.

As for Actaeon, he had never chosen a conventional path for himself. He had made the conscious decision not to undergo the Trials, a rite of passage for all Raedellean youth. Nor did he join his local warband for a period of service, which was the norm for his people. Instead, he dreamt of opening his own workshop to explore the secrets of Redemption and invent solutions that would help people live better lives. It was a dream that he managed to fulfill with astounding success. Through his many deeds and inventions, Actaeon secured enough funding to construct his workshop in the Outskirts near the Pyramid.

With help from Eisandre, Trench, Wave, and Lauryn, and using his new workshop as his base of operations, Actaeon felled great towers, exploded slug monsters, incapacitated deathcrawlers, invented grenados, fought cross-faced raiders, retrieved a relic that inspired the formation of a cult, and even discovered and deciphered some of the inner workings of Pyramid itself. He won the support of high-ranking officials in the Dominions of Shield and Ajman, earned the trust of the Order of Arbiters, and even attracted the attention of the enigmatic Loresworn. Actaeon wanted nothing more than to continue his escapades and explorations in his workshop, but his path took an unanticipated turn. He had fallen in love with a Knight Arbiter who then became the Princess of Raedelle. And so, Actaeon became her Prince Engineer, for he could no longer imagine any life that was not by her side.

But, as we know, one thing is certain in Redemption: everything comes with a cost.

The new Princess and her Prince Engineer soon learned that a full tribal invasion of Redemption was underway, and the Pyramid lay under siege. Thus, married life for them began with being separated immediately to face the biggest challenges of their generation. With the future of Redemption at stake, the Lost Princess and her eccentric Prince Engineer will attempt to save their civilization as they know it.

The Dark Heart of Redemption awaits them.

PROLOGUE: THE BLADE THAT FALLS

"**G**ORGRIAN KERIC, YOU HAVE BEEN found guilty of treason to your country, and for this you have been sentenced to die. If you have any final words, speak them now." The Princess of Raedelle unslung the greatsword Caliburn from her back and held it aloft. The coldness in her voice matched the ice in her eyes. The white gold disk of the sun, high in the azure sky, reflected bright light from the artifact blade.

Gorgrian growled at the newly anointed Princess Eisandre Rellios Caliburn and spat at her feet. The man had been a Companion, once a member of Raedelle's most elite group of warriors, sworn to serve and protect the ruler of Raedelle. Now he stood like a shadow of his former self before the youngest sister of the Prince he had betrayed. He was unshaven and bruised, filthy and with dark hollows under his eyes, as if he had not slept since his capture several days earlier. He wore only a tattered brown sack with holes cut for his head and arms to make disposal of his body easier.

"Only I'm glad I'll not live to see yer pathetic reign. I'd rather serve the worms." Gorgrian gave the young Princess a hard stare, meant to intimidate. But her iron gaze held his own, unfaltering.

"Then may you serve them better than you've served Raedelle," the Princess replied evenly. Her solemn voice carried clearly across the silent crowd of Raedelleans that had gathered upon the grassy hill just outside of Caliburn Castle to witness the execution.

Gorgrian's jaw dropped open at her words. Before he could stammer out a response, Companions Wayd and Brigert stepped forward and drove him to his knees. The Companions' expressions were grim in the harsh light of the day as they bent him forward painfully until his head rested on one ear atop an old bucket.

That a Companion would betray his own Prince had brought a deep shame to them all. And now the Prince was gone, having disappeared inside a pillar artifact on the Wall.

The Princess stepped forward, her sturdy boots sounding on the boards of the small wooden platform that had been hastily constructed for the execution. She regarded the back of his head for a long moment – there was something wrong about it.

"Turn him so that I can look into his eyes," Eisandre said levelly.

The Companions twisted Gorgrian's head and slammed it down against the bucket again. He felt warm blood fill his mouth as he bit through his tongue.

The disgraced Companion looked along the length of the legendary blade and showed the Princess a bloody smile.

She looked down at the man before her for long enough to draw an anxious murmur from the crowd. Then she raised the greatsword high and brought it down to neatly sever the traitor's head from his body, with barely a whisper as the razor-sharp artifact blade sliced through air, flesh, bone, and the bucket below.

Some of the people gathered gasped at the gory sight, some cheered at the sentence served, and a few others stood in thoughtful silence. Only yesterday there had been a wedding on a similar hill nearby, where the grave young woman before them who had just become their Princess had taken a peculiar engineer as her husband. Five had stood before her in the line of succession. She was the youngest of the Caliburns – it should never have come to this.

And yet here she stood before them, with her bright blue Caliburn eyes and her fair Caliburn hair cropped short atop her head, meting out justice as her brother, Prince Aedwyn, would have done. As their father would have done before him and all their Ancestors right back to Raedelle herself.

The Voice of the Ancestors in attendance, Ithelie, stepped forward to close the dead former Companion's eyes, careful not to get any of the blood on her green robes. When she stood, she cleared her throat and addressed the crowd. "This man's soul will not dwell among the Ancestors, but may the Fallen guide him nonetheless to realize the err of his ways and guide us to walk a nobler and more righteous path."

"It is done?" Eisandre asked her quietly, following a pause long enough that it had started to become awkward.

Ithelie looked genuinely confused at the question. "Aye, 'tis done."

Eisandre wiped her blade with a cloth until the shine had been restored and reslung the blade on her back. Then, without ceremony or statement, she turned away from the dead man, the spreading pool of blood, and the many eyes of the crowd upon her. She started back toward Caliburn Castle alone.

But one man, the new Prince Engineer, detached from the group and moved to walk at her side.

When he held out his hand, she clasped it firmly in her own, and they made their way back to the castle together. Once there to finish the preparations for the war and more death to come.

ACT ONE: INVASION

TRAVAIL

"**T**HIS IS AN UNBELIEVABLE WASTE of time. We should be marching right now. The Lakehold warbands are counting on us to get into position!"

They stood before the unyielding doors of Travail; metallic blue doors that locked together along a jagged seam that failed to budge no matter what force was applied.

Travail was a massive building that rivaled some of the biggest Ancient structures in Redemption. The building was defined by sixes. It had six sides that reached toward the sky like massive fin-like blades, though the southern side, opposite where they now stood, was dominated by massive blue doors that could swing open to allow entire ships inside along a canal that was dug from the River of Arches itself. Six levels were apparent from the outside of the building, roughly identified by zig-zagged lines of inset luminaries that glowed with an eerie purple luminescence. There were no windows on the outside walls, which left the building as closed and mysterious as its former Loresworn inhabitants. Atop each fin-like blade there was a tremendous, six-sided, red elderglass frustum. Each of the frustums had an organic elderglass protrusion that twisted outward and extended to join with its counterparts above the center of Travail. Much of this could only be seen partially at the right locations on the fern-covered clearing in the surrounding jungle.

Unlike many of the other buildings of the Ancients, Travail had almost entirely escaped the ravages of time and destruction. Only a section in the southwest corner – a part of the top cornice – had crumbled to the ground, littering the field of ferns at the muddy riverside with large elderstone blocks. At the base of each of the six blades that made up the building's walls there were stalagmitic rock formations where centuries or millenia of raindrops had fallen from the building to leave their mineral deposits behind. One point along the western wing appeared blurred and distorted as though one were gazing at it through an unfocused lens.

It was this strange blurry spot that Actaeon Rellios Caliburn, the new Prince Engineer of Raedelle through his marriage to the Princess, stared at through the scope on his recurve bow. "Now *that* is truly perplexing."

The Lord Arcady folded his arms across his chest, regarding the Prince Engineer with burning hazel eyes. He was decidedly unhappy. "You've been trying to get in for hours now. We need to set out once again. I didn't come here to watch you poke and prod at the Loresworn's nonsensical fortress," he said.

Gunther Arcady was the older Lord of Shore with a hooked nose and slick black hair that had a smattering of gray in spots. He was also Eisandre's uncle, and the person who, Actaeon suspected, but could not prove, had recently tried to have them killed by tribals on the Wall. The force led by Eisandre had barely made it to Raedelle with her brother's artifact sword in hand so that she could be anointed as Princess.

It was for just that reason that Actaeon had decided to take him along with the force he was now leading northward to break the tribal siege of Pyramid.

"Yes, yes. Your point is a valid one, Gunther," said the Prince Engineer, causing the Lord to cringe at the casual use of his first name. "And yet, this is a worthwhile endeavor if we can open the way. The artifacts inside might turn the tide of battle, after all." He shouldered his bow and accepted his halberd back from one of the nearby Companions.

"And you think that *you* of all people will figure out how to unlock Travail? I'm sure they've taken better precautions at securing their fortress than you could break through in a day, or else every Dominion would've been knocking down these doors years ago," Arcady spat.

"The key to Travail is a heart's blind trust," Actaeon said enigmatically, as he ran a hand through the disheveled black hair behind the goggles he wore atop his forehead. They were words that the Loresworn leaders had told him before he'd left the Pyramid. "Through those words lie the answer we seek to this riddle."

Arcady scowled. "Fine! I'll give you an hour more, that's all! After that, the Blackstone warband will continue our march." He stomped off, leaving Actaeon to his work.

Actaeon watched him storm off and grinned. "Companion Yanelle, give the Lord Shore a few moments to calm himself and then kindly remind him that he is under my command and will leave when I decide it to be best."

Yanelle smirked. "Aye, Prince Engineer. As you say." One of the two Companions that had been assigned to him, she had red hair down to her shoulders, striking eyes, and a lithe, but fit, figure.

"You can just call me Actaeon, Yanelle."

"Aye, Prince Engineer. I'll call you Actaeon." She set out to give the reminder to Arcady.

"I still don't get why you had to bring that man along, Act," said Wave, regarding the departing Lord warily with his single eye.

"Would you have preferred he leave Arcady with Eisandre?" asked Trench, nudging his friend roughly. "Or in Raedelle to spread unrest among the people?"

Wave thought about that for a time and then turned to Actaeon. "By the Fallen, Act! You're a damned genius."

"Keep your enemies close," Actaeon said. "I feel like that is something I learned from you two."

"Hey! What're you trying to say?" Wave asked, feigning outrage.

"At least someone is learning something," muttered Trench.

The two old mercenaries were seasoned veterans that Actaeon had hired when he first started his work around Pyramid. Trench was a veritable giant with a hideous scar that ran across his face, running from the top of his right brow through his nose and continuing well into his left cheekbone. Wave, on the other hand, was the polar opposite – short and roguishly handsome with his hair tied back in a neat queue and a patch worn over his left eye. Actaeon had come to trust both men with his life. Plus, they were fairly reliable assistants around the workshop.

"Speaking of learning, how're we supposed to crack this thing, Act?" Lauryn asked. "Arcady's right that we're no closer to a solution than when we started hours ago."

A talented wood carver, Actaeon had hired Lauryn for a few projects at his workshop. He'd been so impressed with her abilities that he'd kept her on as an engineering apprentice.

"A heart's blind trust," repeated Actaeon. "The answer should be obvious. It is likely right in front of our eyes. A heart could be a shape, an organ, or a vital part of something. Blind could be something not easily seen. A trust could be a place where something is held for safekeeping."

"So a hidden place where something is kept for safekeeping," Lauryn said as she tugged on her long braid of reddish-brown hair. "We just need to find the heart then!"

"Precisely, Lauryn," said Actaeon. "And what do we know about hearts?"

"Well, let's see... they push lifeblood through our bodies. They beat in our chests. Without them we'd be dead. They stop when we die. People consider them as love analogues," she trailed off.

"I have an idea," said Actaeon. He turned to Companion Brigert. "May I borrow your shield?"

"Of course, Your Grace," said the stocky, bald Companion. He handed his shield to the Prince Engineer.

Actaeon accepted it and held it firmly in one hand.

The doors before him had no keyhole, no receptacle – nothing obvious that could open it. The jagged seam at the center was so thin that it had turned the points of several daggers they had used to pry at it.

With his free hand, Actaeon pulled his dagger from its scabbard and held it by the blade. Shield in one hand and dagger in the other, he began to strike the shield with the dagger's hilt repeatedly. He quickened the pace to a steady thump that resonated off the tall fortress walls.

"What in shattered Redemption are ya doing, Act?" asked Trench.

"A beating heart!" Lauryn cried out, slapping her hands together.

"Very clever, but... nothing's happening," Wave observed.

"Here, let me help you, Act." Lauryn reached up to touch his neck. She felt for his lifebeat and found it quickly. "Faster. Yes... well, no. A bit too much. Slow it down just a tad. Perfect."

Actaeon grinned and kept striking the cadence at the pace to match the beating of his own heart. "Still no response from Travail, however."

"It's a heart's *blind* trust, no?" asked Wave. "Close yer eyes."

"Now you are thinking, Wave!" said the Prince Engineer. He closed his eyes and continued to hammer out the beat on the shield.

Three sharp clarion notes sounded from high up in the ramparts and the massive doors before them slid open smoothly, the halves disappearing into the walls on either side.

"Damned Loresworn and their tricks," grumbled Trench.

"Nothing is ever simple with them," Actaeon agreed. "I would be quite interested in knowing more about the technology that can simultaneously sense my heartbeat, check it against a drumbeat, and somehow verify that I have my eyes closed. Now, let us go find some damned Loresworn tricks before Arcady needs be restrained."

Actaeon led the way inside and the others followed. Lauryn walked beside him with Trench and Wave close behind. Companion Brigert looked flabbergasted, but he rushed to catch up. Once he did, Actaeon handed him his shield back.

The doors opened to a blue, metal corridor with a hexagonal cross-section. Where each of the corridor surface faces met, was an inset strip of soft, white light – six lines that illuminated the interior and traced a path forward that disappeared around a neat curve ahead.

It was as they rounded the first curve that they saw it. A small pile of metal and fabric lay on the floor in the center of the corridor. As they drew closer, the pile rapidly unfolded a pair of arms and a pair of legs and organized itself to stand before them as what could only be described as a mechanical man.

The man's skin looked like a silver, metal alloy. Actaeon had to look at the others to make sure it wasn't just a trick of the light in the strange place. It wasn't. The mechanical man wore a sleeveless black cloak that was fitted around his muscular figure. The front of the cloak hung open to reveal a form-fitted armor suit a shade darker than his skin. There wasn't a hair on the strange body – his skull was a shiny orb and his face lacked even eyebrows.

It wasn't clear at first that his eyes were closed, but when they snapped open, twin abysses of jet black stared out at the Travail intruders. The man's bare arm snapped out to hold up his palm in warning. "Proceed no further. You are not of Travail." There wasn't the slightest inflection to the voice.

"Looks like we found the real mechanical man, Act," said Trench.

"Aye, and it's much handsomer than the last one," Wave gibed.

Lauryn laughed. "I didn't know you swung that way, Wave. A man of constant surprises."

Trench roared a laugh and Wave's cheeks flushed red as he searched for a retort.

"Sollemnis the Gray sent us here," said Actaeon, addressing the silver guardian. "He thought we might be able to help with the issues at hand. I am Actaeon Rellios Caliburn. Who are you?"

"Quronos," said the guardian simply. "There is no knowledge within these walls of Actaeon Rellios Caliburn. No such information has been given to me. Leave at once, intruders."

"Listen, we just w–" Actaeon's words were cut short as the guardian rushed forward, a sword suddenly in each hand. He hadn't even seen where they had been drawn from before Wave threw him backward down the corridor.

The mercenary's flamberge rapier was out and he parried a stream of thrusts from Quronos' blades.

Trench drew his maul and Brigert his sword. The pair's rush forward was halted as Wave spat over his shoulder, "No! I've got this. Stay outta my way."

As Trench and Brigert slid to a stop behind him, Wave pressed his attack on Quronos. The mercenary's blade was a blur as it flashed to and fro in the artificial light, pushing the guardian to his limit as he fought to ward off Wave's incessant onslaught.

The metallic guardian backed off several steps down the corridor before he charged toward Wave's blind side.

Wave pivoted to compensate, but Quronos was faster and shifted to the other side of the corridor, where he ran up the sloped lower wall and leapt to kick the mercenary solidly in the back. Wave reeled forward to strike the opposite wall, rolling away just as the point of Quronos' blade might have disemboweled him.

The Loresworn guardian followed up with a quick succession of slashes aimed at crippling the downed mercenary. Showers of sparks were thrown when the blades struck the wall after Wave nimbly dodged and rolled away to his feet.

Drawing his companion dagger in his off hand, Wave spun to face the guardian once more, and met the pair of blades with his own. The clashes of their blades thundered down the hall as each searched for an advantage over the other. Neither left an opening, and their blades whirled and arced through the air, performing their deadly dance.

"What *are* you?" asked Wave, breathing heavily from his exhaustion.

"I have the same inquiry," said Quronos as he deftly dodged one of Wave's thrusts. The guardian's own breathing was unlabored by comparison. "Never before has one matched my skill. And while lacking the necessary parallax to determine depth." His next thrust was aimed at Wave's remaining eye.

Wave jerked his head to the side to avoid the blade. His own blades moved instinctively to scissor Quronos' sword and use the guardian's forward momentum against him. It was a risky maneuver that left Wave open to the guardian's other sword. The wild slash came for his exposed neck though, and he was able to duck under it.

As the guardian stumbled forward, Wave kicked hard at his leading shin and connected solidly. Quronos tucked forward as he fell and hit his shoulder hard before rolling and regaining his feet.

Wave didn't give Quronos a moment to recover before he was atop him again, searching for any hole in the guardian's defense.

While the others watched, the battle between the two swordsmen continued unabated for what seemed like an impossible length of time to keep fighting in such a way. It was beginning to grow clear to everyone, including Wave himself, that the mercenary was growing tired and sloppier while the guardian appeared to be inexhaustible.

"By the Fallen... you... can't... be human," said Wave, batting the guardian's blades aside with a growing desperation.

"No less human than you, and more where it counts," replied Quronos enigmatically. He swung one sword at the mercenary's legs.

"Prove it," said Wave, leaping the slash to return several quick ripostes which were easily parried. "You're nothing but a gods damned machine as far as I can tell."

"Blessed, not damned. I've advantages beyond comprehension."

"Naught but a machine, I say! Designed to guard Travail. Unable to provide reasonable discourse," gasped Wave as he backed up several steps against another onslaught.

In one swift motion, Quronos returned both blades to hidden scabbards on his back. The hilts disappeared when he withdrew his hands. He dodged an errant slash from Wave's flamberge before he put his hands together and lowered his head. "I would know my opponent's name."

Wave paused but kept his sword and dagger out, unsure whether to trust Quronos. "You can call me Wave."

"Wave – like the ocean's water against the shore. Like the heat that radiates from the sun-baked sand. Like the motion of leaves in a gentle breeze…"

"More like the relieved gesture made as he departs," Trench said with a chuckle.

"A sentiment most understandable. For he is a most difficult opponent," said Quronos, with no inflection. "My equal on this day. You are welcome to Travail, Wave, as are your companions. Please follow me, I will show the way." The guardian dipped his head once more before spinning on his heel and starting off.

Wave glanced back at the others and shrugged. He sheathed his weapons and started after Quronos. The others followed.

The main hall of Travail was a six-level, cylindrical room that culminated in a luminescent dome that filled the chamber with an ethereal green light. Six equidistantly spaced ramps led up to each level from the last. On each level were six hexagonal doors – most of which would open upon a man's approach. Some of them did not – untold secrets locked behind them. At each level there were also six consoles with lit symbols of the Ancients writ upon them. Above them floated flickering images and apparitions showing figures undergoing various activities.

At the center of the room was a larger version of one of the consoles, six-sided with rounded corners. The image that flickered to life above it was a familiar one.

"Sol," said Actaeon.

"The Engineer, now a Prince, succeeded in unlocking Travail," spoke the shimmering image of the old man with crimson red robes and a gray beard that reached his waist.

Sollemnis the Gray was one of the elder leaders of the Loresworn, and one that had angered Actaeon on multiple occasions in the past when he claimed to be testing him. One time in particular came to mind, when Sol had 'tested' Actaeon by trying to drown him in the Pyramid's control room.

"Prince Engineer," Actaeon corrected him, his face reddening. "And it was not I alone that unlocked Travail, as you undoubtedly watched somehow."

"Watch or no, your ingenuity was the only here to solve the puzzle. Though that one shows much promise," said Sol, his eyes falling upon Lauryn.

Lauryn blushed and looked at the floor.

"Now that you are here," began Actaeon, "it would be helpful if you could show us any artifacts within that might help us in the battle to come. For example, your ability to project yourself to a different place might provide us with a tactical advantage. Or whatever you used to project force from afar."

"And how might our young Prince Engineer know about force projection?" asked the Loresworn hologram, his lips curling into a knowing smile.

"Because I am not daft, Sol," Actaeon said with a grin. "Since you were not physically present in the Pyramid control room when you activated the flood, it did not require one of extraordinary intelligence to figure out that you must have a means to remotely actuate the buttons required to create such an effect."

"That's right. We've been meaning to talk to you about that," said Wave with a scowl.

"Talking wasn't what I had in mind," growled Trench. The giant raised his maul.

Actaeon held up a hand to silence the men-at-arms.

"Also, you could have just told us how to get into Travail, given the other pressing issues at the moment," suggested Actaeon.

"Oh, but a test was needed to assess your worth. One lesser than the task would not have been able to solve the problems that Travail faces," Sol said.

"I'd like to run a test on someone's neck," grumbled Trench under his breath. He clenched his hand into a tight fist, imagining it.

Sol's eyes flicked to Trench.

"Whatever problem Travail faces pales in comparison to those of the realm," Actaeon snapped back, pulling Sol's attention away from Trench. "Will you help us, or will it be nothing but games from you?"

"So quick to jump to conclusions, Prince Engineer. Don't be so sure that

Travail's problems are not the realm entire's. A weakness exists here – one which might spread to encompass all Redemption," Sol spoke enigmatically.

"A problem which matters not if we do nothing to save the civilization which we have worked so hard to build," countered Actaeon. "If you truly care about the realm beyond Travail's ambitions, then you will aid us in our quest."

"You are correct. And we shall. In return we ask the Prince Engineer for just one thing – that you will return to this place to tackle the danger within, before it grows without," said Sol, leveling his wrinkled gaze upon Actaeon.

"And why should you require my help with this problem? Surely a man with the ability to project force and see things in places beyond his sight can work on such problems himself?" Actaeon asked, arching his brow.

"There are limits to any ability, as you well know," answered Sol. "And you have proven to be one of exceptional ability – it is that quality which we believe can overcome the problem at hand."

"I guess you passed enough tests," said Wave with a smirk.

Actaeon grinned at Wave and took a step forward, closer to Sol's projection. "Here is what I will agree to. *If* you help us to find appropriate artifacts in Travail for our quest to break the siege of Pyramid, and *if* those artifacts make an impactful difference in the war effort, then I will return to Travail to help you solve this problem. No more tests though, and no more secrets. If I get the sense that you are keeping things from me, then the deal is off. Got it?"

"I cannot promise that any artifact within will win a war, Prince Engineer," said Sol. "The technology inside Travail might make a difference, but how shall be up to you."

"Well, if we do not win this war, then I do not suspect any of us will be coming back," said Actaeon. He gritted his teeth at the realization of his own words.

"Very well then, Prince Engineer Actaeon Rellios Caliburn. We have a deal," said Sol, with a broad smile. "I will help you with the acquisition of useful artifacts from Travail. There's just one thing that I ask: While your people are here, they should stick closely by Quronos. He is in tune with the specific nature of Travail's problem. I cannot promise that anyone who ventures off on their own will not be lost."

"What are the details of this problem?" asked Actaeon, curious.

"As you said, there are more important issues to attend to," snapped Sol. "Get to work on those. We will discuss Travail's issue upon your return."

At Sol's direction, Quronos took them on a tour throughout Travail. They kept mostly to the east wing of the Ancient building.

When Lauryn asked about the west wing, Quronos' reply was ambiguous, "There the disturbances are turbulent and erratic. I am unable to process the incidences in a manner which produces a discernible pattern. Thus, we should avoid that zone at all costs."

"What is the nature of the disturbances?" Actaeon asked.

"I have not been informed of their nature," said Quronos, turning to regard Actaeon with the disconcerting black spheres of his eyes. "I am simply in tune with the phenomena. Sollemnis will teach you more when you return to help with the problem, I am certain."

The silver-skinned man led them along through the rest of Travail. A wide hexagonal corridor, illuminated in unusual green light, wound along on a gentle slope along the east wing until it reached the end, where it terminated in a switchback that took them back toward the second level of the main hall. Actaeon counted nine switchbacks until the final run of the corridor returned them to the main hall's sixth and final level. Along the corridor at various intervals, the outline of a door would appear as a recess in the corridor wall. Some of these doors Quronos led them into to circumvent sections that he identified as ones to be avoided.

The vast differences in the rooms astounded Actaeon and the others: the first door led them to a room devoid of all light, where they had to hold hands and allow Quronos to guide them through. Another room put them in the middle of a jungle with a clear blue sky – Quronos assured them that they were still inside Travail. One room was filled with water up to their ankles, and had some sort of many-legged, mechanical creatures that swam around them and chirped as though delighted. Yet another room was filled with lines of lit characters that scrolled by in the language of the Ancients. Quronos referred to it simply as 'the archive' – just being there made Actaeon's head hurt. In one particularly dangerous room, they found themselves inside a cylindrical passage that rotated slowly about its axis with tendrils of blue lightning that coalesced along its length. There

Quronos had them stay very close to him and stopped at frequent intervals while the tendrils of electricity worked their way past the group.

Along the way, Quronos paused on occasion to point out various artifacts that might be worth further study in case they might prove useful for the war effort. Actaeon and Lauryn took note of them.

After hours of journeying throughout the Loresworn's abandoned fortress, the group returned to the main hall, where Actaeon spoke to Eisandre through his Thoughtlink Artifact.

The Raedellean advisor, Wise Ambrosius, had given them the Thoughtlink artifacts before their departure. They were a matching pair of polished white, flattened ellipses that the advisor had found in one of the vaults beneath Caliburn Castle. According to Ambrosius, they had been worn by Raedelle herself so that she could communicate with her husband Elphin at the Dominion's very beginning. When placed on the ear, it folded over the lobe and gently clasped itself in place – held there by some unseen force. The artifacts were so comfortable that it was easy to forget they were wearing them. However, when Actaeon or Eisandre directed a thought to one another, it allowed them to communicate no matter the distance.

It took some getting used to, but Actaeon was beginning to find it comforting that he could share his thoughts with his wife at any time.

I intend to leave Lauryn behind with Quronos to study the artifacts here, Actaeon thought to Eisandre. *We need to continue north and rendezvous with the Niwian and Ajman forces in order for our pincer maneuver to succeed.*

Yes, I agree, returned Eisandre's thoughts. *If we don't get your force into position on the east, then the tribal forces will be able to fall back when we attack from the west. Itarik tells me it is critical that you cut them off from the Underforest.*

Aye. A battle there would be long and arduous, thought Actaeon.

I know it must be hard for you to leave Travail, my Actaeon. Thank you for understanding the importance of your presence in the warband's advance.

Of course, love, Actaeon thought with a grin that only he could see. *It is essential that I remain in command. Without me, disputes will arise over who is in charge. Though, I must admit that the mysteries of Travail appeal to my deepest curiosities. Kryo claimed it is one of the places where the Arrival portals originated. Such a place might hold answers to many questions. Plus, there are strange disturbances within that old Sol claims might threaten all of Redemption.*

I will support your return there as soon as we can manage, Act – you know that, she assured. *I'm so very sorry that you must miss this opportunity right now — I know it must be difficult.*

No need to apologize, Eis. Without the success of our current endeavor, there is no safety for such efforts, nor for any others. This we must do, to create a safe place for our future together.

Thank you, Act — for standing by me, and for believing in me. I could not do this without you.

I could echo the same words for you, thought Actaeon. *You have always believed in me as well. We now walk the path of the rest of our lives together and we are stronger and better for it, my wife. Do not forget.*

I won't!

THE ADVANCE

"**T**HEY ARE NOT COMING?"

Three days after departing Travail, Actaeon stood on a rise at the edge of Sunken City with Thernaxis and looked northward.

The new Lord Protector of Memory Keep turned his head and spat in response to Actaeon's question, an action that made his fellow Niwians behind him cringe. "The Ajmani and Shieldian sops are off bickering over the Czerynian lands in the north. Let them think they've gained something for now, Actaeon. We'll divvy up both their pathetic excuses for Dominions once we're done with these tribal scum."

Thernaxis grinned and spat again, gazing out at the hundreds of thin black tendrils that drifted upward from tribal campfires. The Lord Protector wore a full suit of plate armor stained a metallic green color that gleamed like an emerald in the sunlight. His head was shaved aside from two narrow strips of short brown hair that ran front to back along either side of his scalp. A short, cropped beard framed the rest of his face, but what really drew one's eye were his wild eyes that bespoke mental instability in the man.

Actaeon grinned at the man and shook his head. "Raedelle has other goals than that, Thernaxis. Besides, Ajman and Shield are our allies. We all need to work together if we mean to preserve our civilization."

The Lord Protector let out a loud guffaw and slapped Actaeon hard on the shoulder. "Oh, come now, Act! You're the Prince Engineer of Raedelle now – start acting like it! What sort of allies would be up north bickering when you need their help here? Not any ally of mine! Come, let me introduce you to a *real* ally."

The Lord Protector led the way and Actaeon followed with Trench, Wave, and Companion Yanelle close behind him. They descended from the rise and wound their way through the Niwian army's array of tents until they reached a blue tent with a blazing sun embroidered upon it.

"Shattered Redemption..." grumbled Trench. "What's this?"

The flap of the big tent was thrown back and Atreena Covellet marched forth, her sweeping blond hair bright in the sunlight, beautiful in contrast to the brutal efficiency of her heavy plate armor. She strode purposefully up to Actaeon and offered him a complex smile.

"Allow me to introduce Knight Captain of the Keepers, Atree-" began Thernaxis.

"We know who she damn well is," snapped Wave. "The sort of ally that'd sooner stab you in the back."

"They made ya Captain, eh lass?" growled Trench. "Guess there's still some reward in trickery and betrayal in this land."

Actaeon and his associates had dealt with Atreena on several occasions in the past, when she'd come to the workshop to ask for help figuring out an artifact – an unusual request for a Keeper. It was a Keeper's duty to destroy artifacts, not to study them, but Atreena had claimed that she wished to know whether the artifact might have altered a Keeper Initiate. Their work for her had ended after a squad of Keeper Knights attacked the workshop. Had it not been for the intervention of a certain cult, they might have killed Trench, Wave, and Lauryn.

Thernaxis glared at the two mercenaries and his hand raised to the hilt of the big two-hander at his back.

Atreena held up her hand to forestall Thernaxis. "Please, Lord Protector. It is but a misunderstanding. I fear I must take part of the responsibility. There was a miscommunication among the Keeper ranks – "

"A miscommunication that had armed knights attack my workshop and try to kill my associates?" asked Actaeon, no amusement in his tone. "That is a fairly serious mistake for a group that claims to have such divine insight into all the matters of Redemption."

"We are but the human servants of the Allfather, Prince Engineer Actaeon. I ask your forgiveness for our error and offer you congratulations on your new position," said Atreena with a tight-lipped smile. "The Keepers have long been friendly with Raedelle, and we are here now, as always, in Redemption's time of great need, to join you in the breaking of this siege."

She pulled free one of her heavy gauntlets and extended a hand to Actaeon.

Actaeon glanced back at Wave and the one-eyed mercenary shook his head and scowled.

The Prince Engineer took a deep breath and settled his gaze firmly on the Keeper Knight Captain. Her sparkling tan eyes met his own confidently. "Listen, Actaeon – Prince Engineer, I know that I violated your trust by bringing that artifact to your workshop only to have my brethren attack you soon after. You have my word that those actions were carried out without my knowledge and the ones responsible have been dealt with."

"Dealt with how?" spat Wave.

"They've been dealt with," said Atreena. "That's all you need to know. It will not happen again." She returned her gaze to Actaeon. "I've learned to respect you, and your judgment. Your proclivity toward the use and study of artifacts is misguided and unfortunate, but the Allfather sees your talent as a potential asset in his goals."

"That is quite unfortunate in itself," said Actaeon simply.

"Whatever you might think of it, I'm sure you would agree that the happenings up north are most disturbing – the great sphere, the disappearance of the Czerynians, and the rumors of phantoms and strange spirits that even now impede the warriors of Ajman and Shield. Some artifact has unleashed a great evil there, and its destruction might require more than just Keeper military might. We need your help, Actaeon," Atreena said in earnest.

Actaeon nodded slowly and grasped her extended hand. "Despite our disagreements and misgivings, Raedelle is grateful to have you as our ally in the battles to come." He pulled her close to him then and whispered in her ear, "This is your last chance, Atreena. Do *not* test my trust in you again."

She looked him right in the eye and smiled a smile that made Actaeon wonder if he'd made the right decision. "You have my word, Prince Engineer."

As Actaeon, Trench, Wave, and Yanelle walked back to the Raedellean encampment, the giant spun around and stopped in front of the Prince Engineer.

"You gonna let us know what in the Darkest Hour that blue sphere that somehow destroyed Czeryn was, Act?" demanded Trench. "I think it's about time we heard about it, given it might play a role in the battles to come."

Actaeon drew to a stop and looked up at the giant mercenary. Beside him, Yanelle tensed and looked confused – she was assigned to protect the Prince Engineer as a Companion, but Trench had been his hired protector before Actaeon was Raedellean royalty.

"It is alright, Yanelle. As Trench says, I owe you all an explanation," said Actaeon. He'd delayed telling them about the artifact for too long. At the time there had been more pressing matters at hand, but now that they were heading back north, it was quickly becoming more relevant.

"Are you saying you *knew* what that thing was?" asked Wave, looking incredulous.

"Of that, I am not certain, Wave. But I suspect that I do," said Actaeon.

"Shall I excuse myself, Your Grace?" asked Yanelle. She began to inch away, thumbing her sword belt nervously.

Actaeon glanced at Yanelle, then did a double take. "Yanelle, I told you just to call me Actaeon. At least I might recognize when people call me Prince Engineer, but I doubt I will ever recognize Your Grace. I am the last person to require all these formalities."

"My apologies, Your Grace. I'll call you Actaeon instead," said Yanelle, her cheeks flushing a deep shade of red.

"Plus, he's gotta be one of the least graceful people I know. I have to agree with you there, Act!" said Wave with a smirk.

"Careful, Wave. I might just prove you right and slip and poke out your other eye," said Actaeon.

Everyone laughed at that, with Yanelle joining in belatedly. The Companion ran a hand through her shoulder-length red hair and relaxed a little.

"You'd owe me two eyes then, Act. Better be careful – something tells me it'll be a while before we get back to the workshop again," said Wave with a broad grin.

"Aye. Fair enough. But let us get back on topic. I want to tell you what I know about the blue sphere that stole the Czerynians from Redemption. And no, Yanelle – I would like you to stay and hear it too. You all should know the truth," said Actaeon.

"Okay, Your Grace," said Yanelle, prompting a look from the Prince Engineer.

Trench and Wave chuckled.

"Ah, I mean... Actaeon," she corrected.

Actaeon grinned and then began. "Back when the cross-faced raiders captured Lauryn and I, I told you that they had me look at an elliptical cylinder artifact that they wanted me to activate for them. The raiders worked for someone called the Veiled One and it was almost as though they were all possessed. The cross-faced raiders never spoke to me – they used Markor as their go-between. Markor said that the Veiled One needed the device to take back 'his city, for the city is his'."

"Yes, but you told us that you tricked them and didn't activate the artifact," said Wave.

"Let him finish," grumbled Trench.

"Exactly, but what I did not understand at the time was that Lady Lartigan had seen the notes I had taken before Lauryn killed her. If she was also possessed, which I suspect she was given how she turned against us after we rescued her, then I think the Veiled One might have seen the details it needed to activate the device... and use it to somehow obliterate the people of Czeryn," said Actaeon. He scratched his right arm through the thick leather of his jacket.

"By the Fallen!" said Wave. "So, you think a single artifact made all the people in three Holds disappear in an instant?"

"Saints help us," breathed Yanelle.

"And there might be more where that one came from," said Trench.

"Yes, Wave. That is exactly what I am saying. And if it is true, I suspect this Veiled One will strike again and again, until all of Redemption is emptied of the people of the Dominions – our people. Until he takes back what he considers to be *his city* completely."

The bow of the *Glorious Redemption* smashed its way through the first of the waves, leading the Thyrian fleet carrying Eisandre's Lakehold warbands as it started into the choppy waters of the Great Sea. The noonday sun baked the ship's deck, which had started to rock and lurch in the churning waters. The salt spray was a welcome relief in the heat for those on the deck.

Behind them wound the River of Arches all the way back to Raedelle.

Tremendous elderstone structures arced over the waterway like ribs from a long dead creature. All of them were broken in places – missing gigantic fragments that were lost beneath the water. Where the outflow of the river met the currents of the Great Sea beyond there was a dangerous churn of unpredictable waves.

"Bring us straight into the waves, Vash," instructed Captain Harvand Xula, his foot on the quarterdeck railing to steady himself as he scoped out the sea ahead.

"Aye aye, Captain!" came the vigorous reply from the woman at the tiller crank.

The Bosun raised a horn to his lips and blew a quick pattern of long and short notes. The sound carried across the deck but was quickly swallowed by the crashing waves. "Adjusting sails for the wind change, Cap'n!"

The *Glorious Redemption* was one of the largest Thyrian sloops in the fleet. It was a two-masted wooden sailing ship that was manned by a steady crew of fifty sailors, though the vessel could carry as many as one hundred and twenty during times of need. Now was one such time, and the ship was uncomfortably crammed full of warbanders and sailors alike. In addition to a typical complement of marines, which they had left behind in Thyr for this voyage, the *Glorious Redemption* sported ports belowdecks for five massive rolling ballista apparatus which could be moved either port or starboard as required. Five boltspray apparatus were arranged strategically abovedeck, one at the aft rail of the quarterdeck, two to either side of the main deck, and two to either side of the forecastle deck just beneath the fore staysail. Each machine was capable of short-range rapid fire of bolts while the operator cranked a handle and another fed fresh bolts into the feeder. A raised quarterdeck and forecastle deck allowed for better visibility above the main deck whether steering the ship from its big stern wheel or spotting for hazards at the bow. A pair of booms swept back and forth overhead only several hands above everyone's heads as the two largest sails were adjusted to catch the wind. Each mast had a topsail above that, and three additional sails were hung from lines fastened to the bowsprit.

Four other two-masted sister ships followed close behind, along with fifteen more smaller single-masted sloops.

"Excellent, Lucerd!" Captain Xula complimented the Bosun and tugged one side of his long mustache before removing his diamond-shaped quadcorne hat to wipe the sweat from the dark skin of his scalp. He turned to face Eisandre where she stood near the rear of the quarterdeck along with First Companion Itarik, Companion Wayd, Lady Neryl Vanora, and Lord Jad Perth. "I'd recommend you all grab hold of something. It's about to get rough. Come, Lady Vanora, you can take my arm."

The Lady shot the Captain a look with her vibrant brown eyes and leaned back against the railing, taking a moment to adjust her practical gray dress over her matching gray boots. "This isn't the first time I've been on the Great Sea, you know."

The widowed Lady of Whiterose was one of the most eligible bachelorettes in Raedelle. Everyone in the Dominion had heard the story of young Neryl Vanora and her soul match Garvi. After just a cycle of marriage, her father, the Lord of Whiterose, had taken Garvi with him on a hunt with the Duke and two of his sons, Eisandre's father and oldest brothers. The entire hunting party had been ambushed and killed by unknown assailants. Neryl had been elevated to the Lady of Whiterose and months later gave birth to a boy who was Lost. She'd insisted on making the trip to Travail on her own to give up the baby to the Loresworn. In the fifteen years that followed, she had spurned any potential suitors, telling them that her two great loves were gone – there was no more room in her heart.

Captain Xula put his hat back on and tipped the brim toward her. "Suit yourself, Lady. The offer still stands."

As the southerly winds filled the sails, the deck beneath them jerked forward and then upward as they rode another wave.

"I still don't understand. That little earring lets you talk to the Prince Engineer?" asked Lord Jad Perth of Lakefeed in his nasally voice. He was a very short man with a receding hairline and a nose that looked like it'd been stepped on one too many times.

"Not talk, Jad," snapped Neryl. "It allows them to share thoughts. Pay attention."

Eisandre studied the small Lord for a moment and then nodded slowly. "The Lady Neryl is correct. This artifact gives us a strategic advantage as it will allow us to precisely coordinate the movements of our two forces." The deck lurched again, and she paused to steady herself against the railing before continuing. Her gaze wandered to the disconcerting drop to the water below – she'd have to ask Actaeon at some point how such a massive ship could stay afloat. "The information we've obtained so far has already proven useful."

"Useful and worrisome," added Neryl. "Our civilization at the brink of collapse, and two of our supposed allies are up north worrying about their own ambitions."

"Exactly," said Jad. "And why should we be fighting to help Pyramid while the more central Dominions just ignore the siege entirely? We could shore up at home and worry about ourselves."

Eisandre's attention shifted back to the Lord.

Before she could reply, First Companion Itarik chimed in. "The Pyramid is of obvious strategic and political importance to Raedelle's future. Without it, destabilization occurs throughout the entire city, and it is only a matter of time before Raedelle falls."

"And Raedelle might fall anyway with this fool's errand!" exclaimed the Lord. "I was okay with sending warbands to battle with the understanding that our allies would be there too. Without that, I'm not okay with it at all!" He threw his hands up in the air and stumbled as the deck rolled underfoot.

"It is good that you are not in charge of that decision then," said Eisandre simply.

Lord Perth's face reddened at her words.

She continued speaking, "The Thyrian and Niwian Dominions stand with Raedelle on this matter. We don't know what is happening in Czeryn, at present. It's entirely possible that things are worse than the rumors suggest. Pyramid is our place to convene on neutral ground. Itarik is right – without it, the relative peace that we've enjoyed for more than twenty years is gone."

"I just think that you should – " Jad cut his sentence short as Eisandre pushed off from the railing and strode away and down the quarterdeck stairs without another word.

The Princess paused for a moment to steady herself on the rolling deck before continuing on. The two Companions followed on unsteady feet.

Jad glared at Neryl Vanora, and the Lady clicked her tongue. "Watch yourself around her, Jad. She's no sniveling politician like you're used to. That one's been forged in battle. You'd do best to weigh your words around her."

Neryl smirked and walked over to Captain Xula, taking the surprised man's arm. "So, Captain Xula, tell me what you know of the Supreme Captain."

Jad Perth glared at her and turned his head to spit over the railing. Before he could, he jumped in fright as the main boom swung past just overhead in a rush of air as the main sail pivoted to better capture the wind.

THE BATTLE OF GLASS SPIRE

"**T**HE HIGH GROUND IS RIGHT next to that spire," said Thernaxis, rubble crunching under the green-tinged metal of his boots. "We hold that ground and we can push soldiers right down to the Avenue of Glass."

They stood in a clearing in the ruins north of Sunken City – Actaeon, Thernaxis, Wave, and Arcady. Beyond the clearing rose a great, glass spire that sparkled in the light of the dawn's sun. It was a similar spire to those densely clustered in Adhikara to the east, a relic of the Ancients. Actaeon imagined it was designed to make or receive light, for what purpose he didn't know. In the distance behind the glass spire rose the imposing shape of Pyramid, its elderglass pinnacle blazing in the sunlight.

"That place is a damned anthill of tunnels and fissures. We'd be completely vulnerable on the way up there," said Wave, casting a doubtful look at Actaeon.

"And what would you have us do instead? Cower here until the tribals leave out of boredom?" asked Thernaxis. The Lord Protector smirked.

"There are two options the way I see it," began Wave, pointedly ignoring the Niwian Lord's comment. "We can wait here until Princess Eisandre's Lakehold and Thyrian force gets into position. Then the tribals will need to pull back to guard Pyramid and we can work our way forward. Or, we can skirt the perimeter of the Underforest until we reach Redoubt –"

"Redoubt?" blurted Arcady, his sharp hazel eyes narrowed upon Wave. "Haven't you lost enough of your friends there, – what do you call yourself now – Wave? Enough of this nonsense. The sooner that we end this, the better. Things will only continue to deteriorate the longer this takes, for the people inside Pyramid and the people without. We need to take the spire now."

"I agree with Wave," said Actaeon. "It is only logical to wait until the Lakehold forces are in position. Then the tribal forces will be harried on the western front and there is a better chance for us to cross the dangerous terrain unchallenged."

"See, that right there is why you're a Prince *Engineer* and not a soldier," said Thernaxis. He slapped Actaeon hard on the shoulder. "No stomach for it. You don't win battles by sitting still – you win them by keeping your enemies on their toes. The Niwian colors will be moving out either way, Act. I want men up there before the heat of the sun makes things tougher and before they've the time to prepare. You let me know if Raedelle's going to join us, or if it's too hairy for your folk to handle."

The flap of the Raedellean command tent was pulled aside and Companion Yanelle rushed in, her red hair matted against her face with sweat.

Trench, Wave, Actaeon, and Arcady looked up from where they stood at the map table.

Off to the side, away from the others, stood Voice Ithelie, wearing the practical green robes of her station. Ithelie had brown eyes and blond hair that was nearly white in color. Her heavy cotton robes had deep pockets on the sides and a large cowl that could be pulled up to keep rain off her head. During Eisandre's escape from the Wall, the Voice had proven to be an invaluable and courageous ally, speaking the final rites over the dead and encouraging the survivors to continue onward to Raedelle. Actaeon was glad to have her along.

The command tent was in the midst of the Raedellean encampment, which was at the southern fringe of the clearing in the ruins. The Niwians and Keepers had broken camp and left hours before to begin their ill-advised assault on the tribals.

"Prince Engineer, I have a report. Warchief Beiloff has taken a force to join the Niwians," Yanelle said, panting as she caught her breath. "I confronted him – tried to stop him. He wouldn't listen."

"He what?" growled Trench. "That p-kin idiot is gonna lose us this war."

"Who went with him?" asked Actaeon, calmly.

"The Blackstoners and Highwater. Eastern Rim and the Wall Breakers wouldn't follow." She leaned forward to rest on her knees, clearly winded from a long run to the command tent.

"Those warbands were camped closest to the glass spire," observed Actaeon. "That made it easier for them to break camp quickly without us knowing."

"Is there any way to pull them from the field?" asked Trench.

"I don't believe so. I was leading a scouting team to the north when they passed. By the time we get out there, they may already be engaged," said Yanelle. She straightened and used both hands to pull her hair back from her face.

"We must go after them," said Actaeon conclusively.

"You spoke to Eisandre on the matter," said Trench. "She agreed with your decision to hold."

Wave narrowed his remaining eye on Arcady. "Beiloff is *your* dog, Gunther. I don't believe for a moment that this isn't your idea."

"Believe what you wish, Wave," said Lord Arcady with amusement as he looked down his hooked nose at the mercenary. He spun to face Actaeon and surprised everyone with his words. "I agree with Trench on this. If Drystan decided to advance, then we'll deal with *my dog* later. We have a responsibility here, and the soon-to-be-dismissed Warchief put our operation at risk."

Wave slammed a fist against the table. "Says the person who wanted to join the Niwian advance in the first place!"

"Prince Engineer, if you could kindly keep your own *dog* in line." Arcady drawled the word dog. "I have no desire to be spoken to in such a manner by a foreigner in the *Raedellean* command tent."

"Whatever the manner in which this situation has arisen, it does not change the fact that it is before us now, and we must deal with it," said Actaeon. "Rally the other warband Captains. We depart immediately."

His words were met with silence and blank stares all around. Nobody moved.

Ithelie stepped forward and regarded the others one by one with her striking brown eyes. "You heard the Prince Engineer. Our fellow Raedelleans are out there in danger, on the field of battle. What sort of people are we who would leave them to die?"

Trench cursed under his breath. "Aye, Act. We're behind you." He laid a heavy hand on Wave's arm and drew his friend from the command tent.

Yanelle nodded to Actaeon and left behind them, Ithelie joining her.

Arcady rolled his eyes and began to follow.

"A moment, Gunther," said Actaeon.

The Lord Shore stopped and cast a glance back over his shoulder. "What?"

"We need to put our enmity aside and work together on this, for the best outcome for Raedelle. As I said earlier, the circumstances we deal with now trump any previous disagreements we may have had. Raedelle is what matters now," said the Prince Engineer. He scratched his right hand through his fingerless glove.

"If you think I don't know that, then you don't know me at all," spat Arcady, looking at Actaeon out of the corner of his eye. "It's what I've been saying all along. Something your wife's family never understood. I hope she's different, for all our sake."

The Lord turned to walk out.

"One more thing," said Actaeon.

Arcady paused.

"Make sure that your people do not undermine my orders again," said Actaeon. "I may not be a soldier by training, but I am also not a fool. I will listen to your advice, but insubordination can get people killed. You should know that better than most, Gunther. Next time, I will not be giving you a warning."

The Lord Shore shook his head and stormed out, not looking back.

The warbands made good progress into the ruins, but it didn't make a difference – by the time they caught up with Thernaxis' and Beiloff's forces, they found them completely surrounded.

No one among Actaeon's force could actually see the battle as they approached through the several different fissures that led to the Glass Spire, but they could hear the mayhem up ahead. The sounds of desperate fighting and the cries of the fallen echoed along the curved purple elderstone and multi-colored elderglass structures that formed the path which led upward.

In many places, glass rope cables ran over their heads, spots of red light darting to and fro along their lengths – a leftover relic of the Ancients. Massive vines as thick as a man's neck wound their way up to the artificial glass rope canopy and spread their greedy leaves and poisonous purple flowers to the sun, casting pools of shadow down below that made it even more difficult to reconnoiter. As they grew closer yet, they could hear the crackle of Niwian writhe-blades and the twang of Raedellean bowstrings.

Actaeon split his force into three different divisions and sent them forward to break a hold in the southeastern tribal formation so that an orderly retreat into Adhikara could be organized. Captain Varisk Conmara of the Incline warband led the center of the attack with his forces. Veterans of the recent Battle of the Wall, they were quickly becoming known as the Wall Breakers for their actions there. There they fought a running battle to get Actaeon and Eisandre back to Raedelle so that she could arrive at the Conclave and be anointed Princess to succeed her brother. Only fifteen survivors remained from that battle, but they had been reinforced with other warriors from Incline before departing to break the Pyramid siege.

Lord Arcady took half of the Eastern Rim warband to protect the right flank while Actaeon took the other half to protect the left. Eisandre's Uncle, the Lord Gunther Arcady's role in recent events was unclear, though it was quite clear that he would've preferred to have been anointed as the next Prince of Raedelle in Eisandre's stead. Actaeon and Eisandre both suspected that Arcady had played a role in the tribal forces that had unsuccessfully tried to prevent them from reaching Raedelle in time for the convening of the Conclave of Lords. It was purposeful that he was here though. Despite their mistrust of the Lord Shore, it had been decided that it was better to bring him along with the campaign rather than leave him in Raedelle where he could cause unchecked political harm.

As the Prince Engineer's forces approached the battle, it quickly became clear that the center of Thernaxis' forces had fallen to pieces. Dozens of Niwian Greens spilled over the ruins in an effort to retreat from the tribal onslaught.

"Hey! Fall in line! You'd abandon your kinsmen?" Trench shouted at them as they ran past to the south. A few slowed to look, but most kept running.

"Typical Niwian cowardice," spat Wave.

"Let's double time!" yelled Lieutenant Hargum of the Eastern Rim warband to his warbanders. They began to jog forward.

As they advanced steadily, the sounds of fighting intensified to a deafening cacophony amplified by the Ancient structures as they drew closer.

"Ready shields and tighten formation!" called the Lieutenant as they rounded the corner of one of the tremendous purple buildings.

A shout from behind brought the Raedelleans to a halt. Behind them were many of the Niwian Greens that had run past them. They were returning at a run – an arduous task in their dyed green plate armor. At their backs a horde of tribals kept atop them and hacked down the slowest of the bunch.

"Continue forward!" cried Actaeon. "If we can unite our force with Thernaxis', we may yet stand a chance."

As the warband continued forward, a swarm of arrows dropped down upon them from the west. Yanelle shoved Actaeon behind her and two arrows thudded into her upraised shield. Blood splattered into Actaeon's eye, drawn from one of the arrow points that passed through her shield and skimmed her forearm. He wiped it clear and cast Yanelle a grateful look.

"Prince Engineer, we'd best make all haste to close to melee distance," she said.

"As you say," replied Actaeon. "Lieutenant Hargum! Give the order to run forward!"

"You heard the Prince Engineer! Quicken the advance!" yelled the warband Lieutenant. He pointed his spear forward and led the charge. The next two volleys of arrows missed them – both falling short.

"Join up with Thernaxis' forces and push east?" asked Wave as he ran beside Actaeon.

"That was my thought. What do you think?" Actaeon asked in return.

"Seems like the only option. Hope the tribals aren't organized enough to reinforce the center they broke through."

As they rounded the curve of the remaining building, they found the entrenched Niwians. Soldiers in purple and gold armor stood shoulder to shoulder at a low point in the ruins – among them were a handful of Keeper Knights that had escaped the rout at the center. In the middle of their formation, the Highwater warbanders shot their arrows past the Niwian shield wall into the onslaught of attackers.

Actaeon had never seen so many soldiers before. The fighters on both sides numbered in the thousands – all jammed into the wide and ruin-covered clearing between the Ancient buildings from which the Glass Spire arose. It was at once an overwhelming and terrifying sight. By comparison, in the action he'd seen on the Wall, the fighters had only numbered in the hundreds.

Amidst everyone and atop a fallen column stood Thernaxis in his gleaming green armor, now bristling with arrows that had found their way into gaps and covered in dark streaks from the blood of his enemies and his own wounds – the colors mixing on his armor to form an ill grayish shade.

"There you are, Prince Engineer!" bellowed the Niwian Lord Protector, pointing with the long blade of his greatsword. "About time you showed up!"

"I heard things were getting too hairy for you!" called back Actaeon with a grin just moments before his force crashed into the wall of tribals.

Those tribals that didn't get out from between the converging forces in time were quickly dispatched. One of the warriors leapt over the shields of the warbanders and landed before Actaeon. The Prince Engineer impulsively thrust his halberd forward into the man's chest. Blood spilled from the dying warrior's mouth, and he lifted his spiked club one last time to bring it down on Actaeon's head. With no time to react, all Actaeon could do was admire the intricate runes drawn upon his enemy's face, many of which he was familiar with – characters of the Ancients.

Beside them, Companion Yanelle was engaged with another foe, but Trench was there and knocked the club aside with his big maul. The giant mercenary kicked the tribal in the shoulder and sent him flying aside like a rag doll.

"Ruinic Tribals," growled Trench. "Same bastards from the Invasion War."

Wave's heavy crossbow twanged nearby and slammed through another Ruinic tribal's sternum. "At least we know how to kill 'em!" he said as he paused to load another bolt.

Actaeon was thrust into the center beside the Lord Protector as the circle reformed to include the newly arrived warbanders and the surviving Niwian Greens that had managed to arrive behind them.

One of the Greens shouldered his way over to Thernaxis and lifted his visor in salute. "Lord Protector, Captain Reedly reporting for –"

The Captain's words were abruptly abbreviated as the Lord Protector's blade separated his head from his shoulders. The emerald plated body toppled to the side.

"You'd not have had to report again if you didn't run in the first place," said Thernaxis. He spat on the man's corpse. "The Fallen know I hate cowards." He turned his mad gaze upon Actaeon and smiled. "But you're here, aren't you? Soldier or no, you're no coward, Prince Engineer."

The fighting intensified as the tribals that had pursued them from the south arrived and reclosed the noose around them.

Actaeon met the Niwian leader's eyes and shrugged. "We had best discuss our exit strategy, Thernaxis. I propose we push east to rejoin with your eastern forces. Assuming they have managed to hold that location, it is our only hope."

"My thoughts as well. A moment and I'll buy you the diversion you'll need." Thernaxis placed a gauntlet, sticky with blood, on Actaeon's shoulder and smiled. "I'll not have my Niwian Greens remembered poorly."

That said, he raised his sword in the air and shouted, "Greens to your Lord Protector! Fall in on my flanks, wedge formation!" The remaining Greens rushed to take up position, not waiting to test their commander in the face of what had just happened to their Captain.

Once they were in position, Thernaxis shouted another command and the Niwians on the north side of the shield wall staggered apart by one man to allow the Green wedge to pass.

"Good luck, Actaeon! Remember us this day! The Purples and Golds will follow you out." Thernaxis began to laugh and pointed his sword forward, "Charge!"

The remaining Greens charged forward in their wedge formation, weaving seamlessly between the shield wall soldiers and cutting a swathe deep into the enemy to the north.

"Smart son of a bitch," said Trench as he watched the Lord Protector lead the charge with his long blade cutting through row upon row of lightly armored Ruinic warriors.

Actaeon arched a brow at Trench and the mercenary gestured to the east where the tribals began to pull back to reinforce against Thernaxis' suicidal attack.

"Ah, I see," said Actaeon.

"Let's not lose the opportunity," said Trench.

"Agreed. Trench, you take the left. Wave, the right. Lieutenant Hargum will take point. We shall form a wedge of our own and strike eastward," said Actaeon, decisively.

The two mercenaries nodded and rushed off to make it happen.

Yanelle glanced at Actaeon and couldn't contain her smile. "We just may make it out of this, Your Grace."

"We shall see, Yanelle. Especially if you insist on calling me that. I am the least graceful person I know," said Actaeon with a grin.

Yanelle smiled back and gestured to the east, "Hargum awaits your command, Prince E–, er, Actaeon."

"No better time than now, Yanelle," he said. "Charge."

"Charge!" echoed Yanelle.

North and South lines morphed to become Left and Right, and the entire formation became an arrow that drove east. Raedellean arrows were fired en masse to the east to weaken the tribals for the more heavily armored Niwian and Keeper forces to drive through with ease.

As they moved forward and began to pick up pace, Actaeon stole a glance back at Thernaxis' wedge of Niwian Greens as they grew farther away to the northwest. All but the best of his soldiers had fallen under the tribal horde, but he could still see the Lord Protector's blade sweeping bold arcs to and fro as dozens of the enemy were mowed down.

The eastern driving wedge continued to thin the enemy force before them until suddenly they were fleeing away from the allied Redemption soldiers. The Wall Breakers had arrived under Captain Varisk and sent them scattering. Actaeon's wedge began to run then, the volleys of arrows shifting to cover their risky traverse across the battlefield.

Another glance back found the Lord Protector alone and surrounded. Thernaxis' armor was now completely gray with blood and the tip of his sword had broken off in the melee. The shafts of several spears stuck out from the Niwian leader as he continued to fight on. Actaeon imagined he was still smiling his mad smile when the tribals finally knocked him over and fell atop him.

When they reached the eastern flank, they found it intact and strong, led by Lord Arcady, Knight Captain Atreena, and Niwian Red Captain Wronka.

Actaeon allowed some momentary relief to wash over him. That relief was tempered with the knowledge that it was only going to get worse from there. He allowed himself a few long moments to converse with Eisandre over the Thoughtlink Artifact to report their situation.

As the tribal invasion forces began to organize and coalesce against them, the Redemption allied forces conducted an orderly retreat into the Underforest. There they planned to circle north to Redoubt, as Wave had originally suggested.

Eisandre emerged from her tent and shook her head in disgust. They had landed on the Blacksands Beach north of Arena that morning and set up camp. Her boots crunched on the fine black granules as she strode along the beach to approach Companions Itarik and Wayd, the Lady Neryl beside them. A young boy that she didn't recognize stood there as well.

"I gather from your consternation that things on the eastern front are not well," said Itarik.

"There is no eastern front at this point. Actaeon is going to try to reposition the joint forces at Redoubt. It isn't the most direct approach, but hopefully it will be sufficient to break the siege," Eisandre explained.

"And why didn't he wait until we were in position?" asked Neryl Vanora reproachfully.

"He would have waited. The Shorian Warchief, Drystan Beiloff, disobeyed orders and took several warbands north with Thernaxis. Actaeon felt obliged to bring the rest of our warbands to their aid," said the Princess.

"Was that really smart of him?' asked Neryl.

Eisandre stared at the glittering black sand near her boots. The last time she had been here, things had been very different. Actaeon and she had strolled the beach together and sheltered in a nearby rock formation. She had told him that she was Lost, and, amazingly, that hadn't changed how he had felt about her. It seemed like forever ago and just yesterday all at once. In reality, that moment had been only two moons ago – and yet so much had changed. She was a Knight Arbiter then, and he was an Engineer with his workshop and delightful mind full of ideas. She yearned to reach out and touch him – the Thoughtlink Artifact helped, but it wasn't the same.

"Princess?" asked Neryl again. "Do you think that was the right choice?"

"Give her a moment," said Wayd, holding up a hand. "She may be consulting with him now."

Itarik spoke in her stead, "It is likely that we'd have lost all of the warbands if he hadn't brought the remainder to the rescue. If Thernaxis' forces had been defeated, then our Shorian forces would not have been able to mount an offensive alone. Do you agree, Princess Eisandre?"

Eisandre blinked out of her reverie and looked up at Itarik. "Yes. As far as I can discern, Actaeon's actions are the only ones that could have given the eastern offensive a chance to succeed." She glanced at Neryl and hesitated before continuing. "He suspects that the Lord Shore was behind the decision to defy him."

"Of course Arcady was!" said Lady Neryl. "That man thought he was destined to lead Raedelle until you surprised us all. I'm sure he feels great offense at taking orders from the Prince Engineer now. He's likely trying to undermine his position."

"Bastard should've been put to the block before we left. He sent those attackers to kill us on the Wall. I'm sure of it!" said Wayd.

Itarik shot him a look to silence him.

"What? Like you don't feel the same way! Think of all our friends that were killed out there," added Wayd.

"You're unlikely to find any proof in that matter," Lady Neryl said. "The Lord Shore covers his tracks nicely. You'd best listen to the First Companion until you have definitive proof of his actions. Arcady still has much influence in Raedelle, and not just in Shore."

"Who's that?" Eisandre pointed at the young boy. The lad stood there toeing the sand at his feet, trying to remain inconspicuous. He had a mop of brown hair and wore finely made leather armor over his slender frame. He couldn't have been more than thirteen years of age.

"That's your attendant, Princess," said Itarik. "His name is Guybon Hael."

"Why do I require an attendant?" asked Eisandre, looking over the boy as though trying to figure that out.

"To help you put on your armor, clean your sword, and make sure your command tent is properly set up. Among other things," explained Itarik.

"I cannot be trusted to complete these tasks by myself?" asked Eisandre in genuine confusion.

"It's not that you can't be trusted, Your Grace. But you have more important things to attend to," said Wayd.

"What could be more important than ensuring that my weapons and armor are in prime condition for combat?" asked Eisandre. "I've been caring for them for almost my entire life. I have no need of an attendant."

Itarik and Wayd looked at one another, at a loss for words. Guybon looked as though he was close to breaking into tears.

"Well... that's true, but —" Wayd began.

Lady Neryl held up her hand to stop him and stepped forward to slip her hand around Eisandre's arm. "Princess, let us walk along the beach and talk for a while. There are some strange things that people expect of us in these positions we hold. Perhaps I can help to clarify a bit."

Eisandre looked confused and somewhat uncomfortable, but she allowed the Lady of Whiterose to lead her along the beach while the Companions followed at a distance. Lady Neryl cast a smile back at Guybon and winked.

BAD OMENS

"**I** FOR ONE AM GLAD TO have a former Knight Arbiter as part of the force that will break this siege. It will certainly aid my efforts in this matter considerably," said Supreme Captain Amodeus Jarval. He was bedecked in his finest dress uniform – white jacket over navy pants with a crisp white thread running down the outseams. Silvered metal epaulets on his shoulders added to the air of distinction – they matched the curved silver helmet that he wore over sweeping red hair that was tied loosely and hung over one shoulder. The three vertical lines that donated his rank of Supreme Captain were formed with inset jewels into either side of the helm beneath its central ridge.

The Thyrians and Raedelleans of Lakehold were seated at a long table that had been taken off one of the ships and set up on the beach not far from the hide tide line. The Raedelleans were garbed plainly and practically in their thick leather armor and clothing of earthen tones as opposed to the Thyrians, who wore crisp dress uniforms that matched their leader.

Eisandre and Amodeus sat at the center of the table on opposite sides, each flanked by their highest-ranking staff.

"You seem to presume that you have the command of this operation, Supreme Captain," said Lady Neryl, from her spot at the Princess' side.

"Of course I must, given the Princess' inexperience in such matters. Would you suggest otherwise?" asked Jarval, with sincerity.

"Your experience lies at sea, Captain," said Itarik plainly. "Our Princess' experience is on land. We had assumed a joint command, but if you're suggesting otherwise, then Princess Eisandre Rellios Caliburn is the clear choice as we move overland to the Pyramid."

"Do we really want to bear the responsibility of whether this operation is successful or not," asked the Lord Jad Perth from his spot beside Neryl. "I mean, it's all well that we're assisting here, but I don't believe we need to lead the effort."

"An excellent point, Lord Perth," said Captain Jarval. "After all, Pyramid is nestled right beside Thyr. It really is a problem for the central Dominions, is it not? Even if half of them are up north exercising their own ambitions. Perhaps there won't be a place for them in the Pyramid after all this is over."

"There will *always* be a place for every Dominion in the Pyramid, Captain Jarval," said Eisandre. Her tone left no room for argument. "That's the entire purpose of the Pyramid. It's the center of neutrality for all civilized Dominions to gather in pursuit of a peaceful Redemption. This purpose will not change because you say so, nor will Dominions be unwelcome because they refused to help in this time of need."

"I stand corrected, Princess Eisandre," said Jarval with a smile and the slight declination of his head. He ran a hand through the lock of hair hanging over his shoulder.

Eisandre continued then. "I am now the Princess of Raedelle, and Raedelle remains committed to the diplomatic principles of the Pyramid. I will lead my people accordingly. Of course, you are welcome to command your own forces at my side."

The Supreme Captain bristled at her words and delicately cracked the knuckles at the ends of his fingers as he considered his reply.

Captain Xula beat him to it. "There I must disagree with you, Princess Eisandre. We have already heard your account of the Prince Engineer's and Lord Protector's losses on the eastern front. This is precisely why a joint command is ineffective. One commander disagrees with the other, and the forces are split in half and take serious casualties. It's not going to work here either. There should be one allied commander calling the shots."

"Well said, Captain Xula," said Jarval, with a smile.

"Thank you, Captain of All Ships – but you won't like what I'm going to say next." Xula tugged on his mustache and sighed. "Princess Eisandre has an artifact that allows for instantaneous communication with the Prince Engineer, who now basically leads the eastern front. She is a former Knight

Arbiter who knows the Pyramid inside and out – its vulnerabilities and secrets. It only makes sense, Supreme Captain, that Her Grace command the western front – nay! The entire offensive effort."

Amodeus Jarval leaned on the far arm of his chair and gave Xula a look that could strip the bark off a tree. Xula met his gaze solidly and lifted both hands in a shrug.

When the Supreme Captain finally responded, his lips twisted into a smirk. "While I would vastly prefer the glory of commanding this front myself, I cannot deny the points you have just made. Curse your logic, Xula! Here I must embrace humility and realize that I am not the best man for the job. But, Princess Eisandre, you are. The command is yours." He smiled at her across the table and touched the front of his helmet in salute.

Eisandre looked him squarely in the eyes and replied in a most serious tone, "Thank you, but I must point out that I am not the best man for the job. I am a woman."

After an awkward silence everyone at the table burst into laughter at what they took to be an intentional joke. Eisandre smiled as well, though Itarik and Wayd could recognize the confusion in her eyes.

Captain Xula stood up and raised his flask. "Then let us toast the best *woman* for the job. Princess Eisandre Rellios Caliburn, Commander of the Allied Dominion Forces. May you lead us forth to quickly repel this invasion from our beloved city!"

"Hear hear!" said the Supreme Captain. A cheer went up that was quickly drowned out by the crashing of nearby waves.

"There is a messenger from Ajman here to see you, Prince Engineer."

It was Companion Yanelle at the entrance to his tent.

"One moment," replied Actaeon.

I must end our conversation, my love. A messenger from Ajman has arrived in the camp. You have done well, Eis. His thoughts were cast instantaneously to his wife through the Thoughtlink artifacts clipped to their ears.

Go then and speak with the messenger. I hope they bring good news, came her thoughts in reply.

"Send them in, Yanelle," he said.

Yanelle held the tent flap aside and in shuffled a short man wearing brightly striped red and gold pantaloons that he was at risk of disappearing into. He huffed at Yanelle as the top of the tent flap brushed against his carefully arranged pompadour. He cracked his knuckles and made an effort to fix it. Actaeon recognized him immediately as Gaemri Ip Monjata.

"I am *not* a messenger, young lady! As I explained to you previously, I am Portent Gaemri Ip Monjata of the Majestic One, Raja Nadiya Ajman, herself! I have travelled all this way from Adhikara to bring words directly from the mouth of the Raja." Gaemri spat out the words and tugged at the collar of his tunic which clung to his neck in the humid air of the Underforest jungle.

"Then you *do* have a message?" asked the Companion with a barely perceptible smirk.

Gaemri laughed and turned to Actaeon before clearing his throat. "Prince Engineer Actaeon Rellios Caliburn, who surrounds himself with humorous people, the Raja sends her congratulations on your recent marriage and elevation to Raedellean leadership. She is glad to have one so generous as you as a leader in our favorite southern Dominion."

"Is Raedelle not the *only* Dominion south of Adhikara?" muttered Yanelle.

Gaemri shot her a critical look.

"Welcome, Portent Monjata," said Actaeon with a grin at the Companion's words – words which he ignored. "Thank you for coming all this way. The message must be urgent for you to risk coming out into the middle of this conflict. As you can see, we are in a fragile tactical position here. Certainly, you have not come out simply to bring congratulations – though they are appreciated." He gestured to the command table and both men sat down. Actaeon poured them each a cup of warm water from a pitcher on the table.

"Indeed. You are observant as always, Prince Engineer," said Gaemri, gratefully taking a long sip of his water despite the warmth. "She also sends her regrets – not only that she couldn't attend your joining, but also because she is unable to provide Ajmani forces to aid you at this time."

"A fact which disappointed us all, and, along with the absence of Shield, likely resulted in the loss at Glass Spire," said the Prince Engineer. "Knowing the Raja though, I am sure she has good reason."

"Of course the Majestic One has reason. It is this reason she has sent me here to convey to you. As I'm sure you've heard by now, the Czeryn Dominion has been obliterated by some inexplicable cataclysm."

"The blue sphere..." said Actaeon with a frown.

"It has been described as such, yes. After it, the One True Dominion mobilized our armies at once to investigate. Shield also sent their forces into Czeryn. Initial reports indicated that every living Czeryn citizen and slave within a certain radius had disappeared entirely and abruptly. One disturbing account stated that they vanished from within their very clothing, leaving the garments to fall where they stood – a most unpleasant thought."

At the entrance of the tent, Companion Yanelle gasped.

"Was anything else amiss?" asked Actaeon. "Buildings damaged? A crater left behind? Were there survivors?" His mind raced to try and understand the phenomena to the north. It didn't seem possible for what Gaemri was describing to have happened. What sort of technology could cause only biological matter to disappear from within its very clothing? "Did animals and insects survive?"

"Please keep in mind, Prince Engineer, that what we know comes only from scattered reports we have received back from the north. Their veracity stands suspect at this time," Gaemri disclaimed.

Actaeon nodded and sipped his water.

"That said, it sounds as though no physical damage was done to Czeryn. And no, no animals or insects were affected by the cataclysm. The Holds of Ridge, Craters, and Stormstair were affected, with the rumor of a few survivors at the fringes of Stormstair and Craters. Any tales of these survivors appear to be located at the edge of a radius of effect –"

"Centered on where the blue sphere appeared..." said Actaeon, almost at a whisper.

"Indeed." Gaemri paused to sip his water. "And it gets worse."

"Go on."

"Our forces in Czeryn have fallen apart. Many of them have defected and turned. Some of our units have even attacked one another. We fear that Shield has swayed the Kendrans that opposed the Raja to their side in an effort to take all of the Czerynian lands for themselves. There are rumors that Viyudun has returned, having been harbored by Shield for just such an opportunity," said Gaemri, his tone mournful. "Even General Ilugamesh has turned against us. And he was such a firm supporter of the Raja."

"This is all very disturbing to hear, Portent Monjata," said Actaeon as he scratched his right arm through the sleeve of his jacket, his old burn itching as usual when something made him nervous. "You must know though that we cannot provide you with aid at this time. Our forces are committed to breaking the Ruinic tribal siege of Pyramid."

"Oh, of course. Of course! The Raja doesn't mean to imply that she expects you to help with the problems to the north. But the Majestic One understands your situation as well, and furthermore, that you are a friend, and seek to do this thing because you care about the whole of Redemption. She deeply regrets that Ajman cannot help break this siege, and she wants you to know that she feels it is a personal failure of her own. Of course, we have reassured her that such is not the case. Even so, she did not want you to feel that your friends in Ajman had abandoned you. The Raja extends her continued friendship and regret and promises that she will help in the breaking of the siege as soon as she is able."

"Thank you, Portent Monjata. Please let the Raja know that her message is truly appreciated and that we will also endeavor to help her with the Czeryn situation as soon as we are able to. Best of luck to you all in your fight."

"And to you, Prince Engineer," said the Portent as he drew to his feet. "May your battles be swift and effective." The Portent bowed and was gone.

"Are you sure you want to do this, Act?" asked Wave.

Four of them walked through the temporary jungle encampment: Actaeon, Wave, Trench, and Yanelle. The pickets were in place around the resting allied force to keep watch for any tribal attackers. The casualty estimates had come in from the unit commanders earlier. Most of the Keeper 2nd Division and the Blackstone warband had been lost. The Highwater warband had also taken some heavy losses, and the Niwian Greens had all been killed. The surviving forces were heavily beaten and on the retreat in the dangerous and unfamiliar Underforest.

The Underforest was the densest and most mysterious jungle known. At the center of Redemption, it was a circular gulf in the city of the Ancients, nestled between Adhikara and Rust. It was a gap in the ruined structures that was bigger than the entire Raedelle Dominion, with rubble piles that were sunken deep beneath the skeleton of the city. On a good portion of its perimeter, a sheer cliff of fractured structures bordered the Underforest. The cliff face was full of fissures, tunnels, and openings that hid all manner of horrors within. Protected from heavy wind by the deep recess, the tallest trees around Redemption grew there and formed a thick, tangled canopy of branches, vines, and nests that cast an endless night over the Underforest floor. Only occasionally did a ray of sunlight pierce the odd opening above to illuminate the jungle floor far below. A constant cacophony of bird and animal sounds came from overhead that Actaeon found most unnerving.

The Underforest was also the home of the strange Kainai people, or the Children, as many of the civilized Dominions called them. Little was known about them other than they all appeared to be youthful and would disappear into the thick jungle quickly if spotted. They were known to avoid conflict and contact both. In the middle of the Underforest was an Ancient structure known as Temple. The Children allowed the Czeryn to maintain a small base there in exchange for the protection of their Underforest from the other Dominions. It was uncertain how that arrangement had been made, but old legends told of a Czeryn Warlord that took a Kainai as his slave and, after falling in love with her, was convinced to return her to the Underforest and protect all the Children. Actaeon wondered how that arrangement would continue after what happened up north.

"Of course I do not *want* to do this, Wave. But the Warchief's actions have left me with no choice. His disobedience cost many lives," explained Actaeon.

"Yer doing the right thing, Act," said Trench. "If ya don't punish him for it, you'll just get more and more. After all, you're new to this too, so you can't let people under you think such behavior will be tolerated."

Actaeon sighed and drew to a stop in front of Warchief Drystan Beiloff's tent. He lifted his halberd in both hands and steeled himself for the actions to come. "I wish I had a better weapon for this," he said.

"A quick swipe across the front of the neck is all it'll take," said Trench. "Don't sweat it – if ya mess up, Wave and I'll finish it for ya."

Wave looked up at Actaeon and nodded grimly before drawing his flamberge rapier.

Trench unslung his maul from his back and the pair of mercenaries started forward toward the closed flap of the tent.

Companion Yanelle maintained her position by Actaeon's side.

Trench reached forward to pull the flap aside, but before he could, it was thrown open and Lord Gunther Arcady emerged.

"Get that damned sword out of my face," Arcady snapped at Wave as he strode past the pair of mercenaries. "He's gone, Actaeon – I've taken care of it." The Lord Shore pulled his two black leather gauntlets free from his hands and tucked them neatly in his sword belt.

"What do you mean, you have taken care of it?" asked Actaeon, planting his halberd firmly in the ground beside him.

"The Warchief of Shore is the Lord Shore's responsibility, and we cannot have him disobeying either my *or* your orders. I will not have it," said Arcady firmly. "We can appoint a new Warchief in due time."

"So what of it, Gunther? Where is he?" demanded Wave.

Arcady cast Wave an idle look over his shoulder. "He's been dismissed. I've also taken the liberty to tell him not to return to Raedelle. The Princess can make her own decision regarding that in time, but he's no longer welcome in Shore."

"Are you kidding me?" growled Trench. "He should've been executed for what he did!"

Arcady laughed and ran a hand through his slick black hair that had some traces of white. "Typical mercenaries that want to solve everything with the point of a dagger. There are more civilized ways to deal with disobedience than to fill all our tankards with blood. Of course, I wouldn't expect a brute like *you* to understand that."

"It's wartime and he disobeyed his direct commander. You know as well as we do what the recourse is," growled Trench before he spat on the ground between them. "You just wanted to save your friend. Typical gods-damned politicians. You'd know a thing or two about tankards of blood, since all of your drinks are bought with the blood of better men."

"Gentlemen," said Actaeon before anyone else could speak. "While this is unfortunate, it strikes me that it is already done. Let us not argue about it. Honestly, part of me is glad that I need not spill his blood today. Let the Conclave meet after the war is over to decide his fate. As for you, Lord Arcady, know that I will hold you personally responsible for any overt acts of disobedience among the Blackstone or Highwater warbands – or what remains of them. You had best make sure they know that."

Arcady inclined his head at the order, his burning hazel eyes meeting Actaeon's piercing emerald gaze as he replied. "If you insist. When I meet with them, I will also assess the group that remains and appoint the best of them as the new Warchief."

"Oh no, that will not be necessary," said Actaeon with a grin. "I have already selected the new Warchief. Varisk Conmara will fill that role quite well."

"Is that... really the best choice?" asked Arcady, his jaw dropping open.

"The Fallen know it is," came Actaeon's immediate reply. "He brought the Princess and I out of danger on the Wall and he exercised sound judgment in the handling of the entire situation. I trust him completely in this new role."

Arcady clamped his jaw shut and nodded before striding off.

When he was out of earshot, Wave laughed. "Damn, I was hoping his jaw would fall off completely."

Trench chuckled as well and slapped Actaeon on the back. "Nicely played, Act. If the boss keeps it up, Wave, it just may."

Actaeon grinned at them. "Shall we go tell the new Warchief the news?"

87 A.R., the 45th day of Rainbreak

FOOTHOLD

EISANDRE TUGGED HER SWORD FREE of the dying Ruinic tribal and raised it high for the next attacker. That attack did not come, and the dozen or so tribals before her knelt and laid down their spears, then raising their hands into the air.

"A prudent decision," she said. The greatsword Caliburn still hung from the Princess' back as she preferred to use her trusted Arbiter broadsword in battle

A rapid series of twangs sounded beside her, and the surrendered tribals fell dead, neatly skewered by bolts from the Thyrian Flashbolt Marine triple crossbows.

Eisandre spun to look at the marines beside her, led by Major Ainhara Craft. The Major's hair was cut short like the Princess' own, only it was the same white as the Thyrian uniforms, a testament to her age. The white uniforms of the Thyrians were mottled with red splatters from the blood of battle.

"They had surrendered," snapped Eisandre, eyeing the Major and the other marines bitterly as they reloaded their crossbows.

"Yes," replied Craft. "But we have no resources to spare for prisoners. They'd have just been released to join their brethren and fight another day."

"You're right, Major. And we would have fought them again if necessary, but it might not have been necessary. Mercy in battle is what separates us from the barbarism of the tribals. It also serves as an example to the survivors of how to behave in a more civilized manner. Do not do that again," warned Eisandre sternly. A part of her was relieved at the Major's actions though – especially after another glance around at the absolute slaughter of the refugee camp.

"As you wish, Your Grace," said the Major sheepishly as she reloaded the final bolt into place in her triple crossbow.

Companion Wayd arrived at her side then, trailed by Guybon Hael, the young attendant. "Sorry, Princess. We got cut off from you by their last forward drive. Is everything okay?"

Eisandre offered Wayd a blank look before turning about and striding past the fallen tribals. She watched the retreating enemy force as they ran back toward the Pyramid for a long time. Then she closed her eyes.

They stood at the fringes of the Ajman refugee camp that Actaeon had designed for the Adhikarans who had been pushed from their homes during the flooding earlier that cycle. There hadn't been any left alive. The images all came rushing back to Eisandre: the Ajmani that had been pinned by spears to the ground and left to die in the latrine trenches, the ones that had been barricaded inside the large community hall and burned to death as they pounded at the door to be let out, and the large fires in the center of the camp that had scorched human bones scattered about them and little more. The thoughts threatened to overwhelm her. She shuddered where she stood.

How can people do such things? She aimed the desperate thought at Actaeon, seeking any sort of understanding.

They are like animals that would devour another of their kind's young. Willing to destroy everything to gain whatever resources they seek. Opportunistic and brutal – they were not taught the value of human life as we were. It is up to us to teach them, if... His thoughts trailed off.

If we can forgive them, she finished.

Exactly.

From behind her came a muffled yell and she turned to watch as Captain Xula and the Supreme Captain of Thyr tipped over a barrel near the center of the ruined camp. The muffled shouting continued as Supreme Captain Jarval used the hilt of his sabre to knock loose the top ring of the barrel. Xula then stuck the point of his sabre into the lid and used his blade to yank it free.

Out stumbled a person, covered in what appeared to be blood. The red liquid rushed out from the barrel to soak the ground around them.

Eisandre found herself walking in that direction in quiet horror.

The man sputtered and coughed up more blood before the two Thyrians helped him to his feet.

It was only once Eisandre was just a handful of paces away that she realized the man wasn't covered in blood, but, in fact, wine. The rich, sweet smell was unmistakable.

"Oh unholy times of wretch and misery! Deliver me from this, oh Keeper of Light!" the man pleaded. The two Captains released him and he fell to his knees to clasp frail hands before him.

"What is your name?" asked Supreme Captain Jarval.

"Infernal darkness begone now," said the old man, rivulets of red wine running down from the soaked scraggles of hair that remained on his head. He lifted his hands in the air as if to ward away the darkness he spoke of.

Xula nudged him impatiently with a boot. "Speak, old man. You're in the presence of the Supreme Captain of Thyr!"

"Phyrius Ricter," said Eisandre. "First of the First of the Waiting Ones."

The two Captains looked up at her in surprise.

Quite some time ago, when Actaeon had gone in search of what he thought was a mechanical man that he'd spotted from the pinnacle of Pyramid, he'd instead found a large glowing statue that looked strangely similar to Trench. Trench and Wave had transported the artifact back to the workshop. There, Phyrius Ricter noticed it and began to hold a vigil over it. Others came to follow and there was soon a small cult worshipping the statue. It felt like a lifetime ago, but it was only an arc of the moon past.

Phyrius rubbed his eyes with both fists as though he was trying to wipe away a mirage. "You are... you are the Arbiter..." For a moment he was at a loss of words, but then he finally managed. "A friend of the Finder of the Keeper of Light, and the Bringers as well.

"You speak to the Princess of Raedelle," snapped Xula. "Address Her Grace by her title."

Eisandre held up a hand to stall Xula and fell to one knee to speak to Phyrius at his level. "What happened to you, Phyrius? You can tell me."

The old man's lip quivered, and he balled his hands into tight fists. "The coming was foretold. The Keeper of Light gave us warning. And so, we fled to the Boneyards to weather the storm. Only many here did not listen. Some did heed the wisdom of the Keeper of Light to seek refuge with us, but many more did not. And so, one last time did I return to urge them to change their minds and to listen to the Great Keeper's decree." Phyrius shook bodily then and was unable to go on.

Harvand Xula squatted down and put a steadying hand on the old man's shoulder. "Continue. Please."

The Captain's hand helped Phyrius regain his composure and he looked back up at Eisandre. "The demons came then – the demons of the jungle. They rained fire and death down upon us. Those that they did not burn and massacre, they... devoured. The demons made me watch it all. I... I amused them – I think. Once they were done toying with me, the laughter as they locked me within the darkness – it will ever haunt my dreams. May the Keeper of Light sanctify my being against such evil." Phyrius had squeezed his eyes shut again and clasped his hands before him in supplication.

Xula patted his arm and kissed the old man's temple. "Don't worry. We're on our way to make them pay for what they did here."

"May the blessings of the Keeper of Light be with you," said Phyrius.

Eisandre stood and walked several paces away. Her homeland of Raedelle had long suffered tribal incursions, but this was a level of brutality that she had never heard of. It didn't make sense that the tribals would commit such wholesale slaughter with civilians. There was something deeply wrong here.

The Supreme Captain joined her, looking toward the Pyramid – its glass pinnacle gleaming in the sunlight. "Only those too stubborn to leave were killed."

"I am glad some were able to reach safety. But what happened here remains a tragedy," she said, staring off into the distance.

"Victims of their own stubbornness. It was a refugee camp – they should have abandoned it when they had to. How important could it have been?" said Amodeus, doffing his helmet.

"They built this place with their own hands after losing their homes to the Adhikaran floods," she explained. "I imagine it meant a great deal. They didn't want to lose everything again."

"Well, they didn't change that, did they?" he responded, but his voice was sad. He changed the subject then. "We have gained a foothold here, Princess. Your charge was most impressive. They were routed before they could organize any defense. Our next move should be to cut off their supply lines to the north."

"The Boneyards cannot be held by a military force. It would not be a wise direction," said Eisandre.

"We don't have to hold it – just disrupt it. Let's see what the others advise," he suggested.

"Yes," she agreed.

Arrows zipped down the corridor over Knight Arbiter Kylor sof Haringar's head as he manned the first barrier in the Pyramid's sloping eastern tunnel. It was actually the third barrier, but the besieging tribals had long broken through the first two and overrun those there.

The defenders only used arrows that they retrieved intact after raids – their own supply had long run out. In fact, supplies of all kinds were in danger of running low, and Sentinel Arbiter Phragus sof Luep had implemented strict rationing to maximize their chances of survival until help could arrive. Many of the surviving nobles had grumbled about the rationing, but it had been Phragus that had rallied the Arbiters in the Mirrorholds to push back the tribal onslaught and save them in the first place, and so, they were willing to follow his direction – for the moment.

After the initial invasion nineteen days ago, Technical Knight Arbiter Corvin sof Haringar had quickly devised the idea of assembling the barriers made from dismantled furniture from the various Dominional Holds. Each barrier had holes for spears and arrows and ladders to climb to the top and dump boiling water from the baths atop their attackers. Originally, there had been seven barriers in total, each one with a central door from which pins could be pulled if the barrier before it had fallen in order to drop a weighted barricade down. Five barriers remained. Corvin had cursed when the first of the barriers had fallen and the tribals were able to use it to their own strategic advantage.

The defenders still had control of the baths, which were a source of water for hydration and the cleansing of wounds. A makeshift hospital for the wounded had been set up in the vacant Czerynian hold, under the direction of the Althean Healer Seraeta and a few of the other surviving Altheans. Most of the order of healers had been slaughtered in the initial invasion surge.

Thankfully, they also had control of the Terrace of the Stars, a gigantic, open-air garden that jutted from the eastern face of the Pyramid. It quickly became their major salvation as every known type of plant life in Redemption was grown there and tended by the Altheans. One of the

Terrace's tenders, Shard, was an herbalist that became essential in coming up with a feasible ration plan.

"Eyes forward defenders! Here comes the next wave!" shouted the Sentinel Arbiter.

Kylor snapped out of his reverie and pulled his dark goggles down to protect his milky-white eyes. When the wall shuddered, he thrust the spear in his hands forward and felt it hit home into the body of a tribal on the far side of the barrier. He withdrew the spear and stuck it through the adjacent hole.

Two young men, Torot vor Steubick, the one-handed Niwian Lord, and Inditrovalis Jem, the Adept Loresworn, arrived with a pot of boiling water. Since Inditrovalis had both hands, he had the honor of carrying it up the ladder to dump on the attackers. The screams from the other side told him that he'd hit home.

"Take that, you p-kin bastards!" shouted Torot, raising the stump of his arm into the air.

"That's no way for a Lord to speak," said Inditrovalis with a condescending smirk. Just then the entire barrier shook and threw the Loresworn like a ragdoll into his Niwian friend.

A spear was thrust through the barrier and pierced the chest of the Arbiter beside Kylor. The young man turned to face him with a look of horror – blood running down his chin.

"Battering ram," Kylor announced, in his level, clear voice. He raised the whistle to his lips and blew three long tones.

Knight Arbiters Garth sof Belidur and Trello sof Allyk rushed forward from the next barrier back. They both fired several arrows through the holes in the wall and followed it up with further spear thrusts.

Behind them came the giant Tarcy Hael, the Steward of the Raedellean Embassy, Saint Torin's Hold. She pulled a huge ruinblade from her back – it was a large, sharpened shard of metal from the ruins with leather wrapped around its base to use as a handle. With practiced ease, she thrust the weapon forward through the wall to slay the last of the ram-bearers. The thump that sounded told them that the latest onslaught had been prevented – the ram falling to the floor.

Tarcy pulled free the locking bar and lifted the barrier's central door while Garth and Trello dragged over the big log that the tribals were using as a battering ram.

"Another one for our collection," said Garth with a satisfied smile.

Tarcy released the door to slam against the floor and scowled at him. "An' how many more'll come? We'd best make plans ta 'scape. It'll not be long before they best us 'ere."

"There is no escape for us," said Trello. The junior Arbiter threw his spear onto the corridor floor, as if to make the point. "Didn't you listen to the Sentinel Arbiter? We're cut off from the tunnels to Redoubt, and you well remember what happened to those we lowered down to the Open Markets. Don't be daft!"

Early after the invasion had begun, the survivors had lowered evacuees on makeshift ropes down the side of the Pyramid from the Terrace of the Stars to the Open Markets below. Those above had watched as Ruinic tribals arrived in the marketplace to hack apart the evacuees.

"Watch yourself, Knight Arbiter Trello," spoke Kylor sharply. "Steward Hael is our steadfast ally in this endeavor. She is correct — if we can find a means for escape for the remaining survivors, then we shall, but until then, we shall continue to survive here."

"Apologies Knight Arbiter Kylor, and Steward Hael," said Trello, his face reddening as his gaze fell to the floor.

"Yer fergiven," said Tarcy as she narrowed her eyes upon the junior Arbiter. "Jes go an' get that arrow taken care of."

Trello looked at her in surprise and felt his torso, finding an arrow lodged in his shoulder. "Ah, um... thank you, Lady Hael. I'll do just that." He rushed off toward the Czerynian embassy.

Kylor and Tarcy exchanged an amused look as the young Arbiter ran off.

"Alright, lancers! Energize!" cried Lauryn.

Behind her stood the Lady Fletcher with her arms folded. Quronos was beside her, looking on impassively.

Six select members of the Western Rim warband were positioned at the edge of a small copse of trees outside of Travail with the long metal poles held in an upright position. Beside them, Companion Brigert held another of the artifacts. They each placed their hands around the two separate panels that activated the lances and they crackled to life, sending bright orange beams of light almost too bright to look at into the air up to four times the height of their operators.

The lances had been one of the more promising artifacts they had located within Travail. The first one activated had punched a hole into the adjacent room and nearly cut Brigert in half. Now it was time to see if they could be used in a more organized manner.

"Right to left, sweep!" called out Lauryn, wrinkling her nose at the smell of ozone permeating the air.

The lancers lowered their weapons in unison and swept them as directed, the projected beams of light cutting a swath through the small trees before them. Delle Fletcher nodded her approval.

"Left to right, sweep!" Lauryn ordered, and the warbanders stepped forward as a unit. Crackling beams of light swept a clean arc that sliced through the thick trunks of several trees in an instant, sending them tumbling down with thuds that shook the ground.

"Lancers, rest!" she called, and the lance beams all returned to their original vertical state.

"Deenergize," said Lauryn with a shy smile at the Raedellean Lady behind her.

"Well, well, Lauryn – it seems your experiment is a success. These artifacts should be useful in the coming ba-" Lady Fletcher was interrupted by a crash as another tree fell.

Lauryn spun to face the lancers again and frowned. Companion Brigert was advancing forward into the woods, sweeping his lance from side to side in graceful, sweeping arcs as he cut a path into the copse.

"Please deenergize!" called out Lauryn, but the crashing of trees choked out the sound of her words.

"Companion Brigert, you have been ordered to shut that thing off!" called out Delle Fletcher with surprising volume.

"I've gotta see what this thing can do," said the stocky Companion over his shoulder. He stepped forward and swung the lance crosswise again.

The shockwave from the explosion that followed knocked everyone from their feet and left their ears ringing.

Lauryn rolled to her side and stood up. Dust, debris, and smoke obscured her vision as she rushed forward and ran smack into something hard and silver – Quronos. She hit him hard and fell back, but he caught her easily and said something that she couldn't hear. He pointed over her shoulder.

She turned in that direction and ran forward. As she reached the fallen trees, the dust began to settle and revealed that the entire copse of trees had been leveled. Several broken fragments and stumps were on fire.

Upon seeing the crater in the center of the disaster, she felt a scream tear from her throat that went unheard. She fell to her knees, her face wet with tears as she sobbed uncontrollably.

This had been her experiment – *her* fault. She killed someone, someone innocent. Any other time she'd had to kill, her hand had been forced. The Lady Lartigan as she was about to murder Actaeon in the Felmere, or all the tribals during the Battle of the Wall. Those people had been trying to kill her or someone she cared about. The only logical choice was to fight to defend her friends. But this man... this Companion Brigert, he hadn't done anything wrong – hadn't forced her hand. No, he was just helping her test this new artifact, and her lack of preparation had killed him. If only she had done more testing before these trials, then she might have identified a problem and avoided this tragedy. She sobbed again, ears ringing painfully. What would Actaeon think?

A strong hand fell on her shoulder and squeezed. "Get up," said a firm voice.

She looked up to see Lady Fletcher beside her.

"Get up," said the Lady again, her voice cutting through the ringing in Lauryn's ears. "Yes, you killed that man, but he also didn't listen. Give him honor now by standing up and addressing the others. His death will not be for nothing, not while I am here."

Lauryn stood, her hands shaking. "But, Act would –"

"The Prince Engineer would continue with the experiment. It is for the greater good of our entire civilization. That's what he'd want you to do as well. You're his apprentice, aren't you? Didn't he teach you that? Now wipe those tears from your cheeks and get back to work! You have people still breathing that are counting on you. Let the Fallen rest," said the Lady harshly.

Lauryn had a sudden urge to strike the Lady, but as she balled her hands into tight fists the logic of her words sank in, and she nodded. "Aye, Lady." She started toward the warbanders, but paused to turn again. "And thank you."

Delle Fletcher offered her a toothy smile. "Anytime you need me, young one."

The warbanders were gathered loosely at the end of the former copse, a distance away from their lances, which were scattered where they had fallen. Lauryn picked up one of the light lances and hefted it – it really was quite heavy.

As she approached, they flinched, expecting it to explode again. "Who's the senior warbander here?" she asked.

"I am," said a muscular older man with a full head of gray hair. "Name's Brewer, Lady."

"I'm not a Lady – I'm just Lauryn of Lakehold," she said. "And you six are, um... Lauryn's Light Lancers. I know what you're thinking, and yes, what just happened was horrible. But no, I'm not going to let that happen to you. I'm going to train and figure out these artifacts right alongside you. We have to do this – our fellow Raedelleans are counting on us. By the Fallen, all Redemption is!"

Brewer and the others exchanged looks before he turned to regard her. "Okay, Lauryn. We'll do this with you, but I don't trust these artifacts. What's to stop them from doing that again?"

"We're going to figure out every aspect of them, and safely. Then once we understand them completely, we can meet up with the rest of our warbands to aid their fight. Companion Brigert took a risk when he pushed the boundaries of the experiment – we will not be taking unnecessary risks again," she explained.

Brewer nodded, but still didn't seem completely convinced. "Okay, good. I'm not sure how you're gonna do that, but if you can, we'll be behind you."

The others nodded as well and took turns introducing themselves. All were members of the Western Rim warband. There was Hake Rim, a heavily muscular man not quite as tall as Trench, the young twin sisters with auburn hair, Phalto and Phelto, Tacia Fleg, a miserable-looking middle-aged woman with an ugly scar on her cheek, and short, black-haired Varse Perialt, the son of a well-off merchant back on Western Rim, a fact he was certain to share during his introduction.

"Well then, what are we waiting for? Get your weapons, lancers!" Lauryn said with a grin. She still felt sick inside, but it felt good to be doing something.

Her squad of lancers hopped to action and retrieved their weapons.

Just then Jey Vellit, the Captain of Western Rim's warband, approached from Travail, "I have bad news."

"In addition to what just happened?" asked Lauryn, incredulous.

"What just happened?" asked Captain Vellit, looking past her to the devastation with curiosity.

"Companion Brigert didn't listen to instruction and there was an unfortunate accident," replied Delle Fletcher, before Lauryn could answer. "What bad news do you bring?"

Captain Vellit frowned and toed the ground with his boot. "We've lost your nephew, Lady. He ventured into the Western Wing. He was instructed not to, but… I will take full responsibility for his loss."

Delle Fletcher's eyes went dark, and she stared past the Captain at the building of the Ancients.

Lauryn reached up to place a hand on the Lady's shoulder, but Delle slapped it away and stormed off back toward Travail.

Captain Vellit offered Lauryn a sad look.

"I'm going to need some of your warbanders," said Lauryn.

The Captain just nodded.

You have done well to gain a foothold at the western side of Pyramid, thought Actaeon from his hammock. He stared up at the peak of his command tent, arms folded behind his head.

We didn't do well enough. We should have gotten there sooner. If we had, then all those people —

You know not the truth of that, thought Actaeon, interjecting his own thoughts against Eisandre's. *The parlay at Blacksands was essential. You have secured a position of leadership that we will need going forward in this conflict. And your interdominional standing will also serve to strengthen your position back home*, he explained. *These things take time.*

I'm sorry, Act, thought Eisandre, and he could feel the strong sense of sorrow emanating from her through the Thoughtlink artifact.

I know that you are. But you did everything you could to try and save those refugees.

That's not what I mean, Eisandre thought as she paced about furiously in her own command tent. Her anxiety was palpable to him through the artifact. *I am very sorry for them, but I am also sorry for what this has done to you. I know that you'd prefer a thousand times over to be in your workshop, inventing new marvels and solving the problems of the world with your beautiful mind. But, instead, you married me, and then you were immediately forced to lead efforts in this nightmare of a war. We don't even get to be together*

Actaeon paused to consider the alternative, and when he grinned, she could feel his amusement through the artifact. *Had I remained in my workshop to continue my work, the invasion would still have come, and I would have perished when the Outskirts were overrun. You would not have had my help either, in the reclaiming of your brother's sword as the sign of your right to rule Raedelle. No, my place is here, for better or ill. In the eventuality you describe, we both fail, and we both likely die. It was hardly a choice anyway – I love you too much, Eis.*

Besides, he continued. *Unfamiliar as it may be to serve as a battlefield commander, this is the place where I can solve the problems of the world. We break this siege, bring the Dominions together, and create a safe place for our childrens' future – one where I can sit in my workshop and invent to my heart's desire, with you at my side.*

I'm not sure things will ever be so simple, Eisandre thought. She wanted to reach out and touch his cheek. He felt the longing and sent reciprocal feelings back through the Thoughtlink. *I fear we may always be fighting to create or maintain a safe place.*

Nothing worth doing is ever easy.

You've said that to me before. She smiled.

It is truth. Besides, it would be a boring world in which there were no problems to solve, no challenges to overcome, he thought with another grin that brought Eisandre hope.

It always amazes me how you can remain so positive in even the darkest of times, she thought.

Actaeon smiled up at the ceiling of his command tent. *So long as the world has people like you in it, I shall have reason to smile and reason to keep trying in everything I do.*

Eisandre paused her pacing and closed her hand around the pommel of her sword. *Then we will keep striving to create that safer world. I want you to be happy again, with time and peace enough to invent new creations that will help to make the world even better.*

Of this I have no doubt, he thought. *But do not just do it for me. Your people are relying on you, and we must do this thing together, for all of them.*

We will try.

And we will succeed.

You cannot know that, but I hope we do.

Trench tells me there's to be an attack soon. I must go prepare. Actaeon sat up in the hammock and swung his feet over the side, finding the ground with some difficulty. A third rope to stabilize the hammock's lateral movement would be a worthwhile addition, he considered.

Always the Engineer. Eisandre smiled. *Go prepare, my Actaeon. I'm glad you are with Trench and Wave – their experience in this situation is invaluable.*

Of course, my love, he assured. *Without their wisdom in battle and conflict, I should certainly have been killed ten times over.*

THE UNDERFOREST

RENCH THREW BACK THE FLAP of the command tent and hunched over to shuffle inside.

"We've gotta raise this damned tent higher, Act," the giant growled as he stomped over to the standing war table.

Wave trailed close behind. "If you step any harder, you'll dig your namesake and that problem'll soon be behind you."

Gathered around it were the Prince Engineer, Companion Yanelle, Warchief Varisk, the Lord Shore, Voice Ithelie, Captain Wronka – the de facto leader of the Niwians in Thernaxis' stead, and Knight Captain Atreena of the Keepers.

Actaeon grinned at his man-at-arms. "There are many things I aim to improve, Trench. I shall add that to the list. At this moment, however, I am more concerned with the pressing matters of the tribals I hear are ready to attack us at any moment."

"He means he wants a report," said Atreena dryly.

"Trust me, lass, this ain't my first time in a battle council," snapped Trench, his deep scar turning a deeper red.

"Unfortunately," muttered Arcady.

"Care to say that louder?" asked Wave, from his friend's side. His hand fell casually to the hilt of his rapier.

"I prefer not to cross swords with the handicapped," said Arcady, taking a jab at Wave's missing eye without even deigning to look at the mercenary.

Actaeon held up a hand before Wave could respond. "Gentlemen, there will be none of this while I am in command. If you wish to join former Warchief Beiloff as he wanders alone through the Underforest, then please do continue."

The Prince Engineer waited, casting a pointed stare that cycled between Wave and Arcady.

"Sorry, boss," said Wave, leaning forward to rest both palms on the table.

Actaeon shifted his emerald gaze to the Lord Shore alone.

"If you want me to keep the truth to myself, I shall, Your Grace," said Arcady with a smile that morphed into a sneer.

The Prince Engineer uncharacteristically kept his silence and began to strum his fingers on the table impatiently. He kept his intense gaze on the Lord Shore.

"Are you —"

"Lord Shore, please," said Warchief Varisk, interrupting Arcady.

Arcady searched around the table for support from the others and received none. He scowled and then smiled broadly, stepping back to trace a deep bow. "You have my apology, Prince Engineer. I'll not do it again."

Actaeon nodded. "Keep such thoughts to yourself and stay on task. I want to hear your truthful thoughts, Lord Arcady — I want to hear everyone's opinion. If we are to survive this, we must all work together and pool our ideas. We are a team in this endeavor, and insults to your fellows will not be tolerated. Once this conflict is over, you may return to disparaging one another. It is my hope that by then you will learn that each of you has value to our civilized city. Consider my words and let us move on. Trench — your report?"

The giant smiled and nodded. He took a knee beside the table, which put him at a height even with Wave's. "Our perimeter scouts've detected movement on three sides of us, but no regular distribution of forces. A few skirmishes with the tribals have forced our scouts to relocate closer and closer to this camp — which means we're getting less information than we need on movements. One thing's clear though, they're looking to close a noose around us, and it won't be long before it is cinched up tight."

"Sounds as though we had better be proactive in our movements then," said Actaeon. "Suggestions?"

Warchief Varisk piped up first, "The way to the northeast still lies open to us. We must move quickly in that direction. We can send advance scouts forward to find a more defensible location to take on the tribals."

"Deeper into the Underforest?!" exclaimed Captain Wronka. "We are already on terrain that gives our enemy the clear advantage. To commit us farther is madness!"

"Raedelle is more than prepared to fight in the jungle," said Yanelle. "It is something our warbands excel at."

"Perhaps they do, but this jungle terrain is not suitable for the Niwians or my Knights," said Atreena. "So, you're reducing the effectiveness of our force by half if we try to fight pitched battles in the jungle. We need to find some structure to use to our advantage."

"But there is nothing here!" exclaimed Wronka, desperation in his voice. "We should flee south to Adhikara and regroup. The Raja's Portent met with you, did he not, Prince Engineer? If there is any friendship there, then they must allow us to regroup."

"There is something here..." said Ithelie, trailing off. She stood beside Actaeon, looking out of place at the war council – the green robes of her spiritual station at odds with the heavy arms and armor of the others.

"What? There's nothing but jungle in this place," muttered the Niwian Captain, shaking his head.

"Temple..." said Actaeon, with a grin.

"You cannot be serious!" said Arcady. "It's all the way to the northeast of the Underforest."

"No, it makes sense, Gunther," said Wave. He met the Lord's skeptical look with his single eye. "Just hear me out. In pursuing us farther into the Underforest, the tribal forces around Pyramid will be weakened, allowing the Princess to secure a better foothold. We can fight a battle on our terms at Temple and when we weaken them enough, we can work our way along the Rust superstructure to escape to the west."

"You're dead set on the idea of getting to Redoubt," said Arcady, amused.

"Let's not forget that Temple belongs to the Czerynians," said Varisk. "The Children gave it to them as a thanks for Czeryn serving as their Protectors."

"If there's even a Czeryn any longer," said Trench.

"I quite like the idea of reaching Temple," said Actaeon. "Wave makes an excellent point. Separating the Ruinic tribal forces will provide us with an advantage that we need. And any Czerynian forces hiding there may be happy to join our quest. The option of moving south to Adhikara is risky, because without the Ajman army, we may be putting the civilian population at risk. So, we push to the northeast as the Warchief suggests in order to reach a defensible structure that will allow the Niwian and Keeper forces to be more effective. Thoughts on this?"

"Our troops will be happier with a building to garrison – even a strange one such as Temple," said Captain Wronka.

"Great evil lies within that structure, but the wisdom of using it for our strategic benefit, albeit temporarily, is undeniable," said Knight Captain Atreena.

"I suppose we could try it," agreed Arcady.

"It is a sound plan, Your Grace," said the Warchief.

"Fallen watch over us," said Trench.

"I'll be the one to say prayers, thank you," said Ithelie, firing a scolding look across the table at the giant. She raised her hands toward the roof of the tent and spoke. "May the Fallen guide us in our quest. Be with this force as we march onward to preserve the freedom and civility of this land. Grant us wisdom to make the right choices. Grant us calm of mind and steady hand. Grant us courage in the face of death. May our path be the one to victory."

"Well said, Voice," said Actaeon. "Let us make the preparations then to move out."

Later that day, the allied forces marched in a northeasterly direction down three parallel valleys that were carved into the jungle landscape, as though cut by some massive creature's claws. They marched straight into a trap.

Tribals rushed down the embankments on either side to attack the divided forces, inflicting heavy casualties. The commanders rushed to rally their troops as arrows rained down upon them.

"By the Fallen! This is how they hunt. Several parties push their prey into a trap. Damn, we should've known better," said Trench. A tribal broke past the line and rushed toward the giant mercenary, only to have his ribcage obliterated by the spike of the giant's maul.

"Recommendations, Trench?" asked the Prince Engineer beside him.

"We'd best beat an organized retreat. This isn't the terrain we want to fight them on – they've had time to familiarize with it, and we're caught in a tightening noose now," explained the giant before driving a finishing blow down upon the fallen warrior's face.

"Yes, but which direction?" asked Actaeon.

"There's the rub," said Trench with a frown. "We don't know the best option down here. Can't see a damned thing."

"And if he can't see a damned thing, the rest of us are hopeless," said Wave, his blades whizzing to and fro to fell another pair of tribals that had leapt clear over the line of soldiers before them.

"Then we should take that ridge there." Actaeon pointed at the rise to the immediate west. "It is clear, and we can gain a vantage there. Have one of the camp parties follow us up there – we can use the supplies to construct a watchtower."

"A watchtower? While we're surrounded on all sides by attackers?" exclaimed Wave. "No, ya know what, boss? I know better than to ask questions."

"You heard the Prince Engineer!" bellowed Trench. "We take the ridge! Rally to us!"

The giant raised his wicked maul high and charged up the hill past the line of Niwian defenders. One of the Ruinic tribals thrust a spear toward his belly, but Trench slapped it out of the way, grabbed the man by the neck, and held him aloft as he charged upward, using his enemy's body to shield himself from a rain of spears and arrows while he obliterated anyone that got near with his maul.

The line of defenders hesitated until Actaeon followed the big man, Wave and Yanelle to either side of him. The Niwian Purples and the heavily armored knights of the Keeper 2nd Division charged up the incline after the giant.

Both units had trouble maintaining their line in the charge and Actaeon watched as several groups of soldiers were separated from the others and downed by Ruinic tribal spears that quickly located and exploited gaps in plate armor and mail. The Eastern Rim warband rushed to fill in the gaps as they opened.

Actaeon lowered his own halberd before him and raced steadily forward after Trench. Luckily, the angry giant's charge had created a panic in the tribal ranks and many of their numbers fled before him or scattered to the flanks. When an errant warrior came screaming down to attack, Companion

Yanelle's spear quickly pushed the enemy's aside before sweeping across the warrior's throat.

Trench reached the summit of the ridge and roared at the Ruinic warriors that met him there. He casually tossed the arrow-bristled body of the now very dead tribal at them, sending them tumbling over the far side of the slope. More of the enemy rushed forward to attack him from both sides along the narrow rise.

Wave reached his friend's side in time to meet one of the groups while Trench met the other. The juxtaposition of their fighting styles was always amazing to Actaeon.

Wave weaved effortlessly between tribal spears as his blades swept in blurred arcs around him, dropping enemies as he advanced. The dead crumpled to the ground as he passed in a flurry of death.

Trench met his own attackers with frightening furiosity. A roar halted their charge, and he knocked their spearheads aside before swinging his heavy maul so hard that the first warrior's head exploded in a splash of red. A second tribal's ribcage folded around the head of the maul and his body continued sideways to send another three of the enemy flying. Trench swung the maul back in the other direction, which sent the body of the second warrior flying into another row of Ruinic tribals.

The Niwians and Keepers began to arrive atop the ridge to help Trench and Wave push the tribals back. Allied forces from the valley on the other side of the rise had noticed the advance and fought their way up the embankment, causing the tribal ranks to break into disarray as they fled.

"Still can't see anything, Your Grace," said Yanelle.

"We have to get above the underbrush. Have Captain Mirvea bring the Eastern Rim's supplies here so we can build the watchtower." Actaeon placed his hand against the trunk of a tree, relieved that the tribals were on the run. "This one will be perfect – tall, but not too thick. We can lash tent supports here and climb upward. Oh, and make sure the rest of our forces consolidate to this position."

"Yes, Your Grace," said Yanelle. The Companion began shouting orders.

Mirvea rushed up to Actaeon and saluted with fist to chest. "Your Grace, what are your orders?" The Captain's head was shaved to the pate and her features, crisscrossed with many battle scars, were androgynous. The lilt of her voice was the only giveaway that she was a woman.

Actaeon briefed her on the operation, and they set to work with the aid of a few other warbanders.

Tent poles were hastily lashed horizontally against the chosen tree and the one beside it to form the rungs of a ladder. Fighting continued around them as the work progressed, but, aside from the errant arrow, was largely confined to the valleys as the allied forces fought to close their gaps and rejoin.

When the makeshift ladder was completed, Actaeon ushered the warbanders down and tested the first rung with his boot. "Well done. This should suffice."

"Shall I go up, Your Grace?" asked the Captain.

"No, Captain. I will use my scope. Hold this." He handed her his halberd and began to ascend the tree swiftly. Several rungs up an arrow thudded into the tree beside him. The Ruinic archers had begun to target him.

Captain Mirvea and another warbander grabbed shields and rushed upward to protect him as more arrows began to swarm through the trees.

As the Captain arrived beside the Prince Engineer, her outstretched shield arm shuddered from impact and she winced as the penetrating arrowhead sliced her forearm.

"Apologies, Your Grace. I judged you need our protection now," said the Captain with a smirk.

"No need, Captain. You have my gratitude," said Actaeon, meeting her cloudy gray eyes. "Now let us make this quick."

They moved upward as a unit until they reached the top of the tree, where Actaeon unslung his recurve bow and lifted its scope to his eye. Arrows fired from the valley floor fell short of them as he swept their surrounds. From this height, he could see above much of the understory layer of the Underforest jungle, while still being below the thick, light obscuring canopy above. As the attackers moved, he could make out where they were positioned beyond the leaves of the understory plants.

"Whatcha got, Act?" called Wave from below.

"Give me a moment, Wave," Actaeon called back.

"Better make it fast – we're sitting ducks here!"

The answer lay to the west – an undefended ridge that their forces could use to rush past the Ruinic encirclement. Actaeon did a second scan of the surrounds and nodded, satisfied, before starting back down.

When they reached the jungle floor, Yanelle, Trench, Wave, and Atreena were there waiting for him.

"To the west. We break through to the ridge west of us – quickly, and with heavy units at the flanks as we move." When nobody said anything, the Prince Engineer lifted his hands in confusion.

"You heard the man. Let's move!" Trench bellowed.

And they fought their way through to the west.

"They're taking a beating down there," said Captain Xula, as he rushed up the debris pile with his bloody sabre in hand. The blood on his dark skin became visible as he closed in on the command post. Far below him, Thyrian Flashbolt Marines beat a hasty, but organized retreat, pausing intermittently to fire their triple crossbows into the pursuing enemy.

"I told you this strategy would be unlikely to succeed. The Boneyards are a confusing maze," said Eisandre, eyeing Supreme Captain Jarval beside her.

"Cutting off their supply line is an integral step in this operation," asserted Jarval. "We had to try this."

"And now we have tried it and learned the lesson that was obvious in the first place," Eisandre bit back.

"We'll reposition and circle back around to cut them off from the north. Captain Xula, have our forces reorganize for march as soon as they disengage," instructed Jarval.

"No," said Eisandre, lifting her hand to indicate a halt. "To continue this is folly. In the north we risk encirclement. We're done with this effort."

"Excuse me?" asked the Supreme Captain, his jaw falling open.

Eisandre shot him a confused look. "You did not hear what I said?"

"Darkest Hour take us," cursed Jarval.

"I'd prefer it didn't," said Eisandre.

The Supreme Captain threw his hands up into the air. "Do what she says, Xula. She's the Commander, as *you* wanted." He donned his curved silver helmet and stormed away down the pile of ruins.

Eisandre turned to Xula. "I don't understand. He didn't hear me clearly?"

Captain Xula grinned and lifted a kerchief to clean some of the blood from his face. "Oh, he heard you, Princess. And this sort of thing makes me glad I suggested you as Commander. You're right about the position here being utterly unobtainable. He might be pissed off, but he'll come to his senses. Better we hem them in from the other sides that we can actually hold onto."

Eisandre stared at him for several long lifebeats before nodding. "Thank you, Captain Xula."

"No, thank *you*, Princess. Less loved ones I'll need to notify when I get home."

"We caught this child, Your Grace," said Warchief Varisk.

Several hours had passed since their dramatic break from the Ruinic tribal encirclement. Now they were on a steady march northward to put some distance between them and their pursuers.

Behind the Warchief, Jezail and another warbander held a child between them. The child stood in perfect stillness – her gaze focused on Actaeon. It was unsettling – the whites of her eyes had been dyed with something that turned them a dark brown, her iris barely distinguishable from the dye. The rest of the child's exposed skin was dyed a greenish earthen color, though raised lines of brown skin wove their way randomly across her features, like the branches of a tree. Her clothing was colored similarly and cut irregularly, to eliminate any easily recognizable pattern. The girl didn't appear to be older than six or seven years of age.

"Amazing…" said Actaeon, as he looked her over. He planted his halberd in the dirt at his feet and knelt to be on the same level as the captured child. "She is one of the Kainai. Release her."

Jezail and the other warbander released the young girl's arms and the girl immediately lashed out at the Prince Engineer. He winced as her sharpened fingernails opened up several long cuts along his cheek.

Varisk and the others reached for their weapons, but Actaeon stayed them with a lifted hand.

"We mean you no harm," he said sincerely to the girl. He lifted a hand to his cheek and it came away red with blood. "I apologize that my warbanders restrained you. It will not happen again. We are here battling the Ruinic tribal enemy that has invaded Redemption. The help of your people would be much appreciated. Can –"

The girl hissed and recoiled from him before leaping backward and scrambling up the nearest tree with stunning speed. They heard rustling as the girl disappeared into the canopy above, and she was gone.

"We shouldn't have released her," said Jezail.

"No," said Actaeon. "We had to release her. The aid of the Kainai during our stay here would be invaluable. Hopefully we did not upset this one too much." He pulled a bandage strip from his pocket and cut a small piece from it with his hooked dagger to still the bleeding on his face.

"You'd ally with such creatures as they?" asked Varisk, looking mildly disturbed.

"The Czerynians have reaped the benefit of cooperative agreement with them for decades," explained Actaeon with a grin. "We have a rare opportunity now that the northern Dominion has fallen. It behooves us to take advantage of it."

"But the Czerynians have always been the protectors of the Children," said Jezail, using the common name for the Kainai people.

"And now they are without protection, and with invaders on their soil." Varisk nodded with a smile of his own. "Still, it is just more of a burden on Raedelle if we agree to such a relationship with these Children. Protecting the Underforest is a big job."

"Maybe so," agreed Actaeon. "But the benefits are great. Raedelle could use a stronghold near the center of the city. And imagine what we might learn from them? They are better even than our best warbanders at blending into the jungle. Plus, think of the answers we might learn! Why do the Kainai not age? It is one of the greatest mysteries of our time! And Temple too – what secrets lie within that place?"

The Kainai, or the Children of the Underforest, as they were better known, had entered into a protective agreement with the Czeryn Dominion in the early years after the portals had opened to spill forth the new people upon Redemption's soil. In exchange for Czeryn's protectorship, the Kainai gave to them Temple, one of the great structures of the Ancients that stood intact deep within the jungle of the Underforest. There the Czerynians garrisoned a force to protect the Kainai, who were pacifists by nature. The agreement gave the Czerynians a stronghold near the heart of Redemption and gave the Kainai protection they couldn't achieve on their own. And strangely enough, the slaveholding and warlike Czeryn Dominion respected the vulnerable Children and defended them loyally.

Jezail smiled and stepped forward to touch Actaeon's face. "Ah, my friend – some things never change, do they? You're still driven by your curiosity, even in this time of darkness. I've missed your passion for discovery. It makes life more interesting – more than just fighting for survival."

Varisk stepped forward and pulled Jezail's hand roughly from Actaeon's face. "Forget not, Jezail, that our friend is now Prince Engineer of Raedelle."

Jezail shot the Warchief a look that made him take a quick step back.

"Whatever my position may be changes nothing of who I am," said Actaeon, matter-of-factly. "I am only in such a position because the situation demanded it. Eisandre was the next logical leader of Raedelle, and my place is at her side. Aside from those circumstances, I am but Actaeon Rellios Caliburn of Shore."

"And that's why we have something to tell you, Act," said Jezail. "We –"

"We need not waste His Grace's time with this, dear. He has much to consider as we march," said Varisk, interrupting Jezail.

Actaeon laughed and spoke. "I expect that my new Warchief is considering all these details for me. Thus, I will hear what Jezail has to say. Allow her to speak, Varisk."

Varisk chuckled and relaxed a bit. "Aye aye, Prince Engineer. Tell him, Jezail."

Jezail beamed and took Varisk's hand to pull him forward. "We wanted you to be the first to know, Act. Varisk and I have decided to be joined. As soon as things calm a bit, the Voice Ithelie agreed to perform the ceremony."

Beside her, Varisk's cheeks colored a shade of red and he nodded affirmingly.

Actaeon smiled broadly and stepped forward to touch both of his friends' shoulders. "It is about time! I am so happy for you both. We shall make sure to give you a lovely ceremony as soon as we reach a position of relative security."

Jezail rushed forward to wrap her arms around her old friend, tears in her eyes. Actaeon pulled Varisk into the hug and the three childhood friends stood together for several long moments.

When Actaeon stepped back, he grinned at the pair. "You will both do great things together for Raedelle."

TEMPLE

"**H**OLD THE LINE!" SHOUTED VARISK, up to his thighs in muck as he fought. Beside him, one of his friends toppled forward into the morass, an arrow jutting from one nostril.

The Ruinic tribals had outpaced the fleeing allied forces – the heavily armored Keeper Knights and Niwian soldiers just couldn't keep a quick enough pace in the rough and broken jungle terrain. Now they were pinned down, deep in the thick jungle of the Underforest. The clever tribals had waited until the Redemption forces had been forced to pass through a swampy region of jungle. And even then, they hadn't attacked until the allied soldiers had slogged through the bog for much of the evening before. Exhausted, caked with mud, and demoralized, they were in poor condition to fend off an attack.

The Wall Breakers formed a line to protect the lagging units as they passed through the swamp to reach drier terrain ahead. The Knights of the Keeper 1st Division struggled through the mire, holding onto one another to keep their balance.

"Let's pick up the pace, Knight Captain! We're taking heavy losses here!" shouted Varisk, swatting insects away from his eyes.

"Doing my best, Warchief! This damned stuff's impossible!" yelled back Atreena. She paused to clear mud from her visor that had been kicked up by the Knight ahead of her.

Varisk raised his shield to block a thrown spear and grimaced as his eyes swept the field of battle. The Highwater warband guarding the opposite side hadn't encountered much from the Ruinic press yet – mud was inhibiting the progress more, but he knew once the tribals reached them, the line wouldn't be able to hold. On his side, the attackers slogged toward them in steady waves that he held off with his own line of Wall Breakers supplemented by warbanders from the Eastern Rim under the leadership of Captain Mirvea. The volleys of arrows and constant press was beginning to thin their numbers.

"Spin us up a song, Jezail!" he called.

Beside him, Jezail fired an arrow and brushed a lock of red hair from her eyes, which left a streak of grime along her face. She cast him an incredulous look. "You want a song right *now*?"

"As good a time as any. Something to boost our morale and get these sluggards behind us moving faster. This is shaping up to be a battle of time – if we can beat them outta this fen before they reach us with their full force, we just might make it," said Varisk with a smile at his love. "Plus, if I've gotta risk my own hide out here, I might as well hear a song from the loveliest musician I've ever heard."

"Aye, Warchief," said Jezail, blushing. She swapped her bow for her fiddle and began to pluck out a fast-paced melody that carried across the still, muggy swamp air.

Varisk grinned as he felt his heart leap at the notes. Two more tribals approached and he deftly dispatched them, striding forward between thrust spears – the blade of his own spearhead lashed out to find one's heart and another's throat.

Another glance back found that the mired soldiers were indeed picking up the pace. The magic that Jezail's music worked on people really was incredible.

As if in realization that they were losing this opportunity, the Ruinic force hastened its assault. Varisk and his warbanders fought back wave after wave of attackers, and the soldiers behind them continued plodding along to the melody.

Ahead, a small tribal warrior leapt forward and surprised him by hurling his only spear.

Varisk lifted his shield to block it easily and it slammed into the heavy wood with a force that nearly knocked him down. Grimacing, he tossed the shield aside and leapt forward himself to land before the grinning warrior. His spearhead punched through the small man's teeth to sever his spine.

As he waded back through the muck to retrieve his shield, Varisk noticed something had changed.

What happened to the music?

He suddenly felt light-headed and looked down in confusion at where his shield lay – the spear had punched through the wood and its head was covered in red blood. *His* blood.

Suddenly he noticed the warmth soaking his undertunic on the left side. Jezail was running toward him, her mouth hung open in a scream – even her scream sounded like music.

His hand found his throat, felt a warm rush, and he toppled over into the muck and darkness.

Frantic hands yanked him up and onto his back and wiped the mud from his eyes. He looked up at Jezail as she cradled him in her arms.

He opened his mouth to speak – to tell her to be strong, but he only coughed up blood and dirty water.

Instead, he tried to meet her eyes to convey the words, but he got lost in her red curls.

The jungle light shone through them like a beacon.

He felt a moment of thankfulness that this was his last sight. Even the stench of the bog and the flies buzzing around his eyes couldn't take that from him.

And then he was gone.

"Ancestors, I call upon thee to guide the soul of our leader and friend, Warchief Varisk Conmara," intoned Voice Ithelie, arms spread as her nearly white hair blew gently in the breeze that had started, much to everyone's relief. The green fabric of her robes was stained with brown mud.

"Open the doors of the beyond and light a fire to blaze the path for his soul to find those of his spirit family," she continued. "Accept him in reunion and grace, that he may be one with you in wisdom and virtue, to be a guiding energy for our people from this day to eternity. May he guide our other Fallen to their rightful place on this tragic day. I, the Voice Ithelie Faris, through the power entrusted in me by the Ancestors, do now release you, Varisk, from your duty to your people and your Raedelle. Go, our brother, and take your rightful place in legend among our people. May you watch over us always."

Everyone drew silent as Ithelie concluded and stepped forward to lay a single flower upon Varisk's cairn. Though the warbands had scoured the surrounds for stones, there were few to be easily found this deep in the jungle, and so they had piled broken shields with the few stones high atop his body – having smashed them to prevent their use by the enemy.

Pickets had been set up at the edges of the bog they had just exited and their immediate surrounds, to protect those that watched as Ithelie spoke over the dead.

Before the makeshift cairn stood Jezail Vren, hood thrown back to reveal her expressionless face framed in its curly locks of blazing red hair. There was a lifeless look in her eyes, as though her soul had been torn asunder. Her face above the right eye was stretched and rippled from an old burn in a way that tugged her eye open wider. With the blood and dirt that covered her, and the distant expression of grief in her eyes, it gave her the look of a corpse.

Ithelie spun and grasped Jezail's shoulders. "Most of all, watch over your betrothed, Varisk. May your love for her give her continual strength to serve our Raedelle."

She leaned forward until her forehead touched Jezail's, and the young archer let loose a sob before gently pushing past the Voice to kneel at Varisk's cairn. There she bent forward and touched her head to the wood of one of the shattered shields, where she sobbed uncontrollably.

Ithelie searched out Actaeon among those gathered and offered him a solemn nod. "The Prince Engineer will now say some words for our Fallen brother."

Actaeon's eyes widened in surprise – he hadn't expected to be called upon to speak, but he quickly recovered and strode forward to kneel beside Jezail. He embraced her briefly before withdrawing to kneel at her side with one hand on her shoulder and another on the shaft of his halberd.

Around them, the keening sounds of insects began to rise until thousands joined in a cacophonic chorus that filled the Underforest. Massive trees rose out of the thick undergrowth around them, looming over the proceedings like giants standing sentinel.

"Varisk Conmara," Actaeon began, "was and will always be my friend. Without him, I would not be here today." The realization brought tears to his eyes. "He placed his trust in me and gave me the chance to prove myself despite explicit orders to the contrary. It is this sense of right that I would encourage all Raedelleans to follow in Varisk's example – a search for truth at all costs.

"I have had few true friends in my life, and count Varisk among them. A friend from a childhood long ago, turned into a trusted advisor today. A void now remains where he stood, and no one will ever replace him. Today, he cast his place in legend, for he stood fast and defended our retreat to allow the heavy armored divisions of our allied eastern front to escape intact. He did this at the cost of his very life." He paused for a moment to let that thought sink in. "Had he not, we may well have lost half our army on this day.

"The chance he has given us must not be squandered. We will continue forward to victory over these Ruinic tribals who would tear from us our way of life. Our civilization teeters at the edge of abyss, and it is up to us to ensure it may continue for the benefit of our future generations."

A raucous cheer went up among the troops that shook Actaeon at first – it was unexpected at such a solemn ceremony. Beneath his hand, he could feel Jezail shuddering as she cried. He reached down to embrace her, but she pushed him away firmly.

Confused, Actaeon withdrew and climbed to his feet. He reached out for Jezail but found his eyes drawn to the scarred flesh atop her head where her beautiful red locks had never been able to regrow. With sudden realization, he jerked his hand back and strode away. His friend, who he had hurt badly so long ago, now lay at the grave of her betrothed, hurt once again by him. His decisions – his consequences. He wished he were on the western front with Eisandre – perhaps they'd have been better off without him.

"Your Grace, a word?" came a familiar voice behind him.

Actaeon ignored it and continued along.

"Prince Engineer – I am still the Lord Shore, and I will not be ignored," said Gunther Arcady.

Actaeon spun to face the Lord, casting him an uncharacteristic glare. "What is it you would say to me mere seconds after I eulogized my friend?"

"Save me the dramatics, Your Grace," said Arcady with a smirk. He brushed his black hair back and leveled his burning hazel eyes at Actaeon. "This is a time of war. If you aren't up for the task, I'm more than happy to lead in your stead."

Actaeon composed himself and offered the Lord Shore a grin. "Would you care to explain how your fearful and frantic retreat back to Raedelle would help this war effort?"

"Very amusing, Your Grace. But, despite the fact that you failed to heed my advice to distance Raedelle from this conflict in the first place, I would not now dare abandon our brethren to the west," snarled Arcady.

"I am reassured to hear your commitment to our people, Gunther," said Actaeon. "What did you wish to speak about then?"

"Well, Your Grace, contrary to the cheering after your speech about the late Warchief, many of the warbanders are worried as to our direction," the Lord Shore explained. "We have been trapped in this Underforest now for far too long, under constant attack, and on indefensible terrain." He trailed off.

"We have been here for just six days, Lord Shore. What do they wish to know?" asked Actaeon.

"They wish to know what our plan is, Prince Engineer. They are unsettled, you see," said Arcady as he interlaced his fingers and stared into Actaeon's eyes.

Companion Yanelle approached behind the Lord Shore, hand on her sword, but Actaeon kept her at a distance with a gesture.

"They need not be unsettled, Lord Shore," said Actaeon with a grin. "You can tell them we make for Temple."

"Temple still!?" Arcady blurted. "Why, by the Fallen, would we still make for Temple after the heavy losses that we've already taken? Haven't you learned anything from this last battle?"

"As you say, Gunther, we suffer from indefensible terrain and we are trapped in the Underforest," Actaeon explained. "Temple is within the Underforest, further away from our attackers, and it is a defensible structure of the Ancients. Plus, if we are fortuitous, we might find some allies there."

"Allies?" said Arcady incredulously. "If you mean the slaveholding Czerynian picaroons, then I cannot stomach that you'd parlay with such heathens. Do the ends justify any means for you?"

"That is one concept you should be all too familiar with, Lord Shore. After all, you are one who has not hesitated to put the lives of Raedelleans beneath your heel for your ambitions," said Actaeon with another grin. "Besides, the Czerynians are but a key to other resources – we shall see what we discover."

Arcady's face grew red with anger. "Be careful, Engineer! If I challenged you, you'd not stand a chance." His voice trailed off and his hands dropped to his sword belt.

"If you think me a fool duelist like yourself, then you could not know me any less, Gunther," scoffed Actaeon. "That I would sacrifice either of us during such a dire time of need for our people is an asinine posit. Besides, is that not what your hated Czerynians do to vie for leadership – cut one another down? Do not tell me that you would sink to such hypocrisy." He paused to grin as the Lord Shore grew more visibly angry. "No, I did not think so. Now go help get the warbands rallied for the march to Temple – I want us on the way immediately. Dismissed."

Arcady's hands dropped from his sword belt and balled into fists. "You haven't heard the last of this conversation." He stormed off to comply with Actaeon's orders.

"I hope not," called Actaeon after him. He shared a smile with Yanelle. "You are one of my advisors after all!"

Trench knelt beside Jezail. The archer from Incline continued to sob with her head down upon the cairn, the splintered wood of the shields had worn the skin of her forehead until it bled.

"We've gotta leave, lass. The troops are on the march," said the giant, placing a heavy hand on her shoulder.

Jezail reached back and tried to slap his hand away, but Trench didn't budge. She tried a few more times before she shrieked and collapsed atop the cairn. "Just leave me here – I won't leave him!" Sobs racked her body.

"You must, lass. Yer needed with the living. Varisk has passed from this world to be among the Fallen now," said Trench, a rare gentleness in his voice.

Jezail straightened suddenly to face him, her green eyes peering into his own. The blood trickled down her forehead to mingle with the tears on her cheeks. "My place is with him. Damn it, I can still feel him – he can't be gone! NOOOO!"

She shrieked that final word, and it was swallowed by the jungle. Far overhead, birds began to chatter and caw, inspired by her yell. She wanted to pull his cairn apart, to take him into her arms once again, but she was terrified of what she'd find there – terrified of the truth. Strong arms wrapped around her and hugged her close, and she realized that she'd been hammering away at Trench's chest with her fists. She recoiled at the realization and fell forward against him, her sight clouded with red tears.

Jezail pushed away from him and wiped the tears on the sleeve of her tunic to find Trench's distorted face looking back at her, bisected by its hideous scar. "I'm sorry, Trench. I know you're just here to help me. I don't want any help though – I don't want anything anymore. All that I ever wanted has left this world forever."

"I understand, lass," said Trench, and his eyes didn't leave her own.

"How could ya understand? He was to be my husband, the father of my children – my... my future," she sobbed. "How could you possibly understand?"

"Once, long ago, I lost my wife to war. She was... with child," Trench said, turning away to look at the jungle behind her.

"Oh gods, Trench... I didn't know. How did... how did you keep going?" she asked, her voice trembling.

"For a while it was just the rage, lass. The rage kept me going – a desire for vengeance that nearly destroyed me," said Trench. He pointed to the scar that bisected his face from the top of his right brow through his nose and wide across his left cheekbone. "This never lets me forget the wrongness in my mind at the time."

"You regret your vengeance?" asked Jezail, surprised.

"Not for a minute," said Trench, meeting her gaze once more. "Had I not avenged her death, how many more might've died? No... what I regret was the emptiness in my heart – the despair that led me to want to toss away my very life. That's what I can understand, lass. And I'll tell you right now that it's wrong. There's things in this shattered world worth fighting for, and yer a fighter. Yer not to see that for a long time now, but you will. That I promise you. None'll be as precious as yer Varisk, but trust me when I tell you there's things in this world worth your continued fight."

"I'm but a simple warband archer," Jezail said. "How am I to make a difference with my fight?"

"The Wall Breakers," said Trench. "If they lose you and Varisk both, their morale will be shattered. Their leader and his love both lost? It's a curse that'll hang over them forever. But if Jezail Vren rises up from such tragedy to lead them forward it'll inspire them like no song you've ever played before."

"You want me to be Captain of the Incline warband?!" spoke Jezail in what was nearly a shout.

"Everyone wants it – whether they know it yet or not," said Trench. "And if I know anything about Varisk in the short time I've known the lad, I'd say that he'd want that most of all."

Jezail turned slowly away from the big mercenary and lowered her head gently to the sticky, blood-soaked wood of the splintered shield atop Varisk's cairn. She closed her eyes and lay there for a long time. She could feel Trench's hand upon her shoulder as she tried to reach out to Varisk – tried to reach out to make the connection of mind and soul she'd made with him so many times before. He wasn't there though. He was gone.

Jezail sniffled and straightened before she opened her eyes and reached out to grasp the giant's big hand. "What was her name, your wife?"

"Shulaya…" he said, letting the name hang in the air. "Her name was Shulaya."

"I will compose a song for Shulaya," said Jezail with newfound determination. "That she may be remembered even today, so long after you lost her and your poor child. I'm so sorry, Trench."

She leaned forward and wrapped her arms around the giant.

Trench hugged her back, cradling her head against his chest, her red hair against the heavy chain that she'd pounded on earlier. There she cried and cried – for how long she didn't know.

When she pulled away, she wiped the bloody tears from her face and looked up at Trench. "I will do it, Trench. I don't want to, but Varisk loved the warband – I'll not have everything he worked so hard for fall to pieces. I'll do it."

Trench nodded. "I'm glad. And you'll do it well."

"Leave me now, then. It is time I said my goodbyes. I'll catch up with you shortly," said Jezail.

"Aye, lass. I'll be just over past that thicket there if ya need me," said Trench. He stood and strode off.

With a new purpose to continue on, she lay her head down once more on Varisk's cairn to say her goodbyes. And she could feel his presence inside her now.

Warlord Berk was a short and dull-looking man with a strip of tall white hair in the center of his mostly shaved pate. A short, scraggly beard clung to his chin, interrupted by old burns that marred his left cheek like an unsettling mask. He wore a vest of tightly fitting metal scales and greaves to match. The short arming sword strapped to his back had a crude claw at the base of the hilt. He looked at Actaeon with his weary brown eyes. "If what you're saying is true, then all of Redemption is lost."

"If you think that, then you have not been listening to anything I have been saying," said Actaeon with a rueful smirk.

They stood outside Temple. The Ancient building sat amidst a clearing in the jungle, in sharp contrast with the stark wilderness of the Underforest. Its variegated metal shards towered over the clearing like splinters of broken swords, the highest points of which matched height with the tallest trees around it. Where the shards separated, a clear faceted roof could be seen beyond, forming a prismatic structure that capped off the top of Temple. Hewn stone steps created by the Czerynians led up to a wooden defensive scaffolding that had been hung from the main building itself. The scaffolding included heavy shield walls that men could hide behind when Temple was under attack.

At the top of the stone steps was the circular entrance to the Ancient edifice. Something incredibly powerful had melted through the original outer metal shell there. Over it the Czerynians had crafted a heavy wooden portcullis that could be raised or lowered depending on the threat. It was currently in the lowered position.

Czerynian warriors lined the scaffolding above as they watched their Warlord parlay with the Prince Engineer.

The men stood apart from their various forces as they spoke.

"You'll forgive me, I think," said Berk. "We've been through some damned difficult times. Our homeland annihilated by something the likes of which we've never seen. I've watched my friends hack one another apart. There's nothing left to us but this damned creepy Temple. And now you tell me that even the Pyramid is under siege."

"The surviving Dominions are rallying. We have an allied force that has gained a strong foothold on the western side of Pyramid. If we can gain a foothold here and fight our way to the eastern side, they will be trapped between us. We need your help," explained Actaeon.

"I see not one Thyrian, Shieldian or Ajmani fighter with you. Are Niwian and Raedelle the only surviving Dominions?" asked Berk, his eyes narrowing upon the Prince Engineer.

"Thyr has joined us in the west. Your observation is astute, Warlord Berk – the Ajman and Shield Dominions have not joined us. They are tied up with affairs up north," said Actaeon.

"You mean they're divvying up my homeland," stated Berk bluntly. He drew his arming sword and pointed the blade up at the scaffolding of Temple. Behind Actaeon came sounds of consternation and weapons being readied. The Prince Engineer didn't flinch.

Berk continued, the point of his blade sweeping across the Czerynian men high above him upon the scaffolding. "You see here the last bastion of Czeryn. Perhaps the last men, even. And you want us to help you break the siege of the Pyramid for all Redemption, even while half of Redemption fights over our homeland? You'll not be surprised that your offer isn't exactly enticing to us."

"Kindly put your weapon away, Warlord Berk. You have no need of it with me – I can assure you," said Actaeon with a grin. "There does not appear to be a plethora of options for you at this time. Either we sit down and discuss the acceptable conditions to your surviving soldiers joining our allied efforts, or you can continue to enjoy hiding in your 'damned creepy Temple'. Fallen forbid me from preventing your enjoyment." The Prince Engineer hefted his halberd and began to start off.

"You've made your point, Prince Engineer," said Berk with a lopsided smile. "Temple is all that remains for us, and despite its creepiness, it has strategic value. It's my job to see that my people come out on top of this all. So let's sit down and talk, as you say." The Warlord returned the sword to his back.

Actaeon turned back and smiled. He struck out his right hand with its fingerless glove and the Warlord grasped it firmly. "Very good, Warlord."

"Well then, what're we waiting for? Bring whoever you may inside, and we'll continue our jibber-jabber there," said Berk. He turned to lead the way.

Actaeon motioned for Trench, Wave, and Companion Yanelle to join him, and the four followed the Czerynian leader inside.

A fat Czerynian with crisscrossed scars on his arms and face slammed his fist on the table. "You cannot do that, Warlord – it's the Czerynian way!"

Berk stood suddenly, his chair shooting out behind him and tumbling backward noisily. "You use my title well, Strog, and yet you yield no respect for it. The Prince Engineer asked us only to abandon the practice of slaveholding, not our other practices. Do you see many slaves here? If you plan on challenging me to Blood Ascent, then do so now and stop wasting our time!"

Strog's face went red, and he lowered his eyes to the table. "No, Warlord, I'd not dream of it – it's just that it was my livelihood. Without it what will I do?"

"You live yet. Adapt or die, Strog – adapt or die." Berk turned back to Actaeon. "We will do this thing, but I must have your promise that my surviving people will have a place to permanently settle once all is said and done."

Actaeon nodded. "In exchange for the military use of Temple and the aid of your Schiltron in battle, we will allow you independent governorship under Raedelle's protection – though you must abide by Raedellean law whilst under said protection. We will find a place for your people to settle in due course after the conflict is ended."

"And other Czerynian survivors would be welcome in such a community?" asked Berk.

"So long as they agree to the terms we have discussed," said Actaeon.

"We are not in position to ask for more," admitted Berk. "We run low on provisions and, if we are to survive as a culture, this opportunity is too good to turn down. As I said, we must adapt or die – and so we adapt. You have my thanks for your generosity, Prince Engineer. There is one last matter at hand though."

"And what is that?" asked Actaeon.

"You must convince the Kainai that Raedelle will take Czeryn's place as their Protectors," said Berk. "We are no longer in position to provide that protection, but if you can't agree on this with them, they will not allow Raedelle to control Temple."

"I thought the Children were non-violent?" said Wave.

"Aye, but there're other ways to make things difficult, lacking violence," said Berk.

"I am willing to offer Raedellean protectorship to the Kainai," said Actaeon. "Unfortunately, I have been unable to communicate with them. Would you be able to broker a meeting?"

"This I can do," said Berk. "It will take some time."

"Very well," said Actaeon. He stood and extended his hand across the table to the Warlord. Berk stood and grasped his hand firmly. "Now that the jibber-jabber is over," he said, quoting the Warlord from earlier, "What can you tell me of Temple itself?"

Berk grinned and sat back down. "We know less than you might imagine. Most of the building is haunted by the spirits of the Ancients. No Czerynian that I know of has ever explored more of the building than these few rooms near the entrance that we use as a waystation."

"You've been in possession of this place for how long and haven't even seen half of it?" asked Wave. He ran a hand through his long hair and cast Actaeon an incredulous look.

"Oh, we've seen enough of it to know where we aren't welcome," said Berk, narrowing his eyes upon Wave.

"Excuse my friend," said Actaeon. "You claim it is haunted. Haunted in what manner?"

"The spirits of the Ancients roam the halls actively," said Berk. "It weighs heavily upon my remaining men – most don't believe we are wanted here. I'm not sure how much longer I can keep order here."

"You mean like the projections one can find all throughout the ruins?" asked Wave. "Your people are afraid of those? They're all over Redemption!"

"Hush, Wave," said Trench, shooting his friend a glare. "I've seen you cower in the corner when faced with tiny, little slugs – you're not one to question these men." The hint of a smirk could be seen upon his scarred face.

"Little slugs?! Little slugs that stole my damned eye," said Wave, jerking a thumb up toward his eyepatch. "Never seen a ruin apparition steal anyone's eye."

"Enough, little man," said Berk. "I'll tolerate no more of your babble."

Wave blinked his single eye and shook his head. In a flash, he was on his feet and drawing his rapier.

Trench was faster though. With one hand the giant slammed Wave's rapier back into its scabbard, and with the other, he forced his friend down into his chair. "Sit yer arse down, Wave. Unless the Prince Engineer here says so, you'll keep yer sword in its damned sheath."

Wave opened his mouth to protest, but then snapped it shut. "You're right, Trench." He turned to Actaeon. "Sorry, Your Grace."

Actaeon smirked at Wave before turning his attention back to the last known Czerynian Warlord. "So, the projections are more active here? Fascinating. They avoid these waystation rooms though?"

"Much more active," agreed Berk. "And they don't avoid these rooms, though they're seen here much less often." The color drained from his face and he slid back in his chair, bulging eyes staring over the Prince Engineer's shoulder.

Yanelle was on her feet in an instant, her sword drawn and pointed at the shimmering image that stood behind Actaeon. The apparition was humanoid in appearance, its colors fluctuating rapidly, but its details were lost in fuzziness, as though the entirety of it were viewed through a piece of frosted glass.

Actaeon glanced over his shoulder to see what everyone was reacting to. With a grin, he stood up slowly and lifted his hands. "Everyone stay calm. You can sheathe your sword, Yanelle. It is indeed a projection like those that we see often among the ruins – a better one perhaps, but one and the same." He tilted his head to examine the projection. "Are you able to communicate?" he asked it.

The shimmering being's face opened where a mouth might've been, and the room was filled with random bursts of noise that sounded like rain upon a tin roof. The mouth, if it could be called that, opened several times in quick succession, each time accompanied by another burst of the same noise.

"Fascinating," murmured Actaeon. "It is trying to communicate something, though the details are lost for some reason. Some malfunction of Ancient technology. It is able to hear us though. It responded to my question and its arrival corresponded with the Warlord's statement. How curious."

The projection flickered and vanished as suddenly as it had appeared. Behind it stood one of the Shield Wardens of the Czerynian Schiltron, spear and shield in either hand. He banged his spear against the front of his shield. "Warlord, I have news."

Berk shook himself out of his stupor. "What is it Dek?"

"It's the Ruinic tribals, sir – they have us surrounded."

SPIRITS

"**M**Y APOLOGIES, YOUR GRACE. THE men and women of the warbands refuse your orders," said Mirvea. She knelt before him and laid her sword at his feet. "I have failed you."

"Nonsense, Warchief Mirvea. Stand up and look me in the eye," directed Actaeon with a smile. When the Warchief did, he continued, "Why are they refusing?"

Mirvea cleared her throat and licked her lips. "They, uh... They..."

"Mirvea, if you are to fulfill this new role as Warchief, there must be naught but truth between us. Is that understood?" asked Actaeon. He reached out to touch her shoulder in reassurance.

"Understood, Prince Engineer," said Mirvea.

"You may call me Actaeon. We will be working together very closely – no need to inhibit our communications with all these formalities. Now, why are they refusing my orders?"

The new Warchief shifted uncomfortably and lifted her cloudy gray gaze to his. "I will acknowledge your position, Prince Engineer – it is the right way, and that is truth."

Actaeon grinned at that and nodded. "Very well. Then answer the question, Warchief – please. Why will they not scout Temple?"

"Simply put, Your Grace, they're terrified," she explained, looking up at Actaeon with her cloudy gray eyes. "They have heard of the Ancient spirits that haunt this place, and they want no part of it. They don't wish to incur the wrath of whatever unsettled forces reside here. Admittedly, nor do I."

"Not to mention it's a waste of time," muttered Arcady nearby.

"If it finds us a solution out of this present problem, it is not a waste of anyone's time," said the Prince Engineer, shooting Arcady a critical look.

"And what do you propose to do? Enlist the spirits of the Ancients as you have with the handful of Czerynians hiding in this place? As you wish to do with the Children?" sneered Arcady. The Lord Shore brushed his thumb across his hooked nose and shook his head at Actaeon.

"Actually, that is exactly what I hope, Lord Shore," said Actaeon with a broad grin. "If I can find the means to control the projections we see, we might be able to use them to our advantage. I shall be going to scout Temple myself to see if I can procure just that capability. Care to join me?"

The Lord Shore ran a hand through his slick black hair and looked sidelong at Actaeon. "I'll not be gallivanting around Ancient buildings while we're surrounded by the enemy. We need to be prepared for an attack."

"I understand if you are afraid, Lord Arcady. You may remain without," said Actaeon, his emerald eyes glinting with amusement.

Arcady scowled at him and said nothing.

Actaeon turned to the others gathered before him in the largest of the Czerynian waystation chambers. "Who will accompany me then?"

The Voice Ithelie Faris stepped forward and threw back the green cowl of her robes to reveal her striking brown eyes and flowing, nearly white, blond hair. "It is my duty to go with you here, Prince Engineer. I will help you to commune with these spirits as well as I am able." She stepped up beside him. Wave was next to step up. "Can't be worse than anything I've faced beside you in the past, boss. Right?" He shot a questioning look at Actaeon.

Actaeon grinned at the one-eyed mercenary and shrugged. "I cannot promise anything, Wave, except that it should be quite interesting." He turned to the others present, many of whom averted their eyes from his as he looked over the crowd. "Anyone else, then?"

"I ain't afraid of no ghosts," grumbled Trench, and the giant stomped up to stand beside his shorter counterpart.

Actaeon looked at Yanelle and raised a brow. The color drained from the Companion's face, but she stepped up to join him.

"Actually, Companion Yanelle, I would appreciate if you would stay behind to assist Warchief Mirvea in preparation of the defenses," said Actaeon with a knowing smile.

The Companion saluted fist to chest, a look of relief upon her face. "Aye, Prince Engineer."

"Let us depart then. There is no time to waste, as Lord Arcady so tactfully pointed out," said Actaeon.

"Wait!" came a voice, before the group could leave the chamber.

Actaeon paused and looked back.

Jezail marched forth to join them. "I'll be going too."

"Are you sure, Jezail?" asked Wave.

"Yep. Let's move," said the new Captain of the Wall Breakers, and she led the way out of the room.

"By the Fallen!" shouted Trench. He swung his maul at the swirling mist that had blasted forth. It dissipated instantly and the face of his weapon smashed a prism that had been inset into the wall before him. A loud ringing sound pulsed through the wide crystalline corridor. The luminaries flickered before the sound ended abruptly and everything returned to normal.

Wave placed a tentative hand on Trench's shoulder. "Careful, old man. Those things are tough to replace."

"Who're you calling an old man? Yer the same damned age as me," spat Trench. He swatted away his friend's hand.

"Yeah, but I aged much better," said Wave with a smirk.

"Maybe on the outside, but not on the inside," countered Trench with a grin.

"Oh yeah? Thought you weren't afraid of ghosts," prodded Wave.

"Never seen a ghost that looked like that before," said the giant.

"You've seen many?" asked Jezail, reaching out to touch a shard of the prism still sticking out from the wall.

"More'n I'd care to relate," said Trench.

"Not a very friendly way to treat the dead," said Ithelie.

"These are likely naught but projections, left behind from the Ancients," said Actaeon. "Let us not forget that."

"I cannot agree with you there, Prince Engineer," said the Voice. "How are you so sure there's nothing more to these things you call projections?"

"One cannot easily be certain, Voice Ithelie. However, I have interacted with similar such phenomena all across Redemption's ruins. I have tried to communicate with them on countless occasions. Most simply repeat the same actions over and over, with no sign of intelligence. I believe they are just remnants of old recordings," explained Actaeon.

"Just because they can't hear your efforts to communicate, just because they repeat the same actions, doesn't mean there isn't an energy of spirit behind them – an energy backed by intellect," warned Ithelie. "And, even if you're correct, it doesn't mean these Ancients of Temple are the same."

"Quite correct, Voice Ithelie," said Actaeon. "We cannot be certain that this set of projections is the same as those previously encountered. Though, we should be careful not to make assumptions in either direction. There is no more proof that these are tortured souls of the Ancients than that they are naught but simple projections. We must be careful not to let the fear of the unknown cloud our judgment."

Just then, all the luminaries, including their own, flickered and went out. The only light remaining in the corridor was the very dim, natural light that filtered down through the translucent structure of Temple itself, from high above them.

"Helluva time for the Darkest Hour," said Wave.

"I'll say," seconded Trench.

"Wasn't there just a Darkest Hour only shortly before we arrived here? Seems pretty quick to have it again," said Jezail.

"Curious. I wonder if this is a local phenomenon," said Actaeon. He tried to contact Eisandre through the Thoughtlink Artifact, but received no reply. "The only way to know is to ask the others when we get out of here."

"Shattered Redemption..." cursed Wave under his breath. He was looking past them to the far end of the corridor.

As the rest of their eyes adjusted, they came into focus: dozens of the fuzzy, shimmering humanoid shapes the same as the one which had appeared earlier when they had met with Warlord Berk. They were slowly advancing toward the group, in synchronous step.

Jezail let out an instinctive scream that she cut short, clapping a hand over her mouth.

"Orders, Act?" asked Trench. "I feel like my judgment's being clouded."

"They're probably pissed you broke their prism," said Wave, reaching for his blades.

"Stay your weapons," said Actaeon. "We would do best to try and communicate first. If they are upset with us, attacking them will only make things worse. Plus, the efficacy of our weapons against such unknown phenomena is questionable at best."

"Allow me," said Ithelie, and the Voice strode forth with confidence to meet the hazy group of figures.

"Careful, lass," warned Trench. "There're things in this world yer faith won't protect you against."

Ithelie ignored the big mercenary and continued forward until she stood several paces before the hazy flickering figures. She brought her two forefingers of each hand to her forehead before spreading her arms wide in offering. "Ancients of Redemption, it is I, Voice Ithelie Faris, that stands before you in peaceful friendship of shared humanity. We wish this place, your Temple, no harm, but seek to further our knowledge and understanding through it. Will you be our gu-"

She was interrupted as the closest figure stepped through her and took the breath from her body. She clutched her chest and fell to the floor, gasping for air. Her near-white strands of hair rose into the air like an array of needle-like spikes as the lead figure continued slowly through and then past her, no stay in its momentum.

Jezail's arrow passed harmlessly through the throat of the figure and over Ithelie's head to skitter against the corridor wall beyond. Trench and Wave both had their weapons drawn and raced forward to the Voice's aid.

They were stayed by the Voice's hand, which snapped up in an order for them to halt. "S…" She struggled to catch her breath. "Stop there," she commanded. "I am not finished."

The Voice climbed to her feet with determination and reached out to place her hand inside the head of the figure that had passed through her. Her voice resounded along the crystalline corridor as she addressed it. "In the name of the Fallen, I enjoin thee to heed my words – for I speak on behalf of those who remain and those who have gone before. For those who now dwell in your Ancient city of Redemption, for those who seek to understand and to rebuild this place, I compel you to guide us now, or to forever stand as impediments to life and progress. What choice make thee?" Her final question was a shout and as it echoed down the corridor the luminaries flickered back on erratically.

The figure before Ithelie halted and spun to face her.

Beside Actaeon, Jezail gasped, her second nocked arrow falling to the corridor floor.

"Fascinating," said Actaeon, watching the events unfold before him with intent eyes.

"By the Fallen," said Trench.

"Exactly," said Wave.

The shimmering figure's arm snapped out and reached into Ithelie's head. There the pair stood, each of their hands occupying the space of the other's head. The other figures turned slowly to watch.

"I've never in my life seen such courage," whispered Jezail, awed as she knelt to pick up her arrow. Her eyes didn't leave the incredible interaction before her.

"Something more than projections then," said Actaeon. "The things we might learn here..."

As the group watched Ithelie and the Ancient figure with bated breath, the Voice's hair slowly drifted to rest upon her shoulders once more and the luminaries came fully back to life.

A flash of bright light blinded them all temporarily and when their vision cleared, Ithelie lay upon the floor, unconscious.

Behind her stood one of the apparitions – the others had disappeared. It gestured down the corridor and motioned for the others to follow before it began walking away.

Actaeon rushed past the two mercenaries that stood with their mouths hanging open to check Ithelie. He was relieved to find that she was breathing normally and appeared to be in a deep slumber. "She is alive. Trench, carry her. We must follow the Ancient." He hefted his halberd and started after the retreating figure.

Trench shook his head and snapped out of his reverie. He scooped the Voice up easily in his arms and followed the Prince Engineer.

Jezail nudged Wave on the way forward and smirked at him. "Let's go, tough guy – interesting stuff ahead."

Wave shoved his rapier back into its scabbard and blinked his single eye, at a loss for words.

The Ancient apparition led them through a series of corridors and chambers that would've confused even the best of navigators. It began to move more and more quickly until the group was sprinting to keep pace.

It was a relief once the figure passed through a final portal and blinked out of existence.

Beyond the portal was a gigantic spherical room hewn from the same crystalline material that comprised the rest of Temple's maze-like internal structure. Light from above and from distant luminaries set deep into the material of the structure created an ethereal glow inside the spherical concavity. Aside from the opening entrance, there was no other notable feature within the room.

"A dead end," muttered Wave.

"Or the center of everything in this place," suggested Actaeon.

"We'll go in first and check it out for ya, Act," said Trench as he lowered Ithelie gently to the floor.

"I have to imagine that the entity which Voice Ithelie spoke with intended for us to arrive at this point for a reason. As it stands, I believe myself to be the best choice to enter that room first. I have past experience with the control systems of the Ancients that provides me with an advantage over any of you. No offense meant," said the Prince Engineer, with a grin.

"None taken, Act. But it's not worth the risk to you," said Wave.

"There I must disagree with you, Wave. Our forces stand surrounded in this alien place – cut off from our mission and the resources that we need to continue. If we do not figure out a way to escape this dilemma, then we will fail in our endeavor and, indeed, all of Redemption will suffer," explained Actaeon. "My talent lies in engineering us a way out of this, and here we stand at what might be the center of one of the Ancient wonders of Redemption. It is my duty as your Prince Engineer to try and find us an advantage that will enable us to break this siege and complete our goal of pushing the Ruinic tribals from the east. If I cannot do this, then what worth am I to you all, really?"

"You don't even know if this is the center. For all you know this could be a damned trap, for the Ancients to ensnare you in their tomb," spat Wave. "It's a damned stupid risk, and you know it!"

While they argued, Jezail made up her mind and stepped resolutely forward to enter the chamber.

Trench caught her though, and she grunted as he wrapped his arms around her midsection and yanked her away from the portal. "Uh uh, lass. I don't think so. Yer not throwing yer life away that easy."

"Let go of me, you brute!" she shrieked, attempting to elbow her way out of his grasp. Trench's arms only tightened about her the more that she struggled, and he moved her away from the entrance to the spherical chamber.

Actaeon's gaze settled upon Wave's eye. "It is true, my friend. I know it is a damned stupid risk, as you say. However, in this situation the benefit outweighs the potential risk. The entity that led us here has had the opportunity to watch and understand our present dilemma. It showed true intelligence when it interacted with Voice Ithelie and led us to this location. Its ability to interact with her on that level evinces an intelligence that I never anticipated from these projections. That in turn would indicate that there is a reason for us to have been led to this specific location. I heed your argument that we might have been led here to be trapped or exterminated, but I would refute it just the same by the simple fact of how it rendered Voice Ithelie unconscious. Had these entities wanted to destroy us, could they not have simply done the same to all of us or worse? And yet they did not. It is for this reason that I must now take this risk."

Actaeon reached out and placed his hand on Wave's shoulder. He offered his mercenary friend a grin before stepping forward into the spherical room.

Jezail screamed at him and struggled in Trench's arms. "Damn it, Act! Let me go in there first, you bastard!"

After the Prince Engineer passed through the portal, a curved, crystalline door slid down to seal off the chamber he'd entered.

"Shattered Redemption," muttered Trench. The giant released Jezail and pulled his maul from his back. "Open up, damn you!" he shouted before swinging his maul against the door. The head of his weapon struck the solid surface and the impact reverberated up his arms. He struck the door several more times and kicked it before stepping back and muttering a curse.

Jezail's hand flashed out and smacked Trench across the face, turning the brutal scar that bisected his face a deep shade of red.

She went to smack the giant again and Wave caught her hand. "The hell ya think yer doing, lass?" asked the shorter mercenary.

"He should've let me go in there first," said Jezail. "Instead, he put our Prince Engineer at risk and we may now be leaderless."

Trench scowled down at the new Wall Breaker Captain. "Your life's worth more than to throw it away in a place you barely understand. I know how ya feel, but I ain't gonna let ya toss it away for naught. It might not seem like it now, but yer needed here. Deep down you know the Engineer's the right one for this job."

Jezail opened her mouth to retort, but Trench turned his back to her and strode away, back down the corridor through which they had come.

Actaeon stood alone and utterly enclosed in the crystalline sphere. The spherical room was utterly featureless. Even the doorway through which he had come was now indiscernible from the rest of the room's walls – if you could call the curved surface that. The only light in the sphere was the dim light that filtered down through the structure from high above – there were no luminaries inside.

Actaeon pulled his own luminary from his jacket and stuck it in the strap of his goggles, but the literal light it cast shed no figurative light on the situation he now found himself in. Carefully, he knelt down and lay his halberd on the floor so that its blade pointed toward the direction he had entered through the doorway. At least he'd know where to start looking for the seams of the exit if he couldn't figure out an easier way out.

The sloped floor of the sphere's bottom caused him to stumble forward as he straightened. His recovery brought him down to the center of the sphere, where he staggered to a halt.

Where are you? Eisandre's thought floated into his mind. Her thoughts had been absent since the mini-Darkest Hour they had experienced earlier.

At the center of Temple, locked inside a sphere, Actaeon answered.

Knowing you, I suppose I shouldn't be surprised, Eisandre thought, and he could almost feel her amusement. *I'd tell you to be careful, but I don't imagine that is possible with the present situation.*

Unfortunately, no. However, I believe this might aid us in getting out of here. One of the Ancients led us here – I suspect it might help.

One of the Ancients? The Princess' thought carried surprise and confusion along with it.

Or at least a projection of such, he explained. *It gave the impression of intelligence, if not sentience. It is something I would like to study further when this conflict is over. For the meantime, I will continue to explore here to see if I can find a way to break out from this Ruinic encirclement.*

Then I shall let you concentrate, my Prince Engineer, Eisandre decided. *You will let me know if you need help.*

Indeed I will, my love.

Actaeon frowned then, and knelt to feel around at the bottom of the sphere. There he found nothing noteworthy. He stood up and looked straight up to inspect the top of the room. Nothing of interest there either, but just before him artifacts hung in his vision – artifacts that didn't disappear when he blinked and shifted as he moved his head.

An arm's length above him floated a pinprick point of purple light. He closed the baffle over his luminary to block the light and blinked again to bring it into focus.

The point of light was dim even without the light of the luminary and when he shifted his position within the sphere, it became clear to Actaeon that it floated in the exact center.

"How fascinating," he said aloud with a grin.

He pulled his hooked companion dagger from its belt sheath and held it out to touch the point of purple light. Tendrils of purple lightning struck out and knocked the dagger from his hand. It skittered along the curvature of the sphere and slid to a stop at his boot. He knelt to retrieve it and replaced it in his belt.

"Well, then – a dagger is preferable to my hand," Actaeon said.

If he retrieved his halberd, perhaps he could focus the electrical energy back on the door to trigger its opening.

When he stepped toward it though, the hazy, shimmering figure of the Ancient materialized in front of him and strode forward, one of its arms reaching upward to touch the purple pinpoint of light. The apparition flickered out of existence and reappeared before him once more, to repeat the same action before disappearing for good.

"Not my initial inclination, but I can take a hint," said Actaeon to whatever intelligent force was clearly observing his actions in this place. "Any other pieces of advice that you would care to recommend?"

There came no answer, and so he gritted his teeth and reached out to touch the purple light floating above him. The contact radiated down his arm with a sudden, uncomfortable warmth and he felt all the hairs on his body raise.

It was over in a moment though, and the point of light enlarged until it was a large prism. The purple prism continued to grow until it was larger than Actaeon. Inside it was a tangled insect's nest of twisting corridors and scattered chambers. At its very center was a sphere that glowed a faint blue.

Within the sphere stood a tiny red figure at the very center. When Actaeon raised his arm, the figure's arm also raised – when he lowered it, the figure's lowered as well. Four red figures were just outside the sphere in a nearby corridor – one of them was larger than the others and another lay supine on the floor.

Actaeon recognized them as representations of Trench, Wave, Jezail, and Ithelie. He turned to look behind him and found the entirety of his allied force there at the fringes of the Temple's prism and outside of it. Hundreds upon hundreds of red figures stood in defensive formation near the structure's entrance.

He stepped toward them and stumbled on the curved floor beneath his feet. His hands instinctively reached out to steady himself and the entire prism shifted with them. Experimentally, he shifted his hands left, right, up, and down, and the prism moved accordingly. When he rotated his hands about one another, the prism rotated. And most useful of all, when he brought his hands closer together, the prism grew smaller. Conversely, the prism grew larger when he moved his hands apart.

Actaeon bit his lip in excitement. He'd interacted with plenty of Ancient consoles throughout Redemption, but this had, by and far, the most advanced interface he'd ever interacted with. He wondered what else it could do.

He shrunk the prism and rotated it to see that they were indeed surrounded by thousands of red figures that he presumed to be Ruinic tribals.

They were thoroughly encircled by the enemy.

When the mysterious figure of the Ancient appeared before him again, he was hardly surprised. It pointed to the sphere at the center of the prism.

Nodding, Actaeon enlarged the sphere until he could once again make out the details inside it. His own red representation stood at the center of the sphere, hands spread as he manipulated the prism's position and size. Opposite him though, stood a hazy blue figure – a representation of the very Ancient projection that stood before him now.

"Perfect," said the Prince Engineer. "Now, can I move you?"

The apparition's head dipped forward, and Actaeon could've sworn he saw a smile on its face through the flickering haze.

With the utmost care, Actaeon lowered one hand to his side and, with the other, pinched the blue figure between his fingers. He felt a mild tingling in his fingertips, and he moved the figure to the corridor where his companions waited for him. The projection of the Ancient was swept out of the room before him and he watched as Trench nearly leapt into Wave's arms when the figure appeared before him.

Actaeon couldn't help but to laugh as the red figures of the pair of mercenaries stumbled over one another to get away from the blue figure.

It gave him another idea. But it would depend on whether the apparitions could be projected outside of Temple.

He repositioned the prism until he was looking among the lines of his own allied troops. It didn't take him long to find the red figure with the hooked nose that strode to and fro giving orders. With a grin, he pinched the blue figure near the mercenaries and dragged it over, directly in front of Gunther Arcady.

And the Lord Shore fell backward in surprise, the red mouth of his representative figure agape. Old though he might be, Arcady rolled backward to regain his feet and had his sword out and at the blue figure's throat in an instant.

Actaeon chuckled and dragged the Ancient back to one of the prism's corridors, leaving Arcady to question whether he'd imagined an assailant.

As fun as it had been to scare the pants off of his enemy, it had also proven to be an effective experiment. He knew now that whatever mechanism that Temple used to create these projections was capable of projecting outside of the structure itself. And so, he set about searching the Temple for blue figures, which he collected and deposited in a large chamber near the center of the building.

It took some time, but eventually he'd counted forty such blue figures that he'd managed to gather.

It was time to put his plan into action.

He shrunk the prismatic representation of Temple until he could see the ring of red tribals around it. That done, he cracked his knuckles and set to work dragging the blue figures, one at a time, behind the lines of the enemy. He started with those closest to the allied forces guarding the entrance and worked his way around the perimeter.

The red figures of the tribals began to break formation immediately, and they scattered rapidly from the blue figures as they arrived.

As they fled, Actaeon placed more of the blue figures of the Ancient projections in their path. The action fragmented the tribal forces and spread them out in fatal disarray.

It didn't take long for the allied Raedellean, Niwian, Keeper, and Czerynian forces to realize their advantage. Actaeon watched as his troops struck out and began to cut down the panicked Ruinic forces on that side of Temple.

As the red tribal ranks continued to falter and break, Actaeon placed the blue figures in strategic locations all around the tribal ring, until it was completely shattered and the tribal forces fled in all directions.

When possible, he steered them directly into the waiting blades of his allied forces. As the fleeing red figures were dispatched by the steadfast red defenders, the dead figures disappeared from the field.

Actaeon watched, in victorious horror, as several hundred tribals were killed in a matter of minutes, betrayed by their fear of the Ancient projections.

"What a waste of life," he muttered with a frown. The sentiment didn't stop him from repositioning blue figures to their advantage though. It was either his own troops, or the troops of the invaders.

When the red figures of the tribals had all been slaughtered or fled into the jungle of the Underforest, the blue figures all disappeared as well.

The prism of Temple with all its red figures shrank back to the pinpoint of purple light and before Actaeon stood the shimmering figure of Ancient projection.

Actaeon sighed deeply and stepped forward to address the figure. "You have the gratitude of the people... the current people of Redemption. Your aid has allowed us to break free of this place, which will further our cause to end the siege of Pyramid and restore civilization and order to all Redemption."

The figure dipped its hazy head forward slowly and then swept forward through Actaeon.

A sudden violent nausea overcame him, and his vision narrowed to blackness.

"Wake up, Act. We got 'em," came Trench's gruff voice.

Actaeon blinked his eyes and retched ineffectively. His stomach and throat felt like they'd been burned by the gasses of the Felmere. He took a slow breath and held it, before taking another. "Water?" he asked, hoarsely.

"Here ya go," said Wave, thrusting a canteen into his hands.

Actaeon took a deep swig from the canteen and allowed it to trickle slowly down his throat. It burned all the way down. He took another draught of the water before he leveled his gaze on Trench and sputtered out, "Report?" He recognized the room he was in as one of the side rooms near Temple's entrance.

"Whatever ya did in there worked, Act," said Trench, sounding impressed. "The tribals're routed. Our people cut down a great number of 'em. Several of our warbands are still harrying them in the jungle as they try to regroup."

Ithelie stood over Actaeon then and placed her hand on his chest in a manner that felt simultaneously soothing and excruciating.

"You did it, Your Grace. Your commune with the Ancient spirits of Redemption succeeded in our succor," the Voice said. "Once you recover, our people await a word from you. Such a miracle as this has never been seen in our lifetimes."

"Simply a... a projection controller at the center of Temple. Exceptional..." Actaeon took a deep breath and another gulp of water. "Exceptional in its complexity, but no miracle."

"Ancient spirits assembling to aid us in our quest to liberate Redemption is a miracle if I've ever witnessed one," asserted Ithelie. "You go on believing whatever you might though – it changes nothing."

Actaeon grinned up at the Voice. He handed Wave back his canteen and reached out for a hand up. Trench and Ithelie pulled him to his feet and he leaned against the giant mercenary for a long moment until he felt steady on his own feet once more.

"A miracle is something which cannot be explained by nature or science," said Actaeon. "However, you must recognize our own limited knowledge of the science behind this great city. There are things beyond our technological understanding at work here, and those things may easily be mistaken for the divine. It is important that we recognize our own limitations here and realize that there is much still to be learned."

"Much still to be learned, such as the conveniently timed aid of the Ancients in a moment of true and utter desperation for our people?" Ithelie asked with a smile. "Yes, I think we must recognize our limitations and realize there is so much to be learned about this world we live in."

Actaeon reached out to grasp the Voice's shoulder. "That is one thing we might agree on wholeheartedly."

"They're waiting to hear from you, Act," said Wave, gesturing to the circular tunnel that led to the outside of Temple.

The Prince Engineer nodded and began down the tunnel. Halfway along, he reached Jezail, who was leaning against the wall, and paused. "Listen, Jez —"

"Yeah, Act. I know," she said. "You did the right thing for our people. I'm sorry I tried to stand in your way. It's just that..." Tears welled up in her eyes.

Actaeon stepped forward and drew her into a firm embrace. "I know, Jezail. I am so sorry. I cannot even begin to imagine your loss. Please do not forget though, that I need you and our people need you." He felt her arms tighten around him. "Thank you for going in there with me. You are a true friend."

Jezail's body shook as she silently cried against him. "I'm here for you, Act. It hurts like shattered Redemption, but I'm here for you. Now get out there and address your forces." She straightened and pulled away to give him a playful shove down the corridor.

As he emerged from Temple's entrance, a cheer arose from the forces gathered before him. The men and women of the Raedellean warbands, the soldiers of the Niwian units in their distinctive colors, and the Czerynian schiltron hooted, hollered, and whistled at the Prince Engineer. Only the two Keeper divisions stood silent off to one side of the clearing, looking mostly indifferent, though some of them looked downright furious. While the projections might have benefited the battle, the Keepers could not support such a major use of artifacts of the Ancients.

Actaeon arched a brow and glanced back over his shoulder to see his friends standing behind him.

Trench gave him a nudge and winked. "Ya got this, Act."

"Yeah, Act. You're good at using lots of words — it'll put 'em right to sleep," added Wave.

Actaeon cast a smirk toward Wave and turned back to the gathered soldiery of three Dominions. When he held up his hand, they drew silent.

"Brave guardians of Redemption," he began, "this is just a small win on our path to victory. The artifact projections that aided us from within Temple were a boon, but we wi-"

"All hail Prince Engineer Actaeon Rellios Caliburn, the Conduit to the Ancients!" one of the Niwian soldiers yelled. The others present echoed the words in a roar and a chant began.

"Please!" said Actaeon, lifting both hands into the air to silence the chant. He felt his face redden as he continued. "I am no Conduit to the Ancients. In fact, I suspect any of you could have interacted with the artifacts within Temple in the same manner that I did to direct the projections. If anyone spoke with the Ancients, it was Voice Ithelie. She –"

He realized it was a mistake as soon as he had said it, and the crowd before him was cheering again, this time for "Voice Ithelie, Conduit to the Ancients."

The Prince Engineer shook his head and glanced back at Ithelie.

She stepped forward in a sweep of her green robes to speak into his ear, eliciting a roar from those gathered. "Our people see the truth of the matter, Your Grace. You cannot fault them for that. The Ancients have aided us in this cause at our request. We have the guidance and support of our predecessors to this city, and that gives us divine mandate to pursue our quest."

"You make some great assumptions with this conclusion that you draw," said Actaeon skeptically to the Voice. "There are other possibilities here than that which you seek."

Ithelie smiled knowingly. "I make no assumptions about that which I clearly witnessed here. Now isn't the time for a debate though – the people wait to hear more from you," she said, stepping back.

Actaeon nodded and raised his voice again to address those gathered. "We shall resupply and rest here before we continue onward. Unit commanders, make sure your soldiers are well rested and equipped for a march. You have all done well today, but do not let our success blind us to the dangers ahead. Voice Ithelie Faris, will you give our forces a blessing?"

As Ithelie stepped forward to speak, the gathered soldiery cheered and began their chant once again.

Actaeon stepped back between Trench and Wave.

"First of the First all over again, eh?" said Wave, rolling his eye.

"Let us hope not," said Actaeon with a frown at the memory of Phyrius and the cult that had rapidly formed around an artifact statue they had once found in the ruins.

"I dunno – they come in handy when some people are toying around with artifacts," said Trench, shooting his friend a look.

THE CHILDREN

THE NEXT DAY, BERK AND a small group of Czerynians led Actaeon and Yanelle on a circuitous route through the Underforest.

They trudged along through deep runnels in the earth, beneath massive roots that towered above their heads, and through hollow trunks of fallen trees so large in diameter you could've built a sizable shelter within them.

"I don't like this at all," said the Companion, fingering the hilt of her sword. "We could be ambushed by Ruinics at any moment."

"Trust me," rasped Berk in his gravelly voice. "There'd be signs if it weren't safe ta follow this path. And if they were there, I wouldna be here."

"The only signs I see here are jungle and more jungle," grumbled Yanelle.

"Exactly, and that means we're safe. If ya keep yer voice down, that is," said Berk. He met the Companion's eyes and widened his own wildly.

The party resumed their silent progression through the dark jungle, and they wound their way through a maze of muddy channels cut through the loamy soil. Actaeon found that he had to test every step to make sure his boot didn't sink deep into the mud.

Berk's fist snapped up suddenly, and they halted.

It took a moment for Actaeon to realize that they were surrounded by a dozen or so Kainai – so camouflaged were they to the environment. In fact, one of them was less than an arm's length to his left.

The Kainai were all dyed in similar colors to the one they had encountered several days earlier. Mossy greens and earthen browns with raised lines of bark-like brown crisscrossing their bodies. Clothing of leaves and vines clung irregularly to their heavily modified bodies. The whites of their eyes were all dyed dark brown or black, making them difficult to locate even once you knew they were there. All were small of stature, lending to their more common name – the Children.

"By the Fallen!" gasped Yanelle, clearly shaken at her failure to notice the sudden appearance of the camouflaged Children.

"Leave yer weapons here," said Berk. "No worries, you'll get 'em back." He pulled his own arming sword from his back and handed it to one of the Children.

The Kainai accepted it and hastily deposited it into a hollow in a nearby root.

Actaeon handed his halberd over to them and nodded to Yanelle to do the same. She reluctantly surrendered her own sword.

Once the weapons were secreted away, the Kainai began to lead them along and the group followed.

They were led to a tree that, at first, Actaeon thought was a cluster of trees, so wide was its base. Its grayish-brown form towered above them — the branches a city for birds that stretched to the heavens. The bird sounds coming from above were a cacophony that made it difficult to hear. The trunk was supported by roots that fanned out to the sides like great arches of a castle. Many of the roots originated above the ground so that beneath the tree was a maze of openings and tunnels. It was a massive one of these openings that they were led inside. It made Actaeon feel quite small.

The Kainai guides led the way deep into the loam of the earth, down winding passages of moss and rock and root. As the dim light of the Underforest faded, Actaeon realized that he could still see because of the light emanating from clusters of glowing green, phosphorescent mushrooms that grew in recesses along the passage they travelled. The intervals of the natural light sources were conveniently distributed such that Actaeon imagined they must've been grown purposely in those locations.

The path finally opened to a tremendous room that was brightly lit by thousands upon thousands of the tiny glowing mushrooms. The majority of them grew from above, their roots clinging to the wood of a massive hollow in the tree's trunk. Most of the mushrooms glowed green, but there was a scattering of purple and blue phosphorescence as well.

Actaeon quickly recognized that the purple and blue mushrooms were arranged in familiar patterns. He had seen them often on various artifacts around Redemption – symbols in the language of the Ancients that weren't fully understood.

"This place is fascinating," he whispered.

"You are within Ardianteki, Homeroot of the Kainai," spoke an alien voice ahead of them.

At the center of the room, Actaeon's eyes were drawn to a glowing purple sphere, which he realized was attached to some sort of sceptre made of gnarled wood. The figure that held it was another Kainai, the gender unidentifiable, but this one's eyes glowed purple, like the phosphorescence of the mushrooms. A crown of wide leaves sat upon the sceptre-wielder's head, woven into reddish strands of their hair. They raised the sceptre and pointed its orb at the visitors. They spoke rapid words in a language that made Actaeon's head ache.

"Saundrak, Litomar of the Kainai, requests to know why the Protectors have brought with them strangers," said another Kainai that stood just behind the sceptre-wielder and off to one side.

Berk stepped forward and knelt before the one called Saundrak. "Greetings, honored Interglot Heimgar and Litomar Saundrak. I come to bear unfortunate news to you."

Heimgar spoke rapidly to Saundrak, who pounded the orb of the sceptre roughly into the palm of their hand and rained more strange words down upon Berk.

Actaeon's head pounded as she spoke, and a sidelong glance at Yanelle found the Companion raising her hand to rub at her temple.

"What is she saying, Heimgar?" asked Berk.

"The trust of Ardianteki has been violated. Strangers are here, they are unwelcome," pronounced the Interglot.

"Tell her that these are not strangers – they are your new Protectors. They are from Raedelle to the south. Prince Engineer Actaeon Rellios Caliburn and his Companion Yanelle are here to speak on their behalf," explained Berk.

Heimgar translated for the Litomar, and her phosphorescent eyes snapped to Actaeon's. When she spoke again, it was like a spike was being hammered into Actaeon's head.

"Saundrak wishes for knowledge. Why are new Protectors required?

The Dominion of Czeryn serves that purpose well. They have earned our trust over much time," relayed Heimgar.

"Czeryn. Has. Fallen," Berk said, choking out the words. "Certainly, some of the Kainai bore witness to the blue sphere? It has annihilated my people. Czeryn can no longer protect the Kainai – we can scarcely protect ourselves."

Saundrak spoke again, addressing Berk, and this time her strange words were a shout.

"You have already failed the Kainai in many ways. The recent invaders have slain many of our people. Had you warned us earlier, fewer might have fallen," translated Heimgar. His alien voice carried a sharpness that might've been anger. "Depart us, then."

"But –" started Berk.

"Depart us, then, and never return. As you described, your purpose here has ended," said Heimgar.

Berk stood up and glanced at Actaeon, lifting his hands in frustration. Actaeon shook his head and arched a brow.

The Warlord turned back to Saundrak and narrowed his eyes. "You aren't listening to me. I'm tryin' to tell y-"

Saundrak extended her sceptre suddenly forward and it flashed so brightly that it took Actaeon's eyes a moment to recover. When they did, Warlord Berk lay on the ground at Saundrak's feet.

Four of the Kainai stepped from the shadows at the edges of the large chamber. Each took a limb of the unconscious Czeryn Warlord and they hauled him out of the room.

Silence followed as Actaeon and Yanelle watched Saundrak and Heimgar, who, in turn, watched them.

"Have you killed him?" asked the Prince Engineer, after a time.

"Our people cannot kill – our foremost tenet. The one called Berk sleeps. You will be brought to him when we are finished here," reassured Heimgar. "Saundrak has questions of you – will you submit?"

"Absolutely," said Actaeon with a grin. "May there be naught but truth between us. I hope that I may ask questions of you as well. Your people are fascinating – I hope to learn from you."

Saundrak extended her sceptre suddenly forward again, causing Actaeon to wince. Beside him, Yanelle tensed, but he held up a hand to stay her.

The Litomar's words stabbed at his temples as Actaeon listened to them and tried to make sense of the patterns. If he wasn't mistaken, it seemed that the more he concentrated, the more pain he experienced. But how could that be possible? How could spoken words bring about such a physiological effect? A stolen glance at Yanelle found her brows wrinkling in pain as well. So it wasn't just him.

"Prince Engineer Actaeon Rellios Caliburn, Saundrak asks this of you: Why, if you come as Protectors, have you led this force of death and destruction into our home?" translated Heimgar.

"Please, call me Actaeon," he said in reply. His name was getting much too long for efficient use. "We have not led the Ruinic tribals here on purpose. They have arrived within the limits of Redemption to besiege Pyramid. It is our intention to break the siege and restore order to the city. However, we faced a great loss at the Glass Spire, and it forced our retreat into the Underforest. It was not our intention to bring harm. Our goal now is to root out the invaders from this place and drive them from Redemption entirely. For this we would benefit from your aid."

Heimgar and Saundrak conferred for a long time about this, to the great unease of the two Raedelleans.

Actaeon turned to Yanelle. "Try not to concentrate on what they say. It helps to reduce the discomfort."

The Companion cast a confused glance at him, and he shrugged in reply.

Heimgar spoke. "Our people wish to see these invaders removed from our home as well. The one called Berk expressed that you were here to serve as our Protectors. The Kainai choose their own Protectors, but we are willing to consider your offer. Please elaborate."

Actaeon nodded slowly and stepped forward. "Of course. The people of Raedelle, under the leadership of my wife, Princess Eisandre Rellios Caliburn, and myself, wish to enter the role of the new Protectors of the Kainai. In exchange for the use of Temple as a resupply base and waystation, and your consideration of occasional non-military aid in other matters within the Underforest and Redemption, we will drive the Ruinic tribals from the Underforest and station a garrison within Temple to guard your home from any other invaders. If you do not wish for us to be your Protectors, we will still fight these hostile tribals to push them from the Underforest, but we will respect your wishes and leave Kainai territory as soon as we are able. You have my condolences for your Fallen – this war has been difficult for everyone."

Heimgar consulted with Saundrak at length again before replying. "What is this non-military aid you speak of?"

"We are much less familiar with this terrain than your people are. If you can attach several Kainai scouts to our allied forces, we could use your help in locating the enemy forces and identifying the best plan of attack based on your knowledge of the Underforest," explained Actaeon. "Aside from that, my only other hope would be to learn from you. I have so many questions."

After the pair consulted again, Heimgar replied with a smile that revealed remarkably white teeth. "As you have said: May there be naught but truth between us, Actaeon. We would have you as our Protectors if you can ensure, as our previous Protectors have always done until recently, that you will defend us even at peril to yourselves. The safety of our people must be paramount to Raedelle. Will you pledge this to us?"

"On behalf of Raedelle, I do," said Actaeon without hesitation.

"Then you may occupy Temple and use it how you may," explained Heimgar. "Saundrak offers you five scouts for the duration of this conflict in the Underforest, and I will travel with you as Interglot. The scouts will not enter into any physical conflict and must be protected at all costs – if any are killed, our agreement shall terminate. The Kainai welcome our new Protectors with love. You are welcome as guests of Ardianteki."

In accentuation of Heimgar's words, Saundrak approached Actaeon and pulled his face down to hers. He was surprised as she kissed him solidly on the lips. The Litomar smelled like the damp bark of a tree, Actaeon thought, as the Kainai leader moved past him to plant a similar kiss on Yanelle's lips.

The Companion blushed a deep red and offered him a flustered look when the Kainai leader stepped away.

Actaeon shrugged and offered her a grin in reply.

"Saundrak will hear your questions now," said Heimgar.

The Prince Engineer stepped forward and bowed to Saundrak. "You honor us with your willingness to answer our questions, Litomar. In turn, we shall answer any questions you have of us. My first question is – what is the lifespan of the Kainai?"

Heimgar's dark brown eyes narrowed at the question, and he entered a heated exchange with Saundrak that Actaeon tried to ignore until the interpreter addressed him once more.

"Most Kainai do not live past twelve revolutions. There are exceptions, but few," said Heimgar. He didn't look happy to share the answer.

"And those exceptions – do they live much longer?"

"It has not happened in our recent memory. Legends speak of those that lived for hundreds of revolutions in the past, but we are not certain," said Heimgar.

"Interesting. I should like to hear more about your legends when we have more time. How long have the Chil... the Kainai dwelt in this place?" asked Actaeon.

"Saundrak is the four hundred and sixty-seventh Litomar of our people," said Heimgar without consulting his superior.

Actaeon's jaw dropped at that. He placed both palms on his forehead and ran his hands slowly through his hair. At first he didn't know what to say, so he just stared at the two camouflaged Children before him.

"The Czerynians? They knew this?" he finally asked, incredulously.

The pair of Children consulted one another in their painful language once more.

"They never asked," said Heimgar simply.

"Shattered Redemption," whispered Actaeon. He glanced at Yanelle. "Do you know what this means?"

"The Children go through many leaders, Your Grace?" asked Yanelle, confused at the nature of the question.

"More than that, Companion Yanelle," said the Prince Engineer, flabbergasted. "It means they have been around for thousands of years, assuming their Litomars reigned for even a fraction of their lifespan. They could have been here since before Redemption's fall. They might have known the Ancients. By the Fallen, they might *be* the Ancients."

The Companion didn't know what to say in response. She just shook her head as though it were beyond her conception.

"Do the Kainai remember a time before Redemption's destruction?" asked Actaeon.

"Legend tells of a time at the beginning of memory, where the city breathed and soaked its life from the earth itself," said Heimgar. "There is little remembered from that distant past, but that the first Litomar led us to the safety of what you call the Underforest."

"The language that you speak – is it the language of the Ancients, the language of Redemption?" asked Actaeon, his voice trembling with excitement.

"The symbols of our people are found among the broken city," admitted Heimgar. "The knowledge is incomplete, but the potential exists."

"Will you teach me your language? It will be of much benefit for us to better understand what the Ancients have left behind," said Actaeon.

"This we cannot do," said Heimgar. "Others have tried and failed. Your minds are not designed for it. The attempt will lead to your demise."

"And if I am willing to take that risk?" asked the Prince Engineer.

"It is who we are to bring no harm to life," said Heimgar firmly. He frowned before he added, "We will not aid in your death, Prince Engineer Actaeon Rellios Caliburn, whether you welcome it or no."

They sound very interesting, Act. I am curious to see what you will learn about them, sent Eisandre through the Thoughtlink Artifact. She lay in her command tent, appreciating a moment of quiet. The demands of leadership were constant, and, even as they remained fast in their camp to the west of the Pyramid, there were constant inquiries, complaints, suggestions, and updates. Each of them required her attention and direction. It was sapping. She needed these peaceful moments during which she could converse with her love and her mind could be home.

Actaeon smiled and lay on his cot, looking up at the translucent ceiling in his temporary quarters within Temple. The light was fading from the day and the chamber grew dim.

That the Czerynians never delved into their histories like that is unfathomable. To have such a resource at your fingertips, but not to use it. It is hard to understand, he thought.

Not everyone's mind works as yours does, my love – eager to solve the next puzzle. Most are trying to survive, grow their power, sustain their people, and enhance their resources, she thought.

And yet all those things are related. If only more realized that in understanding our history we better understand how to attain our future, he thought.

I suspect that more people will realize that, as you continue to do your work, thought Eisandre.

Yes, and I will be better able to accomplish my work the sooner we end this invasion, he thought. *The warbanders and other soldiers are impatient to be on the offensive again. They have only tolerated my dalliances with the Kainai because of the recent victory we won. That victory is fading quickly in their minds, replaced with thoughts of how miserable the conditions in this Underforest are.*

She found herself nodding as she replied, *My forces grow impatient as well. Even when I remind them of our heavy losses in the Boneyards, they insist on taking some action rather than to strategically exercise some patience. You'd think that more than four days had passed. The Supreme Captain is furious at my insistence to wait. He keeps hinting that, were he in charge, the war would already be over. So many more people would be dead if he had his way.* She clenched her fists in anger at the thought.

It is decided then, concluded Actaeon. *We must convene a joint war council tomorrow with both our command staffs present. Now that I have the Kainai scouts, my forces should be better prepared to fight their way out of the Underforest.*

I hope you can, thought Eisandre. *The longer we remain here, the more likely that the allies will tear themselves apart before the Ruinic invaders even have their chance. I'm hardly the best person to keep them from each other's throats. I miss you, Act. This is hard.*

It is, he agreed. *Not what I expected to be doing this cycle when I first arrived at Pyramid. A lot has happened in such a short time. When we reunite, I owe you a big hug.*

A big hug? Yes, she agreed, with a hint of amusement. Then, in thoughts beyond words, she sent him images, memories, of their few precious times alone together – wrapped in passion, tenderness, and the bright intensity of their love. *And perhaps more.*

Actaeon felt the blood rush to his cheeks and elsewhere. *We could experience some of that now, you know,* he replied with a grin.

We could? she thought, confused until she felt his fingers slide beneath his trousers as though they were her own to wrap around him. *Oh,* she mouthed wordlessly, before rushing to unlace her own breeches.

And though they were on opposite sides of Redemption, they lost themselves in a flurry of shared thoughts and solitary touch. Their joined energy flared and grew dim. They fell asleep murmuring thoughts of love, at once together and so far apart.

ASSAULT

"SOMETHING'S BURNING," SAID MAERDIA BAZARDJAN, the Ajmani artist.

The artist was helping the Althean healers in the makeshift infirmary that was set up in the vacant Czerynian embassy to tend to the survivors trapped inside the Pyramid. She dabbed at Trello sof Allyk's shoulder wound with an antiseptic treatment.

"I'd best get out there," said Trello, gently pushing past the artist.

"Oh no, you don't!" said Phyvia, one of the Althean healers. She was a small, middle-aged woman, but what she lacked in size, she more than made up for in strength as she gripped Trello's arm to prevent the Knight Arbiter from moving past her.

Trello tried to tug free and winced in pain as Largrival, the Czerynian Attaché, grabbed his injured arm. Together the two Altheans forced him back down into the chair.

The Altheans assigned an Attaché to every Dominion in Redemption, except for Raedelle, who historically never accepted one. With the destruction of the Czeryn Dominion, Largrival's position was now defunct.

"Finish up, Mae, yer doing a fine job," said the Attaché.

Trello opened his mouth to argue, but was silenced by a look from the hardened woman. Scars crisscrossed her face and shaved pate, and a spiked cudgel hung from her belt. The Altheans didn't carry weapons, in general, as they ran counter to their diplomatic mission of advising the various Dominion leaders. But when dealing with the Czeryn, one often needed to prove they were willing to fight. The scars she bore were a testament to the many times Largrival needed to prove herself. The fact that she was still standing was impressive – many of the Altheans were not prepared for such a violent assignment.

Mae smiled and finished cleaning the Arbiter's wound. As she prepared some clean bandages, her nose wrinkled as she caught another whiff of smoke.

"I smell it now too," cried out Cortecha, one of the apprentice healers, from where she stood over a Shieldian that had been stabbed in the belly with a spear. "It's a fire!" Her voice cracked with panic.

The makeshift infirmary erupted into a cacophony of cries and moans.

"I really should go," said Trello, tentatively. "Once you've finished bandaging me perhaps?" He gave Largrival a probing look and turned away when she glared at him and held him down in the chair.

"You'll stay 'till I say so," said the Attaché.

"Everyone stay calm." Seraeta's voice cut through the din. "The Arbiters stand between us and the threat. Our job here is to provide healing sanctuary to those who have been wounded, and we will do just that. So keep quiet, and do your jobs. Our lives depend on it."

Seraeta was the senior Althean remaining in Pyramid after the tribal invasion. An older woman with a plain face and short, severe nose, her graying black hair was tied up into a neat bun. She wore the traditional white robes of a healer, stained here and there with the blood of Pyramid's fallen defenders.

Nobody was sure whether the Althean leaders had been killed in the attack or had escaped, but she had stepped up immediately to put together the makeshift infirmary. She'd passed out assignments among the remaining Altheans, sending some to work with Shard, the herbalist who tended to the Garden Terrace, to gather any vital herbs and foods that could be found there, and the rest to work the infirmary. The surviving civilians she'd put to work as well. The less squeamish tended to the wounded under the supervision of the few healers that remained. Everyone else that could work was sent to Shard to help harvest edibles at the Garden Terrace.

"Once he's bandaged, let the young Arbiter go," said Seraeta, striding over to Trello. "They'll need all the defenders they can rally to fight the fire."

Largrival nodded reluctantly, "Aye, sister." Beside her, Phyvia stepped back as well and nodded to the higher-ranking Althean.

Once Mae had secured his bandage, Trello thanked her and rushed out into the Mirrorholds, his sword in hand.

He ran into Sentinel Arbiter Phragus who slapped the blade out of the way with his open palm.

The Mirrorholds were beginning to fill with a thick, black smoke that roiled up from the eastern tunnels. The reflections in the floor made it appear as though the smoke billowed below and above them simultaneously, rolling like a carpet some distance beneath their feet.

The Sentinel locked onto Trello's eyes with his dull gaze. "Put that damned sword away and go find Knight Arbiter Corvin – he's in charge of the firefighting effort." The Sentinel pointed toward the Skyspiral.

"Aye, sir!" cried Trello. He sheathed his sword and took off.

He found the technical Knight as he led a squad of Arbiters and survivors carrying various containers of water from the Baths.

"Knight Arbiter Trello! Tie this around your mouth and help with one of the barrels." Corvin tossed him a thick, damp cloth and Trello tied it over his mouth before rushing to help one of the firefighting squads taking up the rear with a heavy barrel.

Under Corvin's lead, they rushed through a Mirrorholds filled with heavy smoke. As they ran, they passed Sentinel Arbiter Phragus, who gestured wildly with his sword as though they needed further direction.

When they arrived at the slope of the Eastern Tunnels, they found the last barricade was just beginning to catch fire. Flames and spark-filled plumes of smoke whipped up along the corridor, fed by material from the barricades below and helped to ignite the remaining bulwark. The gouts of superheated smoke made it difficult to make out what was happening ahead.

Corvin tossed the contents of his bucket onto the flames wicking along the improvised structure and pointed for the others. "Dump your water at the base of the flames – no more than is needed to douse it. Quickly!" As the technical Knight spoke, his short, cropped hair began to smoke and smolder from the heat.

As the Knights poured water on the fire, it turned to steam quicker than it could extinguish the flames.

Trello felt his eyes stinging as he followed the others into the smoke. It stung his throat. He couldn't imagine how much worse it would be without the damp cloth over his mouth filtering some of it. As the steam reached him, he lifted his free hand up to shield his eyes. He cried out in pain as he felt the skin of his hand and forearm blister and burn.

He lifted the handle of the barrel to toss its contents against the barricade, but was stopped when the other person carrying it yanked it back.

A glance across found Trello's carrying partner, Inditrovalis Jem – the Loresworn, glaring at him. "This one is out. Let's go on to the next."

They passed the still smoking barricade and had to crouch low to stay beneath the flames that whipped over their heads. Trello felt his hair burning and dipped his hand in the water of their barrel to then cool his head. He screamed and dropped the barrel's handle, spilling the contents to the floor of the corridor.

"Darkest Hour take you – why'd you drop it?" cried out the Loresworn as he knelt to right the barrel to save the rest of its contents.

Trello clutched his hand and raised it to his face to find his skin slaking off, revealing the tissue underneath and even part of the bone of his middle finger. He looked back up for help, but the Loresworn had fled.

A strong, reassuring hand fell upon his shoulder – it was Knight Arbiter Garth. "Draw your sword if you can, lad. They're here."

It was then that he saw them – slithering along the ground like snakes. The tribals had crawled low, hugging the floor under the smoke and flame, and wrapped their heads in wet cloths, leaving only small slits for their eyes.

They stood up and raised their spears, but Garth was among them, cutting down those that stood and pinning others to the ground with the point of his sword.

Corvin rushed forward to help but was struck in the head by a flaming chunk of wood that flew from the smoke. The Knight Arbiter crumpled to the floor, unconscious.

As the tribals moved inward to dispatch the fallen Knight, Garth leapt into their midst to defend his brother. The deft strokes of his blade pushed the enemy advance backward even as his tabard caught fire and it quickly spread up to his hair.

Trello reached down to draw his sword, but found that the painful remains of his hand couldn't grasp the hilt. He grimaced and began to pull the blade free with his off hand. A spearpoint slammed into his hand before he could do anything and pinned it to his side.

The tribal lunged at him from the side with a knife drawn. There was nothing that Trello could do and he knew it. He tensed up for the killing blow, but then the tribal exploded in a splash of warm liquid that cooled his burning skin.

Tarcy Hael kicked the corpse free of her ruinblade and swung it through another two tribals, splitting them in two at their waists. She hefted the blade high and charged forward to aid Garth.

The flaming Knight Arbiter was holding his own still, but beginning to slow as the flames spread. Impossibly, he leapt to and fro amidst the carnage, his momentum keeping the flames from his face and chest.

The Raedellean giantess obliterated several more tribals with quick swipes of her ruinblade. She reached down and grabbed Corvin by the back of his tunic. She flung the Knight Arbiter over her shoulder like a toy doll and began to march back up the tunnel incline.

"Why're ya standin' there? Put 'im out!" she snapped at Trello on her way past.

Trello frowned and nodded resolutely. He tugged at his hand, but it was pinned to his side where the spear still stuck out from the side of his belly. Gritting his teeth against the pain, he pulled his companion dagger from its sheath with his badly burned right hand and used it to cut through the sinews between the fourth and fifth knuckles of his left. The pain was only a different counterpoint from the other pain he felt – his burnt hand around the dagger's hilt, the sharp ache in his side, and the excruciating burning of his scalp as flames swept over his head. Even his chest had begun to hurt with every breath. He screamed as he cut, but he wasn't sure whether he'd already been screaming before he'd started.

Once cut, his hand slid free of the spear and he took hold of the barrel that Jem had righted. He dropped the dagger and hefted the barrel painfully with the remains of both hands, rushing toward Garth, who was still fighting on one knee, the flames now licking up his front.

The young Arbiter dumped the remaining contents of the barrel onto his brother Knight, which extinguished the flames in a burst of steam.

The effort brought Trello to his knees before Garth and a new spear that passed through the senior Knight came to a stop in his own chest. An indrawn breath didn't bring him any air and he felt wet warmth bubbling up into his throat, bringing relief to his burning larynx.

On either side of them, their attackers rushed past now, ignoring the two Knight Arbiters pinned together with a spear.

Trello coughed up blood that burbled up his throat. He felt Garth's hand on the back of his neck, his touch gentle.

"Ya did good, kid. This is death now," spoke Garth between coughs that racked his body. "We die here, in defense of our people," concluded the Knight Arbiter, looking into his eyes with one eye, his other having been melted shut. "You were a good partner. Rest easy now, Trello sof Allyk. I'll make sure we have some company."

Garth lifted his sword once more and Trello saw it flash by his face, and then flash again.

He smiled – his eyes heavy. So heavy. He let them fall shut one final time.

"The time to strike is now," said Eisandre. "Both sides hold the advantage."

"It's high time you said that. My marines grow weary of this waiting around," said Captain Jarval, offering the Princess a knowing look.

"Even the most inexperienced strategist knows that a pincer maneuver is only effective with both sides of a pincer," snapped Lady Vanora, her eyes narrowed upon the Supreme Captain.

"Is that what you are? The most inexperienced strategist?" asking the balding Lord Perth with a laugh. "Maybe you should listen to the rest of us then – gain some experience."

Lady Vanora opened her mouth to retort but was beaten to the punch by the Supreme Captain.

"If we wanted to hear the after-action report from the baggage train, we'd have asked you, Lord Perth. Seeing as we haven't, I bid you keep your mouth closed for the remainder of this discussion," said Captain Jarval with a thin smile. He tugged his mustache and added, "Of course, if you decide to open it, we can finish this discussion in Arena."

Jad Perth's face turned bright red, and he clenched and unclenched his fists several times, but in the end, he kept his tongue.

Seeing that Perth was put in his place, the Supreme Captain turned to Lady Vanora. "My apologies, Lady. You are correct. I have been impatient.

Even my own Captains have been wont to point that out." He cast a smirk at Harvand Xula. "I'd like to see this ended as soon as possible. Our people have suffered enough in this Second Invasion War. Seeing as the Prince Engineer is once more ready to mobilize, Thyr stands ready to help mount the west pincer assault. Isn't that correct Major?"

Major Craft nodded. "The Flashbolt Marines stand ever ready, Captain of All Ships."

"Of course they are, Major. Thank you." He turned to Eisandre. "And your Engineer, Princess? How long before he can bring his forces to bear?"

Eisandre's brilliant blue gaze drifted off toward the sky as she conveyed the question to Actaeon.

Give us until the noon sun and we will be ready, Actaeon replied.

Is that enough time? Eisandre asked.

It must be. If we delay much longer, the Ruinic forces might regain their courage. I am not sure these Temple parlor tricks will have the same effect the second time.

Then so it shall be, she sent him. *I will let my forces know. Tell your people the same. The attack will commence at noon.*

"We will begin our advance at noon," said Actaeon to his gathered command council.

"The Allfather's Children stand ready," said Keeper Knight Captain Atreena.

"As do the soldiers of Niwian," said Captain Wronka.

"The Schiltron stands with the forces of Redemption," said Warlord Berk.

"All Warbands are ready, Prince Engineer," said Warchief Mirvea, her fist to chest in salute.

"The Kainai will find you a path through," said Heimgar with a solemn nod.

"I could not ask for a better group to fight this battle with," said Actaeon wholeheartedly. "I have not in my lifetime ever seen such a diverse force of defenders willing to lay down their lives in defense of our very civilization. Now go, and make sure your warriors are prepared. I will see you soon, on the advance."

"Well said, Prince Engineer," said Arcady with an approving nod before he strode from the command tent.

"If ya can get him to say that, we've got this in the bag," said Wave, with a grin.

"Of that I am not so sure, Wave. These Ruinic tribals are difficult foes – I expect more surprises up their sleeves yet," said Actaeon.

"No doubt about it," said Trench. "But we'll be ready."

"I hope so," said Actaeon under his breath as everyone dispersed.

Eisandre led from the front center, methodically cutting through any attempts for the Ruinic forces to organize a defense. Flanking her on either side were Companions Itarik and Wayd, with Guybon Hael, her attendant, trailing just behind with a pack of essential supplies on his back. The fiercest warband in Raedelle, the Southward warband, was at her back, led by the quiet Captain Oragnar with a series of complex hand signals that Eisandre found fascinating and sometimes also distracting.

They herded the fleeing tribals as efficiently as a shepherd herding his flock. Whenever the enemy turned to rally, they were easily broken apart and pushed along. The Thyrian Flashbolt Marines pushed on the northern flank while the remainder of the Raedellean warbands, Lakefeed, Whiterose, and Bastion, took the south. It was a deadly efficient operation, partially aided by the allied Redemption forces' ability to quickly traverse the Avenue of Glass in tight formation with its center while the wings to north and south swung forward to solidify the hold on the ground that they gained.

When they reached the southern entrance of the Pyramid, a cheer went up among the troops and the Princess' call for a stop was echoed by her two Companions.

Eisandre didn't join in the cheering though – she was too busy watching the Ruinic troops that fled to the south onto the plains of the Windmoor and the Stone Gardens beyond. There were significant numbers of the enemy that vanished quickly among the scattered stones and Ancient statuary. Atop that, more of the tribals than she thought could fit into the Pyramid's entrance had jammed their way inside while fleeing.

"Captain Oragnar," she said. "Stay here and guard the entrance with the Southward warband."

The Captain saluted fist to chest and made a swirling gesture above his head that had his warbanders following in an instant to set up the perimeter at the entrance.

Captain Xula ran over from the Thyrian forces. "Your Grace," he puffed, out of breath. "The Supreme Captain wants to know why we're halting. We have them on the run."

"That's exactly what they want us to do," said Eisandre. "They have forces to our south and north now. If we continue down the Avenue of Glass, they will easily flank us and force our retreat from this position."

Xula turned his sharp eyes to the south and grinned. "Well thought out, Princess. I'd follow you into war anytime. What do you recommend?"

"I hope you never need to follow me into war again," said Eisandre, matter-of-factly.

"Aye, as do I. Well put," agreed the Thyrian Captain.

Eisandre turned to Itarik and Wayd, who awaited her orders. "What do you think?"

Wayd looked flabbergasted at even being asked that question, though he recovered quickly and appeared to be racking his brain for a quick answer.

It was Itarik that spoke first.

"I recommend we begin deployment of our troops to form a line just south of the Avenue," he said. "Then we continue east until we reach the east face of the Pyramid – extending no further than we can while ensuring a firm southern line. If we must, we could rapidly retreat back along the Avenue of Glass, but this will push the remaining invaders either into the Open Markets or further east to meet the Prince Engineer's force."

"All the way to The End then?" asked Wayd.

"To The End," agreed Itarik, referring to the ramshackle tavern at the shattered end of the Avenue of Glass.

Xula laughed a deep belly laugh. "How poetic! I like you Raedelleans more and more as this campaign unfolds. Hopefully it's intact still – I could use a drink at the end of this charge. In fact, we can all have a round on me."

Itarik nodded, unconvinced.

"I'll take you up on that, for sure," said Wayd with a distracted smile.

"Bastion!" cried out Itarik. "Form a southern wall!"

As the Bastion warband moved into position, the remainder of the forces prepared to continue their controlled charge.

"I'll let the Captain of All Ships know what the plan is," said Captain Xula before moving off.

"Shall I clean your sword, Your Grace?" asked Guybon Hael.

"Why must it be clean?" asked Eisandre. "I'm not finished using it."

"The last Lord I served didn't like blood on their sword," answered Guybon, his gaze dropping to his boots.

Eisandre raised her blade to gaze at it more closely. The thick blood of those she had slain already had begun to coagulate and harden. After an awkward amount of time had passed, she responded. "Very well, Attendant. Be swift." She handed him her sword.

"Aye aye, Your Grace," said Guybon. His eyes lit up as he accepted the sword. He knelt and drew a cloth from his pack to polish the metal clean.

"Warbands at the ready, Princess," said the First Companion.

"Then let us continue our march," said Eisandre. She reached out once Guybon was finished, and he deposited the clean sword into her hand.

We're almost there, she sent Actaeon. Seeing the others taking the opportunity for a quick snack to replenish their energy, she took a few moments to chew a slice of lizard jerky from her belt pouch and sip some warm water from her canteen, before stepping off to lead the charge once more.

They reached The End while the sun was still high in the sky and Xula was able to buy that round of drinks for everyone before they continued on. Strangely enough, the inn was still open.

And when the sun set later that evening, the Avenue of Glass glowed red with the blood of the invaders.

Still deep within the unforgiving jungle of the Underforest, Actaeon couldn't reply to Eisandre as he narrowly ducked a spear that sailed over his head and thudded into Yanelle's shield. The lithe Companion pulled it free and nimbly threw it back to lodge in an enemy's hip.

A Ruinic warrior leapt down into the narrow jungle valley they were working their way through and lunged at Actaeon with his spear. The lunge ended abruptly when Trench's maul tore the man's jaw from his skull. The warrior stared wide-eyed at the giant for a split second before his eyes rolled into the back of his head and he fell over.

Several more warriors charged down the slope and kept Trench occupied. Yanelle rushed to his side to aid in the fight.

Before Actaeon, Heimgar crouched motionless. If he hadn't known better, he might have mistaken the Kainai interpreter for a vine covered stump sticking from the valley floor.

The sounds of battle and death were all around them as the allied forces of Redemption desperately fought off the tribal ambush.

Another pair of warriors broke through the thick underbrush and were upon them. Actaeon automatically thrust his halberd toward them and it lodged in the first man's ribcage, tearing the weapon from his hands.

Actaeon desperately flung himself between the second attacker and Heimgar, struggling to yank his hooked companion dagger free. Before he could pull it out, the warrior crashed into him and they both rolled down into the brush in a mess of limbs and warm blood.

Gritting his teeth, the Prince Engineer rolled the warrior off of him and reached for his dagger, only to find that it was no longer at his belt. He swallowed heavily and prepared to fight bare-handed to defend Heimgar. It was imperative that they not allow harm to come to their Kainai allies. Saundrak has made it quite clear that their alliance would be very short-lived if anything happened to the Children aiding their war effort.

By the time he realized that his Ruinic attacker was already dead, killed by a crossbow bolt that had buried itself neatly in the man's heart, there was already another enemy rushing toward him.

With no halberd or dagger available at his disposal, Actaeon reached forward and yanked the metal bolt from the dead tribal's heart. As the tribal lunged at him with the spear, Actaeon narrowly avoided the spearpoint and grasped the shaft with his free hand, pulling it toward him and taking his attacker with it.

As they both fell to the ground under the momentum of the thrust, Actaeon jammed the bolt into the side of the man's neck, aiming for the carotid artery. He was instantly doused in hot lifeblood and the tribal released his spear and fell atop him, head cracking into the Prince Engineer's and filling his vision with stars.

It would be beneficial, Actaeon thought as he laid there, if there was a compact way to fire a single bolt that every soldier could carry onto the battlefield, for use as a last resort in just such an emergency. The dying tribal atop him shook and let out one last agonal breath. Actaeon struggled to lift his head and failed, lolling back against the wet leaves below. The cool leaves were a welcome relief against his aching head and neck.

How he missed his workshop. He'd give much to be able to spend his time there searching for solutions and inventing things like a Boltcaster – yes, that's what he could call it. He'd rather study creepy deathcrawlers and noxious, explosive slugs for the remainder of his life than ever fight in a war again, surrounded by death and horror, where the only way to survive was to resort to unimaginable brutality.

Suddenly there was a weight taken from him and it felt easier to breathe again. He smiled and closed his eyes before he was slapped across his cheek. His eyes fluttered open and he looked up at Wave grinning down at him, heavy crossbow in hand.

"The hell're you doing, Act? The rest of us are here fighting what may be our last battle and yer taking a nap under a dead man?" asked Wave with a smirk. "C'mon, get up. We need yer help, damnit!"

Without waiting for an answer, Wave reached down and yanked him up to his feet. As he steadied the Prince Engineer, he paused to aim the crossbow over Actaeon's shoulder and pull the trigger. There was a sharp twang from the weapon and a dying shriek behind him.

"We're in a bit of trouble here," said Wave.

"Understatement of the cycle," grumbled Trench as the giant stomped over through the brush. "They're behind us too – cut off our path of retreat to the Temple. Maybe you can ask Lord Stump over there if there isn't a better way through."

Actaeon nodded. "I will ask him. Sorry, gentlemen – this is not something I am accustomed to." A steady wind at his back gave him some relief from the sweat that poured down his face.

"You never get used to it, Act. You just get more and more surprised that you aren't dead yet," said Wave.

"Speak for yerself," said Trench. "I, for one, actually know how to fight."

"If being a human battering ram is fighting then I'll just have to give up a lifetime of training under the blade," said Wave.

"Works better than poking people with your tiny needles," growled Trench, amused.

"If ya say so, pal. If I recall correctly, the second time I met you, your battering ram technique was less than successful," countered Wave.

"The amount of bodies that you found there shoulda told you otherwise," said Trench.

"Kill as many people as you want – I never saw a single dead man benefit from a battle being won," said Wave.

Trench's maul caught another attacker full in the chest. "Enough talk, Wave. Time to fight. Lord Stump, Act?"

Actaeon shook his head and grinned. After he found his dagger nearby and pulled his halberd free of the dead tribal it'd been entangled with, he knelt before the Kainai. "Heimgar, we are losing this battle badly. Is there a better path to the west? This valley has us at a pointed strategic disadvantage."

Heimgar's lips parted as he spoke, but otherwise he didn't budge. "The valley continues through much of the Underforest. You would need to go far south to circumvent it. There is a shallower point to the north a bit that may ease your traverse."

"Excellent! We shall make for the shallow crossing of the valley. Thank you, Lord St... Heimgar," said Actaeon, biting back a smirk.

The Kainai still hadn't moved except for the steady wind that gently blew his hair.

"Trench, Wave — guard me. I am going to light a fire," said Actaeon. "Companion Yanelle, inform Warchief Mirvea that we shall pivot north to the shallow point."

"Aye aye, Prince Engineer," said Yanelle, saluting fist to chest before she ran off.

"Now's not the time for camping, Act," muttered Trench.

"That is correct, Trench," replied the Prince Engineer. "I'm thinking something a bit bigger." He continued to explain as he dug the necessary supplies from his jacket pockets. "You see, when I was a boy, we used to wait until the updrafts started from the River of Arches and then we'd light backfires to help clear away the underbrush up along the slope."

Understanding dawned on Trench's scarred features. "Ah, so yer gonna burn 'em out."

"Aye," nodded Actaeon as he pulled a strip of brightweave from his jacket pocket and tied it securely to the bottom of his halberd with a clove hitch. He could hear the sounds of fighting around him as the mercenary duo fought off another tribal charge. It gave him a sense of deja vu as he unstoppered the first of the half-through bottles and scraped a bit of the brown goo from it with the tip of his dagger. He smeared the viscous substance along the length of the brightweave, not worrying about cutting the material – even the sharpest of non-artifact weapons couldn't cut through the Ancient fabric. From the second bottle he shook loose some of the fine purple crystals atop the streak of brown goo.

He cringed as an enemy warrior landed beside him and caught Trench's maul in the back, cracking the spine in half. The man lay there gurgling as he died, but Actaeon tried to ignore it – there was no time to waste. He capped the bottles and stuffed them deep into his jacket before unstoppering the last of the bottles. From this he let fall a drop of water atop the concoction and it immediately began to sputter and hiss before igniting in a brilliant blue flame that ran the length of the strip.

"No!" screamed Heimgar. The Kainai charged at Actaeon, hollering in horrified ululation. Trench grabbed the back of the Interglot's shirt before he could reach the Prince Engineer.

Actaeon hefted his halberd and started along the valley to the north. "Wave, to me. Trench carry him. I do not know how long this will last." As he ran through the forest, he let the flaming brightweave streamer drag along the brush behind him.

The giant threw Heimgar over his shoulder like a ragdoll and carried him, the Kainai still keening with the alien warble.

Wave dispatched several of the tribals and rushed to catch his boss, quickly reaching and surpassing him. He took a position up the incline and slightly ahead of Actaeon, so as to guard him without getting burned as the fire from Actaeon's brightweave spread to the underbrush and up the hill.

As more and more of the forest behind them caught fire, Heimgar's ululation grew louder until it reached a high-pitched tone that pierced all of their eardrums. He squirmed on Trench's back to try and break free, but the mercenary's iron grip held him firmly in place.

The Ruinic tribals realized quickly what was happening and made for Actaeon in a full show of force. The twang of Wave's crossbow and the flashing sweep of his rapier kept them clear on one side while erratic kicks and deadly swings of Trench's maul kept the other side clear.

Companion Yanelle arrived at their side in short order and saluted, sword hand to chest. "Warchief Mirvea has all the allied forces on the move. Orders have been relayed, sir."

"Great, Yanelle. Help on Trench's side. He has a bit of a burden at the moment," said the Prince Engineer as he hopped over tangles in the brush to continue racing along. He followed along the western side of the valley about a quarter of the way up the slope – it was important that the fire didn't spread eastward as well, or else everyone might be in trouble. Luckily, the wind was blowing steadily westward. So long as it didn't shift, they should be alright.

Yanelle nodded and fell in with Trench to guard Actaeon's eastern flank.

"There's not enough of us, Act," called Wave. "They're gonna overwhelm us ahead – they're getting the hint."

As Wave spoke, the Wall Breakers, led by Captain Jezail, crashed into the inrush of tribals ahead and held them at bay.

When the Prince Engineer's band reached them with their flaming blue halberd streamer, Jezail gave the order, and the warband fell in on both sides to defend them.

The warbanders on the eastern flank were able to push the attackers back out of the valley and soon ran along atop the valley edge to protect that side.

The run was an exhausting one, especially in the humid jungle air and with fire licking at their heels, but they finally reached a shallower area of the valley.

Heimgar, who had long since run out of energy to maintain his ululating shrieks, paused in his sobs to speak into Trench's ear.

"Lad says this's it," said Trench.

"Perfect," said Actaeon. He came to a halt to survey the situation. They had outpaced the unprepared tribal forces a bit and now had some room to breathe. Allied forces were arranged ahead and behind their position along the valley floor and the eastern rim. The wind maintained its westerly course and steadily blew the fire up the incline to push the Ruinic forces back on that side. To the west, the late afternoon sun was descending and would create a visual issue for them, as it would be at the enemies' backs. Hopefully, the smoke would dim the light of the setting sun and also give a visual signal to Eisandre's forces so they would know exactly where the eastern army was located.

"What's your plan, Your Grace?" asked Warchief Mirvea as she rushed to his side, regarding him with her cloudy gray eyes.

Actaeon felt his eyes begin to water as the smoke caught up and pulled his goggles down to protect them. He narrowed his gaze to peer into the jungle to the east. Far off in the murky distance, he could see the movements of Ruinic warriors among the trees.

"Have the Czerynian Schiltron set up to protect north and south here. Captain Wronka's Niwians can lead the charge up the valley slope while the warbands and Keepers guard the rear. In the meantime, I will continue onward to light more of this fire to protect our northern flank," Actaeon explained.

The Warchief saluted, fist to chest. "It will be done."

Actaeon nodded and waved his Wall Breaker escort onward.

Upon their return, Actaeon was pleased to see the bristling shield formations of the Czerynian Schiltron. They had broken into two groups and formed what looked like two hairy caterpillars to the north and south of the valley site. The Raedelleans and Keepers guarded the eastern flank as ordered and Captain Wronka was already leading the charge up from the valley floor through the burnt undergrowth.

Gunther Arcady and the Blackstone warband emerged from the jungle to the east and he pushed his way past the pickets to speak with Actaeon.

The Lord Shore was covered in spattered blood and took a moment to pull the leather gauntlets from his hands and wipe the blood from his forehead.

"I'll admit, Engineer, that this approach you have here is a sound one," said Arcady with a begrudged smirk. "It pains me to tell you that based on the numbers we've seen to the east, there's little chance we'll weather this. The Ruinics must've gotten more reinforcements from beyond the city. We're better off trying to hold them at the eastern rim of this valley."

"And fight with our backs to a cliff?" asked Wave. "What're our chances of surviving that? The advantage of Act's fire isn't going to last forever."

"Honestly, Wave," said Arcady, exasperated, "I don't believe we'd survive that position either, but down here we'd be picked off like fish in a barrel."

Many of the other commanders pushed forward to listen to the exchange and most of them looked to the Prince Engineer. To the west, sounds of battle reached them as the Niwian and Ruinic forces met.

"Your decision, Your Grace," said Jezail. "We trust your judgment."

"Given the option, I will always pick the hopeful course of action over the hopeless one," said Actaeon with a grin. "Thus, if the decision is left to me, I say we continue the effort to break through. Even if we fall more easily in this position, none will say we did not try. Think also, on the fact that our brothers and sisters from Lakehold and Thyr await us on the other side. It strikes me that we cannot in good conscience abandon them now. They need us. All of Redemption needs us."

A smattering of rallying cries went up at the Prince Engineer's last words, but it was short-lived.

Mirvea spoke up. "It's not all or nothing, Your Grace. We can place some units up on the eastern rim of the valley. In fact, it's only appropriate that the Ea–"

"Shattered Redemption! That's a suicide run if I've ever heard it. You'll all die up there," said Wave.

"Better that some of us die up there than all of us down here," Mirvea spat back at the mercenary. She turned back to Actaeon. "Put me up there with the Eastern Rim warband, Your Grace. We'll give you all the time we can. I think you know it's the right thing."

"I shall require the continued service of my Warchief, Mirvea," said Actaeon bluntly. "If Captain Hargum or anyone else agrees to it, then I will send them, but nobody goes to their death up there unless they volunteer for it."

"All or none, Prince Engineer. We'll be going," said Hargum, stepping forward to be heard. He tugged nervously on his bushy mustache. "Appropriate that the warbanders of Eastern Rim die on an Eastern Rim." He turned to the others, "You boys and girls with me?"

"Aye," they said, half-heartedly.

"Don't give me that, damnit!" Hargum spun to face his warbanders. "If you can't muster a greater enthusiasm than that, then yer no damned use to me up there. Now, are you ready to die so that our brethren may live?"

"Aye, sir!" shouted the warbanders. Captain Hargum spun and gave Actaeon one final salute before leading the warband to climb up from the valley floor.

"The Keeper 2nd Division will join them as well," said Knight Captain Atreena. She nodded to the officer at her side and the heavily armored knights began to ascend after the warbanders.

"They volunteered?" asked Actaeon, skeptically. He kept the fact that Atreena led the 1st Division to himself.

"Indeed they did," said Atreena. "Let it be remembered that Keeper blood spilled on this day paved the way for our success."

At Mirvea's suggestion, Actaeon sent the Keeper 1st Division and the Highwater warband to back up the Niwian advance. The shallow pass was narrow, so the rest of the allied forces would have to survive on the valley floor until Wronka's charge broke through.

It didn't take long for those that remained below to hear the sounds of clashing up above. The defenders of the eastern rim fell one by one, tumbling down to the valley floor below – though many of them dragged a Ruinic tribal or two with them.

With her green robes fluttering behind her, Ithelie rushed from body to body to invoke the final rites, bidding the Ancestors to accept them in the afterlife. She ignored any protests at her being amidst the danger, and a pair of warbanders followed after her reverently with shields raised to protect her.

Captain Hargum's body was the last to fall. They tossed his head down after. It rolled to a stop several paces from Actaeon, empty eyes looking up at him as if in accusation.

It was over quickly, and for a long span of time the Ruinic warriors stood at the rim simply watching them.

"Shields!" barked Mirvea, her face pale.

And then came the bombardment.

Stones, spears, and arrows rained down upon them and the slaughter of the allied forces began.

"There was no other option. Nothing else that I saw," murmured Actaeon.

Wave grabbed him and pulled him beneath the closest Schiltron. "There's nothing we can do now, Act. It's up to Wronka now."

Trench was also there, hunched beneath the shield vault as he crouched over Heimgar.

The shields shook and quivered as they were pelted repeatedly from above. Occasionally, a bigger stone split one of the shields and pulverized the bearer below it. When this happened, the organized soldiers of the Schiltron ejected the dead man and filled in the gap. Beyond the formation the screams of the dying rose to an ear-splitting cacophony.

"I should not be hiding here, Wave. Am I not their leader?" asked

Actaeon, wincing as another rock smashed through between two shields to slam into the ground, luckily missing everyone.

"You'll be naught but worm food if ya don't sit tight, Act," said Wave.

There was a commotion outside and Companion Yanelle crawled under the Schiltron formation. A stream of blood trickled down her face, nearly matching her dark red hair.

When she reached Actaeon, she propped herself up on her elbows and spat blood onto the ground.

"They're carrying Wronka back down, Your Grace," she cried out over the racket. "He's dead. The Niwians are being routed without him. They're breaking."

At that news, Trench burst his way through the side of the shield formation and charged off with a roar.

"Yanelle, watch Actaeon and Heimgar for me, will you?" asked Wave, calmly. "I have to go with Trench."

Yanelle gave the one-eyed mercenary a dazed look and nodded.

Wave leaned forward and kissed her solidly upon the lips.

Yanelle lifted her hand to smack him, but he caught it first.

"In case we don't get the chance ever again," said Wave, with a smile and a shrug.

"You... you..." she sputtered, at a loss for words.

"Hold that thought, I'll be back," said Wave, and he escaped through the hole that Trench had pushed open to run after his friend.

The screams continued without.

EVENTIDE'S LIGHT

AS WAVE RUSHED DESPERATELY FORWARD to catch his friend, the fleeing Niwians impeded his progress. Soldiers in red, gold, and purple tabards beat a hasty retreat back down to the valley floor, many to be skewered and lanced by the rain of spears and arrows from the eastern rim. The sun's rays streamed through the breaks in the jungle canopy and silhouetted the running figures, some of which tripped and tumbled over the tangled jungle roots and fallen bodies of comrades who had died gaining the ground they were now abandoning in a panic.

"Naught but death lies behind me, fools!" yelled Wave. "Our only chance is to take this ridge – at least we'll die trying." He eyed the fleeing Niwians in disgust as he raced to catch Trench, wondering what sort of coward would run when so much depended on this charge.

Up ahead, Trench barreled through the retreating soldiers, tossing them aside with ease as he charged along. These unfortunate troopers flew through the air and rolled down the steep embankment to jam in amidst the Niwian dead stuck in places where the ground met tree trunks that sprouted along the slope.

Some of the Niwians had begun to take heart after seeing the mad giant storm past and there was a growing force rallied behind him now. The advance was slowed, however, by the amount of bodies clogging up the valley wall. The dead stacked like cordwood, against the uphill sides of the trees and created barricades behind which Ruinic warriors hid and burst out to thrust their spears at the men and women that had joined Trench's suicidal charge.

Wave pulled the trigger of his crossbow and dropped one of several tribals that emerged from behind one such wall of the dead to attack Trench. The giant dispatched the other two with a maul swing to the head and a well-placed kick. He grinned back at Wave before letting out a roar that echoed along the valley and resuming his upward trudge.

Wave caught up with him in several short moments, tossed the unloaded crossbow over his shoulder, and opened the throat of an enemy tribal with his rapier. "Yer supposed to wait for me, you glory hound!"

"Not like anyone will even see you here, my tiny friend," laughed Trench as he swung his maul at an incoming spearpoint, breaking both arms of its former carrier and sending the whimpering man tumbling down behind them.

"You forget who's always keeping you alive," Wave spat back as he bobbed and weaved between spears and sharpened shards of artifact steel, his flamberge slicing its way through his foes.

"More like who's stealing all my kills," growled Trench with amusement. His maul lodged itself in the ugly face of an attacker that had skewered a Niwian Gold beside him.

"Mostly you just toss them about and I have to finish 'em off anyway," said Wave with a grin. "Problem ahead."

"I see it," said Trench, and they began to work their way up toward it. Wave picked up a fallen Niwian shield while Trench used the lightly armored body of his most recent kill to block the arrows that fell upon them.

Ahead there were two tribals taking turns hacking with their axes at the gnarled roots of the trees on a particularly steep section of the slope. Beyond the trees was where the Niwians under Captain Wronka must have been stalled and stopped. The pile of bodies that had rolled down to pile against the base of the trees was taller than a house. A mix of tribals and allied forces that had lost their lives and fallen back along the incline, all coming to a stop against the copse of trees that the tribals were now working to fell.

One of the trees gave way as the mercenaries and their diminishing force of Niwians made their way up from the valley floor and several bodies rolled down toward them. The tribal axeman moved to join his comrade at the last tree holding up the grisly pile.

Wave leapt his way clear of the rolling corpses and dropped the shield to sprint the remainder of the distance up the slope.

The tribals turned from their task at the last moment as Trench slammed into one of them and Wave's blades made quick work of the other.

The pair took a moment of respite as the pile shielded them from projectiles and grinned at one another.

"This makes fighting giant slugs with Act seem pretty damned good," said Wave, catching his breath.

"I'll second that, my friend," said the giant as he leaned against the tree. He squinted into the sun as he looked back up along the ridge. "I don't think we're meant to get through this one."

"Odds don't appear to be in our favor. The last of our brave charge either perished or fled again too," said Wave. "How long are old soldiers like us meant to last anyway, though?"

"By the Fallen, too long already," said Trench. "We did a lot of good though, in our borrowed time."

"We did, didn't we?" said Wave. "One last charge then? Something to make Glaive proud..."

"Aye, something to make Glaive proud," echoed the giant. He straightened and took his weight off the tree to ready his weapon.

The two men had a split second to look at each other in shock at the next sound.

The tree cracked.

The bodies fell.

The space under the schiltron was dwindling, the surviving Czerynians clustered closely together to protect themselves with their shield formation. A half dozen injured soldiers had been pushed roughly beneath the shield turtle for protection.

The constant barrage upon the shields from above created an earsplitting din. Actaeon watched the shield arms of the Czerynians shudder each time a heavy stone or spear landed atop them. Raedellean warbanders joined the formation to replace the Czerynians as they fell.

"Ancestors' tears! I should be out there, no?" Actaeon asked. "A coward would crouch under here while his soldiers die in battle. I should be out there." He felt conflicted – on one hand, he knew his abilities could not possibly make a difference in this situation, but on the other hand, he knew that a leader shouldn't behave thusly.

"Only if you want to die more quickly, Your Grace," shouted Yanelle over the racket. The blood on her face had dried into a cracked stream that ran downward, parting around her nose before rejoining at her lips. "If there's a chance for rescue, we'd do best to keep you alive under here as long as we may. Besides, if they see you fall, even the formations that remain might break."

"You are right, of course, Companion Yanelle," said Actaeon. "We shall hold here then, and pray for the best outcome. Speaking of, where is Voice Ithelie?"

"Without, speaking the rites of the dead to those newly fallen," said Yanelle. "We tried to bring her under, but she said she'd break anyone's arm that tried to take her away from her duty."

"Extraordinary," said Actaeon, in awe.

A sudden silence punctuated his remark and left everyone's ears ringing painfully. The cacophony of objects crashing against the schiltron was suddenly gone and replaced by a different sound – the ground shuddered under distant thuds that sounded like a behemoth's footfalls.

Actaeon's eyes widened as he met Yanelle's gaze and he reached out to grasp her hand and pull her along. Together they squeezed out from the schiltron and stood to gaze up at the valley's eastern rim.

Ruinic tribals no longer lined the valley edge, but could be heard in the distance rallying against whatever monster was approaching. The thuds were getting closer now and they could feel the forest floor shake under their feet.

Actaeon pulled his recurve from his back and lifted his scope to assess the scene around them. The western ridge was littered with countless corpses – more than he had ever seen in one place, and most of them his people. There was a section of the slope where hundreds upon hundreds of the dead had spilled down, even felling trees somehow. Here and there, scattered groups of allied soldiers still fought skirmishes with the Ruinic enemy, but both sides had taken such heavy losses that the effort was half-hearted.

On the eastern rim, the enemy had almost entirely retreated from the valley edge, though he could make out a handful of tribals that stood with their backs to the valley, preparing to face whatever monstrosity approached.

In the valley itself, the two Czerynian Schiltrons remained, locked in their disciplined protective formations. Several other clusters had formed as well. Actaeon was glad to see that a large warbander formation was led by Captain Jezail, who had also stepped forth to survey the sudden change. Another large shield wall under the command of Knight Captain Atreena was standing fast near the base of the western slope. It comprised a mixed force of heavily armored 1st Division Knights, Highwater warbanders, and Niwians – all survivors of the western charge.

It was from that last group that Warchief Mirvea approached. The bald and scarred commander stepped up to Actaeon and saluted fist to chest. She looked as though she was about to vomit on his boots.

"Warchief, I am glad to see you alive," began the Prince Engineer.

"Well that makes one of us, Your Grace. I watched every last one of my Eastern Rim warbanders die while all I could do was sit down in this damned valley," she said, disgusted. "Now we get to wait down here until whatever Cracked Redemption sent after us next arrives to finish us off."

"Watch your tone, Warchief," snapped Yanelle. "The Prince Engineer is in the thick of this with us, and he's done right by us all."

Mirvea winced at Yanelle's words. She toed the ground with her boot before looking Actaeon in the eye with her cloudy gray gaze. "The young Companion's right, Your Grace. Apologies."

"You are forgiven, Warchief," said Actaeon, sympathetically. "I am sorry also, that I could not let you fight with your brethren. But you are needed here more urgently. For the same reason, I had to hide beneath a shield turtle while the invaders rained death down upon us and killed so many others."

Mirvea bowed her head at his words, but kept her silence.

"I would have your report," said Actaeon.

"Aye, Your Grace," said Mirvea. "The three Niwian divisions are down to one, with a smattering of survivors from Red, Purple, and Gold. Captain Wronka isn't dead, despite initial reports. He took an arrow to the chest, but the cutters tell me it missed his heart. Still, his lung was pierced, and he might not survive the ordeal. Half of the Highwater warband, which was only at half manpower to start, has perished. The Keeper 1st Division lost a quarter of their Knights and Captain Jezail lost several of her Wall Breakers. Believe it or not, none of the Blackstoners died."

"And what of the Kainai?" asked Actaeon.

"All five scouts are safe," said Mirvea. "I'd reports that the Interglot was with you?"

"Aye, he was, Warchief," said Actaeon. "Good job keeping them safe. Our partnership with the Kainai absolutely depends on their safety."

The sounds were closer now and clearly coming from the southeast. Actaeon looked through his scope again and could see now the source of the thuds. He could also smell upon the air the same scent of ozone that writheblades created, carried along by the gentle breeze. "Some sort of artifact is felling the trees."

"How could you know that?" asked Mirvea.

"It smells like a writheblade, and I can see the treetops falling down through my scope," explained the Prince Engineer. "Some sort of similar artifact, I would imagine, but to cut through that many trees so quickly, the blades must be tremendous. Let us hope that they are on our side."

"We've no idea whether that's the case," said Mirvea. "Suggest we prepare to make our own stand if need be. I recommend spreading the troops thin, seeing as our shields can't block what can fell trees so easily."

"My thoughts exactly," said Actaeon with a grin. "Make it happen, Warchief."

The Warchief began shouting orders and the surviving allies spread out along the valley floor. Archers and spear-throwers made ready for volleys.

Screams could be heard over the eastern rim, floating through the air with an odd combination of smells – ozone and fresh loam kicked up by the fallen trees.

The first wave of tribals that came over the edge took everyone below by surprise as the enemy plummeted to the valley floor. One Keeper Knight was struck directly and crumpled to the floor beneath the fallen Ruinic warrior. Two fellow Knights pulled their comrade away to the west, a stream of bright blood pouring out from the helmet's visor as they dragged the injured Keeper between them.

"Get those people outta there!" bellowed Mirvea, gesturing for everyone to pull back to the west.

The forces moved quickly at the Warchief's order, and just in time as a second wave of fleeing tribals came crashing down. Behind them came the first of the trees to topple over the eastern rim. Nature's giants fell to the valley floor, shaking the ground like an earthquake.

The final Ruinic line had backed up against the edge of the valley and was now visible as they made their stand against whatever killer artifact had annihilated their forces.

Blinding orange projections of light cut a swathe through the jungle and swept in neatly spaced arcs as they sliced the remaining Ruinic warriors into pieces, taking the nearest trees along with them. The last of the eastern enemy tumbled to the ground in a mix of gore and vegetation and a terminal thunder of trimmed trees.

As the dust cleared, Raedelle's Western Rim warband came into view atop the valley's eastern rim. Among them, spaced equally, stood a dozen warbanders that held thick staff-like artifacts at their side. At their center stood Lauryn of Lakehold, with her own artifact staff in hand. Beside her was the silver machine man from Travail, Quronos, his twin blades dripping with blood.

"Hi, Act!" called Lauryn down from above. She raised her free hand shyly in greeting. "Sorry we're a bit late."

At that, Actaeon burst into laughter, and a cheer went up from the allied troops that rivaled that of the falling trees from a moment ago.

Down on the valley floor, Lauryn told Actaeon all about her experiments with the light lances. She had discovered that using the light lances for more than thirty lifebeats would cause the lance to explode. Following their use, they required a thirty-lifebeat cooldown period before they were once more ready for operation.

Lauryn had run controlled remote tests on several of the artifacts to determine these limits after the unfortunate death of Companion Brigert. As she relayed those details to Actaeon, her hands began to shake.

Actaeon reached out to take her hand. "It is an unfortunate aspect of what we do, Lauryn. Our experiments and research are not without risk. We must understand these risks and seek to mitigate them whenever possible, but whenever others are involved that do not understand the danger, there is an increased chance of loss. From what you have described, you did everything you could to conduct these tests safely, and the Companion failed to heed your direction. You did a good job, Lauryn. Without your help and haste, we would all have died here today."

Lauryn nodded and reached out to wrap Actaeon in a fierce embrace. Tears ran down her cheeks as she spoke. "Thank you, Act. I needed to hear that. I've been unsure how to take it. Lady Fletcher's been giving me firm kicks in the behind ever since and that's been keeping me going, but I still can't help but to think I could've prevented Brigert's death if I'd approached the problem differently."

"You may have prevented it. And you also may well not have reached us in time to help," said Actaeon sincerely. "It was an urgent problem that you needed to solve with haste. When I was a young boy, I hurt one of my friends badly because I failed to take proper precautions for an experiment that had no urgency. From this mistake I learned an important lesson that I know now I have succeeded in conveying to you so that you need not suffer the same error as I did.

"It is still not easy," he continued, releasing her from the embrace. "You lost someone under your direction and that will be difficult for a long time – perhaps forever. I am learning to deal with that very fact now on a scale that leaves me utterly astounded. The only thing that keeps me going now is the knowledge that if I give up it may all fall to pieces, and all these lives lost may have been for naught. Thus, we must march on, because it is about more than just us, it is the whole of Redemption that depends on us now."

"Thank you, Act," said Lauryn. She reached up to wipe the tears from her cheeks. "You are a good teacher. I am glad to have had the chance to learn from you."

"And you are a good Engineer, Lauryn Light Lancer," said Actaeon with a grin. "I am proud to be your teacher. Now let me see that artifact of yours – it is fascinating."

Lauryn blushed and handed him the light lance.

Actaeon examined it closely, turning it over in his hands to inspect every detail.

The lance was a long pole with two spaced apart panels that activated a beam of orange light five times the height of a man in length. As Actaeon scrutinized the artifact, Lauryn explained that the beam could cut through every material they had tested it with. She had devised a formation where the unit of Light Lancers was broken into squads of three – spaced apart by twenty meters. Each squad rotated the front lancer every twenty lifebeats to prevent the weapon from exploding.

"How can the light beam simply end at a distance?" asked Actaeon, arching a brow. "In every instance I have examined light, it continues to propagate forward unless absorbed or reflected into a different direction."

Lauryn shrugged as she watched her mentor turn the device over in his hands. "I asked Quronos the same thing. He just replied with something cryptic: 'It is hard light – most unlike the soft light you are familiar with. At the terminus of the lance beam, the photonic molecules combine until they acquire too much mass, whereupon they fall free and scatter.' I couldn't make much sense of it myself, and he didn't offer up much more than that."

"Incredible," said Actaeon. "One day we shall figure it all out, Lauryn. With both of us working together on Redemption's secrets, there is no telling what we might uncover."

"Let's get this darn war over with first," said Lauryn with a smile.

"Indeed. And we shall need the continued services of your Light Lancers," said the Prince Engineer.

Up along the western slope, squads of allied soldiers walked the piles of corpses, looking for signs of any living.

Ithelie walked among them, speaking the rites of the dead, that the Ancestors might guide them in the afterlife.

As she passed one particularly morbid spot, she heard what sounded like grumbled curses from beneath the bodies. "Over here!" she called out. "I think there might be somebody alive."

The Wall Breakers rushed over under the direction of Captain Jezail to begin moving the bodies aside to search underneath. In short order, they had uncovered the pair of mercenaries and pulled them to their feet.

Jezail steadied the giant as he staggered out from beneath the corpses. "You okay, Trench?"

"Aye, lass," said Trench, looking down at the dead at his feet. "Better than many others."

Wave straightened and adjusted his eye patch over its empty socket. "Thanks for digging us out."

Companion Yanelle strode purposefully up to Wave.

The one-eyed mercenary smirked at her and dipped his head politely. "You were saying..."

The Companion's punch to his empty eye socket caught him off guard and landed him back in the pile of bodies.

"Maybe you should've stayed there, Wave," suggested Trench.

"Aye," said Wave, shaking his head to clear the stars from his eye.

"I'm not so sure even the Fallen could've helped you from her," said Jezail.

Wave smirked and accepted Jezail's hand to help him back up.

With the help of Lauryn's Light Lancers and the Kainai scouts, the allied forces on the eastern front were able to quickly and efficiently root out the remaining tribals from the Underforest. With the Ruinic invaders on the run back toward Pyramid, Actaeon's forces pursued close on their heels.

We're making quick progress in the west, thought Eisandre to Actaeon as she led the steady march to complete the pincer movement pinning the retreating tribal forces between her western allies and Actaeon's eastern force.

The formation marched at double time, with the Ruinic warriors fleeing eastward several hundred feet ahead. The Flashbolt Marines marched at the fore and whenever the enemy began flagging Major Craft would call the command to fire. The rapid fire of bolts from the triple crossbows dropped dozens of the Ruinic rearguard.

Early into the march, many of the tribal forces had split off into the confusion of the marketplace and the Warrens beyond. The marketplace grew more and more confusing as one got deeper into it, and the Warrens were an impossible hive of tunnels and chasms carved out of the Redemption ruins. Many of the poorer and unsavory living around the Pyramid called that place their home. Eisandre hoped that they'd had a chance to escape before the invaders arrived.

The Whiterose warband split off at the instruction of Lady Vanora to guard the marketplace from the high ground.

Same here. They are quite afraid of these Light Lances that Lauryn brought. We should meet you south of Redoubt, sent Actaeon. *I cannot wait to be together again.*

We must wait, but not for long, Eisandre replied.

The forces met just as the sun was skirting along the western horizon, casting reds and purples beneath the fluffy, white clouds. The looming shape of Pyramid cut the sunset neatly in two.

Eisandre had her soldiers encircle the fleeing invaders. At Actaeon's instruction, she kept them from closing in too much – just out of range as the Light Lancers cut the survivors to pieces. It was a brutal one-sided slaughter, where the allied forces took no losses at all. The only surviving tribals fled northward into the ruins of the Boneyards.

Uncharacteristically, several of the Ruinic warriors surrendered. Not that it would do any good. None of the allies understood the tribal language. Still, they would try to interrogate them to see what information they might glean from sketches.

The Princess and her Engineer met amidst the carnage and, heedless of those around them, they embraced firmly, their foreheads touching.

"You don't look well," she said to him.

His hair and face were caked with blood, some his, but most from more unfortunate souls. One of his goggle lenses was cracked and the arms of his ribbed jacket and trousers were caked with dried mud.

"Oh believe me, I am extremely well at this moment, my love," he said with a bright grin.

"So many died," she said, her brilliant blue eyes searching his own for an answer to that statement.

"Too many," he said. "But we did it. We routed them, and now we command the battlefield."

"It's not over," she said.

"I know. But we shall liberate Pyramid soon enough, for better or for worse," he said.

"Let's hope for the former," she said.

"Agreed. And I shall hope to never have to do anything like this again," said Actaeon. "It is not my forte, for certain."

"I'm sorry," Eisandre said simply and with heavy sorrow.

Actaeon took her face gently in his hands and kissed her tenderly before resting his forehead against her own once more. "If it is what I must do to secure a life at your side, then I will do it as often as necessary. Let us only hope that the need is sparse."

With the marketplace encircled by the Whiterose warband, the Keeper 1st Division and the remaining Niwian forces and the southern entrance to the Pyramid secured by Captain Oragnar's Southward warband, the only remaining entrance to Pyramid was the shattered Northern Descent.

Eisandre dispatched First Companion Itarik to secure it with the Lakefeed and Bastion warbands, and the Thyrian Flashbolt Marines.

The remaining units set up a camp at the eastern end of the Avenue of Glass.

Late into the night, runners returned to report that Itarik found the Northern Descent had already been secured by a force of rogue Raedelleans that called themselves the Fist of Arandel. It was led by a former Companion named Geodric Caider.

"A band of traitors!" said Eisandre, her brow furrowed in concern. They stood beside the map table in the command tent.

While Eisandre and Actaeon had worked to break the artifact sword and symbol of Raedellean power, Caliburn, out of the pillar artifact that had vanished her brother, Caider had instead chosen to betray Raedelle.

"Yes, but things were uncertain at that time," said Actaeon.

"They stole weapons from Saint Torin's Hold in a time of great need for Raedelle," said Eisandre. "If it hadn't been for Balin and the others that replenished our arms, my Uncle would now be Prince in Raedelle. Of course they were uncertain – and all the moreso because of the treason committed by Geodric Caider and his rebels."

"You are correct, of course," said Actaeon. "But, in this time, we need everyone that we can get on our side."

Eisandre looked displeased. "And when they decide to steal from us again when times are rough? Next time we will be the fools."

"So, how'd ya survive, Oril?" asked Trench, gulping from his tankard of ale. "I hardly expected you to be here after all that happened with the Ruinic invasion."

"Yeah, there's gotta be some helluva story there," said Wave, raising his own tankard. "Let's hear it so we can drink to it."

They sat at the bar in The End, the ramshackle tavern at the broken eastern end of the Avenue of Glass. Around them was a collection of artifacts, old and eccentric, unknown and broken, curious and droll. It was a veritable analogy to the ruins themselves, with one of the most extravagant collections of the inexplicable and the useless hanging from the walls and ceilings. It had been around since before the Dominions had been established. In the best of times The End was a melting pot of visitors to the Pyramid. Now it was just a few weary soldiers seeking solace at the bottom of a tankard.

"I'm sorry to disappoint you fellas," said Oril as she poured another tankard out for Jezail, who sat at the far end of the bar. Trench had insisted she come along with them, and she assented – it was better than lying in her tent and imagining the moment her life had been ruined over and over again. "I survived because I kept serving them drinks," Oril was saying. "Everyone needs a tavern. And The End's here, so ya might as well stop for a drink."

The bartender ran a hand through the curl of raven hair at the side of her head and winked at Wave, who nearly fell from his stool.

"Careful there, pal," said Berk. The Czerynian Warlord steadied Wave and gestured to the seat beside him. "Mind if I join you?" The Warlord sat down without waiting for an answer and motioned for another ale. "Heard you two got buried under a pile of the dead."

"Better than the alternative," said Wave. "And what if I said no?"

"Then I'd not be buying the next round," said Berk with a smile.

"In that case, you're most welcome, good Warlord," said Wave with an exaggerated dip of his head. "So, did you hear? It sounds as though the Ruinics and us share one thing in common at least."

"Aye," said Berk, raising his tankard. "We could all sit down and share a fine ale. Perhaps next time we could just invite 'em by for a drink instead of all this damned drama."

"Let's not go that far," said Oril. "I said I served 'em drinks, not that they enjoyed any of my fine ales. Naw, I served 'em some of the worst swill I could dig outta my cellars."

"And they didn't lop yer head off?" asked Trench with a touch of amusement in his tone.

"On the contrary, they loved the foul stuff. Guess they didn't have anything like it in the jungle," said Oril. She filled up the mercenaries' tankards and poured out a fresh one for the Czerynian.

"I hear that Czeryn's buying rounds of drinks now," said Captain Xula as he strode up to the bar. "Wouldn't miss that for the smoothest seas." With him were Major Ainhara Craft and Companion Wayd.

"Aye, well things are different now with me in charge," said Berk. "Pull up a chair. I consider anyone a friend's fighting the real war instead of up north invading my home. Just don't spread the word too far – there's not much left in our coffers. In fact, there's not even any coffers!"

Xula removed his diamond-shaped hat to reveal his dark, bald pate and dipped his head politely. "Then I'd presume you are Warlord Berk. I am Captain Harvand Xula of the *Glorious Redemption*. The old lady is Major Ainhara Craft of the Flashbolt Marines and our Raedellean friend is Companion Wayd Arbrigel, one of the Princess' personal guards."

"This old lady'll knock you right off the stool, if ya don't watch your tongue, Xula," snapped Craft as she yanked aside the tankard of ale that Oril had just poured out for the Captain and took a great gulp from it.

When Xula smiled at her, she offered him a smirk of amusement.

"I'm surprised you three are here drinking at all, based on what I heard about the last battle you fought," said Wayd.

"Somebody's gotta have a round in honor of the Fallen," said Wave.

"Aye, and we'll be here all night given the number of rounds required," grunted Trench before he gulped down his tankard and slammed it back on the bar for a refill.

Xula arched a brow at Wayd.

"The Prince Engineer's mercenaries," the Companion explained. "Trench and Wave. Trench is –"

"The handsome one," chuckled Trench, pointedly running a finger along the deep scar that bisected his face.

"And Wave's the smart one," said the smaller mercenary with a wink of his single eye.

"Bah! Maybe the unfortunate day my brains get smashed in," bellowed Trench with a guffaw.

"Don't mind him," said Wave to the others. "He's already had most of his gray matter knocked from his ears."

Trench placed a heavy hand on Wave's shoulder. "Need a pirate, Captain? Wave here's already got the eyepatch. He's all ready to go!"

Everyone laughed at that, including the Thyrian ship Captain.

"No thank you," said Xula. "One-eyed pirates are always running aground. I need all my sailors with both eyes." He placed his hat on the bar beside him. "I've heard a great many things about the pair of you. Not sure how much of it I should believe."

"Believe all the good stuff and doubt all the bad stuff," said Trench with a lopsided grin.

Wave laughed and clanked his tankard against Trench's. "Well said, my friend. I take back what I said before. Perhaps you've got some matter left up there after all."

"Stories I've heard, I'd more readily do the opposite," said Craft with a shrug. The Major took another sip of her ale and shot Trench a challenging look.

"I'll vouch for some of them," said Wayd, drawing to his feet and lifting his tankard into the air. "They aided the Princess after her brother was lost in the pillar artifact, helped her rescue her Prince Engineer, and then joined Raedelle to help us retrieve the Caliburn and fight our way across the Wall and back home. They're true heroes in my book." The Companion lifted his tankard high and then drank from it, looking confused when nobody else lifted theirs.

"I appreciate it, lad," said Trench. "We're no heroes though – just doing our jobs."

"Enough of this talk of us," said Wave. "We're here for those that couldn't be here. If ya wanna bash us, save it for another day – just cover the rounds." He glanced at the bartender with his single eye. "Pour out another round, will ya, Oril?"

"Coming right up," said Oril. She filled up a large pitcher at the keg and poured out another round into everyone's tankard, foamy ale splashing onto the bartop.

Xula yanked his hat out of the way to avoid the spillover.

Once the tankards were all full and Oril poured one out for herself, Wave lifted his into the air. "For the Fallen." Everyone lifted their tankards as the mercenary let the words hang in the air. "Men and women better than us, one and all. They fought and died at our side and got us to this point. Without their sacrifice, we'd not have made it to the Pyramid. They died so that we might continue the mission, so that we might restore civilization to Redemption. So let us drink tonight, to them, because they couldn't be here to join us."

"To the Fallen!" Captain Xula said firmly.

"And to those who are yet to fall before this war is over," said Trench.

A look passed between them all at Trench's words, their thoughts on the matter unspoken: that any among them might die before the conflict was over.

"The Fallen," echoed Major Craft.

"For the Fallen," said Warlord Berk.

"Remember the Fallen," said Companion Wayd.

"For Varisk," said Jezail, who had remained silent at the far end of the bar up until that point.

And so they drank.

SHULAYA'S LAMENT

"THE FIST OF ARANDEL IS prepared to serve Raedelle, Your Grace." Geodric Caider stood before Eisandre and Actaeon, outside of the command tent.

The former Companion was a short but muscular man with thick, unruly hair and rugged features that were enhanced by a rough stubble that clung to his cheeks and chin. He wore the finely crafted lion-lizard leather armor of a Companion and wore a short arming sword at his belt in addition to a collection of throwing knives.

"Are you going to steal our weapons again?" asked Eisandre bluntly.

Caider's cheeks reddened visibly underneath his brown stubble. "Uhm, my Princess... it was an uncertain time. We did what we had to do. It wasn't personal. It was for Raedelle."

"'Darkest Hour take the Caliburns,'" spoke the Princess, staring at him with a cold gaze.

The traitorous Companion's eyes widened and he ran a hand through his tousled hair and down over his face. "Why'd ya say that, Your Grace?"

"That's what you told the attendant that tried to prevent you from robbing our armory in our time of great need," said Eisandre levelly.

Caider's jaw fell open and he stared blankly at the Princess for several long moments. He shook his head several times and looked to Actaeon for help. When he found no succor there, he threw himself to the ground before the Princess and clasped his hands together. "Your... Your Grace. I –"

"The Darkest Hour didn't take all of the Caliburns," she reminded the man at her feet. "It left one behind to cut off the heads of those who betray our homeland." That said, the Princess turned and walked back into the command tent, leaving Caider to swallow her words.

Caider looked as though he was about to vomit. All the color had drained from his face. He shook his head several times and then pulled himself to his feet. He shot one last appealing look at Actaeon. "Act, brother... you've gotta help me. Things were falling apart here. I didn't want the arsenal to fall into the wrong hands. It was all for Raedelle. I did it for our Dominion."

"You sure have a strange sense of service, Caider," said Actaeon with a grin. Upon their reunion, Eisandre had insisted that he bathe and get a much-needed rest after the trial of the day before. Thus, he was rested and prepared to deal with his misguided friend. "Stealing from Saint Torin's, assaulting and tying up the attendants, and wishing ill upon the family you once served. Heck, the last time I saw you, you called my wife a rather nasty word after telling her that her brother had died. I am fairly new to this whole service thing, and even I know better than that."

"Listen, Act. You know me. I'm sorry, brother. Would I ever do something on purpose that I didn't think would help my friends?" He leveled his gaze to Actaeon's and spread his hands.

"When we needed your help, you were not there. In fact, you hurt our efforts and almost put Arcady in charge. If it were not for Balin and the Raedelleans from the marketplace, we would not have had enough weapons to arm our party," said Actaeon, leaning forward against his halberd. "You have to consider Eisandre's perspective as well. She is charged with upholding Raedelle's justice now and the acts you committed can only be described as treasonous, whatever were your intentions."

"Did she mean it? She'd really lop off a brother's head?" asked Caider, fear in his tone.

"We found proof of Companion Gorgrian's betrayal, and she insisted on carrying out his sentence herself," said Actaeon. He frowned to himself, remembering how difficult it had been for her to carry out the execution.

Caider stood silently for a long while before he straightened and spoke again. "If that's her decision, then I'll face the consequences. I just ask one thing, Act."

"What is that?"

"Don't kill me just yet. While I still breathe, I can help ya fight," he said, clenching his fists. "I don't want to die while the Pyramid is still under control of the invaders. Plus, I can translate for you."

"Translate the Ruinic tribal language?" asked Actaeon, arching a brow in genuine surprise. "I had thought nobody knew their tongue."

"The Prince had me tasked with learning more about the Ruinic people. So I went there and hid and spied on them until I knew their tongue and customs. Once I did, I came outta hiding and joined their community for a time," said Caider. "When you found me on the Avenue of Glass and saved my life, I'd been outed and barely escaped with my life. They caught me leaving notes in a hidden cache and I was forced to flee."

Actaeon nodded slowly, reaching over to scratch his right hand through its fingerless glove. The old burn up his arm always seemed to itch when he was preoccupied with something. "Fascinating story, Caider. You shall have to tell me all the details one day soon. Tell me though, what exactly were your intentions when you put that force together and raided the armory in Saint Torin's?"

"Honest, brother?" asked Caider.

"If you know me at all, you know I would not have anything less," said Actaeon, raising his brow in expectation.

"Alright, brother. I thought Raedelle was falling apart. It wasn't the place I signed up to serve under Prince Aedwyn, and the Duke before him. It's been that way some time now – starting with Aedwyn's absence and also with Eshelle's nonsense and posturing in her brother's place. She didn't listen to anyone. Now Prince Aedwyn, he could be a right stubborn brother, but he had sense – he was a guy I could follow. An' when Eis, er... the Princess told me she was just gonna go back to the Arbiters after everything that happened, I figured there was nobody left," said Caider.

"There *were* some people left. Remember the ones that you stole the weapons from?" asked Actaeon with a grin of amusement.

"Yeah, I remember 'em. It don't make me feel any better 'bout what we did, but I thought it needed be done," said Caider firmly. "So I took the Fist and we went to try an' make a place for Raedelleans that didn't want to live under that bastard Arcady. We went north into the desolation of Czeryn to see if we could carve out a place for a Raedellean resistance."

"I could make an educated guess that your plan did not work out as expected," said Actaeon.

"Nay, it was bad up there. Place is cursed, I tell ya. People were driven mad. Some of 'em from the Fist... they had to be put to death. Ajmani fightin' Ajmani, with Shield's help, and then more from Shield comin' to fight all of 'em. There's something wrong with that place, brother. I think we should all just stay away." There was genuine fear in his tone.

"Fascinating," whispered Actaeon. "The influence of the Veiled One is spreading more widely. They mean to take the city from us."

"Cracked Redemption's the Veiled One, brother?" asked Caider.

"What it is I am not sure yet, but I believe it has the ability to invade and control minds. Do you recall the cross-faced raiders that were pursuing me?"

Caider nodded.

"I believe they were all under the control of this Veiled One. They captured Lauryn before Aedwyn's disappearance and held her hostage, demanding my presence, alone. When I went out to find her, they captured me as well and tried to manipulate me into activating an artifact for them. They had the Lady Lartigan captive as well."

"By the Fallen, Act," breathed Caider. "Don't tell me you helped them with the artifact. Is that what turned Czeryn into a zone of damnation?" He took a step toward the Prince Engineer and clenched his fists.

Around the corner of the command tent, Yanelle's sword slid from its scabbard and she cleared her throat loudly in warning.

Caider glanced at the Companion and then returned his gaze to Actaeon's, demanding an answer.

"Of course I did not. But I made a mistake all the same. When we made our escape from the raiders, we took Lady Lartigan with us. In the confusion of our escape into the Felmere, she managed to put a dagger to Lauryn's throat and demanded to see my notes on the artifact. I had to show her and then, in the distraction," Actaeon hesitated for a moment, "Lauryn and I killed her. And yet the blue sphere appeared not long after, as though a device was activated of such destruction that might have warranted the relentless pursuit of me by the cross-faced raiders all these years."

"Saints, brother," said Caider, his mouth hanging open. "So you're saying there's something out there called the Veiled One that could do to the rest of Redemption what was done to Czeryn?"

"That was my conclusion as well," said Actaeon. "It is just one of the reasons that we all need to unite now, more than ever, to protect our home. If we fail, then we may all fall."

"Maybe the Keepers were right," said Caider, looking bewildered. "These artifacts may lead to our downfall again."

"The Keepers are correct about one thing," agreed Actaeon. "Such technology should be feared, but not destroyed as they preach. It must be explored and understood, and, in some cases, secured. However, it is the nature of humanity to explore, discover, and seek out advancement. The evolution of technology cannot be stopped any more than the rise and fall of the sun or the determined proliferation of life itself. It will arrive, often sooner than we are prepared for it, sooner than we know how to handle it. But it will always arrive, despite any effort to impede it. It is necessity that brings about the human drive to invent, and there will always be needs.

"The important thing for us," he continued, "is to make sure we are as prepared for its arrival as possible. And I believe that entails the sharing of knowledge, the open education of all our people, and making a quest for truth in all things our priority. It stands to reason that, properly armed with knowledge and truth, humanity might weather the advancement of technology and continue to grow and prosper."

"Alright, alright, brother," said Caider, holding up his hands in appeal. "I take it back then. The Keepers aren't right. So, as I was saying to ya, we left the northlands and returned here to find you tryin' to liberate Pyramid. Tried to help a bit, but this is like nothing I've ever seen, Act. You and Eisandre put a force together that will go down in the histories. More than even Duke Macsen's force in the First Invasion War. It's something I want to be a part of – something that the Fist can help with."

"I will speak with Eisandre, but I cannot guarantee she will accept your service. She may well decide that your actions need bear consequence," said Actaeon, spreading his hands. He lifted his halberd and turned to reenter the command tent. "Wait here, Caider. I will return shortly."

Actaeon was in the command tent for nearly an hour before he emerged once more.

Caider looked at him with pleading eyes.

"The Princess has made her decision," said Actaeon.

Caider knelt and nodded. "Whatever it be, I'll accept it."

"Very good," said the Prince Engineer. "Her decision is that you shall never again serve as Companion of Raedelle." He pulled a sheet of paper from his pocket and began to read off of it. "The Fist of Arandel will remain operative. However, you will relinquish your command to your most trusted Lieutenant. You may continue to serve with the Fist until this conflict has ended, at which time you will continue to serve in whatever capacity the Princess decides for the next five years. The Fist of Arandel will be responsible for the replacement of the following stolen equipment to the armory at Saint Torin's: thirty-seven bows, eight hundred thirty-six arrows, fifty-eight spears, fourteen swords, and three barrels of ale."

Caider looked dazed as he responded. "Act, brother... you mean I can't lead the Fist?"

"Trust me, Caider, it is better than the alternative," said Actaeon. "It gives you the opportunity to continue to serve Raedelle. It addresses the crimes you have committed against Raedelle fairly while still recognizing your worth to the Dominion. I would take it, Caider."

Caider nodded slowly. "Aye, Act. Like I said – I'll take it. Damn, but I'll take it."

"He accepted," Actaeon said as he stepped back into the command tent and leaned his halberd near the entrance flap.

Eisandre did not reply. She stood before the map table, looking at the placement of troops without really seeing them.

Actaeon pulled the goggles from his head and moved to stand beside her. He rested a hand on her shoulder. "You are preoccupied, my love." He began to massage her shoulders, the tension there palpable.

"I am not trained to command a force of this size. Perhaps a squad or two of Knight Arbiters, if necessary, but not an army," she stated. "This task is beyond me."

"And yet you have come this far and accomplished this much. The Pyramid is under our siege now, and we are perhaps days away from defeating the Ruinic invaders. Not to mention that you have solidified your position as the commander of what may be the most impressive multi-dominional force in our peoples' short history with Redemption," Actaeon explained as he worked her stiff muscles. He felt her shoulders begin to relax under his ministrations. "Is there really anyone trained for such a thing in all Redemption?"

"Maybe not, but there are people that have commanded the armies of Dominions in the past. They are better trained than I am – are they not?" she asked, letting out a sigh. "I missed your touch."

"As did I," Actaeon agreed. "And I am not sure as to whether they were better trained than either of us. There was a time when I used to be convinced of the truth of that, but we have both seen how some of the other commanders behaved during this ordeal. Their actions were often not strategic in nature. If they had remained unchecked, they may have easily lost us the entire war. Many times, such action was taken only to earn themselves glory, not for the benefit of our joint efforts. I can say with relative certainty that both of us acted in the higher strategic interests of Redemption, and that is what matters the most in this circumstance."

"Thank you, Actaeon. Your words make sense, although they don't change the fact that I feel completely unprepared for all this," said Eisandre, turning around to step into his arms. She met his emerald eyes with her brilliant blue gaze. "Now, it has been too long. I wish for us to step beyond words." She reached up to touch his cheek lightly and gave him a pleading look.

Actaeon grinned. "Aye, I shall endeavor to stop talking now." He drew her close and their lips met in a passionate kiss.

Eisandre tugged his jacket free of his shoulders, and it landed behind him with a heavy thunk.

As they continued to kiss, with such familiarity as though they'd known one another forever, Actaeon worked at the thick laces of her leather cuirass to pull it free.

She doffed the cuirass and broke their kiss to unbuckle her sword belt and lay her sword carefully on the map table, in case she might need it. Her eyes locked with his. "Will we be left alone?"

"Aye. I told Yanelle to give us some time for private discussion, barring an emergency," said Actaeon.

The look Eisandre gave him was grateful as she pushed him back against the map table and knelt to unlace his trousers. He gasped as she took him into her mouth.

After so much time apart, Actaeon couldn't endure such attention for very long and he pulled her up to kiss her lips deeply before he guided her to the cot.

And twenty-two days after they had wed and promptly were forced to separate to mobilize Raedelle's warbands, they joined once again – their foreheads touching as they gazed into one another's eyes, thankful and full of love.

Captain Oragnar snapped his fingers loudly and pointed to the Pyramid's entrance.

"Ready yerselves! They're coming out," shouted Areyna. She quickly pulled her many dark braids back into a queue to reveal the shaved sides of her scalp. Black woad streaked her face, confounding her expression.

The Czerynian Schiltron had joined them under the command of Shield Warden Dek, a young warrior with a hint of madness in his eyes. He shouted orders to his men, and they formed a tight shield wall at the base of the broad steps that led up to the Southern entrance. Behind them, the Southward warbanders readied their spears. Trench and Wave stood among them, Wave with his crossbow cocked and loaded.

There was movement in the shadows and then a single figure was shoved roughly forward, his hands bound before him. It appeared at first that the man's tabard was red, though on further observation it became clear that his tabard was actually gray, but was soaked through with blood.

A pair of Ruinic tribals stepped up behind the captive and brought him to his knees with a firm kick. The man leaned forward and vomited blood. There were dark red marks on either side of his head where his ears used to be. He raised emotionless eyes to look at the assembled forces below and began to laugh.

"By the Fallen, Wave – that's Sentinel Arbiter Phragus," muttered Trench.

"Shattered Redemption," cursed Wave. "We gotta do something."

"I know," said Trench.

As they spoke, one of the tribals stepped forward and began to shout loudly in their alien tongue. While he spoke, the second tribal withdrew the Arbiter's sword and lifted it to swing at Phragus' neck. There was a twang and Wave's bolt struck the tribal's shoulder causing him to drop the sword and scream out in rage.

Wave put his foot in the stirrup to reload his crossbow, but before he could get the second bolt seated, the first tribal had picked up the sword.

The Ruinic warrior swept it forward to remove the Arbiter's head from his shoulders. He stooped to retrieve the rolling head and lifted it to drink the blood pouring from Phragus' neck.

Wave's second shot went wide and struck the Sentinel's headless body in the chest, knocking it backward. The mercenary shouted in anger and leapt the shield wall, dropping his crossbow and drawing his flamberge rapier and companion dagger as he ran up the stairs.

The Ruinic tribal shouted something and, with a laugh, tossed Phragus' head down the steps at Wave before helping his companion back into the Pyramid.

Trench crashed through the shield wall and yanked one of the shields out of an unsuspecting soldier's hands. The giant whipped it forward like a discus. It struck Wave in the back, sending him sprawling forward.

When Trench reached his friend, Wave was crouched over the Arbiter's head, which had rolled to a stop against his boot.

Wave looked up at the giant, the color drained from his face. The one-eyed mercenary opened his mouth to speak before closing it again in a scowl.

"I know, Wave," growled the giant, wrenching his hands on the haft of his maul. "It ain't right what they did. We'll make 'em pay before this is over."

Wave shook his head and looked like he was going to be sick. "It's worse than that. Phragus' ears — there's bite marks where they were."

The doors to Saint Torin's Hold shuddered under another strike from the Ruinic battering ram. They held in place, backed by the heavy hewn timber tables that the Raedelleans had held their communal meals on in normal days. Now they lay on their backs, one atop the other, perpendicular to the doors and with most of the other furniture jammed strategically in place to hold the doors shut. Kylor and Corvin, two of the surviving Knight Arbiters, both drove wedges into strategic places to help reinforce the barricade. The young Niwian lord, Torot vor Steubick, was helping them as best as he could with his one good arm.

Tarcy Hael had taken command of the remaining forces since the loss of Phragus and the fall of the Mirrorholds to the invaders. The giantess had been left in charge of Saint Torin's Hold by the Princess Eisandre before the Princess had even departed on the journey that led to her anointment to her present position. In fact, she wasn't even aware that Eisandre was now the leader of Raedelle. When she saw the state of the battle for the Mirrorholds and the ensuing fire, she had recognized immediately that they were going to fail. The last, desperate option then was for all of them to consolidate their efforts to defend a single room and hold it until rescue arrived.

Shard had brought the good news from the garden terraces that allied Dominion forces had made it to the Pyramid's doorstep – arriving on the Avenue of Glass south of the marketplace. Unfortunately, the old Althean tender to the gardens had still been there when the Ruinic forces had broken through.

Tarcy had been the one to suggest – no, to order all of the remaining survivors to barricade themselves inside Saint Torin's. Kylor had agreed to the logic, since, as Tarcy had pointed out, Saint Torin's had the heaviest furniture to barricade the doors with. Thus, the Altheans had moved their wounded from the old Czerynian embassy, and the remaining survivors had brought as many rations and supplies as they could quickly gather.

Still, that didn't leave much, and now they were starving. There was no escape and nothing to do but survive and keep the tribals out.

Maerdia Bazardjan knelt upon a folded cloth to whisper prayers. She closed her eyes and began to murmur them in earnest. "Gods of the old and gods of the new, we call upon you. Your blessings we do seek, and to our spirits may you speak. Our hands are yours to guide with our minds open wide. Watch over these people in their time of greatest need. Give them the strength to survive until our friends without can bring us rescue. Guide our rescuers in their decisions so that they may bring us quick succor."

"Hmmph," huffed someone nearby.

Mae opened her eyes to find the Loresworn, Inditrovalis Jem, arms crossed as he leaned against the nearby wall. His face was blistered and burned and most of the hair atop his head had seared away.

The artist offered him a genuine smile. "Will you join me for this prayer, Adept Jem?"

"Ha! Your prayers mean nothing. Do you really think there are gods of old and new watching over you?" The Loresworn Adept sounded drunk, and when he nearly slipped to the side, catching himself to recover quickly, it confirmed her suspicion.

"I know there are, Adept Jem," said Mae. "My prayers are heard even now. Even with death at the door and our time running out. In fact, especially now."

"If you say so, Lady Bazardjan," said Inditrovalis with a sneer. "Whatever makes it easier for you."

"It is times like these that we must have faith," asserted the artist. "We must trust that our friends will make the right decisions to reach us in time. With my prayers I hope to bolster their spirits and ours to give us the strength we need in these dark times."

"Tell that to Garth," spat the Loresworn. "Tell that to Trello and Phragus. To Shard. Did faith help them?" He scowled, disgust written upon his features. "I'll tell you right now that it did not. Their blood paints the halls of the Mirrorholds as we speak. Their lives meant nothing – their deaths came regardless of whether they had faith in gods or man or anything else. How do you account for that, Lady Bazardjan?"

Maerdia smiled up at him and spread her hands. "They gave their lives for us, did they not? Their lives and their deaths were spent so that others might live on to accomplish great things. That was their fate and role in the grand plan of the gods."

"And if all of us die then, Lady Bazardjan?" asked Jem. "Then were their sacrifices worth anything? Or is it rather a matter of chance, of probability, and of circumstance?"

"Of course they were worth something, Adept Jem," said Mae gently. "Those who find us will know what they did to defend the survivors of the Pyramid. Their actions will inspire generations to come. Nothing is meaningless. Nothing is for naught."

"And if the Ruinic tribals destroy our friends on the outside?" asked Jem. "Will there be anyone left to remember? To be inspired?" His words slurred as he spat them out.

"You are scared, Inditrovalis," said Mae. "It is alright to be scared. I am too. Come join me for this prayer. You need not believe in it, but you are not here alone. We are all in this together." She reached up toward him, palm upward, offering her hand.

The Adept Loresworn started to reach out, but recoiled suddenly, as though shocked. "Say your prayers, Lady Bazardjan. You'll learn before too long that there's no one listening."

He stormed away and Mae watched him go.

She wiped a tear from her cheek and closed her eyes once more, spreading her hands. "And give my friend, Inditrovalis, the courage to find his faith in you, in his people, and in himself."

It was then she caught the smell of burning flesh. Her nose wrinkled and she recoiled.

Behind her, someone yelled, "They've lit fires. Get down low – they've lit fires!"

"I've always known they were cannibals, brother," said Caider. The former Companion crossed his arms over his chest and leaned against one of the support poles in the command tent.

Assembled around the map table were all the commanders of the allied forces – Actaeon, Eisandre, and Warchief Mirvea represented Raedelle while Supreme Captain Jarval, Captain Xula, and Major Craft were there for Thyr. Captain Wronka of the Niwian Dominion leant heavily upon the table, his chest wrapped with bandages and the dry wheeze of his breathing audible amidst the tension of the room. Warlord Berk of the few remaining Czerynians stood on one side of him and Keeper Knight Captain Atreena stood at the other side, in her full plate armor.

Interglot Heimgar stood between Trench and Wave at the other side of the table. Quronos and Itarik stood beside Wave while Gunther Arcady and Neryl Vanora stood next to Trench. Along the perimeter of the tent stood another dozen people, including Lauryn, Wayd, Yanelle, Ithelie, Jezail, and Jad Perth, who had tried to shoulder his way to the table at the onset of the discussion and had been instructed to the back of the room by the Lady Vanora, no uncertainty in her tone.

"Then why didn't you say anything about that?" asked Wave, the mercenary's remaining eye narrowing on Caider.

"Didn't come up," shrugged Caider.

"Is 'ere anything else that hasn't come up that ya think might help us?" asked Berk in his gravelly voice as he tugged at his scraggly white beard.

"Ya wanna hear about what I found out, or would ya prefer to rehash this 'till nightfall?" asked Caider. He shrugged nonchalantly.

"Caider has interrogated the Ruinic captives," explained Actaeon. "He has some information we might find useful."

"Let's not waste time then. Out with it, Geodric," said Arcady.

Caider shot the Lord Shore a nasty look. "It's Caider, thank you."

"I know your name, Geodric. Now out with it," said the Lord with a devious smirk.

Caider took a step toward Arcady and the Lord turned to face him, arching a brow as his hand came to rest gently upon the pommel of his sword.

"Settle your squabbles later," barked Atreena. "I, for one, want to hear what he has to say."

Arcady spread his hands apologetically to Caider and turned back to the table.

"Let us hear it," said Wronka, the effort causing his body to rack with coughs. He lifted a cloth to his mouth and it came away red.

Caider leaned against the tent support again and folded his arms once more. "Very well, brother. I spoke with them about why they invaded Redemption and what they intend to do here. They say they were sent by the Devourer, whatever the heck that is, to give him the sacrifice that he demands. They're here to do this Devourer's bidding until it has enough energy that it'll tell them to return home."

Trench exchanged a disturbed look with Wave, both of their faces draining of color. "Thought we killed that bastard in the First Invasion War..."

Wave shrugged. "Guess not."

Trench shook his head and looked down at the table, at a loss for words.

"What sort of sacrifice does this Devourer demand?" asked Actaeon with a frown.

"The souls of Redemption dwellers," said Caider.

"You can't be serious," said Captain Xula. "Are you really saying these nuts were sent by a mad god to harvest our souls?"

"I didn't say it, brother. They did," said Caider. He reached up and ran both hands through his unruly hair. "I'm just relaying the message."

"And how are the sacrifices made?" asked Lauryn from the back of the tent.

Caider swallowed and frowned, looking bothered for the first time in the discussion. "They eat the dead."

"Shattered Redemption."

"By the Fallen."

"Darkest Hour take us."

The sudden murmur of curses and exclamations was cut short by Ithelie. "Let us pray for their souls."

A hush came over the tent and everyone's eyes turned to the Voice.

She raised her hands up and tilted her head toward Companion Yanelle and Jezail until the women both took her extended hands. Ithelie waited for the others in the tent to follow suit before she spoke.

Arcady and Trench exchanged a comical look before the two men clasped hands firmly. Itarik reached past the silver-skinned Quronos to take Wave's hand. Even Atreena took her neighbors' hands.

"Ancestors heed our prayers. Guide the souls of the Fallen during this conflict, that they stay safe from this ancient evil brought to our city by invaders. Bolster them in their time of separation and counsel them against the lies of this Devourer. Help carry us to victory over this great threat to our civilization so that we may free our city and live in peace once more." Ithelie's voice trailed off and one by one, those present unclasped hands, some much more quickly than others.

Eisandre was the first to speak, hands still joined with Actaeon and Mirvea. "Prayer will not help those still trapped within the Pyramid. We must act quickly."

"Exactly," said the Supreme Captain. "We must throw all our forces at the Pyramid to destroy these tribals once and for all."

"And lose how many in the process?" asked Wronka. The Niwian coughed again and was careful to keep his tissue better hidden this time. He looked as though he wanted to say more, but he kept silent, perhaps to avoid another coughing fit.

"It matters not," said Arcady. "What sort of people are we if we do nothing? Our options are to lose more soldiers to prevent a fate worse than death for those trapped inside, or to stand outside and watch them be... devoured."

Wave shot Arcady a look. "The Lord Shore's right on this one. We can't let any others die that way. By the Fallen, they're eating them alive!"

"They've already been doing it," said Caider. "Charging in now changes nothing. Now that we know it, it's time for bad tactics? Nah! Captain Wronka's right, a lot of us will die charging straight into Pyramid – is it really the smart choice?" The former Companion turned to Princess Eisandre. "Whaddaya think, Princess? You were an Arbiter."

The Princess stood for a long while looking down at the map table in disturbed silence. "The Pyramid was never defensible. We will be able to invade it easily, but with very heavy losses. Heavier than we've had yet, perhaps. And yet, I don't see how we have another choice. Still, I fear we will not reach those trapped before the Ruinic tribals have a chance to kill them in their desperation."

"It is decided then," said the Supreme Captain with a victorious smile.

"We should make our charge first thing in the morning," agreed the Lord Shore.

"It's a damned stupid idea," said Captain Xula. "We're sure to lose more people than we save."

Supreme Captain Amodeus Jarval cast a sidelong look at his fellow Thyrian Captain, tugging his red mustache in annoyance. "Your thoughts are beginning to become onerous, Harvand."

"Perhaps if –" the other Captain started.

"There may be another way," blurted out Actaeon.

"What is it, Act?" asked Trench.

The Prince Engineer held up a hand and began digging through his pockets. He pulled out dozens of sheets of vellum with sketches and notes scrawled upon them and emptied them upon the map table. Finally, he found the one he had been looking for and, with a grin, he unfolded it and spread it upon the table. He tapped it with two fingers and nodded. "Yes."

"Yes what?" asked Warlord Berk. "That a map?"

"Aye," said Actaeon. "It is a map of the tunnels beneath Pyramid." He looked up at Trench and Wave with a grin. "Remember the map that Shar Minovo drew for us?"

"The lift she claimed brought her up right in the center of Pyramid's Sun Chamber?" asked the giant, though he was slowly nodding.

"Wait a sec, Act," said Wave. "Didn't she get caught in a big collapse in the tunnels before that part? That's not exactly a direct route – we gotta retrace her steps through a collapse. It might not even be accessible anymore."

"Who is Shar Minovo?" asked Atreena.

"She was a Shieldian Adjunct," explained Actaeon. "She was killed by deathcrawlers."

"Hold on, brother," interrupted Caider. "Wasn't she the one that the deathcrawlers devoured from the inside at the feast where the Prince General's son was made Governor?"

"Well, I suppose that is technically correct," said the Prince Engineer. "Their eggs hatched inside her after an incubation period. The young were just emerging."

"Wait a moment," said Lady Vanora. "Why did this Adjunct have eggs inside her?"

"I believe it is likely that the Adjunct had them injected into her system during the failed expedition where she found the lift," said Actaeon.

"By a deathcrawler?" asked Major Craft, horrified.

"By a deathcrawler," confirmed Wave.

Everyone was silent as the information processed.

"So let me get this straight," began Captain Xula. "You're proposing going into the tunnels underneath the Pyramid to follow a map drawn by a dead woman, along a path that may or may not be blocked by a collapse, through an area known to be inhabited by one of Redemption's deadliest creatures, to get to a lift that nobody but you's ever heard of before now?" The Thyrian searched Actaeon's face, his eyes so wide they looked as though they'd fall from his head.

Actaeon blinked and scanned those assembled at the table before his gaze settled on the Thyrian Captain. He scratched his right arm through the thick material of his jacket and shrugged. "That is correct, Captain."

Xula's mouth slowly curved into a wide smile and he slammed his fist down on the table. "Well, damn! Count me in then."

"And once you're in there – then what?" asked Warlord Berk.

"Well, once we are in there, then we flush them out," stated Actaeon matter-of-factly.

"You cannot possibly fit this entire army down there," said Arcady, frowning.

"Obviously not, Lord Shore," said Actaeon. "We will flush them out with water. Many of you will remember the boiling flood that came out of the Sea Lounge and killed many innocent citizens."

"How could we forget?" asked the Supreme Captain.

"I will make that happen again," said Actaeon. "I will need just a small force to help me make it through the tunnels and to Pyramid's control room. Once there I can flood the corridors and create a diversion. When the flooding has done its job, then the Princess will lead the waiting army to rush in and wipe out any remaining invaders."

"There's a lot that can go wrong," said Wronka, followed by a coughing fit.

"Agreed," said Atreena. "And if any part of this plan fails, we will succeed in nothing. Some secrets are best left buried deep down beneath the bones of the city."

"You forget – we have the Thoughtlink Artifacts," countered Actaeon. "If the Princess loses contact with me, you know the plan has failed and then we are not any worse off than we were before."

"We'll be short one engineer," said Jezail.

"You do not require an engineer for a frontal assault," said Actaeon. "My skills are better used infiltrating Pyramid and flushing out the invaders. If we succeed in this, we will save a great many lives. Besides, the Ruinic tribals might just kill any survivors at the first signs of a frontal assault. We give everyone a chance this way."

"It is a good plan," Eisandre said. She looked up at Actaeon with sadness in her eyes. "We will carry it out at first light tomorrow."

Jezail Vren plucked a slow, cheerful melody on her fiddle in the back corner of The End. The tavern was full of allied force troops gathered to celebrate what they hoped would be the last night before victory could be declared.

At the opposite side of the establishment, Actaeon, Eisandre, Trench, Wave, Lauryn, Wayd and Yanelle sat together nursing tankards full of drink that Oril had just brought to their table.

"Drink up," said Wave. "I've a feeling tomorrow's gonna be a long day."

Everyone lifted their tankards to meet in the center of the table before taking sips of their drinks.

"You know that you need not accompany me in this, gentlemen," said Actaeon to the pair of mercenaries with a grin.

"Bah, who ya kidding, Act?" asked Trench before giving the Prince Engineer a rough slap on the back that caused him to spit some of his next sip out onto the tabletop. "You know 'swell as we do that ya don't stand half a chance without us. Course we're going! 'Sides, we started these adventures with you in the tunnels – might as well end 'em there too." He caught Eisandre's cold gaze and offered her an apologetic look before taking a swig of his ale.

"You know that I would prefer to join you in this," said Eisandre, looking to Actaeon.

"Yes, I know," said Actaeon, placing his hand on hers. "You also know this is the way it must be. I am the only one here that knows how to use

Pyramid's control room, and you are the foremost expert on the layout of Pyramid itself. Plus, we are linked by our Thoughtlink Artifacts, so it will be as though we are functioning as a single unit, but in two different places."

"It's a logical arrangement, but I don't have to like it," said Eisandre. "We are finally in the same place again, together. I don't want to have to go in separate directions again so quickly."

Actaeon wrapped an arm around her and pulled her close to kiss her forehead. "I know, my love. I feel the same." With a sad smirk, he raised his tankard to Trench and Wave. "Still, gentlemen, I appreciate your company, if only for the comedy you're certain to bring to the expedition."

That brought a round of laughter from the table.

When it died down, Lauryn spoke. "I would join you as well, Act. I've got a good chance of figuring out the control room in case you are..." she glanced sidelong at Eisandre, "diverted elsewhere. Plus, my light lance might come in handy."

Actaeon shook his head. "I cannot risk losing both of us, Lady Lauryn. If both of us fail to return, who will be left to unlock all of Redemption's secrets?"

The compliment made Lauryn blush. "That's what I thought you'd say. That's why I asked one of my light lancers if he'd join you. Hake Rim'll be joining your party, and, before you say anything, I will not be taking no for an answer."

"Companion Wayd will be joining you as well," said the Princess. "I've asked him to make sure you reach your goal safely."

Across the table, the auburn-headed Companion smiled. "Don't worry, Prince Engineer. I'll not allow any harm to come to you."

"I am counting on it, Companion Wayd of Arbrigel," said Actaeon with a grin. "I shall be glad to have you at my side." He turned to Yanelle. "And just because you've been assigned to me, Companion Yanelle, doesn't mean that you need to accompany me on this mission. It is too great of a risk to expect you to join us out of duty."

Yanelle spun her tankard slowly on its base and cast a sharp look at Actaeon with her striking eyes. "Permission to speak freely, Your Grace?"

"Of course, Companion Yanelle," said Actaeon.

"Then don't be an ass, Your Grace," she said with a hint of humor in her voice. "As if every single battle on the eastern front of this damned war wasn't nearly the end of us. I'll be at your side as usual – it's my job."

"Hoo – she told you boss," said Wave. He shot Yanelle a wink.

"You know, it just looks like you're blinking when you do that," said Yanelle with a smirk.

"I've been telling him that for a while now," said Trench.

"Hey, it's not my fault I only have one eye. Act owes me one. I still gotta be able to wink," countered Wave.

Actaeon smiled and raised his tankard. "Well, Wave's eye aside, I'll be glad to have you with us, Companion Yanelle. Thank you for telling me, as Wave said."

The Companion clanked her tankard against his and they both drank.

When they were done, all eyes turned to a figure that had approached the table and now stood silently.

Quronos met their stares with his blank, black gaze. Reflections of the overhead luminaries could be seen in the shiny metallic skin of his head. "I will accompany you in your venture."

"The machine that can fight," said Wave. "Come join us for a drink."

"I require no such nourishment," said Quronos. "At first light I shall be there." The silver man turned and exited the tavern as quickly as he had arrived.

Another metallic figure strode up to the table, this one a human in full plate armor. Atreena's sweeping blond hair was free of her helm and tumbled about her steel pauldrons, echoing the blazing sun of the Allfather etched upon her breastplate.

"Amazements never cease," muttered Trench.

"May I join you all for a drink?" asked the Keeper Knight.

Actaeon nodded curtly. "Lady Knight, please do." He waved for Oril to bring another tankard. "What brings you into our company?"

"I will be joining you as well," said Atreena as she pulled up a chair.

"The last time you joined us, I had to hack my way through a squad of Knights," said Trench in clear disgust. He narrowed his eyes at her from across the table, his scar turning an angry shade of red.

"And I apologized for it," said Atreena. She gave him a hard look. "And now I intend to make good on my apology."

"Ha!" The giant took a deep draught from his tankard and slammed it down on the table.

"Knight Captain, aren't you better suited to lead your division?" asked Eisandre.

Atreena looked squarely at the Princess. "Your Grace, respectfully, I have been to this control room before. I know better than most how to get back there, and I will help get your husband in place."

"Forgive me for my lack of understanding, Lady Covellet," began Actaeon, "but why would you help me access a form of technology reviled by the Keepers and that I fully intend to use in order to kill with?"

"Because, as I've told you in the past, someone needs to keep an eye on what you're doing with it," explained Atreena. "The Keepers cannot well destroy all the Pyramid now, can we? So the next best thing is for us to ensure its artifacts are not used for ill against the people of Redemption."

"So you would have me believe that now your people will police the use of artifacts instead of just destroying them?" Actaeon arched a brow. "You must understand my skepticism at this sudden change of intent on the part of the Keepers."

"There are those with different schools of thought within our ranks," said Atreena. Oril handed her a tankard, and she slid the bartender several copper bits and took a sip of her ale before speaking again. "It is my hope that you can learn to trust me once more."

"Shattered Redemption, we will!" roared Trench.

Atreena startled at the giant's yell, but managed to maintain her composure.

Actaeon raised a hand to his friend. "Trench, please. If the Knight Captain wishes to join us, then we will accept her help. She and her people have done nothing for the whole of this conflict to give us doubt about her motives."

Trench gave Actaeon a hard look and opened his mouth to argue.

"If we wish to overcome this disaster, we must accept help and work together with all the civilized peoples of Redemption," said Actaeon, beating him to the punch. "And that is just what we will do."

"And if that trust is betrayed," said Eisandre, "we will not be so forgiving again."

Atreena nodded to them both and raised her tankard. "To trust."

"To trust," the others echoed. Everyone raised their tankard, including Trench after a moment of hesitation, and they all drank.

The music stopped and from the far corner of the tavern, Jezail spoke, her voice carrying over the conversations in the room.

"This next song is a special one. I call it Shulaya's Lament."

The room drew silent as Jezail drew her bow slowly across the strings of the fiddle. The End was filled with a mournful low note that reverberated as Jezail's fingers slid along the strings. It was followed by several lengthier notes that bridged the gap to hopefulness as her fingers teased sound from the instrument's strings. She then led into a melody that was joyful, yet, somehow, forlorn.

The audience in The End was captivated. All eyes turned to the fiddler as she began to alternate between a series of short, plucked notes and longer ones drawn out with the bow. Any conversations had been cut short to listen.

Jezail stood as she played, and, lifting her face to the heavens, she began to sing. Her words came softly at first, but grew in power as she sang them, her melodic voice carrying throughout the tavern and onto the Avenue of Glass beyond.

> *Life is a chance we are all given —*
> *A chance for love, a promise of ambition.*
> *And some doth seek, though others doth not,*
> *The reward of devotion and a life begot.*
>
> *And though the seasons keep cycling past,*
> *The hopes we wrought will far outlast.*
> *Dreams we share upon a hill*
> *Conceived with warmth we share at will.*
>
> *And yet some wishes fail to thrive.*
> *Shulaya knows, Shulaya tried...*
> *A love so true was with this one,*
> *And for a man so near the sun.*
>
> *A man who worshipped her bright smile,*
> *And gave her all that he could find.*
> *Shulaya gave to him their future aim.*
> *Yet fate does not heed a mother's pain...*

Shulaya knows.
Shulaya tried...
Shulaya died!
Shulaya tried...

Jezail built up to a crescendo of notes on her fiddle as she continued to sing the next verse.

Shulaya knows now in her sorrow,
To give of love is to one's tomorrow —
A light to feed the fire of chance.
To summon life's fragile dance.

And though our time is fraught with peril,
We must but try to ring hope's bell!
Shulaya knows, she gave her soul —
That one might breathe and see this world.

Our land is rough and full of trials,
But Shulaya tried all the while.
And in so forth, she gives us hope...
That a future bright we may invoke.

A light for all Redemption's ruin,
To throw us clear the Ancients' doom!
So listen well, Shulaya dear —
Guide us to find our new frontier!

Shulaya knows.
Shulaya loved...
Shulaya tried!
Shulaya lives...

In all of us...

Jezail ended the song with a whisper and the same mournful note she began it on. Her fingers worked the strings carefully to draw the note out until those present didn't even notice it was gone.

There was silence in The End, as though everyone present were waiting to see if the song might continue.

The legs of a chair slid across the floor, creating a torturous scraping sound that contrasted so sharply with Jezail's melodic song it was painful to the ear.

The giant stood there, tears streaming down his face, and regarded the young Raedellean woman with her blazing red hair and her fiddle for a long moment. Then he crossed the room to stand before her.

Jezail looked up at him and offered a soft smile.

Trench sketched a bow, as graceful a motion as anyone had ever seen the giant make. He knelt then and took her hand to kiss the back of it gently, tears running freely down his face to pool in the chasm of his scar. "Thank you, lass."

Jezail nodded to him, now eye to eye with the horrifically scarred giant. "No thanks are needed. Just come back safe from what you are about to do."

INTO THE DEEP

WAVE AND ACTAEON INCHED FORWARD on their bellies to peer over the ledge on the north boundary that rose high above the marketplace.

Below was a disaster.

The Open Market was normally a chaotic arrangement of hastily constructed wooden stalls and many different colored tents designed to draw the eye of passing shoppers. In the best of times, there were meandering and narrow paths between the varying merchants and depending on the time of day, progress could be quite difficult to make with so many shoppers stopping randomly to gaze at the wares.

Now it looked as though one of Actaeon's grenados had been set off in the midst of that chaos. Many stalls were splintered and crumpled. Untended, tents had collapsed from rains and now sat, squat and waterlogged like so many flattened bugs. The fabric of other tents had blown free to become entangled in the structure of nearby stalls and torn to shreds by the wind. The occasional corpse of a hapless market dweller could be made out sprawled amidst the aisles, bloated and swollen in the sun. Ruinic tribals moved throughout the rubble, picking it apart in search of supplies.

Actaeon unclasped his recurve bow from his back and set the scope to his eye to survey the scene below.

"By the Fallen," whispered Wave. "I don't even have to look through your scope to see there's a lot of tribals down there."

"Let us hope the Wall Breakers set up a nice diversion for us then," said Actaeon.

"Forward!" cried First Companion Itarik as he led the charge, Princess Eisandre at his side. The line of warbanders from Whiterose and Lakefeed streamed into the marketplace behind them, rushing into the narrow lanes between the various shop stands as they advanced. Squads routinely split off from the main onrush at intervals to search adjacent stalls in order to make sure there was no Ruinic ambush lying in wait for them.

To the west, Lord Arcady led a similar charge with the Wall Breakers and the Thyrian Flashbolt Marines at his back. Instead of splitting off, the marines simply fired their triple crossbows into the tents and stalls to ensure that any lurking ambushers were taken care of.

At the eastern end of the marketplace, Supreme Captain Jarval led a third charge. With him were the remaining Thyrian fighters and the Keeper 1st Division.

The western front was met with resistance first. Panicked tribals crashed into them in an effort to flee from the marketplace. Arcady and the Wall Breakers efficiently cut down the unorganized, fleeing enemy and the next rush was stopped dead in their tracks by the barrage of bolts from Major Craft and her Flashbolt marines.

"Here comes our group," said Itarik.

Eisandre drew the arming sword at her hip, leaving the greatsword Caliburn in its scabbard on her back. "Bring everyone to a halt. We stand our ground here."

"Halt!" echoed Itarik, raising his off hand fist even as he struck down the first of the arriving Ruinics with his sword.

Eisandre skillfully swept her sword to and fro, blocking a spear thrust, killing one attacker, and maiming the next.

Together the Princess and the First Companion made quick work of the initial tribal charge. The warbanders of Whiterose and Lakefeed formed a line to either side of them, shoving broken stalls out of the way to make room for the defensive formation.

The tribal advance stopped short in its tracks several paces away, kicking up a cloud of dust.

At Eisandre's direction, the Raedellean line lunged forward as a unit, under the cover of the dust cloud. It caught the tribal line by surprise and saw most of the front line fall under warbander blades and spearpoints.

The survivors staggering backward and tried to regroup as the Raedelleans continued to press their attack.

Out of the corner of her eye, Eisandre could see that Jarval's unit had also engaged the enemy.

They are fully engaged now. You should make your move, she told Actaeon through the Thoughtlink Artifact.

"It appears as though we have our opening," said Actaeon, lowering the scope from his eye and pushing back from the ledge. Any tribals lingering around the tunnel openings directly below them had left to join the effort to stop the allied advance.

"Alright, let's just keep in mind this is a one way trip," said Wave as he secured the last of the three ropes around one of the shattered elderstone pillars a dozen or so paces back from the ledge. "We won't be able to scale these lines again quick enough to avoid their arrows."

"If all goes well, we'd better not need to, right?" asked Companion Wayd, though he sounded unsure of himself.

"If we need to then all of this is for naught," said Actaeon. He returned the bow to its clasp on the back of his jacket and fastened his halberd into place for the descent.

Yanelle nudged Wayd. "Let's go – we're going first."

"Us? Why?" asked Wayd.

Yanelle shot him a critical look.

"Oh, yes," said Wayd. "Of course we'll go first." He stepped in front of Actaeon and Wave. "Sorry, Your Grace, Wave – we will go down first to secure the way. It's what we do."

"Oh, is it?" asked Wave with a smirk. "Try to control your descent. I hear the ground can take the unprepared by surprise."

Wayd gave him a confused look in return and nodded. "Good thing I came prepared then."

Quronos was past both Companions in a flash. The silver man whipped the rope around his waist and disappeared over the ledge without a second of hesitation.

Wayd blinked and peered down over the ledge.

"Better hurry if yer gonna be first," said Trench with a lopsided grin.

Yanelle smiled and slid the rope around her waist to descend after the Loresworn guardian. She took her time to carefully approach the edge and let some rope out slowly so that she was perpendicular to the wall before she started her controlled descent downward.

Wayd followed close behind.

Wave nodded to Trench. "We're next."

"I'll go last. Take up the rear," said the giant.

"And have your huge ass land on me?" asked Wave. "I don't think so. Let's go, my friend." The one-eyed mercenary glanced at the Keeper. "Same with you, Lady Atreena. I don't need you taking half of us out if you slip with that full suit of plate."

Atreena offered him a sneer. "That's Knight Captain Covellet to you, sellsword. And you'll be glad to have me at the fore with my suit of plate when we run into one of those deathstalkers."

"Deathcrawlers? I'll be glad to have anything between me and one a' those damned things, to be honest," said Wave. He instructed her with the rope and helped talk her over the edge.

Once the Keeper was over, Wave turned to his friend. "I've shown you how to do this plenty o' times."

"Aye aye. I'm going, I'm going," said Trench, eyeing the edge mistrustfully. He wrapped one of the free ropes around his body and started on his way down, the rope straining under his weight as it drew even tauter around the elderstone pillar.

Wave saluted Actaeon and went over himself.

"I suppose we are the last ones," said the Prince Engineer with a grin. He looked at Harvand Xula and Hake Rim before him.

The bulky light lancer slung his lance across his back – he had fashioned a crude leather sling for just the occasion, and once the first rope went slack, he took it up and started his descent.

The dark-skinned Thyrian Captain approached Actaeon and placed a firm hand upon his shoulder. "Listen, Prince Engineer, I don't know how this mad plan of yours will turn out, but I want you to know that you've my respect for doing this. They'll tell of us in songs for this day, whatever may become of us."

"Your words are appreciated, Captain," said Actaeon honestly. "So long as there are songs to be sung in the future, then I believe we have done a good job here, however this may turn out."

"Don't be silly," said Xula. "You've got ta get back to your woman. We'll make it turn out just fine." He bared his white teeth and turned to slide down his rope.

When Actaeon made it to the bottom, all hell had broken loose.

"It's Ancestors' tears down here! Hurry up, Your Grace!" Wayd shouted.

They were heavily engaged with Ruinic tribals that had come out from the openings to the Warrens to attack them. Thus far, the small squad was holding them off, but more were approaching quickly.

Actaeon dropped down the last length of rope too quickly and fell onto his back. Trench yanked him up and he pulled his halberd from the clasp on the back of his jacket.

"This way," cried the Prince Engineer. "Follow me to the tunnel entrance."

Actaeon started off at a run, and the others followed him with weapons drawn, Trench and Atreena taking up a rearguard. The tribals pursued them closely as they ran.

"I hope you know which tunnel opening we've gotta go into, Act!" shouted Wave. The mercenary aimed his heavy crossbow over one shoulder and squeezed the trigger, sending a bolt into the face of Trench's closest pursuer.

"Even if I fail to pick the correct one, it should be close enough to converge with the others," said Actaeon, huffing as he ran. "Only a few terminate abruptly."

"Well ya better not pick one of those, or *we're* gonna terminate abruptly," said Wave as he fixed another bolt into place.

"I'll second that notion," said Wayd.

When Actaeon reached what he thought was the correct tunnel, the bottom of which was some distance above the ground, he tossed his halberd up and leapt to pull himself onto the ledge. He helped Wave and Yanelle climb up next, and the pair ran past him to secure the tunnel beyond.

In a feat of inhuman agility, Quronos leapt clear over Actaeon's head to land beyond him and quickly joined the others.

Actaeon helped Wayd up and then stood, retrieving his halberd. He pulled out his luminary and stuck it into the strap of his goggles which he pulled down over his eyes. He winced at the remembrance of how Wave had lost his own eye from the expelled offspring of one of the giant slugs they had battled in these very tunnels.

As the others scrambled up, he pulled free a copy that he'd sketched of Minovo's map and began to follow the tunnels at a jog.

The tunnel entrance was lined with vines as thick as a man's thigh that had worked their way within in search of nutrients and light. Once Actaeon had passed the end of the vines, he felt his boots sticking in a substance at the bottom of the tunnel. A foul odor rose to wrinkle his nose.

"Act, this isn't good!" said Wave from up ahead.

"No, Wave. It indicates some poor fortune for us," said Actaeon with a frown.

"At least you'll be able to make some more grenados," said Trench as he climbed into the tunnels at the rear. "Better get moving, Act! They're right at our heels."

"Understood, Trench," the Prince Engineer called over his shoulder. He picked up the pace, Wave and Yanelle leading the way before him, with the bolt of the mercenary's crossbow and the point of the Companion's sword.

"Which way, Act?" asked Wave. The light from their luminaries splayed across a t-shaped intersection in the tunnels.

"Straight. Go straight ahead," instructed Actaeon, holding the map before his luminary with one hand and his halberd pointed forward with the other.

When the tunnels next split, they went to the left at Actaeon's instruction. The floor tilted dramatically downward after they made the turn and all of them spilled forward and slid down the incline.

At the bottom of the slope, the party all slammed into one another. Luckily, all of them had the presence of mind to point their weapons to the ceiling. Even so, it was miraculous that nobody had been skewered by the time Trench and Atreena slammed into the back of the party.

"Thought I said I didn't want your huge ass landing atop us, Trench," said Wave as he lifted himself up from the slimy muck that he had landed in face first after being struck by the others. "Same thing with the plate, Atreena."

"Fine," said Trench, spitting some of the muck from his own mouth. "Switch. We'll take point."

Trench and Atreena passed the others on the sides of the tunnel corridor and led the way as the point guard, Actaeon following closely behind them with his map.

"Split coming up, Act. Which way?" asked Trench.

The Prince Engineer frowned and wiped some of the muck from the map with the back of his sleeve. The unfortunate action left even more muck on the map. "A moment," he said as he pulled some felt cloths from his pocket and tried to wipe the vellum sheet clean. The loose lenses that had been wrapped in the cloth spilled free to scatter and disappear on the floor of the dark tunnel.

"We don't have a moment, Your Grace," called Captain Xula. A clash of arms sounded from the rearguard as the pursuing tribals crashed into their weapons.

"Left. Go left!" shouted Actaeon. He shouldered Trench and Atreena forward and the party broke into a run once more, keeping several paces ahead of the tribals.

"'Nother one, coming up!" called Trench.

"Another left, and then a right," said Actaeon. "That will bring us to the place where –"

The creature before them brought the entire group to a sudden halt.

Its bulk filled up most of the tunnel ahead. An identical version to the one that Actaeon had encountered in the past – only bigger. A garden slug from a child's nightmare with row upon row of curved, jagged teeth filling a maw that dwarfed Trench. Behind those lethal teeth were hundreds of smaller slugs, a writhing mass that Actaeon knew it could expel at a moment's notice. Snapping tendrils bristled from the monster's mouth and along the rest of its body – tiny growing versions of itself sticking out in a thousand deadly projections.

Three large stalks, as thick as a large man's thigh, extended from its body and the ends opened to reveal hundreds of tiny black eyes. One cluster looked at Trench, the other at Atreena, and the final one regarded Actaeon, unblinking.

Trench reflexively swung his maul and smashed the eyestalk before him against the tunnel wall.

The creature recoiled and a shrill hiss filled the entirety of the tunnel. The open maw enlarged to an impossible size.

"Back up!" shouted Actaeon. "Go right. Go right!"

The party backed up rapidly, crashing into their Ruinic pursuers in the process. After a brief clash and a blur of blades from Wave and Quronos, they broke free and began to flee down the right branch of the tunnel.

Behind them came a rush of air and numerous dull, slimy thumps as the contents of the nightmare creature's mouth struck their pursuers.

They broke into a flat out run down the right tunnel with the remaining tribals chasing after them, though more to flee the now pursuing giant slug than to attack them.

Actaeon noted the absence of the gentle flow of air as the creature slid into the branch of the tunnel behind them, its bulk completely filling the passage. Screams came from the rear as, one by one, the fleeing tribals began to be devoured by the pursuing monster.

"Shit, it's gaining on us!" yelled Wayd.

"It's too fast," said Atreena, breathing heavily as she ran in her armor.

"Please tell me there's something ahead we can use to our advantage," said Wave.

"I have no idea of what lies ahead, Wave," said Actaeon. "The map only showed where the Adjunct had gone, but she went left at that junction, not right."

"Call a halt an' I'll skewer it with the lance," suggested Hake Rim.

"No, you may well collapse this entire tunnel if you use the lance," warned Actaeon.

"Please don't do that," said Yanelle.

"Fine, then get me a wider spot," said Hake Rim. "I ain't letting that big bug eat me."

Behind them came another scream, followed by yet another. Their pace was beginning to wane as they sprinted down the seemingly endless tunnel.

"There is a chance that the tunnels come together as we continue on," said Actaeon. "Perhaps we can make it back to our goal via a different route."

"How much of a chance?" grunted Trench.

"Not a good one, I suspect," admitted Actaeon.

"I've still got my grenado, Act," said Wave.

"So do I, Wave," said Actaeon. "It is the same problem though – the tunnels may collapse under the force of the explosion.

Another blood-curdling scream ripped through the air behind them.

"Option's starting to look better an' better," said Trench.

The tunnel canted suddenly downward again and they all tumbled forward and slid down the incline, a mess of limbs, weapons, and armor.

The passageway opened up into a vast chamber, but the incline continued, and the party slid down, spreading apart until they came to a stop on a level floor near the center of the chamber.

"That's more like it," said Hake Rim, his light lance crackling to life as he swung it upward along the incline, slicing several sliding tribals to pieces.

The group of remaining tribals managed to control their descent enough to steer clear of the crackling length of the light lancer's beam. They lifted their spears and one of them shouted something in their language.

Hake Rim swept the lance's beam back and forth to keep them at bay. "Twenty," he cursed and then shut off the lance, leaving the chamber dark except for pools of light created by the few remaining luminaries.

Actaeon thought he had seen some strange lumps on the ground out of the corner of his eye in the bright light cast by Hake's lance. He turned in that direction and lifted the baffle that had fallen forward to cover the luminary in his goggles.

The light revealed the lumps, and they looked like bodies.

"Yanelle, Wave, come with me," the Prince Engineer ordered, and started across the empty expanse of floor between him and the body-shaped lumps.

The Companion and the mercenary fell in beside him, their swords held at the ready.

Actaeon knelt beside the first one. It was a Ruinic tribal covered in ornamental tattoos and torn leather armor. When he felt at her neck, the lifebeat was still palpable, but just barely, and very slow.

"By the Fallen," said Actaeon. He lifted his head to look at the other lumps and the light of his luminary revealed dozens of bodies, all laid out in a neatly spaced line.

The terror was clear in Yanelle's voice as she asked, "What is this? What's happening?"

"Deathcrawlers," said Wave.

"Deathcrawlers," echoed Actaeon. He tilted his head back to look at the ceiling and his luminary shed dim light on movement far above.

Hake's light lance crackled to life again, filling the massive chamber with a smell of ozone and revealing hundreds of them far overhead – brown and black carapaces gleaming in the light. The insectoid creatures sped at impossible speeds as they rippled across the ceiling, floating on thin legs that moved so fast they looked like fluttering hairs.

At that moment, the giant slug emerged from the tunnel opening and slid down the incline into the chamber, leaving a trail of brown slime behind it. It paused and contracted before it uttered its shrill hiss once more. The slug's jagged maw opened again, and it spewed a cluster of projectiles at the group of tribals.

Several of the tiny slugs struck Hake Rim, knocking him to the floor. His light lance shut off.

The chamber plunged into darkness.

And the screaming began.

Something slammed into Actaeon from behind, throwing him into Yanelle and sending them both reeling to the floor. He managed to keep hold of his halberd and, once the Companion helped him regain his feet, he held the halberd point forward before him in the bubble of light cast by his luminary.

"Wave?" called Actaeon. He could feel Yanelle's back against his.

A surge of motion came at his back, accompanied by a set of raspy chirps. Yanelle swung her sword and he could feel it connect with one of the deathcrawlers through their joined bodies.

Companion and Prince Engineer were both knocked to the floor as the deflected creature ran past them, chirping as it went.

The sudden return of light was blinding as Hake Rim activated his light lance once more. Smaller slugs still writhed where they had latched onto his body and the light lancer sliced through the carapace of a deathcrawler that had pinned him against the floor. Its pincers bit through his thick leather armor, injecting paralytic venom into his thighs.

The lancer struggled to his feet, resisting the venom for a moment, and Trench knocked the head of the creature from him with a swing of his maul.

As the slug continued to advance its tremendous bulk, the lancer, the giant, and the Keeper Knight placed themselves in its path, their weapons ready.

"I'm outta time," said Hake, and he shut off the light lance.

The chamber fell back into darkness.

At that moment, a large luminary slid forward from behind the slug and cast fresh light upon the battle.

"Hoo yeah, brother! Let's do this," yelled a man as he ran forward and leapt upon the slimy back of the creature. At first Actaeon thought it was one of the tribals – the man was certainly dressed like one. The fact that he spoke their language was a giveaway though. It was Geodric Caider, dressed in full tribal guise. The ex-Companion straddled the monster and lifted his spear into the air to plunge it repeatedly into the beast.

A pair of deathcrawlers slammed into one side of the slug and latched onto it with their lethal pincers. The slug hissed and opened its mouth to eject more of its young into the faces of another pair of deathcrawlers approaching its other flank.

Trench and Atreena leapt between the slug and its attackers. The giant brought his maul down to shatter the carapace of one creature while the Keeper's blade shattered the snapping jaws of the other and sent it reeling onto its back where it curled into a tight ball and rolled off into the shadows.

The two Companions along with Captain Xula and Quronos formed a loose circle around the Prince Engineer to protect him. They swung their blades to deflect the charging deathcrawlers that emerged spontaneously from the darkness surrounding the pools of light cast by their luminaries.

Hake Rim activated his light lance again and fell forward with a curse – his legs were failing as the deathcrawler's paralytic began to set in. The beam of the lance sliced through the floor before he could deactivate it, and a section fell away to crash down somewhere below.

The slug altered its forward momentum to avoid the newly created hole, which sent the two deathcrawlers that were latched onto it tumbling over the edge, bodies writhing as they fell.

Caider was tossed from the slug's back and landed on his feet. The heel of his rear foot slid right up to the edge of the broken floor.

The bulky creature slid away and charged straight at Actaeon's group.

"Ready yourselves. It approaches," said Quronos emotionlessly.

"Shouldn't we run?" asked Wayd.

"No way we'd outrun it," said Xula. "I'd rather die with the enemy on my sword than at my back."

"I would rather not die at all," said Actaeon.

They all laughed at that – nervous laughter.

"Then let's not die," concluded Yanelle. She extended her sword forward in a long guard position as the slug picked up momentum.

The slug's maw opened as it drew near, presumably to hurl more of its offspring at them. Before it could do so, a heavy spear slammed into its back – Caider's.

It recoiled and hissed before circling back in a tight loop with surprising speed. The remaining eye stalks extended to regard the ex-Companion with hundreds of eyes.

Caider slid to a stop and glared right back at the monster. "Alright, brother – let's see what you're made of." He pulled his long knife from his belt.

The slug's mouth opened again, revealing the rows of deadly teeth and hungry, snapping offspring.

And Caider surprised them all by smiling and leaping straight in, past the rows of teeth.

The slug writhed spastically and shook, sliding back and forth in a manic effort to dislodge the unexpected arrival of the stabbing Raedellean warrior in its gullet.

It slid onto its back and the length of its body followed in a violent flip that slammed into the side of the formation protecting Actaeon, which sent them all reeling.

Trench and Atreena each grabbed one of the light lancer's arms and dragged him past the struggling creature to rejoin the rest.

When they stopped, Hake Rim placed his hands in the appropriate locations and his lance crackled to life, once more casting brighter light throughout the chamber.

Twenty paces to the side of the party, the Ruinic tribals stood in abject terror. Several of their dead surrounded them, and some of those still upright had either fallen to their knees or had writhing slug appendages sticking out from their bodies.

Along the incline beyond the struggling slug were hundreds of tiny eyes, glowing in the light of the lance. Each pair of eyes was supported by hundreds of thin legs.

"This ain't good," muttered Trench.

"Suggestions?" asked Actaeon as he levered himself back to his feet and pointed his halberd forward defensively.

"I'll say it again," said Wayd. "Shall we run?"

"Where's Wave?" asked Trench.

"He disappeared after the first of the deathcrawlers crashed into us," said Actaeon.

"Shit," muttered Trench.

"I'll second Companion Wayd on running," voiced Captain Xula.

"And I'll third it," said Atreena.

"Twenty," whispered Hake Rim under his breath, and the light lance shut off again.

A strange sound began, which it took Actaeon half a moment to identify as the skittering of thousands of legs charging forward.

"Run," agreed the Prince Engineer. And when he felt the others hesitate, he said it louder. "Run!"

The remaining members of the party fled into the narrow pool of light cast before them by their luminaries. Screams behind them told of when the deathcrawler legion slammed into the remainder of the Ruinic tribals.

Hopefully the uninjured ones had gotten away, thought Actaeon, noting how strange it was that the situation now had him rooting for their enemy. Nobody deserved to die at the hands of these horrors of the deep.

The chirps of the creatures drew rapidly closer as they ran.

Actaeon fumbled for the grenado clipped to his jacket.

"Yer gonna throw that thing, Act?" asked Trench, huffing as he carried the partially paralyzed light lancer over his shoulder.

"Unless you have a better idea," said Actaeon.

Quronos stepped to the side and stopped before spinning to face the onslaught.

A glance back cast luminary light upon the silver guardian of Travail as his pair of swords formed a fan-like blur that obliterated the first of the deathcrawlers that met him. Others swarmed in from the sides and over the dying bodies of their brethren and Quronos disappeared underneath the mass of chirping insectoids.

"Nope. Throw it!" shouted Trench.

Actaeon brought the grenado to his weapon hand and twisted the pin ninety degrees to pull it free. He switched his halberd to the left hand and the grenado to his right. He hefted it for a moment, judging its weight – it had been some time since he'd thrown one, and those had been trials.

"It's Ancestors' tears in here. Throw it already!" The giant's shout echoed in the cavernous chamber.

Actaeon grinned nervously and lobbed it over his shoulder.

For a moment nothing happened, but then the shockwave from the explosion threw them all forward. It had been way too close, thought Actaeon.

The sounds in the chamber were replaced by a singular ringing in their ears that drowned out everything else.

Actaeon rolled onto his back and peered into the light cast by his luminary – somehow still in the strap of his goggles.

There was nothing but darkness. No charging deathcrawlers, no pursuing tribals, no struggling slug. The explosion had worked – at least for now.

Actaeon felt his stomach lurch as the floor beneath him gave way.

MAD FLIGHT

THE FLOOR STRUCK ANOTHER SURFACE below and shattered into hundreds of pieces.

No sooner had they begun to breathe again, than they started sliding downward rapidly. Fragmented bits from above pelted them painfully.

Actaeon felt another body slam against his own and tried, but failed, to grab onto whomever it was before they were yanked away by the rapidly crumbling remains of the floor.

"Saints, what do we do, what do we do?" Wayd cried out from nearby, cutting through the ringing in their ears.

"Try and keep yer head up and hold onto yer weapon," instructed Trench. The giant still clutched one of Hake Rim's arms as they slid. Atreena grasped the lancer's other arm firmly.

"Allfather help us," shrieked the Keeper Knight Captain.

"The end approaches. Brace for impact," instructed Quronos enigmatically.

"How the – " someone began, but their words were cut off as they all slammed to a stop at the bottom of whatever incline they had been sliding down.

Floor fragments tumbled over them and rained down from above in a chaotic maelstrom.

Then there returned the comparative silence of their ringing ears.

Actaeon's body racked with coughs. He methodically checked himself for injuries and found a sizable lump on his left knee. Touching it made him wince and feel faint.

He grimaced and carefully planted the butt of his halberd down to help lever himself to his feet. The pain in his knee was tremendous and when he put weight on it, he nearly passed out. He found that he could hold himself upright if he supported a portion of his weight with the halberd.

Next was the problem that he couldn't see anything and his ears were still ringing from the shock of the explosion.

Actaeon reached up to check the luminary and found that the baffle was still raised. With his right hand he felt his eyes and found that his goggles were still there and intact over both eyes. Which meant he hadn't been blinded, but that – yes, he could see it now, the momentary swirl of dust as he waved a hand before his face.

The dust from the collapse was so thick that even the light of his luminary couldn't pierce it.

It was that dark.

He found a sizable chunk of debris and settled down heavily upon it to wait for the dust to clear. He continued to cough as he breathed in the settling dust. From the top left pocket of his jacket, he pulled a small roll of brightweave free and tied it about his face to filter the dust. He immediately felt a pain in his chest ease as he breathed.

In the lower right pocket of his jacket he found his bandage roll, which he wrapped tightly around his left knee to compress the injury before securing it with a knot.

As the dust began to settle, he could make out some of the space around him through the haze by the light of his luminary.

Several thick vertical columns came into view – the floor between them covered in the debris that had fallen from far above. Any ceiling was far above his head and lost in the settling dust of the collapse.

A desperate groan to his right drew his attention and he used the shaft of his weapon to help himself to his feet and investigate.

He found Atreena there and pulled some of the debris from atop her. The Knight wheezed and pulled back the visor of her helm to regard him. She rasped something that he couldn't make out and he lowered himself to his good knee and leant forward to hear her better.

"Can't... breathe..." rasped the Knight Captain, the color drained from her face. She searched his face frantically. "Help... please!" She gasped for air and clutched at Actaeon's arm in terror.

Actaeon placed his hand over hers and grinned, his expression hidden by the brightweave cloth. "Do not worry, Lady Knight. We will figure this out."

Gently, he removed her hand from his arm and moved down to investigate her chest. The problem was immediately evident – her breastplate had a large bend in it that was preventing her chest from expanding.

"Found it. Your plate is bent. I will have to remove it so you can breathe," he explained.

"Just... do it already!" she gasped. She pulled off her gauntlets and began to work at one of the leather straps that held one shoulder in place.

Actaeon followed her lead and worked on the other side.

Next they moved down to another set of straps under her armpits.

When they had those straps undone, Atreena pushed the breastplate forward and sucked in a deep breath.

"Allfather help me!" she said as she took in another deep breath and began to cough.

"Seems as though Act helped ya, not yer Allfather," said Trench as he emerged from the gloom of the settling dust.

Hake Rim leaned on Trench's shoulder, using his light lance as a crutch on the other side.

"Good to see you, Trench. Hake, I take it the paralytic is wearing off?" asked Actaeon.

"Aye sir – I ken feel my legs a bit more now," said the lancer.

"That is good." Actaeon finished untying the final straps on Atreena's breastplate and set it down on the floor before Trench, inside up. "Trench, would you mind banging out that dent?"

"Not at all," said the giant with a smirk. He swung the wicked head of his maul down to strike it with a sound that resonated far above them.

"This chamber is quite large, judging by the noise that made," said Actaeon.

"That's fine armor! How dare you batter it like that?" cried out Atreena.

"If ya'd prefer, I'll bend it back," said Trench. "I think I liked her better when she couldn't breathe."

"Very funny," said Atreena. She yanked the breastplate out of Actaeon's grasp and began to refasten it back into place.

"Where are the others?" asked Actaeon.

Just then the sound of clashing weapons started nearby.

The four of them rushed over in time to witness Yanelle yank her sword free from the chest of a dying Ruinic warrior. The dead man collapsed atop another of his unfortunate friends.

Harvand Xula stood shoulder to shoulder with the Companion in front of four of the enemy slain, blood dripping from his sabre.

A fifth Ruinic tribal – a young woman with a shaved pate, sharpened teeth, and a face covered with Ancient ruins painted with dark woad – stood before them. She hissed at them and tossed her spear to the ground, lifting her hands in the air – the universal sign of surrender. Whatever she said next in the strange Ruinic language was a mystery to everyone. She knelt then and made a crude chopping motion at her neck.

"I'll not be the one to hack down a prisoner of war," said Xula. "On your feet."

When the tribal didn't move, Yanelle reached forward and yanked her to her feet.

The tribal woman hissed at her only to have it cut short by the Companion's fist, which dropped her back down to her knees. Blood streamed from the Ruinic warrioress' broken nose, and she bared her sharpened teeth at Yanelle.

When Yanelle made to strike her again, the tribal's mouth snapped shut and she held up her hands.

With a wince, Actaeon knelt on his good knee and picked up the tribal's spear. He hefted it in his hand and regarded it closely before he spoke. "Listen, Lady Ruinic, the way I see it, we all have a common enemy in this place. Either we work together to survive, or they will find our remains down here one day long after we are gone. If I give you back your weapon, will you promise not to try and kill us until we escape this place?" He let his words hang in the air for a moment before he extended the spear to her.

The woman nodded and accepted her weapon back. She drew to her feet and wiped the blood from her face, the action causing Xula and Yanelle to step between her and Actaeon.

"Your Grace," said Yanelle. "With respect, there's no way she understood what you just said."

Actaeon levered himself to his feet. "Sometimes context and action speaks louder than words, Companion Yanelle. I believe Lady Ruinic understands the gist of what I aimed to communicate with her."

"If not, she'll understand what my maul feels like as it enters her brain," said the giant.

"Always good to have a backup plan," said Actaeon with a grin. "Now, we are still missing Companion Wayd, Quronos, and Wave."

"Not to mention Caider," said Trench. "Wherever in shattered Redemption he came from."

"Not to mention Caider," agreed Actaeon. "Let us start our search at the bottom of the slope we came down and we can branch out from there."

"We'd best be quick, lest those deathcrawlers return," said Xula.

"I would guess they will be back once the dust settles from the collapse – they are predators after all," said Actaeon.

"I'm hoping they're all dead from yer grenado," said Trench.

Xula, Yanelle and Atreena spread out and led the way while the others followed.

They shortly reached a taller pile of rubble consisting of the fragmented floor from above. A massive column protruded from the collapse, rising into the chamber high above and out of sight of their luminaries. Chunks of stone were piled higher around the column, having slammed to a stop against it.

Companion Yanelle was there first.

"Saints…" she whispered. She sheathed her sword and began to pull rocks from the pile.

The Thyrian Captain and Keeper Knight joined her and soon they had him uncovered.

A large chunk of stone had smashed him against the bulk of the column. He lay flat across the top of the stone, his rough-cut auburn hair splayed out on the stone surface, caked with blood.

"Wayd." Actaeon winced and knelt beside the Companion's body.

Together, Actaeon and Yanelle lifted their kinsman up from the stone so that his back was against the column. Wayd's head flopped lifelessly to the side, grossly malformed from one of the chunks that had killed him.

"Cracked Redemption," mouthed Trench.

"May the Fallen guide him," said Hake Rim.

Actaeon motioned to Yanelle and together they laid him forward back upon the stone that would be his final resting place. He found suddenly that he deeply missed Voice Ithelie. She would know the right thing to do in this terrible moment.

"We should cover him, Your Grace," said Yanelle.

Actaeon nodded. "Yes."

They gently piled the stones back upon the Companion. When they were finished, they stepped back. Everyone turned to Actaeon expectantly.

"Companion Wayd Arbrigel was a loyal friend of the Caliburns and a brave warrior right until the end," said the Prince Engineer. He took a deep breath and felt Trench's big hand on his shoulder. "He was a Goader too – a specialist trainer of the lion-lizards that help defend Raedelle. He fought and died in this conflict so that all of Redemption may continue to grow and prosper. May he join the Fallen in guiding us on our path to protect and defend Redemption. I will remember Wayd Arbrigel. He was a friend."

"I will remember Wayd Arbrigel," echoed the others.

Nearby, the stones shifted and tumbled free.

Actaeon turned to regard the moving debris and the light of his luminary reflected from a silvery surface behind the fragments. "Quronos," he said.

"That is c – correct, Prince Eng – Engineer," said the guardian of Travail, stuttering his words. He pushed more stones away until his head was free. There was a large dent in one side and one of the guardian's jet-black eyes was missing. In the empty socket, sparks arced across the void as if trying to inject life into something no longer there.

Quronos lurched forward and dislodged more of the debris that held him in place. With difficulty, he pushed his way out and climbed free of the collapse. His left arm was missing at the shoulder where cords of glass rope hung loosely, red and purple lights traveling down them to culminate in a shower of sparks that rained down to the floor.

"Looks like ya got the mechanical man you were always looking for right here, Act," said Trench with a grin that tugged at the giant's deep scar.

"It's an artifact..." murmured Atreena.

"Don't get any ideas, Knight Captain," said Harvand Xula.

"Neither should you," retorted Atreena. "If you think this *artifact*," she sneered the word, " is a friend, then you are truly delusional."

"Say what you will," said Actaeon. "We are all in this together. Artifact or no, we welcome Quronos' aid in this mission."

"You – You – u've my th – thanks, Prin – Prince Engineer," said Quronos. "I w – will help as long as I – I – I'm able to." With his remaining arm, the guardian reached up and drew one of his thin swords from some hidden compartment within his back.

"And we are honored to have your help, Quronos. There is much I hope to learn from you after we survive this ordeal," said Actaeon with a grin.

"I – I – I hope to tea – each you the – the – the things you wish to learn," said Quronos.

"For that I am grateful. We had best continue on," Actaeon suggested. "There is no knowing when the creatures from above will resume their pursuit."

Actaeon led the group away from Wayd's improvised tomb and the slope they had slid down after the collapse. The others followed, spread wide and at intervals, with the tribal he'd named Lady Ruinic at the distant rear – her spear held ready for anything they might encounter.

They smelled it long before they came upon it. The scorched giant slug lay deflated on the ground amidst the scattered debris. Flames licked along its sides.

It spasmed suddenly and the blade of a long knife emerged from within the dead creature. It sliced its way upward in jerky motions that eventually parted the monster's slimy flesh. The widened opening revealed the muscular figure of Geodric Caider, his flesh blackened with thick burns in any places not protected by his lion-lizard armor.

The ex-Companion opened his bewildered eyes to regard Actaeon. It took him a moment to recognize the Prince Engineer, and he smiled a satisfied smile. "I did it, Act. I killed the thing. Wasn't so bad."

Xula and Trench pulled Caider free of the dead slug's body and laid him carefully on the floor nearby.

"You did well, Caider," said Actaeon. "I certainly did not expect you to leap within its maw like you did."

"Yeah, brother. Showed it who's boss, eh? Too bad I ain't gonna make it. Wanted to see this whole thing through with ya."

Actaeon reached out and grasped Caider's hand. "You did good, Caider. I am glad you were here to help us."

"Thanks, Act," said Caider. "Means a lot to me." He looked over Actaeon's shoulder to the tribal warrioress. "See ya made a friend. That's good. Maybe things can be sorted after all." He spoke to Lady Ruinic in her language.

Lady Ruinic stepped forward and bared her sharpened teeth before replying in turn.

"What does she say?" asked Yanelle.

"She'll not fight with you anymore," said Caider with a smile. "There's worse things in Redemption worth fighting – she sees that now." Caider's head lolled to the side and he regarded Actaeon with a weak gaze. "Listen, brother. I ain't long for this world. Let the Princess know I'm sorry for what I did. Couldn't let ya go it alone. Sorry I couldn't do more, but I'm finished."

"You are not done yet, Geodric Caider," said Actaeon firmly. "For the Princess Eisandre Rellios Caliburn would elevate you back to a Companion."

"Ya can't do that, brother. Only the Princess can, and she's not here," said Caider.

"Oh, but she is," insisted Actaeon. "She speaks with me through the Thoughtlink Artifact. Eisandre knows the sacrifice you made on this day, and she asks for your service. Geodric Caider, I ask that you defend the Rellios Caliburns and thereby defend Raedelle. Would you accept?"

Caider smiled up at Actaeon in the dim light of the luminaries. "Aye, Act. Tell Her Grace that I will be her stalwart defender, in life... and in death."

Actaeon nodded and lifted his halberd to touch its shaft to Caider's forehead. "Then rise, Geodric Caider, as a Companion of Raedelle."

"Thanks, Act. You're a good man. Miss you... brother." Trench and Xula helped the Companion to his feet, and the life faded from his eyes – his head lolling back.

"Lay him down and cover him," instructed Actaeon. "His actions on this day will not be forgotten."

As the others covered Caider's lifeless form with more broken bits from the collapsed floor, a sound came to their ears from far above and behind them.

It was a series of shrill chirps.

"We'd best move, Your Grace," said Hake Rim.

"Aye. Let us move, and fast," said Actaeon.

And so they ran along the vast floor of the chamber, away from the slope they had slid down and the debris of the collapse – away from the predators that still pursued them.

The seven survivors ran as fast as they could, despite their smattering of injuries, through a seemingly endless chamber, past hundreds of the massive elderstone columns that held it up. The chirps were growing closer behind them and occasionally on their flanks.

"Sorry about Wave," Actaeon said to Trench. "I wish we could have found him back there."

"Can't see how it matters, Act," admitted Trench. "I'm not sure many of us'll make it outta this one, if any at all."

"We knew this would be a desperate mission from the start, with little chance of success," said Actaeon. "Still, we would not have attempted it if we didn't think it was at least possible. And with most of us still on our feet – we have to believe it is."

"We just have to find this mysterious lift that a dead girl told you about," said Captain Xula with an unseen smirk of amusement.

"You make it sound as if she was not alive at the time," said Actaeon.

"Was she?" asked Xula, baring his white teeth in a big grin.

Quronos' head swiveled to regard behind them as he ran. "Th – they will be – be – be upon us in sev – seventy lifebeats."

"How can you see them, Quronos?" asked Actaeon.

"I c – c – can image on n – non – non-visible wavelengths," asserted the artifact man.

"Well that would have been good to know," Actaeon said. "Do you see any places that we could reach in time where we could hold them off?"

"Y – y – affirmative," said Quronos. With his remaining arm he pointed forward and to their left with the tip of his blade. "You w – will – will not like it."

"Let's go then!" shouted Atreena. The heavily armored Knight began to run in that direction and the others followed.

Quronos picked up speed and ran past them all to grab the Keeper Knight and stop her.

"Unhand me, you abomination!" she shrieked, she brought her free hand down to knock the guardian's arm from her own. The crosswise slice of her broadsword was easily parried by Quronos' own blade.

"I – I – I merely wished to st – s – stop you before you passed – passed –

passed it," said the artifact man. He gestured with his silver arm toward the nearest column, which had a man-sized portal in its face.

Somehow, even though he was holding his sword, Quronos grabbed Atreena and flung her into the opening. Her armor clattered as she crashed into the column's interior and her scream of protest disappeared with a rush of air.

"Go – g – go inside," said Quronos. "I sha – shall – sha – hold them until you are through."

"Where does it lead?" inquired Actaeon.

"Dest – destinate – destination unknown," Quronos responded. He took a step past them and pointed his blade forward toward the approaching chirps that were growing in volume.

"I'll go first to clear the area," growled Trench. He clutched his maul tightly and leapt inside to be swept away in a rush of air.

The light lancer and Thyrian Captain wasted no time in leaping into the column behind him.

"After you, Your Grace," said Yanelle, saluting Actaeon fist to chest.

Actaeon nodded and stepped into the portal, keeping a tight grip on his halberd.

He was swept upward with a warm rush of air that took his breath away, sucking the air from his lungs.

The experience was over in the blink of an eye, and he was tossed by the air current upward and to the side in a much smaller room. He landed squarely on Hake Rim.

Hake gasped as the wind was knocked out of him. As the light lancer recovered his breath, he cried out. "By the Fallen, get off me. What d'ya think yer – oh, sorry Yer Grace. Glad to 'ave broken yer fall."

"Sure you are, warbander," said Actaeon with a grin. "Thanks for being there to break my fall." He rolled off of the light lancer and pulled himself to his feet to assess the room, wincing at the ache in his knee.

It was a junction of some sort, with a plethora of openings in the floor, walls, and ceiling – some of them much bigger than the one they had been pushed up through. The inside of the chamber was multi-faceted – comprising adjacent squares and hexagons that it took Actaeon a moment to realize formed a truncated octahedron. In actuality the floor and ceiling were square sections with no openings.

They had been spat out of an orifice in one of the hexagonal faces of the room and ejected toward the square floor in its center. The entire chamber felt like the inside of a giant bellows, with air being alternately injected and ejected from it. The constant change in pressure made Actaeon's ears pop repeatedly.

In the center of the room were human bodies spaced at equal intervals and all oriented in the same direction.

As the remainder of his allies were tossed unceremoniously into the room along with puffs of air that made his head pound, Actaeon moved to investigate the bodies.

The majority of them were tribals, but one of them stood out from the rest. The long, black hair tied into the neat queue, the eyepatch, and the loose finespun cotton tunic – still showing white in some places where it stuck out from his dyed blue leather armor, despite the dirt and grime – were a dead giveaway.

Actaeon rushed over to Wave and, with some difficulty, knelt by his head.

The mercenary was still conscious and looking around, his eye flicking about frantically. The finely wrought crossguard of his flamberge rapier shone in the luminary light – he must've managed to sheath it before he was fully paralyzed. His eye bulged wide when he saw Actaeon above him. For a moment he looked panicked, but he quickly composed himself and rolled his eye toward the top of his head. He repeated the movement a second time, deliberately.

"They come in and out from above your head?" asked Actaeon. "Blink once for yes, twice for no."

Wave blinked once, slowly.

Actaeon nodded. "Yanelle, Quronos, Atreena – guard that opening." He pointed to a larger orifice into the room that was directly above Wave's head. "That is where they come in and out."

"Aye aye, Your Grace," said the Companion. The three of them quickly took up a defensive position.

Trench rushed to Wave's other side and knelt next to his friend. "Don't worry, Wave – we'll get you outta here."

Wave squeezed his eye shut and when he opened it again, he gave the giant a long, hard look.

Trench turned to the Prince Engineer. "He gonna be okay, Act?" His voice quavered with concern.

Actaeon looked into the giant's eyes and shook his head. "Get him out of here, Trench. We will worry about it when this is over. Every problem has a solution." Despite his words, he couldn't help but think of how, so long ago, his mother had died of Rogue's Bane. There had been no solution, even with his every effort.

"Whaddaya mean, Act?" asked Trench, concerned. "Speak to me straight about it. Can we fix whatever's happened to him?"

"I said just get him out of here, Trench!" snapped Actaeon uncharacteristically. "Let me worry about the rest." He reached down to pull Wave's grenado free of the mercenary's sword belt, clipping it to his own jacket in case he might need it.

Trench's expression grew dark and he glowered at the Prince Engineer, though he kept his silence.

Behind him, Lady Ruinic dispatched her fellow tribals with quick slashes that opened their necks with the tip of her spear. Before ending each of their lives, she muttered something in her language.

"Apologies, Trench. I –" began Actaeon.

He was interrupted when Trench noticed Wave's eye widen so far it nearly bulged from its socket.

The giant grabbed the shaft of Lady Ruinic's spear a split second before she could open Wave's throat with it. His swift kick caught her mid-chest and sent her flying to land atop her dead brethren.

Trench spun the spear around in his off hand and threw it so that it buried itself in a dead tribal's belly just a handspan from Lady Ruinic's head.

She hissed at him, and he narrowed his eyes at her.

"Come near my friend again and that'll find yer eye socket," Trench growled.

Lady Ruinic looked away and scrambled to her feet before pulling her weapon free.

"Sorry, buddy," said Trench to his friend before he yanked Wave from the floor and tossed the smaller mercenary over his shoulder. "You'll thank me later – I hope."

There came chirping from the mouth of the tunnel the others were guarding.

"We'd best get out of here," suggested Atreena.

"Which way?" asked Xula.

"Toward Pyramid, of course," said Actaeon, rummaging in the pockets of his jacket.

Everyone turned to look at the Prince Engineer in surprise.

"Ya can't be serious ya still've got yer sense of direction," said Hake Rim.

Actaeon pulled his directional finder from one of his pockets and set it carefully on the floor. The pointer spun rapidly about the center as if it couldn't make up its mind. "That is unfortunate. Too much metal here." He regarded the device for a moment longer before scooping it up to return it to his pocket.

"The m – m – most direct route toward the Pyramid is thr – thr – through that orifice," stated Quronos. The artifact man pointed toward a downward sloping opening in one of the lower hexagonal facets on the opposite side of the chamber.

"Let us not waste any time," said Actaeon.

The chirping was getting louder.

Actaeon crouched and led the way into the tunnel. It was narrower and, with any hope, would stop the larger of the deathcrawlers from following them that way. He shuffled his way downward as quickly as he could manage, with his halberd pointed forward into the claustrophobic bubble of light cast by his luminary. He could hear the others making their way behind him.

When the floor leveled out, three more tunnels branched out before him.

"Most unfortunate," he muttered.

Quronos arrived at his side and turned to regard him with the jet-black abyss of his remaining eye. "The left is the – the – the most direct approach." A spark shot across his empty eye socket.

"You had best lead the way then," said Actaeon. "We shall follow."

"Aff – aff – affirmative," said the mechanical man.

Quronos wasted no time in plunging forward into the darkness of the left branch.

Actaeon ran after him, still crouched, trying to keep the Travail guardian at the edge of his luminary's reach.

They weaved and wound a deliberate path through the featureless cylindrical tunnels.

"How is the rear?" called Actaeon at one point.

"Clear," shouted Trench, his voice carrying loudly down the narrow enclosure. "Nothing following yet."

Quronos took another turn and the tunnel began to widen gradually until they had enough headroom to stand and then, suddenly, much more above them. They ran past several more branches of similarly sized tunnels, making much quicker progress with the level floors and larger passageways.

Quronos stopped so suddenly that Actaeon slammed into him.

The artifact man stood as solidly as a stone and the Prince Engineer bounced backward and began to fall. His fall was arrested as Companion Yanelle ran smack into him and someone else into her.

A litany of curses arose from the rest of the party as they all crashed to a halt.

"Where are you going?" exclaimed Yanelle. The Companion shoved Actaeon to the side of the tunnel as Lady Ruinic slid past her, the tribal's spearpoint forward.

Yanelle interposed herself between Lady Ruinic and Actaeon, but the tribal warrioress wasn't interested in the Prince Engineer.

Lady Ruinic barked something vicious at them and ducked below Quronos' remaining arm as she ran into the junction beyond him.

"I – I – I," began the guardian, but he didn't have the chance to finish his sentence.

Lady Ruinic was caught off guard as the massive slug slammed into her with its open mouth, crumpling her body like a rag doll before the pair slammed into one of the junction walls. There was a loud crack as her limbs snapped.

The slug recoiled and its body widened dramatically in the open space of the junction to swallow Lady Ruinic, spear and all.

It let out a hiss that almost sounded satisfied, before it turned to Quronos and the others and opened its now bloody maw once more. Dozens of horrible tendrils that grew from its body snapped at them hungrily.

Quronos lowered his blade and prepared to face it. Just behind him, Yanelle held her own sword in a guard position, determined to defend her ward even in this desperate situation.

The slug's massive body enlarged and drew away from them before it let out another hiss and lunged forward.

The multiple deathcrawlers that slammed into its side from another opening in the junction saved them.

Instead of obliterating the survivors, the slug's momentum caused it to crash into a wall of the junction, shattering many of its teeth.

It writhed backward and, with its maw, latched onto one of the deathcrawlers just behind the creature's neck. The deathcrawler spasmed back and forth in an effort to escape, the action sending many of its legs flying free.

"N – N – Now," began Quronos.

"Now is our chance," cried Actaeon. "Follow Quronos!"

The silver-skinned artifact man ran into the fray, ducking beneath the thrashing form of a deathcrawler and leaping lithely over another.

Actaeon followed with Yanelle at his side. In the chaos, he forgot all about the pain in his sprained knee.

A deathcrawler lunged toward them, its twin pincers spread wide to either side of its gaping jaws. Yanelle's blade took off half of the creature's jaw and one of its pincers. It let loose a high-pitched shriek and flipped onto its back, writhing and kicking at them with its legs as they ran past.

Quronos' blade cut another of the monsters to pieces before him before he leapt clear over it and made for the tunnel beyond.

The others scrambled past the unfolding battle between the giant slug and the arriving swarm of deathcrawlers. More of the creatures latched onto the big slug, their pincers injecting paralytic poisons into its bulk. It managed to swallow its first attacker and expanded rapidly forward to tear a chunk from the middle of another, missing Atreena by a hair as she took up the rear behind Trench, who was carrying Wave.

They all made it to the tunnel that Quronos had selected in one piece.

There Hake Rim turned to face the dueling nightmares. The muscular warbander grinned and readied his light lance. "Go on, the rest o' ya. Gonna show these abominations who's boss."

The others looked back at him and hesitated before running after Quronos.

Several deathcrawlers charged Hake Rim, and ozone filled the air as his light lance crackled to life. The center creature was obliterated by the long beam cast forward by the device. The monster to its left lost its head as it reeled away from the beam and Hake Rim swept it to the side, cutting through biological matter and structural stone alike.

A third deathcrawler slammed into Hake Rim's chest and pinned him against the wall. Hake cried out and neatly sliced through its body before dropping the heavy artifact's shaft down onto its head to knock it free.

"Eleven, twelve," said the light lancer as he waded into the chaos of the junction, sweeping the beam left and right to obliterate the monsters.

At the far side of the junction he spotted the giant slug struggling beneath the writhing bodies of a dozen deathcrawlers and grinned as he raced toward it and swept the artifact beam down to slice it in two.

The impact of the lance caused an instantaneous detonation that vaporized the slug, any deathcrawlers, Hake Rim, and the entire junction in an explosion that dwarfed that of the grenados that Actaeon had created.

The resulting pressure wave burst down the tunnel and flattened the remainder of the fleeing party to the floor. There was a sickening sensation as the corridor's floor fell out from below them. They slammed into it once more in short order, with a jarring thud.

His ears ringing, Actaeon climbed to his feet to assess the situation.

The pressure wave had caused the tunnel to fracture in half – the bottom falling down and landing some four times the height of a man below. Ahead of them was a near vertical section of semi-circular corridor, high above which was an intact portion of corridor they had fallen from. Back behind them another fragment sloped upward dramatically back toward the blown apart junction.

Quronos stood near the collapsed vertical section, gazing up at the intact corridor above. Behind him, Captain Xula and Companion Yanelle regained their feet unsteadily. Xula lifted a hand to his left ear and it came away with blood.

Behind Actaeon, Knight Captain Atreena sat up and yanked her helmet from her head to toss it aside. Lines of blood trickled down to her neck from both ears and she yelled out, clawing at her ears with both hands. "I can't hear," she said softly at first and then yelled, "Can't hear!"

Trench placed a heavy hand on her shoulder and lowered his face to hers. She recoiled momentarily before she realized who it was. "Yer ears burst in the blast. You'll be alright in time. In the meantime, cool it." The giant turned to Actaeon. "What happened, Act?"

"Your guess is as good as mine," said Actaeon in a louder voice than necessary – his own ears still ringing from the explosion. "If I had to hypothesize though, I would say that Hake's light lance beam met that slug."

"Cracked Redemption," said Trench. "Thing's like a thousand grenados."

"Probably more," admitted the Prince Engineer. "Hopefully he bought us some time with his sacrifice. Now the question is, how do we get up there?"

"Wave's got his grapple and rope," said Trench, gesturing to the unconscious form of his friend.

"Pass it forward," said Actaeon.

"Aye," said Trench, unwrapping the coil of rope from Wave's body and passing it forward to Actaeon.

"Gi – give – give it to me," said Quronos. The silver man still stood gazing upward, but he held his remaining hand out behind him. His blade was gone, perhaps returned to its compartment in his back.

Actaeon gladly dropped the line into Quronos' hand.

The artifact man leapt upward with surprising agility and landed on his feet an impossible distance above. Once there, he quickly unwound the rope with rapid motions from his single hand and let it dangle to the collapse below.

Yanelle looked up at the rope and then back at Actaeon questioningly.

Captain Xula shook his head in disbelief and sheathed his sabre before taking hold of the rope and beginning to climb. "Just amazing," he said as he climbed. "Too bad this is all too inconceivable for anyone to ever believe."

Actaeon grinned up at the Thyrian. "With any luck at least one of us will survive to verify your story," he said, before nodding to Yanelle. "We had best follow."

"Let's hope so, Prince Engineer," called down Xula. "Because I don't want to have to recount this tale by my lonesome."

Yanelle went next, followed by Actaeon and then Atreena. Then Trench tied the rope about Wave and motioned for them to yank up the unconscious mercenary.

Once they'd hauled Wave to the intact part of the tunnel, Actaeon threw the rope back down to Trench. "Your turn."

"I hate p-kin ropes," muttered the giant. He took the rope in his hands and tried to walk up the wall before him, but he slipped and landed heavily upon his back. Trench roared in anger and slammed his fist into the floor.

"Tie it around yourself like you did with Wave," instructed Actaeon. "We will haul you up."

"Forget it, Act," said Trench. "Leave me. I'll work my way up some other way."

"By the Fallen, I will not," said Actaeon with a smirk. "Cut the nonsense and tie the rope, Trench. We shall wait right here until then, so it is up to you whether you or the deathcrawlers reach us first."

"Darkest Hour take you!" cursed Trench. But the giant took the rope and tied it in a makeshift harness about his body. When he was finished, he tugged the rope. "Fine, haul me up like a baby in a cradle."

"It will add to Captain Xula's tale – that time the two legendary veterans of the Sustenance and both Invasion Wars needed to be tugged up like babies in a cradle," joked Actaeon. He shared a grin with Xula.

And, as if on purpose, they began to yank Trench upward just as he opened his mouth to retort.

Once he was up, the party began once more to walk the length of the corridor, following the shower of sparks from Quronos' missing arm as he led the way. Everyone was silent as they walked.

The tunnel went on for a very long distance, with no further turns or junctions.

It finally opened up into a large, pyramidal-shaped, cavernous room.

Actaeon led them to the center of the room, where a triangular shape was inset into the floor. Once they reached it, a short triangular post rose from the ground. Atop it was a singular glowing symbol of the Ancients. It was a symbol that he recognized – one that activated something.

Actaeon turned to the others and grinned, feeling tears at the corners of his eyes. "My friends, I believe this is it. We have reached our goal – the lift that Shar Minovo used to return to the Sun Chamber of Pyramid after her own ordeal. If this brings us there, we have but to reach the Sea Lounge and Pyramid's Control Room above that to complete our plan."

"Then the lives lost will not have been in vain," whispered Yanelle.

"Indeed," said Xula.

"Listen," said Trench.

And so they did. It was unmistakable. The distant sound of chirps – thousands of them.

"Let's leave this place," said Atreena, sensing something was wrong.

"Second that," said Xula.

They all gathered inside the large triangle that was set into the floor. Trench set Wave down in the center.

Actaeon grinned and placed his right hand with its fingerless glove atop the glowing symbol. The triangular inset shifted and began to rise, causing everyone's stomachs to lurch.

As it rose, deathcrawlers burst into the chamber and rushed toward the center. Trench, Atreena and Xula each took places at the points of the triangle, their weapons ready. The creatures scrambled underneath, but were unable to reach the lift. In short order, the floor below transformed into a writhing mass of thin legs and snapping pincers, hunting for prey.

The group collectively held their breath as the lift continued to rise until it reached the pinnacle of the chamber. The top of the chamber opened to allow the lift to pass through.

The light that filtered down through the opening temporarily blinded them all, with the exception of Quronos.

When their vision finally cleared it became apparent that they stood within the vast Sun Chamber at the center of the Pyramid. The winding staircases of the Skyspiral reached to the heavens above them in chaotic helixes that converged and diverged at intervals. Far above, the natural light of the day's sun filtered down through complex prisms that spread the light downward uniformly throughout the chamber.

Once the artifacts of that light had sufficiently cleared their vision, they saw it – the hundreds upon hundreds of Ruinic tribals that presently camped in the Sun Chamber. The looks upon the closest of which, just an arm's length away, proved that they were just as surprised as the new arrivals were.

ASCENT INTO CHAOS

AN UPROAR ECHOED THROUGHOUT THE Sun Chamber as the Ruinic tribals took up their arms at the arrival of the strangers within their midst.

The six survivors still on their feet formed a tight defensive circle with Wave on the floor at the center.

The nearest tribals began to probe their defenses carefully with their weapons as others rushed to equip themselves.

Some of the tribals attempted to lure them into an attack.

"Hold fast," barked Atreena. "Don't break rank."

Thinking quickly, Actaeon pulled the starsphere artifact from his jacket and touched it twice with both hands before lifting it with one hand high above his head. Suddenly there was a spinning sphere of projected stars floating around them.

The closest Ruinic tribals backed away from the projections, hissing and growling at them as they swung their weapons ineffectively at the tiny pinpoints of light.

"Allfather help us," gasped Atreena. Actaeon could feel her against his shoulder as she backed away from the stars herself. "Such evil – at what cost?"

"If the Allfather has any better ideas I welcome them," Actaeon said levelly.

"Once that stops scaring them, we're finished," said Xula. "Hope you've got another plan, Prince Engineer."

"I've got one," said Trench before stooping to lift Wave and toss him over one shoulder. "Follow me. We make for the nearest Skyspiral stair."

Without waiting for a reply the giant roared at the closest tribals and charged forward.

Actaeon ran behind Trench with the starsphere held as high as he could manage so the stars could project past the giant's body. The others followed close on his heels.

Any tribals that didn't leap out of the way were devastated by Trench's maul.

They reached the nearest staircase quickly and without pause. Trench bounded up, leading the way.

Actaeon paused near the base of the stairs to continue projecting stars from the starsphere artifact.

Yanelle stopped beside him while Xula and Atreena rushed after Trench.

"Out of the way, you brute," Atreena ordered. "I know the best route to the Sea Lounge. Follow me!"

At the bottom of the stairs, Quronos came to a halt and held his blade out toward the boundary of the rotating stars projected from Actaeon's artifact. "G – go – go. I will hold them."

"Are you certain?" asked the Prince Engineer. "I cannot imagine you could handle them all, despite your abilities."

"You must – must – must survive to return to Travail," said Quronos as a shower of sparks fell from his empty eye socket. "Remember upon your return: The halls are naught but a re – re – re –"

The malfunctioning artifact man was unable to complete his sentence as the Ruinic tribals surged upon him. His blade was a blur that left behind a red mist and falling bodies of the enemy. One spear managed to sneak through his defenses and bury itself partially into his chest before it broke. Quronos was forced to fall a step back at the onslaught.

"Naught but a what, Quronos?" demanded Actaeon. "Naught but what?"

But Yanelle was tugging him up the stairs. "Your Grace. Your Grace. We must go."

Actaeon hesitated still. "Quronos, tell me."

More Ruinic warriors filled in behind their dead brethren to take their turn being cut down by the strange guardian of Travail. Several spears were thrown – one which would've struck Actaeon if not for a well-timed swing of Yanelle's sword.

"Act!" shouted the Companion. "Let's go!" She yanked him harder.

Actaeon snapped out of it when she shouted his name. He grinned and began to follow her up the helical staircase that ascended toward the top of the Sun Chamber.

The staircase began to curve back on itself as it wound its way through the vast void above the Sun Chamber's floor. A glance back down showed that Quronos was still holding off dozens of attacking warriors. To the sides of the stairwell, several Ruinic tribals were springboarded by their brethren to leap up and climb over the elderstone railings to attack Quronos from the sides. Once the first tribals had leapt upward, others quickly followed behind.

It was only a matter of time before those on the sides swarmed him. The artifact man attempted to back further up the stairwell to gain a better defensive position. It was too late however, as the main force of tribals making the push up the staircase surged over him and knocked him onto his back.

Ruinic tribals ran up all the other staircases, rushing to intercept Actaeon and his quickly dwindling party of allies.

The tribals atop Quronos began to stab him violently with their spears.

When they parted for a moment, Actaeon could see the silver man's face, the emotionless black eye staring up at him. He thought he saw Quronos smile before a spear thrust took off the artifact man's jaw with a shower of sparks. Then the staircase's curve wound back on itself as they ran and Quronos was out of sight.

The explosion that came next shook the entire Pyramid.

The stairs rushed upward toward Actaeon and slammed into him so hard that he blacked out momentarily. There was nothing beneath his feet and he kicked out into empty space, looking for a purchase. He slid first down one stair and then another, toward the void, but then Yanelle yanked him back upward, her fists gripping his jacket on either side.

The red-haired Companion yanked him atop her before letting out a sigh of relief.

Actaeon offered her a bewildered look, and she shook her head in return, blinking rapidly.

A quick glance over his shoulder told him that the staircase beyond their boots was gone.

"Thank you, Companion Yanelle," said Actaeon, meeting her gaze. "I am honored to have you at my side as my protector. I am also alive," he added with a grin.

"It is my job to protect you, Your Grace, er... Act," said Yanelle with an awkward smile. "I don't need thanks." She gestured for him to climb off of her.

"Ah, yes. My apologies." Carefully, Actaeon lifted himself off of her and stood on shaky legs – the pain in his left knee was still flaring bright and he winced. He still had his halberd, though Yanelle had lost her broadsword in her effort to rescue him.

Yanelle took his offered hand and carefully climbed to her feet.

Their staircase had been obliterated up to just a few steps below where they stood. It gave the illusion that they were floating in the air above the floor – the support structure of the staircase being far above them. The other helical staircases that comprised the Skyspiral had also lost their lower sections, though not as badly as the one they stood upon. Far below them, was a crater filled with debris and bodies alike. The detonation had ablated a significant area of the Sun Chamber's elderstone floor.

"Unanticipated," said Actaeon. "Quronos must have had an explosive mechanism within him. Either that or a power source so massive that it could explode in such a manner upon failure. Likely both, come to think of it. It makes sense that he would be designed to trigger his power source to detonate in such a situation. Absolutely fascinating. I wish I had had more of an opportunity to know more about him."

On adjacent staircases, the surviving Ruinic tribals were beginning to recover and pointed at Actaeon and Yanelle before starting to climb their respective stairs once more. One of them threw a spear toward them, but it fell far short.

"We'd best move. The tribals are trying to intercept us above," pointed out Yanelle, her brow raised at the Prince Engineer.

"Agreed, Companion Yanelle," Actaeon said. "Plus, the Skyspiral is likely to be unstable after the blast."

"Lead the way then, Your Grace," said Yanelle.

"Good idea," said Actaeon. "I forgot you lost your weapon."

The Companion blushed with shame and drew the long knife from her belt.

Actaeon led the way up the stairs as quickly as he could manage with his injured knee.

Trench and the others were waiting at a wide landing where two of the staircases met.

Captain Xula pulled Wave's flamberge rapier from the unconscious mercenary's belt and passed it to Yanelle. "There you are. He won't be needing this any time soon. You know how to use one of those?"

"Of course," said Yanelle. "It's a blade."

"Lighter though," said Xula. "You've got to use the point to your advantage and look for vulnerabilities in armor. You'll not be bashing your way through armor with that blade."

"If I ever decide I need more sword lessons after this is all over, I'll be sure to find you," said Yanelle sarcastically. "If that's all for now, let's get moving. We can both take point."

"I have the point," said Atreena, louder than necessary. The Keeper Knight Captain began to charge up the stairs, moving nimbly in her heavy plate armor.

Companion Yanelle followed behind her and Xula took up the rear while Actaeon and Trench, still carrying Wave, stayed in the middle.

A group of five tribals reached the next landing before them. Atreena and Yanelle didn't hesitate or slow their pace as they continued upward.

Atreena broke two of the enemy spears with her blade. Her next two sword strokes decapitated one tribal and opened the chest of the other, slicing easily through his leather shirt.

Companion Yanelle parried one spear thrust with Wave's rapier. She gracefully dodged a second spearpoint and took the shaft in her hand to pull the attacker toward her and rake the flamberge blade across the woman's throat.

Another tribal, seeing an opportunity, stabbed at Yanelle's off hand side but his actions were brutally abbreviated by Trench's maul.

Yanelle stabbed the final enemy in the side as he turned to flee. Trench swept his maul beneath the tribal's legs to send him tumbling over the railing to the floor far below.

The Companion offered the giant an appreciative look and Trench simply nodded in return.

The opposition eliminated for the meantime, they raced to beat the other ascending tribals to the far landing that jutted high from the chamber's western wall. What remained of the helical stairwell wound them through two more landings where other staircases joined with theirs.

They beat the tribals to both and Atreena led them onto a different staircase that curved upward toward the far landing.

There, Atreena and Yanelle ran ahead to the massive open portal to check the western tunnel that would take them to the Sea Lounge. The tunnel sloped gently downward and terminated at the Way of Pillars before the Pyramid's southern entrance out of sight around the curve and far below.

Actaeon followed the group at a jog as Trench kept pace with him. Every other step caused a flare of pain from his left knee. He switched his halberd to his left hand to compensate, but he was having trouble keeping up. A glance back revealed that a small group of pursuers had reached the landing behind them.

"Better get moving faster, Prince Engineer," said Atreena. "We'll defeat that group if they catch us, but that'll give time for more and more to show up and ensure our eventual demise."

Actaeon grinned. "I do not suppose you would be willing to carry me, Knight Captain? If not, I fear this is my quickest speed for the immediate future."

Atreena raised her visor to glare at him with her intense tan eyes. "What did you say?"

"He said ya could carry him," Trench answered loudly so that she could hear despite her injured eardrums. The giant offered her an ugly smirk.

Atreena scowled and let her visor fall back down. "At a time like this you would make jests?"

"I see no better time than the present. To laugh in the face of great risk. Is there a greater act of defiance?" Actaeon chuckled and winced, though he increased his pace as much as he was able.

As a unit, the six of them, Trench still carrying Wave, started at a steady jog down the wide, elderstone tunnel that curved along in the western side of Pyramid. Luminaries inset into the ceiling lit the way as they proceeded with no opposition down the slope of the tunnel. It curved gradually to the left as they progressed. Various doors and portals were set into the walls at intervals, but the party ignored them and attempted to move as quietly as they could in case Ruinic enemies were in those rooms.

"There's bound to be a force down in the Way of Pillars," said Xula in a hushed tone. "They've got to guard the southern entrance."

"Undoubtedly," said Actaeon. "This plan should take care of them."

"Huh?" said Xula, still suffering the effects of his burst eardrum.

"If they don't prevent us from getting there," said Trench.

"Strange, these halls. Not sure I've ever seen 'em empty like this," said Yanelle.

"Aye, and it don't feel right," said Trench.

The group drew silent once again as they continued on, weapons ready for a sudden attack.

There was none, and at long last they came to a halt before the Sea Lounge. Its twin wooden doors were closed. The wood was still freshly hewn as the Arbiters only had them installed as recently as the collapse and floods that had killed many denizens of the Pyramid, washing them down the slope of the western tunnel in a torrent of boiling water. The memory made Actaeon shudder. He had barely escaped that death himself.

The collapse of the Sea Lounge's ceiling had also revealed a control room of Pyramid – perhaps the only one of its type. Actaeon had deciphered the controls and fixed a major problem with the overheating baths higher up. The Arbiters had been forced to post a guard here afterward, since open access to the control room was deemed too dangerous.

It had felt like a chaotic time back then, but now, by comparison, it seemed like such a calm and stable point.

We made it to the Sea Lounge, Eis, Actaeon sent through the Thoughtlink Artifact.

I am glad. Eisandre's thoughts came into his mind as naturally as though they were his own. *The allied forces stand at the ready at both Northern Descent and the Avenue of Glass, just out of sight of the enemy. We await your intervention.*

I will see you soon, Eis.

Soon, Act.

Actaeon grinned and strode forward to push the heavy doors open. They swung wide to reveal the interior of the Sea Lounge.

It got its name from the aquatic creatures and plants that lived within its three inner walls. A massive chunk of elderstone sat atop what used to be the Sea Lounge's bar – a single, solid piece of wood that lay splintered and warped under the fallen piece of ceiling. Above the bar was a large hole from where the fragment had fallen. A hastily constructed wooden staircase led upward into it.

None of these things were what Actaeon noticed though. What he noticed was the twenty or so Ruinic tribal warriors gathered inside. They appeared to be having a meeting of sorts, judging by the rough semi-circle they stood in around the broken bar. Their spears, bows, and various other weapons were all leaning against the translucent walls. Clusters of fish tried to nibble at some of the spearpoints.

The Prince Engineer's first instinct was to pull the doors back closed. His actions were cut short, however, as Trench barreled past him and ran into the room, knocking the doors back open with his shoulders.

The giant roared and charged into the middle of the Sea Lounge. The tribals, still shocked at this sudden interruption, just stared in disbelief as the giant leapt atop the chunk of elderstone. Trench wasted no time in bringing his maul down atop the head of the tribal in the center, obliterating it in a shower of gore. It was only then that the others snapped into action, yelling in their foreign tongue as they rushed to retrieve the weapons they had placed behind them against the walls.

Atreena raised her sword and charged in after Trench. Captain Xula was right behind her. The Keeper went left while the Thyrian went right.

Companion Yanelle hefted Wave's rapier and shot a look at her ward.

"Go," urged Actaeon. "I shall guard Wave." He motioned to his unconscious friend whom Trench had unceremoniously dumped near the doorway.

As Yanelle ran to join the fray, Actaeon lowered himself to his good knee, resting his halberd across his bad one. He unclasped his strung recurve bow from his back and put the first arrow to string.

Trench hurled the headless body across the room, knocking down several tribals. As the next closest warrior reached his spear, the giant mercenary ended him abruptly by driving his head into the wall. Fish rushed forth to peck at the glass on the other side of the red stain left behind.

By the time Xula reached the closest Ruinic warriors, they had retrieved their weapons and turned to face him. He surprised the lead one by tossing him his diamond-shaped hat. The tribal ducked and the warrior beside him dodged to the side. Xula took advantage of the opening and a quick sweep of his sabre opened the throat of the first warrior and eviscerated the second.

On the other side of the room, Atreena knocked several spearpoints aside with her sword and crashed into a cluster of Ruinics in her full plate, knocking them to the floor. She made quick work of the fallen lightly-armored tribals with the point of her broadsword. Another tribal lifted his spear to throw it at the Keeper Knight but stiffened and fell as one of Actaeon's arrows lodged in his lower spine.

Yanelle arrived at Xula's side and they moved so that they were back to back to hold off the tribals attacking them. The Companion had difficulty blocking the spear thrusts with the light rapier and kept pushing back against Xula in retreat. The Thyrian Captain was pushed toward more spears, which he was able to shatter with a quick motion of his sabre.

"Ho! Watch it there," warned Xula. "Nearly skewered me."

"Sorry," said Yanelle. "Not used to fighting with this hairpin that Wave uses."

"Maybe time for that last grenado, Act?" yelled Trench as he swung his maul to paint the wall with a large red streak.

"And bring the entire ceiling down?" called Actaeon as he let an arrow loose to lodge in the belly of another enemy.

The surviving Ruinic tribals turned to flee, having witnessed more than half of their brethren cut down or disabled in such short order.

Unfortunately, there was only one way out of the room, and so Actaeon counted seven tribals running at him with spearpoints lowered as they hollered in their native tongue.

Actaeon's eyes widened and he released his third arrow prematurely, sending it wide of the charging enemies.

Undeterred, they continued to charge at him across the Sea Lounge.

"My apologies," he said to his friends, before he rose and lunged forward to pull the doors shut.

This time he succeeded in closing them a moment before the tribals slammed into the doors with a loud bang.

The wood splintered, but the doors held under the impact. Actaeon was able to slide the reinforced shaft of his halberd through the heavy handles before the tribals attempted to pull them back open.

There was intermittent commotion on the other side of the thick wood as they began to yank desperately at the doors. Then followed screams and a clash of weaponry, after which came silence.

Far away, along the downward slope of the western tunnel, there was the sound of more Ruinic enemies approaching, responding to the sounds of fighting.

Behind him Wave groaned.

Someone banged on the inside of the doors.

"Open these damned doors!" bellowed Trench from the other side.

"A moment!" called Actaeon. He slid his halberd back out from the door handles and pushed the doors open.

Before him stood a blood-spattered array of fighters, including the Keeper Knight, Companion, giant mercenary, and ship's Captain. They glowered at him, one and all, as blood dripped from their weapons. At their feet lay seven dead Ruinic warriors.

Actaeon grinned at them all. "I had the utmost confidence in all of your ability to finish them off." When they said nothing in response, he added, "I could not say the same for myself."

Xula leaned back and let loose a big belly laugh. "Well said, Prince Engineer Rellios Caliburn!"

The others smiled and laughed. Even Atreena lifted her visor to grin at him.

Actaeon retrieved his bow and then knelt inside the doorway behind the doors.

"What are you doing, Your Grace?" asked Yanelle.

Actaeon pulled a spool of thread from his jacket and broke a piece of string from it with a yank. He began to tie it around the inside door handle.

"Act?" asked Yanelle.

"Oh," Actaeon said. "Apologies, Companion Yanelle. They are coming up from the Way of Pillars. I plan on leaving a present for them." He unclipped the grenado from his jacket and tied it to the other end of the string.

Trench dragged a moaning Wave into the Sea Lounge and slammed the doors shut. "Thought you said that'd bring the ceiling down on us?"

"Precisely, Trench," said the Prince Engineer. "Only, I do not plan to be here when this goes off. When they throw the doors open, they will slam into the alcove wall and hopefully set this last grenado off."

The giant grinned and slapped Actaeon on the shoulder. "I like the way ya think, my friend."

"Be careful, Trench – I am about to pull the pin." Actaeon turned to the others. "Get up to the control room. I will follow."

"Now ya tell me," said Trench. The giant lifted Wave and carefully placed him over his shoulder.

"Follow me," said Atreena. The Knight Captain led the way up the makeshift stairs that took them to the corridor above the Sea Lounge. Trench and Xula followed close behind.

Yanelle hesitated. "Please don't delay, Actaeon."

Actaeon grinned at her. "Go ahead, Companion Yanelle. I shall be right behind you."

When the Companion was gone, he turned his attention back to the grenado. Careful not to move the device, he twisted its pin and carefully tugged it free while holding its body against the bulk of the door. Once it was free, he shuffled carefully back and used his halberd to leverage himself to his feet.

Actaeon jogged to the makeshift staircase, wincing at every other step. He climbed the stairs and found himself in a familiar cylindrical passage through solid elderstone. It felt good to be in a place that he knew well after so long away from everything he'd once known.

The passageway was longer than he remembered, and just when he hit a rhythm with his forward pace, it shook violently.

Actaeon staggered painfully and kept jogging onward. The grenado must've exploded. Hopefully that meant that their pursuers would be unable to continue.

After a long while, he reached the rope ladder that led up to the control room and began to climb.

When he reached the top, Yanelle helped pull him up and he emerged into the tremendous chamber. It was filled with multi-colored tubes that he knew contained liquids. They traversed the room on horizontal, vertical, and diagonal paths. He recalled the three enormous spheres overhead that were held in place with some sort of translucent blue material. The northern sphere and, indeed, the uppermost northern side of the chamber was fractured. The light that streamed in from outside of the Pyramid told him it was late afternoon.

Trench stood nearby over Wave, cradling his maul in both hands. Yanelle joined the giant, her dark red hair backlit by the sun's rays.

"Finish it, Act," said the giant. "We'll stand guard."

"Aye, Trench," said Actaeon. "I will. Thank you both."

He limped his way along the luminary path until he reached the square column that supported a familiar cubical room far above.

Atreena stood nearby, her helm under one arm. Captain Xula stood next to her, his hat beneath his own arm to reveal the dark skin of his bald pate.

"Will you be joining me?" asked Actaeon.

"Wouldn't miss it for the world," replied Xula.

"I must ensure you don't do anything unseemly up there," said Atreena with a weary smile.

"Of course," said Actaeon with a grin. "Let us proceed then."

He reached out toward the face of the column and a circular symbol flared to life. He pushed it and the floor began to shift. Sections of it rotated upward to lock together and form railings.

The three of them gripped the railings as the lift began to move upward steadily, on its way to the cubical room above.

It came to a stop at the entrance to the small room, where hundreds of symbols of the Ancients flickered to life. The room consisted mostly of windows to allow the viewing of various symbols on the hollow pillars in the room without. A semi-circular desk stood in the center, covered in a multitude of glowing symbols and changing images. More symbols were on the walls and on the ceiling just above the windows.

But there was one element present that Actaeon didn't recall being there last time. Above the desk, there floated a small, silver orb with a ring of illuminated blue dots around its horizontal circumference.

"Hello, Kryo," said Actaeon. "Quite the strange place to meet, I must say."

The bottom of the sphere slid open and a dull blue light projected downward. Unfocused at first, the projection gradually sharpened to reveal the Loresworn leader. The short man stood before him in a full brightweave outfit of shimmering black with silver edging. His scalp was shaved clean and a thick frame held lenses on his face that made his eyes look like tiny beads. On his feet were matching faceted silver artifacts.

Atreena drew her sword, but Actaeon held up a hand. "It is alright, Lady Knight. He is an acquaintance of mine."

"Ill company you keep," said Atreena, but she sheathed her broadsword.

"Actaeon Rellios Caliburn," began Kryo. "Prince Engineer... Breaker of Pillars, Unlocker of Travail, Projector of Ancient Spirits, Friend of the Children, Infiltrator of –"

"Enough," said Actaeon with a smirk. "I imagine you are here to assist me in this effort?"

"Indeed I am," spoke Kryo through his projection. "Though, I must say I am both surprised and thrilled that you made it here today."

"I have powerful friends," Actaeon said.

"I see that," said the Loresworn. "And you have another friend in myself. I shall help you in this endeavor."

"Help in the effort to free Redemption from its Ruinic invaders is always welcome," said the Prince Engineer. "Tell me though – why would you not utilize the projected force ability that the Loresworn have to accomplish this? The lives of many of my friends might have been saved."

"Alas, only Sol has the ability to harness such forces," explained Kryo. "And Sol is busy."

"Of course he is," said Actaeon, skepticism oozing into his tone. "I am certain he is busy working on that Travail issue he needs me to solve."

"It is more complicated than that," said Kryo.

"Many things in this world are more complicated than we might imagine once the truth is revealed to us," said Actaeon. "Is that not a novel thought? Having the truth revealed to us? Though I am certain he is doing important work."

"I will be honest with you, Engineer," said Kryo.

"That would be a welcome start," agreed Actaeon.

"Sol's presence is required at Travail. Without his efforts, the cataclysm that approaches would have already occurred," explained the Loresworn leader. "It is why we require your aid. He may only prevent it for so long."

"Then we had best finish this so that I may help you prevent whatever this mysterious cataclysm is that you are referring to," said Actaeon. "Though I must say that I fail to see how I would have the ability to do this thing over the rest of your Loresworn."

"Very well," said the projection. "I assume your plan here is to flush them out. It is the only logical course of action, after all."

"You surmise correctly, Kryo," said Actaeon. "I plan to flush the eastern and western tunnels simultaneously. And the Sun Chamber, if possible."

"Might I recommend you superheat the waters as well?" suggested the Loresworn.

"If I can decipher the symbols well enough to achieve that, it is a sound idea," said Actaeon as he stepped up to the console and began to tap the symbols.

"Oh, I believe I can help you with that," said Kryo, adjusting the lenses over his eyes to peer down at the console. He gestured to several symbols in quick succession. "That one. And that one there will build the pressure. And this one will siphon the cool water away."

"Am I correct that these two will open valves to flood the eastern and western tunnels, respectively?" asked Actaeon, after following Kryo's instruction.

"Most certainly. A very capable deduction from the Prince Engineer," said Kryo.

Actaeon, came a thought from Eisandre. *The top of the Pyramid is beginning to glow.*

Fascinating, he replied. *We are about to unleash the torrent. Tell your forces to stand ready.*

I will, thought the Princess. *Please try to keep the Pyramid mostly intact.*

Aye aye, sent the Prince Engineer with a grin.

"And if my less capable deductions are correct, I would hazard to guess that these three symbols will flood the Sun Chamber from above." Actaeon gestured to the symbols and turned to regard the projection.

"Your less capable deductions are no less correct," said Kryo. "And how would you like to know how to activate all the symbols you need simultaneously?"

Actaeon arched a brow and noted several glowing arcs on the desk that had begun

to climb when he'd touched the symbols indicated by Kryo. "Show me, if you please."

Kryo gestured to another symbol on the board. "Touch this, and again when you're ready to activate everything."

Actaeon nodded and touched the symbol, followed by one each for the eastern and western tunnels and two for the Sun Chamber. He reached to touch the third and then withdrew his hand to look at Kryo and grin. Instead, he pressed the Ancient symbol to activate everything and a deep rumbling sound filled the chamber.

"Quite wise," said Kryo.

"And you would have let me flood this entire compartment with boiling water?" asked Actaeon. "Your definition of friendship is clearly different than my own."

"Had you made such a mistake, we'd surely have no use for you in the succor of Travail. Plus, knowledge such as yours untempered by wisdom is better off being driven from this world," stated Kryo, matter-of-factly.

"Tell me he jests, Your Grace," said Xula, raising his sabre.

It is working, Actaeon. The Princess' thought entered his mind. *The floodwaters run from the southern entrance.*

Excellent, he replied. *We have issues up here.*

What is it?

Loresworn, he stated simply.

Be careful, Act.

You too.

I am afraid I cannot, Captain Xula," Actaeon said aloud.

"You p-kin varlet! I'll have your head for this," exclaimed Xula. The Thyrian strode forward and placed his sabre at the projection's throat.

"I am not here in reality, Captain Harvand Xula of *Glorious Redemption*," stated Kryo.

"I'm no fool, you Loresworn sop. Just giving you a taste of what you're soon to experience when you come out of hiding," growled the Captain. He pulled the sabre back and struck the floating sphere with the side of his blade, sending it careening to the right, where it struck a window and bounced back. Kryo's projection flickered back to life in the new location.

"That is long enough, I think," said Actaeon and he began to push the appropriate keys to return the Pyramid's systems back to normal.

"I pray you'll keep your promise, Prince Engineer Actaeon Rellios Caliburn," said Kryo. "Travail needs your intervention. All Redemption does."

"I shall keep my promise," said Actaeon. "But I promise you no protection from the wrath of my friends here. Your actions have earned you no respect among the people of this city."

"That is for the —"

The lights in the chamber all died at once, the projection of Kryo disappeared, and the artifact sphere clattered to the floor.

Atreena punctuated the sphere's fall by smashing it to pieces with the pommel of her sword.

"What a waste," said Actaeon. "I could have learned much from that artifact."

"Allfather take that damnable thing," said Atreena.

"I'll second the Knight Captain," said Xula. "Good riddance."

The Darkest Hour had begun.

MOPPING UP

WITH THE LIGHT OF THEIR torches to guide them, the allied forces simultaneously rushed into the many openings of the broken northern descent and the southern entrance through the Way of Pillars. Eisandre had given the order from the southern side and Itarik had given the command to the horn blowers to signal the attack for the soldiers stationed on the northern side.

They swept into the Ancient structure largely uncontested. Clusters of Thyrian Flashbolt Marines and Lauryn's Light Lancers led the way through the hallways, leaving any Ruinic tribal still breathing full of crossbow bolts. The rare instances of organized resistance were quickly wiped out by careful sweeps of the light lances.

The Way of Pillars was a massacre of boiled bodies – their skin rolling off like wax sheets to reveal bright red muscle tissue underneath. The stench of boiling death was overwhelming. All along the slopes of the eastern and western tunnels lay scattered tribal bodies. Every surface was hot to the touch, as though it had spent time being heated in an oven.

Eisandre followed the advance up the eastern tunnel toward the Mirrorholds, surrounded by Wall Breakers and with her First Companion at her side.

Together they passed the burnt-out remains of the barricades. Under the force of the deluge, most of them had been pushed to the side or had broken into pieces, and they had to pick their way past them with some difficulty. Lifeless bodies were piled up against the substantial barricade sections that remained.

The dead here were burnt past the point of recognition. It was impossible to tell whether they were friend or foe, except by the armor that still clung to bodies or the weapons frozen in place in their melted hands.

Guybon Hael tripped over one of the bodies and scrambled away from it. The Princess' attendant wretched and covered his mouth with his leather gauntlet as he vomited, the foul liquid exiting his mouth in streams between the fingers of his glove.

Itarik yanked the boy to his feet and scolded him. "Pull yourself together, young man. You are the Princess' attendant. Act like it."

"Saints, Act," whispered Jezail, her face aghast at the horror. "What have you done here?"

"May the Ancients help whoever stands in the path of your Engineer, Your Grace," said Ainhara Craft.

Eisandre didn't hear the Thyrian Major though. She had spotted something up ahead that was familiar and horrifying.

The sword of a Knight Arbiter, with its pyramidal pommel and the crossguard ending in short points to make it difficult for an enemy to disengage their weapon. It was the same as her own sword, which the Arbiters had allowed her to keep despite her expulsion from the Order. Only on this sword, one of the crossguard points was broken in a specific way that she remembered.

She found him nearby – her former partner, Knight Arbiter Garth sof Belidur. He was pinned to another Arbiter with a Ruinic spear that passed through them both. The only way that she could tell it was him was that the other Arbiter still had their sword in its leather sheath on their sword belt. Both bodies were burnt beyond recognition and curled around one another in a fetal position. Oddly, a small tuft of unburnt sandy hair still clung to one side of Garth's head.

In a flash, she remembered the way he would smile at her as he cracked jokes that she often failed to understand, that sandy hair glowing in the sunlight that streamed in through the Pyramid's Pinnacle while they walked their patrols. Remembered sparring with him in the training circle – he had been a challenging opponent that she often couldn't best. Remembered when they would take turns cutting one another's hair – his sandy hair falling to the floor. She knelt and reached out to touch the remaining tuft, feeling hands tugging at her that she shrugged away. Distant voices thundered in her mind, but she paid them no heed.

A thousand thoughts flowed, streaming around her in bright happy colors. Eisandre gasped as the rainbow of thoughts began to darken, burning in an invisible flame. They blackened and cracked, crumbling to pieces which landed all around her. More tugging, more voices – though more distant now, fainter.

Through the haze, one voice came into her mind. *Eis, it is Actaeon. I am here with you. Garth fought and died to protect the people trapped inside Pyramid. He would have wanted you to continue on and liberate them. Finish what he could not.*

"He didn't have his partner," choked out Eisandre.

You took the path that you needed to bring him help.

"I wasn't able to help him," said Eisandre, rocking back and forth on her knees. "I wasn't there." Behind her she could hear the First Companion say something, but he was too far away for her to make out what he was saying.

He was not alone, came Actaeon's thought. *He and the Arbiter he died with gave their lives to save the people in Pyramid. Those people may yet need you now. Go find them, Eisandre.*

"Part of me was here," whispered Eisandre. She shut her eyes tightly and clenched her teeth until her jaw hurt. But she placed one foot under her and then the other. The colors all around her continued to burn.

Itarik was behind her and helped her to her feet once more.

And then, suddenly, she was wrapped in a gentle embrace. It made her recoil at first, but the touch was light and strangely comforting. Ithelie pulled back, and the air around Eisandre felt colder as the Voice's green robes pulled away. The burning colors of her thoughts were gone.

"Their names, Your Grace?" asked the Voice simply.

"Garth sof Belidur, a Knight Arbiter who died protecting the Pyramid," said Eisandre. "The other I don't know, but they were a Knight Arbiter as well."

Ithelie nodded solemnly and removed the green cowl of her robe to reveal her blond, nearly white, hair. She approached the pair of Arbiters and spread her arms to the heavens beyond the fire-darkened eastern tunnel.

"Ancestors, I call upon thee to guide the souls of these Knight Arbiters that lay before us, including Garth sof Belidur. Guide these and all the

Arbiters that are now counted among the Fallen, having done their sworn duty to protect this Pyramid and all it represents to the people of Redemption." The Voice paused for a moment to let those words hang in the air. "Open the doors of the beyond and light a fire to blaze the path for their souls to find those of their spirit families. Accept them in reunion and grace, that they may be one with you in wisdom and virtue, to be a guiding energy for the people of Redemption from this day to eternity. May they guide the other Fallen to their rightful place on this tragic day. I, the Voice Ithelie Faris, through the power entrusted in me by the Ancestors, do now release these Fallen from their duty to all Redemption. Go now, our brothers and sisters, and take your rightful place in legend among our people, and forever be remembered as guardians of Redemption. May you watch over us always."

The Voice then knelt to place her hands upon the heads of the fallen Arbiters. She whispered something else inaudible before rising again and offering the Princess a solemn nod.

"He didn't have his partner," breathed Eisandre.

"His partner stands here before me, finishing the task that he gave his life to accomplish – the surest way to honor his life and sacrifice," said the Voice, and she gestured up the slope of the tunnels toward the Mirrorholds.

Eisandre nodded, at a loss for words, and led the way up.

They found the survivors in Saint Torin's Hold. The battered and exhausted group rushed to dismantle the barricade they had hastily constructed from the furniture inside the embassy.

Unfortunately, all their allied rescuers could do was wait until they finished. Eisandre sent Major Craft onward to finish clearing the eastern Pyramid while she, her attendant, the First Companion, the Voice, and the Wall Breakers awaited the survivors.

Once the barricade was removed, a giantess emerged. Bald and scorched, Eisandre at first mistook her for Trench, but quickly realized it was Tarcy Hael – the big woman's hair and eyebrows had been burnt away. She wore her familiar ruinblade upon her back, a sharpened piece of debris from Redemption's ruins.

Tarcy snapped to attention and saluted, fist to chest. "Held the Hold, m'Lady Caliburn."

"You are now speaking with Her Grace, Princess Eisandre Rellios Caliburn," announced the First Companion.

The giantess grinned. "Good. Got da sword ah see."

"Yes, Steward Hael of Bastion," said Eisandre. "You've done well here."

Behind Tarcy the survivors poured out of Saint Torin's. All in all there were less than a hundred people left alive.

Two Knight Arbiters approached and saluted Eisandre.

Kylor lifted his dark goggles to reveal his milky, alien eyes. "Knight Arbiter Eisandre. We are most relieved to see you here."

"I am no longer an Arbiter, Knight Arbiter Kylor," said Eisandre, matter-of-factly. "Are there other survivors left elsewhere?"

"Apologies. None that we are aware of," said Kylor.

Corvin sof Haringar stepped forward, his eyebrows and hair burnt away and a bandaged lump on his forehead. "Do not apologize, Kylor. Eisandre is here. She returned with a force to liberate us all. Where is our Order's leadership? She's as much of an Arbiter as we are, as far as I'm concerned."

Kylor turned to Corvin and cast him a blank look with his empty-looking eyes.

"Let's not question the Order's leadership, Knight Arbiter Corvin," spoke Eisandre sternly but gently. "We are taught early on that the Pyramid is indefensible. In case of invasion, the Order's main directive is to preserve itself until such a point as the Pyramid is liberated. It has always been the Order's responsibility to maintain neutrality here, not to defend."

"He knows this," said Kylor. "But clearly he needed a reminder."

"You've my apologies, Eisandre," said Corvin. "I should not have criticized our leadership – for that I am wrong. However, I stand by my other statements."

"Eisandre has been cast from the Order, Corvin," said Kylor. "A denial of that is yet another criticism of our leadership."

"Kylor is correct," said Eisandre. "I have accepted the judgment of my commanders. If I can accept that judgment, then you must as well. My duty now lies with Raedelle."

Corvin lowered his head. "Aye, Eisandre. Your point is noted and I rescind my earlier comments. Still, we are glad to see you."

"I am glad to see you as well," agreed the Princess.

The Lady Bazardjan stepped forward as well to address Eisandre. The

Ajmani artist sketched a graceful bow, her purple and blue silks flowing about her body.

"Your Grace has answered my prayers," said Maerdia.

"We came as soon as we could," said Eisandre.

"The gods were on our side," said the artist.

EISANDRE'S REDEMPTION

You appear as a sun on the top of the shadow hill (broken mud and twisted mirrors(far faces fading)) I hear your laugh like a shining joy starburst of all light (clouds reflecting sky into bright solemnity, spreading illumination seeking) but the gravelly crunch of metal glass under your boots roots me to your (every) direction so I rise and spread my wings toward the bright beacon of your eyes (familiar in a crowd of ghosts) then words move between us, shapes of sounds, slightly conveying thoughts I think we share on a string that stretches and then increases our proximity (etiquette, (rules that run together), racing, returning, retreating)

you present your hand that remembers the secret
of my name and I answer with a touch

(solid stop)

peace
calm
clarity
a circle of knowing
a place to rest

my anchor of a thousand lifetimes, Actaeon, my love.

ACT TWO: ULTIMATUM

RETURN TO THE WORKSHOP

IT TOOK THE BETTER PART of the Pyramid's liberation day and the entire next morning to excavate the Sea Lounge sufficiently to allow Actaeon's team to escape from the control room. The grenado that Actaeon had left for the Ruinic tribals had successfully mitigated their threat, but the unfortunate and unanticipated consequence was that most of the Sea Lounge's ceiling had caved in. When they followed the tunnel back down to get to the Sea Lounge, they found it blocked by massive chunks of elderstone debris.

At first Actaeon had considered rappelling down the broken northern face of the Pyramid using Wave's rope, but the rope turned out to be much too short for such an endeavor. Instead they got some much-needed rest on the floor beneath the control room after Eisandre confirmed for Actaeon that, under Lauryn's direction, a team was hard at work to make a way out for them.

Knight Arbiters Kylor and Corvin, helped Lauryn as she made careful cuts with her light lance to break up larger pieces of debris. The Southward warband helped with hauling the pieces out of the Sea Lounge and into the western tunnel. Lieutenant Areyna directed the muscular red-headed twins, Torg and Cafry, in their removal. Many of the pieces were large enough to require ropes to haul them out.

"You needn't stay and help me," said Lauryn to the two Knight Arbiters. "You must've had a difficult time trapped in here – I'm sure you need your rest."

Corvin smiled at her and shook his head. "We'll not be resting until the Prince Engineer and the others that liberated us are freed. We would be in even worse shape if not for what they did."

Lauryn offered him a smile in return. "I'm glad to have your help, but the instant I see you wavering, I'll send you off to get some rest. This is dangerous work."

"Aye, Lauryn of the Light Lancers," conceded Corvin.

Lauryn nodded and her light lance crackled to life as she cut another sliver of elderstone free. The remaining piece, unhindered, slid past her and tumbled to the floor. It scraped against one of the translucent walls of the room but failed to leave a mark.

"A fascinating material," said Lauryn. "It survived the explosion of Act's grenado and these impacts don't even abrade the surface. I wonder if the light lance would cut through it."

"It would be best if you avoided that test," suggested Kylor, before indicating the next cut.

Lauryn laughed, "I'll see what I can do."

Her light lance crackled to life again.

"It would be a fitting day to emerge into the world from this control room," said Actaeon with a grin. "For myself, at least."

The group sat around in a rough circle on several horizontal cylinders. Wave lay nearby, breathing shallowly – still unconscious.

"It's your emergence day?" asked Harvand Xula. The Captain leaned back against an adjacent vertical cylinder, his diamond-shaped hat in his lap.

"Aye," said Actaeon with a smile. "Twenty-six cycles ago. The First of Reap's Call. My parents always said it was a lucky day. Though it is doubtful that any day portends better things than another."

"I, for one, am glad for your emergence, Prince Engineer Actaeon Rellios Caliburn," said Yanelle. The Companion stood and saluted him, fist to chest.

Actaeon grinned and blushed. "I would not have survived if not for all the times you skillfully prevented my death during this war, Companion Yanelle. I am glad to have your sword at my side. Or... at least, Wave's sword in your capable hands."

"Ah, but my friend here deflects," said the giant as he stood. Trench's grin tugged at the deep scar that bisected his features. "We're talkin' about you, Act."

The Keeper Knight Captain stood up and drew her sword to raise it to her forehead in salute. She had removed her helmet and let down her sweeping blond hair. "That's right, Prince Engineer. And we are thankful for what you've done for the realm. Whatever I might feel about your methods, you have saved many lives."

"I'll add to that sentiment," said the Thyrian Captain, rising to his feet to join the others. He swept a graceful bow, his hat in hand. "I'm glad to have joined you on this fool's errand."

"Not a fool's errand," said Trench. "A genius' master plan."

Actaeon stood as well, leaning heavily on his halberd. "Say what you will about it, I would never have made it here without your help. On this twenty sixth cycle since my emergence, let us remember those Fallen that brought us to this point. Companion Wayd Arbrigel, Companion Geodric Caider, Light Lancer Hake Rim, and, of course, our artifact friend Quronos, guardian of Travail and now of Redemption entire."

"May they rest well, those Guardians of Redemption," said Captain Xula.

"Aye. They and all the others who got us to this point," said Trench. The giant cast a look toward his unconscious friend.

"We will do everything we can to help Wave. That I can promise you." Actaeon reached over to touch the big man's arm.

"Everything's not always enough," said Trench.

"Everything is all there ever is," said Atreena.

"Aye," said Trench. "Just so."

"Wave'd tell you all to stop stating the obvious and get his sorry ass outta here," said Yanelle with a smirk.

Trench cracked a sad smile at that. "Yes. That he would."

As if on cue, the rescue party emerged from the tunnel that led to the Sea Lounge.

Lauryn climbed up first, followed by the pair of Knight Arbiters and the Southward warbanders.

The Light Lancer leader and apprentice engineer squealed with delight and ran over to give Actaeon, then Trench, a hug.

She sobered up quickly when she noticed Wave on the ground. "What happened?"

"Deathcrawlers got 'im," said Trench.

"We have Altheans with us," Eisandre interjected into the conversation. "They may be able to help him." She had arrived behind the others, the Supreme Captain of Thyr beside her and three Altheans in tow.

Actaeon's face lit up, and he rushed over to sweep the Princess into an embrace.

Eisandre pulled him against her fiercely in response. When they separated she said, "Please do not put your life at such great risk again."

Actaeon laughed. "I will do my best not to."

Eisandre nodded and turned to the others. "You have saved many lives this day. Your actions and those of your fallen comrades will be remembered with great honor and gratitude. Thank you."

"Indeed. You have saved many lives," echoed the Supreme Captain, removing his jeweled silver helmet to address them formally. He swept his shock of red hair back from his eyes and regarded Xula. "I had to see this for myself. These deeds will go down in legend."

The ranking Althean, Seraeta, swept past both Dominion leaders and knelt beside Wave. She gestured for Cortecha to join her.

After a brief assessment where she looked into the mercenary's mouth and nose, checked his ears, and felt his chest, she looked up at Actaeon. "Her Grace told me that the Deathcrawler creatures you contended with injected him."

"Yes," Actaeon said. "With some sort of paralytic agent. And I have reason to believe they laid eggs inside his body."

"Saints," breathed Lauryn, dropping to her knees at Wave's side next to the Altheans.

"I have nothing to deal with the creature's young," admitted Seraeta. "But our herbalist, Shard, believes there might be something that will slow his body's processes. With any luck, it will slow the growth of the eggs as well and give you some time to figure out a solution."

"Shard is alive?" asked Knight Arbiter Corvin, surprised.

"Yes," snapped Seraeta, glancing sidelong at the Arbiter, as if annoyed. "Shard was found hiding in the Terrace Gardens." She returned her attention to the Prince Engineer.

"Whatever time you give me would be appreciated," said Actaeon. "Thank you."

"Very well. We will administer the remedy as soon as Shard retrieves it," said Seraeta. "Where will we find Wave?"

"In my workshop, on the Outskirts of Pyramid," said Actaeon. "I will need the facilities there to carry out the necessary experiments."

"Very well," said Seraeta. "Cortecha will accompany you. She is an apprentice healer – though after her recent experience, I'm sure she won't be an apprentice for much longer."

"I will also join you," said another of the Altheans that stepped forward. There was no room for argument in her tone. Her face and shaven scalp were covered with a variety of scars.

Actaeon cast an uncertain glance at the spiked cudgel hanging from the woman's belt. "An armed Althean? How curious…"

"I have accepted Largrival's service to serve as the first Althean Attaché to Raedelle," said Eisandre.

"She was formerly the Czerynian Attaché," explained Knight Arbiter Kylor.

"Ah." Actaeon nodded. "Quite appropriate then, given our arrangement with the Temple Czerynians." When the new Attaché offered him an unimpressed look, he continued. "You see, we found them during our time in the Underforest. Warlord Berk helped us make contact with the Kainai. Part of the agreement necessitated that Raedelle agree to take Czeryn's place as the Protectors of the Kainai and that the surviving Czerynians would join Raedelle. Oh, and to find a place for the surviving Czerynians to settle."

The Attaché's eyes narrowed upon the Prince Engineer. She said nothing.

"Of course, they decided to abandon their practice of slavery," explained Actaeon. "It will be a challenge to integrate them into Raedellean culture – one that we will appreciate your help with."

The Attaché remained silent.

"Torg, Cafry, and I will accompany you as well, Your Grace," said Lieutenant Areyna. "There may well be more scattered tribals about."

"Thank you, Lieutenant," Actaeon said to the warbander.

Actaeon looked to Eisandre then. *Will you be alright here, love?*

I will manage what needs to be done. Eisandre nodded to him reassuringly. "Go and figure out a way to help Wave."

The Princess and Prince Engineer shared another tight embrace. They separated quickly, with urgent matters weighing on both of their minds.

Xula touched Actaeon's shoulder. "Luck, my friend. If you need my sword, I'll be here for some time."

Atreena saluted Actaeon as well. "Same with my sword, Prince Engineer of Raedelle."

Actaeon nodded solemnly to them both, and led the way from the control room.

The Outskirts was a ghost town. Those who had lived in the small community at the western end of the Avenue of Glass had yet to move back into their homes. Many of the buildings had been obviously ransacked and some of them razed.

Actaeon's stone workshop, however, was intact where it stood on the southern fringe of the community. The massive wooden door was shut tight. The carved relief that had been fashioned by Lauryn depicting the Engineer and the two mercenaries doing battle with the first of the giant slugs they had encountered was untouched.

Most of the other buildings' doors were ajar.

The group came to a halt a short distance before the workshop.

"A trap?" suggested Trench.

"What would they gain with such a trap?" asked Actaeon. "More likely they avoided the building for some reason. Perhaps Lauryn's relief, or the presence of artifacts."

"Maybe Phyrius Ricter and his cult scared them off," Lauryn suggested with a chuckle, referring to the Waiting Ones – the group of religious fanatics that had arisen around a statue that Actaeon had found out in the ruins of the Boneyards.

Actaeon grinned and led the way to the door. "Only one way to find out." He removed the cast iron key from his jacket and turned it first in one keyhole and then another. Strangely, he felt no click from the tumblers, and when he pushed it, the door swung open. He strode inside. A quick inspection found that the door had been forced open, breaking both locks.

The twin warbanders, Torg and Cafry rushed in on his flanks. Yanelle and Areyna were close behind them.

Before they had departed to free Prince Aedwyn's sword nearly an arc of the moon ago, they had closed all the shutters and covered all the luminaries, so the interior of the workshop was covered in a blanket of darkness, excepting the tall rectangle of sunlight that poured in through the entrance.

Torg reached out with his spear to probe something against the wall near the doorway and leapt backward when a giant slug fell down to the floor. The costume quickly flattened and the warbander's face glowed red enough to match his beard once he realized what had scared him.

"Seems strange," said Lauryn from where she stood in the doorway beside Trench, the giant cradling Wave in both arms. "So quiet."

"Aye," said Trench. "Like something's missing."

Actaeon dusted off his luminary and stuck it in the strap of his goggles. He flipped back the baffle to cast light upon the far wall.

There was dried blood spatter on the stone there and the Prince Engineer stepped forward to inspect it. "The Ruinics were certainly inside," he said, wincing as he knelt to examine the pool of blood on the floor. "It appears that someone fought them over it."

"Can we have some more light in here?" asked Cortecha. "And a place to put our patient?"

Lauryn gathered the scattered sketches and notes from atop the nearest workbench and Trench laid Wave down atop it.

After her eyes adjusted, Largrival spotted one of the larger luminaries glowing under a sheet and crossed the workshop toward it.

"Hold," instructed Actaeon, suddenly recalling why the workshop sounded so quiet. "Everyone exit the workshop, calmly."

The Attaché yanked the sheet from atop the luminary, filling the eastern end of the workshop with the glowing artifact light. "For what purpose?" she demanded, spinning to face Actaeon.

Behind her, illuminated by the newly uncovered light and clinging to the wall, were three deathcrawlers – larger than Actaeon had remembered them, and much quieter.

"Turns out they are not missing, Trench," said Actaeon.

"Thanks, Prince Obvious," said Trench.

Largrival followed the others' gazes to the wall behind her and the color drained from her face until it matched her gray scars. She pulled the cudgel from her belt and swung it at the trio of creatures.

By the time it hit the wall, all of them had already scattered in every direction, moving so quickly that they were difficult to track.

Areyna raced forward with her spear and managed to impale one of them against the side of the wooden stairway that led up to the loft.

The deathcrawler writhed and snapped at the air inches from the warbander Lieutenant's face, but the twins each pierced its head with their own spears and struggled with it as it tried to rip free.

Another many-legged monster made a beeline for the center of the room.

Lauryn activated her light lance and deflected the deathcrawler, cutting a wide gash in the stone floor.

It emitted a high-pitched chirp and skittered away, leaving many of its legs behind as it retreated, its carapace smoking.

"Getting real tired of these bugs!" growled Trench, pulling his maul free and watching the third one zip upward into the underside of the vault above the loft.

"You and I both," said Yanelle, her sword in one hand and her other hand on Actaeon's arm.

Cortecha began to shriek uncontrollably. The apprentice healer crawled beneath the workbench where Wave lay, her screams echoing throughout the workshop.

Actaeon tugged Yanelle. "Follow me." His halberd brought to bear, he led her over to the western side of the workshop. There stood the laboratory tables, fume hood, and shelves stocked with many of the semi-transparent artifact half-through bottles filled with a wide assortment of chemicals and substances.

One of the deathcrawlers zipped by along the wall as they arrived at the shelves. Actaeon reflexively stabbed at it with his halberd. He cringed as the blade missed the lightning-fast creature and struck the wall, sending up a shower of sparks that cascaded down upon the bottles of volatiles.

"Here, take this." Actaeon thrust his halberd into Yanelle's free hand. "It has a longer reach than your sword," he explained in response to her blank look. Without awaiting her reply, he spun and selected three bottles from the shelves.

He drew the appropriate arrow from his quiver – an arrow specially designed for the purpose. Attached to its shaft was a small leather pouch, the thickness of which Actaeon had selected to contain his blue fire long enough for him to fire off the arrow.

Into the pouch he poured a glob of the viscous brown material, upon which he sprinkled several purple crystals from the second half-through bottle. To the mixture he added a drop of water from the third bottle and the concoction began to smoke and sizzle before flaring to life.

Actaeon drew the strings tight to close over the blue flames that leapt up just as Yanelle backed against him while deflecting another deathcrawler charge.

Deftly, he removed the recurve bow from its clasp on his back and strung it, placing the smoking arrow to the string. He drew the bow and held it, sweeping the workshop with the light of his luminary as he searched for one of the deadly creatures.

Over by the loft stairs, Areyna stabbed the deathcrawler repeatedly as the twins fought to hold the writhing creature in place, dismembered legs flying in all directions as it struggled with desperate chirps.

One of the free deathcrawlers charged at Trench and he struck it so hard with his maul that the creature flew aside and crashed into the wall beside the door where it landed in a flurry of legs and curled into a protective spiral. The giant rushed after it and began to hammer away at its carapace.

Actaeon spotted the third deathcrawler as it skittered down the wall on the far side of the workshop. It rushed the table with Wave, guarded by Largrival.

The Prince Engineer released his arrow, which zipped across the workshop spinning heavily through the air with its unbalanced load. The arrow lodged into the creature's side where one of its legs connected with its carapace and the contents of the pouch flared to life and splashed upon the deathcrawler's body.

It lifted into the air as its front legs began to pop off – replaced by gouts of blue flame. The deathcrawler reared up as the flames consumed it. It changed its direction and charged toward the laboratory shelves – like a giant running torch of blue fire.

Yanelle tackled Actaeon out of the way a lifebeat before it reached them and crashed into the shelves of chemicals.

The laboratory setup erupted in a conflagration of rainbow flames, sputters, sizzles, and intermittent explosions. The multi-colored flames fanned until they reached the stone vault above, bursts of purple and green smoke mingled with the black smoke from the burning shelves.

Actaeon and Yanelle shuffled away on their backs.

The Prince Engineer pulled his goggles down to protect his eyes and looked on in fascination. "Amazing. The plethora of effective combinations we are witnessing is quite promising for future study."

The Companion brushed her red hair from her eyes and offered Actaeon a wide-eyed look.

"Maybe not all at once next time, Act," suggested Lauryn. She approached the pinned deathcrawler cautiously and skillfully separated its head from its body with a quick sweep of her light lance, ending its struggle.

"Of course," said Actaeon. He stood up as the multi-colored show began to die down to reveal a scorched and broken deathcrawler carcass against the blackened shelves. Most of its legs had burnt away. "It shows much promise though." He pointed to the bellows near the laboratory setup and pulled a lever that opened the vents built into the vault high above. "Lauryn, if you close the door and reverse the bellows through one of the floor vents, we can push this smoke out of here."

"Aye aye, Act. I'm on it," said Lauryn. She set aside her light lance to do so.

Trench continued to hammer away at the deathcrawler near the door.

"I believe it is wholly dead, Trench," said Actaeon.

"Just making sure," said the giant.

"Just so," said Actaeon. "But please stop. We may need these bodies as intact as possible to study in order to save Wave."

Trench slammed his maul against the flattened head of the monster one last time. "Aye, Act. Happy Emergence Day."

Actaeon laughed and clapped Trench on the forearm. "Thank you, my friend. An interesting choice of gift."

ANATOMY OF A MONSTER

"IT APPEARS TO BE WORKING," said Seraeta, her ear pressed to Wave's chest. Trench had moved one of the beds down from the loft to the workshop floor so that Wave could rest more comfortably while being monitored. "His lifebeat has slowed significantly."

"How long do we have?" asked Actaeon from where he stood on the other side of Wave's bed.

"I haven't used Maiden's Sleep but for a few times," Seraeta explained. "And then only for several days to prevent the spread of necrotic tissue before the cutters could do their work. One time to slow the effects of a terminal disease in a Shieldian noble to give him a chance to see his child born. With other cases I've heard of that extend past that timeframe, irreversible damage occurred."

"What manner of damage?" asked Actaeon.

"Their mind was not in correct order," said Seraeta. "Almost as though they had become Lost, but without the extent of psychosis."

"And we have no indication as to whether it will be effective in slowing the growth of deathcrawler eggs within his body," said Actaeon.

"True," stated Seraeta, considering. "But I've reason to suspect it may have a chance of doing so. It was used when I was a young Althean to try and delay a pregnant woman's death to allow her enough time to give birth. The remedy slowed the baby's development as well, however. In the end the woman died before the baby was born and we needed to cut it from her."

"That's horrible!" said Lauryn, looking up from the next table over where she was sawing through one of the deathcrawler carapaces with a pair of knives. Her apron was spattered with bug guts.

"It would have been worse if we'd allowed the baby to expire in the womb," snapped Seraeta.

"I meant that it was horrible the poor baby had to be cut from its dead mother," said Lauryn, eyes narrowed. She used a large pair of forceps to crack free one of the carapace plates.

"Life is not always easy," said Seraeta.

"I didn't –" began Lauryn, her face turning red.

"Should we attempt to locate the eggs in him?" interrupted Actaeon.

"I'm loath to dig around the site of the injection since the areas affected by the creature are prone to infection," said Seraeta.

"Certainly we could apply a local antiseptic?" suggested the Prince Engineer.

"Where would you go, Your Grace, were you a larval deathcrawler?" asked the Althean, her brow raised as she awaited a response.

"Indeed," said Actaeon, considering. "The bowels or the chest then. I see the problem – cutting into those locations would certainly kill him."

"That is correct. And had they tried for the brain, we'd have certainly noticed," said Seraeta. "And I hope you now see how your solution must be twofold."

"Inhaled and ingested both, yes," said Actaeon with a frown. "A liquid solution might be aerosolized."

"Got it!" exclaimed Lauryn. There followed a wet crunch and a sploshing noise as she rummaged about inside the carapace.

"Yes," said Seraeta, wrinkling her nose in disgust. "I will leave you to it then. Cortecha will do what she can for your man. I must tend to those in the Pyramid."

The Althean turned on her heel to stride from the workshop.

"Thank you, Seraeta," said Actaeon genuinely. "Your aid here will not be forgotten."

"The eggs, Act. I've found 'em!" said Lauryn, holding a glittering mass of yellow goo aloft in one hand.

"Keep them warm," said Actaeon. "Now we just need locate the seed in the other one to fertilize them. Hopefully it is male."

Trench made a gagging sound where he worked on his gear near the back of the workshop. "I'll be outside if ya need me." The giant couldn't stumble out quickly enough.

"I think it is," said Lauryn, excitedly. "There are significant differences in what was left of the body."

Companion Yanelle stood beside the door, the color drained from her face as she struggled to maintain her composure.

"Yanelle, would you please double check that the perimeter is secured?" suggested Actaeon with a smirk.

"Yes, Your Grace!" The Companion was outside the door before she even finished the statement.

Lauryn and Actaeon shared a grin before they went to work on the second deathcrawler.

The Felmere was its normal hazardscape of fetid chemical pools, corrosive clouds of various colors, and loud sputtering interactions where two or more chemicals flowed together.

Actaeon led a meandering path that Yanelle and Trench followed carefully, as they had been instructed. The landscape had changed vastly since he'd last traveled there, as it always did. He paused from time to time to collect samples in empty half-through bottles.

The sample collection itself could be hazardous. Sometimes he could use his halberd to dangle a bottle with a leather cord. He would not risk his primary weapon with the chemicals he knew to be corrosive. For those, he had brought a broom handle along and used that to extend the bottle for collection.

All three of them wore kerchiefs over their mouths to filter any errant plumes of acrid smoke that drifted their way. Actaeon wore his goggles over his eyes and had insisted that the other two wear spare goggles from the workshop.

"We looking for something specific, Act?" asked Trench.

"Aye," said Actaeon as he knelt to extend a bottle out over a pool of dark, shimmering liquid. "I want to recreate two compounds that we had success with before the war. If I am correct about the missing parts of my notes, then we should be able to retrieve everything we need for them."

"Missing parts?" asked Yanelle.

"The notes I had taken on the compounds were an unfortunate casualty of our flaming deathcrawler friend," explained the Prince Engineer. "Luckily, enough of them remained that I think I can decipher what was missing."

Yanelle nodded. "And what are these compounds?" She regretted the question as soon as she'd asked it.

"A good question, Companion Yanelle," said Actaeon as he retrieved the half-through bottle. He cleaned the outside with a cloth, stoppered it, and placed it carefully in one of his many jacket pockets. "The first one I named Shimmering Oil, mostly for the visual appearance. It caused the deathcrawlers that ingested it to fall asleep for a period of several hours. The second one I called Dragon's Milk, on account of how hot the milky compound became when first mixed. Dragon's Milk caused severe seizures in the deathcrawlers we experimented on.

"Both compounds are promising as they will hopefully have a more profound effect on the deathcrawler in its larval stage. However, the greatest risk is whether they will prove harmful to human physiology. It then becomes a challenge of dosage and –"

"Too much and Wave's dead," growled Trench. "Too little and the deathcrawlers live – Wave's dead."

"Unfortunately, yes," said Actaeon. "That is –"

"'Nuff talk then. Let's get moving and get what you need," said Trench.

Actaeon nodded and stood. "This way."

He probed the terrain carefully with the butt end of his halberd, testing the stability of the ground. Quicksands and quagmires were common in the Felmere as one chemical or another bubbled to the surface.

As he walked, he thought back to the events at the workshop. Lauryn had been thankful that she didn't have to join him in the Felmere. She had stayed behind to work with Cortecha on fertilizing the deathcrawler eggs. Once fertilized, the eggs would be injected into chickens. It was those chickens on which Actaeon would test his compounds. With any luck, the compounds would kill the eggs but not the chickens.

There would only be a limited number of eggs though, and therefore a limited number of chickens to experiment on. More deathcrawler traps would need to be set in the tunnels beneath the Pyramid, but even if they caught more and managed to fertilize more eggs, the Maiden's Sleep would only give Wave so much time.

After everything Wave had given for him, Actaeon had to find a way to save him.

His thought was interrupted as the ground spasmed beneath his feet and rushed upward to greet him with a faceful of contaminated dirt. A gush of warm blood spilled from his nose down his neck to the tunic below as he rolled onto his back. A quick glance behind him found the Companion and mercenary similarly arranged on the ground.

Trench climbed to his feet behind Yanelle and followed the point of her sword up to the tremendous blue sphere that grew massively to the northeast.

The closest side of the sphere rushed toward them with improvidence. As it grew closer, it became a great blue wall that surged nearer and nearer with a frightening speed.

The rumbling of the earth itself swept away Yanelle and Trench's defiant cries. Actaeon's statements as to the intrigue of the moment were similarly drowned out by the roar of the ground beneath them.

The body of the translucent sphere approached as though it would envelop and destroy them, but at the last lifebeat, a mere hundred paces from them, it paused.

It shattered into infinite pieces before their eyes and in a blinding flash of light, was gone.

Twinkling fragments of light floated to the ground from where the sphere had once been.

Actaeon pulled himself to his feet and ran toward the event, ignoring the yells behind him and the pain in his injured knee.

The giant tackled him to the ground and pinned him there. "Fuck if imma let you run off to yer death!"

Actaeon coughed and struggled beneath Trench's weight. "If I could just get a sample…"

"Cracked Redemption take yer samples," growled Trench and the giant put more of his weight atop the Prince Engineer.

Actaeon gasped for air and struggled beneath the mercenary. "Trench – crushing –"

"Get off him," demanded Yanelle.

"Shut yer yap, lass," said Trench.

Yanelle drew her sword and held it to the giant's neck. "I will not ask you again."

With a jerk, Trench grabbed the blade and ripped it from her hand, flinging it into a pool of steaming green chemicals. Rivulets of blood ran down his palm, but the giant didn't seem bothered by it in the least as he stood and yanked Actaeon to his feet by the Prince Engineer's collar, ignoring the series of blows that the Companion landed atop his back.

Trench turned and threw Actaeon against Yanelle, sending them both tumbling to the ground.

The giant unslung his wicked maul from his back and held it aloft.

"Wave might die, Act!" roared Trench. "And fer what? He risked his life to protect you – yer plan. Yer his only hope an' yet ya'd risk yer life for an Ancient-damned sample of something that may well jus' kill ya."

Trench stomped his foot in his rage and pointed behind him with his weapon.

"An' what in shattered Redemption is that anyway? How many jus' died, Act? How many more? When's it stop? You activated that gods' damned thing!" The giant squared off and clutched the maul in both fists. "I'll tell ya this much – yer gonna hafta fight yer way through me if ya wanna throw away yer life like that."

Yanelle leapt to her feet and began to rush the giant, but Actaeon grabbed her arm and yanked her back.

"Hold Companion," he said firmly. "I will answer him."

Yanelle snapped her head back in a flurry of red hair and glared at Actaeon, her eyes wild with adrenaline.

The Prince Engineer grinned at her and used her arm to pull himself to his feet. He took several steps forward until he was in range of obliteration from the giant's weapon. Then he spread his hands.

"You are right, my friend," Actaeon said. "I showed the Veiled One how to activate that device. Unknowingly, but all the signs were before me. It was right here that I made that fatal mistake and showed the Lady Lartigan the answer to the artifact's riddle. There were enough clues for me to conclude that she was under the Veiled One's control, but I was too ignorant to see them.

"And so an entire Dominion died," he continued before pausing to take a deep breath. "An entire Dominion dead on account of my failure. I had thought that I faced failure before, far in my past, but I had not the faintest idea of how greatly I could let all of Redemption down. It is because of me – my ability, my knowledge, my failure – that a weapon more powerful than all the Dominional armies combined now stands ready to erase us from the very face of this city."

"No..." breathed Yanelle behind him. "It can't be true."

"Oh, but it is," said Actaeon. "It is true. It is the ruin that the Keepers warned of. The ruin that the Loresworn hid their knowledge to protect all humanity from. By my own hubris, brought about."

Trench spat at his feet and snarled at the Prince Engineer.

"You are right to doubt me, my friend." Actaeon bowed his head. "It is my error that has brought this peril upon us. Had it not been I though, it would have been another – of that I am sure. Perhaps even Lauryn, for she possesses the skill, whether or not she yet realizes it.

"If I am to repair the damage I have done I can tell you one thing," he continued. "I will need the help of all my friends in the process." Actaeon lifted his eyes to meet the giant's and then turned to meet Yanelle's for a long moment before turning back to Trench. "Without your help, your guidance, your strength – all my ideas are nothing but dreams scattered to the winds. But together we might accomplish anything. We might unite the Dominions, restore Redemption, and solve the great mystery of the Ancients. But first I must gather the rest of the chemicals to save our friend Wave, that he might help us in our quest to defeat this Veiled One and keep all Redemption safe."

Actaeon drew silent then and waited for Trench.

The giant mercenary took a deep breath and tilted his head to regard the man he'd served since Actaeon's arrival at the Pyramid on the fateful day that the Engineer had found him and Wave in The End and hired their services.

"The Fallen know you talk too much, Actaeon Rellios Caliburn of Shore," said Trench.

Actaeon grinned up at his friend and lowered his hands.

"Less talking," said Trench. "More gathering chemicals. Wave's waitin'." He looked past Actaeon to Yanelle. "Sorry 'bout yer sword."

Yanelle brushed her hair from her eyes brusquely and raised her brows at the mercenary. "Apology accepted. Do it again and I'll be the one to finally slay the legendary giant."

Trench roared a laugh at that. "Now that I'd pay to see!"

A FUTURE'S CONCEPTION

THE WORKSHOP WAS ABUSTLE WITH activity when Mae walked in, her elaborate silks flowing behind her with each graceful step.

Lauryn, Trench, and Largrival were busy moving pre-built sections of the new deathcrawler traps outside to load in old Vez' cart. Trench had stumbled upon the old carter and his grandson rolling back along the Avenue of Glass with his rickety cart. Vez had been more than happy to sign up for work so soon after hearing of the Pyramid's liberation.

Cortecha had the two warbander twins, Torg and Cafry, running back and forth to rotate the cool cloths that covered Wave's body. Repeated doses of Maiden's Sleep had begun to take its toll on the mercenary. "His body tries to fight it like an infection," she explained with her thick Shieldian accent. "If we let the fever take his body it will reverse the effects of the Sleep and his biological processes will resume at normal pace. Hurry now! We need to keep rotating these out." The healer laid a cool cloth across his bare chest.

"If my timing is poor, then I can return later," said Mae.

"Nonsense," said Actaeon. He gestured her over to where he stood working on mixing chemicals under the laboratory's fume hood.

Nearby, Areyna pumped the bellows to evacuate any harmful gasses, looking nonplussed about it.

The artist offered her a genuine smile that was met with a scowl.

"Delicate work, this," said Actaeon. "Although I am certain you have your share of such work, Lady Bazardjan."

Mae wrinkled her nose and inched closer to regard the chemicals. "Yes, Your Grace. Only I cannot fathom how you 'see' your work coming together. I can see what I want to carve from a stone, or mold from a lump of clay, or paint upon vellum. This though – how do you even know what you're producing?"

Actaeon poured the final ingredient into the flask and grinned as the dull red compound changed from transparent to milky. "With much experimentation, Lady Mae. In fact –"

The artist stepped back to offer him a flowing curtsey.

"Oh, no need for such courtesies," he said, waving his hand. "Nothing has changed. You should still call me Act."

"If naught has changed, then who was it that led the bravest heroes the world has ever seen on a deadly mission to rescue us survivors of the Pyramid's siege?" asked Mae. "From the stories I heard, it was the Prince Engineer of Raedelle that answered our prayers for succor. The Prince Engineer who cleared the way for his Princess to break the siege and save us."

Actaeon blushed and lifted his goggles from his eyes. "I merely activated a sequence in Pyramid's control room to gain a strategic advantage for our side."

Areyna dropped the bellows arm and stepped forward. "Oh please, Your Grace. Had we attempted to break the siege without your 'strategic advantage' we'd 'ave lost many warbanders in the effort. I'm probably only here pumping away at this Saints-damned bellows 'cause of you."

The warbander Lieutenant shook her head and walked out from the workshop.

Mae smiled up at Actaeon and nodded. "Your warrioress speaks truth. Captain Xula told me the story. I prayed that someone might come and do what you did. The gods are at your back, Prince Engineer Actaeon Rellios Caliburn. May you long stay in their favor."

"I would prefer if they would stay where I could see them," said Actaeon with a grin.

Mae took his hands in hers and met his eyes with a joyful gaze. "I would craft a piece in honor of your deeds. You are humble – that much is clear, but some were lost in the effort, no? And some might yet be..." She trailed off and glanced over her shoulder at Wave. "I would sketch the one called Wave. Sketch him and hear of the others that were lost – Hake

Rim, Geodric Caider, Wayd Arbrigel, Quronos of Travail, even the one you called Lady Ruinic. I would know their faces and their souls, that I may do them justice."

Actaeon lowered his head for a long moment before he lifted it again to meet the artist's gaze. "Of course you are welcome to sketch Wave. And I am happy to answer any questions you might have of the others. No questions now though, Lady Mae, for it is now my duty to save my friend from this ailment. I must continue to work."

Mae smiled and squeezed his hands before releasing them. She knelt before him then and extended her hands up toward him.

The Prince Engineer hesitated for a moment before grasping her hands in his own.

"Gods of the old and gods of the new, we call upon you," began the artist. "Your blessings do we seek, your guidance we ask that you speak. Our hands are yours to guide with our spirit open wide. Foremost, I ask that you guide this man's hands – that he may save his friend Wave from the ailment he has incurred by saving people of Redemption."

Actaeon lowered himself painfully to his good knee as he listened to the prayers of the Ajmani artist, her eyes closed as she called upon her gods.

"With the ill omen of another blue sphere to the north," she continued, "protect us from more such events. And guide the Raja of the One True Dominion and the Prince General of Shield in their safe withdrawal from the assailed realm. May all of us learn to live in peace and prosperity despite our differences. Lastly, give us the strength to rebuild that which we have lost in this conflict. Allow us to rebuild stronger and greater than ever before."

Finished, she squeezed Actaeon's hands and released them before rising to her feet. She offered Actaeon her hand.

Actaeon grinned and accepted it. The artist helped him to his feet.

"I gather by your prayers that Shield and Ajman are withdrawing from the north?" he asked.

"Yes, they have both withdrawn to protect their Holds," explained Mae. "The accursed phenomena that is the blue sphere has driven terror into the forces of both Dominions and caused their retreat. Rumor has it they have both lost large portions of their armies."

"And any word on what they have learned about the remains of Czeryn?" asked Actaeon, a brow arched.

"Only that there were none left alive there, and no bodies even. It was as if every Czeryn living there simply vanished to the winds." Mae paused and shuffled her feet. "It all sounds so... horrifying."

"Fascinating," said Actaeon.

Trench came to a stop nearby. "Yer the only person who'd ever say the disappearance of an entire people was 'fascinating'." The giant grinned his lopsided grin and shook his head.

"No really," said Actaeon, in seriousness. "If the rumors that the Lady Mae has heard are true, then the Czerynians disappeared much like the Ancients themselves. Gone without a trace and even their bodies missing – their things left behind as though they did not anticipate leaving. There is a possibility that the artifact that creates the blue sphere is the same artifact that caused the Ancients to vanish."

"You think it an artifact?" asked Mae. "Not the wrath of the gods? Such would be no surprise, given their sins of violence and slavery."

"Perhaps they are one and the same," suggested Actaeon. "There are artifacts in this city that might take generations of study to understand completely. How much do those in Redemption really know about what they worship?"

Mae gasped and took a step back from the Prince Engineer. She recomposed herself and brushed the wrinkles from her silks. "I pray for thee, Prince Engineer Rellios Caliburn. May you find the truth of the gods, old and new, in your lifetime."

"If your prayers will guide me to that goal," said Actaeon with a smile. "I will gladly accept them."

"I am glad," said the Ajmani artist. She pursed her lips. "And now, with your permission, I will sketch your friend."

"Of course, Lady Mae," said Actaeon. "Let us know if you will require anything."

"Good timing to sketch 'im while he's like this," said Trench. "We don't need it goin' to his head."

Mae offered another curtsey and then mounted a stool beside Wave's bed. She withdrew a piece of vellum backed by a wooden tablet from within her silks and began to sketch upon it with a charcoal stick.

She sketched with broad and thoughtful strokes as she regarded him. The artist paused frequently and on occasion stood to pace around the bed he lay upon, adding a stroke here and there as she walked.

Cortecha regarded her with irritation and took the time to mop Wave's brow with a cool cloth.

The warbander twins rushed to and fro to replace the cloths with fresh ones as Mae worked. She didn't appear bothered by the activity at all – simply continuing her sketch.

During one of her circuits, she paused near the mercenary's head and lowered herself down to place a light, lingering kiss upon his lips.

Trench caught the act and nearly dropped the piece of the deathcrawler trap he was carrying past. "Well then, now I've seen everything," he muttered to himself.

Mae touched her forehead gently to Wave's then. "May the gods of the old and gods of the new give you the strength to get through this," she whispered in his ear. "Thank you for what you have done for us, brave warrior."

She straightened and offered Trench an innocent look.

The giant mercenary's eyes widened. He shook his head and continued on his task.

The artist continued her work, her skilled hand capturing every detail of the sick man, excepting the signs of his current ailment. She could picture him in her mind's eye without his symptoms and so she sketched accordingly.

Her thoughts were interrupted as Wave began to cough, a few times at first, but then more and more, until he was heaving in violent coughs that sent spasms throughout his entire body.

Cortecha frowned and shooed Mae back. Surprisingly, for a woman of such small stature, the Althean quickly maneuvered the mercenary onto his side as he coughed. She began to massage his back with one hand while she dabbed his forehead and temples with a cool, wet cloth.

The coughs continued to wrack Wave's body as the Althean worked.

Mae leaned forward to whisper to him again. "May the gods –"

She was interrupted as Wave promptly vomited all over her slippers and the silks of her lower dress.

Horror overcame her as the ejected deposits at her feet began to wriggle and squirm along the workshop floor.

Mae opened her mouth and the scream came a moment later, followed by her rapid departure from the workshop.

"I'd rather not go in there again," said the mercenary.

"You've gotta do it," said Lauryn heartily. "Your friend is counting on you!"

The giant's eyes narrowed upon her and he scowled, the action tugging at the scar bisecting his face. "Look lass, you weren't in there with ceilings full of deathcrawlers faster 'an my eye can track and toothy slugs that fill the entirety of tunnels and spit smaller, slightly less toothy slugs at ya."

Lauryn just crossed her arms from where she stood in the bed of the old carter's wagon and smiled at Trench – a rare moment when her eyes were at level with his own.

"Alright, ya know I'll do it. But only 'cause that bastard's still making women run away screaming even in his sleep. Rather we get him conscious so I can talk some sense into him." The giant glanced over his shoulder at one of the nearby tunnel entrances in the lower marketplace and shuddered.

"Don't forget I've got my light lance," said Lauryn. "I can protect us." She unslung the artifact and hefted it.

"Oh, 'cause that helped so much the last time!" exclaimed the giant.

"I can use it even better than Hake could," said Lauryn.

Trench eyed her skeptically.

"Don't give me that look! I figured out *how* to use it," argued Lauryn.

"If you say so. Just don't cut the floor out under our feet," muttered Trench. He continued to grumble as he lifted several sections of trap out of the wagon bed. The plan was to deploy the traps at intervals throughout the tunnels to catch more deathcrawlers in case they were needed for Actaeon's experiments.

"A light lancer wouldn't never do that," said Lauryn as she tugged another section free for the mercenary.

"So you admit it – ya would do it," snapped Trench with a victorious smirk that distorted his features.

"I said I wouldn't!" she argued and threw the next section at him, which he caught with ease.

"Wouldn't never's what ya said," said Trench. He paused to chuckle after he set aside the last section.

"Not true!" said Lauryn, her fair skin blushing a deep red. "Tell him, Vez." She looked to the old carter for help.

"Young mistress'll forgive me if'n I dunna take a side. Yer not payin' me well 'nuff fer that," mumbled Vez. "Yep, no deathstalkers, no 'un dem sluggos, an' no settlin' yer squabbles fer ye."

Lauryn looked taken aback and narrowed her eyes upon the old carter. "How much extra, then?"

"No 'un 'mounta bits in 'demption gonna make me face 'em those three. 'Pologies, young mistress." Vez offered her a toothy smile and removed his worn hat from his head to reveal thinning wisps of white hair.

"That settles it then," said Trench. "Last I checked, I've been fighting in battles since before yer mama was in nappies, so I'm in charge in these situations. Keep that thing off unless I tell ya to use it. I like a floor under my feet." He hefted the pile of sections onto one shoulder then and strode off easily toward the opening.

Lauryn sighed in exasperation and rushed to catch up with him.

"Hold it absolutely still. I do not wish to spill any," said the Prince Engineer as he held the half-through container aloft.

The chicken squawked and fluttered away from Yanelle, leaving a pile of feathers and excrement on the workbench in its wake.

Actaeon grinned and blew a feather from his nose. "The exact opposite of that would be appropriate next time, Companion Yanelle."

"Your Grace, er... Actaeon. This isn't my area of, uh... expertise," said Yanelle, brushing feathers free from her red locks of hair.

"I assure you that administering chemicals to chickens that have been injected with fertilized deathcrawler eggs in order to see if they can be used to save my friend who is actively working on dying is not my area of expertise either," said Actaeon with amusement. "Nonetheless, we appear to be the ones with the best chance of saving him. Trust me – if there were someone more qualified in this matter, I would be more than happy to request their assistance."

"Apologies, Actaeon," said Yanelle. She brushed her hair back from her eyes. "Um... what next then?"

"You should probably go get the test subject before it finds the exit to the workshop," suggested Actaeon with a smile.

"Oh, yes!" The Companion saluted, fist to chest, and rushed off to catch the chicken.

After Yanelle got the hang of holding the chickens still, they began to administer the chemical doses down the poor animals' beaks. Each test subject was then deposited into a labeled cage and they were lined up for monitoring. They had ten subjects in all – five each for various doses of Dragon's Milk and Shimmering Oil.

Cortecha administered another dose of Maiden's Sleep to Wave. When she saw Actaeon had finished his present task, she motioned him over.

"I'm worried to give him more," she said as the Prince Engineer arrived to look down on his friend. "Even this – his lifebeat is so slow. Is it too much? Any more and I fear he'll just fade away."

Actaeon lifted his goggles from his eyes and regarded his friend gravely. "In this situation, we have little choice. Without the Maiden's Sleep, the deathcrawlers destroy him. Thus, you must continue to administer it until I find a way to mitigate this dilemma. If I fail, Wave dies."

Cortecha placed her hand on his. "That's too much pressure on you. Don't feel this is all on you."

Actaeon lifted his eyes to hers and smiled before gently pulling his hand away. "And yet I am the only one working to find a solution. Whether or not you say that, the truth is that it *is* all on me." He gestured to the one-eyed mercenary before unconsciously scratching at the back of his fingerless glove. "This man has saved my life countless times. Is it too much to ask for me to save his just once?"

Wave coughed and sputtered just then. His lips moved, and he began to whisper.

They both leaned forward to make out what he was saying.

"Arandel on his sword," the mercenary muttered, the words barely audible. "Dead to trust the man. Dead to trust the man! No! No!" His voice was louder now – a rasp. "Fallen on his sword! Paladin dead to trust the man."

Actaeon placed a hand on Wave's forehead. His temperature was high. "He is hallucinating from a fever."

Cortecha snapped her fingers and whistled. "Torg! Cafry! Bring more cool cloths."

The red-headed warbander twins snapped up from where they were idling by the door and rushed to follow the Althean's orders.

"You'd better have a good reason to have called me here," scolded Seraeta as she strode into the Arbiter Pyramid Command chamber. "I've still many injured to attend to." She regarded those present coolly, waiting for their reply but poised to walk out if she didn't hear a proper explanation.

"Lady Seraeta, please sit. You will wish to hear what these gentlemen are proposing. Allow me to introduce Sollemnis the Gray and Kryo of the Loresworn." The man who spoke was none other than Paladin Arbiter Cignith sof Iarnus. The leader of the Arbiters wore the plain gray uniform of his Order, with a red badge displaying interlocking shields pinned to the front of his tabard. The one difference between the Paladin Arbiter and the other Knights was that he wore the crimson red cloak of command over his uniform and steel shield pauldrons polished to a mirror finish on his shoulders. Cignith had a hawkish look about him – aged but ready to pounce. Vigilant gray eyes above a long, crooked nose, and white sideburns that reached down to his chin. He gestured to a seat at the table with slender, gnarled fingers.

The Paladin Arbiter sat at the head of a long, rectangular table. Opposite the table from Seraeta was one man she had seen before and another she had not.

The one she had seen was known as Sollemnis the Gray – an ancient-looking man with a tremendous gray beard that grew to his waist. He grasped a walking stick with a green crystal shard at its apex. A silver belt fastened red robes with silver ropework about his body. Attached to the robes was an assortment of strange artifacts. He stood a distance behind the table, smiling to himself.

The one she had not before seen – Kryo – was extremely short with a frame upon his face that held a lens before each of his eyes. His head was completely shaved. About his body he wore a brightweave outfit, the shimmering black artifact cloth covering him from the shoulders down to the table where he sat.

Seraeta sighed and pulled out one of the chairs to sit down. "I am but an Althean Healer. Why would you require me to hear a proposal?"

Kryo leaned forward and adjusted the frame on his nose. "The Althean Order is bereft of its leadership. With the Matron's life lost to the Ruinic invasion and your elder sisters missing or deceased, the leadership of the

Altheans is all but certain to fall into your hands. There may be no formal mechanism for you to assume the role, but whether or not you continue to deny it, your Order will eventually need a new Matron. You are the obvious choice in the matter."

Seraeta blinked and narrowed her eyes upon Kryo. "Well then, you waste no time in throwing the Fallen of my Order aside so that whatever agenda you Loresworn have might be addressed."

"Hear him out, Matron," suggested Cignith.

"Don't you dare call me that," snarled Seraeta. "If anyone is to decide on the next Matron of the Altheans, it will be done internal to our Order. No Arbiter or Loresworn or any other outside person will decide the fate of the Altheans. Is that clear?"

The Paladin Arbiter's thin lips curled slightly and he nodded. "There was no intent of dishonor in our dialogue here. Please forgive my presumption."

Seraeta nodded, satisfied. "Very well. You are forgiven. That said, you are most likely correct that they'll choose me as Matron, but the Order as a whole will be a part to that decision. I will not presume to lead."

"The Loresworn acknowledge that as well," said Kryo. "Even so, I ask that you hear out our proposal. In the event that you do not rise to Matron, you can pass it along to whomever does. Though what I am about to propose might hasten along whatever selection process you determine."

"Tell me this proposal of yours then. And be quick – there are many injured to attend to, as I've told you," said the Althean.

Old Sol broke his silence. "A momentous occasion in history and one of the framers seethes in impatience. A bedside manner wholly unsuited to any caretaker of the injured. Oh, Redemption! May this one find the patience to heal you."

"Bah!" Seraeta scoffed at the old Loresworn's words. "Get to the damned point already. Enough with the riddles and conjecture."

Kryo nodded and slid his chair closer to the table. "That I will, Seraeta of the Altheans. It is an idea that was first broached to us by the one now known as Prince Engineer. That the Orders of Arbiter, Althean, and Loresworn together join for the betterment of our great city. At first, I dismissed the idea as nonsense. But now... now what is happening across Redemption – the damage from Second Invasion War, the destructive forces to the north, the in-fighting between Dominions, and, most importantly, the issue at Travail. We will better combat the threats to our city if we work together directly. The Arbiter strength and discipline, the Althean influence and healing, the Loresworn knowledge and discretion. With the talents of our Orders combined, we might shape the future of Redemption in a way that will assure security, safety, and freedom. It is this alliance, this joining – a TriForge, that I lay on the table before you. A TriForge in the service to Redemption."

"Three Orders standing tall so that none shall see them fall," intoned Sol.

"The Arbiters are interested in this proposal, so long as the TriForge is led by a Trifold Council – a leader from each Order represented, wherein a majority vote rules," said Cignith.

"Our thoughts as well," seconded Kryo.

"I will discuss it with the Sentinels then. If their feedback is sound, then we will so join the TriForge," said the Arbiter leader.

All eyes turned to Seraeta.

She sighed. "I suppose I will have to address the lack of leadership in the Altheans sooner. That said, you have my attention. It is a proposal I will consider if I become Matron and I will pass along to the next Matron if it is not myself."

"Excellent," said Kryo. He removed the lenses from his eyes and wiped them with a cloth. "Might I suggest we reconvene in two days' time? Give you both time to do what you must."

The Paladin Arbiter dipped his head. "We will meet again in two days."

"I'd better get to work then," said Seraeta. She drew to her feet.

"A force to forge the peace that Redemption long deserves. Long live the TriForge of Redemption," said Sol, the top corners of his beard upturning in a smile.

"Hold's back 'an runnin', Yer Grace," said Tarcy. "If'n ya need ta attend ta other matters, I ken manage."

"Your effort is appreciated, Lady Hael," said Eisandre, her cool blue gaze surveying Saint Torin's Hold.

Much of the furniture had been restored, and many Raedelleans were hard at work, restocking the food and supplies and washing clean smoke-stained walls near the entry doors.

"M'not any Lady, Yer Grace," said the giant warrioress. "Jus' Tarcy'll do fine."

"I've been told of your valor in the protection of the people here," said the Princess.

"Doin' me job, Yer Grace," said Tarcy simply.

"Your job was to protect this embassy," countered Eisandre. "You did much more than that, from what I've heard. It sounds as though all the Pyramid survivors owe their life to your quick thinking and bravery during the siege."

The giantess turned a deep red, her eyes searching for the door.

"I've spoken with the Prince Engineer and the First Companion," said Eisandre. Behind her, Itarik nodded. "We're in agreement that we'd elevate you to Companion. I'd be foolish not to have your strength and loyalty at my side."

"I... er..." Tarcy stumbled over her words. "I ain't no Companion, ma'am – er, Yer Grace. Jus' Tarcy. Nuthin' special."

"Your Princess sees things differently, warbander," said Itarik, in a gentle but firm tone. "Are you suggesting she is incorrect?"

"No, ah... I'd a ne'er!" said Tarcy. Embarrassed, she knelt before Eisandre. "Fergive me, Yer Grace – me blade's at yer service, course." She reached up to tap the ruinblade strapped to her back.

"Then I ask that you defend the Caliburns and thereby defend Raedelle. Will you accept?" asked the Princess.

"Um, aye, Yer Grace," said Tarcy. "You'll 'ave me blade."

Eisandre reached out to touch the woman's forehead, nearly level with her own.

"Then rise, Companion Tarcy. I will need your continued service."

A sudden wave of nausea struck Eisandre as the giantess rose to her feet and she felt the room spinning around her. Uncharacteristically, she reached out to steady herself on the new Companion's arm. "I must attend to other matters now. Excuse me."

The Princess rushed past a bewildered Itarik to the door and the Mirrorholds beyond.

She walked swiftly to the Caliburn quarters, biting down the rising bile in her throat as she did so.

At the edge of her hearing, she could vaguely make out the First Companion announce that he was right behind her.

When she entered the quarters, she slammed the door shut and promptly vomited in the nearest plant pot. She noted the plant had withered and died in neglect since the siege had begun, and the vile liquid from her stomach seemed somehow appropriate, given its fate.

The Princess' head spun, and she landed hard on her backside, somehow placing the plant pot aside in an upright orientation.

Act, I don't feel well, she thought, and the Thoughtlink Artifact carried off her thoughts.

Actaeon paused as he poured the Dragon's Milk down Wave's throat. It was the second attempted treatment.

The Shimmering Oil had been an utter failure, having no effect at all on the deathcrawler larvae. Wave's lifebeat had become thready – it was scarcely audible, even with an ear pressed to the mercenary's chest. If the Dragon's Milk failed to exterminate the deathcrawlers within him, Wave would certainly die.

It was his last chance, and Actaeon knew it as he poured the dose of the liquid down his friend's throat.

But then his beloved's thoughts found their way through the Artifact clipped to his ear. They brought with them nausea and worry.

Eis, he thought back. *What is wrong?*

I don't know, she admitted. *I'm nauseous and dizzy. I had to leave the Hold very quickly.*

A sudden thought entered his mind, and he felt a sudden horror as he stared down at his mercenary friend. *There was no way you could have encountered a deathcrawler, is there?* As though in effort to combat the sudden concern, he tilted Wave's head back and carefully poured the remainder of the Dragon's Milk down the mercenary's throat.

Deathcrawlers? came Eis' confused thought. *Why would a deathcrawler have made me feel this way? No, I have not been near one.*

Actaeon finished pouring the concoction and began to massage the cartilage of Wave's throat gently to aid in his swallowing of the liquid. *Yes, I know. My apologies, love. It is just that working on this problem with Wave has me on edge. The symptoms you mentioned are among those that Shar Minovo had experienced before her –*

But I didn't encounter a deathcrawler, Eisandre reminded him. *These symptoms could be associated with a great many ailments. We've both been through a lot. I most likely caught some more mundane illness.*

You are correct, Eis. It could be a normal illness — or even a product of anxiety after a period of prolonged stress.

I feel much less anxious than I did when everything was at risk, she rationalized.

Perhaps, considered Actaeon. *I will head to Pyramid to be there with you. I should be there in an hour or two.*

No. Her thought was gentle but commanding. *Wave needs you more. You stay there and do what you can for him. I have others who can help me.*

Actaeon nodded slowly, concern creeping into his mind as he noticed his friend wasn't experiencing the immediacy of reaction that his chicken test subjects had demonstrated. *Yes, love. Please keep me apprised of your condition.*

I will. And you do the same.

When the next morning came, Wave had still not shown any improvement after the Dragon's Milk.

Lauryn came down the stairs from the loft to find Actaeon poring over papers at the workbench nearest Wave.

"Act, you'd better get some rest. You've been up all night," said Lauryn, concern in her tone.

Actaeon glanced up from his notes to offer Lauryn a bleary-eyed look. "Wave's time is very short, Lauryn. And if I spend less than every waking moment trying to help him, then that will never be enough for me."

The sudden memory of his mother sprung into his mind, unbidden. She had told him to get his rest too, as he struggled to find a cure for the Rogue's Bane that took her life. One evening he had smiled at her and assented. "Yes, mother."

The next morning he woke to find her dead.

That was why he couldn't rest now. The old memory came back through time to haunt him. That and the knowledge that Wave wouldn't survive another dose of Maiden's Sleep – Cortecha had assured him as much.

Lauryn's surprisingly firm hand on his shoulder snapped him out of his reverie. She looked down into his eyes. "Act?"

"You are right, Lady Lauryn of the Light Lancers," said Actaeon with a

weak smile. His emerald eyes gleamed in the dim light of the workshop –
most of the luminaries still covered for the night. "And yet, I cannot rest –
not while there is yet hope that I might discover some solution, however
evasive to my mind."

"Then at least go take a walk," suggested Lauryn. "Don't you always say
that the best way to solve a tough problem is to take your mind away from
it? Your own thoughts are circling around the same failed solutions. Go and
take a stroll. See if those ideas come to you. Leave Wave to his dreams of
ladies' kisses and epic sword fights."

Actaeon offered Lauryn a vacant look that at first worried her, but then
his lips curled into their characteristic grin. Excited, he leapt up to hug her
close and kissed her forehead. "You are a genius, Lauryn of Lakehold!" he
announced. "Ladies' kisses, indeed. Watch after him, I will be back as soon
as I am able."

With that he hastily tugged on his jacket and raced to the door to
retrieve his halberd. He unlatched the workshop door and flung it open to
race into the dawn.

AROMAS AND ASHES

ACTAEON BURST INTO MAE'S CHAMBER in the Hives, having run there all the way from the Outskirts.

The artist gasped and covered her breasts with her arm – caught by surprise in the middle of cleaning herself with a damp cloth. "Your Grace doesn't knock?" she managed before slipping behind a curtain.

The Prince Engineer averted his eyes. "My apologies, Lady Mae. It is just that I had a revelation."

"A revelation that has you barging into my chamber in the early morning without even an announcement?" she scolded. "What would Her Grace, your wife, think?" She peeked out at him around the curtain and offered a stern look.

"I imagine she might be as excited as I am," said Actaeon. He began to pace to and fro near the entryway to her apartment.

Maerdia's eyes widened and she withdrew back behind the curtain. "Excited!?"

"Indeed," he said, unable to hide the elation from his tone. "I believe I may have an idea about how to cure Wave."

In the center of the room was an unfinished sculpture showing several rough figures in combat with creatures that looked like chunky versions of a deathcrawler and a giant slug. One of the figures was leaping toward the open maw of the slug. Leaning against the sculpture was a pair of different sized writheblades in their ceramic scabbards.

Actaeon scrutinized the details of the statue as he paced.

Mae stepped out from behind the curtain at that, a thin silk wrap clinging to her damp skin. It would've left little to the imagination had Actaeon's mind not been entirely elsewhere. "You're serious? That's tremendous news! But wait... why would that bring you to my chamber? Certainly there's nothing I could do to help. What is this cure you have in mind?"

Actaeon stopped pacing and turned to face the artist. "A kiss."

Mae's jaw fell open and she offered the Prince Engineer a blank stare.

"Do you remember what happened after you kissed Wave?" asked Actaeon.

"It just... it was only... I kissed him because..." she stammered, turning her head in shame.

Actaeon grinned and held up his hand to forestall her explanation. "The reason matters not. The only thing that matters was the outcome. Do you remember that?"

Mae thought about it for a moment and shuddered as it came back to her. Her eyes rose to meet Actaeon's and she nodded. "I remember."

"However the manner, the kiss caused the larvae inside him to revolt and expel from his body," he explained, leaning heavily against his halberd. "If we can somehow replicate the effect and enhance it, we may yet be able to save him."

"So you want me to kiss him again," ventured Mae.

"Not necessarily, Lady Mae," began Actaeon. "I do not believe it was the kiss itself, but rather some other factor in the kiss. A paint upon your lips, a cosmetic upon your skin, the odor of something recently ingested, or even a perfume worn about your body. If you could part with some samples of what you wore that day, I can test it out on Wave."

Mae crossed her arms and regarded Actaeon with skepticism.

"If you please, Lady Mae," said Actaeon formally. He placed his fist to chest and bowed to the artist. "Without Wave, I would not be standing before you today. I owe him my life many times over. You would have my utmost gratitude if you would help me with this. I am shorn of ideas – this is perhaps his final chance."

Her feet bare, Mae approached Actaeon and gently took his shoulders in her hands to raise him up from his bow. "Your Grace should not bow to me. As I said to you several days earlier, I owe you my life for the risk you and your team of heroes took to save those trapped in the Pyramid. I will do whatever I can to help."

"You have my thanks, Lady Mae," said Actaeon. "We must exercise haste."

"Yes," said Mae. She stepped back from him and looked thoughtful before rushing behind the curtain once more. When she emerged, she was wearing a more substantial cotton robe, her hair in a wrap, and soft leather shoes upon her feet.

She moved quickly about her chamber that also doubled as her studio. "This was the perfume," she said as she thrust a bottle into Actaeon's hands.

"And this incense I burned that morning," she said, snatching several sticks from a container and handing them to the Prince Engineer.

She rushed to just before her privacy curtain and snatched a bar. "I freshened with this soap. Oh, and I worked on a sculpture of clay that day. Here, I'll make up a sample for you."

She lifted a pail and spilled some clay from it onto her worktable, then retrieved a bottle of water to splash upon it. With urgency, she began to knead the chunk of clay, working the water into it until it was a malleable ball. She tossed it to Actaeon, who caught it awkwardly, nearly dropping some of the other things in his hands.

"I believe that is all," said Mae. "We should depart at once!" The artist led the way purposefully from her chambers out into the Hives beyond.

Startled, Actaeon watched her rush by. He grinned and stuffed the variety of items into his jacket pockets before running to catch the artist.

Artist and Engineer burst into a somber workshop.

Trench and Lauryn both stood on the far side of Wave, heads lowered. The Althean stood on the other side, gently mopping his forehead with a cool cloth.

One of the warbander twins – the one without the beard, nearly bowled over Actaeon in his rush to retrieve another cloth. "Sorry, Your Grace," he managed, before skirting past.

Cortecha spun to offer Actaeon a grave look. "He hasn't long, Your Grace."

"Before it happens, we've gotta burn 'im. He'd not 'ave wanted the damned things to hatch," said Trench. His deep scar was shiny with fallen tears.

"Nonsense," said Actaeon. "No time for that sort of talk. Here. Bathe his chest, arms, and face in this soap, Cortecha. Lauryn, spray this perfume about his nose and mouth. Trench, grab a flint and light this incense stick." He handed out the items and gave Maerdia Bazardjan her ball of clay.

The artist immediately approached the unconscious mercenary and began to alternately knead the ball of clay and rub her hands upon his face.

The others just stood there and offered Actaeon a blank look.

"You want him to live, do you not?" scolded the Prince Engineer. "Then get to work," he said without awaiting a reply.

Cortecha opened the ties on Wave's shirt and used the damp cloth she held to moisten the soap before lathering it on his chest and neck.

Lauryn nodded and sprayed the perfume around the mercenary's face.

The three women worked, and Wave remained unmoving.

Actaeon felt the man's neck for his lifebeat. It was barely there.

"Why won't this Ancient-damned thing light?" cursed Trench from a nearby bench where he tried to spark the incense.

"What's supposed to be happening?" asked Lauryn.

"If I am correct, then he will vomit up the remaining creatures once exposed to the correct chemical," explained Actaeon. He reached up to scratch his right arm.

The three women all took a step back from Wave, but when he didn't vomit, they returned and continued with their ministrations.

"Finally. P-kin thing!" snarled Trench. The giant approached with his lit stick of incense and held it near Wave's nose.

The smaller mercenary's nose wrinkled as he breathed in the incense.

"That is it," said Actaeon. "The incense!"

Wave's shoulders and neck spasmed and his eyelid fluttered open, revealing the white of his rolled back remaining eye.

"Get him on his side," commanded Cortecha.

Trench helped the Althean turn Wave on his side just as he began to bring up the lethal contents of his stomach and lungs.

Wave's entire body shook, retched, and spasmed as he expelled the deathcrawler larvae from his body and onto the workshop floor.

Actaeon and Lauryn scrambled to collect the agitated larvae in some of the larger half-through bottles using tongs.

Trench continued to wave the smoking stick of incense back and forth before Wave's face so that the smoke washed across his pale features.

Wave continued to spasm violently as he coughed up his body's invaders.

Trench held him in place with his free hand while Cortecha used a pair of forceps to quickly remove any larvae that became stuck in the mercenary's throat.

The larvae were nearly mature, with little nubs where the legs would eventually emerge. Some of them already writhed and fought back with underdeveloped pincers.

It was at that moment that the Shieldian Lord chose to step into the workshop. The young Lord took one look at the writhing larvae upon the floor and all of the color left his face. He gagged and covered his mouth with a gloved hand before averting his eyes. "Master Rellios – what in shattered Redemption are you doing now?"

"Ah, Lord Zar," said Actaeon. "I am glad you are well. Come in, I should like to hear what you have been up to."

The Lord Enrion Zar, son of Prince General Indros Zar – the leader of Shield, took one look at the scene in the workshop and fled back to the relative peace of the Outskirts to lose his morning meal.

"I hope your man returns to good health," said the Lord Zar.

The two men leaned against the outside workshop wall, watching the activity of the Outskirts as residents moved back in and reestablished themselves in the ransacked buildings. Off to the side and a short distance away, a sizable squad of Shieldian soldiers stood at attention.

"Indeed," said Actaeon. "There stands a good chance that the deathcrawler threat to his body is over. Only, now his body must recover from what it has been through."

"I pray the blood of Wardens flows through his body," offered Enrion.

Actaeon offered the Lord a skeptical look but kept his thoughts to himself.

"So Master Rellios is now Prince Engineer Actaeon Rellios Caliburn," marveled Enrion, brushing a stray lock of his wavy black hair from his face. "It was Monsoon's Dawn when last we spoke, if I recall correctly. So much has changed in less than three cycles of the moon."

"A strange turn of events for me," admitted Actaeon. "Leadership was never an ambition of mine. A distraction from where I would rather spend my energy – deciphering the secrets of the city and inventing solutions to new problems. And yet, lacking stability in Redemption, none of that would be possible. And so it must be."

"Never an ambition," mused Enrion with a smile. "And yet so many follow you without question. An entire team at your beck and call to help you with the same monstrosities that I once paid you to destroy." The Lord Zar turned to regard Actaeon, envy in his narrow black eyes. "Care to switch places?"

"While I would gladly switch places were it simply a choice of position, I would not choose to be anywhere other than by Eisandre's side," said Actaeon. "It is for that reason, among others, that I am now a Prince Engineer instead of a simple Engineer."

"Oh, but I jest," said Enrion, laughing it off. "If I am to ascend to such a position, I will earn it of my own accord. The Prince General has made me Lord of Holdfast, you know? No longer a mere Governor of a fledgling Hold, but a Lord of an established Shieldian Hold."

Actaeon smirked inwardly when Enrion referred to his father by rank. "A position you have earned – especially in showing how you could successfully manage your fledgling Hold. Something tells me that you did not come here just to receive my congratulations, however."

"Perceptive as ever, my engineer friend," said Enrion. "I come seeking your expertise. The situation in Czeryn grows dire. We fight an enemy we don't understand and weapons that the Ancients themselves must have constructed."

"From the little insights I have gleaned, there is no enemy left to find in Czeryn. Which leaves me curious as to what enemy you are fighting," said Actaeon.

"As curious as I am, Mast... er, Prince Engineer. At first, we had thought that Ajman had declared war on us to fight for the territory. Both Dominions had initially brought troops to the former Czeryn Holds to claim territory, but there was no violence until we reached Craters and Ajmani soldiers began attacking us. They refused to parlay with us, and we were forced to cut them down in some places and retreat in others.

"My father was about to call for an invasion of Kendra when one of our elite units from Rust attacked Endira's base camp," Enrion continued. "It was a massacre. In the end, the Steel Rose was victorious," he said, using his sister's nickname, "but the Amphis' Ledge forces were cut in two by the end of it. Soon after, scouts spotted a joint force of Ajman and Shield advancing on our position, led by the General of Ajman. We managed to join up with another Ajmani force led by the Raja's woman, Calisse T'ra Coletka. Together we broke free in time before another of those Ancient-damned blue bubbles happened."

Actaeon let out a low whistle. "You are lucky to have survived. I am glad to hear that the rumors of war between Shield and Ajman are untrue – though it appears that the truth is even worse."

"So much worse," admitted Enrion. "A war with Ajman we know we could win. It might be difficult, but, in the end, the Shield always holds. Now you know why I am here. We need your intuition and engineering know-how to combat whatever is going on up there."

"The enemy is taking over the minds of your soldiers – turning them against you. Some form of mind control," explained Actaeon.

"Our thoughts as well," said Enrion, turning a critical eye on the Prince Engineer. "But how could you draw that conclusion so easily?"

"The Veiled One," said Actaeon. "That is what the enemy calls itself. We have had encounters with it before. Do you recall the cross-faced raiders that had pursued me across the Redemption ruins?"

"That sounds vaguely familiar," said Enrion. He pushed off the wall and turned to face Actaeon fully.

"Yes, well, they never managed to capture me, but they captured Lauryn," explained the Prince Engineer. "In order to free her, I surrendered myself to them. The Lady Lartigan was there as well."

"Wait," interrupted Enrion. "Gretchen Lartigan, from Niwian? The same one who disappeared from the Monsoon Festival? How come you never told me about this?"

Actaeon arched a brow at the Lord. "I might have been just a little bit busy. I went to tell the Lord Protector, but he had been assassinated."

"Ah yes, the Keepers disposed of Garizo Fothrakas," said Enrion, matter-of-factly.

"The Keepers disposed of him?" asked Actaeon, surprised. "Why would they do such a thing?"

"In an effort to increase their influence and control of Niwian," said Enrion. "Very clever of them. Become a Niwian Protectorate, remove the Niwian leader to make way for a suicidal Lord Protector like Thernaxis, and once he manages to remove himself, to help a new leader elevate to power – one that will provide them with far more influence in return for their support."

"You have proof of this?" asked Actaeon, raising a brow.

"Of course not – not that it would matter," said Enrion with a thin smile. "But it is politics, the course is obvious when one considers the motivation."

"There is a logic to it," said Actaeon. "And, with the mainstream recognition of a Dominion, comes more freedom to spread the message of the Allfather."

"Now you're thinking like a politician, Actaeon," said Enrion with a grin. "You've nothing to worry about in your new position – just keep thinking that way, and learn to anticipate."

Actaeon frowned and shot Enrion a look. "I will keep thinking like an engineer, thank you. Logic will always reveal the truth, and the truth is what we need to lead our people."

Enrion smirked. "You'll find that the truth isn't always fit for the people. Sometimes we must tell them what they need to hear so that they may do what we know to be right and just."

"Then that is where we shall differ," said Actaeon with a grin.

"So will you help us with this Veiled One?" asked Enrion, changing the subject.

"I will provide any insight that I can," began Actaeon. "But I have just returned from a war. My people are weary, and we must needs help rebuild here now. I cannot commit to fighting more battles, but, as always, you will have my support in any way possible from Pyramid and its surrounds."

"I see..." said Enrion, unable to hide the disappointment in his tone. "I rather preferred it when you were just a Master Engineer."

"That makes two of us, Lord Zar," admitted Actaeon with another grin.

"Will you at least speak with the TriForge?" asked Enrion. "They haven't granted me an audience in the matter," he admitted reluctantly.

"The TriForge?" The Prince Engineer raised his brow.

"You haven't heard? The Arbiters, Altheans, and Loresworn have joined together as the TriForge – an organization dedicated to Redemption," explained the Shieldian. "The Healer Seraeta was elevated to Matron of the Altheans and together with the Paladin Arbiter and Kryo, they formed a Trifold Council to collectively help Redemption with its troubles. We could use the help of the Loresworn, if not your own. Might you speak with them about it?"

"Excellent news," said Actaeon, nodding emphatically. "I am glad to hear they have taken this important step. It will serve all of Redemption better to have those Orders aligned thusly."

"So you'll speak with them about this?" asked Enrion impatiently.

"I certainly will speak with them," said Actaeon. "In fact, I believe I will go do that right after I check in with my wife."

"Actaeon Rellios Caliburn," said Kryo. "Prince Engineer… Influencer of Orders, Slayer of Deathstalker Brood, Unlocker of the Ve-"

"Stop it, Kryo," interrupted Actaeon. "I have had enough of your nonsense."

He'd just gotten back from checking on Eisandre, who was feeling much better since her sudden and unexplained illness. Actaeon was still worried about her though, even though she had insisted she was better.

The Prince Engineer now stood before the new Trifold Council of the TriForge – its three members seated at the table within the spartan Arbiter Pyramid Command chamber.

"Aye, it don't appear you've got yer little toy ball for me to smash," said Trench from his spot at Actaeon's side. The new Raedellean Attaché, Largrival, stood to the Prince Engineer's other side. "If ya piss off Act enough, I'll have to smash *you* this time instead of the ball."

Kryo leveled his gaze upon Trench and pushed his lenses up along the bridge of his nose.

Trench smiled at him, the expression tugging at his wicked scar in a manner that made him look truly mad.

Kryo recoiled and shook his head before returning his gaze to Actaeon. "Very well. I shall cease with the honorifics. What is it that brings you before this Trifold Council today?"

Actaeon took another step forward and addressed them. "Paladin Arbiter Cignith sof Iarnus. Matron Seraeta. Master Loresworn Kryo. It gladdens me that you have decided to form this TriForge. Much good will come of it for Redemption, I believe."

"Prince Engineer Actaeon Rellios Caliburn," began the Paladin Arbiter in his gravelly voice. "If Master Kryo is to be believed, you have our thanks for the suggestion that resulted in this Trifold Council sitting before you."

"It was the logical course of action for your Orders to pool their resources," said Actaeon.

"Logical, and yet not obvious to a great many others," said Cignith, looking down his hawkish nose at the Prince Engineer. "I understand you have your differences with my Loresworn brother. I hope you can overcome them."

"Aye," said Actaeon with a grin. "He tried to boil the infiltrators of Pyramid to death, myself included. We overcame it alright."

"It was a –" began Kryo.

Trench moved forward in the blink of an eye and slammed his fist on the table, the sound echoing throughout the sparse chamber. "– a mistake," he finished for the Loresworn leader. "Aye, it was." After another of his twisted smiles, the giant stepped back from the table.

Cignith turned his vigilant gray eyes on Kryo to give him a long and deliberate look. "Sounds like a mistake for certain," said the Paladin Arbiter at last. "I'm sure it will not happen again." The Arbiter leader turned his attention back to Actaeon. "So, as my Loresworn colleague asked – what brings you before our Trifold Council today?"

Actaeon gestured to a chair. "May I?"

Cignith nodded. "Of course."

Actaeon leaned his halberd against the table and sat down in the chair. He glanced up at Trench and Largrival.

"Nah, I'm happy to stand, boss," said Trench. "Thanks, though."

Largrival nodded her agreement.

Actaeon nodded and turned his emerald gaze upon the leaders of the three Orders. "I bring the first suggestion for your new TriForge. You stand in a great position with your newfound Council, and I cannot imagine a more appropriate time. Redemption has just countered one of the greatest threats to its security and faces yet another dire threat to the north. The Dominions must join together to fight these threats or die. There must be a permanent peace between the Dominions at worst, an interdominional alliance at best. The Dominions must be able to work together against the forces that threaten this Ancient city. However, it is not my place to call a meeting to discuss such things – no, that must come from a neutral source. It must come from your TriForge. It must be *overseen* by your TriForge.

"Yours is the Council that will forge a new interdominional alliance, if it is ever to be," continued Actaeon. "So I ask you to attempt just that. To endeavor to unite all Dominions into a single solemn cause – to the guardianship of all Redemption from forces that would seek to destroy its people, its humanity. For asunder we will certainly perish, but together we will flourish. It is this great goal that I task your new TriForge with, if you choose to accept it."

"Big ideas that you bring to this chamber, Prince Engineer Rellios Caliburn of Raedelle," said Cignith.

"Big ideas are what will differentiate our people from the ruination of the Ancients," Actaeon asserted. "Without such ideas, I am certain that we will meet the fate of the Ancients, or worse. Will you attempt what I suggest?"

Cignith looked to Seraeta.

"Yes," said the Matron. "It is what the Althean Order was originally formed for, after all."

The Paladin Arbiter turned to Kryo next.

The Loresworn pulled his lenses from his eyes and wiped them with a cloth before replacing them. "An ambitious endeavor, but, nevertheless, one we will support. We shall see if it will succeed."

Cignith nodded and turned to Actaeon. "You have all three votes of the Trifold Council, Prince Engineer. We will try to do as you suggest and bring all of the Dominions together for a meeting. We shall see what the leaders decide."

Actaeon nodded and stood from the table. He retrieved his halberd and raised the blade to his temple in salute.

"There is one more important issue which must be addressed before you depart," said Kryo.

"I am listening," said Actaeon.

"The matter of Travail's weakness grows in urgency," said Kryo. "Until now you've ignored it, but it is a matter that requires your attention."

"And what was it? Eight days ago?" asked Actaeon. "If I had pushed the incorrect sequence and boiled us all in Pyramid's control room, then what? What was your fallback plan for Travail? Or did you not consider that?"

"Yet another example of your singular talent," countered Kryo. "If you were to fail, then you would not have been the correct choice to face

Travail's dilemma. But you did not fail, and in doing so, you have proven that you are the one to solve the quandary."

"So certain you are, both you and Sol, whenever we speak that I am the solution to your problem. And yet you continue to test me at every chance you get," said Actaeon, letting out a laugh. "I will not go to Travail based on your conjecture. I have a sick friend to tend to, a Dominion to secure, and all of Redemption to put back together after the greatest war in my lifetime. You have repeatedly demonstrated your uncertainty about my abilities and now I doubt the validity of your very dilemma. Can you blame me? So no, I will not be rushing off to save Travail. Save Travail on your own, since you know so much."

Actaeon turned and began to stride from the chamber, Trench and Largrival following.

Kryo stood and shouted, his voice cracking. "You come here asking us to unite Redemption against forces that seek to destroy it and then walk away from one of the greatest threats in our people's history. Uncontested, it will spread to encompass all of Redemption. I'll remember this day, Prince Engineer – the day that you invented one groundbreaking idea, and turned your back on another."

Actaeon turned to glare at Kryo. "If you speak truth, then you have your own lack of transparency to thank for it. The Loresworn have never been open and honest with the people of this city – not as recent as eight days ago. If you speak truth, then it is your own doing, and so you can own the responsibility. Fix it yourself, Kryo."

That said, the Prince Engineer strode purposefully from the chamber.

Drystan Beiloff, the former Warchief of Shore, watched the workshop in the Outskirts from a distance and smiled.

The warbander Lieutenant Areyna and her stupid-looking twins, Taffee and Corg – or something, were leaving – headed toward the Avenue of Glass.

Beiloff waited as the warbanders retreated into the distance, filled with half regret. He hated Areyna's attitude – too bad he couldn't take her out with the rest. He hadn't lived so long by being stupid though, and he wanted to make sure he took out Actaeon and those two damned mercenaries. The three warbanders would decrease the chance of that.

When they were far enough away, he cracked his knuckles and lifted the hefty bundle under his arm. Once he reached the workshop, he knelt to the side of the door and unwrapped it. Inside was a length of heavy hewn timber and several glass bottles filled with oil incendiary. The Ajmani apothecarist in the Warrens had assured him that they would shatter easily and burn hot.

Beiloff smiled and lined them up before striking his flint to light the soaked rag fuses that stuck out from the bottle tops. "I'll bet the Engineer screams like an ugly tavern wench as he burns," he muttered to himself with amusement.

Once the bottles were all lit, he stood, satisfied. The door to the workshop swung open at that moment and a small woman walked out, wrapped in the white robes of an Althean.

"What do you think you're doing? There's a sick man in there – put those out at once," commanded the Althean in a thick Shieldian accent. A moment later her eyes widened in understanding and she tried to get back inside the workshop.

Drystan's reflexes were faster though, and he kicked the door shut before she could get back inside. She opened her mouth to scream and he covered it with a gauntleted hand and shoved her backward violently until her head crashed into the stone wall of the workshop behind her. His dagger was in her belly a lifebeat later. He twisted it and pulled it out to stab her in the heart.

"Shut up, you bitch," he whispered in her ear – the last words she ever heard as the life faded from her eyes.

He let the Althean fall and kicked her in the side for good measure. If she was going to ruin everything, at least she paid the price.

That done, Drystan opened the workshop door and quickly threw in the incendiaries one by one, making sure to hit the wooden stairs with one and the bottom of the wooden loft with another.

Without waiting to see if they caught, he slammed the door closed again and wedged the long timber length between the ground and the door, pinning it shut.

The pounding against the door and the screams within told him that the incendiaries were working.

He smiled and pounded back on the door. "Tell the Engineer to enjoy the warmth!"

As much as he wished he could stay and listen to them burn to death, he backed off to the fringes of the Outskirts to watch from a distance. He hadn't survived all these years by being a fool.

Wave awoke as his body racked with a fit of coughing. He doubled over on the cot upon which he lay and felt a burst of heat upon his face so hot that he impulsively rolled in the other direction and fell to the floor.

A burning beam crashed down upon the cot he'd lain upon and showered him with embers. He could feel his hair burning, and quickly patted it out.

The realization came to him suddenly: he was in the workshop – the workshop was on fire.

A thick black smoke was all around him, making it impossible to see, or breathe. He lowered himself until his face was pressed to the stone floor and pulled his undertunic up over his mouth to filter some of the smoke.

Wave felt around him and found his sword belt beneath the smashed cot. He slipped it over one shoulder and continued to feel around to try and find his boots.

Another beam crashed to the floor beside him. The loft above must be on fire. He gave up on the boots and rolled away from the remains of the cot just as a large section of the loft came down atop where he had been, showering him in a fresh deluge of embers.

The mercenary scrabbled away until he smacked his head against a wall. He cursed under his breath and peered under the smoke – looking for the way out.

Back past the collapse, he thought he could make out daylight through the swirling smoke.

No time to waste, he lifted himself up to a low crouch and ran for it, the heat from above baking his back through his thin undertunic.

He found Lauryn lying unconscious there, beside a triangular hole she'd cut with her light lance in the wall of the workshop.

Instinctively, Wave grabbed a fistful of her tunic with one hand and her light lance with the other and dragged them both out through the hole.

He pulled Lauryn several paces away from the workshop before dropping her and the light lance. He collapsed to the ground in another fit of coughing. At first he rolled onto his back, but he flopped back onto his stomach after the heat from his undertunic seared the skin of his back.

Boots crunched against gravel nearby and Wave heard the soft sound of a blade being drawn from its sheath.

The mercenary was up in a flash. Barefoot and with his under-clothing still smoldering, he drew his flamberge rapier and parried a downward thrust aimed for his head. His lightning quick riposte struck his assailant in the shoulder, punching through leather armor to create a flower of red.

Wave pulled his companion dagger free and rolled his arm to launch the sword belt from his shoulder toward the enemy.

The attacker slashed wildly at the belt, knocking it aside. He scowled at Wave, looking down his crooked nose at him. Woad markings spanned both of the man's bare arms and extended up his neck from beneath his thick leather armor.

Wave spat and laughed at the disgraced Warchief. "Vain..." he said, letting Actaeon's old nickname for the man hang in the air for several long moments. "Arcady's dog. You've not sunk low enough in your life? Did Arcady send you, or was this your own brilliant idea?"

"I'll be remembered long after your corpse has rotted away," retorted Beiloff.

"I'll bet," said Wave with a smirk. "As the saddest sop Redemption's ever seen."

Beiloff snarled and swung his broadsword, which the mercenary easily deflected. The pair exchanged a series of quick blows and parries.

"I typically enjoy a challenge when I fight," said Wave. "Do keep that in mind."

"Say all you want," growled Beiloff. "Meanwhile yer master and friends burn up in the workshop."

"If anyone else said that, I'd be worried," said Wave with a sly smile. "But Vain is sure to have screwed it up. I'm sure everyone was away."

"I'll gut you!" screamed the former Warchief. He lunged forward to stab at Wave's heart, but his sword was batted easily aside.

Wave laughed as his counter-slash opened up the forearm of Beiloff's off hand. A sudden wave of nausea hit him though and he keeled over and retched, producing nothing but bile from his empty stomach.

Drystan Beiloff took the opportunity to press his attack upon the mercenary.

His body revolting, Wave was still able to parry the blows as he retreated hastily. The press of Beiloff's attacks combined with the weakness of his own body caused him to lose his footing.

The disgraced Warchief took the opportunity to stab Wave's leading ankle, drawing blood and sending the mercenary to the ground hard.

Wave's head lolled backward and his eye closed. When he opened it, he could see Lauryn's still form lying beside him. The hiss of a blade brought his sharply honed reflexes back to life and his flamberge blade met Beiloff's straight blade just a finger's span before it would've sliced open Lauryn's neck.

Beiloff staggered back and lifted his blade high. "Any last words from the lame swordsman?"

"I dunno, you tell me," said Wave with a smile.

"You overconfident cad," belted out Beiloff. "I've bested Duke Branwyn himself. Gawyn and Owayn too. And you think you're special. I've slain royalty without batting an eye! You're nothing to me. Nothing!"

"Good to know, Vain," said Wave. He rolled backward and regained his feet before lunging forward. He balanced his weight on his uninjured leg and pressed a rapid assault upon Beiloff that the former Warchief couldn't possibly keep up with. His two blades became a blur of death-bringing steel.

Wave first cut his opponent's left lower bicep tendon and then his right. Beiloff's sword clattered to the ground.

The smoking mercenary smiled and swept his flamberge low, severing one of Vain's achilles tendons.

The former Warchief collapsed to his knees and fell forward, scrambling for his sword. He managed to grasp the hilt, but failed to lift it.

Wave stepped on his opponent's blade with one bare foot and kicked him in the face with the other, sending him to land upon his back.

Stars floated at the edge of his single eye's vision as pain lanced up his injured leg, but he limped forward to finish the job.

"Farewell, Vain," Wave said with a grin. "Remember – saddest sop Redemption's ever seen."

As Beiloff opened his mouth to protest, Wave swept the tip of his blade to open the man's throat and release a flood of red.

"Still got it," Wave said with a smile. Then he coughed up his blood onto his gray undertunic and promptly face-planted into the ground beside the dead former Warchief.

A NEW DAWN

WAVE AWOKE WITH A START and sat up to smack his head against the slanted window directly above. He blinked and shook his head as he gradually became aware of his surroundings.

"Yer fine," growled Trench. "Just don't sit up again."

He was lying in bed in Actaeon's old room in the Song of the Sisters, a restaurant and inn at the pinnacle of the Pyramid. The headboard was adjacent to a slanted window that was part of the Pyramid's translucent top. Rays of morning sunlight streamed through the window into the room beyond – filled with scattered sketches and notes from the Engineer.

Trench sat in a chair beside the bed, watching over him.

"This bed's in a damned stupid location," grumbled Wave as he peered, bleary-eyed, over at his friend.

"Tell me about it," said Trench. He had slept there earlier in the cycle after recovering from their first encounter with a giant slug. "Glad to see yer alright."

"I gather those twisted things didn't hatch inside me?" asked Wave. "So, he did it?"

"Aye," said Trench. "With a treatment from the Altheans that slowed the progress. He figured out a way. Go figure – a lady's kiss saved the lady's man."

The hazy memory of his duel with Beiloff came back to him suddenly, and, with a start, Wave sat up and cracked his head on the window again. He clutched his head and grimaced. "Lauryn – is she…"

"The lass's fine," said Trench. "Ya saved her from the fire. She's out and about with the boss."

Wave let out a sigh and fell back onto his elbows.

"The Althean that helped save you didn't make out so well," said Trench. "Her name was Cortecha. Don't soon forget it. Without her, you'd have died, I'm certain."

Wave nodded slowly. "I will not. She die in the fire?"

"Nay, 'twas that disgraced Warchief killed her before lighting up the workshop. Skewered her with a knife while she did naught to fight back. I shoulda killed that p'kin sop the first time we ran into him." The giant looked down at his hands with regret.

"And you'd have been a fugitive around the Pyramid," said Wave. "We couldn't have known he'd do those things, Trench. You know that. The Knight Arbiters would've had your head for it."

Trench nodded, his eyes still in his lap. "Yer right. Sometimes it just feels like we can't protect our own friends."

"Nonsense," said Wave. "It's the fight that never ends, but if we hadn't fought it all these years, how many more would be lost? Someone's gotta fight it, my friend – and who better than the pair who have nothing left to lose?"

Trench raised his eyes to look at his friend. "But we don't have nothing left to lose. In this fight we've found a new family – and everything to lose once again."

Wave's mouth curled into a smile. "Well then, let's be sure we don't fuck it up again, eh?"

Trench grinned, the effort tugging at the brutal chasm that spanned his face. "Aye, let's."

Wave held out his hand and the giant reached out to grasp it firmly.

The mercenaries' gazes met and they shared a nod.

Wave released Trench's hand and laid back down upon the bed. "So we saved the Pyramid?"

"We all did," said Trench. "But we lost Geodric Caider, Wayd Arbrigel, Hake Rim, Quronos, and Lady Ruinic."

"Shattered Redemption," breathed Wave. "That's half of us. Wait... who's Lady Ruinic?"

"A tribal that joined with us for a short time," explained Trench. "Before getting eaten by a slug."

Wave nodded solemnly, processing the information. He'd shared drinks and adventures with Caider, fought alongside Wayd in the Battle of the Wall, and battled Quronos to a stalemate in Travail. "They'll be missed," was all he could muster.

"Aye," seconded Trench.

"And the workshop burned down," said Wave.

"Just the loft and much of the contents," said Trench. "Act had the place built for fire. It stands still, but there's much repair work that needs be done. A crew's fixing it up as we speak."

Wave nodded slowly. "So what are Act and Lauryn up to?"

"Out on the Felmere," said Trench. "There's some sorta plague of monsoon bugs that's been destroying food stores and crops," he explained.

"Without us?" asked Wave. "That's a dangerous place."

"Aye, but Yanelle's with him," said Trench. "They'll be fine."

Wave nodded and then smiled. "So tell me more about this kiss that saved me."

"All signs point to gravidity," said Seraeta.

"Gravidity?" asked Eisandre. She offered a confused look to the new Althean Matron.

The Princess had sought out Seraeta to ask about her recent bout of nausea and dizziness. It would not do to have that occur again, especially with everything that needed to be done after the Second Invasion War had ended.

"Gravid," said the Matron. "Gestating, expectant, with child, pregnant," she rattled off.

Eisandre blinked and looked at her belly with confusion. "A baby?"

"Yes, a baby – that's what one becomes pregnant with," said Seraeta sternly.

Eisandre was silent for a long moment. Then she asked, "How can you be certain?"

"When did you first have relations with your new husband?" asked Seraeta.

The Princess blinked and fixed her blue eyes on the healer.

"Well? Out with it. When did he first put it inside you?" she demanded bluntly.

"Our wedding day," said Eisandre, undisturbed by the question. "The thirtieth of Rainbreak."

"Hmm," uttered the Matron, counting the days in her head. "Past the five week mark. It is certainly possible that you'd experience those symptoms already. I've seen them as early as four. I will have some Piegroot delivered discreetly to Saint Torin's for you. Brew a cup of tea from it. Three cups a day should help reduce the symptoms."

Eisandre looked at her with concern and then down at her still flat belly. "Will it..." She trailed off.

"It'll not harm the baby," said Seraeta. "Am I correct in assuming you'll want it?"

"Want it?" asked Eisandre, clearly lost in these matters.

"Want to keep the baby," said Seraeta, as though it were obvious.

"Keep the baby?" repeated Eisandre. "You mean, as opposed to giving it to the Order?"

Seraeta narrowed her eyes upon the Princess. "Oh you poor dear, none of the Arbiters ever taught you, did they?"

Eisandre looked past the new Matron of the Altheans, her mind swirling with unfamiliar thoughts.

Seraeta put her hand gently on Eisandre's shoulder. "Come walk with me in the gardens. I will teach you all about it, and we can gather some of the Piegroot there ourselves."

The Portent had come first, sent by the Raja, and found Actaeon in the Mirrorholds, where he was staying with Eisandre while the workshop was repaired. The tiny envoy from Ajman with the disproportionately large pompadour had informed them that a plague had arrived.

Some monsoon bugs often made a showing after the rains. They'd vexed farmers since the first portals had opened and a new people arrived in Redemption. The bugs liked to feed on vegetables, especially leafy crops, and, after the rains, field tenders needed to constantly patrol the plants and pick the pests off before they did too much damage.

Old stories told of the plague of monsoon bugs long ago in 12 AR and the period of starvation that had followed, but the few elders that remained to tell of those times were just children when it had transpired. As such, little was remembered of the event, and many took it to be an exaggeration.

The story that Gaemri Ip Monjata told was no exaggeration though. The swarm of monsoon bugs had swept in from the north, down through Kendra and Amphis' Ledge and on past Rust to Pools of Light.

Lord Enrion found Actaeon shortly thereafter to tell him that Holdfast was similarly inundated with the pests. To the Lord's disgust, one of his retainers handed Actaeon a large half-through bottle full of the big sapphire bugs. Their bodies were slender, the length of a human hand with three sets of long triangular wings along its segmented body which culminated in gnashing jaws. They snapped at one another as they flew about the large container, looking for something to eat.

A newly promoted Colonel Wronka had come next to tell of the pestilence's arrival in Sunken City. The Colonel came at the bidding of the new Lord Protector of the Niwian Dominion, a Faschin vor Steubick. In addition to a plea for the Prince Engineer's help, the Lord Protector gave thanks for the actions that saved his only surviving son, one of those trapped within Pyramid during the Ruinic invasion.

Much of Redemption's food supply was at risk. If the plague made it to Raedelle and the Colonies, starvation was all but certain across the entire city.

Actaeon figured that some presently unknown factor must have altered with Redemption's ecology to have caused such an inordinate amount of monsoon bugs to thrive. It might even be related to the blue spheres over Czeryn, or the migration of tribals during the siege.

And so Actaeon Rellios Caliburn had ventured out into the Felmere once more to replace the inventory of chemicals that had been lost in the workshop fire.

Accompanying him were Companion Yanelle and the newest Companion, Tarcy Hael, along with Lauryn and two of her light lancers, Tacia Fleg, the scarred, middle-aged warbander, and Varse Perialt, the handsome merchant's son.

The Companions flanked the Prince Engineer until they reached the fetid chemical bog, at which point Actaeon instructed them to follow his exact path.

"Shoulda have yer flank, Yer Grace," argued Tarcy.

"In normal circumstances, I would agree with you, Companion Tarcy. But in the Felmere, one wrong step could immerse you in poisonous quicksand from which there is no escape," explained Actaeon nonchalantly. "Follow my path closely – I am well versed in the traversal of this place."

Tarcy scowled and fell in line behind Yanelle.

"I still don't understand how you're the only person in the city that can deal with any of these Ancient-damned creatures," said Yanelle as she carefully followed Actaeon's footfalls with her own steps.

"You get used to it," said Lauryn with a giggle. "Act's got a methodical approach to these things. Eventually you'll start to see things the way he does and you'll be exterminating these sorts of pests on your own."

Yanelle's eyes widened at the suggestion. "I'll just stick to my sword, thank you." Her eyes swept the landscape carefully, looking for hazards amongst the multi-colored chemical pools and the drifting clouds of smoke that blew across the terrain. She pulled the kerchief that Actaeon had given her more tightly about her mouth. "So you really think that you can find something here to kill these bugs?"

"In the Felmere lies a plethora of chemicals seen no other place in Redemption," explained Actaeon. "It is important that we collect the largest variety we are able. Then we can test out the various combinations and compounds to see if any have efficacy against the monsoon bugs."

"If you say so, Your Grace," said Yanelle. "As I said – I'll stick with my sword."

"Fallen know we may need it," said Lauryn as she forced a smile at the Companion. "Last time I was here, we had to stab a possessed woman in the eye with a pencil and skewer her with Act's halberd."

Yanelle's eyes widened. "What do you mean, a possessed woman?"

"Possessed by the 'Veiled One,' as it fashions itself," explained Lauryn. "It's what we think may have caused the blue spheres that annihilated Czeryn."

"Doubtful," said Varse Perialt as he strode along at the rear of the group, his light lance held as one would a staff. "Sounds more like a cult to me. Possession... what nonsense."

Tacia Fleg shot her fellow light lancer a critical look.

Varse smirked back at her and shrugged.

Actaeon came to a stop between two chemical pools before a thicket of dead brambles and held his fist up. "Your doubt is understandable, Light Lancer. However, I must assure you that the Lady Lartigan's behavior was wholly abnormal to us. We had encountered her before –"

"*Wave* had encountered her before," corrected Lauryn with a smirk.

"Well, I did have a few interactions with the Lady Lartigan myself," answered Actaeon. "But you are correct that Wave had the closest encounter with her. We had known her to be a typical lady of the Niwian nobility. Her behavior while under the influence of the Veiled One was anything but typical. She threatened to kill the Lady Lauryn at one point in order to extort from me the analysis of the artifact we believe caused the Czerynian disaster. It was not the normal behavior of the woman we had come to know through Wave – a woman who had screamed when costumed revelers dumped slime on her during the Monsoon Festival. And yet, when stabbed in the eye and impaled by my halberd, she made not a single sound."

Varse shrugged and offered Actaeon a critical smirk. "Still, Your Grace, I say it's a cult follower. One's behavior can be altered quite significantly when they believe in something. The idea of possession is utter nonsense."

"Keep yer tongue, lad," snapped Tacia Fleg. "It's royalty yer addressin'."

Varse glared at the scarred, older light lancer. "And I meant no disrespect, old woman." He sneered the last two words. "If I choose to share my thoughts with the Prince Engineer, I'll be free to do so without your comments."

Tacia stopped in her tracks and spun to face her fellow light lancer.

Varse offered her a smug look and swept a hand through his wavy mane of red hair, brows raised as if in challenge.

"Both of you can it and get moving!" barked Lauryn as she spun to address them. "Unless you want me to pull your lances and find someone more worthy of the position. I'm sure the Western Rim warband would be happy to have you back."

The pair of light lancers both snapped to attention and fell back into the line snaking along carefully behind Actaeon.

Actaeon turned to offer Lauryn a grin. The young woman was coming into her own, both as an engineer in her own merit and now the leader of a band of light lancers. He couldn't help but to feel a twinge of pride at how far she had grown since joining up with him.

He led them on a winding march until he stopped and turned to the right on a path that led between a yellowish bubbling pool and a steaming green one. As a cloud of green smoke drifted past the narrow dirt path between the pools, it unveiled a thicket of dead brambles.

There was a tiny opening in the center of the barbed thicket that was large enough for someone to crawl through.

"Kerchiefs up," said the Prince Engineer as he pulled his own up over his mouth and nose. "Through there is one of the more useful chemicals."

The others did the same but before Actaeon could lead them onward, Tarcy Hael set her hulking frame between him and the remainder of the path.

The Companion set her hands on her hips. "Ar'l a lead, Yer Grace," she said, her tone brooking no argument.

Actaeon leaned heavily on his halberd and grinned before gesturing forward. "Please do, Companion Tarcy. And, thank you."

The giantess lowered herself down and crawled forward through the opening on all fours. The Prince Engineer followed, Companion Yanelle behind him and Lauryn behind them with her light lancers.

They emerged in a circular clearing amidst the thicket of dead plants, at the far side of which was a pool of thick black liquid, its surface shimmering.

The rest happened so fast.

Actaeon first noticed the blotch of red to his left, the color incongruous with the rest of the colors in that particular section of the Felmere.

The creature, a giant, feathery thing with a beak twice the size of a man's head, tilted forward and ran straight at them.

"Terror bird," managed Actaeon before the creature leapt clear over Tarcy, whose weapon was already drawn.

It landed beside him and he felt a searing pain in his belly that brought him to his knees and then his back, clutching his halberd to his chest.

The creature bounded along in a red flash and, with a crunch, removed Tacia Fleg's head with a single snap of its huge beak.

Behind her, Varse let out a scream and spun to run face first into the wall of dead spiky plants behind him.

The terror bird fled for the opening through which they had entered, but Yanelle was there faster and her sword bit into the creature's flank. It flared open its wings and raised one of its feet toward the Companion defensively, the three curved talons on its foot dripping the Prince Engineer's blood.

Lauryn's light lance crackled to life and she sliced off one of its wings in an explosion of flaming red feathers.

It recoiled and shrieked, a sound which echoed throughout the deadly

Felmere. Tacia's head tumbled to the ground from its open beak before it raced back into the clearing, still shrieking its rage.

The newest Companion lumbered forward to place herself between the Prince Engineer and the threat. She leveled her massive ruinblade at the wounded terror bird.

The gigantic monster finished its shrieking fit and leveled its head at the giantess, snapping its beak violently before charging her, moving forward at a frightening speed, its taloned feet thudding heavily against the soft ground.

With one swift swing of her ruinblade, Tarcy cleaved the creature in half. Its momentum carried both of its halves well past either side of the Companion. Red feathers rained down upon the now blood-drenched woman as she turned to survey the damage.

The bottom of the creature continued to kick and thrash, crashing into the brambles beside a pale Varse until Lauryn's lethal beam brought it to a dead stop.

Yanelle and Lauryn both rushed to the fallen Prince Engineer's side. They opened his leather jacket and lifted his vest and tunic to reveal three gashes across his belly from the terror bird's wicked talons.

"Make sure you get a good sample of that black liquid," said Actaeon with a faint grin. "It would not do for us to have..." His voice trailed off and his eyes fluttered.

"I'll get it, Act," said Lauryn. She left his side to go collect the sample.

Actaeon blinked and his eyes focused on Yanelle. He lifted his right arm to reach for something but winced in pain. "A vial in my left inside jacket pocket."

The Companion nodded and fumbled inside the indicated pocket until she held a small half-through vial.

Actaeon blinked. "Very good. Pour it in... in my mouth," he managed.

Yanelle removed the stopper and poured the contents down the Prince Engineer's throat.

Actaeon felt an immediate warmth suffuse his body, spreading from his belly and outward until it encompassed all of him. It felt like he was hovering outside of his body then – just observing.

Eis, he sent through the Thoughtlink Artifact. *I may be a bit injured. Can you send help to the workshop?*

Act? Eisandre's thought came through immediately and he could feel her concern. *I will do so right away. What happened?*

I am fine, love. Just a terror bird caught us off guard. Must have hit me with its talons. Sorry...

Don't be sorry, she thought. *Just return to me in one piece. I'll see you very soon.*

Aye aye, Princess, he thought with a grin.

His head lolled to the side then, and he saw Varse cradling the dead light lancer's head in his arms, tears streaming down his face. "I'm so sorry, Tacia. I'm so sorry."

Actaeon felt his vision narrow on that horrible sight before darkness overtook him.

THE MAD HISTORIAN

ACTAEON COUCHED HIS HALBERD AND charged forward to impale the deathcrawler that had latched onto Yanelle.

The creature fell away, but warm blood sprayed from the Companion's ripped open throat to soak him. She fell into his arms and mouthed dying words that were lost to him.

They were in the catacombs below the Pyramid, fighting for their lives against the hellish creatures from the abyss.

An ear-piercing scream drew Actaeon's attention and he looked in time to see Caider leap into the tremendous dripping maw of a giant slug creature. Trench and Wave ran forward, each grabbing a leg, but Wave split in half in an eruption of small deathcrawlers that swarmed the giant, bringing him to his knees.

Dazed, Actaeon looked down at the woman in his arms, but it was no longer Yanelle – it was Lady Ruinic with her sharpened teeth and woad-painted face. She hissed at him and bit into his shoulder with those fangs.

He shoved her away and scrambled backward, but she lunged forward to land atop him where she hissed and bit his cheek before she pulled his own dagger from his belt to stab him in the belly.

Actaeon fought through the pain and stretched to retrieve his halberd. He closed his hands around its shaft and slammed the giant blade through Lady Ruinic's sternum.

Only it wasn't Lady Ruinic any longer.

It was Eisandre.

"Act," she said, blood gushing past her lips. "Act."

He screamed then.

The floor shook and then fell away beneath them.

Actaeon continued to scream as the life left his wife's body.

"Act!" she said again, this time a shout.

The Prince Engineer awoke and sat upright in a feverish frenzy. He was still screaming as tears streamed down his sweaty face.

"Act!" shouted Trench. "Act, yer fine! I gotcha, bud. 'Twas naught but a dream. Yer fine." The giant wrapped massive hands around his shoulders and shook him, as if to emphasize each sentence.

"Eisandre?" Actaeon cried out, glancing about the workshop with wild eyes. He was in a cot in the corner of the workshop's ground floor. He saw the loft, rebuilt with fresh timber and it all came rushing back to him.

The end of the war, saving Wave, the fire in the workshop, rebuilding, and the terror bird. All of the things that had happened in the past arc of the moon.

He reached down to where Lady Ruinic had stabbed him in his nightmare and found the tightly bandaged wound from the terror bird's talons. It was tender to the touch, and the skin around it was inflamed. He remembered Seraeta stitching up the wounds and applying a salve after Tarcy had carried him back from the Felmere – Eisandre had been there with the Althean.

"Eisandre is fine, lad," assured Trench. "She's leading the warbands to flush out some of the Ruinic remnants that were making trouble in the Boneyards, but she'll be back in the afternoon to see ya." He released Actaeon and sat back down upon the stool at his bedside.

Actaeon took a deep, painful breath and nodded to his friend.

Trench recognized the bewildered look in his friend's eyes and smiled sadly. "The dreams'll come like that for a time, but it'll end eventually, Act. Consequence of what we've been through. The shock of war and death."

Actaeon listened, his emerald eyes settled upon his friend's scarred face. "Does one ever feel safe again afterward?"

"Can't say it ever'll go away," said Trench, honestly. "Things don't get any easier either, but I'll say I've found one thing to be sure. The flashbacks and dreams get less frequent in time – they won't always dominate the world for ya."

"You spent your whole life fighting battles. How have you coped?" asked Actaeon.

"Share the load," said Trench. "There's a time in the past where I didn't think I should tell such things to others, but now I realize – the more I share with others, the less hard it hits me."

"And how does one go about sharing such a mental load, as you put it?"

"Just gotta tell the stories, my friend," explained the giant. "Not to everyone, but the ones that've been there with you – fought the battles. You've heard Wave and me batting old stories back and forth. We ain't no storytellers, but that's what helps us cope with what we've been through. Makes it real, makes it manageable somehow. That's all I know, Act. That and I'll be here for you however ya need."

"Thank you, Trench," said Actaeon. "I am lucky to have found such a fine friend in you."

The giant grunted out a laugh. "Last I remembered, ya paid me to be yer friend. And aside from that, we've been through Ancestor's tears together – I might need lean on you myself now."

"I'm certain he couldn't support your weight – especially under his current condition," said Wave from the workshop entrance. The mercenary waved an envelope in the air and made his way over to Actaeon's cot, leaning heavily on a crutch.

"You are looking much better," said Actaeon as he watched his friend approach. "Even with the crutch."

"Aye, thanks to you," said Wave. He placed a hand on the Prince Engineer's shoulder and looked him in the eye. "Thanks for not giving up on me, Act. I heard about how hard you worked."

"You have never given up on me, so why should I give up on you?" asked Actaeon with a weak grin.

"True. Well, you aren't done yet," said Wave.

"I am not?" asked Actaeon, genuinely confused.

Wave smirked and gestured to his eyepatch. "Aye, you still owe me an eye. I didn't forget your promise."

Trench roared with laughter. "That's right, Act. Better get working!"

Actaeon began to laugh too. He stopped as quickly as he started, clutching his bandaged side as tears rolled down his cheek.

"This guy jinxed you, ya know." Wave pointed to Trench.

"Oh, not this again!" said Trench.

"He said you'd be fine out in the Felmere without us," said Wave, undeterred. "I'd hold him entirely responsible. It's like he knew it'd happen, but did nothing about it!"

"Nonsense!" barked Trench.

Actaeon held up a hand and shook his head. "Wave, Wave... it is not like that at all. You see, after the lengthy period of time trying to decipher a solution for your deathcrawler babies, I came to a certain realization."

"Ha!" laughed Trench. "Deathcrawler babies!"

Wave put one hand on his sword belt, ignoring Trench. "Oh, and what realization was that?"

"It must be much easier to just lie in bed while everyone else scrambles around for you, than to be the one doing the scrambling," explained Actaeon. "Thus far, my hypothesis holds true. My empirical observations assert as much."

Trench roared with laughter and had to stand up to walk away.

Wave just shook his head and tossed the envelope atop Actaeon's blanket. "Here, wise guy. Open your damned letter."

Trench patted the other mercenary roughly on the shoulder. "Sorry about yer babies, my friend. If it's any recourse, they were damned ugly. Uglier than me if I don't say so myself."

Wave spun and punched Trench in the arm, immediately regretting the action as he stepped back to shake his throbbing hand.

Actaeon broke the wax seal on the envelope and pulled the letter free. He carefully unfolded the vellum and silently read it. "Oh... curious..."

"Aw, c'mon boss, don't hold us in suspense," said Wave.

"Well, it says that the Raja is to be wed in ten days' time," said Actaeon. "To the grandson of the old Raj's brother. Very smart – that will help her consolidate power throughout Ajman."

Trench scowled and looked down at his feet. "If ya say so. Marriage should be about more 'an political inclinations though."

"Oh no. Poor Trench is jealous," said Wave with a smirk. "He'd hoped the Raja'd fancy him after seeing his likeness matched the statue we found." The smaller mercenary was referring to the glowing artifact statue they had found two cycles earlier. It had a face that looked remarkably like Trench's without the scar, which led Actaeon to postulate whether the piece of Ancient technology had the ability to assume a nearby face on its own. Phyrius Ricter and his Waiting Ones cult had taken possession of the statue.

When the giant looked up, there were real tears in his eyes — they dripped down to settle in the deep horizontal scar that crossed through the features of his face. "You were there, ya idiot. Don't ya remember Shulaya?"

Wave wiped the smirk from his face. "Shulaya? Your wife? Of course I remember her."

Trench bared his teeth and narrowed his eyes at Wave. "And ya don't recall her face? Ya don't remember what she looked like?"

Wave blinked his single eye. He stood there silent for a long moment, looking at his friend on the stool beside the Prince Engineer's cot. Finally he shook his head. "I'm sorry, Trench. I don't."

Trench swallowed and nodded somberly.

Silence hung heavily in the workshop as the three men regarded one another.

It was Actaeon who finally spoke. "The Raja looks like her, am I correct? She looks like your fallen wife?"

"Oh shit..." breathed Wave.

The giant simply nodded. He lifted his hand up to cover his face.

Actaeon met Wave's eye and nodded for him to go to his friend.

"I'm so sorry, Trench," said Wave. The smaller man hobbled over to his friend where he perched on the tiny stool and wrapped an arm around him. "I didn't know."

Trench put a big arm around Wave. "I know yer just bustin' my balls on it, an' ya probably didn't realize. It's been buggin' me for a time now though. A stupid thing, but it has me thinking — what if things could be different for me?"

Wave nodded and clutched his friend to him with his free arm. "The Raja ain't Shulaya though, and she won't bring her back to you, however she may look."

Trench jerked back suddenly and pulled away from Wave's embrace. "Ya think I don't know it? My mind's playing me a damned fool."

"Trench," said Actaeon.

The giant stood and held his hand up. "No more. I'll speak no more of this. Time for yer treatment, Act."

Trench lumbered over to the forge and heated up a small kettle until it was steaming. When it was finished, he poured a bit of liquid from it into a tankard and brought that back to Actaeon.

The Prince Engineer accepted it graciously and then looked back to his friend. "So what is this?"

"An herbal remedy that the Althean Matron told me to have ya drink," said Trench. "She said it'd help stave off any infection."

Actaeon probed the swollen area around his bandage with his free hand and nodded. He lifted the tankard to his lips and began to sip the herbal concoction slowly.

"Listen, Act," said Wave. "There's something we've got to tell you."

"Oh?" The Prince Engineer raised a brow as he continued to sip the steaming beverage.

Trench narrowed his eyes on Wave.

"Something I hadn't thought about in a long time," said Wave. He turned to Trench. "Remember Paladin Arandel?"

"Quill?" asked Trench.

"Yes," said Wave. "You'd have heard of him, Act?"

"Indeed." Actaeon set the tankard aside on a workbench that had been pulled up beside his cot to serve as a bed table. "One of the Arandel brothers of legend. The mad historian. They taught children the old stories. He went crazy and tried to kill Ambrosius – fell on his own sword in the process."

"Only he wasn't mad," said Trench.

"How could you know that?" asked Actaeon. "Paladin Arandel is a figure out of legend. He killed himself when I was... what, three... four years old?"

"We worked with him, boss," said Wave.

The giant turned to Wave and gave him a hard look which they shared. After several long lifebeats, the pair of mercenaries shared a solemn nod – the unspoken sentiment passing between them that they would share a piece of their history with their new friend.

"Fought alongside him, learned from his wisdom, witnessed some a' the histories he penned with our own eyes," admitted Trench as he turned to meet the Prince Engineer's eyes.

"We knew him well, Act," said Wave. "Well enough to know he wouldn't have taken his own life. Well enough to know he'd have had a damned fine reason to try and kill Ambrosius."

Actaeon took another sip of the herbal concoction and took a deep breath before arching a brow at his two friends. "So you are trying to say that he had a reason to try and kill Ambrosius?"

Trench grunted and crossed his arms over his chest.

"Paladin Arandel was one of the sharpest men we've had the pleasure to know in our lifetimes," said Wave, looking to the giant for help.

"Aye, that's the truth of it." Trench smiled sadly, twisting the deep scar that ran across his face. "If the ol' historian tried to kill Ambrosius, which all accounts say he did, then Ambrosius needed be killed. I know not why, but I know the hard truth of it."

"And now he's advisor to you and your Princess," said Wave. "Plus, I saw him conversing with Arcady before we left for the front."

"Conversing about what?" asked Actaeon, arching a brow.

"Yeah, how come we're just hearing this?" shot Trench.

"I dunno. Slipped my mind, I guess. There were some... distractions." The mercenary grinned to himself.

"Spit it out," growled Trench.

"Well, Arcady was barking at him like a chained up dog," began Wave. "I couldn't hear much of what they said, but I did hear one thing Ambrosius said back to him. It was, 'The moment she showed up here there was no choice.'"

"So Ambrosius supported Arcady initially then," said Actaeon. "I wonder how deep it went."

"Ancient-damned bastard!" shouted Trench. "I bet he did everything. Sent the tribals after us. Tried to turn Raedelle against Eisandre. The whole damned lot of it!"

"Let us not jump to conclusions, Trench," said Actaeon. He blinked and shook his head. "So what should we do with this information?"

"I guess that..." Wave trailed off and looked at the floor.

"What you are saying is that I should not trust him," said Actaeon.

"We ain't tellin' you what to do, Act," said Trench.

Actaeon grinned. "No, you are just telling me what to do."

"I..." began Trench.

The Prince Engineer's grin broadened and he slapped the giant's arm. "Listen, gentlemen – I am so far out of my league in this new role that it is ridiculous. You both know that. It is your advice and candor, and that of others whom I trust, that I must rely on if I hope to survive this unanticipated endeavor – and I do plan to survive it. I will heed your caution and consider what to do about it. It is a worrisome revelation, indeed. I had thought we could at least trust those who Prince Aedwyn considered his trusted allies."

"Yer not outta yer league, lad," said Trench. "We both fought with ya through Ancestor's tears in the Underforest and if it weren't for yer leadership, we'd not have made it. Pyramid'd still be under Ruinic control. So many more'd be dead."

"He's right, boss," said Wave. "We'd follow you into any situation after what you've done."

"Well, hold up. Maybe not any." The giant chuckled and held up a hand.

"True, true," said the one-eyed swordsman. "Any situation so long as it's not beneath the Pyramid again."

They all shared a laugh at that.

"Well, gentlemen," said Actaeon. "I appreciate your confidence in the job that I have done so far. Without your advice and expertise, I would have not had a chance in shattered Redemption to succeed. For that you have both my thanks and my friendship. I owe you both my life... many do."

Trench stood and moved to stand beside Wave at the foot of Actaeon's cot. The two mercenaries looked at one another and nodded before Wave tucked his crutch under his armpit and they both saluted fist to chest – a Raedellean salute.

Actaeon lifted his own fist to his chest and laughed, causing him to immediately clutch his side. "Enough of that now. Time for me to get some rest – Althean's orders!"

The mercenaries laughed and turned to leave Actaeon in peace.

Actaeon dreamed of using a device he'd imagined during the Second Invasion War campaign. It was a handheld mechanism that could launch a single bolt using a spring coil, many of which could be found amidst the ruins. Whenever things looked hopeless, he'd pull the apparatus from a holster on his leg and quickly fire off a bolt to fell one of his enemies.

When he awoke, Lauryn was there, working at the new laboratory bench on compounds to defeat the monsoon bugs. At his behest, she brought him several sheets of vellum and a sharpened charcoal stick so he could begin sketching his designs for a new invention – one that he thought of as a boltcaster.

He sketched a split barrel that could accept a standard crossbow bolt. The spring coiled around the barrel itself. In a pinch, Actaeon felt he could make his own coiled springs. It would take some experimentation. With the correct heat treatment, the coil would be able to return to its previous shape even after being compressed.

The spring supported a sliding piece that fit inside the split barrel with tabs through either side to engage the coil. A locking mechanism would engage the sliding piece when a bolt was loaded into the firing position and a trigger positioned within a handle angled ergonomically with respect to the barrel could release the slider to fire the bolt.

Actaeon added a lock that would swivel into position using a linkage when the bolt was loaded into place. The lock protruded partially into the barrel and would provide retention for a loaded bolt, so that it wouldn't simply fall out from the barrel upon the device being drawn from a holster. Custom bolts with a detent could be made for the device to take advantage of the lock mechanism, although, even without a detent, there would be some friction to hold a standard bolt in place.

The spring, of course, would not be easy to compress. It would need some sort of mechanism to squeeze it down into the firing position. A crossbow-style stirrup was too unwieldy for something which he intended to be a compact device to fit into a holster on one's belt.

In the end, after multiple iterations through the design, Actaeon found that a lever could do the trick. It would stand up perpendicularly from the barrel, and, when cranked backward so that it was in line with the barrel, it would compress the coil spring when properly pinned to the sliding piece.

Lauryn took his drawings and began to carve the complex wooden shapes needed for many of the parts that would eventually be casted with metal. She broke frequently from her work with the chemicals at the laboratory bench to relax and make the carvings.

Trench worked on coil extrusions at Actaeon's behest, all the while under the bedridden Prince Engineer's guidance. Along with a plethora of curses, the giant toiled along at the forge to give coils the right heat treatment so that they would be durable enough but also would return fully to their original shape after compression.

Wave was charged with setting up a test rig and target for the boltcaster which could trigger the device remotely to minimize risk in case of catastrophic failure.

Companion Yanelle helped the swordsman with the design of the fixture, using the opportunity to tease the man relentlessly, much to the amusement of Trench and Actaeon.

"No, no, no," scolded Yanelle with a devilish smirk. "It has to be easy. If you yank too hard, you'll tug the whole thing off-canter and put a bolt up through His Grace's new loft. Surely, I thought a man with your reputation would know a thing or two about finesse. I guess it's true what they say – reputation's not everything."

Wave rolled his eye and gave her a look. "Ya know, I think I liked you better when you were a nice, deferential Companion."

Yanelle arched her brow mischievously. "Oh, so that's how you like your women? Deferential? Well you won't be finding that from a Raedellean woman. Best stick to your fancy ladies from the central Dominions. I'm sure they're taught to behave in the bedroom in a way that helps men low on their confidence."

There was a crack from the forge as Trench broke a spring coil free. The giant's laugh resounded throughout the workshop and spread like an infection to the others.

Yanelle's mouth curled into a smile before she also began to laugh.

Wave smirked and gave her a playful shove. "If you're all finished picking on the disabled guy, I could use some suggestions on how to improve the trigger."

Yanelle's eyes widened. "Disabled guy? You wouldn't know it to see you in battle. And last I checked, neither your missing eye nor your injured ankle plays any factor in a battle of wits."

"Ah, so the fine lady Companion *does* know how to make a compliment," said Wave with a chuckle.

"If I pay you a compliment, there won't be any doubt about it," said Yanelle. "So you need to adjust the tension on the pull trigger. You can't have it so stiff as to tug the boltcaster's aim, but you also don't want it to shoot off prematurely." She took Wave's hand in hers and guided it to one of the wooden parts on the test rig. "Try shaving away a tad at this part – it'll move a bit more smoothly."

Wave turned to her and smiled, reaching up to brush some stray hairs from his face. "Fine advice, Lady Yanelle. Your thoughts are most insightful." He turned his hand to grasp hers, but the Companion had already withdrawn her hand.

"Better get to work then, pal," said Yanelle. She punctuated her remark with a slap on Wave's shoulder before turning on her heel. "I'd best do a patrol outside the workshop in the meantime." As she turned to walk out, she grinned at Actaeon. "Tough to find good hired help these days, eh Your Grace?"

Actaeon struggled to suppress his laughter and nodded to the Companion.

After she strode out, Wave said to no one in particular, "She fits right in."

"Ain't that the truth," said Trench as he doused the coil in a bucket of cool water, sending up clouds of steam.

"May I have a word with Actaeon?"

All eyes shot to the doorway where stood the Princess, the hilt of the greatsword Caliburn extending out over one shoulder while her Arbiter arming sword rested upon her left hip. Sunlight backlit her blonde hair and glinted off Elphin's Torc about her neck as she took another step into the workshop. "I wish to speak with him alone."

Actaeon's emerald gaze shone with love.

"Of course, Your Grace," said Lauryn with a smile. She doffed her goggles and placed them atop the laboratory bench. "Let's get some fresh air, gentlemen," she said to the two mercenaries. As she walked past Eisandre she reached out to gently squeeze her hand.

"Nice ta see ya, lass," said the giant, placing a loving hand upon the Princess' shoulder as he passed by with Wave close behind, still limping along on his crutch.

When the workshop was clear except for Actaeon, Eisandre looked around as if to confirm the fact and hesitantly stepped farther inside.

"Come, love," said Actaeon. "I have missed you."

At his words, Eisandre rushed to his side. "Seraeta said you should recover quickly." She took one of his hands in hers.

"Indeed. I feel much improved already," said Actaeon, squeezing her hands with his own. "I have much to do which I am already hard at work on – helping to defeat this plague of monsoon bugs, and making prototypes for a new boltcaster weapon that I devised."

"I'm so glad that you have time now to rest and do the work you enjoy," said Eisandre.

"Well, I would prefer not to be resting," said Actaeon. "Though it has not been so horrendous to be injured. My team is doing quite well in helping me develop the ideas I have had. So tell me, what did you want to talk about?"

"I consulted with Matron Seraeta, and she is fairly certain," said Eisandre, her voice quavering. Her grasp tightened on his hand.

"Certain of what, my love?" Actaeon sat up and took both of her hands in his. "You need not be nervous to speak with me. Whatever it is, we shall get through it."

"She says…" began Eisandre, clearly struggling with her words. "She says that I am…" *with child,* she sent through their Thoughtlink Artifact, unable to complete the sentence aloud. Her blue eyes searched out Actaeon's, not sure what to think.

"W… with child?" asked Actaeon.

Eisandre nodded, and tears fell down Actaeon's face, unbidden.

Uncharacteristically without words, Actaeon pulled Eisandre down to him and embraced her tightly. He sobbed against her at the incredible nature of the news.

"That is extraordinary," he said, after a time. "The most incredible creation of our lives. I am so happy."

"I'm scared," admitted Eisandre, in a small whisper.

Actaeon hugged her tightly. "As am I, love. Scared, elated, flabbergasted. I can tell you this much though – we have gone through difficult times beyond imagining to get to this point, and we will get through more."

"I hope you're right, Act," said Eisandre. "There's a tiny life inside me, growing. When I close my eyes and concentrate, it's as if I can feel it – intensely beautiful but so very fragile."

"And we shall protect it," assured Actaeon. "And ensure that our little one has a bright future in this world."

They held one another close and shared a long cry of complicated emotions.

After a time, Eisandre spoke. "I hope you are right, Act. I hope that we can carve out a future for our child in this world. It all feels so uncertain."

"And yet it is in our hands," said Actaeon. "More than ever, the future lies within our own control. We have the power to shape our Raedelle, to shape Redemption itself. It is a frightening responsibility, but we know what we want for our child, and we have the power to make it so."

"Then I hope we have the strength to make those dreams come true," said Eisandre.

"May we have the strength to make our dreams come true," seconded Actaeon. "May we have the strength to carve out a home in this world that brings hope for many generations to come."

"Here it is, Act," said Lauryn as she handed the first working prototype to him.

Actaeon was doing some light stretches and exercises outside the workshop at the instruction of Largrival.

He had wanted to stay to supervise the various experiments and testing being done, but the scarred Althean's tone had brooked no argument.

And so, much to his perturbation, the Prince Engineer did jumping jacks under the strict eye of the new Raedellean Attaché. It had been ten days since his injury, and therefore, he reasoned, her advice was logical, if vexing. He continued to exercise, despite the pain in his side, and his mind's urge to get back inside the workshop to keep working on the problems at hand.

Lauryn's arrival was a much-needed interruption, and he offered her a thankful grin. He accepted the boltcaster, the first device of its kind, from her and turned it over in his hands, analyzing every detail. "It has been tested?" he asked.

"It's been tested several times," said Lauryn, her freckled face glowing as she looked on. "You're holding the most reliable model. It's consistently fired in the test rig without any issue, even after remaining loaded for several days to determine whether the spring coil fatigued, as per your recommendation."

Actaeon smiled at her and turned his attention back to the weapon in his hand. The young woodcarver he'd found in the marketplace earlier that cycle was quickly turning into an engineer in her own right. "It is always an amazing feeling, is it not? To hold a finished design in your hands after so much work and refinement. An idea from your mind's eye, made real by your own knowledge, capabilities, and craftsmanship."

Lauryn smiled and nodded quickly. "'Tis, Act. I love it." She shook her head and thrust a bolt out toward him. "Go ahead then, try it. You invented it, so you oughta do the honors."

The Prince Engineer accepted the bolt and inserted it into the boltcaster's barrel after tilting it upward slightly. With his off hand, he cranked the lever back, in line with the body of the weapon and it snapped into place with a satisfying click. He grinned. "I see you improved the retention mechanism."

His apprentice placed her hands on her hips and cocked her head at him. "Get on with it already. I want to see it in real action, not a test rig."

"Aye aye, Lady Lauryn," said Actaeon, amused.

Largrival crossed her thick arms over her chest. "Don't be hurting yerself with that thing. We can't have ya set back."

Actaeon ignored the Althean. His emerald eyes alit upon the perfect target: a burnt segment of the old loft that had been left leaning against the side of the workshop.

He pulled his goggles down over his eyes, aimed the boltcaster at one of the most intact sections of the lumber structure, and, without hesitation, pulled the trigger.

There was a crack as the bolt tore through the wood target to strike the workshop's stone wall behind it. The bolt spun off to the side and landed in the grass nearby.

Actaeon lifted his goggles and approached the loft segment.

Largrival cleared her throat as the Prince Engineer began to haul it aside. "Be careful."

Actaeon paused and chuckled. "And here I thought you wanted me to get my exercise, Lady Largrival!"

Anger flashed in the eyes of the bald and scarred woman for a moment before it was gone. "Apologies, Yer Grace. Carry on. And please don't call me Lady. I'm an Attaché, not a member of the sniveling nobility."

"Now now, Attaché Largrival," scolded Actaeon. "After all, I am a member of the sniveling nobility now. A title like 'Prince Engineer' puts me in that category, I figure, whether I like it or not."

Largrival grunted her assent and Actaeon shoved the burnt wreck of the loft aside and knelt to inspect the deep chip that the bolt had taken from the workshop's wall.

Actaeon rose and turned to smile at his apprentice. "A remarkably successful design, Lauryn of Lakehold — or should I say, Lauryn the Engineer." His smile broadened.

Lauryn brushed the loose locks of her hair back from her blue eyes and her face turned a deep red. She clasped her hands together before her and then rushed to wrap Actaeon in a tight embrace. "Thank you," she said, her voice muffled against his jacket.

"No, thank you," he said, returning the embrace. "Keep up the excellent work." After a few lifebeats, he added, "We are not done after just one success. There are always more aspects of a design to refine. We must prove that we can repeat this success with a second boltcaster. And, most importantly, I would like to see where you are with the monsoon bug experiments."

"Of course, Act," said Lauryn, stepping back. She ran excitedly back into the workshop. "C'mon, I'll show you!"

"If you will excuse me, Attaché Largrival," said the Prince Engineer. "I must attend to some things now. Thank you for getting me out here to exercise. You should come along – some of this might interest you."

Largrival grunted her disapproval and stomped after Actaeon as he made his way back into the workshop.

NOT TO BE

"LADIES AND GENTLEMEN OF ALL the Dominions of Redemption. We welcome you bear witness on this most transcendent of occasions," announced the tiny Portent, his brightly striped red and gold pantaloons threatening to swallow him. His hands traced a flourishing path through the air toward the tallest spire behind him. Gaemri himself stood atop a spire just beneath that one. "The Majestic One's Joining to one of whom the gods of old and the gods of new sincerely bless."

The feast was like none that had ever been seen before. Multiple spires of different heights had been built within the Pyramid's Sun Chamber, reaching up into the winding staircases of the Skyspiral toward the midday light streaming down from the Pinnacle. Atop each of the spires was a table reserved for honored guests, while staircases that spiraled around the outsides of each spire wound down to hundreds of tables below, occupied by those guests that were not specially recognized. Amongst the lower tables, musicians, dancers, and servers moved to and fro in a chaotic weave. Troops of musicians stood arranged on the various staircases of the Skyspiral above, playing melodies that sometimes competed and sometimes cooperated. Of course, all had fallen silent as the Portent began to speak.

The area where Quronos had exploded was covered in large canvas sheets that were pinned to what remained of the staircase above, effectively hiding the damage. A small troop of Ajmani soldiers in their red and gold attire stood at attention around the canvas, as if to defend the damage from discovery.

Actaeon and Eisandre occupied one of the taller spires, along with the Companions Itarik, Yanelle, and Tarcy, the mercenaries Trench and Wave, the Voice Ithelie in her plain green robes, and Largrival, the new Raedellean Attaché.

Lauryn and her squad of light lancers held a place of honor at another nearby spire.

Other spires were occupied by honored guests from among the Ajmani, Thyrians, Niwians, Shieldians, Altheans, Loresworn, and, Actaeon noted with amusement, Phyrius Ricter and his Waiting Ones.

Portent Monjata continued. "The gracious leader of the One True Dominion has decided to make her special day a day of recognition as well. Recognition of the heroes that liberated our great city from the evil of tribal barbarism. Many came together to help free our great Pyramid from the savage siege. But in the end, just a handful of heroes pulled together to inspire us all. These heroes broke the siege and rescued those who survived the horrors that unfolded within these walls. And so, we recognize them on this day – a day which will commemorate not just the Raja's love, but also the heroism that saved so many treasured lives."

"Oh no," muttered Wave as he listened to the Portent's words.

"This ain't gonna be good," seconded Trench.

"So thus," continued the Portent. "Without further ado, I introduce Her Greatness, the Raja Ajman, who has asked you all together this evening to celebrate love, our faith in the gods of old and the gods of new, and the heroes of Redemption."

As he spoke, the Raja somehow rose up from beneath the floor of the tallest spire, carried by some mechanism from below, her arms lifted in supplication toward the rays streaming down from the Pinnacle. She wore a thin crown of colored jewels atop her head of flowing dark curls. Gold-fringed red silks highlighted the curves of her body while remaining modest and regal. An overabundance of purple eyeshadow with golden accents at the corners that sparkled in the sunlight drew every eye present to her own.

"This, our eighty-seventh cycle in Redemption, may have been our hardest yet," said Nadiya, her voice filling the chamber. "Czeryn has fallen, Travail lies abandoned, a Prince of Raedelle lost to an artifact, the Pyramid besieged by barbarians, two Lord Protectors of Niwian lost to us, and now a plague to steal our harvest, just as the Reap's Call sounds. Hunger's Spur this coming cycle shall be especially poignant. And yet, we are not without blessing – not without light. For any darkness is only in time filled with light.

"Bright heroes strode forth to beat back the invaders, and a chosen few even risked everything to enter the Pyramid and flush out the barbarians so that the lives of survivors might be saved. One such survivor was a daughter of Ajman – an artist and sculptor, Maerdia Bazardjan. Lady Bazardjan, would you do us the honor of unveiling your latest work?"

All eyes fell to the center of the Sun Chamber, where the heavy tarps covered the place where Quronos had exploded amidst an army of Ruinic tribals. Actaeon felt a pang of regret in his gut – there was so much he'd wanted to ask of the mechanical man from Travail.

Mae was recognizable below, with her deep russet skin and simple purple and blue silks. She strode forth toward the Ajmani soldiers in their pantaloons and they parted before her. She directed them to grasp the carefully arranged sections of canvas and, at her command, they tugged them free.

The crowd gasped.

The missing staircase had been rebuilt in shining marble steps up to the remaining section of original elderstone staircase above it. Rising up to either side of the stairs were carved statues of the team that had infiltrated the tunnels underneath the Pyramid.

To the left of the stairs were the survivors. Actaeon with goggles atop his head and a grin on his face, halberd in one hand and a grenado in the other. Behind him was Companion Yanelle with her sword held over Act's shoulder to fend off some unseen enemy. Next in line was Wave, hair tied back in a neat queue, the point of his flamberge rapier in a frozen lunge toward a deathcrawler as its tremendous pincers were about to close around his waist. Captain Xula was next, with his sabre held to the ready. Then Knight Captain Atreena in her full plate armor, piercing another deathcrawler with her sword. Last in the group was Trench, the giant's wicked maul on a downward swing to smash the carapace of one of the creatures.

To the right of the stairs were the fallen. Quronos was first, the carved stone especially fitting for the silvered mechanical man with his two swords held crossed before him. Just behind him was Companion Wayd Arbrigel, pulling a fierce-looking Lady Ruinic out of the way of a giant slug. Hake Rim blasted apart the ground before the slug with his light lance, an effect that Mae had crafted in exquisite detail from the stone, beam and all. And lastly, Geodric Caider was frozen in a leap forward toward the creature's gaping maw.

"Incredible," mouthed Actaeon. The likenesses were stunningly accurate.

"Now the First of the First won't know which statue of Trench to worship," added Wave with a chuckle. His words were met with a shoulder punch from the giant.

"May this statue represent not only the heroes that saved so many on that day, but all the Guardians of Redemption," continued the Raja. "To those who keep our civilization whole and safe for future generations. I dedicate my day of Joining to all of you. Without you, this day would not be possible."

Eisandre clasped Actaeon's hand and leaned in close to him.

Actaeon grinned and touched his head to the Princess' as they continued to watch the Raja.

They continued to hold one another close as they watched the wedding ceremony. As a High Priestess of the Ajman Dominion in her own right, the Raja took the unusual step of conducting her own ceremony, with the aid of her portly Portent and her bodyguard, the Warrioress Calisse T'ra Coletka.

A cadre of Ajmani priestesses dressed all in white escorted a similarly garbed Selnij sil'Mujarba Tri'akala, the grand-nephew of the late former Raj. The young man wore a self-satisfied smirk as he ascended the stairs that wound about the spire, escorted by the priestesses before and after him. He ran a hand through oil-slickened black hair that hung loosely to his shoulders and took his time to wave at everyone as he climbed to the top. The priestess directly behind intermittently prodded him to move faster, and Selnij turned to waggle a finger at her.

When he reached the top, he sketched a flourishing bow toward the Raja and nearly tumbled over. Calisse caught him and roughly lifted him upright. Whatever she whispered in his ear next caused all the color to leave his face. She nodded to him and stepped back to the side, watching him with stern eyes framed within the same purple eyeshadow as the Raja.

After the Raja gave her opening incantations and her cadre of priestesses echoed her words, the Portent and Warrioress lit a ring of fire at the center of the spire before stepping aside and dropping to their knees. The priestesses ringed the perimeter of the spire's top and knelt, heads bowed in supplication.

The Raja gestured for her groom to begin and the pair began to walk around the fire in opposite directions. They went around the fire three times. Each time they passed they grasped hands lightly.

Finally, on the third pass, Selnij spun and began to pursue the Raja in their circuit about the fire.

The fire shifted colors now – from orange to blue, blue to purple, purple to green, and finally to red.

"Huh. Funny," chuckled Trench.

"How so?" asked Actaeon, watching intently.

"Typically the bride turns to pursue the groom," explained Trench with amusement. "But the Raja – she commands."

Selnij pursued the Raja around the fire, and on the third circuit he reached her and dropped to his knees, taking her hands in his own.

The Raja whispered words to him that went unheard by the majority of the chamber.

The groom nodded and, at her gesture, rose to his feet.

They went arm in arm then, about the fire once more. Three times again, but this time as one. On the completion of their third circuit, the fire extinguished and they stepped into the center of the circle.

Selnij knelt and bowed his head before the Raja.

The Raja touched his forehead and intoned the invocation in a voice that resonated throughout the chamber. "And so, these two souls are now bound inextricably into one. May you support and cherish one another together for eternity, or, otherwise, together be damned. This I entreat to you both. A life spent in service to one another so that both may grow."

"I shall do just so," answered Selnij without hesitation.

"And shall I," answered Nadiya with a smile.

The Raja drew her new husband to his feet and touched her forehead to his. They remained as so for several long lifebeats until she stepped back and smiled gently.

Both knelt and grasped hands while the cadre of Priestesses rose and reached over to touch above their heads. They began to hum – a deep warbling sound – while rotating around the newlywed couple. Three revolutions in one direction and three in the other, before they separated and resumed their places at the perimeter.

The Raja Nadiya Ajman and her Consort Selnij Ajman then rose hand in hand to greet those present.

"We thank you for bearing witness to our union," began the Raja. "It honors our Joining and strengthens our bond – the presence of friends and heroes of our city, both those of the One True Dominion and those without. And so, I ask that you all rise so that I may say a blessing over us all."

The Raja paused while everyone in the Sun Chamber rose to their feet. She lifted her hands toward the Skyspiral.

"Old gods and the new, give your wisdom and guidance to all those present this day to celebrate. Guide the warriors' hands in every strike of the blade, every thrust of the spear. Guide the artisans' hands in every stroke of the brush, every shape of the chisel. Guide the statemens' hands in every decision for the future, every appeal to the people. Guide the healers' hands in every stitch to close a wound, every poultice applied to ease pain. Guide the farmers' hands in every tilling of the soil, every spreading of seed. Guide us all in our quest to make a better Redemption, a Redemption worthy of our people. With your wisdom, may we thrive!"

Nadiya lowered her hands and smiled over at her new husband.

"And now," she continued. "May you all enjoy the feast and be merry!"

Raucous cheers went up, and the musicians began to play lively melodies once again.

Servers carrying platters loaded with all sorts of meats, cheeses, fruits, and vegetables strode into the chamber. They first brought food to the tables atop the various spires, and then to the tables below.

As the first of the platters was set before the Raedellean entourage, Actaeon spoke. "Is such a feast really a responsible idea given the monsoon bug plague?"

Trench snatched up a large chicken leg and took a bite out of it. "Let me know what ya decide, boss," he mumbled through a mouthful of meat. "In the meantime, I'll just start sampling."

"Ah seckin dat," chimed in Tarcy before she tore into a chunk of cheese.

Wave shrugged. "When in Pyramid…" He began to pop some grapes into his mouth.

"As the food is here now, I would not suggest allowing it to go to waste," said Actaeon. "I merely wished to express my doubt as to the soundness of the decision involved in its origination."

Nobody answered the Prince Engineer – they were all too busy eating.

Actaeon grinned and began to collect an assortment of food for his own plate.

As they ate, Calisse T'ra Coletka, the Raja's Warrioress, ascended their spire. She wore red and white silks wrapped tightly around her body, over which was her thick leather armor, dyed red for the occasion. A more conservative touch of the same purple eyeshadow with gold flecks as the Raja wore adorned her face. At her side was her wide falchion with its downwardly curved hilt.

Wave's eyes widened and he stood from his chair to trace a graceful bow. "Why, Lady T'ra Coletka, don't you look lovely tonight. For what do you grace us with the honor of your presence?"

Trench coughed and nudged Wave. "Maybe tone it down a notch?" he suggested in a whisper.

Wave smirked and ignored his friend.

"Actually, the honor is all mine," countered Calisse. She bowed formally to the Princess and her Prince Engineer. "Tonight I dine to celebrate my Raja's Joining, and I do so in the presence of great heroes of our time. The Raja sent me to see that you were adequately served."

Eisandre swallowed a bite of bread and spoke. "Please extend our congratulations to The Majestic One. The ceremony was lovely, and we are honored by the statue that commemorates those who helped break the siege."

"Yes, it was very impressive," added Actaeon. "Please give our compliments to the Lady Bazardjan."

"I will do just that," answered the Warrioress. "I trust that the serving staff has not left you wanting?"

"Not at all," said Actaeon. "The food is delicious, and the music is delightful."

"It gladdens me to hear it, Your Graces."

"Come," said Wave, pouring out an extra tankard of ale. "Join us. Let us drink to the Raja and her new husband's health and good fortune."

Calisse smirked at the mercenary and sauntered forward to accept the tankard.

Wave lifted his own high. "To the Raja and her new husband. Long may they live and bring prosperity to Ajman Dominion and all of Redemption!"

"Hear hear!" cried the others before everyone drank.

Calisse lifted her tankard again. "And to the guardians of Redemption. The ones that broke the siege of Pyramid and restored the safety of our civilization. May their services not be needed again for a long while."

"I'll second that," said Trench.

Everyone drank to that as well.

Calisse set down her tankard and smiled. "The Raja hopes that you will be able to greet her personally later on. Now then, I must check in with the other heroes present. Would anyone care to escort me?" She offered Wave a lingering look.

Yanelle stood up and brushed aside her shock of red hair. "It would be my honor to escort you, Lady T'ra Coletka." She smiled over at Wave, whose jaw had dropped open, and offered him a wink.

Calisse blinked in surprise and nodded. "I would be most grateful, Companion..."

"Yanelle," answered the Companion. "You may call me Yanelle."

"Pleasantly met, Yanelle," said Calisse.

"You've no idea," said the Companion as she rounded the table. When she reached Wave, she gave him a light kiss upon the corner of his lips. "In case we don't get the chance ever again," she whispered with a smirk.

"But... but..." stuttered Wave, his face turning a shade of red that nearly matched Yanelle's hair.

"Hold that thought until I get back," Yanelle said. She took Calisse' arm gently and led her away down the stairs. Whatever she whispered into the Warrioress' ear made the Ajmani woman blush.

"I'm really starting to like that lass," said Trench with a big grin that tugged on his deep scar.

"She certainly fits right in," said Actaeon with a smile.

Trench slapped Wave on the back. "Sit down, Wave. Yer food'll get cold! 'Sides... whatever she told the Raja's Warrioress on the way down tells me they're gonna be awhile."

Wave's surprised expression slowly morphed into a smirk of amusement. "I think I'm in love," he said.

"Aren't we all?" asked Trench. He raised his tankard again. "To love!"

The others raised their tankards.

Eisandre and Actaeon shared a loving glance.

"To love," they echoed and drank.

The conversation dissolved into laughter and feasting that mixed with the music. And with the drink, the time passed quickly.

When most of the others had gravitated down to the floor of the Sun Chamber to join in the revelry, Actaeon placed something into Eisandre's hand.

She opened it to find his Thoughtlink Artifact. She was about to speak, but Actaeon put a finger to his lips and gestured for her to remove the sister artifact from her ear.

She did so and Actaeon upturned a bowl of bread, dumping the contents on the table before he used it to cover the two artifacts. That done, he began to tap out a random rhythm upon the underside of the wooden bowl using his fingers.

"What is it?" Eisandre asked, distracted and confused by his tapping.

"Ambrosius... we may have reason not to trust him," said Actaeon.

"Wise Ambrosius?" asked Eisandre. "He was advisor to my brother and my father before him. And he voiced support for my own claim to Raedelle."

"Yes, and come to think of it, both Aedwyn and Branwyn met their ends in ways that remain shrouded in mystery," said Actaeon. "Your father ambushed and killed on a hunting trip and your brother trapped inside the pillar artifact, which could have been orchestrated. It remains curious to me that nobody was trapped inside with him. There stands the possibility that Wise Ambrosius had something to do with both incidents."

Eisandre tilted her head to one side as she listened to her husband. "Do you have any evidence to support your suspicions?"

"No," admitted Actaeon. "I realize that this is strictly conjecture at this point. However, Wave and Trench told me something which has me worried." His eyes met the brilliant blue of her critical gaze and he continued. "They knew Paladin Arandel well. Do you remember the legend?"

"Of course. It was the cycle I was born," said Eisandre. "The mad historian tried to kill Wise Ambrosius and ended up dying upon his own blade."

"The mercenaries tell a different story." Actaeon continued to tap randomly on the underside of the bowl. "They describe a Paladin Arandel that was a master of his mental faculties and a warrior who would not have fallen upon his own sword. Trench said that if Paladin tried to kill Ambrosius, then he thinks the old historian had a good reason to do so – a reason that was lost when he died."

Eisandre found herself staring at Actaeon's fingers as they drummed a pattern that filled her mind with distraction.

"The rest is intuition on my part, but conjecture at this point," continued Actaeon. "There may be reason not to trust the man, but I have no proof that he had anything to do with the unfortunate death of your father or disappearance of your brother. It may be that they are not related at all, but your mention of the fact that Wise Ambrosius served the two previous leaders of Raedelle, and they both met mysterious ends, raised my suspicion. Of course, correlation does not infer causation, so no conclusion can be drawn. Though of course, causation cannot be ruled out without more information either."

Eisandre frowned slightly. "Do you need to do that?"

Actaeon raised a brow. "Do what?"

"Tap like that," she said.

He followed her eyes to the bowl. "Uncertain. It is a precaution."

"Could you stop tapping, then?" she asked. "I'm having trouble concentrating on your words."

"I could," said Actaeon. "But it is not advisable. If I do not tap like this, we might be eavesdropped upon through the Thoughtlink Artifacts."

Eisandre looked genuinely confused. "Who could eavesdrop upon us? There's only two of them."

"Are there?" Actaeon asked, looking skeptically at the bowl as he continued to tap. "Remember who gave them to us."

Eisandre lifted a hand to cover her mouth, concealing a deeper frown. "Wise Ambrosius. Do you think there could be more?"

"It is certainly possible," he said. "Is anything known of how they ended up in Raedellean hands?"

Eisandre shook her head. "Not that I've been told. I could ask my mother."

Actaeon narrowed his eyes. "Do you trust her, Eis? She supported Arcady's rise to the leadership of Raedelle."

"I trust you," Eisandre admitted. "And Trench and Wave and Lauryn. And Itarik – some of the other Companions too, Yanelle and Tarcy. Anyone that fought on the Wall with us as well – Jezail, Ithelie, and the others. I trusted my brothers and my sister, but they are dead or missing. I trust the Arbiters and Altheans, but now many of them have died as well. No, I'm not sure that I trust my mother. I don't know her well enough. I don't understand her."

Actaeon took her hand in his free hand and offered her a broad grin. "More people to trust than I have ever had in my life. And all because of you."

Eisandre smiled and slowly traced the inside of his palm with one of her fingers, feeling all of the creases there.

"There is one more thing I must tell you," he said. "Before we left Caliburn Castle to fight the war, Wave saw Arcady arguing with Ambrosius. He did not hear much of the conversation, but he did hear one thing. Ambrosius said to Arcady, 'The moment she showed up here, there was no choice.'"

"So he was for my uncle then," she said.

Actaeon nodded and squeezed her hand.

"That is understandable given that he likely knows I am Lost. Were there any other reasonable choice, I would have chosen them over myself also," said Eisandre. "There's no way to be sure that he had anything to do with the terrible things that my Uncle did, or for my brother becoming trapped inside the pillar artifact in the first place. But I agree with you, Act. We cannot trust him."

"I am sorry to have to tell you this, Eis," Actaeon said with a sad smile.

"There is no need for an apology," said Eisandre. "But what do we do about this?"

"I had considered that, actually," began Actaeon. "If we simply cease the use of the artifacts, it would be suspicious. What if instead we choose a codeword? When either of us says the codeword, it can mean that we wish to remove the artifacts because of some confidential discussion that is about to take place."

"Agreed," said Eisandre. "And we could decide upon other codes as well, so that we might discuss places and people over the artifact without any eavesdroppers being able to understand."

"Fantastic!" said Actaeon. "I like that. For the main codeword, how about Boneyards?"

"Boneyards?"

"Aye." He grinned. "What easier topic to work into a conversation than the place we first met?"

"May I have the next dance?"

Trench towered over the Raja and her new husband, where they stood in the center of the Sun Chamber, conversing with guests.

The song had just ended and the musicians were ramping into the next melody.

Selnij opened his mouth to object, but his new wife spoke first.

"For one of the Guardians of Redemption, it would be my honor," said the Raja. She smiled at her new husband and excused herself.

Selnij gave the giant a suspicious look before he sauntered away and snatched up one of the priestesses to dance with.

Trench bowed until his head was below the Raja's. He extended a hand which she took without hesitation.

"Rise, Trench," she said, gently lifting his chin with her palm. She drew him toward an area where others danced and guided his hands to the appropriate locations.

The giant blushed a deep red that accentuated his hideous scar. "The honor's all mine, Yer Greatness."

"Position and rank are not all that is important in this world," said the Raja. "Accomplishment, merit, and skill warrant even more respect, I'd venture."

Trench smirked. "Says a woman that's won control of her Dominion and commands the respect of them outside of it. A woman who looks out for her people, from what I've seen."

The Raja led the dance, drifting to and fro gracefully.

It was all Trench could do to avoid stomping upon her delicate slippered feet.

"I do care about the people of my Dominion and of Redemption entire," admitted the Raja. "And I know you do too. The fact that you serve the Prince Engineer tells me so much about you as well. For the work you are doing helps to build up our city and the people within it. I hope to call you a friend, Trench."

"Of course ya may, Yer Greatness," said Trench.

The Raja smiled and led him to twirl her as the music began to crescendo.

As she twirled back into his arms, she dipped her head elegantly and spoke. "So what is it that you see in me, Trench – if that is your real name? I am not unmindful of the way you gaze at me."

"Atrilles," said the giant. "And I see a ruler that can truly lead her people. A Raja for Ajman that will finally put the good of the people before prestige."

"Tell that to the soldiers whom I've sent to their deaths in the north," said the Raja, her brow creasing in pain.

"I would in a lifebeat," said Trench. "I've seen what ya've done for the common people during the floods earlier this cycle. You'd not have wanted those soldiers to die. A leader's got tough decisions to make. I trust ya make 'em with the best interests of yer people in mind."

"Indeed I do," she agreed. "But that's not the whole truth, is it, Atrilles? There's something else you wish to tell me."

"Aye, Yer Greatness," admitted the giant. "It's that..." She led him to twirl her again. "...That yer the spitting image of my late wife, Shulaya. It's why I can't take my eyes off you. You look like the love of my life."

"My, what a beautiful name – Shulaya. And a lucky woman, to have had such a man as you, even if her life were to be cut so short," said the Raja. "Alas, it is not to be – you and I. As much as we both might want it to be." The Raja lifted Trench's big hand to her mouth and kissed his knuckles. "You are a good man, Atrilles of Ajman."

The side of Trench's face stung suddenly, and a moment later, he realized he had been slapped. He turned to find the Raja's groom winding up to hit him again. The wrist he caught in one hand and the neck in the other. The giant lifted Selnij from the floor by his neck and growled down at him.

The music died abruptly, and the Sun Chamber drew silent with a collective gasp.

"Be good to yer wife. The Fallen know, ya don't deserve her," said Trench before he dropped the groom to the floor.

Selnij fell to his knees and grasped his throat, gasping for air, his face red with rage.

Trench bent in a stiff bow toward the Raja. "Many blessings upon yer marriage, Yer Greatness. I wish ya much luck and happiness."

The Raja smiled a smile that reached her eyes. "Thank you for your well wishes. We shall remember them."

Trench rose and offered her a smile that tugged painfully at his scar before he pivoted and walked away.

The giant ascended the Skyspiral with determination. The music had begun again a short while ago, but he continued on – away from the woman who looked so much like his dead wife and the angry husband that could never treat her as well as she deserved.

At one point he passed several Ajmani soldiers in their red and gold pantaloons. They looked unsure as to whether they should try to apprehend him, so he smiled one of his terrifying smiles at them.

They averted their eyes and continued on their way.

Trench stormed up the spiraling stairs, a man on the run from his past, until he finally found his way to the Garden Terrace. There he took a deep breath of fresh air and strode out among the amalgam of plants from various regions throughout Redemption.

He brought a hand to his face and shook his head. "Idiot," he said of himself as he continued along one of the winding paths on the open terrace through the fragrant red plants of Adhikara's Flamewoods. How appropriate, he thought, that he would march straight into the section of terrace flora that would remind him of what he was running from.

With heavy footfalls, he continued on until he was past the plants from the Flamewoods and into an area rife with the fronds and sparse ground cover of southern Thyr.

"Slow down, would you?" came a familiar voice.

When he turned around, there stood before him a woman with curly locks of blazing red hair that hung down to her chest. Her green eyes looked up at him – the skin above her right eye stretched and rippled from her old burn.

"Jezail," he said. "What're ya doin' here, lass?"

"What in Cracked Redemption do ya think I'm doing?" retorted the Captain of the Wall Breakers. "I'm looking for you, ya idiot... your word, not mine." She smirked and placed her hands on her hips.

"Why would ya be lookin' for me?" asked Trench.

Jezail stepped forward into his shadow and cast a determined look up at him, her green eyes sparkling. "Because I want you, you fool."

Trench let out a guffaw and slapped her roughly on the shoulder. "Oh, please. I'm way too old and ugly for ya."

Jezail slapped him right back on his shoulder and grinned. "Fortunately for me, you don't get to decide that."

Before Trench could react, the much younger woman stepped forward. She wrapped her arms around his neck and climbed up into his arms to kiss him.

Trench felt his lips open to her kiss, unbidden, but then he shook his head and stumbled back, away from the warbander. "But, lass, it hasn't yet been an arc of the moon. Yer still in mourning."

"And you're not?" Jezail stripped away her jerkin to reveal the hard nipples on her bare chest and tossed it aside into the field of ferns. The redhead smirked and began to unlace her trousers. "You said it was rage that kept you going after she died. I don't want rage, Trench. I can't do rage. I want something else. Give me something else."

The giant trembled and looked back down at the archer as she kicked free of her trousers and boots. He couldn't help but admire her naked body – the twisted burn scars that ran down the right side of her to end at her hip only made her more real and lovely in his eyes.

"Ya sure, lass?" he asked.

Jezail stepped forward to take his trembling hands in her own and grinned up at him. "Damned right, I am."

Trench smiled a soft smile and leaned forward to wrap her in his arms and kiss her tenderly.

And there in a field of soft Thyrian ferns, high up in the Pyramid's Garden Terrace, he gave her several somethings else.

SABOTAGE

ALL THE MOST POWERFUL LEADERS in Redemption gathered in the sparsely furnished Arbiter Pyramid Command chamber.

This was the first time Eisandre had been there since she'd been expelled from the Order. Now, instead of being an Arbiter, she sat as a Princess, representing Raedelle. It was a strange feeling to be there now in such a different capacity. The last time she had been in this chamber, she had been stripped of her title of Knight Arbiter.

Beside her at the rectangular table was Actaeon, his arms folded and his halberd leant against the table.

To her other side was Faschin vor Steubick, the new Lord Protector of Memory Keep and the Niwian Dominion. The Lord Protector's dark brown coif of hair was carefully arranged in a large arc that started at the top of his head and looped around to end in a clip on his collar below his chin. Every time he turned his head to look around, his hair came uncomfortably close to the Princess' face.

Next to Faschin was Fatuan Molvich, the Elocutor of the Allfather. The old, frail man in his blue plate armor was the effective leader of the Keepers, and rumor had it that he was the real power behind Faschin's rise to Niwian power after the death of Thernaxis. A heavy wooden cudgel sat on the table before him, its head covered with old red stains and its handle wrapped in well-worn strips of leather. Broken luminaries were inset at random intervals into the head of the weapon.

To his left was Supreme Captain Jarval of Thyr. Amodeus wore his dress uniform – his queue of red hair standing in stark contrast with the white jacket. His curved silver helmet rested upon the table before him atop a scimitar with jewels set into its hilt.

At the other side of the table sat the Raja with her Warrioress, Calisse.

Next to them was Indros Immerai Zar, the Prince General of Shield, who sat stroking his long beard of thin black hair shot through with gray as he regarded those present with jet-black eyes that peered out from under his tall black and red mitre. The writheblade at his hip could be heard crackling even as it hung hidden beneath the table. He was joined by his two children, Lady Endira and Lord Enrion.

Lady Endira, who was known as the Steel Rose, was dressed in a scale mail dress that was tightly fitted to the curves of her body. She folded her arms under her bosom and cast a scornful look across the table at the Prince Engineer.

Actaeon noted her glare and grinned before raising a hand in greeting.

The Shieldian Lady harrumphed and turned her head away.

Her brother, mistaking the greeting for him, smiled at Actaeon and dipped his head politely.

At the head of the table sat Paladin Arbiter Cignith sof Iarnus, garbed in his plain gray uniform, but he had a presence that commanded attention even despite the plethora of high-ranking officials present.

At his one side sat Matron Seraeta of the Altheans, and on the other was Kryo of the Loresworn. The spectacled man's head was barely above the table – of his torso only the tops of his shoulders were visible, garbed in shimmering brightweave cloth.

"I thank you all for attending today," said the Paladin Arbiter from the head of the table. "It is with singular purpose that we have asked you here, and we hope that you will heed our words and weigh their importance for the future of Redemption."

"This meeting is timely, for it is overdue that the Ajmani are held accountable for their actions against Shield," intoned Indros, settling his jet-black eyes upon the Raja.

Calisse stood up, her hand falling to the hilt of her falchion. "Retract your words imm-" She was interrupted by the Raja's gentle touch upon her hand. The Warrioress quickly returned to her seat.

Nadiya smiled thinly at Indros. "Prince General, you know as well as I that our own soldiers have turned against us. We've borne witness to as many instances of Shieldian soldiers killing Shieldians as we have Ajmani soldiers killing Ajmani. There's a force up north that is beyond both our comprehension – it has obliterated the Czeryn, and now it has taken control of our soldiery. Our greedy attempt at expansion has cost us too many of our peoples' lives."

Indros looked at the Raja, expressionless.

"I do hope you don't mean to tell me that your intelligence reports from the field are so incomplete," said the Raja, meeting the Prince General's gaze, unphased.

"We should be open with her, father," said Enrion.

"Hush," barked Indros. "I'll be the judge of what we should do."

"He's right, for once," said Endira with a condescending look toward her brother.

"Forgive my children – they are naive and disrespectful," said Indros. "This time, however, they are correct. We have encountered the same. We know not what to make of it at this point. At first we were convinced it was an Ajmani deception, but now we are quite certain it was not."

The Raja nodded slowly. "I hope then, Prince General, we can work together to decipher this great mystery. I have been nothing but honest with you, and I hope you can give me the same honor."

"Hmm," grunted Indros. The Prince General of Shield turned to Paladin Arbiter Cignith. "What are we here for anyway? This had better be relevant."

Cignith steepled his fingers together and looked down his hawkish nose at them. "As relevant as it ever has been, given your discourse. As the leaders of the newly formed TriForge, we wish to establish this as the first meeting of a Redemption Interdominional Council. It is our hope that such continued meetings can help the Dominions organize together and resolve any differences with everyone present. Eventually, it may even result in an Interdominional Alliance."

"Very smart," said Amodeus. "You've succeeded in subjugating the Altheans and the Loresworn and now you wish to crown yourself King is it?"

The Prince General stood abruptly, the crackling from his writheblade rising in volume, no longer hidden beneath the table. "Shield will bend the knee to none," said Indros.

"Nor will the One True Dominion," seconded the Raja.

"One True Dominion," scoffed the Niwian leader, Faschin. "Ha! What a story! Hear that everyone? Go home – our Dominions aren't even real."

Most of those present stood to leave along with Indros.

Actaeon slammed the butt of his halberd against the floor with a crack. When everyone paused, he stood slowly, sweeping his emerald gaze across those present. "This idea was mine. Would you do me the honor of hearing it out?" He waited.

The Raja folded her robes and returned to her seat. "Of course. The Prince Engineer is a friend of Ajman."

Indros cocked his head to the side and regarded Actaeon critically before shaking his head and returning to his seat. "The Prince Engineer has aided us on more than one occasion. Shield will hear what he has to say."

Beside his father, Enrion nodded approvingly.

"As will Thyr," said Amodeus. "Raedelle led and organized the effort to break the siege of the Pyramid. We'd all not be sitting here now if not for your effort, Eisandre and Actaeon Rellios Caliburn. Please speak."

"And you'd listen to this... this... Prince of blasphemers?" shouted the Keeper Elocutor. "Look at him and behold! Adorned with artifacts from head to toe. Is this the evil influence we deign to allow in our midst?"

Actaeon grinned. "I have zero artifacts on my toes."

The Niwian Lord Protector spun to face Actaeon, the culmination of his outlandish arc of hair striking Eisandre in the chin. "I agree with the Elocutor. Why should we listen to you?"

The Princess grimaced and swatted the hair from her face.

Faschin thrust himself to his feet. "Well then, I've been insulted enough for one day. You can take your petty Council and choke on it! The Niwian Dominion will not abide such uncivilized behavior."

The Lord Protector spun and nearly ran straight into Endira and Calisse, the two women having circumnavigated the table to block his egress.

"Sit down," said Endira. "You'll hear what he has to say."

Fatuan opened his mouth to protest, but the Raja's Warrioress spoke first. "You too. Don't make me see if that armor is real."

The Niwian and Keeper leaders retook their seats. Both of them glared at Actaeon.

Behind them, both Shieldian Steel Rose and Ajmani Warrioress folded their arms and barred the way out.

"Oh, come now," said Actaeon with a smirk. "Do not offer me your disdain. I fought beside Thernaxis at the Battle of Glass Spire. I saw the last of the Greens fall. Were you there, Lord Protector Faschin? I think not. You were safe in your home, awaiting your rise to power when the Lord Protector who led his troops aggressively from the front inevitably fell.

"I only stand here in this room because the Keeper Second Division was part of the force that held back the enemy long enough in the Underforest for Lauryn and her Light Lancers to save us. You will not see anyone from the Keeper Second here though – they all perished that day. Something that you undoubtedly already know, Elocutor Fatuan, especially if you indeed speak with your Allfather about the truths of this realm.

"In fact, one of your Keeper Captains was an essential member of the team I brought in to infiltrate Pyramid and break this siege. An effort that, I have been told, managed to save a large group of survivors holed up in the Mirrorholds – Saint Torin's Hold specifically. One of those survivors, Lord Protector, and correct me if I am wrong, was your son, Torot."

The Lord Protector looked down at the table. Beside him, the Keeper Elocutor continued to glower at Actaeon.

"So for all those who have died and all those who have lived among your people in this Second Invasion War, I ask that you hear out what I have to say," concluded Actaeon. He leaned against his halberd heavily and raised one brow.

"Your words do naught to mask the ev-" began the Keeper, but Faschin cut him short.

"Enough, Fatuan," said Faschin. He lifted his head up to look at Actaeon. "You've made your point, Engineer. Go ahead then. Speak. And make it good."

"You have my thanks," said Actaeon. "And I shall try my best to do just that."

The Prince Engineer met Eisandre's gaze for a long moment, and she nodded her approval before he stepped away from the table to pace the length of the room. As he walked, he spoke. "Why an Interdominional Council? And why might we eventually hope for an Interdominional Alliance? Not, my friends, to allow any one of us to control Redemption. Let us face it, each Dominion is much too powerful for the others to eliminate it. And why shed such needless blood upon the foundation of our city? No, we should be working together to make Redemption better, not separately, and certainly not opposingly. A Dominion has been eliminated, and even erased much as the Ancients were from the bones of their very city. An alien force powerful enough to do this exists to the north, and it takes control of Ajman and Shieldian troops alike, forcing them upon those who once were their brethren.

"And yet we fight on, because this city which once belonged to the Ancients now belongs to us. Because we represent humanity, and humanity stands for discovery and exploration and understanding and love, and we need more time for that – to uncover all the great mysteries of Redemption. Because, whether prisoner or warden kin, or both, we are the same as the Ancients by all evidence that we have thus discovered, and because we refuse to accept the same fate that they succumbed to. Because we battle for a future where our children can thrive and survive and become more than we could ever have imagined." Actaeon smiled at Eisandre then.

"Together," he continued, "we are better able to combat plagues, pestilence, dangerous artifacts, outside invaders, and alien beings that can take control of our very armies. Working together we are better able to find and understand and employ the artifacts that can serve to make Redemption what it once was, to feed and shelter all our people – regardless of belief or culture or birth. And to finally uncover the secret of our own origin – why we were sent here, where we came from, and what this place is."

"Some ambitious plans, Prince Engineer," said Thyr's Supreme Captain. "I like it, but it sounds unrealistic. How do you propose we do all this?"

"I shall second that question," sneered Faschin.

"An excellent question, Supreme Captain Jarval," said Actaeon. He paused his pacing to grin at the Thyrian. "Perspectives. It is all about perspectives. In brainstorming the various problems I have encountered as an engineer, I have found that perspective is the most effective approach to uncovering the solutions I have required. And is that not what we have here? The most diverse set of perspectives ever assembled – that and the most powerful leaders of our realm. But our ability to set into effect the solutions we need lies not in our wealth, nor our power, nor our strength, but our different approaches to life, our disparate ways of looking at things.

"And yes, I include the Keepers in that statement, Elocutor. There is a particular Knight Captain that I have had the pleasure to share much conversation with. In speaking with her, I have come to realize that even the Keeper's aversion to technology can help us, by tempering this group with a perspective of caution toward many artifacts, because some are dangerous, and could doom us all if used the wrong way. And so I ask you all, lend your perspectives to this Council so that we may all share in the benefit. To carve out a lasting home for ourselves in Redemption. To make a tomorrow that our children will thank us for."

The Loresworn leader, Kryo, pushed his lenses up along the bridge of his nose and cocked his head. "Then allow me to lend my perspective, Prince Engineer Actaeon Rellios Caliburn. It is high time you heeded the warnings of the Loresworn. Travail needs your —"

He was interrupted by a voice at the door to the command chamber.

"Excuse me, Paladin Arbiter, there is a visitor for you," said Corvin sof Haringar, one of the technical Knights. The Arbiter had a strange look in his eyes.

Cignith stood up so quickly that his chair nearly toppled backward. "I thought I left instruction that this meeting was not to be interrupted!"

Actaeon's jaw nearly hit the floor as the next man stepped into the room. A man with a clean-shaven pate wearing a ramshackle mix of leather armor and pieces of hammered metal from the ruins. He wheeled a large, canvas-covered object into the room on a rickety dolly, but that wasn't what drew Actaeon's attention. It was the black cross that was painted on the dark skin of his face, dividing it into four neat quadrants.

Eisandre was beside Actaeon in an instant, her sword drawn and raised before her.

Actaeon touched her wrist. "The Veiled One has the Arbiter too."

"I know," she murmured.

Behind them Indros stood from his seat. "What is the meaning of this intrusion?"

The cross-faced raider wheeled the dolly to the side and began to speak in monotone. "You will leave my city at once, or meet the same fate as those known as the Czeryn."

"And just who do you think you are?" asked Faschin.

"The Veiled One," said Actaeon.

"This one knows," said the raider, gesturing to Actaeon. "This one, who activated the device which will bring your demise should you fail to heed my words." The raider opened his mouth and the next words seemed to blast, like a spike, into the minds of all those present. "LEAVE MY CITY!"

Indros calmly strode from his spot at the table and walked past where Actaeon and Eisandre stood, his iron shod staff clicking with every other step. "Shield does not respond kindly to threats." The Prince General pulled his writheblade free of its ceramic sheath and in a crackling blur, swung it upward through the raider, slicing him into two neat pieces.

The dead man's blood splattered all over Corvin's plain gray tabard and face. The Knight Arbiter didn't even flinch.

The smell of ozone permeated the room, accompanied with another nauseating smell – that of burnt blood, bone, and flesh.

The room was still for a lifebeat, then another.

The Knight Arbiter reached for his sword and Indros swung the crackling writheblade toward him.

Eisandre stepped forward and in a fluid set of motions, she drew her two-handed sword, Caliburn, and struck forward with the pommel of her arming sword.

Corvin crumpled to the ground like a sack of bricks, having been struck in the temple by Eisandre's pommel.

The outer half of Indros' writheblade went flying across the room and fizzled out – cut in two by the artifact sword Caliburn.

The Prince General cried out as the remaining half of the artifact blade overheated in his hand. He dropped it to the floor and it began to smoke.

A hush fell over the room as everyone waited to see what would happen next.

Indros leant his staff against his shoulder and clutched his burnt hand. "So the legend is true. You may be thankful I like your husband so much."

"And you may be thankful that you didn't kill this Knight Arbiter," retorted Eisandre.

"Touché, Princess," said the Prince General. "Now, let's discuss what this previously whole man meant when he said, 'This one, who activated the device which will bring your demise.'" Indros lifted a crooked finger and jabbed it toward Actaeon.

Actaeon ignored Indros and walked over to pull the canvas from the dolly. What he saw there caused the color to leave his face.

Underneath, tied to the dolly with hemp rope, was a smooth elliptical cylinder with two spherical ends. It tapered more narrowly at the top and there were seventeen Ancient symbols on it, all glowing red and blinking in steady synchronization. The symbols were arranged in concentric circles – a single symbol in the center, six in the first ring, and ten in the outermost. As he watched, he noticed the blinking was steadily increasing in rate.

Kryo was at Actaeon's side in short order. "Not good – this is not good. Is there a way to deactivate this? Are you aware of one?" The Loresworn knelt down and hit several sequences of symbols in quick succession, but there was no response from the artifact. The symbols continued to pulse faster and faster.

"None that I am aware of," said Actaeon. "It may not have been designed with a deactivation method in mind. Or at least not an obvious one." The Prince Engineer knelt and pulled several folded pieces of vellum from his jacket. He rifled through them until he found the correct one. He laid it on the floor and began to touch the symbols in the activation sequence order that he had deciphered long ago when the cross-faced raiders had kidnapped Lauryn and him. When that failed, he tried the sequence in reverse, to no avail. The blink rate continued to increase.

"Stand back, I'll smash it open," said Fatuan, the Keeper lifting his heavy cudgel.

"I had a similar thought," said Actaeon. "But not in quite that manner. Not even a sword will pierce the material of this artifact."

"What are your thoughts, Prince Engineer?" asked Kryo.

"There should be a seam at the bottom," explained Actaeon. "It is likely that the Ancients loaded the payload into this device from that end. If we can open it there, perhaps we can separate it into pieces and render it inert."

"And if not?" asked Amodeus Jarval.

"Then we shall meet the Czerynians," said Actaeon.

Kryo ran his fingers along the smooth cylindrical bore until his fingernail clicked against the seam Actaeon had described. "Yes, it is here."

"How can we possibly open it? You yourself said even a sword wouldn't do it," said Enrion Zar.

"With your father's writheblade," said Actaeon. "Or what is left of it. Quickly, someone cut some strips of material so that we might wrap the hilt."

"We should flee while we still can," suggested Faschin.

"Then you are as daft as you look," spat the Steel Rose. "One of these things eliminated everyone in Czeryn. How far can you run before it finishes whatever it is doing?"

The Niwian Lord Protector offered her a pale look in return.

"Enough arguing with that sop, Lady Zar," said Calisse, the Raja's

Warrioress. "Unlace me!" She approached Endira and turned her back so that the Lady could access the laces of her leather cuirass.

Endira arched a brow and smiled seductively. "I suppose that's one way to spend our final moments."

"Oh stop it, woman," snapped Calisse. "Get this off of me so we can wrap the hilt for the Prince Engineer."

The Steel Rose pouted, but then promptly hiked up her scale mail dress to remove a dagger sheathed at her thigh. With a careful tug and stroke, she deftly sliced through the laces of Calisse's cuirass.

The women laid the cuirass on the table and began slicing it into strips, which they tossed toward Actaeon.

"Alright, let us get the artifact up on the table," said Actaeon. He used his hooked dagger to cut through the hemp ropes tying it to the dolly.

Together, Eisandre, Fatuan, Amodeus, Enrion, and Cignith hefted the device and placed it carefully on the table.

Actaeon wrapped several of the strips carefully around the hilt of the smoking lower writheblade half. More smoke began to rise and fill the room as the leather burned.

"I'll fetch some water," offered Seraeta, and she stepped from the room.

Actaeon nodded and hefted the writheblade, which crackled and sputtered intermittently as it struggled to keep operating, filling the room with a sickly ozone scent.

"Hold the device still, and be prepared to start rolling it away from me," said Actaeon.

Eisandre climbed onto the table and took up position on one side of the artifact while Amodeus held the other.

Enrion flinched away as the Prince Engineer held the writheblade aloft.

Just before Actaeon could make a cut, Kryo placed a hand on his shoulder. "Are you certain this will work? What if you inadvertently pierce the contents?"

"I am certain of nothing, except that if we try nothing we will die," said Actaeon. "If I pierce the contents, it will do one of two things: activate the contents if they are volatile on their own, or have no effect if the contents in that portion are inert and require mixture with another solution or energy source. Here is hoping that it is inert and that the writheblade energy does not activate it."

Kryo nodded in agreement. "It must be done. I agree it is our best option."

"Less talking and more cutting?" suggested Amodeus.

Actaeon grinned nervously and began to slice into the artifact's housing along its seam, the fractured writheblade jerking in his hands as he cut when it lost power at intervals. He guessed that the thickness of the smooth metal material would be no more than a finger's width based on his experience with similar artifacts. With any luck he would be correct.

When he was a quarter of the way through, Eisandre and Amodeus began to roll the device away from him while he continued to cut.

The overloading heat from the writheblade began to burn through the leather wraps on the hilt and the smoke began to sting his eyes.

"Pull down my goggles," Actaeon ordered, and Kryo pulled them down.

Just as the heat began to grow to a level that was too much to bear, Seraeta arrived with a pitcher of water and began to pour it slowly over Actaeon's hands.

Actaeon loosened his grip on the hilt as he cut to allow the water to wick the heat away from the broken artifact.

The broken, sputtering writheblade carved a jagged path through the device as he cut. The smoke from it continued to fill the room and was banking down from the ceiling when tiny cylinders dropped down from overhead and it began to rain inside. The rain soaked them and the smoke in the air disappeared, but the cooling relief of it was welcomed by Actaeon, whose hands felt as though they might catch fire at any moment.

Everyone present watched, rapt, as the operation took place amidst the growing chaos of the room. When two Knight Arbiters poked their heads in to see what was going on, Cignith ordered them to remove Corvin and secure him.

Eisandre and Amodeus continued to roll the device slowly as Actaeon sliced through it in jerky, sporadic movements.

As the symbols rolled upward so that they were visible once more, everyone gasped. They were blinking with incredible rapidity now, perhaps three flashes per lifebeat – and everyone's lifebeat was faster in that moment, for certain.

Just as they were about to complete the circumferential cut, the writheblade sputtered one last time and died in Actaeon's hand. Along the seam there was but a single thin piece of material still attaching the top cylinder to its bottom sphere.

Actaeon tossed the dead artifact aside and plunged his hands into Seraeta's quarter full pitcher, sighing at the cool relief on his skin.

"Cracked Redemption, what do we do now?" asked Enrion.

The Raja brought her clasped hands to her chest and began to pray.

"We need a sword – the strongest one here," Actaeon looked at Eisandre.

"But didn't you say a sword couldn't pierce this thing?" asked Enrion.

"I did say that," said Actaeon. "Let us try it now."

Eisandre stepped down from the table and pulled the greatsword Caliburn from her back once more. She blinked as the rain from the ceiling ran down her brow and into her eyes. Without hesitation, she carefully swung the blade toward the sliver of material that held the two halves together.

There came a sharp pop and her blade recoiled. When she blinked the water from her eyes once more, she saw that the sliver had been broken.

Actaeon took her face in his hands and kissed her. "You are amazing, Eis. Thank you."

"I am?" asked Eisandre, confused.

Actaeon grinned and gestured to the bottom of the artifact. "Alright, let us pull it free."

Actaeon, Eisandre, and Calisse held the main body of the device still while Enrion, Cignith, Amodeus, and Fatuan pulled the bottom free, working their fingers into the cut that Actaeon had made.

The bottom came free to reveal a cluster of silvery-white hexagonal rods sticking from the bottom.

Everyone turned to look at Actaeon, including Kryo.

Actaeon shrugged. "Pull them free?"

They began to slide the rods out, one at a time, until they were all out – seventeen in all. Although they were still connected to the artifact by glass ropes that were somehow fused to their ends.

"What's next?" asked Enrion.

"Everyone out of the room," said Actaeon. He rolled the artifact along the table a bit so that the glass ropes were spun into a tight bundle and then he stepped off of the table to retrieve his halberd.

Everyone began to file out of the room, except for Eisandre, who shook her head. "I will not leave you."

Actaeon kissed her forehead and touched her belly. "You have more than just us to think about now, love. Please – I need to know that you are both safe. I do not anticipate a major issue with this."

Eisandre grabbed him by his jacket and kissed him hard. "Come back to us."

Actaeon grinned. "Yes, my love. Now go, before none of us come back."

Eisandre reluctantly left the room.

The moment she was clear, Actaeon wasted no time. He hefted his halberd and brought the blade down heavily upon the bundle of glass rope.

"The Prince Engineer should most certainly go, since he is responsible for our present dilemma," said Indros.

The device sat in pieces upon the table, rendered inert, as all of the soaked Dominion leaders stood around it in the puddles of water that had rained down from the ceiling, deliberating their next actions.

"Being held against one's will and forced to study an artifact in order to rescue a friend is not the same as being responsible," countered Eisandre.

Indros stroked his beard, miming a thoughtful expression. "Ah, so the value of two lives outweighs the value of all lives? I hadn't considered that."

"I'm sure he did what was necessary, father," said Enrion.

"Tell that to the families of our dead soldiers!" snapped his sister, Endira.

"Enough bickering," said the Raja. "Prince Engineer, will you tell us your side? If you knew the risk to all Redemption, why did you show them how to use this device?"

Actaeon nodded. "Thank you, Majestic One. I did not know the extent of the risk, but I suspected the device was dangerous. The cross-faced raiders always pursued me with indifference to their own safety and indeed to their very lives. It struck me that they needed me for something of the utmost importance to them. Of course, it was possible that they required some sort of succor from a device, but that didn't seem likely since the raiders took their own lives before being captured by myself or my friends. That left something nefarious."

The Keeper Elocutor slammed his fist against the table and shouted. "And you helped them! Blasphemer!"

Actaeon grinned over at Fatuan. "Lord Protector Faschin, I believe we would all appreciate it if you would heel your lapdog."

"The Keepers are no one's lapdog, you ruinthrall!" shouted the Elocutor, slamming his fist against the table again.

Faschin kept his gaze firmly fixed upon the table.

Paladin Arbiter Cignith was not so quiet. "I'll have no quarrel at this table. We are here to work together for the betterment of Redemption. Cease your shouting, and let the Prince Engineer finish, Fatuan."

The old Keeper threw his hands up in the air, rolled his eyes, and turned to stride a few paces away from the table. "Fine, Cignith. Have it your way."

Actaeon continued. "My plan was to escape with fellow Engineer Lauryn, my notes on the artifact, and Lady Lartigan too, once I found that she was being held there. We managed to escape and flee south into the Felmere, but that was when Lady Lartigan stole my dagger and held Lauryn hostage. She asked to exchange the notes for Lauryn's life. At that point, it was obvious that she was under the Veiled One's control. I could not allow her to escape. Together Lauryn and I fought her to recover the sketch. She did not survive the encounter, but it always worried me that she had seen the contents, since her mind appeared to be not her own. Clearly, I was correct to be concerned, for somehow she relayed the information back to the Veiled One before she died."

"Is that all then?" asked Matron Seraeta.

"No, it is not," said Actaeon. "I agree that I am responsible for this, even though I fought to prevent the secret from slipping into evil hands. I am deeply sorry that I could not have done better. There is nothing I can do to bring back the people that were lost in the artifacts' cataclysms, but I will help you now. I will help you defeat the Veiled One.

"I only ask one thing in return." The Prince Engineer scratched his right arm through his jacket. "I need all of your help in this endeavor. Give this Interdominional Council a chance. Let us work together from this day onward."

"Ajman will be a part of this Interdominional Council," the Raja chimed in first.

"As will Thyr," said the Supreme Captain.

"And Raedelle," asserted Princess Eisandre.

Indros steepled his fingers together. "Shield will not turn their backs on such an effort."

All eyes turned to the Niwian Lord Protector.

"Oh, you're waiting for an answer?" asked Faschin. He was working, and failing, at arranging his hair back to its previous state before the ceiling's rain had soaked it. Now he looked like a waterlogged rat. "Yes, yes," he said, waving a hand dismissively. "Niwian will be a part of your little meeting."

"Then so shall the Keepers," said Fatuan.

"Very well then," said Cignith. "Let the records show this to be the first official meeting of the Interdominional Council." He gestured to the table before him. "And quite a successful one, if I might add. We closely avoided total annihilation. What will our next actions be?"

"The Veiled One is cornered," said Indros, stroking his beard. "Shield and Ajman sweep in from the east. Raedelle and Niwian from the south. Thyrian ships prevent any escape into the Great Sea." He raised his hand into the air and clenched it into a fist. "We choke the life from the snake."

The Supreme Captain nodded. "Our ships will be ready."

"As will the soldiers of Ajman," said the Raja.

"You are neglecting one very important factor," said Actaeon.

Indros' eyes narrowed upon the Prince Engineer. "Oh no, as I said earlier, you will accompany the advance in case any similar tricks as the one which played out here earlier occur."

Actaeon grinned and waved his hand dismissively. "Of course I will be there, as I already said. However, do not forget that this Veiled One has somehow taken control of countless of your people already. In fact, it has just taken control of Knight Arbiter Corvin sof Haringar, as we witnessed – and I know the Knight Arbiter to be a sharp-witted individual, not one to lose control of his mind easily. It would be best if we arrive prepared."

Indros offered Actaeon a rare smile, his lips curling thinly around his mustache. "Your time on the battlefield has paid well, Prince Engineer. What did you have in mind?"

"Keep to the same plan as you described, only use those forces as diversions," explained Actaeon. "In the meantime, a hand-picked team will attempt to locate the Veiled One and destroy it – whatever it is. I believe that once the source of the Veiled One is defeated, the rest of its forces will revert to whatever previous state they once held. Also, if you allow me one week, I will attempt to create a method to block the ability for this hidden enemy to take control of our minds."

Kryo pulled his lenses from his eyes and wiped them with a cloth. "And how could you possibly know how to do such a thing?"

Actaeon grinned. "I have an idea. You shall be the first to know if it succeeds."

Kryo grunted and replaced his lenses.

"I will accompany your elite team, Actaeon," said Enrion.

Endira blinked at her brother, her mouth twisting into a scowl, "And why should you?"

"Because," said Enrion, "I am the most familiar in Shield with the way the Prince Engineer works. So I'll be the best equipped to help him."

"I've helped him too!" snarled Endira.

"Hush," said Indros. "It was the boy's idea. He will go." The Prince General cast a doubtful look upon his son. "Do not mess this up."

Endira huffed, but kept her tongue.

"You've my word, father," said Enrion, though the color had already left his face.

The Raja's Warrioress, Calisse, looked at the Raja, who smiled and nodded, before she stepped forward. "I will also join you on behalf of the One True Dominion."

"It is a good idea to have a representative from each of us to make sure of the mission's success," said the Paladin Arbiter. "Might I recommend we all provide at least one representative to the Prince Engineer's force?"

There was a scattering of assent throughout the chamber.

"Very good. Please provide the names to Prince Engineer Actaeon Rellios Caliburn by the end of this week," said Cignith. "There is much now to be done. Let us adjourn."

PREPARATIONS

CAN YOU HEAR ME NOW?

I can, responded Eisandre, before removing the cast metal pot from her head. "How do you know this is even possible? We've tried hundreds of ideas at this point." She scrutinized the heavy cast pot in her hands and added, "Besides, it would be very difficult to wear something like this in the field, especially if one expects to do important things like, for example, see."

Actaeon smiled and took the pot from her to set it aside on a workbench. He placed both of their Thoughtlink Artifacts inside it. "Anything is possible, Eis. Likely is a whole other story. It may be quite the unlikely solution, in which case we shall most surely fail to find it before the expedition. And further, we must consider that even if we find a method to block communications through the Thoughtlink Artifact, it does not mean that it will also block the Veiled One's attempts to control our minds."

"Why do you believe them to work in the same manner?" asked Eisandre.

"In both cases, thoughts are being sent through the air somehow. If we can find a way to block or disrupt one, then it stands to reason it may block the other one with the same method," explained Actaeon.

Eisandre's brilliant blue eyes lit up with an idea. "We could test the solution on Knight Arbiter Corvin to see if it is effective."

Actaeon grinned and reached out to brush her cheek gently. "You will be an Engineer yet, love."

"But I am the Princess of Raedelle," said Eisandre, confused.

"No reason you cannot be both," said Actaeon. "And, yes, the thought to test it on Corvin occurred to me as well, but whether or not it is successful might alert the Veiled One to what we are trying. It might then have the advantage over us. So, no, we shall have to go in with the solution blindly, unfortunately."

Eisandre smiled over at him, with fondness. "Your mind is remarkable. I marvel at how you consider so many possible factors all at once."

"I have just had time to think about it, is all," said Actaeon, blushing.

"You're modest too" The Princess reached out to touch his cheek and was surprised at what she found there. "You have whiskers!" She pulled her hand back and then reached out to brush his cheek again, feeling all the little hairs.

"Have I?" Actaeon grinned and lifted his hand to hers. "I suppose I have forgotten to shave them with all the distraction of late."

"May I... kiss them?" she asked, surprised at her own spontaneous request.

Actaeon laughed, a bright and happy sound that he realized he hadn't heard in much too long. "Of course!"

The Princess leaned forward to kiss his cheek and was caught by surprise as her husband swept her into his arms and kissed her deeply. She opened her mouth to him to kiss him back, but he was already nuzzling her cheek with his and kissing her earlobe.

Eisandre laughed and half-heartedly pushed his face away. "Act, that tickles! And you know what your kisses there do to me."

Actaeon continued to nibble at her lobe as she squirmed in his embrace. "We have the workshop to ourselves for now," he whispered in assurance. "Everyone is out on errands at the moment."

"But what about when they return?" she offered, casting a worried look at the door.

"We shall have more than enough time before they get back," he assured his wife again.

She felt his stubble brush against her other cheek as he shifted to kiss the lobe of her other ear. The familiar warmth arrived in her belly, although now she was keenly aware of the life in there as well. She gasped as Actaeon ran his hand down her body through her clothes. The sensations somehow felt more intense than ever. "Oh…"

Actaeon smiled and kissed her again. He lifted her to sit upon the clear part of the workbench and ran both hands down her body to the laces of her plain gray trousers, which he quickly worked free.

With the laces out of the way, he tugged her trousers and undergarments down. She lifted her hips to help him with them and he pulled them down to her boots.

The Prince Engineer wasted no time in kneeling before his Princess, and the feeling of his whiskers against her thighs made her giggle uncharacteristically. She reached down to push him away, but then came another sensation that made her fingers knot in his unruly hair and pull him hard against her.

"Saints, Act," she murmured, and it wasn't long before her body tensed and she lost control, falling backward onto the, thankfully mostly clear, workbench. Her shoulder, however, caught the edge of the cast pot, and it crashed to the ground in a cacophony of sounds that covered her own cries as it rolled away.

Unsatisfied, Eisandre pulled him up along her body to kiss him hard. "I need you," she informed him, in between kisses as she kicked her legs free from her boots and trousers. "Hurry!"

Actaeon grinned as they kissed and worked his own trousers free.

And just as she felt him at her entrance, she pushed him away. "Wait!"

Actaeon stopped, a confused grin upon his face. "I thought you said to hurry."

"I did, but…" Eisandre searched out his emerald eyes with her own. "Is it safe for the baby?"

"Yes, love. The baby will be fine," said Actaeon with a loving smile.

"You're sure?" she asked, still concerned.

"Indeed. I am sure," he said.

Eisandre nodded quickly, accepting his assurance. "Then hurry up," she said, once more pulling his hips against her own.

"Yes, Your Grace," laughed Actaeon, before complying and leaning forward to kiss her again.

And outside the workshop, a red-faced Companion Yanelle sent the returning mercenary duo away so that the Princess and her Prince Engineer could continue their experiments uninterrupted.

"Ah, just the man I'm looking for."

Actaeon came to a stop and turned to find Warlord Berk standing before him, reflected a dozen times over in the floor, ceiling, and walls of the Mirrorholds.

The last Czerynian Warlord tugged on his scraggly white beard and regarded him with weary brown eyes. "I hope you've some time fer an old friend. You see, there's some business I'va been meaning to discuss with you."

"Of course, Warlord Berk," said Actaeon, leaning forward against the shaft of his halberd. "What is it you wish to discuss?"

"Well, ya see I know Czeryn's a part of Raedelle now as per our little agreement, and so I've come to you in search of an answer," explained Berk.

"Warlord, I can assure you that we are still seeking a long-term location in which your people might settle down," said Actaeon. "Much has been afoot, and so –"

"Let me interrupt you there, Prince Engineer," said Berk, raising a hand. "I trust that you're looking, and I know that events have slowed the process down. It's those events I came to talk about. Not to worry."

Actaeon arched a brow. "What about the events?"

"Ah, see, now there you're playing stupid," said Berk. "Everyone an' their grandmammy's talking about this Veiled One. Forces are on the move. Activity in your workshop's picked up. I'm no slouch, much I may look like one. I know you plan to move against him – against the enemy which destroyed all my people."

Actaeon nodded slowly. "You surmise correctly, Warlord. I take it you wish to be involved?"

"Ah, the insightful Prince Engineer..." said Berk with a smirk that tugged at the burn which covered his left cheek. "I'll owe ya an ale next time we drink together. Ya see, there aren't many of us Czeryns left in Redemption. We mayn't 'ave lived the best lives, but we were people too, and so were the slaves we kept. An' if I might say so, I'll be seeing to it we have our vengeance for all those dead."

Actaeon nodded and grinned. "Then you will join my group during the assault, Warlord Berk. And if I have anything to say about the matter, you can plunge your blade into the heart of whatever the Veiled One ends up being."

"Aye, that's the way of it," said Berk, putting an arm around Actaeon's shoulders. "I knew ya'd come 'round. Just you let me know the time and place."

Actaeon came to a halt before a certain set of quarters in the Mirrorholds and rapped against the door several times with the butt of his halberd.

The door opened shortly and Enrion Zar poked his head out. "This better be – oh, Prince Engineer Rellios Caliburn, it's a delight to see you. One moment." He withdrew his head. "Kiroko, dear, put on a robe, we have a guest."

"If I am interrupting you, I would be happy to return later," said Actaeon with a grin.

Enrion opened the door fully. "Nonsense. Come on in, Actaeon. There's someone I'd like you to meet."

The Shieldian Lord led the way inside the quarters. Unlike Eisandre's spartan Mirrorhold quarters, this room was adorned with lavish tapestries, strange artifacts, and painted wooden furniture of the finest craftsmanship. Ornamented blades of various lengths and shapes were displayed in a half dozen weapon racks arranged throughout the chamber.

Upon a settee sat a young woman with eyes that projected wisdom. Her black hair was pulled back tightly in a bun and held in place with a set of piercing metal sticks arranged in a broad star pattern. She stood and drew her white and black striped robe tightly about her before dipping her head politely to Actaeon. Her eyes, however, never left his face and her lips scrunched together in a funny smile.

"Lord Zar, please introduce me to this intriguing man who wears goggles atop his head and carries so many interesting things," she said.

"Lady Kiroko Xan, might I present to you Actaeon Rellios Caliburn of Shore, Prince Engineer of Raedelle. This is the man who helped me with my plans to make Lazi's Tomb defensible," said Enrion, beaming.

"Prince Engineer, allow me to introduce to you my betrothed, Lady Kiroko Xan of Amphis' Ledge. Her family is one of the great benefactors that have supported our efforts to create a permanent Hold in Lazi's Tomb," explained Enrion.

"Ah, the one who toppled the towers," said Kiroko, sounding impressed.

Actaeon bowed his head politely. "A pleasure to meet you, Lady Xan. And congratulations are in order on both of your betrothal."

Kiroko walked up to Actaeon and gingerly took his hand, which she lifted to her lips to kiss lightly. "The Engineer who helped make our Lazi's Tomb a place of hope for the future is always welcome in our home."

Actaeon blushed and looked over at Enrion. "It was my pleasure to be of assistance in the matter."

Enrion smirked and waved Actaeon over to a nearby sitting area with several couches. "Come, my friend. Sit and join me for a drink, will you?" Without waiting for an answer, the Lord began to pour out several glasses of rice wine.

Actaeon lowered himself into one of the couches and let his halberd rest against his shoulder.

Enrion first offered him a glass and then handed another to Kiroko.

Actaeon accepted it graciously and when everyone held a glass, he raised his. "To your betrothal."

Enrion and Kiroko joined him in a drink before Enrion sat on the opposite couch and Kiroko retook her seat a short distance away on the settee.

"So, my friend. Congratulations are in order for you as well," said Enrion. "To have risen so quickly and so unexpectedly to power in Raedelle. You have done quite well."

"It is certainly not a position I ever aspired to," admitted Actaeon. "Nor really even desired. If I were not in love with the Princess of Raedelle, I would have gladly turned down such power."

"Oh, come now, man!" said Enrion with a broad grin. "You cannot tell me that you don't revel in the ability to make the right decisions for your Dominion. I'm sure you're just being humble about it."

"I should much prefer to spend my days in the workshop, inventing solutions to problems and studying the artifacts of Redemption to try and solve the city's mysteries." Actaeon took a long sip of his wine and felt the liquid warmth spread in his belly. "And yet, the quandaries of our realm are multifarious and unflagging. It is not yet a safe place for one to freely accomplish such work. Not yet a safe place for our children to live in."

"Will it ever be really?" asked Enrion.

"I am beginning to realize that the battle to keep Redemption safe is a never-ending one," said Actaeon, cradling his glass in both hands. "It is something which we must fight for unceasingly, lest our apathy allow corruption and danger to seep back in unchallenged."

"And what better place to be than leading such an effort?" asked Enrion in seriousness.

"Perhaps you are right, Enrion," said the Prince Engineer. "Politics and war were never my strength though."

"Says the man who helped lead the liberation of Redemption from Ruinic tribal invaders and then somehow got all of the Dominion leaders to sit down for the first time in who knows when." Enrion smirked and sipped his rice wine.

"The Lord Zar speaks truth, Prince Engineer," said Kiroko, from her settee. "You underestimate yourself."

"I would always prefer to underestimate myself and seek improvement than to overestimate myself and meet my demise," said Actaeon.

"Such wise words," said Kiroko. "You don't help your case."

Actaeon looked over at her and grinned.

"So, Actaeon," said Enrion. "What brings you to my humble quarters? Is there something I might do for you?"

Actaeon leaned forward and set his glass on the low table between the couches. "Actually, yes. There is something."

And as Actaeon told him, all of the color left the Lord Enrion Zar's face.

"You'd better not be avoiding me."

Trench looked up from the foundry where he was pumping the bellows as he worked to heat and then hammer rivets in place to attach the strange form that Actaeon had cast to the back of the open-faced helm.

The giant let the arm of the bellows fall and set down his workpiece. "Course not, lass. It's just –"

"Just I haven't seen you in ten days!" interrupted Jezail. The redheaded Captain of the Wall Breakers put her hands on her hips and tilted her head to cast a dour look at Trench that was only enhanced by the way the burnt skin was drawn widely around her right eye.

"Act's had us busy, lass," said Trench, spreading his hands.

Jezail stepped forward and took those hands in her own. She looked up into his eyes and smiled faintly. "That's not it, old man. It's not it at all. No, I think you're scared."

Trench chuckled at that, his lips curling upward to push against the ugly scar that bisected his face. "I ain't scared, lass. That's the truth of it. It's just that I didn't know what that night meant to ya is all."

Jezail smirked and cocked her head to the side in a way that sent a flurry of red curls tumbling. "You weren't sure if it was just a rebound from Varisk for me, is that it?"

"Cuts right to the point this one," said Trench with another chuckle. "If'n that was the case, I'd reckon you'd not want to have big ol' Trench chasing you about with flowers."

"Aw," said the archer, bringing one of his hands to her breast. "What I'd not give to have the gentle giant chase me with flowers."

"I'm not exactly known for being gentle, lass," said Trench.

"You're gentle when it counts," said Jezail in a tone that made the giant blush. "And stop calling me lass. If you can lay with me, you can call me Jezail, or did you forget my name already?" She gave him a searching look.

Trench's jaw dropped. "I... I..." He looked momentarily flabbergasted, but then he shook his head and set his jaw. "I ain't Wave, ya know. I remember yer name, Jezail. Jezail Vren, Captain of the Wall Breakers."

Jezail let out a musical laugh and playfully shoved the giant. "I'm just breaking your balls, big man. I know you know my name. And no, you're not just a rebound from my beloved Varisk. You're one of the kindest, most beautiful souls I've ever met. You make me feel safe and loved and beautiful and like a woman again. I'm glad you've got that scar on your face." She reached up to touch it – to trace its brutal path with her finger. "Because, Trench, without it, too many others would so easily see what a beautiful person you are inside, and I'd not stand a chance of having your arms around me."

Tears crept out from Trench's eyes to pool down into the deep scar. "It ain't so easy, lass, er – Jezail."

"Because of Shulaya?"

"Because of Shulaya," admitted Trench, and he began to sob.

Jezail gently pulled him down to his knees and held his head against her breast while the giant cried.

"Hush, my sweet Trench," she whispered. "You will never forget your

Shulaya just as I will never forget my Varisk. I have room in my heart for you both. I only pray that you can say the same."

Trench lifted his head to look into her shining green eyes. He nodded. "There will always be a place for you in my heart, Jezail."

On his knees the same height as Jezail, Trench took her face into his big hands and kissed her ever so gently, while beside them the fires of the foundry sputtered and died out.

"I've brought it, Act."

Lord Enrion Zar motioned to the four Shieldian soldiers behind him just outside the workshop. Two of them carried a strongbox between them. One of the soldiers moved to open it.

"Stop!" shouted Enrion. "You will not open that in my presence. Have I not made that clear?"

The soldier snapped back to attention. "Sorry, My Lord."

"Don't be sorry," snapped Enrion. "Just remember your orders. Is that too much to ask?"

"Aye, My Lord," came the reply.

"It *is* too much to ask?" asked Enrion, rolling his eyes.

"No, My Lord," responded the soldier as he maintained crisp attention.

"Then do not make me ask again, lest you be dispatched to patrol the lower sections of the Rust superstructure." Enrion cracked his knuckles and regarded the soldier with an impatient look.

The soldier let out an audible gulp. "Aye aye, My Lord. I will make certain."

"Good," snapped Enrion before he returned his gaze to the Prince Engineer. "I do not wish to be here when it is opened. You understand, I am sure."

Actaeon nodded and took a step closer. He could hear the violent and steady hum from within the strongbox. "Yes, I understand, Lord Zar. I am concerned though."

"Concerned about what?" sneered the Shieldian, in an outright failure to hide his disdain for the situation.

"What if this turns out to be the solution we are searching for?" asked Actaeon. "You have already volunteered to be a part of the force that will utilize said solution. If this proves to be the answer, you will need to wear it quite closely to be protected from the Veiled One."

"I'll do what I must," spat Enrion. "But I pray to the Wardens of old that your testing fails in this case. You still have time. You'll find something else – I'm certain of it."

"I cannot promise you that any solution would be better than this one," said Actaeon.

"Well I can promise you that *any* solution would be better than this one," said Enrion. The Shieldian Lord turned and began to stride away. He glanced over his shoulder. "I'd wish you luck, but in this case I do hope that you fail."

Once Enrion Zar was well away in the distance, the previously scolded soldier looked up at Actaeon questioningly.

Actaeon leaned upon the shaft of his halberd and nodded. "Go ahead."

The soldier clicked open the latch of the strongbox. Slowly, he lifted the lid to reveal a pair of writheblade daggers. The artifacts crackled and sputtered as the smell of ozone permeated the air around them.

Actaeon nodded. "That will do. Please, bring them inside."

The soldier snapped shut the strongbox and they brought it inside and set it down upon one of the workbenches at the center of the workshop.

"Thank you," said Actaeon. "You may go."

The soldiers saluted sharply and spun to leave.

Companion Yanelle shut the door behind them. "Do you wish me to stay, Your Grace?"

"Of course you may, Companion Yanelle," said Eisandre. She was seated on a stool at one of the workbenches beside the laboratory shelves, cradling her now slightly rounded belly.

Actaeon carefully reopened the strongbox to reveal the writheblades, crackling with their pent-up energy.

Yanelle brought over the two prototype helms that Trench had made and Actaeon carefully lifted each writheblade and inserted it so that the crossguard was between the two protrusions in the custom casting that was riveted to each of the open-faced helms. Once they were in place, with the blade sticking up from the back of the helm, Actaeon slid a pin in place to retain them and secured the pin with a length of twine.

The first helm he donned himself before passing the other to the Princess.

Eisandre inspected the crackling artifact blade before lifting the helm to don it herself.

Alright then. Can you hear me, love? inquired Actaeon through his thoughts.

He received no reply.

"It seems you can no longer hear my thoughts," said Eisandre, after some time.

"I cannot," said Actaeon excitedly. He offered her a broad grin.

Nearby, Yanelle clapped her hands together. "You've done it?"

"Perhaps we have," replied Actaeon.

He tried several more times to send thoughts to Eisandre, to no avail.

As an additional test, Actaeon gave his Thoughtlink Artifact to Yanelle, and after confirming that her thoughts were sent to Eisandre correctly, they added the helms. The reception of their thoughts was still blocked by the presence of the writheblades.

"Absolutely fascinating," said Actaeon. "The energy of the writheblades either absorbs or otherwise blocks the thought transmissions from the Thoughtlink artifacts. I would say that this is a successful test. If our assumptions are correct, then wearing the writheblade helms will prevent the Veiled One from invading our minds in similar fashion."

Yanelle reluctantly handed Actaeon back his Thoughtlink artifact. "That really is an amazing thing, Your Grace," she said. "You're lucky to be able to share your thoughts like that."

Actaeon shared a knowing look with Eisandre. They both knew that there was a distinct possibility that their shared thoughts were not as private as they once had thought.

"Perhaps you are right, Companion Yanelle," he said. "But perhaps you are not."

Actaeon made his way into the marketplace in the company of Wave.

He was pleasantly surprised to see that Balin's shop was still there, despite the Raedellean blacksmith having died on the Wall.

Instead it was manned by the blacksmith's widow, a round, gruff woman with wispy gray hair and intricate woad markings worn upon both sides of her face.

"Whaddaya want?" she snapped at the pair. "Buy something or move along now!"

Actaeon dipped his head politely. "Greetings, good lady. We require your assistance with the manufacture of a set of custom helms to a certain specification."

"Whatcha see's whatcha get. I ain't in the business of takin' requests," spat the woman as she glowered over the counter at the men. "An' name's Grameera, I ain't no fancy lady."

"That much is certain," muttered Wave under his breath.

"What'd that one say?" Grameera snapped at Actaeon. She narrowed her yellowed eyes at Wave. "Dun be makin' me come o'er there and skewer yer other eye."

Actaeon grinned. "Please do not. It would not do to have to make him two eyes. One alone is an impossible enough task."

The Prince Engineer's attempt at humor was met with a scowl.

Actaeon wiped the grin from his face and shrugged. "Come Wave, let us find another smith that can make what we need. This one must not be as talented as old Balin was."

As Actaeon began to turn away, Grameera reached across the counter and spun him back around with a heavy hand.

"Who'd you thunk taught 'im everything he knew?" asked Grameera. "Balin was a lousy cook 'fore he met me." She spread her lips in a toothy grin that had more gaps than teeth. "Quit seemin' so surprised – I dun saved many a man from spilling the contents of 'eir gut afer eatin' his gruel."

Wave chuckled. "Balin a cook – I'd never have guessed."

"So ya knew me husband well then?" asked Grameera.

"Aye, we did," admitted Actaeon. "He has helped me with no small number of projects since I first settled in the Outskirts."

"Balin was a good friend and a hero 'till the end," Wave added.

"Yes, he was," seconded Actaeon.

The countertop creaked under her weight as Grameera leaned heavily upon it to peer at them.

"Wait a beat," she said. "Yer that anyneer he's a always got ta talkin' about. Arn't ya?"

"Engineer, yes," said Actaeon.

"Then you'd be in' the ones 'at got 'im killed in the end," she snapped. The fat woman's eyes narrowed upon them.

Actaeon met Grameera's gaze and opened his mouth, not sure what to say.

"Aw, dun go lookin' like a sad lil' laddie," said Grameera with another gap-toothed grin. "He twas a gonna git 'imself dead 'venchly one way're another. Best he die fightin' alongside some 'un he believed in."

"Balin saved many lives that day on the Wall," said Actaeon, finally finding his words. "My own included. Without his aid, the Princess may well have not reached Raedelle."

Wave nodded solemnly. "Your Balin fought on even after the enemy struck him a killing blow. They'd knocked our line to pieces with a charge and would've slain us all had your husband not leapt into certain death to give us the time to regroup. I could only hope to find as worthy an end as he."

Grameera sniffled and wiped a tear away from her eye. She shook her head and looked down at the countertop, her head hanging heavily. "He always were makin' me proud, my Balin. I miss 'im e'ry day."

Actaeon stepped forward to rest a gentle hand on her shoulder.

The blacksmith swatted his hand away and smirked, wiping the last tears from her eyes. "He'd not 'ave 'ad us standin' 'round cryin', would he?" She turned around and when she turned back, she deposited three tankards full of warm ale onto the countertop.

"Drink up, lads," she said, lifting a tankard. "Ta my Balin!"

"To Balin," echoed Actaeon and Wave.

The three of them drank deep draughts of the ale.

Actaeon's eyes widened at the wretched taste of the spoiled ale and looked over at Wave who nodded in emphatic, unspoken agreement.

They set the tankards back down quickly.

Grameera continued to take sips from her tankard. "So a' what's this helm ya want made? I'll be makin' it fer ya afer all."

Wave untied a sack from his belt and dumped the prototype helm upon her counter. Beside it he placed an ample pouch of copper bits.

Actaeon grinned. "I am truly glad that you will help us, Grameera. We will need twelve more of them."

"Twelf!" she exclaimed, nearly spitting out her last sip of ale.

And Actaeon explained the rest of the details of the job to the widow of the man that had saved them all.

Actaeon and Wave strode through the sweltering midday market on their way to the Warrens.

"Are you sure this dealer's going to have them, Act?" asked Wave, wiping the sweat from his brow. "By the Fallen, the marketplace smells worse than when the tunnels were all kludged up."

"I fail to believe your memory is correct in that conclusion, Wave," said Actaeon as he trudged along between the stalls, leaning heavily upon his halberd's shaft. "Lauryn insists that they have some of the rarest artifacts. If we are to find twelve more of them, we must hope that she is correct in the matter."

"I hope so too, Act," said Wave. "But what're the chances? I think it's wishful thinking."

"We shall see," said the Prince Engineer.

The pair continued on in companionable silence, both wishing they had something to wash the vile taste of Grameera's ale from their palates as they continued on their way to the Warrens. There lived the worst of Redemption. The criminal underworld of the city operated out of the maze of tunnels directly adjacent to the marketplace. Smugglers, thieves, black market dealers, and assassins. Rumor was that they'd take on any job for a price, and they'd slit your throat and take your bits for free.

After tipping the 'protection' thugs at one of the main entrances, Actaeon and Wave made their way along a main tunnel, lit dimly by staggered luminaries. They strode past darkened alcoves with shady characters that peered out at them. Past chambers whose entryways were illuminated with a faint red light and moans of ecstasy coming from within. Past ramshackle box-like structures built against the cylindrical tunnel walls – some silent, others with groans or sickly snores or disturbing laughter coming from within. Past piles of detritus and refuse stacked at intervals away from the other structures, where nobody bothered to ever clean them up.

It was out of one of those piles that the gang of thugs sprang at them.

Actaeon was caught off guard, but Wave had expected it.

The mercenary guided one approaching dagger neatly into the throat of another assailant. He spun clear and slid his companion dagger between the ribs and into the heart of the third.

Two of the attackers dropped dead without more than gurgling noises and when the last one opened his mouth to protest, Wave slapped him hard.

"You make sure nobody else bothers us while we're here and I'll neglect to tell them about how you shivved your fellow gang member in the neck," said Wave. "Got it?"

The man nodded hurriedly and bent down to retrieve his dagger from his dead friend's neck.

Wave's boot caught the man in the side of his head and sent him reeling into the refuse. "I didn't say you could have your blade back, friend. Now get on ahead of us and make sure the others know that we're under protection, before I decide to have a little practice with my sword."

The man scrambled out of the refuse pile and staggered down the tunnel without a word.

Ahead in the dimness there were the hushed whispers of many voices and some curses that echoed along the corridor.

Actaeon arched a brow at Wave. "You are sure that will not make them angrier?"

Wave shrugged. "Most likely they'll leave us be by the time we're out of here. If not, I could use a bit of practice with my blades. I'm a bit rusty after my injury."

Actaeon shook his head and continued on. "Just see to it that I will not catch an errant blade edge in the process, Wave."

"You got it, boss," said the mercenary with a smirk.

They made a left at the next junction and ducked down under an Ancient gate to step into a large chamber that was filled with so many artifacts and chunks of debris that it reminded Actaeon of the Boneyard ruins.

He pulled out his luminary to shed some light on the room. A light smoke hung in the air that occluded their view of the ceiling and limited the distance they could see into the cluttered chamber.

"This appears to be the place," said Actaeon.

"Who's asking?" came a gravelly voice.

Actaeon aimed the beam of his luminary up at the source.

A figure in a heavy black cloak took several big steps down from one of the stacks of artifacts and paused to blow a cloud of smoke from their mouth.

"We come in search of artifacts," said Actaeon.

"Of that I've got aplenty," said the mysterious figure. "You intend to pay?"

"Well. Provided you have what we need," said Actaeon.

"Glad to hear it," said the figure in their gravelly voice. They approached more closely and lit another linreed stick with the one that they had been smoking. "Care for a smoke?"

"No, thank you," said the Prince Engineer.

"I'll take one," said Wave.

Actaeon arched a brow. "I thought you had stopped, Wave."

"Only because it's nigh impossible to get linreed sticks in the middle of the jungle," said Wave. "Now that the war's over, I might as well start again."

The cloaked figure lit a second stick and passed it to Wave, who gladly accepted and took a deep puff off of it.

"So what brings the new Prince Engineer and one of his mercenaries to my humble shop?" asked the figure.

Wave took another puff off his linreed stick. "Seeing as you already know us, ya mind telling us who you are, friend?"

"Ah," came the raspy reply. "Where are my manners?" The figure lifted their hood to reveal the feminine features of a young woman. She had short, cropped hair and wore shimmering artifact goggles over her eyes. "You can call me Rin."

"A pleasure to meet you, Rin," said Actaeon, dipping his head politely. "As I see you already are acquainted with us, I shall cut right to business."

"That's usually for the best," said Rin as she lit yet another linreed stick off the one she'd been smoking and began to puff on that one, tucking the finished one within the folds of her cloak. "Tell me what you're looking for. I've got everything you need, right here."

"I doubt that," said Wave. "You don't know Act."

"Doubt away," responded Rin, her face hidden momentarily behind another puff of smoke. "It's your own loss."

"If what you say is true, and you can provide me with what I seek now, I expect I will be back in the future," said Actaeon.

"I don't get many repeat customers here," said Rin with an expressionless gaze.

"That sounds rather ominous," said Actaeon.

Rin shrugged and took another puff. "Maybe. Now, what's it to be?"

"Twelve writheblades," said Actaeon simply.

"Gonna cost ya," said Rin nonchalantly, as if people came to her shop requesting the rarest and most deadly artifact blade in Redemption every day.

"Unsurprisingly. I come prepared to compensate you fairly," said Actaeon.

"Here's how it's gonna work," began Rin. "I get you one blade at a time. You pay me for each one."

"Understood," said Actaeon.

Rin lit another linreed stick and stuck it in her mouth before she reached within her cloak to withdraw the first writheblade in its ceramic sheath. She pulled the blade partially free to allow them to witness the crackling of the artifact and the smell of ozone that accompanied it.

"One down," said Actaeon. He reached into one of his pockets and tossed her a large silver coin, which she snatched out of the air before passing him the artifact in its container.

She leapt nimbly up to one of the piles and ascended it with practiced ease. She tossed random artifacts down and out of the way before digging out yet another artifact blade. This one she displayed for them in the same way and Actaeon paid her again before she set out to retrieve another and then another.

Wave took one final puff and flicked his linreed stick away. "Strange one you found here, Act."

Rin was in front of him a lifebeat later, another writheblade held aloft.

Wave's hand fell to his rapier and he took a half step back.

"As much as I appreciate your sentiment, Wave, I'd appreciate if you'd not so carelessly discard your smokes," said Rin, her face devoid of emotion. "I'd not wish for it to inadvertently react with anything."

"Um, uh... yes, ma'am," said Wave, at a loss for words.

After accepting payment for another blade, Rin once again disappeared among her piles of artifacts, in search of the next one.

"Careful what you say, Wave. This one is sharp," said Actaeon with an amused grin.

"How do you know of us anyway?" asked Wave, addressing the question to the chamber at large, having no idea where the artifact dealer was at that moment.

"Who doesn't know two of the gentlemen that helped liberate the Pyramid?" asked Rin. "I'd still be hiding deep in the Warrens if it weren't for you two and the others."

Actaeon shrugged and leaned on his halberd. "It does not appear that many others in the Warrens know who we are."

"Their loss then," said Rin, appearing before Actaeon with another writheblade. "This one's on me, for what you did." She handed it to the Prince Engineer and was off again to locate another.

Actaeon shared a look with Wave.

Wave shook his head and shrugged.

"Where are my manners?" came the dealer's voice from some distance away. "Another smoke, Wave?"

"No thanks," said Wave. "There's enough hanging in this room that I don't even need one."

"Suit yourself," came the reply, followed by a crash of falling artifacts.

The fourteen gathered in The End at the agreed upon time on the evening prior to their departure.

Actaeon had paid Oril handsomely to reserve the tavern at the east end of the Avenue of Glass for the gathering and she had been more than happy to oblige.

The Prince Engineer stood leaning against his halberd with his back to the bar, facing the doorway as he watched everyone arrive. To his right stood Yanelle, the Companion wearing a grim look upon her handsome features. To his left Lauryn was seated at a barstool, her light lance lying across her lap. He hadn't wanted to bring her along, but she had confronted him with the sound logic that she was the only other one who had seen the encampment of the cross-faced raiders. If anything happened to him, Actaeon made it clear that it was Lauryn who would take charge of the mission.

Trench and Wave sat at their typical table in the corner near the door, already several tankards of ale along.

The Arbiter was the first to arrive. Kylor sof Haringar was dressed in leather armor, covered by a plain gray tabard and bearing the crimson cape of his order about his shoulders. Dark goggles hid the milky-white pupils of his eyes.

"Prince Engineer Rellios Caliburn," he said formally, before he moved to stand stiffly off to one side against a wall.

The Raja's Warrioress arrived next, representing Ajman. She wore thick leather armor dyed with intricate red patterns and had a wide-bladed falchion at her hip. Calisse joined the mercenary duo at the corner table. Wave offered her his tankard and she gladly accepted, taking a swig of ale.

Wronka was next through the door, wearing the bright white plate of a Niwian Colonel. He surveyed the room with his long face and offered respectful nods to those present before he took a seat at the bar.

"Hope ya didn't start without me!" cried Harvand Xula as he burst through the door. The Thyrian Captain twirled one end of his long mustache as his sharp eyes swept the room. "I wouldn't miss this for the world." He removed his diamond-shaped hat to toss it onto the mercenaries' table before he spun a chair around backward and joined them. "Pass me an ale!" he demanded, wiping the dark skin of his bald pate with one hand.

Largrival was next, the new Raedellean Attaché's face and bald head crisscrossed with scars. She nodded curtly to Actaeon and took her place beside Yanelle.

The bartender, Oril, began to deliver fresh tankards of ale to the new arrivals. When she offered one to Kylor, he raised a hand in refusal.

They could hear the clatter of armor from the Keeper Knight Captain even before she entered. Once inside, Atreena Covellet pulled off her helm and shook free her sweeping locks of yellow hair. Her tan eyes narrowed at the retinue present and she saw herself to the bar to sit next to Colonel Wronka.

The young Shieldian Lord came moments later. Enrion Zar nodded politely to Actaeon and took a seat at his own table.

Warlord Berk sauntered in next and scowled at Enrion and Calisse in turn. "'Spose one can't be too picky about company these days." He was wearing his vest of tightly fitted metal scales and matching greaves. After a moment's hesitation, he picked a spot at the opposite side of the bar from Wronka and Atreena and started over toward it.

"Who invited a Czerynian?" asked Enrion, wrinkling his nose in disgust at the man with the white strip of hair down the middle of his head and the burn scars on his left cheek. "Last I checked that Dominion was no more."

Berk spun around to face Enrion and smirked. Noting the open revulsion in the Shieldian's expression, he changed his mind and sat down right across from him. "Never heard of a wee thing called vengeance?" He snatched up the tankard that Oril placed before Enrion and took a deep draught from it. "Ain't a great many left to affect it are there now?" He gulped down the rest of the ale and set it down hard on the table. "Uh oh. Don't tell me I drank yours. Oh well."

"I don't drink such swill," countered Enrion. "Bartender! Some rice wine here." When he saw Oril move to complete his order, he returned his gaze to the Warlord. "And what exactly is it that you plan to avenge? A culture of brutes that hack each other's heads off to assert leadership? Or perhaps you seek requital for the loss of your precious thralls? If I were you, I'd thank this Veiled One for freeing you of a culture of bondage and savagery. Good riddance!"

Berk took a deep breath and held it. A silence fell upon everyone in The End so that all that could be heard was a muffled crackling from behind the bar.

And just before the Warlord was about to launch himself across the table at Enrion, he felt Actaeon's hand on his shoulder. The Prince Engineer plunked down another tankard of ale. "Here is another drink, Warlord. And I would recommend that you share the same sentiments with those present that you shared with me several days prior."

Berk slowly let out his breath, his eyes locked onto Enrion's. "Aye, Yer Grace. You've the right of it." When he spoke, he spoke to everyone in the room, though his eyes, unblinking, never left the Shieldian's face. "As I said to the Prince Engineer, we mayn't 'ave lived the best lives, but we were people too, and so were the so-called thralls we kept. An' if'n you all don't mind so terribly, I'll be seeing to it we have our vengeance for all those dead. Call it my redemption, if ya will."

"I'll drink to that," said Trench, lifting his tankard.

"As will I," said Xula, raising his in turn.

Enrion lifted his rice wine glass and toyed with it for a moment before raising it. "I'll drink to your taking responsibility to avenge your dead."

"That's right." said Berk. "Glad you came 'round." He raised his tankard. "To vengeance!"

"To vengeance," echoed Wave.

"May the Allfather's justice sow death among them," said Atreena.

"To the protection of our civilized Redemption," said Actaeon.

"To taking down that twisted maniac," said Lauryn.

"To liberating the lands that belong to the civilized people of Redemption," said Calisse.

"Maybe it be we come together for different reasons," said Berk. "But let that not stop us from one singular goal: to wipe the Veiled One from the face of this city – our city!"

They all drank to that, and a long silence followed.

"So what's the plan, Act?" asked Wave, finally breaking it.

Inditrovalis Jem, the Adept Loresworn, chose that moment to stride into the tavern.

"Nice of you to finally show your face, Ruinthrall," said Atreena.

"My apologies for being late," said the Loresworn. He held in his hand a satchel, which he hefted into the air. "I brought some artifacts that might be of aid to our efforts."

"What manner of artifacts?" asked Actaeon, his curiosity piqued.

"You'll see when the time is apparent," said Jem. "Kryo's orders."

"Of course it is," said Actaeon sarcastically. "Well then, let me not delay further. I dare not share the plan until we are enroute to the north. However, we have devised a mechanism that we hope will block the ability of the Veiled One to take possession of our minds."

"You *hope* it will?" asked Calisse, doubtful.

"There is a good chance," said Actaeon. "It has been tested alongside an artifact that makes communication with the mind possible. I posit that it is likely that the Veiled One uses a similar mechanism to enter an individual's thoughts and thereby take control of their mind. If I am correct, these helms will protect us from that mechanism."

Actaeon nodded to Lauryn and Yanelle and they began to hand out woven bags from behind the bar to all those present, except, of course, Oril.

When Enrion opened his bag to peer inside, his face went pale and he quickly handed the bag back to Yanelle. "I cannot stand these things. Just give me this on the morrow. I need not carry it about."

The Companion offered him a confused look before she shrugged and handed the bag to Berk instead.

The Warlord dumped the contents of the bag onto his table and an open-faced helm rolled free, a humming writheblade affixed to the back of the helm's base with a bracket, arranged to point upward when the helm was worn. The blade was protected with its ceramic sheath, although the sheath slid open when it struck the table to reveal the crackling blade and unleash the smell of ozone upon the room.

Enrion bounded back from the table, knocking his chair over in his haste to get away from the artifact. Actaeon wondered why the Shieldian Lord was so afraid of writheblades. He'd have to ask him at some point.

Berk chuckled at the Shieldian and lifted the helm to inspect it more closely. He pushed the ceramic sheath back down to muffle the crackling and then set the helm upon his head. "Well, I must say it quite suits me."

"Of course you will have to remove the sheath in order to reap the ability of the writheblade and effectively block the probes of the Veiled One," explained Actaeon.

"I will not wear this... abomination," asserted Atreena, tossing the bag back to Lauryn.

"Then you'll not go with us," Lauryn snapped back.

"I will so," said Atreena. "The agreement of the Interdominional Council was for a representative from each Dominion and Order in Redemption to go north."

"Then go north," Lauryn returned. "But not with us."

"You'll not dictate to me what to do, girl," said the Knight Captain.

"I'll do just that," countered Lauryn. "I'm the second in command of this expedition. You –"

"Lauryn, hold," Actaeon interrupted her softly. The Prince Engineer approached the Keeper Knight Captain. "I understand that you eschew all artifact technology, Captain. However, our plan hinges upon this working. I must know that you will cooperate with this team. Does not your Allfather have words about the greater good where technology of the Ancients is concerned? You yourself have brought me artifacts to analyze."

"But only to understand how it had affected a member of my Order," explained Atreena. "It's a slippery slope. The Allfather has never approved of using artifacts to fight artifacts. It runs against everything I believe in."

"I am not asking you to use it to fight," said Actaeon. "Only to wear it. A writheblade is designed to cut, to pierce, to slash. You shall do none of those things. If it makes it more acceptable, one of us can put the helm on for you and remove it when we are done."

Atreena offered a pleading look to those present, but it was met with dismissive headshakes from the others.

Finally, she turned to Wronka and the Colonel shrugged. "He's right, Atreena. If you don't wear it, you cannot join us."

Atreena scowled and stomped her plate clad boot upon the ground. "Fine. I will comply. But only under the condition that I not be required to touch that cursed artifact."

"You have my word," said Actaeon.

"Good," said Atreena. "Then I'm in."

"Terrific," said the Prince Engineer. He returned to his former place with his back against the bar and leaned his halberd upon his shoulder. "As you well know by now, the armies of Raedelle, Ajman, Shield, Thyr, Niwian, and the Keepers stand ready to launch their assault on the former Czerynian Holds. Once they attack, we will steal north to find the encampment in which Lauryn and I had been held, locate the Veiled One, and destroy it."

"May the Ancestors guide us," said Yanelle.

"We're with you, Actaeon Rellios Caliburn, Prince Engineer of Raedelle. And honored to fight beside you," said Captain Xula.

The others chimed in with their assent.

"You all have my gratitude," said Actaeon. "This will not be an easy task. But it is an essential one if we are to make Redemption safe for our progeny."

Berk raised his tankard and smiled. "Let's go kill a god!"

THE VEILED ONE

W**HEN DAWN CAME ON THE** fifty-fifth day of Reap's Call, the armies of Redemption charged into the field. The Raedelleans and Thyrians invaded Craters from the Boneyards. Ajman and Shield assaulted Stormstair from the north and south, respectively. Joint Niwian and Keeper troops attacked Ridge from the south. All the while, Thyrian ships sailed around the coast to the north to provide support.

All of the attacking forces faced incremental resistance as their own soldiers randomly turned against them on the field. The allied troops were prepared though, and those soldiers were disarmed, bound, and placed into wagons that followed each army.

Still, the cross-faced raiders used partisan tactics against them, drawing them deeper and deeper into the former Czeryn Holds. Many of the enemy wore the uniforms of Shieldian or Ajmani soldiers, but bore the black cross upon their face that showed they now served a different master.

As the joint armies of Redemption fought a desperate and impossible battle in the north, the interdominional force led by Actaeon headed north through the Felmere.

"You're sure we can't take these infernal things off for at least a short time?" asked Enrion as he trudged along closely behind Actaeon.

The group had broken into two columns – one which followed Actaeon, and the other which followed Lauryn, since both of them knew how to find the safest paths through the dangerous chemical bog. The two columns of seven were forced to separate by quite a distance by the various spiked brambles, chemical pools, and quicksand they encountered.

"I am quite certain, Lord Zar," answered Actaeon. "In fact, if any of us remove our helm, our position may immediately become known and the entire plan will have been for naught."

"Remind me why I signed up for this," grumbled Enrion.

"I've always wanted a writheblade of my own," said Berk, next in line behind the Shieldian. "Good a way as any ta earn one."

"Well you are welcome to mine when this is done," said Enrion.

"Granted I don't destroy them all at the terminus of this mission," said Keeper Knight Captain Atreena with a smug smirk.

The Loresworn, Inditrovalis Jem, snorted his derision. "Absurd! One of the very Ancient forces of Redemption has awoken and means to kill us all and you're concerned with a few writheblades. Typical Keeper…"

"Say what you will," responded Atreena. "But your little dalliances with writheblades eventually lead to the likes of this Veiled One. It is all one and the same, in either case leading to our destruction. Typical Loresworn, blinded to the truth by your shiny artifacts."

"Ha!" scoffed the Adept Loresworn. "For Keepers, the truth is subjective."

Atreena halted dead in her path and spun to face the Loresworn. "There is nothing subjective about the word of the Allfather." Her hand fell to the hilt of her blade.

"Alright, alright," said Wave from the rear. "Get moving before we end up sinking into an acid pit, or get suffocated by a drifting cloud of gas, or, worse yet, we all die of boredom from listening to you two bicker all day." He motioned with the point of his crossbow bolt for them to keep moving.

Atreena made a point of lifting her blade slightly out of its scabbard and slamming it back home. "Very well, but only because the tiny mercenary makes a sound point or two."

"Agreed," said Inditrovalis with a smile. "Do lead the way, Knight Captain."

"Who're you calling tiny?" asked Wave with a snort. "It's not the size of the mercenary, it's –"

"Not the same thing," said Companion Yanelle, from farther up ahead in the column.

"It could be," Wave called ahead.

"Not in this lifetime," said Yanelle, smiling to herself.

The going was long, and the day was hot with stagnant air that made each draw of the breath feel as though one were trying to suck the air through a layer of mud. They made slow and miserable progress through the Felmere until they reached the northern fringes.

That was when the fog drifted in from the north, reducing their visibility so much that they had difficulty seeing their hands in front of their faces when their arms were fully extended.

"By the Fallen, you've gotta be kidding me with this," muttered Wave.

"This cannot be coincidental," said Actaeon, calling a halt for his column.

"What do you mean?" asked Enrion.

"The same deep fog descended upon me when I had gone to rescue Lauryn from the Veiled One," explained Actaeon. "It is too unusual a coincidence – as if the Veiled One can control it at will."

"Well there, now yer soundin' crazy, Yer Grace," said Berk.

"Even so, we cannot rule out the possibility," said Actaeon.

"I thought you were always saying, 'correlation doesn't in for something or another'," said Wave.

"Correlation does not infer causality," said Actaeon. "It is true. It does not. However, there are clear signs here that indicate this fog is unnatural. A total lack of breeze and yet a fog drifts in. No significant rain in at least a week. Even if it had rained last night, the fog should have risen earlier in the morning, when we left. And yet, here we are in mid-afternoon with a fog descending upon us. Such a heavy fog that we cannot see."

"What are you saying, Your Grace?" asked Yanelle.

"They know we are coming," said Actaeon. "They likely know exactly where we are."

"Better join up with the others then, Act," suggested Wave.

Actaeon nodded and pulled his Arbiter prototype whistle from his jacket. He blew three short, low notes out with it – the agreed upon signal.

A lifebeat passed with nothing.

But then came Kylor's whistle blowing the same three note pattern.

"Come, Prince Engineer, it is time to use the artifact I brought for us," said Inditrovalis Jem. The Loresworn knelt in the sticky mud and laid his satchel down before him, pulling several objects from it.

Actaeon turned and followed the column back until he reached the Adept. "What is it?"

"The eyes of a bird in the palm of one's hand," said Jem, enigmatically.

"Ever full of riddles," said Actaeon. "When will you Loresworn ever speak frankly?"

"Here," said Jem, lifting an artifact shaped like a tiny club to Actaeon. "Try it for yourself."

Actaeon accepted it and lifted the object to inspect it more closely.

Instantly, another artifact buzzed upward toward his face.

Actaeon stepped backward out of the way just in time as it shot up past him and into the air.

The artifact in his hand showed a shifting image that began as a white cloud and soon expanded to show the land beyond the cloud – beyond the fog. It showed the ruins in the distance and the multi-colored pools of the chemical bog. The view continued to expand rapidly until it displayed a decent area of the northern Felmere and the ruins to the north.

"A flying machine that can project its visions down to my hand..." breathed Actaeon. "Fascinating."

When they came into view, Actaeon recognized the domes immediately as the ones from the cross-faced raider encampment from which he had rescued Lauryn and the Niwian Lady who had betrayed them, Agarine Lartigan, from the clutches of their captors. They had relied upon one of the Veiled One's own men, Markor, and his proclivity to slam doors to create an explosion using the contents of several grenados in order to escape. Actaeon thought he could still see the blast radius near the domed building they'd been held inside.

The view continued to expand rapidly until parts of the Great Sea were visible.

Instinctively, Actaeon jerked the artifact he held downward and the view began to contract.

It took him a few tries where he raised and lowered the artifact, but eventually he was able to find and hold a good elevation by holding the artifact level with his upper chest.

Actaeon grinned nervously at the image before him. "Shattered Redemption, we are in trouble."

"What is it, Act?" asked Wave. "Whaddaya see?"

Actaeon watched as several clusters of what he presumed were cross-faced raiders swarmed into the fog, headed in their direction.

"They are coming... the cross-faced raiders," said Actaeon. "Form a perimeter. Get Lauryn's column over here at once."

"We're here, Act," came Lauryn's voice. "You heard the man – spread out! Form a perimeter. Prepare for immediate attack." She joined Actaeon and looked down at the artifact in his hand. "Ooo... you found their base!"

"That much is certain, but I am not sure how we will get there," Actaeon said. "We are outnumbered at least three to one by their forces and it is clear by this image that the fog obscures only an area around us. It is by design, I am certain now – some unknown artifact technology."

"Not to worry," came Captain Xula's voice from the fog. "That's why we're here. We'll tear 'em to pieces, be it fog or be it clear."

"That's right – let them come," said Calisse, the Raja's Warrioress. The sound of her falchion being drawn was dampened by the thick fog.

The pounding of boots sounded all around them until it was clear that they were surrounded. The enemy halted several paces away on all sides, just out of sight.

"Hello, old friends," said Actaeon with a grin. "Now may we finally settle things."

"Boss, you've got that artifact in the sky," said Wave. "What's our best way outta this?"

Actaeon studied the image and considered Wave's question. "Their base is to the northwest of us. However, I see they hold several units in reserve to prevent us from reaching it. Our position remains heavily shrouded in fog, so I cannot discern much more than that. South of our position there is another group of the raiders forming up to prevent us from leaving. Unfortunately, I cannot recommend a push in any specific direction as of yet."

"Might I recommend we make a push for their encampment?" suggested Colonel Wronka. "It is our best chance of ending this swiftly."

"Cover!" shouted Atreena.

Everyone with shields raised them and bolts thudded into them from all sides. The group contracted to take cover behind the limited shields.

Trench grunted as a bolt buried itself into his left shoulder, but the giant barely budged.

It was then that the attack came. The cross-faced raiders fell upon them from all sides.

Completely silent in their charge, the raiders wielded clubs and sharpened blades crafted from the ruins of the Ancients themselves.

Lauryn stepped between Trench and Wave and activated her light lance, projecting a deadly beam of light that turned the fog a pale orange as she swept it through the enemy.

Several bodies fell to the ground with a disturbing lack of screams, severed in two.

The surviving raiders fell back in perfect unison, hidden in the dense mist.

They waited several long lifebeats before charging in again and being repulsed once more.

"They're toying with us," said Wave.

"Shall we toy back?" asked Trench.

"My thoughts exactly," said Wave.

Trench lifted his maul high into the air and let out a roar that blasted through the silence like a battering ram.

The mercenaries charged outward, weapons swinging, and the others followed suit.

Only Actaeon and Inditrovalis Jem remained at the center, still watching the image on the artifact that the Prince Engineer held in his off hand.

Actaeon could hear the rustling as cross-faced raiders slid past their expanding defensive circle. He tossed the artifact to the Loresworn, who fumbled it and dropped it to the ground. With both hands, he lowered his halberd toward the sound of the rustle just in time. The weapon was nearly shocked loose from his hands as one of the raiders impaled themselves on the blade

Jem dove after the artifact, but when he reached out for it a club shattered his arm. He screamed out in pain and rolled onto his back, clutching his broken arm in his other hand.

Two boots stepped to either side of his head.

"Gods, no!" Jem cried out. His uncharacteristic last words were cut short as the club caved in his head.

The raider impaled on Actaeon's halberd continued to push forward until Actaeon tripped and fell onto his back. The butt of his halberd buried itself into the ground beside him and he still felt pressure against it, though he couldn't yet see the raider that was stuck on the blade.

The first part of the raider he did see were the bloody hands that grasped the halberd's shaft to pull them closer to the Prince Engineer, impaling them farther on the weapon. Next came into view the black cross on the face, and then the eyes, driven by their singular purpose.

Actaeon shook his head and fumbled for the hooked dagger at his belt. He pulled it free and jammed it into the raider's neck up to the hilt. Life drained from the raider's eyes as he watched and he stood to pull his halberd from the dead opponent's back – its entire shaft wet with warm blood.

Several paces distant, Knight Captain Atreena fought for her life. Her tower shield had been torn from her hands and now she stood with only her sword. Her plate was actively battered by unseen assailants as their weapons lashed out at her through the fog. She'd lost count of how many had fallen under her blade, and yet they continued coming at her, leaving dents in her previously pristine armor with their heavy clubs.

When a face appeared from the fog, the point of her sword quickly dispatched it, leaving another body to crumple to the ground in eerie silence.

But the next club that swung out of the mist took her sword from her hands. She drew her short dagger and her hand with it was smashed by the next swing of the club. The one after that caught her in the side of the head.

Atreena fell heavily to her side and spat blood and loose teeth from her mouth. Weaponless and gravely injured, she picked herself back up so that she might die on her feet. She did have a weapon though, she remembered. She lifted the helm from her head and regarded the crackling writheblade mounted to its back for a single lifebeat before she tossed it aside.

She was a Keeper. She'd not die with an artifact in her hands.

Nor would she live.

The arc of a blade took her head from her shoulders and she toppled over in a clattering of plate armor.

"To the northwest," cried Colonel Wronka, rallying the survivors. He cut his way past two more raiders. "To the enemy's encampment!"

Lord Enrion struggled to keep up with the Niwian as he rushed forward. There was haze and confusion all around him. Cross-covered faces emerged from the fog to either side, dispatched by the blades of his allies, or maybe his own – he couldn't tell. The fog flashed the sickly orange color again as the nearby light lance did its work, leaving behind a heavy smell of ozone and burnt flesh. All that coupled with the constant crackle of the writheblade just behind him was too much to bear.

Enrion screamed and fell to his knees. He reached up and wrenched the helm from his head to toss it away. The crackle disappeared, but everything else remained. The noise and cacophony, the flashes of death and light and horror – it was all too much.

But then came an alternative. A feeling of relief came over him, and he felt a force gently wrap him in a blanket of darkness, warmth, and safety. With relief, Lord Zar gladly gave himself to it.

Using a dead raider's body to shield himself from the enemy blows, Wronka nudged Enrion. "To your feet, Lord Zar. We must keep moving!"

Enrion regarded the Colonel with expressionless eyes before calmly sliding the point of his sword home beneath the white metal of his pauldron.

Wronka's eyes widened momentarily when it reached his heart and then his lids fell heavily. He fell to the side, dead.

A possessed Enrion turned toward Calisse next, but the Warrioress batted his sword aside and struck him solidly in the temple with the ornate pommel of her falchion to send him crumpling to the ground.

"The Veiled One has him," called Calisse. "He took off the helm."

Berk emerged from the swirling mist and put the edge of his arming sword against Enrion's neck, grasping the possessed Lord's hair in his other fist. "Cracked 'demption. Bastard's killed Wronka. I'll end him so he can't kill any more've us."

Wave put the point of his rapier to Berk's throat. "Lemme guess, you'll give me the same kindness if my helm falls off? Get yer damned blade off his neck, Berk."

"Oh, is the little man gonna make me?" asked the Warlord, unflinching at the feel of cool steel on his own neck. He smirked up at Wave, an unsettling look from the man with the twisted burns on his cheek and the strip of white hair in the center of his otherwise bald head.

"May I dispatch this picaroon, Act?" asked Wave in a level tone, as one might use over a cup of tea.

The survivors came together around Berk, Wave, and the unconscious Enrion to form another defensive circle.

"Get your blades off one another's throats immediately," snapped Actaeon. "Are you utterly oblivious to the quite real and persistent threat all around us? If we fail to work together, we will die. In fact, even if we do, the prospect of our survival is not good."

Berk and Wave lowered their blades and stepped back.

"Good," said the Prince Engineer. "Now, Trench and Wave, I need you to get Enrion back to safety. The rest of us will continue to the northwest."

"You've gotta be kidding, boss," said Wave. "You'll need us at your side to protect you."

"I have Companion Yanelle," said Actaeon. "And one of the finest fighting forces ever assembled."

"What's left of it," said Wave with a scowl.

"You two are the best chance he has of making it back," said Actaeon. "Plus, Trench is already injured. He will have to carry him while you clear a path. Now go – there is no time for argument."

Wave rolled his eye and assented. "Fine, Act. But we're coming back as soon as we're able." The mercenary offered Yanelle a pleading look. "Please look after him."

The red-headed Companion met his look with annoyance. "Is that not my job?"

Wave bit his lip and nodded.

"Let's go," said Trench, lifting Enrion easily onto his good shoulder. He switched his heavy maul to the other hand, grimacing in pain at the bolt still lodged in his arm.

Wave led the way to the south and back into the deadliest parts of the Felmere, his blades a blur as he cut them a path through the enemy.

The giant followed at a run.

"Onward," said Actaeon to the others. "But let us keep this formation tight."

Shoulder to shoulder, the remaining eight of them staved off sporadic raider attacks until they reached the bottom of a steep embankment that marked the northern extreme of the Felmere.

"This would be an optimal location for them to ambush us," suggested Knight Arbiter Kylor. The dark goggles that covered his eyes made him look like an apparition in the mist.

"What's the eye in the sky show, Act?" asked Lauryn. She eyed the embankment skeptically and aimed her light lance up along it.

Actaeon shook his head and leaned heavily against his halberd, It was still slippery with blood which he wiped on his heavy trousers. "Adept Jem had it last. If I witnessed accurately, he is no longer with us."

"Gods of old and gods of new, help us in this moment of desperation," said Calisse.

"No 'un ever said this'd be easy, lass," said Berk with a shrug. "Way's open to the south if ya lack the nerve."

Calisse flipped the tight queue of her hair that had worked its way free of her helm over her shoulder and gestured with her blade. "Please, do lead the way. I'd never take the opportunity for retreat from a Czerynian."

"Shut yer traps, both a' ya," snapped Largrival. "Eyes ahead. 'Less you wanna be slaughtered."

"Our Althean friend is correct," said Harvand Xula. "Now's not the time. We'll argue it out over a fine ale at The End after this is all over."

The group stood with their weapons ready for the impending attack.

But none ever came.

Actaeon grinned. "Perhaps they forgot about us."

"That or they left to pursue the mercenaries and the Lord Zar," said Kylor.

"For their sake, let's hope not," said Lauryn.

Actaeon shrugged. "Alright then. Up the hill we go."

With the point of his halberd's blade forward, he led the way up the embankment. They did their best to keep a tight formation on the ascent. When they reached the top they closed in so that they were shoulder to shoulder in a tight arc with Actaeon and Lauryn at the center.

Still, no attack came.

"I never thought I'd be doing this when I first joined you in the workshop," admitted Lauryn.

"I never would have wished it upon any of us," said Actaeon.

A strange voice sounded then, raspy and dulled by the fog

"Old boy!" it said. "I knew you'd come. Knew it, indeed. Lower your weapons – lower them. There's nothing to fear – well, nothing and everything. But you know the drill. Talk we will, let's talk. Yes."

"Markor," said the Prince Engineer. He raised his blade and set the butt of his weapon to the ground. Beside him, Lauryn gasped.

The fog blew past them and into the Felmere, revealing a one-armed man with the leather sleeve of his coat rolled up to the stump of his right arm. The man was hideously burned – the skin pulled back around his left eye to leave it unnaturally wide. Tufts of unkempt hair stuck up at intervals between scorched portions of his scalp. His leftmost teeth were permanently exposed as his lips had been seared away on that side. He wore a smirk like a shield with the remainder of his mouth – an affectation that made him look monstrous.

Behind him and forming a ring to block off any movement to the north stood a sizable force of raiders, crosses on their faces one and all. Each of them leveled a crossbow at the eight remaining members of Actaeon's interdominional force.

"Oh don't look so shocked, old boy," said Markor. "Thought you killed me, you did. But you failed, oh you failed. And here I am, even better than before. Even better."

"Do not pretend like you were not holding us against our will," said Actaeon. "We did what we had to in order to escape. I suppose you have come to gawk at us now as these mindless drones shoot us full of bolts?"

"Oh don't you fret, old boy. Don't you fret," repeated Markor. "I come to make you an offer. Not a threat. An offer."

"And what could you possibly offer us?" shouted Lauryn.

Markor lifted his remaining hand. "Why, to serve. To serve, as Markor does. The Veiled One takes pity on you. He knows you'll die here. But why? Why, when you could serve? Serve Him in His City. He can use ones such as you. Oh, forsooth."

Xula arched a brow and glanced over at Actaeon. "Say the word, Your Grace, and I'll happily oblige you his head from his shoulders."

Actaeon grinned over at Xula. "Hold off on that for the moment, Captain." He stepped forward to address Markor and felt Yanelle's hand on his elbow. "Serve your Veiled One and what? Murder everyone in the city? Is he not satisfied with what I unwittingly gave him already?"

"Serve or die. Serve or die, it is!" Markor exclaimed, pointing his finger into the air with exuberance. "This city belongs to the Veiled One. You will see it – if you live, yes, you will. The choice is clear, the way is set. There is naught more to discuss. Your technical expertise – the Veiled One wants it. Would you rather die, or serve? For that is the choice. The choice it is."

"And what about you, Markor?" countered Actaeon. "The Veiled One clearly cares nothing about you. You are but a tool to him. It matters not to him if you live or if you die."

"Clever old boy, trying to deceive me," said Markor. "And yet He has given me everything. Everything, you hear me? And you have given me nothing at all. Nothing. And yet I am to believe your lies? Lies."

"Was not the Lady Agarine Lartigan under the possession of your Veiled One?" asked Actaeon.

Markor blinked rapidly with his remaining eyelid. "Your point, old boy. Get to your point! I lose my patience."

"Had it not occurred to you that since the Lady Lartigan was with us before you triggered the detonation, the Veiled One knew it was about to happen?" asked Actaeon. "And yet, he let you into that room, even though he knew you would likely be killed in the explosion I had set for your return. I am no expert, but that does not sound like the actions of someone who cares much about you. You are a tool, Markor. Naught but a tool."

Markor's jaw dropped open and the burned man stared at Actaeon for a long while. After a time he began to shake his head. "No. Not true. It is not true. It cannot be. Cannot."

"And yet you know it is," pressed Actaeon. "You are no fool, Markor. You know that the Lady Lartigan was possessed by your god. He knew what she knew, saw what she saw. He knew that you would likely die when you came into our room and slammed the door. And yet he said nothing to you. Some god, this Veiled One. If you ask me, I would rather worship a latrine."

Markor hung his head heavily and said nothing, his eyes searching the ground for answers.

"Perhaps he wanted you to die," suggested Actaeon. "After all, why did he not just possess you as with everyone else? Is it because your mind is different, Markor? Is it because he could not possess you? No wonder that he would want you out of the way then. The one element he could not directly control. The one person who could potentially stop him. How convenient an opportunity it must have been to have you perish in an explosion."

Markor screamed, a shriek that pierced their eardrums painfully and echoed across the Felmere.

"Stop it! Stop it," the burnt man demanded with a shriek. He covered one ear with his remaining hand. "I will not turn on my master, not for you, not for nothing." He took a step forward until he was right beside Actaeon. He offered the Prince Engineer a terrifying gaze, which Actaeon met.

Yanelle stepped forward until she was right at Actaeon's side. Her sword was between him and Markor.

"Alright," said Markor in a rasp whisper so that the raiders couldn't hear him. "You've convinced me, old boy. Let's take him down. Let's do it. Only he's not here, not in this place. You'll have to follow me, follow me you will. And quickly. Quickly, yes. I know the way, old boy. Let's go. Go!"

The last word was a shout, and the one-armed man ran to the west, barreling between two of the cross-faced raiders. He bumped into the shoulders of both, spinning them sideways.

Captain Xula was right on the man's heels. His sabre whipped from side to side and both of the raiders' heads toppled to the ground.

"Go!" cried Actaeon to the others.

They pushed through the hole that Xula made and chased Markor to the west.

The cross-faced raiders followed close on their footsteps.

Wave ran like the wind, reassured by the pounding footfalls of his best friend just behind him.

He retraced the path that Actaeon had led them on, guided from memory and the occasional set of footprints in the muck.

Together the pair of mercenaries weaved through the chaos of the Felmere. Past lethal chemical pools and under clouds of deadly vapor as they fled.

The boots of the cross-faced raiders thumped behind them and in the distance off to either side, in relentless pursuit.

Wave was ready as those footfalls came nearer from either side. He moved both of his blades instinctually, dismantling the raider on the left. The point of his flamberge rapier took the raider's inner arm, the companion dagger knocked free the ruinblade, the rapier swept across the attacker's chest, and the dagger opened the throat.

Not a second later, he was ready for the man on his right. The cross-face came out of the white fog. A parry with both blades sent the weapon sidelong. He used the cross as a guide next, one blade coming down vertically and the other across horizontally.

The raider fell away, splashing into a pool. Acidic droplets stung the back of Wave's neck.

"By the Fallen, Wave," growled Trench as he stomped along heavily with Enrion on one shoulder. Several of the droplets had landed on his face and he tried to wipe them off with the fist that clutched his maul. "Be careful."

Several footsteps were getting too close, and the giant swung his wicked maul behind him, spinning in the process.

The weapon struck home once and then twice, eliciting a wince from Trench each time as the strike resonated through his arm and triggered a spike of pain where the bolt still protruded from his shoulder. Trench continued on in his lumbering run.

Three more raiders intercepted Wave from the front, emerging from the fog. He weaved quickly around them, slicing tendons and cutting throats in a flurry of his blades as he kept up his forward momentum.

Trench barreled through them with considerably less grace. He swung his maul behind him again painfully, striking one pursuer's head and sending them flying into another pool with a splash.

"I don't think I can keep up this pace," said the giant, breathing heavily as he ran.

"You're not the only one, my friend," said Wave.

There were numerous footsteps just at Trench's heel now.

Wave sidestepped and ducked down before spinning an about face.

Trench rushed past him with Enrion on his shoulder.

The half dozen raiders that came next didn't see what hit them as Wave put his blades to work. He dismantled them methodically, parrying weapon blows, dodging and ducking where prudent, and slicing through critical muscles when the opportunity arose. In short order, the six lay dead or bleeding out before him and he spun around and ran to catch up to Trench again.

As one of the cross-faced raiders stepped before him, Trench pointed the head of his maul forward and shattered the attacker's jaw like a battering ram. The incapacitated man spun off to the side and the giant continued on.

"Darkest Hour take these bastards," huffed Wave. "It's like all of them followed us." He sidestepped a blow from a ruinclub and slashed the offending inner elbow.

"Bet they did," said Trench. "They don't want us to escape." He swung his weapon wildly, catching another of the raiders in the temple.

The giant lost track of the trail they had been following and crashed bodily through a dried-up thorny bramble. He pushed his way through it, feeling all the little spikes cutting into the skin of his face, hands, and arms, wherever he wasn't protected by his leather armor.

On his shoulder, Enrion groaned at the impact.

"Don't wake up, lad," said Trench. "I'd hate to have to put you out again."

Several paces behind the giant, Wave wasn't so lucky. He tripped over one of the roots and fell forward. On instinct, he tucked and rolled, holding the blades perpendicular to the roll direction to prevent injury. Several thorns raked across his face dangerously close to his remaining eye.

"Shit, Trench! Watch where you're going," shouted Wave as he rolled back to his feet.

Wasting no time, the mercenary swordsman spun and effortlessly dispatched the next several raiders that attempted to pass through the hole in the brambles that Trench had created. When he was satisfied that the hole was clogged with bodies, he turned and made a mad dash to catch the lumbering, unstoppable giant.

The footfalls of pursuing raiders could now be heard to either of their flanks, on the far side of the nearest chemical pools that they weaved between as they ran.

And then they burst from the fog into the comparably clear atmosphere of the Felmere, which still had its drifting vapor clouds and smoking actinic puddles.

There were five raiders closing in on them from the right. Seven from the left.

"The odds are against us," said Wave.

"Ain't they always, my friend?" asked Trench.

"More now than usual," said Wave. "Shall we?"

"Let's," said Trench. He dropped Enrion to the ground like a sack of potatoes and lifted his maul high into the air.

Wave turned his back to Trench with the unconscious Shieldian between them and crouched low, pointing his flamberge rapier and dagger forward in a ready stance. "Worse odds than this've befallen us."

"Aye, 'tis the truth of it, but how many others fell on those days?" asked Trench.

"We could always make the Lord Zar a nice pincushion," smirked Wave.

Trench grinned at him over his bloody shoulder. "Steady hand and level gaze..."

"...may our strikes fall true..." continued Wave.

The raiders weaved their way nimbly through the chemical quagmire as they now closed the distance to the old mercenaries.

"...and our enemies part before us, my brother," finished Trench.

"My brother," echoed Wave.

They tensed as the creepily silent, cross-faced raiders closed the rest of the distance.

And stopped.

Far off to the north, a horrific shriek echoed across the Felmere.

Never ones to let an opportunity pass by, the mercenaries rushed forward in opposite directions.

Trench's maul shattered the skull of the first raider on his side and Wave's blade deftly opened the throat of the first on the other side.

But the other raiders were already retreating. The remaining ten of them angled northward at a jog without any of them looking back even once.

"That's right. Run away," taunted Wave.

"I've a feeling there's forces well beyond our understanding at work here," said Trench. "Let's hope Act and Lauryn can figure them out."

"We should go back to them," suggested Wave. He gestured toward the crumpled form of Enrion. "We got him far enough away. He'll live."

"And what if this Veiled One still possesses him and walks him into a pool of acid?" said Trench. "Nah. Act told us to get him to safety. That means the whole way."

"I know," said Wave, sheathing his dagger. "It just feels wrong, not being there with them."

"For me too," agreed Trench, bending to pick up Enrion again. He put the Shieldian Lord over his shoulder as a parent might a small child. "But it's the task we've been given."

"Aye," said Wave in assent. "Let's do it right."

The mercenaries continued on their way out from the Felmere.

Markor led them to the west and then to the north along the cliffs that terminated at the Great Sea with an endurance that was unexpected of a man in his condition.

The surviving members of the force; Actaeon, Yanelle, Lauryn, Largrival, Berk, Kylor, Xula, and Calisse all ran to keep up with him.

They had gained some distance on their pursuing raiders, who now marched along steadily behind them, just in visual range.

"How can we be certain he is not just leading us away from his master?" asked Kylor sof Haringar. He glanced over at Actaeon through the darkened lenses of his goggles.

"We cannot be certain at all," admitted Actaeon. "However, I am hopeful that when presented with my argument, he has decided to aid us."

"And if not?" asked Warlord Berk, skeptically.

"If not, then we are in quite an incredible amount of trouble, the likes of which has never been witnessed, perhaps since our people arrived here through the portals," said Actaeon with a nervous grin. "However, I am not so certain that the outcome would be better if we did not take this risk now."

"That's why we're behind you, Act," said Lauryn as she dashed along, her light lance over her shoulder.

"Aye, Your Grace," seconded Xula. "We'll see this through with you 'till the end."

"Indeed, Your Grace. We'll not let you down," said Calisse.

"I know that rank and position carries with it the prestige of title," said Actaeon, huffing as he ran. His recently injured belly had begun to cramp up. The three scars from the terror bird began to burn as though they were new. "However, given all that we have been through together, it would please me greatly if you called me Actaeon, or just Act if you would prefer."

"Whatever you might wish, Actaeon," said Berk.

"Act it is," said Largrival.

"Of course, Your Grace," said Yanelle.

Calisse cast a sidelong glance at the Companion and saw the redhead smirk. She offered one of her own in return.

They ran along the cliffs until they reached a point where the ancient ruins cascaded down to the water. There Markor began to gingerly pick his way along through the rubble and the others followed closely behind.

Long rusted fingers stuck out from the cliffs to extend into the water like the claws of some great mechanical beast. Far below, the Great Sea's waves hammered against the broken coastline. Out farther into the sea, like a pox upon the very waters, were hundreds of transparent domes, many of them shattered in places. A few of them flickered eerily with flashes of images that disappeared so quickly that they were impossible to make out.

Farther ahead, the natural cliffs jutted out from the ruins once more, although instead of the dirt and hard-packed clay, there were brown, rocky formations riddled with openings. In more than one place, the stone of the caves was significantly undercut by erosion and jutted out a dozen stories above where the waves crashed against rocks below.

When they reached the far side of the ruins, Actaeon stopped and gestured the others past him. He buried the butt of his halberd into the dirt and pulled free his recurve bow, which he'd already strung for the occasion.

The pursuing raiders all had to weave the same precarious path through the ruins. In several places they were forced to traverse wide beams that crossed over ruinslides that led down to the beach far below. In that position, thought Actaeon, even he should be able to hit them. He put an arrow to the string, drew it back, and let loose.

The Prince Engineer's first arrow caught the lead raider off guard and lodged itself in his chest. The cross-faced raider looked down at the shaft before falling off the beam to hit the ruinslide below and tumble down to the narrow beachhead.

The remaining raiders turned and began to retreat the same way they came.

Actaeon launched four more arrows at them in quick succession. The first went wide, but the next three managed to lodge themselves in the backs of two more raiders, knocking them off the beams.

"Act, let's go!" called Lauryn.

Actaeon turned to find that Companion Yanelle stood just behind him. Lauryn was at one of the holes in the rock formation. She waved a hand in the air and when she saw that Actaeon had seen her, she ducked inside.

Once they were all inside, Markor led them through an intricate network of sandstone sea caves. Many of them had been deliberately carved out to create sitting areas, alcoves, steps, and enlarged doorways. Many of the chambers they passed through had openings that offered a remarkable view of the sea outside. The natural walls in the caves were speckled and pitted with holes.

Their path took them into a large hexagonal chamber that had been hewn from the stone. Narrow vertical holes were cut high in the walls on the seaward side to let some light in. Otherwise, luminaries had been set into the stone at intervals to light the way. A narrow staircase wound its way down along the perimeter to the bottom of the chamber, but it had no railing and they were forced to hug the wall as they followed Markor. The burnt man led the way without hesitation, as though he'd descended the stair a hundred times before.

Lauryn screeched as she nearly toppled from the stair. Her light lance fell and landed with a bang below. "Shit," she muttered.

"Don't look straight down," cautioned Xula.

"By the Fallen, that is some drop," said Actaeon, looking straight down.

"Don't be thinking about becoming a Fallen now," said Berk, followed by a gravelly chuckle.

"This way, this way," said Markor, his voice echoing within the chamber. "Don't dally. They're coming for you. Oh, they are!"

When the relieved group finally reached the chamber floor, Lauryn ran over to her light lance and tested it. The lance crackled and shot a beam of energy straight upward, knocking a piece of the stair free and sending it crashing atop one of the artifacts below.

"Excellent," she exclaimed, happy that the lance still worked.

"Lauryn, please think about what you are doing," said Actaeon. He scratched his right hand nervously through its fingerless glove before pointing with his halberd toward the artifact that had been struck by the chunk of stone debris.

Lauryn gasped as recognition dawned on her. It was one of the elliptical cylinders that the cross-faced raiders had used to destroy Czeryn. Surrounding it were an additional nine of the devices. Some of them were open and had pieces missing, but the majority were intact.

"Gods of old and gods of new protect us," breathed Calisse, also recognizing the devices.

"We shall have to protect ourselves," said Actaeon. "Starting now. Starting here."

"Look at this," said Kylor. He lowered his goggles around his neck to reveal his milky white pupils and approached a small artifact box on a pillar in the center of the room. "This must be it."

"That's it. Yes, that's it, indeed," said Markor. "The Veiled One resides in there. And everywhere. But there is most of him. Open it if you dare. I dare not. No, not Markor! Have at it, old boy!" The scorched husk of a man backed away from the artifact box in fear and reverence.

Actaeon and Lauryn joined Kylor by the device while the others took up a defensive perimeter around the room.

"What should be our next course of action, Prince Engineer?" asked Kylor.

"We should investigate to see if it can be disabled," suggested Actaeon. "Alternatively, we simply destroy it."

"There appears to be a lid," said Kylor.

"Shall we open it?" asked Lauryn.

"I have no better idea," said Actaeon. "And our time is limited."

"Smash the cursed thing and be done with it," said Berk.

"I'll open the lid," said Kylor, offering Actaeon a questioning look.

Actaeon nodded and the Knight Arbiter carefully lifted the lid to the box.

It floated upward wondrously and levitated toward the ceiling high above. Red luminescent particles emerged from within and followed the box up to expand outward into the chamber until it was flooded with them. They spiraled gently around the hexagonal room before pausing sharply and lancing through Kylor sof Haringar at a thousand different angles.

The Knight Arbiter fell to pieces beside Actaeon and Lauryn, his body diced into a thousand tiny parts by the red particles which now swirled around his body like a tornado. The pieces fell to the ground in a mixture of clattering armor and the more grotesque sounds of his body parts. A pool of blood quickly expanded around their feet.

Actaeon and Lauryn backed away hastily in opposite directions, both in shock.

Lauryn leveled her light lance at the whipping tornado of red lights, but Actaeon snapped out his hand and shook his head.

"Well I've had just about enough of you," shouted Berk. The Warlord drew his arming sword and charged the box atop the pillar, intending to slice it in two.

The particles lanced from where Kylor once stood to slice through Berk similarly.

The last Czerynian Warlord blinked and his eyelid fell to the floor, followed by the rest of his body, in tiny pieces.

Lauryn screamed and fell to her knees.

"Get down!" shouted Xula.

Everyone but Markor threw themselves to the floor as the red particles began to whip violently around the chamber's periphery.

Markor shrunk back against the wall in one corner. "Forgive me, My Veiled One. I have betrayed you. Forgive old Markor."

The red lights whipped past Markor's eyes and he screamed, bleeding red voids where his eyes once were. He clutched at his bloody face and fell forward, unconscious.

The particles continued to speed around the room in a violent whirlwind that threatened to destroy them all.

Actaeon noticed that they carefully avoided the cylindrical artifacts. "To the artifacts!" he yelled over the maelstrom.

And they all scrambled over to the artifacts, hugging them as tightly as they dared.

The whirlwind of red narrowed down until it was only a thin rotating tendril above the artifact box. The particles lanced downward at once until they were all inside the artifact. The lid slammed shut atop the box.

The chamber was silent then except for Lauryn's sobs.

Largrival frowned and put an arm around the young engineer.

"They're here," Calisse announced, scrambling to her feet.

Sure enough, the footfalls of the cross-faced raiders could be heard upon the stairs.

Actaeon set his halberd aside to take up his bow. He nocked an arrow and pulled back, aiming upward in search of a target.

"On your feet the lot of ya!" commanded Xula.

Actaeon began to fire his remaining arrows upward, sending bodies to rain down around them.

Lauryn stood next and her light lance crackled to life as she began to slice apart the lower sections of stairs that the beam could reach.

More bodies fell, and more chunks of sandstone crashed to the floor in clouds of dust that occluded their view of the chamber above.

His arrows spent, Actaeon shouldered his bow and picked up his halberd. Reaching under the helm, he pulled his goggles down atop his eyes.

Lauryn continued to haphazardly slice upward at the stairs with her lance.

Yanelle tackled Actaeon aside as two raiders dropped toward him. The raiders struck her instead and she disappeared under them in a cloud of dust and debris.

Calisse let out a warcry that echoed throughout the chaos and battled her way through the two raiders that had landed atop Yanelle. It was with an unbridled fury that she fought and quickly dispatched them both. She knelt then beside Yanelle and lifted the Companion's head carefully into her lap, shielding her from further impacts with her body.

Ropes unfurled to the floor then and cross-faced raiders slid down them to flood the room.

Several of them closed in on Actaeon and lifted their weapons.

Actaeon pulled the boltcaster from the holster on his thigh and shot one of them through. He threw the device at another.

Largrival's cudgel sent the third reeling and swung back to kill the second.

Three different ruinblades emerged from the Althean Attaché's torso. She scowled and swung around in one final, desperate action. The raiders' blades were pulled from their hands and Largrival's spiked cudgel caught two of the three in the head, shattering skulls before she released her weapon and fell atop the third raider, wrapping her big hands around his neck and choking the life from him as she died.

On the other side of the chamber, Lauryn fought intensely, the beam of her lance filling the room with orange madness and ozone as she slashed through any raiders that approached her. Cognizant of her proximity to her friends, she swung the weapon to and fro from a kneeling stance, the beam aimed upward so that any allies wouldn't be killed accidentally — only raiders intent on killing her were dispatched. She pushed the lance to its absolute limit, counting up to twenty-nine lifebeats. She remembered Brigert's explosive death on every second over twenty.

At twenty-nine, she shut the lance off and rolled aside, smack into a raider. She fell onto her back, feeling the wind of the raider's blade as it whipped by her face.

But then the raider fell atop her, dead.

Captain Xula rushed past her, and she could hear the clangs of his sabre fending off the blows of more raiders.

Actaeon backed up against one of the artifact cylinders and held his halberd like a couched lance. A raider slammed into it and tore the weapon from his hands.

"Lay down your weapons!" shouted Actaeon.

"You can't be serious," cried Xula.

"Lay them down and remove the helms," repeated Actaeon. "It may be our only hope."

And with that, he lifted the helm from his head and tossed it away.

Instantly, he felt thoughts in his mind that were not his own.

The alien thoughts probed and searched until they found what they were looking for and pushed Actaeon's consciousness into the deep recesses of his brain.

But not before Actaeon was able to do one last thing.

STRIKE AT THE HEART

PRINCESS EISANDRE RELLIOS CALIBURN CAME to a sudden halt as her forces charged past her.

She gasped and nearly dropped her sword as the thoughts flooded her mind.

Suddenly, she knew exactly where Actaeon was, where the Veiled One was, and that her love was in grave danger.

What came next was confusing and invasive and not from her husband.

With a wince, she pulled the Thoughtlink Artifact from her ear to free herself from the alien thoughts.

Her mind reeled and she saw a swirl of images, interleaved with colors and a madness that threatened to consume her. She fell to her knees and felt a hand at her shoulder.

"Your Grace. Your Grace, are you okay?" came a distant voice.

Complex patterns and symbols drifted before her. All things that she had never seen before, and yet they were familiar. It was soothing to watch, comforting.

But Actaeon needed her. He was in more trouble than he'd ever been in, and it was up to her to save him. She was the closest person who could. She had to help him.

The Princess shook her head and the confusing thoughts, the thoughts of the Lost, all scattered to the winds. She stood then, surprised to find the boy – her attendant, Guybon Hael clutching her shoulders.

"I am fine," Eisandre answered him before swatting his hands away from her shoulders. "Halt the charge. We're going elsewhere."

Guybon snapped a sharp salute, fist to chest, and ran off. "Halt the charge," he yelled. "Halt the charge by order of the Princess!"

Ainhara Craft, the Thyrian Major of the Flashbolt Marines, slid to a stop beside Eisandre and used her foot to cock her triple crossbow. She loaded three more bolts and arched a white brow. "What's changed, Your Grace?"

"I know the location of the Veiled One," said Eisandre. "And I know how we can defeat it. Gather the leaders."

"Now that's what I like to hear," said Major Craft with a grin.

In short order, the collective leaders of the joint Raedellean and Thyrian force stood before Eisandre. First Companion Itarik, Major Craft, Captain Oragnar of the Southward warband, and Captain Jezail of the Wall Breakers. The remainder of the Thyrian leaders were on their respective ships.

Eisandre briefed them on Actaeon's surrender, the location of the Veiled One in sea caves along the western coastline, and the number of artifacts standing ready to purge the rest of life from Redemption.

"It now falls to us to finish the task," she explained. "There are none other closer. We must prevent those artifacts from leaving the caves."

"We'll stop them, Your Grace," said Jezail.

"You'll have our bolts to pave the way before you," said Major Craft.

Captain Oragnar shook his head and whispered in the ear of his Lieutenant.

Areyna looked at her Captain and shrugged before stepping forward. "The Captain brings up a good point. What's to say the Veiled One won't see us coming and possess most of us?"

Eisandre nodded. "A valid concern, Major Craft. Don't worry, Actaeon is keeping the Veiled One distracted. He has a way with words."

Areyna nodded and looked back at her Captain.

Oragnar offered a thumbs up.

Areyna returned her gaze to Eisandre. "Very good."

Companion Tarcy spoke then. "'En we'd best get a move on 'fore he runs out of 'em words."

Jezail laughed. "You don't know Actaeon. He doesn't run out of words."

Eisandre smiled faintly, a smile that quickly drifted away to be replaced with thoughts about how her husband was now in the hands of the enemy.

The feeling was, unfortunately, a familiar one, but this time she didn't have Trench or Wave to guide her through an improbable rescue. Now she had only herself.

Her thoughts shifted to the time when she had prepared to assault Blackstone Fortress to rescue Actaeon, hiding in a thicket with Trench while Wave ran reconnaissance. To the moment when Actaeon had shot his arrow at the pillar artifact and had been hit by the resulting energy. To how her brother had disappeared into that artifact, never to be seen again.

"Aedwyn," she breathed.

And her brother stood before her, in her mind's eye, with his sharp blue eyes, like her own but sparkling with life and charisma. He reached out to touch her cheek and opened his mouth to speak. But his words came out ragged and choppy, his lips unmoving. "...andre, bring them... ...together." But then the world began to swirl and Aedwyn smeared into that swirl. It drew him farther and farther away until she could barely make out the yellow of his hair in the center of the spiraling. Away, away...

"Aedwyn, don't go..." she whispered.

But a heavy hand clamped down on her shoulder. And there before her was Itarik, the First Companion. The man who had run all the way from the Wall to the Pyramid to tell of Aedwyn's capture. The man who had returned with them to try to rescue him, without rest. The man who had fought at her side after her brother was lost to ensure that she would reach the Conclave in time to be anointed Princess. She focused all her attention on him, and that helped.

"Now we go," said Itarik, regarding her with his serious brown eyes. "Now we go, Princess Eisandre. Actaeon awaits you."

Eisandre slowly nodded. "Yes." Then she had a sudden thought. "Major Craft, can you signal your ships? Have them meet us at the sea caves?"

"Consider it done," said the Marine Major. She cocked her crossbow again, spilling the bolts to the ground. This time she loaded a single bolt, which she lit with a careful strike of flint.

When she fired it into the air, it traced a line of thick black smoke that cut upward into the sky.

"I'll keep firing those shots as we draw near," said Ainhara Craft. "They'll know what to do." She stooped then to gather up her bolts and reload her weapon.

"Very good," said Eisandre. "Let us strike at the heart of the Veiled One. Lead the way, Companion Itarik."

"Aye aye, Princess," said the First Companion. He bellowed out orders and the forces of the two Dominions set out to the west.

By the time they arrived at the sea caves in the early evening, the sun was setting over the western horizon of the Great Sea and the cross-faced raiders had managed to bring several of the deadly devices to the surface from the deep chamber.

They lowered the makeshift litters they had made for the artifacts when they saw Eisandre's forces approaching from the ruin field. The raiders drew their weapons and dropped down into the ruins to meet them in battle.

Companion Tarcy drew her ruinblade and charged ahead to meet them.

The others joined her, her brother Guybon at her heels.

Tarcy stopped abruptly and lowered her weapon before she did an about face and lifted her blade once more.

Guybon bounced off of her and was caught off guard as the hilt of his sister's weapon came down to crack him in the skull. The young attendant crumpled to the ground at her feet and his sister stepped over him and made straight for the Princess.

Eisandre was ready. She raised her sword and widened her stance to cushion the blow that the giantess brought down upon her.

She grunted and deflected the ruinblade away and to the side before lunging forward to try to strike Tarcy in the skull with her pyramidal pommel.

The giantess' fist took her unawares and stole the wind from her lungs, sending her plunging to the ground hard.

Eisandre rolled backward as she fell to regain her feet quickly and place some ground between them. A sharp piece of debris bit into her shoulder as she rolled, and she felt warm blood.

Rapid fire snaps sounded all around them as the first of the cross-faced raiders entered the range of the Flashbolt Marines' triple crossbows.

Eisandre sought to regain her feet, but Tarcy was already atop her, the deadly ruinblade swinging in from the side toward her neck. She brought her sword over to parry, but the contact never came.

Instead, Itarik arrived from the side like a bolt of lightning and leapt forward to kick Tarcy with both feet.

The move sent the giantess tumbling head over heels down an embankment of ruin scree.

Itarik landed hard on his back and when he tried to stand, he realized that he could not – a sharp piece of metal had impaled his thigh and left him pinned to the field of rubble.

"Sorry, Princess," said the First Companion.

"We need a cutter!" cried Eisandre.

Another series of sharp cracks sounded as the second volley of bolts was sent forth to thud into the closing lines of the enemy.

In another lifebeat, the raiders were upon them.

Oragnar and Areyna leapt before Eisandre to defend her from the onslaught, having just managed to disarm and tie up the twin warbanders, Torg and Cafry, who had also been possessed.

Music began to play then, bizarrely – a steady and fast-paced melody.

"Listen to my music and let not the Veiled One draw you from it," ordered Jezail as she plucked the tune on her fiddle, Varisk's sword held in the same hand that she plucked with.

As though reanimated by the tune, Tarcy shambled back to her feet – the same dead look in her eyes as before. She wasted no time in lunging forward to slice at Eisandre's feet with her ruinblade.

Eisandre leapt clear of her own Companion's blade and into the path of two raiders. She was forced to fend off their blows cross-body, one wielding a club and the other a crude dagger fashioned from the ruins.

The one with a dagger left an opening for the point of her sword to stab beneath his armpit and into the heart, dropping him.

The club-wielder then struck at her again and she dodged to the right, grabbing the handle of the club to pull the raider into a decapitating blow from her arming sword.

In her peripheral vision she could see that Tarcy had climbed up to her level again and was charging straight at her.

Instinctively, Eisandre threw the raider's club, which had come loose from his dead hands.

The club tumbled through the air and neatly beamed Tarcy in the center of the forehead.

The giantess blinked once, blood running down her face before she tumbled forward to land upon it.

"Let's go, Your Grace. We've got the upper hand," called Lieutenant Areyna.

Eisandre inspected the battlefield and saw that two warbanders were binding Tarcy's hands and that cutters were tending to First Companion Itarik and Guybon Hael.

She spun back to Areyna. "Forward. Into the sea caves."

"Aye aye," said Major Craft. She loaded another signal bolt into her triple crossbow and lit it before firing another smoke trail into the sky. "Ships'll be closing in by now."

"Good," said Eisandre.

And they rushed forward then, Oragnar and Areyna at the front and the Thyrian Marines to the flanks.

"Let us lead the way from here," said Ainhara Craft as they arrived at the first opening to the caves.

Eisandre nodded and Major Craft led her marines into the first room.

There came the sounds of a few snaps and then Craft shouted, "Clear!"

Eisandre and the warbanders entered to find dead cross-faced raiders and another of the elliptical artifacts which had tumbled onto its side.

"By the Fallen," said Areyna. "Enough to wipe us all from the city."

"Not anymore," said Eisandre.

They continued on as the Flashbolt Marines cleared out the rooms ahead of them. Most of the rooms were vacant, but the cross-faced raiders clashed with the marines in a few tight places, only to be quickly taken down by their bolts.

Eventually they reached the large hexagonal chamber that Actaeon had described over the Thoughtlink Artifact. They descended the staircase until they reached the floor below.

There amidst death, destruction, and debris, surrounded by piles of dead raiders and bodies cut to horrible pieces, stood three figures, guarding the artifact box that Actaeon had told Eisandre would contain the Veiled One.

It was none other than Actaeon himself, halberd held in a defensive posture.

On one side of him was Lauryn with her light lance pointed at them, her thumb over the second activation panel of the artifact.

At Actaeon's other side, was Calisse T'ra Coletka, the Raja's Warrioress. Her wide-bladed falchion was held high.

Eisandre raised a fist. "Nobody fire. These are allies." With her other hand, she clipped the Thoughtlink Artifact back to her ear and cringed as the alien thoughts of the Veiled One flooded back into her mind.

Lauryn's thumb came down then and the orange beam of the light lance crackled to life and pierced through one of the Flashbolt Marines directly to Eisandre's right.

She swept the beam up the stairs, cutting down two more marines.

A dark-skinned body leapt up then – a body with a quadcorne hat and a sabre in hand.

Xula tackled Lauryn to the ground and wrenched the light lance from her hands before kicking it clear. He restrained the young engineer in a tight bearhug.

Actaeon, no, sent Eisandre through the Thoughtlink, along with the bright radiance of her love.

Actaeon grinned and dropped his halberd before falling to his knees. He let out a defiant cry of anguish that resounded throughout the chamber, shattering the Veiled One's hold upon him.

Before Calisse could react, Areyna and Oragnar were atop her. The two leaders of the Southward warband quickly had her disarmed and restrained, her face pressed to the ground.

"How come it didn't possess you?" Areyna asked the Thyrian Captain as he held a struggling Lauryn in place.

Xula shrugged. "Not a clue. I just laid there and played dead. Thought about how the rolling waves felt while lying in my bunk."

Eisandre rushed to Actaeon's side and he nodded at her, relief in his eyes. Next, she spotted the unconscious Companion Yanelle to one side of the chamber and gestured to her. "Cutters, tend to the Companion."

A pair of the warbander field surgeons made their way down the stairwell to tend to the Companion.

Surveying the rest of the chamber, Eisandre picked it out then – the Arbiter's blade in pieces with its pyramidal pommel. Beside it were a thousand chunks of gore in a neat little pile above a puddle of coagulating red blood. Among the chunks of gore were pieces of what she recognized to be Kylor sof Haringar's goggles.

"Kylor," whispered Eisandre, struck numb with shock at the particularly gruesome loss of her former Knight Arbiter colleague. Kylor had also been Lost, so that was a struggle they both had to overcome to succeed as Arbiters. It was something that they had shared, in mostly silent solidarity, each drawing strength from the other's success.

She frowned and sheathed her own Arbiter sword. The legendary Caliburn blade still hung from her back, but she reached over one shoulder to draw it before approaching the artifact box that contained the Veiled One – whatever it was.

Eisandre raised the blade high into the air. Before she brought the blade down, she looked to Actaeon for confirmation.

He nodded weakly. "Do it, Eis."

Without further hesitation, she brought the blade down hard upon the box.

Sparks flew and the artifact tumbled from its podium to land on the floor. Now dented where Caliburn had impacted it, the box shook and vibrated violently where it lay, struggling to open once more and unleash its violence upon the room.

Eisandre looked at her blade and then to the box with a frown. Actaeon had told her that this would work. She looked at him then, uncertain of how to proceed.

"Unanticipated. But there may be another way," said Actaeon. The Prince Engineer looked over at Harvand Xula. "How quickly can your ships get here, Captain?"

Major Craft hurried to the nearest portal and gazed out onto the Great Sea beyond. "They already are."

Actaeon grinned. "Good."

"It's a royally mad plan if I say so," said Harvand Xula. "A shame I hadn't come up with it myself."

The Captain stood on the rocking deck of the *Glorious Redemption* as it tacked southwest off of the cold northerly winds of the late season.

"Ya ken always take credit for it, sir," called down Vash from the sterncastle as she adjusted the ship's wheel to ensure the sloop would get the most out of the wind.

Xula narrowed his eyes upon the helmsman and shook his head. "Ya know I'm a man of humility, Vash. I'd never take credit where it's not due."

"Ya wouldn't?" asked Vash with a smile, doubt in her tone.

"Alright alright," said Xula. "Enough with your insubordination. Lest I keelhaul you!"

"Not sure who'd keep her on course, Cap'n, but whatever you like," retorted Vash.

Xula grunted and smiled. With heavy boots he strode across the deck to where one of the the strange ellipsoid artifacts was strapped to the main mast – the same as the artifacts which had destroyed the Czerynian people. Beside it was fastened one of the writheblade helms with the Veiled One's dented box stuffed carefully within to protect his crew from possession.

Striking his monocular open, he then gazed through it to the east and judged the distance by eye.

"That oughta do it," he said before collapsing the monocular and restoring it to its pouch. "Bosun, douse the sails!"

The Bosun stepped forward and began to call a series of commands to the ship's crew. "Man the gear!" The crew scrambled up into the rigging to comply. "Mainsail clew down! Tauten the leech! Mainsail clew up! Ease the sheet and nock! Foresail clew down! Round the jib! Round the staysail!"

Sailors rushed to and fro upon the deck and swung from ropes in the yardarms between the sails to quickly douse them all.

Xula lifted the worn piece of vellum on which the Prince Engineer had hastily sketched his instructions and tacked it to the main mast with his dagger. He reviewed the paper carefully and compared the sketched symbols to those on the artifact.

Lucerd kept shouting orders until the sailors had all of the sails down. The Bosun looked to the Captain then. "All sails doused, Cap'n."

Xula met his eyes and nodded. "Drop anchor. Man the longboats."

"You'rd the Cap'n!" called the Bosun, and began to relay the instructions.

Sailors scurried across the deck. The anchors dropped and longboats began to drop down into the choppy waters.

Xula waited until all but one longboat was down. "Ya'll only have one shot at this, Xula," he said to himself. "Don't sod it up." If the Prince Engineer was correct, it should give them enough time to get clear. He punched the progression of symbols from Actaeon's notes into the ellipsoidal device.

The artifact began to emit a buzzing sound and whirred loudly from somewhere within.

Captain Xula didn't wait to see what might happen next. He snatched his dagger from the main mast and stuck it between his teeth before taking off at a run across the deck. On the way, he motioned for Lucerd to drop the longboat.

The longboat slid neatly into the waters, where it bounced far below as Xula deftly slid down the line and dropped into the boat beside Vash.

"Take us out, Vash," he snapped. "Get us clear."

"Aye aye, Captain!" she replied.

Some of the sailors began to row as the others raised the longboat's mast into position and hoisted its small sail.

Vash used the tiller to steer them away from the ship and to the southeast, getting a boost from the wind as the sail went up.

Xula put one boot up on the rear gunwale and folded his arms over his chest. "We just may have done it."

Back on shore, atop the sea caves and high up above the waters of the Great Sea, Eisandre and Actaeon watched the *Glorious Redemption* race into the distance until it was naught but a tiny dot on the horizon. And then it was gone completely.

"Do you think it will work?" asked Eisandre, taking Actaeon's hand.

"We shall see," said Actaeon, interlacing his fingers into her own. "It was capable of eliminating all life from the Czerynian Holds. If the Veiled One is a life form of any similarity to our own, then it should be similarly destroyed."

"And if not?" Eisandre wondered.

He squeezed her hand. "If not, then we keep on fighting until our city is safe for our future."

Eisandre placed a hand upon her belly, protectively. Then, her thoughts on a different note, she spoke. "Too many have died. When will it stop?"

Actaeon looked to her then with his piercing emerald eyes. "I am not sure that it ever will stop entirely. For all of our history, and likely for all of history before us, people have fought and died so that others might live. It is always too many, I think, but because of them some of us continue to breathe and have the opportunity to leave the world better than we have found it."

Eisandre nodded solemnly. "Then let their sacrifice not have been in vain."

"Aye," agreed Actaeon. "Let us live our lives to make them proud."

Their gazes were drawn back to the Great Sea once more then as the tremendous, blue, translucent sphere rose out of the ocean on the western horizon. It grew bigger and bigger with increasing speed until it threatened to envelope the very land that they stood upon.

Both of them flinched backward, drawing one other close in the process.

But the bubble had grown to its apogee. It hung in the air for a breathless moment. And then it shattered into trillions of tiny pieces before disappearing in a flash of light.

Where the sphere had been, blue sparkles floated down into the sea to disappear forever into the waves below.

ACT THREE: CALAMITY

ARRIVAL

THE RECLAIMED ARTIFACTS FROM THE Veiled One were brought back to Actaeon's workshop to be systematically dismantled and destroyed. Representatives from each Dominion watched over the process to make sure that none of the deadly devices were lost. The writheblade daggers that had been brought back from the assault on the Veiled One were used to cut open the artifact casings.

From there, the artifacts were separated into their base components — the hexagonal rods, the casings, the control panels, and finally the dense bundles of glass wires with lights racing along them. The latter Actaeon thought must serve as the brain of the device, controlling it during its horrific task.

The components were sent to the far corners of the city, again with representatives of each Dominion to oversee the process.

The rods were taken far out into the Great Sea by Thyrian sloops, where they were dumped in the deepest waters known to the sailors.

The bundles of lighted wires were lowered into the bubbling acid baths of the Felmere.

The control panels were brought by the Shieldians deep into the depths of Rust's superstructure, where they were tossed down into shafts that went so far down into the earth that nobody had ever seen the bottom and returned to tell about it.

The casings were diced into tiny pieces with the writheblade daggers, until they were naught but a pile of useless shards.

Just one of the casings was set aside. The Ajmani artist, Maerdia Bazardjan, took that casing and incorporated it into a new stone sculpture, one that showed a writheblade wielding figure with ornaments and clothing from each of the remaining Dominions worn about their body as they sliced the casing in two. The split open casing revealed within it a deceased Czerynian Warlord, arms crossed over his chest and a peaceful look upon his face. The Warlord looked strikingly similar to Berk.

The statue was unveiled to the public several weeks after the new cycle's celebration on the first day of Arrival.

The Arrival Celebration was traditionally a solemn affair, and the eighty-eighth celebration was no different. There were reenactments of the Prisoners and Wardens coming through the portals into the new world of Redemption – a new world for them, but an immemorial world for the Ancients that came before them. The Arrival was a time of difficulty, where people searched to find their place, sought food to survive, and formed the friendships and allegiances that would forge the Dominions of Redemption. Thus, instead of feasting, the people of Redemption exchanged gifts and made meals for one another to celebrate acts of sharing, friendship, and solidarity.

This cycle was different though. Everyone was aware of how close they'd come to extinction at the hands of the Veiled One.

And so, when Mae's statue was unveiled on the Avenue of Glass just before the entrance to Pyramid, the spiritual leaders of Redemption gathered together to pray and give thanks to their respective gods.

A few days after the Arrival celebration, everyone had been happily surprised when Captain Xula had returned, sailing in with *Glorious Redemption*. He'd anchored the ship off Blacksands Beach and had rowed to shore with some of his crew.

Arbiter lookouts up in Pyramid's Pinnacle spotted the ship and a large multi-dominional contingent quickly assembled to greet them.

The longboats beached along the Blacksands to cheers from those gathered. Though some present were more concerned with what had happened to the artifact box that contained the Veiled One.

Xula assured them that he'd pried open the box after returning to the ship and no dangerous energies had emerged.

"After that, I dumped it into the Great Sea, so that it might be swallowed up forevermore," Xula said.

The Captain had been insulted when Lord Enrion Zar insisted on searching his ship to confirm that the box was not there.

Despite the insult, Harvand Xula escorted a contingent of Shieldian soldiers back aboard his ship to substantiate his claim. When he returned to shore, he had a few choice words for Enrion.

Actaeon had found the young Lord Zar still tied up in his workshop when he arrived several days after the conclusion of the battle with the Veiled One.

Enrion had been full of vitriol and anger toward the two mercenaries that watched over him.

Despite his extensive pleas that he was no longer possessed, Trench and Wave had refused to release him. They didn't trust that it wasn't simply a ruse from the Veiled One to allow a possessed Enrion to escape.

Enrion's pleas had soon evolved into sharp orders and then devolved further into threats of incarceration and other punishments for the mercenary duo.

By the time Actaeon walked into the workshop, the Lord Zar was using language that was most unlordly.

Trench and Wave sat across from him at a workbench, sharing their tankards of ale with him, which he alternatively spat at them and swallowed gratefully, much to their amusement and his continued consternation.

"I'll have you both thrown from the Suntower!" cried the young Lord after he swallowed down a gulp of ale. When Actaeon swung open the door, he looked up. "At last," he breathed a sigh of relief. "Prince Engineer Rellios Caliburn, will you kindly order your two brutes to untie me at once!"

At Actaeon's instruction, the mercenaries untied a red-faced Enrion Zar. The Lord rubbed his wrists and looked as if he were about to hit them, but then he thought better of it and stormed out of the workshop.

Actaeon arched a brow at the pair, standing in uncharacteristic silence.

"We could've sworn it was just a trick of the Veiled One to get us to cut him loose," said Wave in response,

"Aye, and he sounded less and less like the Lord Zar as time went on," said Trench.

Actaeon just stared at them for several long lifebeats before he burst out laughing. "Of course he sounded less and less like himself. He is most furious with you for keeping him restrained like that. Nevertheless, you did the right thing in this situation."

The mercenaries joined him in laughter.

"I ain't goin' to the Suntower anytime soon, boss," said Trench.

Later that arc, work was completed on rebuilding the inside of the workshop. The smoke was scrubbed from the stone walls, the remaining ash and debris cleared, and a new loft was erected to Actaeon's specifications.

In addition to reconstructing the library, office, and bunk areas, Actaeon also had an enclosed room constructed for Eisandre. She would need more privacy as she progressed through her pregnancy, he figured. He also had extra bunk areas installed for the Companions that would be assigned to them.

The loft was framed this time from heavy metal girders that had been carried in from the ruins and cut to length with writheblades. The floor atop the new girders was still wooden, but the loft should not collapse as easily during a fire, or at least Actaeon hoped so.

The triangular opening that Lauryn had cut in the wall with her light lance to escape the fire was now a small escape hatch that could be barred from the inside.

Actaeon conducted his final inspection of the repairs and nodded to Garrag, the talented one-armed carpenter he'd hired to do the job. "Perfect. It is all perfect." He handed the man a hefty sack of copper bits. "There is a good amount extra in there. Be sure your crew is compensated well."

Garrag accepted the sack and bowed his head. "Methanks, Yer Grace. 'Twas me pleasure. Keep me in mind when next ye need sumpin' built."

"I certainly shall," responded Actaeon.

Garrag exited the workshop then, leaving the Prince Engineer alone.

Actaeon put his hands on his hips and smiled, surveying the workshop. It was finally back to normal. "Well then," he said to himself. "Let the work begin again."

There came a sharp rap on the door and then Yanelle let herself in. "It is time, Actaeon."

He grinned over his shoulder at the red-headed Companion. "I shall be there in but a moment, Companion. Thank you."

The execution was a big event, and many had gathered along the Avenue of Glass to bear witness to it. People from all of the Dominions had lined the Ancient causeway to see a servant of the Veiled One be punished.

Actaeon thought it morbid to do such a thing right in front of the beautiful statue that had just been unveiled, but he had to admit there was a certain poetic justice to it.

The Prince Engineer leaned heavily against his halberd where he stood on the hastily-erected dais before the new statue with Trench and Wave to one side and Eisandre to the other. Companion Itarik, with his injured leg still covered in a heavy bandage and splint, and Companion Yanelle guarded the left and right flanks of the group. They scanned the crowd attentively, on the lookout for any threats.

Across the Avenue, at the front of the crowd, stood leaders from all of the Dominions to ensure the execution was carried out.

"Offer still stands, lad," said Trench. "I'll do it, if you want."

"Thank you, my friend," said Actaeon. He turned to smile up at Trench. "It is not your battle though – it is mine. It has been since I was a young man. The cross-faced raiders have pursued me all of my adult life. They forced me to unlock an artifact that unleashed unimaginable death upon our city. And they would have done more if we had not stopped their abominable plan. All this because one man put them on my trail. Thus it falls to me, and I will be the one to do it, even if I do not want to."

"If it weren't you, they'd have found someone else," said Wave.

"But it *was* me," said Actaeon.

"I am sorry that you must do this," said Eisandre, with the burden of personal experience. She reached out to squeeze his hand. "It will not be easy."

"Nothing worthwhile ever is," he replied with a sad smile. He squeezed her hand in return.

The Princess nodded and met his gaze with sad eyes.

Actaeon let go of her hand and reached over to touch her cheek. "I shall be fine, my love."

Eisandre stood at a loss for words before she found the ones she wanted to say. "I adore your bright optimism, your constant smiles, the way you approach every problem with boundless energy and innovation. I fear that these experiences will change you. That isn't what I wanted."

"War changes us all, lass," said Trench. "That's the only certainty to it. Those of us that live'll never be the same as we were before. Naught to be done 'bout it."

"Trench is correct in the matter," said Actaeon. "It is not like I could have sat this out in my workshop unscathed and unchanged. In fact, had I remained there during the events that had transpired, I would almost certainly have died. No, I must needs have changed in order to do what had to be done to protect our future."

Eisandre nodded solemnly. "I understand." Her eyes became lost in the crowd then as they flitted from face to face. So many people just to come and watch someone die.

Just then, Paladin Arbiter Cignith sof Iarnus emerged from the Pyramid's southern entrance. Behind him came a pair of Knight Arbiters, a captive held between them, one gripping the captive's arm and the other his stump. They walked the man out onto the Avenue of Glass and up onto the dais.

Actaeon noted that one of the Arbiters was Corvin sof Haringar, who had always worked closely with Kylor sof Haringar. Both had trained under the same Knight Arbiter, thus the shared surname of their Order.

The pair of Knight Arbiters marched Markor up to Actaeon. They pushed him roughly to his knees and then pulled the small sack from his head to reveal the man to the crowd.

Groans and shrieks of disgust sounded from those gathered as the prisoner's hideously burnt face was exposed to them. Both of the man's eyes were missing, leaving two gaping sockets, one stretched and surrounded with old burns. Tufts of unruly hair sprouted like weeds between the burned portions of his scalp. His leftmost lips were seared away to reveal the half grin of the skull beneath. The remaining portion of his mouth was twisted into a monstrous smirk.

The Paladin Arbiter raised his hands to quiet the crowd before he spoke. "We gather here to bear witness to the execution of Markor, a servant of the Veiled One, who sought to kill all the denizens of Redemption and claim the city for himself. The judgment has been passed, and so it shall be. Markor will die on this day."

The cheers that went up from the crowd sent a chill down Actaeon's spine.

With that said, the leader of the Arbiters strode from the dais platform and stood beside the Dominion leaders.

Actaeon stepped forward and Markor's smirk grew, twisting his face all the more. The man looked up to regard him with his empty eye sockets.

"Markor," said Actaeon.

"Ah, old boy. So you'll be the one to do it, will you? You will! Try not to mess it up this time, eh? Last time it didn't go so well. Oh no, it didn't!" Markor cocked his head to one side and laughed at Actaeon, a horrible rattling sound that shook the man's body.

"I shall let you choose, Markor," said Actaeon. "Either by bolt, or by blade. What shall it be?"

"Ever a gentleman," smirked Markor, continuing to regard Actaeon with his empty eye sockets. "So did it mean nothing, old boy, that I led you to the one you sought in the end? Nothing at all then?"

"It did not mean nothing," said Actaeon. "It meant that you can rest somewhat easier knowing that you found some measure of redemption in helping us defeat the threat to all of our civilization."

"Not sure that it'll make a difference to the worms that eat me, old boy. Not sure at all," said Markor. "Eh, give me a bolt then. A bolt it'll be. Better than you hacking at my old neck."

"Very well," said Actaeon. He handed his halberd to Trench and drew the boltcaster from its holster. "Goodbye, Markor."

"Goodbye, old boy. Hope ya don't take this too hard in the end. I hope ya don't, really." Markor smiled up at him.

Actaeon aimed the boltcaster at Markor's chest, toward the left side where the heart was. But then he thought better of it. He shifted the boltcaster to aim at the center of Markor's skull and pulled the trigger at point blank range.

The bolt lodged itself through Markor's skull, completing the death sentence. The back end of the man's skull exploded with the force and the body toppled from the dais to land atop the Avenue of Glass, blood from his brain spurting from the entry and exit wounds as it turned the transparent elderglass a bright shade of red.

Actaeon returned the empty boltcaster to its holster and frowned down at the dead body that he'd created – oblivious to the cheers of the crowd.

"I'm sorry," he said, shaken to his core. He turned and strode down the steps of the dais.

Eisandre joined him, and they walked together in silent companionship until they were back in the workshop.

Once back in the workshop, Actaeon threw himself into his experiments with Eisandre finding ways to be helpful.

There was still the major problem of the monsoon bugs that were destroying Redemption's crops. If there was anything to be done, he would put a stop to it.

He sat down at the laboratory workbench and set some promising half-through bottles before him. The large, sapphire bugs flitted around the half-through jug in the center of the workspace, looking for food.

Actaeon pulled the stopper halfway and slid some leafy greens in for them. A frenzy of flapping triangular wings began as the bugs fought over the scraps of food, their jaws mincing the leaves with ease until it was a fine pulp.

It wasn't until he felt Eisandre's gentle hand on his shoulder that he realized he had stuffed the bottle almost completely full of greens. The monsoon bugs struggled with indecision in the narrowing space left at the bottom of the bottle, alternating between munching on the sudden plethora of leaves and frantically trying to escape.

He had been back at the execution again, staring into Markor's empty eye sockets just moments before he killed him.

"You can't work effectively right now," said Eisandre gently.

"I must solve this issue," argued Actaeon, though his words were half-hearted. "Redemption is counting on my efforts here."

Eisandre touched her forehead to his and pressed a light kiss to his temple. "I recall you saying something about no solution being better than one wrought by an overworked mind. Surely that applies to your own mind as well?"

Actaeon grinned and slumped a bit over the workbench. "You have me there." He fished most of the leaves out of the bottle, much to the relief of the captive subjects, and replaced the stopper.

Eisandre began to massage his shoulders but stopped when she realized he was still distractedly looking at items on the workbench. She took his face in her hands and turned him toward her. "Come," she said simply.

The Prince Engineer followed his Princess' order and followed as she took his hand and led him upstairs to their alcove in the loft. She closed the door behind them.

"Lie down on your belly, please," she said as she unslung Caliburn from her shoulder and leaned it near the door. She removed her bulky armor and placed her swordbelt beside the bed where she could reach it quickly if she needed to.

After Actaeon laid down on the bed, he felt his wife straddle his back. This time when she began to knead his shoulders and back, he had nothing but his thoughts and the feeling of her touch to distract him.

At first, as she massaged him, he found his mind playing out different scenes in his head – the execution of Markor, the manner in which Berk and Kylor had been obliterated by the Veiled One, the chaos of the battle in the fog, and even back to the war when the giant slug swallowed Lady Ruinic whole. There was so much he wished he could've learned from the tribal woman about the tribal motivations to attack Redemption, about their mad god – the Devourer, and even about their origins. Were they Ancients that had devolved into madness, or were they like the Wardens and the Prisoners, but somehow driven mad? It would not be easy to learn those answers now.

As Eisandre worked the tension out of his neck and back, he gradually felt his thoughts ease as well. Instead his mind drifted to the weight of her hips on his, to the feel of her calloused hands on his neck, her breath on the back of his ears, and the endearing way that she grunted softly as she shifted to work on a particularly difficult knot.

When he shifted beneath her to flip onto his back, she looked down at him seriously and nodded. "If you wish, I can massage your front now."

Actaeon grinned and reached up to pull her down to him where he kissed her hard.

"Oh," said Eisandre, caught off guard by the sudden change in direction. The kiss made her breath catch in her throat and it didn't take long before she was kissing him hard in return and they were pulling off each other's clothes.

Actaeon gasped as she let out another of the sounds she had made earlier, but this time it was because she had shifted to take him inside her.

And there, in each other's arms and away from the horrors of the world, they lost themselves and found each other again in the sanctuary of their love.

A long while later, they returned to the workshop floor, where Actaeon was able to work with a clearer, albeit distracted, mind. Eisandre didn't want to leave, so he gave her tasks to help with the process.

"Are you okay, Act?" asked Lauryn behind him. Eisandre looked up from where she sat grinding herbs with a stone mortar and pestle, surprised that the apprentice would ask that question when the answer was obvious.

Actaeon jumped. "Ah, Lauryn. I did not know you were there."

Lauryn stepped beside him and knelt to peer at the bugs. "Sorry, I didn't mean to scare you."

"I was distracted by this problem," said Actaeon. "What approach to take is uncertain. And even if I find an appropriate pesticidal agent, then by what means could it possibly be distributed freely so as to cover all of Redemption? And what if the agent lacks an availability in the amount required? And how can we be certain that it will not harm any people?"

"You sure end up working on a ton of bug problems, Act," commented Lauryn.

"Unfortunately, I cannot appear to escape the reputation I managed to gain following the elimination of the first giant slug in the market tunnels," said Actaeon with a grin. "I would be lying if I said it did not bug me."

Lauryn smirked. "At least this one isn't big enough to kill you."

"Not directly anyway," said Actaeon, returning his gaze to the bugs. They fought and postured with one another over the remaining pulp.

"I'd meant if you were okay after the execution, you know," said Lauryn. With the nail of one finger, she tapped the jug several times to see if the creatures would react.

Actaeon offered a look of appreciation to his young apprentice. "It is most kind of you to ask." He let out a heavy sigh. "I am not okay. It is an event that will haunt the remainder of my years. But so will the time that I saw the blue sphere rise over Czeryn and with it take the lives of an entire Dominion. Whether or not I had a choice, I played an essential role in those deaths. My mind deciphered the secrets of that artifact. Had I not existed, tens of thousands of hearts might yet beat. The Dominion leaders were right to send me out there to destroy the Veiled One. As difficult as that was, and, as difficult as it was to take a man's life, it was still the conclusion of a horror that has weighed heavily upon me for some time now. I am not sure that I will ever be okay, Lauryn. But because of what I did today... because of it, I think I will be better. Every day. One day at a time."

Lauryn smiled and laid her hand on his shoulder. Her eyes met his gaze directly. "Everything that you might hold against yourself for what happens, know this: there was once a terrified young girl, kidnapped and held against her will by an enemy so terrifying that she felt as though she'd be swallowed by eternity and disappear from the world. That girl was me. And where most men would've turned their backs on the impossible odds, there was one man that set everything aside and risked it all for me. A man that I once thought had hired me just for my woodworking skills, but I now know brought me into his fold because he realized my potential and wished to make me greater than I was."

Eisandre spoke up from where she sat at a nearby workbench grinding up some leaves with a mortar and pestle. "And had you not existed, the Pyramid would still be under siege. My Uncle would be in charge of Raedelle. When the Veiled One finally figured out how to activate those artifacts, all of the Dominion leaders would have been destroyed. You were the one to stop that. Without you, countless more would be dead and dying."

Actaeon's cheeks burned red at their words. "You both seek to flatter me."

Lauryn's eyes narrowed then. Her hand tightened upon his shoulder. "I seek to tell you the truth of my experience, Prince Engineer, Your Grace – if you will."

Actaeon chuckled and nodded. "The truth is something I shall never deny. Thank you – both of you. My apologies. Do continue. And please, stop with the Prince Engineer nonsense."

Lauryn laughed and rolled her eyes. "Well, it weighs heavy on me too, you know. If you hadn't come out to help me, then so many lives may've been saved. But I agree with the Princess – I think they'd have found another to help them activate the artifact. A Loresworn maybe. A technical Arbiter perhaps. Maybe a Niwian that spent a lot of time studying at Memory Keep. You're not the only one who could've figured it out, you know. But if you hadn't come for me, I'd have ended up just like that Lartigan Lady – a plaything for Markor and the Veiled One. If you hadn't come for me, I'd effectively be dead. But you did, because you're a good person, Act. So chin up. It's hard what you've been through. I won't deny that. But I'm here right now because you acted in the moment to do what you thought was right. And I don't intend to waste the opportunity you've given me. Not ever."

Actaeon placed his hand atop hers and nodded. "You are correct, of course, Engineer Lauryn. Thank you for sharing your perspective. It changes my own."

Lauryn smirked and then yanked her hand out from beneath his. "Good. It better. Now let's get to figuring out a way to dispatch these damned bugs efficiently and thoroughly. Is there any history of similar bug issues in Redemption? Maybe we start there."

Actaeon snapped his fingers. "Of course! The Garden Terraces."

"What about them?" asked Lauryn. One of the monsoon bugs spread its triangular wings and launched itself toward her, only to strike the inside of the jar. It was still frightening to have a hand-sized insect jump at you and Lauryn shrank back.

"They are tended by someone," explained Actaeon. "Certainly they have had to keep insects at bay from their many varieties of plants. Let us go see if they can offer us any insight."

Lauryn nodded enthusiastically. It would be good to retreat away from the jar with the gnashing, aggressive monsoon bugs.

They found Shard at the topmost level of the Garden Terrace.

The squat herbalist knelt beside a scraggly mat of weeds, yanking out blue and white flowers and tossing them to the side. They muttered curses that scarcely remained under their breath.

Lauryn giggled. "Aren't you supposed to pull out the weeds and not the flowers?"

The garden tender turned a massively wrinkled face toward them. It wasn't clear whether they were a man or a woman – so lost were their features in the wrinkles and folds of age. Dark eyes were sunken into a mass of creased flesh which narrowed upon them as they looked upon the two engineers. The eyes darted back and forth, taking in their strange equipment.

Shard grunted and their lips twisted into a smile that revealed the few teeth they had remaining. "Not Loresworn, then what?"

"I am Actaeon Rellios of Shore, and my colleague is Lauryn of Lakehold. We are engineers," said Actaeon with a grin. "Tasked with solving the problem that these have created." He lifted a half-through bottle containing one of the sapphire bugs.

"Ah," said Shard, waggling their finger. "Why'nch ya say so." After what seemed like an epic struggle, they rose atop stumpy legs. They took the time to carefully brush the dirt from the bottom of their brown Althean robes – robes which had once been white judging from the pattern of stains. "Come, come, come." The herbalist started off.

Lauryn looked at Actaeon and attempted to arch her brow.

Actaeon chuckled and arched his own. "We had better follow her – er... uh, them?"

"Aye aye, boss," said Lauryn with a chuckle of amusement at Actaeon's uncertainty. "Lead the way."

Shard led them on a meandering path through the Garden Terrace. The gardener trotted along in no apparent rush.

Actaeon and Lauryn followed a few steps behind. Shard's heavy breathing was easily audible as they stumped along. They went past coastal plants with their single trunk and clusters of leaves at the top, past rare plants of the Felmere – their colors as bright as they were deadly, past jungle trees so thick with vines that their trunks weren't visible, and past the scraggly brush and fleshy-leafed plants of the Flamewoods.

Shard cracked their knuckles and slowly settled to their knees in a section of garden that featured a variegation of different mushrooms. They withdrew a knife and scraped some black fungus from the bottom of one of the caps, offering it to Actaeon. "'Ere, give this an' watch a few days."

"Terrific," said Actaeon. He handed Lauryn his halberd and accepted the blade. Carefully, he uncorked the top of the bottle and scraped the mold from the blade of the knife so that it fell into the neck. It showered the creature below in a cloud of dust.

The monsoon bug began to flap its wings frantically, but Actaeon had already plugged the bottle once more.

"It didn't like that stuff," said Lauryn.

"Indeed it did not," said Actaeon as he handed the blade back to the herbalist. "Is it harmful to humans?"

"Not 'nall da cycles I been tendin' 'ese gardens an' sprayin' it ta kill dem bugs," said Shard.

"So how much of that stuff can we get from you?" asked Lauryn.

Shard shook their head and shooed them away with wrinkled hands. "No no no. Not 'nuff ta spare 'ere."

Actaeon accepted his halberd back from Lauryn and leant upon it. "Then where might we find more?"

"'Neath Rust you'll find it," said Shard.

"The Rust superstructure?" asked Actaeon. "These mushrooms grow there?"

Shard rolled their eyes in exasperation and nodded. "Aye. 'Ere 'ave one." They uprooted a mushroom and handed it to Actaeon. "Now go go go." They waved their arms in an attempt to shoo the two engineers away. "I've work."

"You have been most kind, Lady Shard. You have our gratitude," said Actaeon, with a polite dip of his head.

"Ain't no Lady," admonished Shard. "Now lemme be."

Actaeon's eyes widened. "My utmost apologies. I did not mean offense."

But the herbalist was once more deep into their work – now stooped and tending to the mushroom garden.

The pair started away, and when they had left earshot of the Althean, Lauryn laughed. "You should've seen the look on your face, Act. It was priceless!"

Actaeon monitored the exposed monsoon bug for the next few days. Sure enough, curly black tendrils began to emerge from the unfortunate creature's carapace. By the second day the tendrils were wrapped so far around its body that it could no longer fly – several of the phagic appendages even had pierced through its wings. By the third, it was dead, its body lost in a veritable thicket of tendrils.

He ground up the tendrils and subjected more monsoon bugs to the powdered result, but there was no similar effect. No, he realized that he'd have to go retrieve more of the fungal mold himself.

"I shall have to travel to Rust in order to retrieve more of the substance," he said as he lay in bed in their new room in the loft one evening after a long day's work.

Beside him, Eisandre rolled onto her side to wrap him in an embrace. Actaeon could feel the gentle swell of her belly at his side – she had just begun to show with baby. "We are not surprised. Still, I wish that you didn't have to go."

Actaeon smiled and drew her closer to him. "I shall not be overly long. Just off to Rust and back as soon as I find the substance."

Eisandre stared into his emerald eyes with her own brilliant blue ones. She pushed forward until her forehead touched his. "Is this a task that Lauryn can handle, perhaps?"

"Lauryn may yet be able to, but it is a task that I want to personally oversee. After all, our food supply depends on this project. I intend for this little one to have plenty of food to help them grow," he said, reaching between them to touch Eisandre's tummy, where the baby was doing just that.

"Very well," she said. "But I will miss you. I don't suppose we can use the Thoughtlink?"

"I will miss you as well," said Actaeon, his hands running lower down her body to caress her thighs. The close proximity of her body was beginning to excite him. "And actually I do think we should use the Thoughtlink Artifact. It is important that we do not arouse suspicion. But let us avoid discussion of my location or any progress in the journey. We do not want to make it easy for Ambrosius to have us ambushed."

Eisandre felt a pleasant shiver move through her body as he touched her, and she lifted a leg over his hips so that they could be closer. "I would certainly feel better if we could maintain contact," she admitted. "Do you know what else I would like right now?" She bit her lower lip and looked into his eyes.

The expression made Actaeon's breath catch in his throat. "Uh... well, I would be most happy to oblige your request, my Princess." He leaned forward to kiss where her neck met her shoulder, an action that he knew would continue to turn her on.

"Thank you," said Eisandre, her eyes fluttering as he kissed her neck like that. "I would very much like to have some tangleberries to eat right now."

Actaeon pulled his head back and offered her a look of surprise. "Oh," he said.

Eisandre shifted to get dressed and pull on her boots. She considered her armor for a moment and then shook her head – it would only be a short walk. "I saw some bushes just south of the workshop near the edge of the

Windmoor so it shouldn't take long. I find I have the strangest desire to eat some right now."

Actaeon laughed and stood to pull his pants and jacket on. "I can gather a basket of them for you myself if you would prefer to stay," he offered. The Matron had mentioned that Eisandre might have strange cravings during her pregnancy and had instructed Actaeon to make haste in the fulfillment of said urges for the best health of the baby.

She looked perplexed at the suggestion. "Why would I prefer to stay? The sooner I reach the bushes, the sooner I can eat some berries," she said as she buckled her swordbelt in place.

Just as they reached the door, Eisandre spoke again. "Oh, and Act?"

Actaeon turned to her. "Yes, Eis?"

"Let's hurry back so we can have sex." She smiled at her boldness and actually blushed, which Actaeon found to be quite attractive.

He blushed his own shade of red and grinned from ear to ear. "We shall gather a basket of tangleberries faster than anyone in Redemption has ever seen."

"I don't believe people in Redemption typically keep track of how long they take to gather berries, much less log these times for comparison," said Eisandre, confused as she tried to imagine why that would be done.

Actaeon's grin broadened and he leaned forward to kiss her before taking her hand to guide her from the workshop.

Distracted by his kiss, she followed eagerly, and they grabbed a basket on the way out into the night.

When they arrived at the cluster of tangleberry bushes at the edge of the Windmoor plain, Eisandre began to pick the big berries and eat them immediately, as if they were the most delectable treat in Redemption.

The night was quiet with the exception of insects chirping and the cool air was still about them. The bushes towered well over their heads, dotted with bright pink berries that were visible even in the dim starlight.

Actaeon took a moment to admire the bright field of stars that canvased the sky all around them before he began to fill the basket with berries. He smiled as he watched Eisandre's obvious enjoyment.

After a short while, Actaeon showed her the basket, which he had managed to fill with several hundred of the bright pink orbs. "Do you think this is enough for now?"

Eisandre narrowed her eyes and knelt to get a closer look in the basket in the dim light. She took a few berries and popped them into her mouth. "I don't think that we should wait until we get back to the workshop," she said.

"You have already been eating them, have you not?" he said with a grin.

The Princess surprised him as she undid the clasp on his belt to pull his pants to the ground with a heavy thunk. When she took him into her mouth, he gasped and dropped the basket. It fell to the side and many of the berries he'd gathered rolled out. Actaeon attempted to stoop to pick them back up, but she balled his shirt in her fists and held him in place.

"Oh..." said Actaeon, for once at a lack of words. So that's what she didn't want to wait for. He looked up from his wife and at the few luminaries of the Outskirts, both stunned and excited by her sudden boldness.

She stopped then and looked up at him, her blue eyes reflecting the starlight. "Is it okay?"

Actaeon nodded. "Very okay."

"Good," she said, before continuing where she left off.

"Incredibly okay," he said, gasping again.

She smiled and pulled him down to her. When she kissed him hard, he tasted the strangely sweet and deep rooty flavor of the tangleberries on her tongue.

Actaeon grinned and fed her some more berries from the capsized basket before kissing her again.

He helped her out of her trousers, and Eisandre had to bite her lip to avoid waking everyone in the Outskirts as Actaeon filled her.

Much later, as they both lay hand in hand below the infinite canvas of stars, Eisandre wondered aloud, "I wonder what it will be like, having a family together." She found that she enjoyed the feel of the cool grass under her body – it provided a nice contrast to the warmth she felt from their lovemaking.

Actaeon grinned and passed her a berry, which she gladly accepted. "The possibilities are as endless as the stars, I believe. But when we meet our little one, I imagine it will feel as though there was never a life before them. Despite the challenges of being parents, I believe it will make our lives feel perfect."

"Could I possibly be a good mother to the child that is coming?" mused Eisandre. "It isn't even just that I'm Lost. I also never had a real mother figure in my life. I was young when my parents sent me to the Arbiters –

and there I was brought up by men to be a disciplined warrior, not someone who would be prepared to raise a child."

Actaeon squeezed her hand. "If there is one thing that I have known about you since we first met, it is that you can do anything at all which you put your mind to. In fact, it is surprising to me that you still are not convinced of that yourself. You led the largest interdominional force in our generation to liberate Pyramid. You came to rescue me, for the second time, in fact! And in the process, you struck the final blow against the Veiled One, thus saving Redemption from the fate of the Czerynians. Not to mention I have seen you go toe to toe with some of the most powerful Dominion leaders and show them that you are not to be trifled with. You continue to inspire people, lead people, protect people, and love people in ways that extend far beyond your Arbiter training. And so you see, I have no worries about what sort of mother you will be. For I know you will put every part of your being into the task."

"Raising a child isn't the same as leading Raedelle or fighting in battles," pointed out Eisandre. She reached over for another tangleberry and her hand found Actaeon's with one of them already in hand for her. The way their minds could align so closely made her smile.

"Is it not, though?" suggested Actaeon. "The stakes are the same, after all. Only the future that you will be fighting for will belong to that one child. And that child's actions will serve to shape our very world. There is one thing that I know – the world will not be the same when it meets Eisandre Rellios Caliburn's child."

"Look!" said Eisandre as a shooting star darted across the night sky.

It was followed by another, and then one more.

And there they remained in silence for some time, fingers intertwined and together marveling at the infinite canvas of possibilities that lay before them.

The journey beneath the massive superstructure of Rust was not for the weak of heart or the claustrophobic. It was a veritable maze of corridors, girders, and beams stretching between metal floors and walls. And everything was in various states of rust and degradation.

"I still fail to believe that this was the only location where these mushrooms are found," said Lord Enrion Zar as he inched along one particularly perilous beam. He clung to the rope that Wave had tied across the chasm. The Lord dared not to look at the eerie drop below, but the light cast across the walls from the swinging luminary at his belt kept pulling his eyes there.

Finally, he stepped onto relatively solid ground at the other side. Enrion grimaced when it creaked beneath his feet.

"This Shard's right. Lots of mushrooms like the dank darkness down here. We'll probably find it," said Peirxon Hyk. The dark-skinned, lanky man had an absent look in his red eyes as he spoke, puffing on a linreed stick.

The farmer had been reluctant to guide them beneath Rust, especially after Actaeon had caused the 'incontrovertible and utter annihilation' of his farm when he'd toppled the towers of Lazi's Tomb and one had unintentionally fallen atop the man's Guaraja Root farm.

But when Actaeon had explained that the substance they sought would kill monsoon bugs, Hyk's eyes had lit up, and he had readily agreed to help them locate it.

Enrion slapped the linreed stick from Hyk's hand. "Quit smoking those down here. Not all of us want to breath in your foul smoke."

Hyk looked displeased, but bit his tongue and nodded.

"Yes," agreed Actaeon. "Plus there might well be pockets of flammable gas down here. It would not do to inadvertently light one of them."

"Lovely," said Companion Yanelle as she arrived on the ledge, bringing up the rear.

Ahead, Wave had been about to gesture them forward. He hastily put out his own linreed stick against a rusty section of girder. "This way, boss. I think I see a way down."

"Isn't there something aside from this mold that we could use to kill the bugs?" asked Enrion. "Fire perhaps?"

"It isn't mold!" snapped Hyk. "Uh... respectfully, Lord Zar, it is fungus."

Enrion offered the farmer a sharp look that shut the man up and caused him to look at his toes.

"I thought mold *was* a type of fungus?" asked Lauryn, following Wave as he descended a series of rungs.

Hyk remained silent.

"You are quite correct, Lauryn," said Actaeon. "There are a wide variety of fungi, including molds, yeasts, and mushrooms, of course. In fact, our target fungus is likely a type of mold that finds a home beneath the cap of the mushrooms we seek."

"Double the fun... guy!" joked Lauryn with a giggle.

"Exactly," said Actaeon with a chuckle.

The mercenary checked each rung for stability before trusting his weight to it. "Perhaps you guys could cut this conversation short? I'd prefer not to fall asleep and end up at the bottom of Redemption."

Yanelle laughed. "For once, I agree with you, Wave."

"Glad to hear it," said Wave. "Wait. Whaddaya mean, for once?"

It was Yanelle's turn to remain silent as they climbed downward.

Enrion slipped from a slimy rung and barely caught himself on the next one down.

His luminary broke free and tumbled down to a floor far below.

The light illuminated thousands of grayish bumps that spread out along the floor.

"That's it. More mushrooms," said Pierxon Hyk. "Should be at around the depth we're looking for too."

"Terrific," said Actaeon with a grin. He reached up to flick the half-though bottle that dangled by a wire from the top of his halberd. The monsoon bug inside flitted about in reaction. "Wake up in there – you are about to be needed." He looked down over his shoulder. "Wave, do you think we can reach it?"

Wave wasted no time in tying off the remaining length of rope that he wore cross-body. Carefully, he unraveled the loops from his chest and let it fall. "Aye, Act. The rope'll reach the rest of the way. I'll slide down first to check the stability."

The mercenary slid nimbly down the rope and gingerly tested the floor with the toe of one boot. When he was confident it was solid, he tested the rope to make sure it was still secure and stepped back. "Alright. It's safe. C'mon down."

The others slid down the rope one after the other until everyone stood among the mushrooms.

The bulbous caps stood on stalks that nearly reached their knees. Enrion looked particularly disgusted by it. He eyed the rope nervously. "Let's make this quick, please."

Actaeon handed his halberd to Yanelle and knelt to cut one of the caps free with his hooked dagger. He returned the dagger to his belt and turned over the severed mushroom head in his hands.

Sure enough, there was a black, fuzzy mold clinging to the bottom of the cap.

The Prince Engineer pulled out his dagger and scraped some onto the blade before setting the cap aside. He stood then and reached for the bottle dangling from his halberd. "Alright, little guy. Let us see whether this is the correct substance." First uncorking the bottle, he then slid his blade against the neck to shower the bug in a cloud of black dust that settled at the bottom and then quickly flared up into a cloud as the creature frantically flapped its wings. Actaeon recorked the bottle. "And now we wait on our friend and gather as much as we can."

The group set to filling all of the bottles that they had brought with the black mold. Each one of them had carried a backpack full of the half-through bottles.

"Remember, I want to bring back several intact mushrooms as well," said Actaeon as he methodically filled one of his bottles. "Set aside some healthy-looking specimens for me. I want to see if we can't grow these in the cellar of the workshop."

"I hope these are the right ones, Act," said Lauryn.

"Same here," agreed Enrion. "I won't be coming back here."

"Worry not," said Actaeon with an amused grin. "I am fairly certain that these are the same as the ones which Shard had shown us. If I am correct, then all that remains is to run some tests to make sure that it isn't lethal to humans and figure out a method of distribution to kill these pests across all Redemption."

"Oh, is that all?" asked Yanelle with a smirk.

By the time he arrived back at the Pyramid, Actaeon had an idea.

They had spent the night in Rust before returning. Just long enough to see the first of the lethal tendrils emerge from the monsoon bug's body. Actaeon had kept the creature dangling from his halberd as they travelled back to Pyramid by way of Stormstair and past the Arbiter stronghold of Redoubt. He figured it was good for everyone to see what their discovery beneath Rust could do to help them defeat the pestilence.

Enrion had insisted that Shield keep two of the backpacks – his and Hyk's, and Actaeon figured it was only fair.

They returned with four backpacks full of the mold powder. He would have to determine the efficacy to see how far the substance could be stretched.

Before they left Shield, they had also exposed several creatures with similar respiratory systems to humans to the powder. A chicken, a rat, a pig, and a long-legged canopy dreezer were among the test subjects.

Lord Zar had sent Shieldian soldiers along with Actaeon's crew with the sole task of transporting cages with the creatures in them. The soldiers carrying the pig and the dreezer had a particularly miserable time. The dreezer was especially difficult, as it liked to swing manically back and forth from its three hairy arms during the more dangerous traversals in the ruins, as though it were trying to cause its carrier to take a tumble.

When the soldier shouted at it, the dreezer just stared back with an everpresent frown above its eyes on the bulge under its body that served as a head.

Upon their arrival back at the workshop, Actaeon left Lauryn with a half-through bottle of the mold. He tasked her with determining the minimum amount needed to kill one of the creatures.

In the meantime, he went to the Pyramid with Yanelle to pay a visit to the Arbiters.

When he arrived in Arbiter Pyramid Command, the Knight he was looking for was already there.

"Greetings, Your Grace," said Corvin sof Haringar. "It is good to see you."

"And you, Knight Arbiter Corvin," said Actaeon. "I hope you have recovered well."

"Indeed I have, Prince Engineer," said Corvin. "I have Knigh... I mean, Her Grace, the Princess Eisandre Rellios Caliburn, to thank for that. It would please me if you convey my gratitude when next you see her."

"You can do that yourself when next you see her, Knight Arbiter," said Actaeon with a grin. "I am sure that will be soon. For right now, I need your technical expertise."

"Oh?" asked Corvin, curious. "For what, Your Grace?"

"Please, call me Actaeon. We have worked together much, so there is no need for such formality," said the Prince Engineer. "How much do you know about Pyramid's ventilation system?"

"Quite a bit, actually," said Corvin, looking excited about the topic. "I have been working on a means of using it to deliver various gaseous compounds to invading..." The Knight Arbiter trailed off.

"What is it?" asked Actaeon.

Corvin looked at the floor, embarrassed. "I really shouldn't be discussing these things with you. No offense, Actaeon, er... Your Grace."

"None at all taken, Knight Arbiter," said Actaeon. "I understand that my new position creates some political awkwardness for discussing such strategies for the protection of Pyramid. If you need any help with the project, you could always consult with my associate, Engineer Lauryn of Lakehold. It is something entirely different for which I wish to utilize the ventilation system though."

"I, uh..." stammered Corvin. "Perhaps I shall do just that. So what interest do you have in the Pyramid's ventilation system?" The topic piqued his curiosity, helping him to overcome the awkwardness of the interaction.

"We have located a substance that will exterminate the pestilent monsoon bugs," explained Actaeon. "If we can design a method of distribution for it using Pyramid's ventilation system, then we might distribute the pesticide across Redemption with the changing winds."

"Ingenious!" exclaimed Corvin, excited at the idea. "So you mean to expel air from the system to the outside. I wish I'd have thought of that myself. The intake vents are located near Pyramid's pinnacle, just below where the elderglass part of the structure ends." He looked at Actaeon, clearly impressed.

"Not to worry, Knight Arbiter," said Actaeon. "I will be sure that you have full credit as a part of the team that achieves this task. And the vent locations would be perfect to allow the wind to take the substance across the city. It makes sense for the Ancients to have designed it that way too. To draw in fresher air from well above the city infrastructure."

"Oh, no," said Corvin, shaking his head. "I need not have any credit. I'd simply like to be a part of it."

Actaeon grinned. "That would make two of us then. Could you show us where some of the main vents might be accessed?"

Corvin nodded eagerly and motioned for Actaeon and Yanelle to follow him.

They spent the rest of that day touring the various cylindrical ventilation shafts of the Pyramid, standing in the largest sections, crouching in the middling-sized sections, and even crawling in some of the smaller sections.

In these explorations, they were able to determine what were likely the best locations to place the substance in order to maximize the delivery. At each of these locations, Actaeon drew large X's with the blunt end of his charcoal stick.

Late the next day, when Actaeon and Corvin arrived at the workshop, Lauryn had a full report for Actaeon on the efficacy of the substance.

"It worked!" she exclaimed. She jumped up and down with barely contained excitement and clapped her hands together.

Actaeon grinned. "Meritorious news, indeed. Would you mind explaining your findings in greater detail, Engineer Lauryn?"

Lauryn blushed and looked at Corvin. She offered the Knight Arbiter a shy smile before she nodded. "Yes, yes, of course. So, I figured out a few things, actually. Firstly, the mold can be diluted into water with surprising efficiency. I have tested out three hundred parts water to one part fungal dust and it manages to kill the creatures." She led them over to the laboratory workbench where she lifted a perfume sprayer. "Lady Mae was kind enough to let me borrow one of these. I had the idea to use it as a delivery method."

"Very smart, Lauryn," said Actaeon.

"Yes, smart indeed," seconded Corvin, looking quite impressed.

Lauryn blushed again before grasping the t-shaped handle that came out of the back of the piston cylinder. She pushed it once and sent a vapor cloud into the air. "This spray is concentrated more than enough to kill the bugs."

"An atomization of the substance," said Corvin. "Fantastic."

"An admirable method of delivery that will be quite effective in spraying crops by hand," said Actaeon. "However, it will be difficult to create enough of a spray to spread across Redemption."

"I'd the same thought, Act," said Lauryn. "And knowing what you intended to do in the Pyramid, I tried boiling some of the compound. It requires a bit of a higher concentration, but when I boiled it and left the plugs out of several half-through bottles with monsoon bugs inside, they were all killed by the vapor, no matter where in the workshop I placed them."

"The dust can ride the vapors. Fascinating. Soon you shall require a workshop of your own Lauryn," said Actaeon.

"Oh, I'd never want that, Act," said Lauryn, blushing a shade deeper. "We work better together, after all."

"Indeed we do. Two minds are better than one," said Actaeon. He walked over to the place where the four test subjects they had brought from Shield were caged.

The dreezer swung back and forth from the top of his cage causing it to slide back and forth on the workbench. The strange canopy-dweller offered him a frown and a blank stare from its beady eyes.

The pig snorted.

"Our test subjects all appear unscathed," observed Actaeon.

"Yes, and I made sure they were exposed to the latest concoction along with the monsoon bugs, so we'll be able to see if that effects them negatively as well," said Lauryn.

"Did you expose yourself as well?" asked Actaeon.

Lauryn offered him a sheepish look. "I didn't think of it until afterward."

"We must think of all the variables in any problem. Even one failed consideration might result in death when dealing with matters such as these," said Actaeon.

Lauryn nodded. "I'm sorry, Act."

Actaeon grinned and put a reassuring hand on her shoulder. "You will not forget this lesson next time. Plus, congratulations are in order – you are now officially part of this experiment. Your respiratory system is much more like a human's than the dreezer's, after all."

"You mean it isn't human?" asked Corvin.

They all laughed at that.

"Let us get started then," said Actaeon.

And so they set out immediately.

First, they distributed the bulk of the pesticide using the Pyramid's ventilation shafts. Lauryn and Corvin would set the substance to a boil in the appropriate location amid the intricate network of shafts. A relay of Arbiters was positioned between them and where Actaeon stood by in the Pyramid control room. They blew their whistles once the mixture was boiling and Actaeon touched the correct symbols to expel the vapor from the appropriate vent in order to take advantage of the wind.

Overall, the process took them several weeks.

During that time none of the test subjects, including Lauryn, developed any negative symptoms as a result of the exposure.

For the distribution, they needed to wait until the wind was blowing in the correct direction and there was no precipitation. But eventually, reports came trickling in that the monsoon bugs were dying in Lazi's Tomb and Amphis' Ledge. In Holdfast and Kendra. In Sunken City and Canal Keep. In Arena to the west. In Adhikara and Pools of Light to the east.

When finally the reports came back from Raedelle's Holds of Lakehold and Shore that monsoon bugs were dying in droves, they knew that their work was complete.

The second front was to utilize the perfume sprayers. The Arbiters had impounded any and all of the devices that could be found. A call sent out to the various Dominions yielded yet more. And Actaeon began a full-fledged effort to build as many of the atomizers as he could in the workshop.

In the end, three hundred and fifty of the devices were stockpiled. These were distributed to the far edges of Redemption. Raedelle received one hundred, the southern Colonies one hundred and fifty. The remaining hundred were split between the other Dominions.

With the devices, farmers treated their crops by hand in places where the wind had failed to bless the plants with its monsoon bug-killing payload.

All in all, the monsoon bug plague was brought under control.

And by Hunger's Spar, the people of Redemption were more hungry than usual, but they did not starve. Rations were put in place. Portions were reduced. The people were fed.

And in places scattered about the city, the rare, unfortunate individual died – coughing up blood from their lungs as they spasmed in a desperate attempt to get enough air. The instances were so infrequent though, that nobody figured out that the solution to the monsoon bug problem which saved so many from starvation also sentenced a chosen few to a horrible death.

WITHER

THE DISSONANT PAIR OF SHIELD Wardens burst into Saint Torin's Hold just as Actaeon was making his way out.

"Just the man we're seeking," said Strog, the rotund Czerynian with a matrix of scars that marred his arms and face. "We need you to make a choice, Your Grace."

Beside him, the younger Shield Warden named Dek nodded, a hint of madness in his eyes. "Aye, we've decided you're to pick the next Warlord among us, now that Berk's gone on to the Hall of the Dead."

Actaeon arched a brow and leaned on his halberd. "Correct me if I am wrong, but is that not something you typically fight about?"

"Only when challenging a living Warlord," said Strog, spewing spittle as he spoke. "Shield Wardens don't fight amongst themselves."

"Aye, it doesn't make sense when a half dozen Shield Wardens might need to fight to the death over it," said Dek. He smirked. "Plus, Strog knows I'd skewer him in a lifebeat. He hopes you'll just pick him and have it over with."

Strog glared at the younger Shield Warden.

"But what would prevent you from skewering him after I chose him?" asked Actaeon in seriousness.

"Precisely," said Dek, offering Strog a wink.

"The young sop thinks he'd stand a chance," said Strog with a chuckle. "I was making his mamma squeal when he was still in diapers."

"A… lovely image, Shield Warden," said Actaeon sarcastically. "So where do I fit into this decision-making process?"

"Typically a different Warlord will appoint the next Warlord from amongst the Shield Wardens," said Dek.

"Or just absorb them into their own command if they've the balls," said Strog. "We talked it over and both of us agree. Seeing as you brought us into Raedelle's fold, then it stands to reason you're the closest thing we have to a Warlord. And so you should make the decision."

Actaeon looked back and forth between the two men and they looked back at him expectantly.

When it was clear that they were not going to go away, Actaeon let out a sigh and spoke. "This is quite a big decision you have both put upon me. You surely will understand that it is not something I intend to rush."

"But how are we to manage until we have leadership?" complained Dek.

"You will work together to provide that leadership jointly until I have come to my decision," said Actaeon. "Which, am I correct to assume, you have been doing since Warlord Berk gave his life in the fight against the Veiled One?"

Strog nodded quickly. "Of course, we have, Your Grace."

"I am glad to hear it," said Actaeon. "Allow me a week and you shall have my decision." He stepped between them then to continue out from the Hold.

Dek's hand fell upon his arm, stopping him.

Behind Actaeon, Yanelle's hand fell to her blade, and there it stayed, awaiting the Shield Warden's next move.

Actaeon arched a brow and looked down at Dek's hand on the arm of his jacket.

"You know, Your Grace," began Dek, his eyes blazing. "We haven't forgotten your promise to Berk. That you'd find our people a place to settle as a part of our agreement."

Actaeon grinned. "No, Shield Warden. I have certainly not forgotten. That is an issue I intend to discuss in great detail with the next Warlord." That said, he jerked his arm from the Czerynian's grasp and continued out from the Hold.

Yanelle followed him out, making a point to knock Dek roughly aside with her shoulder. "Touch the Prince Engineer again like that and you'll have to find a new arm," she said and then was gone.

Strog laughed at the exchange and shrugged at Dek's glare. "That'll have won him over for sure!"

"Like he'll pick a fat p-kin bastard like you to be a Warlord," scowled Dek. "Dream on."

The younger Shield Warden stormed out and Strog took a moment to let out a hearty laugh. "The position's as good as mine after that little exchange."

As Actaeon descended from the Way of Pillars past the new sculpture commemorating the defeat of the Veiled One and down to the Avenue of Glass, he was met by a familiar, gray-eyed face.

"Just the man I'm seeking." An ancient figure stood in the middle of the Avenue and pointed the end of his walking stick with its green crystal shard at Actaeon. The man was bald and wore a gray beard that was tucked into the silver belt at his waist that held his crimson red robes about his body.

Actaeon rolled his eyes and looked back at Yanelle. "How many times will I hear that phrase today?"

Yanelle offered him an understanding smirk, but kept her silence.

Actaeon turned to narrow his eyes on the old Loresworn. "What is it now, Sol? Do you wish to test me again? Perhaps this time you shall have the Avenue of Glass melt beneath my feet." He gestured with his halberd to the elderglass causeway that spanned to the east and west.

Old Sol stepped forward and spread his hands. "I come to reason with you, Prince Engineer. For the weakness grows yet stronger, and yet... none contest it."

"Last time I spoke with Kryo, I told him to fix it himself," said Actaeon, feeling short on patience. "Has he done nothing in the time that I have spent doing so much?"

"Kryo does all he can to contain the weakness," said Sol. "As for yourself, your friend is no longer ill, the Veiled One's pieces have been scattered to the aether, and the pestilence is no more. Surely, you might entertain an old man's request? After all, it is only our entire reality that hangs in the balance."

A crowd had begun to gather at a distance to watch the two men's confrontation.

Actaeon shot Sol a skeptical look. "And how am I to know that these *requests* of yours are not an attempt to simply destroy me? After all, how many times have you tried to kill me already? Oh, but I suppose I should just trust you and walk back into Travail? I am sure that you will not have any more trials there for me – no more puzzles. It is all just a game to you. That much is clear." He turned to walk away then.

"Have I not given you Quronos? Have I not given you light lances?" shouted Sol, his voice echoing with surprising volume. "Have you no gratitude?"

Actaeon spun back around and slammed the butt of his halberd against the Avenue of Glass. "Gratitude? Gratitude! Surely you jest, Sol. Quronos would have killed us upon our entry into Travail if it were not for Wave's skill with a sword. And you told us nothing of the light lances, as per the usual Loresworn methodology of keeping all your knowledge to yourselves. And guess what? A Companion died because of it. Companion Brigert. Do not forget his name, for his blood is on your hands, Sol." He slammed his halberd down again and reached over to scratch his right arm through the leather of his jacket. "How many more, Sol? How many more must die because you cannot share the truth with others?"

"The truth is not for the heedless many. Not for the ones who, through precipitous action, would use it to destroy the fabric of our world," boomed Sol tilting his head.

"Thirty lifebeats," shouted Actaeon. "No more than thirty lifebeats. A simple fact, given freely, could have saved a man's life from being lost in the blast of a light lance. A warning that a deadly guardian lay inside Travail would have prevented a group of those who only sought to protect Redemption from nearly losing their lives." The Prince Engineer hesitated then, but, in his anger, he continued on with his train of thought. "A known cure for the Rogue's Bane could have saved a very special woman's life when her son pleaded for help at Travail's gates. And yet, you gave nothing. You give nothing. You never will. And now you come with a plea for help from the very person you would have let perish on so many occasions." He shook his head. "No Sol, I will not help you. Not when I know not when next will come another attempt to kill me or the people I love. As I said to Kryo – fix it yourself." He began to turn away but stopped at the Loresworn's next words.

"Your mother had to die, Actaeon Rellios of Shore," said Sol. "She had to die so that you might learn failure."

"Say that again," Actaeon said, his hand falling to the grenado clipped to his jacket.

"Your mother had to die," Sol said. "The knowledge of the Ancients is not for just anyone."

Actaeon's hand tightened around the cold shell of the grenado, but he thought twice about it. "Let us go, Yanelle. There is no need for us to remain." He turned then and started to the west along the Avenue of Glass, his Companion a step behind him.

"Dare you walk away from me?" Sol called, his voice booming. "I've not finished with you yet, Engineer."

When Actaeon didn't stop, Sol pointed his staff at him and muttered something.

The energy wave that emanated from Sol's staff caught Actaeon by surprise. The concussive blast knocked him and Yanelle down and sent them sliding along the smooth surface of the Avenue of Glass.

Yanelle was up in a lifebeat, her sword in hand. She rushed the Loresworn and leapt into the air, her blade poised high to slice through old Sol.

But Sol reached into one of the pockets of his robe and Yanelle paused in mid-air and simply hung there. Sol aimed his staff at her chest and fired another concussive wave that sent the Companion flying clear off of the Avenue of Glass.

Yanelle let out a muffled cry as her sword was ripped from her hand and she landed hard on her boots. She tumbled onto her back and clutched at her chest, gasping for air.

Actaeon only hesitated for long enough to see that the people in the crowd nearest Sol had also frozen, but not the ones further away.

Before Yanelle even hit the ground, he switched his halberd to the other hand and drew his boltcaster. When he pulled the trigger, the bolt lodged itself into Sol's gut.

The old man reached down and his hand came back with blood. "You should not have done that." Sol took several steps forward and aimed his staff toward Actaeon.

"The Fallen know that I tire of these games of yours," said Actaeon with a grin. He holstered the empty boltcaster and ripped his grenado loose, backing away as he twisted and pulled the pin.

"It's no game, you fool! The fate of us all lies in your hands." Sol fired a series of concussive waves that struck Actaeon with the force of a powerful wind.

Actaeon slid backward along the elderglass surface and continued to back away.

Sol reached into his pocket and withdrew another artifact. This one was a metal sphere, similar to the one Actaeon had seen project the image of Kryo. The sphere flitted through the air, quickly closing the distance between them.

Actaeon threw the grenado before the sphere could reach him. A lifebeat later the sphere was in his face. He batted it away with the blade of his halberd. The sphere recovered and sped back. Lightning arced out of the artifact and struck him in the right arm. He dropped the halberd and fell to the elderglass, stars in his eyes as darkness threatened to bring him down into unconsciousness.

He blinked and struggled up onto his elbows in time to see Sol aim the staff at the grenado which hung suspended in midair three quarters of the way between them.

Actaeon spun and flung himself facedown, covering his head with his arms.

The small concussive thump of Sol's staff sounded next, followed by the near instantaneous sound of the grenado's detonation. The blast shook the Avenue itself with a violence that lifted Actaeon several inches into the air. He could feel the impact and the heat through his clothes as it pushed him back down against the elderglass.

Actaeon lifted himself slowly to his feet, his right arm still partially numb from the shock. There was a shallow crater in the elderglass beneath where the grenado had exploded. Fragments had been taken out from the sculpture, leaving one of the writheblade wielding figure's arms missing and a chunk gone from the face of the Czerynian Warlord.

Beyond the crater lay Sol, smoke rising from his scorched robes.

Actaeon stood unsteadily, blinking the stars from his eyes. With an arm that felt like a sack of dead weight, he yanked his recurve free of the clasp on his back. Without taking his eyes off of Sol, he stepped inside the curve and flexed the bow to string it.

After putting an arrow to string, he approached the old Loresworn slowly, careful not to get close enough to be frozen by Sol's artifact.

Sol stirred and blinked his gray eyes open to settle upon the point of

Actaeon's arrow aimed at him. He let out a deep sigh and shook his head slowly in disappointment.

"My mother did not have to die," said Actaeon. "And neither do you, even if I should kill you. Let this be a lesson to you. I do not intend to play your games anymore. Next time I will do what I must to ensure this never happens again."

"Go then," said Sollemnis the Gray, spitting blood that trickled into his beard. "And leave Redemption to its doom. I see now... I see now that you're not the man I thought you were, Engineer."

"Good," said Actaeon with a grin. "And do not you fail to remember that." He backed away from the Loresworn until he reached the Companion. "Yanelle, are you alright?"

"Aye, Act," said Yanelle, gasping for air still. "Sorry."

Actaeon shook his head and released his draw on the bow to offer her a hand. "Nonsense. Next time just remember not to rush the man with the plethora of artifacts on him that we know nothing about."

Yanelle took his hand and regained her feet with a smile. "I will, Your Grace. And... nice work here."

Actaeon grinned. "Let us go."

And so they left the smoldering and bleeding Loresworn to his fate.

Lieutenant Areyna of the Southward warband burst into the workshop. "Your Graces, there are tribals from the far south gathered on the Windmoor. And they're asking for you."

Actaeon and Eisandre both looked up from what they were doing. He had been excitedly showing her how a boltcaster was assembled from a batch of new parts.

Eisandre had been listening with interest. She loved to listen to him talk about his inventions – his passion and enthusiasm were delightful.

In the meantime, Lauryn, Trench, and Wave were busy fabricating batches of the parts for the devices at the foundry end of the workshop. They had assembled nearly a hundred already, and were planning on making at least five hundred of the devices before they would stop. The Arbiters would get the first hundred, followed by the warbands.

After word of Actaeon's confrontation with Sol on the Avenue of Glass had come out, both Shield and Ajman had made offers for the boltcasters and the grenados. Actaeon had agreed to make them fifty boltcasters each, as long as they provided him with feedback on their operation. However, he'd outright refused to provide them with grenados, much to the dismay of both the Raja's Portent and Lord Enrion Zar.

Actaeon arched a brow and set the boltcaster down on a workbench. "Tribals are asking for *us*?" It didn't make any sense. They had just pushed the Ruinic tribal forces out of Redemption. Why would tribals want to speak to them now? "Which tribals exactly?" he asked, after considering further.

Areyna shrugged. "Looked like Lake Tribals to me."

Eisandre stepped forward. "Show us the way, Lieutenant."

And so, Areyna led them out onto the breezy plain of the Windmoor. It was a cool, cloudy day and a chill breeze cut through the early afternoon air. The Princess and Prince Engineer were accompanied by their full complement of Companions – Itarik, Tarcy, and Yanelle. The rest of the Southward and Incline warbands came with them as well. Most of the warbands had returned to Raedelle by now, but Southward and the Wall Breakers had remained behind just outside of Pyramid to protect their Raedellean leaders.

The tribals were encamped on the plains of the Windmoor, their animal skin tents set up in tight defensive rings at the fringes of the Stone Gardens' various rock arrangements. Smoke trails wound their way into the overcast sky from dozens of campfires.

As the Raedellean delegation approached, the tribals emerged from their tents to assemble outside. The tribals wore thick paint upon their faces. Most of the painted faces were blue with wiggly black lines. Some others wore blue with slanted black lines, while a chosen few wore yellow face paint with the same slanted black lines.

"The yellow ones are the leaders," said First Companion Itarik.

"Let's hope this isn't another invasion," said Yanelle.

"I sincerely doubt it," said Actaeon. "It is not a very effective method to begin an invasion. Camping in a location of questionable defensibility and requesting a parlay before initiating an invasion? No, I believe they want something else entirely."

"Yes, but what?" asked Eisandre, curious.

They came to a halt some ten paces from the line of tribals.

Everyone gathered stood in silence for several long lifebeats. The tension in the air was palpable.

Eisandre was the first to speak. "We've come as requested." She stepped forward of her own line, her hands resting easily on her sword belt as she swept the line of painted tribals before her with cool blue eyes.

"I had to see it for myself," came a familiar voice. The tribal line parted and a woman stepped forward, her face painted the same yellow color as the leaders, although the black lines on her face were vertical. Instead of the rough-cut skins of the tribals, she wore the practical leather armor of the Companions and, strangely, wore a sword at her hip. Her blue eyes fell upon Eisandre and her lips curled into a smile. "My little sister. The Princess of Raedelle. The position suits you, I think."

At first, Eisandre was stunned by this unexpected turn of events. She neither moved nor spoke for several long moments that started to become awkward. Recognition slowly dawned on Eisandre, followed by acceptance and a powerful wave of emotion. She let out a sob and rushed forward to Eshelle. Her big sister wrapped her arms around her and pulled her close.

"Eshy..." Eisandre whispered, "You're alive! You're here! It's been so long. I thought..."

The Companions tensed up, but Itarik recognized Eshelle and held up his fist.

"Thought I was dead?" asked Eshelle. "I don't die that easily, little one."

The sisters shared a long embrace there out on the Windmoor as the gentle breeze whipped through their hair.

There were tears of happiness in Eisandre's eyes when Eshelle finally stepped back, clasping her sister's shoulders to appraise her. "Oh, Sandre... we have something to celebrate, I see!"

The Princess gave her older sister a confused look.

"Why, you're with child!" said Eshelle, beaming. "Do you know the baby will arrive?"

Eisandre stepped back and touched her belly, looking down at it thoughtfully. "Midway along Torrentfall is what the Matron says."

"Two more arcs of the moon! I'm so very happy for you, Sandre," said Eshelle. "I can't wait to meet my little niece or nephew." She squeezed her sister's arms and smiled. Despite four older brothers and Eshelle, Eisandre's child would be the first born of the next generation of Caliburns. "Will you and your husband please join us at my fire?" When Eshelle noticed the concerned glance from Itarik, she added, "Bring the Companions along, if you like, but better to leave the warbands here for now."

Eisandre nodded and allowed Eshelle to lead her into the encampment. Actaeon and the three Companions followed closely behind. The tribals parted to allow them through.

Eshelle, Eisandre, and Actaeon all took seats around the fire upon large, overturned buckets. The Companions positioned themselves a short distance behind the Princess and Prince Engineer.

"It is good to see you well, Lady Eshelle," said Actaeon after he'd helped Eisandre down to her seat. He settled down on his own makeshift chair, letting his halberd rest against his shoulder. "I cannot help but notice that you have quite the unusual and inexplicable escort."

"Oh, I assure you it is perfectly explicable, Master Rellios," said Eshelle, using Actaeon's old title. "The Witherians wouldn't allow their leader to come here alone. And I didn't dare bring them to Raedelle. The warbands might've attacked first and asked questions later. Once I'd learned that you were still near the Pyramid, I set out to meet you here."

"We are both Rellios Caliburns now, Eshy," corrected Eisandre. "We've taken each other's names. And I've conferred the title of Prince Engineer upon him – it seemed more appropriate than Prince Consort."

Eshelle seemed amused and a little perplexed. "Interesting that you took his name too. You know you needn't have."

Eisandre shook her head. "I wanted to. We rule as equal partners. Without Actaeon by my side, I could not be Princess of Raedelle. Our Uncle Arcady would have been anointed Prince."

Eshelle wrinkled her nose in disgust. "I'd rather a Water Goblin be Prince than that old man." She looked over at Actaeon. "Very well, Prince Engineer Rellios Caliburn it is."

"How about simply Actaeon, or Act?" he suggested. "After all, we are family now, are we not?"

Eshelle nodded approvingly. "That is appreciated, Actaeon. But I will respect your full name and title when appropriate, as my sister suggested."

Actaeon grinned. "If that matter is settled, then I believe you have quite the incredible story to tell."

"As do you both," said Eshelle. "But, very well. Since I've been absent for so long I will tell my story first."

Eshelle told them about how she had led an elite force of Companions across The Wall to thwart Arcady's plans. They had been ambushed by an overwhelming tribal force before they could reach Shore. The Companions had fought bravely but were ultimately killed by the attackers. Their sacrifice had given her time to flee.

With a head start over her attackers, Eshelle had fled through the ruins of The Wall and attempted to reach Shore herself, but every step of the way the tribals had remained between her and her homeland. They drove her steadily toward the River of Arches.

"They had me cornered at a cliff beside the river, and I leapt from it," continued Eshelle. "Such was the drop that I blacked out when I hit the water."

She awoke in a ruined chamber of the Ancients hidden away on the southern shore of the river. She was in the care of a tribal warrior that had distinctly different markings from her pursuers. When she attempted to escape, she found she was too weak and lapsed into unconsciousness.

Over the next several weeks the warrior nursed her back to health. She had broken an arm and a leg and had come down with pneumonia, most probably from a broken rib suffered during her long fall to the River of Arches.

In that time, the warrior taught her his language and she taught him hers. She learnt his name was Milopitas and that he belonged to one of the tribes around Lake Wither. As he nursed her back into health whilst hidden in the jungle just south of the River of Arches, Eshelle realized that she'd begun to fall for the man who had shown her such kindness and devotion even after her numerous attempts to fight him and escape. Every time, he simply laughed and waited until she tired herself out before helping her back to their hidden camp in the ruins.

After she recovered from her illness and her injuries had healed, Milopitas brought her back to his people. They were at first quite skeptical of the Raedellean woman that had been brought among them. After all, Raedelle had been their enemy for generations.

But Milopitas was the son of an elder, and so her presence was tolerated, even if there was rampant mistrust among the Witherians.

Eshelle described winning their trust somehow, though she glossed over the details.

"The deeds I performed for them left them in awe at my proficiency as a warrior," she explained vaguely and with no small amount of hubris. "After that, there was no question. They trusted me implicitly."

She and Milopitas were joined then, in the loose fashion that the tribals were married. She began to train the tribals in Raedellean tactics and weapons skills. They learned language and Raedellean culture from her. In turn they taught her their language, customs, and how to survive in the jungle wilds.

It had become clear to her that the tribes of the Tribune waters farther to the south controlled the tribals around Lake Wither. It was there that Eshelle realized she could make the greatest difference for her new allies and for Raedelle Dominion at the same time.

She trained the tribe in tactics to more effectively fight as a unit. And with her new husband, she travelled to the other tribes around Lake Wither. She taught them all the same tactics and skills. With Milopitas' help, Eshelle brought together the tribes of Lake Wither into a single allied force. She and her husband led this force to attack the tribes of the Tribune waters and pushed them far to the south.

It was during these engagements that she lost Milopitas. A spear caught her husband in the eye whilst they rushed a Tribune encampment together. He'd died instantly as she held him in her arms.

From that point on, there was an unease among the Witherian tribes. They had followed Milopitas and the elders of his tribe, but now Milopitas was dead.

In mourning, but nevertheless undeterred, Eshelle continued to lead the joint forces of Wither into battle against the Tribune tribals. Again and again they won, and she led them to victory after victory.

For the first time, the tribes of Lake Wither realized that by working together they could control their own fate instead of being subject to the Tribune bullies which had always kept them weak and dependent.

The elders of the tribes understood that Eshelle had guided them to this point. And when Milopitas' father was fatally injured during another battle, he declared his wishes to have her be their next leader.

"There was one factor that helped along their decision," said Eshelle.

"Oh?" asked Eisandre.

"Milopitas' child growing inside me," said Eshelle. "That fact, more than any other, made it certain that I was one of them." She smiled at

Eisandre's look of wonder. "That's right, Sandre – your child will have a little cousin, the Fallen willing."

"That is wonderful news, Eshelle," said Actaeon. "But I do not understand. Why would you not send word to Raedelle in all that time?"

"Because by the time I was healed, it was too late," said Eshelle with a scowl. "A new Princess being anointed is big news. Even the Lake Tribes heard of it. It didn't make sense to me, to be honest, that they'd choose a... That they'd choose Sandre. I figured that somebody was behind it and was manipulating things. That we'd lost, and that I'd been betrayed. At first I planned on crafting the Witherians into my own private fighting force, to retake Raedelle from whatever enemy was controlling my baby sister, if need be.

"But then," she continued, "I heard more news. News of a Princess of Raedelle leading an entire interdominional force to liberate the Pyramid. News of Eisandre Caliburn leading an army to bring down a demon that had destroyed Czeryn."

"Eisandre Rellios Caliburn," the Princess reminded her sister.

"Yes, that," said Eshelle with a smirk.

"And so you changed your mind and decided to seek us out to find out the truth," said Actaeon.

"Indeed," said Eshelle. "So, enough of my news. You've got a story to tell now."

Actaeon then told of how they had freed the sword Caliburn from the pillar artifact. How Eisandre led the Wall Breakers to reach Shore and Raedelle in time to be at the meeting of the Conclave. He told of how the Conclave had selected Eisandre as the next Princess of Raedelle and how Eisandre had selected him to be her husband.

Once he'd answered all of Eshelle's questions about those events, he told of how they had then led Raedellean forces to break the siege of Pyramid. Of how they'd ended up as the leaders of the allied forces on their respective fronts. Eshelle was particularly impressed to hear about how Actaeon had led a small force into the marketplace tunnels to infiltrate Pyramid from below.

He also told her of the destruction of Czeryn and his involvement with the cross-faced raiders. Next, he detailed their efforts to defeat the Veiled One far to the north.

"I clearly misjudged you, Actaeon Rellios Caliburn," said Eshelle. "I am truly sorry that I didn't take you more seriously when you first approached me in Saint Torin's Hold. It will not happen again."

Actaeon blushed and waved away the suggestion. "It matters not, Eshelle. What matters now is that we have you at our side, for we will need you in the battles to come." He gestured to the gathered tribals that listened intently around the fire. "You and your new friends, I hope."

Eshelle narrowed her eyes upon Actaeon. "And why shouldn't my little sister step aside now that I've returned? And not only returned, but pacified half of the neighboring enemy tribes. I should be Princess!"

"Should you?" asked Actaeon. "And after everything that Eisandre accomplished, despite everything she has overcome..." he paused and shot her a knowing look then, before continuing, "you would cast your little sister aside then so that you can rule? Do you think that the people of Raedelle would be fine with the Liberator of Pyramid being replaced? The one who slayed the northern demon, as you call it. The leader who organized all civilized Redemption to fight off the worst invasion in our lifetimes. Do you think your beloved Witherians will ever really have a chance of joining Raedelle without her help?"

"I —" began Eshelle.

Actaeon interrupted her. "The way I see it you have two choices. You can either cast Eisandre aside and give Redemption a weaker Raedelle for it — there are many out there who would thank you for such a favor. Or you could throw in your support with us and, in turn, strengthen Raedelle and solidify our Dominion's place as the leader among Dominions."

"If you want to be Princess —" started Eisandre.

"You think Raedelle would really be willing to accept Wither?" Eshelle asked, interrupting her sister.

"We shall have to bring it before the Conclave, but I do not see why we could not." Actaeon arched his brow and looked to Eisandre for confirmation.

Eisandre took a moment to absorb the implications. "The Conclave is not likely to be receptive to the idea."

"Not at first," said Actaeon. "But when they consider the positives, I believe they may be more open-minded. A new territory, the mitigation of an old threat, easier access to the Colonies for trade, more arable land, new warriors to form new warbands in order to reinforce Raedelle after the losses of the Second Invasion War. And all that under the control of your older sister, one of the legendary Caliburns."

Eisandre nodded as she thought about his suggestion. "It will still be a challenge to convince them, but your arguments are strong enough to give them pause."

Eshelle smiled and tucked a lock of stray red hair behind her painted yellow ear. The smile faded from her face at another thought. "But the Conclave will never trust having only me in charge of such a large Hold, with no other means of Raedellean control. If something were to happen to me, the alliance would never last. They won't allow it."

Actaeon grinned. "Not to worry. I have some ideas on how to mitigate that concern."

"They're here, boss," said Wave.

The mercenary led the pair of Czerynians into the workshop and over to where Actaeon was showing Eshelle one of the new boltcasters.

She turned it over in her hands, admiring the lightweight design.

Actaeon looked up and motioned the two Shield Wardens over. "Gentlemen," he said. "Come join us. Thank you for coming."

Actaeon led them over to a different workbench, where he poured out several tankards of ale from a fresh keg that had been placed there for just the occasion. Each of the Czerynians quickly accepted an offered tankard, as did Eshelle, who followed them over.

"It's been longer than a week, ya know, Yer Grace," said Dek, before taking a deep draught from his tankard.

"Indeed it has," said Actaeon with a grin. "You have quite the astute powers of observation, Shield Warden. And I am pleased to inform you that I have made my decision."

Strog stepped forward, his eyes waggling to and fro nervously. "The decision for the next Warlord?"

"That is correct," said Actaeon.

"Don't get too excited," said Dek, to his older kinsman. "It ain't gonna be you."

Strog's face grew red and he clenched his fist. The rotund Shield Warden kept his tongue though, and alleviated his anger with a swig from his tankard.

"Dek is correct, Strog," said Actaeon. He took the time to take a slow sip of his ale. "I must regret to inform you that you are not my selection for Warlord of the remaining Czerynians."

Dek stepped forward and lifted his tankard into the air. "That's right, Strog, you sorry sop. Here's to the new Czerynian Warlord! Get yer drinks up there. That's right."

"But Dek, how could you properly toast the new Warlord when you do not even know who I have selected?" asked Actaeon with a mischievous grin.

Dek lowered his tankard. "Whaddaya mean? If'n not Strog, then it's me, clear's day."

"I never said that," said Actaeon.

"Then who?" shouted Dek. He slammed his tankard down on the workbench surface, sending a geyser of ale into the air to splatter down upon the table and his leather vest.

"Why, the Lady Caliburn, of course," said Actaeon. He gestured to Eshelle. "I take it you have not met, so allow me to introduce the Lady Eshelle Caliburn, my sister-in-law and the new Warlord of the former Temple Czerynians.

Dek's jaw dropped.

Strog laughed. "Ridiculous."

Eshelle's lips twisted into an amused smirk.

Dek shook his head and then shook it again more passionately. Then he hurled his tankard against the wall where it fractured into a dozen pieces. "A *woman?* A woman *cannot* be Warlord."

"And yet that is my decision," said Actaeon quietly. He took another slow sip from his tankard.

"Go clean up your mess," muttered Eshelle under her breath.

"And a damned stupid decision," said Dek. "Clearly a jest. Who's yer real choice then? C'mon. I'll even accept this fat shit if'n ya say so." He gestured to Strog.

"Watch yer tongue, lest I make a new necklace of it," snapped Strog.

"You are welcome to challenge the new Warlord, if you think you might be her better," suggested Actaeon with a shrug.

Dek looked at Eshelle and rolled his eyes.

"I said to go clean up your mess," repeated Eshelle. This time her raised tone filled the entire workshop.

"Sod off, woman," snarled Dek. "The men are talking."

Eshelle's fist caught him in the face before he could react and Dek found himself on the cool floor before he knew what happened. Pain flared on the right side of his face, and he lifted a hand to find a trickle of blood there.

Dek opened his mouth to protest, but another jolt of pain from his jaw prevented it from opening fully.

"I'll say it one last time for you," said Eshelle with a chuckle. "Clean up the Prince Engineer's workshop before I break the other side of your jaw. I guarantee I can find a new Shield Warden quicker than you can make a fool of yourself further."

Dek scrambled to his feet, his eyes wide with fear. "Aye, Lagy Shell," he said, his words slurred as he rushed over to the wall and began to pick up the pieces of the shattered tankard.

Strog laughed. "That's Warlord Eshelle to you, ya brat."

"Um'l... Aye Warlorg," Dek slurred as he gathered the shards.

Eshelle smiled. "I think I'm going to enjoy this."

CHALLENGE

I T WAS A BEAUTIFUL CLEAR day, with just the hint of a chill breeze when Lord Enrion Zar was joined with Lady Kiroko Xan. The ceremony took place in the Stone Gardens. The normally tall grasses had been cut for the occasion, allowing guests to traverse freely between the Ancient statues and carved stones that littered the plain at the fringes of the Windmoor.

Only the closest of friends and family were invited for the occasion.

"Strange," said Wave, as he strolled along with his group of invitees. "I'd have expected Lord Zar to use the opportunity to woo the neighboring Dominion leaders."

"He'll be busy enough wooing his betrothed, don't you think?" asked Jezail from where she walked at Trench's side.

Wave shrugged. "Never seen a good Lord or Lady of the nobility miss the chance to make things political."

Actaeon grinned. "There have been enough political events as of late. It shall be refreshing to set that aside for our friend's special day." He and Eisandre walked hand in hand. They were closely trailed by two Companions – Itarik and Yanelle.

"That's right, Wave. Just enjoy the day," said Jezail with a smirk.

Wave made a show of lifting his eyepatch to peer at Jezail with his empty eye socket. "Yes, ma'am. So how do you know Enrion Zar anyway? I don't recall you spending a particular lot of time with him."

"I don't," admitted Jezail shyly. She brushed her locks of red hair behind her ears. "I'm here as a guest."

Wave looked around, confused. "A guest? Of whom?"

Jezail smiled a shy smile and reached out to take Trench's big hand.

The giant raised his brows at his friend. "She's my guest. Got a problem with that?"

Wave's jaw dropped. "Oh…" He snapped his mouth shut and quickly shook his head. "Not at all. And might I say – nicely done, Trench!"

Trench grinned, the action tugging at his deep scar uncomfortably. "Don't worry, Wave. I'm sure there'll be some single Shieldian ladies looking for attention after they see the happy new couple joined."

Wave smiled. "I'm counting on it." He glanced at Yanelle then and the Companion rolled her eyes and shook her head before looking away.

After a time they arrived at the reception site. It was a broad spiral formation several hundred paces in diameter, consisting of six spiral arms of stone columns. Actaeon noticed that the columns all varied in their number of sides, from three at the very ends and increasing up to the center of the arms until there were too many to count. The central stone was, appropriately enough, a cylinder. Here and there scattered stones had been broken or crumbled, the remnants lying in the grass nearby.

Harvand Xula was the first to greet them. "My friends! So good to see you all." He hugged Actaeon tightly and slapped the Prince Engineer hard on the back. "Glad you came, Act."

Next, he turned to Eisandre and grasped her shoulders in a warm greeting. "Princess, it is always lovely to see you. I'm hopeful this time that you won't need to rescue me."

Eisandre took an abrupt step back out of Xula's grasp, an action that didn't appear to phase the Thyrian Captain despite the awkwardness. "I too hope that is not necessary," she replied.

Enrion greeted them next. He was dressed in an outfit of shimmering blue. Even the gloves on his hands and the slippers on his feet were the same shimmering blue as the rest of his outfit. Over his trousers, he wore a matching blue skirt that ebbed and flowed with every step he took. "My honored friends. It gladdens me that you could be here today. Come, the ceremony is about to begin."

They joined the rest of the assembled guests to kneel in a large circle with the center of the spiral in the middle.

After everyone was kneeling, one figure rose. It was that of Indros

Immerai Zar, the Prince General of Shield. He levered himself to his feet with his iron shod staff.

Beside him, his daughter, the Lady Endira Zar, also known as the Steel Rose, stood. She was dressed in a snugly fitted dress of silver and black, over which was a cuirass of intricate banded metal strips that crisscrossed her body down to her hips. Her signature pair of thin swords was strapped over her left shoulder.

She lifted her father's red and black mitre to place it upon his head and handed him a long wrapped bundle of white cloth, which he clutched to his chest as he stepped forward. "His Most Venerable Grace, Indros Immerai Zar," she announced before returning to her knees.

"And now we bear witness as two of the chosen are joined on this day, the twenty second of Monsoon's Dawn," intoned Indros, a series of echoes resounding from the stones around him. "Marriage is a battle," he continued. "And what better sacrament to undergo than that for a people who are warriors in blood and warriors in mind."

Indros unwrapped the bundle and tossed aside the cloth to reveal a pair of decorative single-edged swords with characters of the Ancients etched into their blades. The pommel of each sword had a light blue streamer of fabric tied to it. "Now... to the point," he said. "Who is it that would join my son on the field?"

"It is I, Your Most Venerable Grace," came a voice. "Lady Kiroko Xan of Rusthaven." Kiroko wore a shimmering blue outfit to match Enrion's. Her black hair was tucked neatly into a bun that was held in place by several loops of metal that passed through it.

Indros threw one of the swords at her, blade first.

The Lady weaved to the side effortlessly and snatched the blade in midair by its pommel. She straightened and saluted the Prince General by touching the pommel to her forehead. "I stand ever ready."

The Prince General nodded and turned to survey the circle of kneeling attendees. "And where is he who would join this Lady on the field?"

Enrion stood. "It is I, father. Enrion Zar, Lord of Holdfast, Governor of Lazi's Tomb – your son."

"Very well then," said Indros, coldly. He threw the second blade at Enrion even harder, but this time pommel first.

The hilt struck Enrion in the shoulder and he nearly stumbled backward. But his hand whipped out and he snatched the blade from the air not a moment before it would have been beyond his reach.

The Shieldians present let out a collective gasp. If he'd have dropped the sword, the ceremony would have been off.

Enrion recovered and saluted his father with the sword. "I stand ever ready."

Indros nodded slowly and stroked his thin, graying beard as he pondered Enrion with beady black eyes from beneath the tall mitre. "Just so. Then let the battle commence." He strode purposefully from the circle.

Enrion and Kiroko bowed to one another slowly. When they rose, each offered the other a salute. The pair began an intricate dance, weaving throughout the stones as they moved. The blue streamers from their swords whipped and wound their way behind them as they toyed with one another through the spirals.

Gradually they came closer and closer together in their dance, each's movements a reflection of the other's. Until at last they arrived at the center cylindrical stone. There they danced around it on opposite sides, their shimmering blue skirts fluttering as they moved.

It was Enrion who finally closed on Kiroko.

She tried to block his blade, but he batted it aside and pushed her against the stone. He put his free hand beside her head and met her eyes with an intense gaze.

Kiroko smiled and leaned forward to kiss him.

Enrion's eyes closed, but before their lips could meet, she ducked under his arm and pirouetted around his back.

Kiroko's blade arced toward Enrion, but the young Lord's blade met her own and he pushed her in the opposite direction.

Kiroko fell then, and Enrion caught her in his arms. But when he leant down to kiss her, she spun away again.

The full battle ensued then – the pair pressing one another back and forth amidst the many-sided stones.

At some point the sounds of stringed instruments began, played by musicians hidden out of sight beyond the Ancient stone formation.

Sparks showered from their blades at every clash as Enrion pressed Kiroko until her back was against another stone.

Enrion reached out to gently grasp her neck. His hand slid downward and he ripped her blue tunic and skirt away to reveal a shimmering silver outfit beneath.

Someone threw Kiroko another sword with a light gray streamer. She caught it and brought both of her blades together to trap Enrion's. She spun beneath his arm and leapt into the air before rolling away. Once she regained her feet, she saluted Enrion first with one sword and then the other.

Enrion smiled and caught a second sword that was thrown to him. With both blades, he saluted her in return.

Both spread their blades and began to circle one another with slow, methodical movements.

The hidden music of the strings slowed along with them, but as the tempo increased, so did their pace.

It was Kiroko who finally leapt to the attack, the strings of the musicians aflutter with activity right in step with her.

Enrion brought both blades forward and a shower of sparks like none seen on any real battlefield came off of their blades.

The blades were a blur then. They whirled and spun and rolled and leapt amidst a maelstrom of clashes and sparks, flashes, and clangs.

Those motions morphed effortlessly from those of combat and chaos to those of love and affection. Where they once were swinging blades, they were now caressing one another with love. And where they once sought to repel, they now sought to draw the other in.

Their swords were held to the side then and the dance became one of celebration. The pair began to move as one, helping each other into the next dance movement. Eyes locked together.

The melody shifted to a jovial one.

In time they halted all movement and drew one another close. And they kissed.

"Witness on this day!" intoned Indros once more. The Prince General had reemerged from the circle of kneeling attendees. "As Enrion Zar and Kiroko Xan are joined as one."

The couple paused in their kiss and released their embrace. They both saluted Indros with their swords.

Indros waved dismissively. "Let the celebration commence."

"Does it hurt?" Jezail felt Trench's shoulder where it had been pierced by the bolt.

The bulk of the celebration had passed and Jezail had led Trench away to the edge of the Stone Gardens where she had spread a tablecloth that she'd stolen from the reception. And so, on it they both sat – their backs against a stone pyramid as they faced the Windmoor and looked up at a staggering field of stars.

"Not so much as you'd think, lass," said Trench. "I've had so many worse ones."

Jezail leaned into his side and reached up to trace the deep scar on his face. "Like this?"

"Aye," said Trench. "I don't remember much about it until well after it happened. I probably should've died after gettin' that one. I wanted to at the time."

Jezail slid her head down to his chest and looked up at him, her red hair splayed out across his lap. "I'm glad you didn't."

Trench smiled, the effort tugging at the deep scar bisecting his face. "Me too, Jez." He ran his big fingers through her soft hair, playing with it gently.

She continued to trace the lines of his face. "You're worth my continued fight. I know that now. We never know where life will take us."

"Whaddaya mean, lass?" asked Trench.

"That's what you said to me when Varisk died. 'There's things in this world worth your continued fight.' Well you're one of them, and I'm so glad I kept fighting," said Jezail, smiling up at the giant. Her giant.

"You honor me, Jezail," said Trench. "I don't deserve yer love, but I'm glad to have it." He smiled down at her again.

"Nonsense," said Jezail. "You deserve everything." She ran her fingers along his lips. "You know, it is beautiful, your smile."

"Yer blinded by feelings, lass," said Trench with a grin. "I've nothing to do with the beauty 'neath these stars. It's all you." He traced the old burn that stretched the skin around her right eye with surprisingly gentle fingers for his large hands.

Jezail's cheeks flared red, emphasizing her freckles.

Trench chuckled.

"What's so funny, old man?" asked Jezail, making her lips pout.

"Yer just cute when the lifeblood runs to yer cheeks, young lass," said Trench with a chuckle.

Jezail smiled mischievously and took his hand from her face. She guided it gently down into her trousers. "Not the only place my lifeblood runs to, ya know."

Trench's eyes widened as he felt her arousal.

Delighted, Jezail let out a musical laugh, followed by a low moan. "Still cute, am I?"

"Naw lass... yer... yer..." stammered the giant.

Jezail grinned and rolled beside him onto the stone's slope to pull him over into a deep kiss.

And there, underneath the canvas of stars, with the cool winds of the Windmoor upon their bare skin, she took him to a place where no words were needed.

"You have been avoiding me, Gunther."

Gunther Arcady paused midstride just before the Mirrorhold entrance to the Shieldian Hold and pivoted to face his addresser, daring him to say more.

Ambrosius the Wise threw back the hood of his gray and green robes. He met Arcady's gaze with his own, devoid of all emotion. The Raedellean advisor turned to watch a passing Niwian nobleman before lackluster eyes snapped back to the Lord Shore. "You have been avoiding me, Gunther," he repeated.

"I've business to tend to, Ambrosius," snapped Arcady with impatience. "Have you ever considered that the failure to find me is your own?"

"You've not kept up your side of the bargain," said Ambrosius. The silver-haired man shook his head in disappointment. "Not one bit. Letting the Engineer and that Lost child meddle in affairs much beyond Raedelle's. It is not their place, haven't I told you that?"

Arcady narrowed his eyes. "Oh, and I suppose you also expect me to birth the royal successor too? The last I checked, you supported my niece's anointment to Raedelle's helm, not mine. Oh, and might I add – I'm not certain how you convinced Beiloff to burn the Engineer's workshop, but that was a bad idea."

"I convinced him of nothing," said Ambrosius. "But thank you for revealing that you weren't the ideator behind what I thought was the sole worthy act you had accomplished in the last few months."

Arcady's mouth twisted into a wry smile. "While nothing would make me happier than to have seen the Engineer's workshop burn with he and his new wife inside, I am neither so stupid nor so impulsive. I did not get to my position by being vacuous."

"That is true," agreed Ambrosius, bringing his hands together before him. "You achieved your position because I *let* you achieve it."

The Lord Shore closed the distance to the advisor and growled his next words. "Cut the trumpery and get to your Ancient-damned point, Ambrosius. My patience is wearing thin."

Ambrosius arched his brow. "And my own has not? I am particularly displeased with what happened with The Veiled One. I expected you to at the very least put up an argument against their campaign in the north. Instead, I find that you said exactly nothing."

Arcady felt anger rising in his chest. "You would have had me argue against a campaign to destroy a lunatic who would have murdered all of the people in Redemption? It is clear that you are becoming mad, Ambrosius. I've had enough of this conversation. The Veiled One should absolutely have been killed, and I wouldn't have lifted so much as a finger to stop it."

The Lord Shore pivoted on his heel and strode away. But then, sudden and unbidden, there came the urge to stop and he turned around again to face Ambrosius the Wise. Arcady shook his head and struggled to turn back. And failed.

"You will not defy me again, Gunther," said Ambrosius.

Arcady looked at the floor and nodded, blinking in surprise as he did so. "I will not defy you again," he said, the words not his own.

"From hereon in, you shall do your utmost to prevent the Princess and her meddlesome Engineer from interfering in any foreign affairs. Enough damage has been done. And if you cannot prevent them, you shall notify me," explained Ambrosius. "Do you understand?"

"I do understand, Ambrosius," said Arcady, his eyes fluttering in surprise as words that were not his own came from his mouth. "You have my deepest apologies. I will not let you down again."

"Good, my child," said Ambrosius, resting a hand lightly on Arcady's shoulder. He squeezed so hard that it left a bruise. "And do not forget the promise you made me long ago. You work for me. Will you remember?"

"I will... remember," said Arcady, flabbergasted.

"Very good." Ambrosius patted Arcady's cheek and offered an emotionless smile. "I'll hold you to that."

And with that, the Raedellean advisor strode off and left the Lord Shore standing there for an awkward while.

Wave awoke with lips wrapped around him in the most delightful manner.

He tilted his head back and sighed, trying to remember where he was and how he'd gotten there.

The last he remembered, he'd been at Enrion's wedding. He remembered being disappointed when he saw Calisse and Yanelle dancing together. He'd been keen on both women, but they seemed more interested in each other. Even when he tried to join them, they'd just laughed teasingly and danced away from him.

As he'd withdrawn, he watched Jezail lead Trench off toward the Windmoor.

"Good for him. It's about time," he'd said before leaning against one of the stones in the spiral formation.

It was then that the Steel Rose wrapped her hand around the hilt of his rapier. "Come with me, mercenary," she said, her tone brooking no argument.

She'd led him into the Pyramid and up into her private room in the Mirrorholds. There she'd had her way with him multiple times until they'd both fallen to sleep, exhausted and drunk from rice wine.

Wave winced as sudden teeth on his skin snapped him out of the recollection. "By the Fallen! Watch it, woman!"

Endira Zar stood up and slapped him lightly. "Shut up, mercenary. I don't pay you for your lip."

"Pay me?" asked Wave, woozy and confused. He lifted a hand to his stinging cheek.

The Steel Rose put a hand over his mouth and climbed atop him. She had her way with him until she was well and thoroughly pleased.

Once they both were through, she climbed off and wrapped a sheer robe about her body. "You may leave," she said, tossing a pouch of bits atop the bed beside him.

"That's it?" said Wave. He looked down at the bits spilling from the pouch onto the silken sheet, bewildered.

"Do not make me call the guards," snapped Endira. "You've served your purpose. Now get dressed and get out."

Wave shook his head and shrugged. "If you say so, Lady Zar." He pulled on his trousers and boots. Next, he shrugged into his tunic and pulled on his jacket. "Though don't mind my saying that I'd be more'n glad to come back when next you find you might need my services."

Endira didn't even turn, but her hand snapped out and she pointed to the door. "Out!"

Wave let out an exasperated sigh and quickly fastened his sword belt around his waist. "Yes, Lady Zar. But be warned – next time might not be so satisfying for you, after last night and this morning. When that happens, I'll just be a simple summons away."

"Did I not say out?" asked Endira. "Else I'll lop it off and you'll never use it again."

"Um," said Wave, looking down at his crotch. "Point taken. And with that said, I'll be off."

The Steel Rose turned her back on him and retreated behind the divider to her wash area to clean herself.

Wave rolled his eye before striding out into the Mirrorholds.

He came to an abrupt halt in Endira's doorframe when he glimpsed Ambrosius the Wise and Gunther Arcady, the Lord Shore. The pair were engaged in a heated dialogue.

It was a conversation that he didn't want to miss. He pulled Lady Zar's door mostly closed behind him and watched the pair carefully from behind the pair of Shieldian guards that stood at attention several steps beyond the door's alcove.

Talk of the burning of Actaeon's workshop piqued his interest and he strained to hear the details over the clamor of the echoic Mirrorholds. Nearby workers were cleaning soot from the mirrored ceiling facets – eliciting a steady squeaking sound that only left bits and pieces of the conversation audible at his distance.

Wave overheard mention of the Veiled One next and then watched as Arcady began to storm off. Strangely enough, the Lord Shore turned back around and had another exchange with Ambrosius. The old advisor patted Arcady's cheek and walked off.

"Can I help you, sir?" asked one of the Shieldian guards who had finally noticed him in the doorway's alcove.

Wave smirked and disregarded the man's suggestion with the wave of a hand. "Nah, I've got this from here. Thanks though." He closed Endira's door the rest of the way and started over, making sure his sword belt was properly cinched as he did so.

Arcady still stood, looking astonished, in the center of the Mirrorholds when Wave arrived before him.

The back of Wave's hand across his face took the Lord Shore off guard and he staggered back several steps.

"Shattered Redemption's wrong with you?" snapped Arcady, his hand falling to the hilt of his sword.

"By the Fallen, man! You should ask the same of yourself," barked Wave. He spit at the Lord's feet. "Bet yer regretting sending your dog to burn me up in the workshop. Perhaps next time you'll send someone who can actually do a job the right way. Only there won't be a next time when I'm through with you, you cad!"

"How dare you speak to your better that way," retorted Arcady, his hazel eyes burning with controlled rage. "I'd nothing to do with your precious Engineer's workshop catching fire."

"Sure..." said Wave. "And I'm an Ancient. Don't play me a fool, Arcady. I heard you speaking of it with Ambrosius. You've done nothing but try and ruin the Princess and the Prince Engineer since the beginning."

A crowd had begun to gather and Wave raised his voice so that everyone could hear. "You kidnapped Act to force him to free that damned sword for yourself and then when we rescued him, you murdered all of the guards that we'd rendered unconscious and tried to blame it on us. Then you paid off tribals to chase us across the Wall, all so that you could stop Eisandre from reaching Caliburn Castle so you could claim the throne for yourself. How could you do that to yer own niece, you monster of a man?" Wave didn't allow him a moment to respond to that. "When that didn't work, you had your dog burn down the workshop to try and kill them. And what's this I hear now? You were on the side of the Veiled One? Yeah, I overheard that too."

The gathered crowd began to murmur, many of them pointing at the Lord Shore.

"I don't have to stand here and listen to baseless accusations and slander from a simple sellsword like you," said Arcady. "Especially not one whose murder of so many innocents at Blackstone Fortress was swept under the rug to protect your employer. And now you try to turn that on me?" He shook his head in disgust. "Enough of this. You struck me – do you plan on following up on that challenge or are you naught but a coward, Gavid?"

Wave met Arcady's burning eyes with his lone eye and laughed. "It's time that Redemption is rid of one more person like you, Gunther. I challenge you to the death. You can pick the time and place. Unless, of course, you're the coward here."

There was a collective gasp from the crowd gathered to witness the altercation.

Arcady's lips twisted into a smirk and he ran a hand through his slick black hair. "Now there's something we may finally agree on. Redemption is better off without you breathing your lies and slander to all who would listen. I shall call it in four days' time, at the sun's apex, in the Stone Gardens."

"Funny how you're more concerned with the purported slander than the purported murder," noticed Wave. "Anyway, best get yer things in order. Maybe choose a successor? I'll see you four days hence. I look forward to killing you – should've done it decades ago."

"As I recall," said Arcady, "your chaperone had to step in before I could kill you."

The Lord Shore turned on his heel and strode off.

"It must be nice to constantly live in a delusion of your own making," said Wave with a smirk. He turned to leave the Mirrorholds in the other direction.

"I'm not sure this is the best idea, gentlemen," said Wave.

Actaeon and Trench had brought him to The End the night before his duel with the Lord Shore. He'd argued with them about it and they had assured him that there would only be one drink. They were currently well into their fourth.

"Another round?" asked Oril, the bartender.

"Bring it on," said Actaeon with a grin.

Wave raised his hands. "Not for me. I've got to have my wits about me on the morrow."

"Aw, come now, Wave!" said Trench. "The duel's not until noon. You'll be fine for a few more drinks."

Oril dropped three fresh tankards on the bartop.

Trench shoved one of them into Wave's hands and lifted his own. "To a world without Gunther Arcady, startin' on the 'morrow."

Actaeon lifted his own tankard. "I shall second that toast."

Wave shook his head and downed the remainder of his fourth tankard in order to take up the fifth. "Fine. I've gotta toast that one." He lifted the new tankard into the air.

They all clanked their tankards together and drank.

"If only I was there ta see the looks on everyone's faces when you called 'im out like that," said Trench.

"It was glorious," said Wave with a smirk. He took another deep draught from his tankard. "They were all whispering and pointing at him. Those rumors won't die anytime soon, I think." He set his tankard down then. "Excuse me, gentlemen. I've need of the facilities." The shorter mercenary stood and, though a bit wobbly, strode off to go relieve himself.

Once Wave was gone, Trench cast a look at Actaeon. "Ya think it'll be enough?"

Actaeon shrugged and met Trench's concerned gaze with a mischievous grin. "Oril has been giving him her heaviest alcohol while she has been watering our own drinks down. Another drink or two, perhaps? And then we can put the plan into effect."

Trench shook his head, upset. "I wish we didn't hafta do this, Act."

"You said it yourself, Trench," Actaeon reminded him. "Wave has one less eye and his leading ankle still is not the same after Vain injured it. He will not stand a chance against Gunther Arcady. Thus, we come in."

"I hope yer right," said Trench. "Else we're setting him up to fail by getting him drunk like this."

"Just intoxicated enough to set our plan into effect," said Actaeon, lifting his tankard. "Enough talk about it. Wave returns."

Trench forced a smile that tugged on his deep scar and lifted his tankard to Actaeon's before taking a sip.

"I miss anything?" asked Wave as he sat back down at the bar. He lifted his tankard. "What're we toasting?"

"May yer blades strike true," said Trench.

"And without hesitation," added Actaeon.

"Aye! I'll drink to that," said Wave.

And so they did.

Later that evening, Actaeon and Trench carried a drunk and unconscious Wave between them as they walked along the Avenue of Glass.

"I just hope he wakes 'fore the duel tomorrow," said the giant.

"Matron Seraeta gave me a potion that should wake him easily," said Actaeon. "It will stimulate his senses and better prepare him for the duel as well. Best that we administer it just a short while before it begins. He may be stressed that he is late, but his reflexes will be optimal for the event."

"Yer a devious fella, Act," said Trench. "Remind me never ta cross you."

"Very well," said Actaeon with a grin. "Never cross me, Trench."

The two of them laughed.

When they arrived back at the workshop, they brought Wave up into the loft. There they tucked him into his bed.

"Sleep well, old friend," said Trench. The giant patted Wave's forehead affectionately before he stood and glanced back at Actaeon. "It's time, Act."

Actaeon nodded and headed back down the stairs. There he looked through the chemicals of the laboratory until he found the correct one – a small half-through vial that contained a clear liquid with golden flakes suspended within it.

As he made his way back to the stairs up to the loft, he nearly barreled into Yanelle.

The Companion wore naught but a simple shift, her sword belt loosely wrapped about her waist. The cold stone floor against her bare feet didn't appear to bother her.

"Ah, Yanelle," said Actaeon with a smirk. "We must have woken you with our late arrival. My apologies." The Companion often stayed up in the loft when she was there guarding Actaeon – Lauryn had built her a partition to sleep in.

She crossed her arms and offered him a stern look. "It's not right what you're both doing to him, ya know."

Actaeon arched a brow. "And the alternative would be better?"

Yanelle shook her head groggily. She cast a disappointed glance back up the stairs. "Best would've been if he weren't dumb enough to make the challenge in the first place."

Actaeon grinned and put a hand on her shoulder. "Now that is where we can both agree. Believe me, Yanelle, I did not save him from one wretched creature only to have another type of wretched creature kill him."

Yanelle looked up at the ceiling, still conflicted. Finally she nodded.

"You're a good friend, Act. I still don't agree with it. But you're a good friend."

Actaeon smiled and met her gaze. "Thank you, Yanelle. That means a lot coming from you."

She smirked at him and offered him a playful elbow in the side, causing him to wince at his still tender terror bird injury. "What're you wasting time talking to me then? Better get upstairs 'fore he wakes."

Actaeon grinned and brought the bottle back up to Trench.

The giant leaned over his friend's bedside as he applied the liquid.

Once the task was completed, Trench turned to Actaeon and nodded solemnly.

Their work done, they both retired to bed.

Tomorrow would be a busy day.

DUEL

"I NEVER SHOULD'VE GONE OUT DRINKING with you pair of idiots," grumbled Wave. He rubbed his pounding head as he walked through the knee-high grasses of the Windmoor between Actaeon and Trench. Yanelle travelled some distance behind them. Lauryn had refused to join them – she was furious that Wave would risk his life over a duel.

"And miss what could be the last chance ta drink with ya?" asked Trench. "That'll be the day!"

"Bah!" Wave turned and spat into the grass. "As if I'd let a spoonfed noble like Arcady get the best of me. That'll *really* be the day."

"Do not fail to forget what that man is capable of, Wave," said Actaeon. "Remember the Fallen of Blackstone Fortress whom he murdered after you sought to simply render them unconscious. Arcady is a conniving soul. He is as inventive at death and destruction as I am at any engineering construct."

Wave halted and offered Actaeon a hard look in return, his headache momentarily retreating. "I don't forget them for one moment, Act. That's why I'll paint these grasses red with his blood. For those murdered at Blackstone, including young Olli the page, for all the brave Wall Breakers we lost on the Wall, and for poor young Cortecha, who nursed me back to health only to have her life cut short by Arcady's dog. Yeah, Act, I know what he's capable of. And it stops now, it stops here. I'll not abide another death at his hands."

Actaeon took a deep breath and nodded. "I understand, Wave. This is your way of fixing things."

"That's right," said Wave. "Just do me a favor?"

"Anything," said Actaeon.

Wave smirked. "If I lose, toss a grenado into the ring and send us both to shattered Redemption."

Actaeon grinned. "You have my word, Wave. Only..."

"Only what?" snapped Wave.

"Do not let it come to that," said Actaeon. "We need you in intact Redemption."

"I'll not forget, Act," said Wave. He continued on.

They could see the scattered stones ahead when they ran into Eisandre.

The Raedellean Princess waited for them with First Companion Itarik at her side.

Wave took a knee and offered the Princess a flourishing bow. "Your Grace."

Eisandre stepped forward. "Stand up, Wave."

The one-eyed mercenary stood and Eisandre embraced him uncharacteristically. "You should not have done this. There are better ways. We need you with us."

Wave looked surprised and hugged her lightly in return. "I appreciate that, Princess. But the behavior of this animal must be stopped. And I intend to do just that."

Eisandre released him and stepped back. "Return to us. This world needs you. Don't throw that away."

Wave's single eye drifted to the trampled grass between them. "Aye aye, Your Grace. I'll not forget that. Thank you for being here."

When Wave looked back up, the Princess had stepped aside. She watched him with uncertainty. He sucked a deep breath and continued forward.

Wave smiled as the crowd came into sight. It was a larger crowd than he expected. It appeared that most of the nobility in and around Pyramid had come out to see the contest between the two veterans. "You guys know I've been through much worse than this. You should stop worrying so damned much."

"Who said we're worrying?" asked Trench, slapping his friend on the shoulder.

Wave shrugged. "You're a mite too quiet for a group that has confidence their friend'll win this round of life."

"Yer lookin' too far into things, my friend," said Trench. "We're just givin' you the space ya need ta sort out any final thoughts."

"Final thoughts?" said Wave. "What're you trying to say?"

"Final thoughts before the duel, we mean," said Trench. "Nothin' special. Just giving ya time to think 'bout how ya wanna kill the man's all."

Wave paused and narrowed his eye upon his large friend. After a moment he shook his head and continued onward. "Just don't forget to toss a grenado in if it looks like things are going downhill."

"A grenado, aye aye," said Actaeon with a grin. "I doubt you will need it though."

Wave kept onward and as the people at the fringes of the crowd noticed him an excited cheer went up.

"Gee, they're damned excited to see one of us die, eh?" said Wave.

"Always are," said Trench.

A heavy hand fell upon his shoulder and spun him around.

Companion Yanelle stood before him. She regarded him for several long lifebeats before she smirked and pulled his head to hers, kissing him hard upon the lips.

When she broke the kiss, a bewildered Wave was at a loss for words.

"In case we don't get the chance ever again," said Yanelle with a smile, echoing his own words once spoken in a moment of desperation in the Underforest.

"You..." Wave said, blushing. "I thought..."

"Don't think so hard about it," said the Companion, brushing a lock of red hair from her eyes. "Just go win your duel, alright?"

"Alright," said Wave. The mercenary smiled and turned about. With a newfound confidence, he strode forward.

The crowd parted to allow him into the circle of trampled grass they had gathered around. There were many more people than anticipated — there must've been half a thousand spectators present for the event. Those gathered drew quickly silent now that both combatants were in the ring.

"Typical of a sellsword like you to keep me waiting," said the Lord Shore as Wave arrived at the center of the gathered crowd.

A wide berth was left for them to fight amidst the scattered formations of the Stone Gardens. A Sentinel Arbiter, Mitrius sof Cignith, stood within the space that remained, presiding over the duel.

Wave was surprised that such a high-ranking Arbiter had been sent out. It showed how important a political event this was, he supposed.

"I figured you'd enjoy the extra few breaths of life it'd allow you," Wave retorted.

Arcady ran a hand through his slick black hair and smiled at Wave. "Without Glaive to intervene do you really think you stand a chance?"

Wave smirked and tied his hair back into a neat queue. "Now we get to see what would've happened without her saving your throat from my blade."

Arcady laughed. "Ha. Go on believing that, Gavid. The only throat she saved was your own."

"Just be sure to listen to the Arbiter, Gunther," said Wave. "You don't have Daddy around to keep you in line this time."

Gunther rolled his eyes and offered a sidelong glance at Mitrius. "Let's get this over with already. My patience for this rogue has more than run its course."

Mitrius stepped between them and blew a note from a piercing whistle that Actaeon had designed.

The crowd drew silent and the Sentinel Arbiter raised both of his hands.

Once he was satisfied with the silence, Mitrius spoke, his voice echoing among the many stones. "These two gentlemen have agreed to a duel to the death and have requested arbitration by the Order of Arbiters, as is law in neutral Pyramid and its surrounds. Each of their dueling swords will be allowed. No other weapon shall be present in the ring. If I blow my whistle, both combatants will pause the fight. Once the killing blow has been established, I shall call the match. None outside of the ring shall interfere or else be held in contempt by the Order of Arbiters. This duel shall not end until I so deem it ended. Do you both understand and agree?"

"I agree," said Wave as he handed his companion dagger to Trench.

"Yes, let's get on with it," said Arcady as he slipped on his blackened lion-lizard leather gauntlets.

"Very well then," said the Sentinel. "Gentlemen, draw your weapons and begin."

Wave slid the length of his flamberge rapier free of its scabbard. He took some practice swings with the weapon before pointing the wavy blade and looking along it at his opponent. "Been thirty years coming, old man."

The Lord Shore's hand came to rest gently upon the filigree basket hilt of his dueling sword. He leveled a positively malevolent smile upon Wave. "Thirty years have been much kinder to me than they have to you." He winked at the mercenary in emphasis to his point. "And it's about to get much worse for you." Arcady slowly drew the sword and held it out to the side, as if daring Wave to test his defenses.

Wave began to circle toward Arcady's off hand side. "If your idea of the years being kinder involves the opportunity to paint your lands red with the blood of your kin, then you've got me there, ol' Gunny-boy. I've not been so lucky as that." He smiled and offered him an exaggerated one-eyed wink.

With an exasperated sigh, Arcady rolled his eyes and gave an appealing look to the Arbiter, who shrugged and gestured for him to continue with the duel. The Lord Shore shook his head and lowered his eyes upon Wave once more. "Will you get this over with already, I've got better th-"

But he was interrupted as Wave shot forward in a flash.

Arcady easily met his blade with his own blow for blow across his body as the mercenary sought to flank him.

When Wave was at his left shoulder, Arcady took the opportunity to press his own series of rapid attacks at the mercenary's off hand side.

Even lacking his eye on that side, Wave fended off the blows without slowing.

Their blades and movements quickly became naught but a blur for most of the spectators.

"You've adapted well," said Gunther as he pressed the attack. "I shall give you that much. You would have gone great places in your life had you not been such a blackguard."

Wave nimbly moved to and fro in order to cause Arcady to overreach and used the opportunity to press his own series of attacks. "In case you've not noticed, I've gone great places despite your trying to stop me. In fact, I made it all the way to Lakehold to help a true leader take Raedelle's throne instead of an unscrupulous pretender who'll soon feed the trees."

Arcady's hazel eyes narrowed and burned into his opponent at those words. And when the right opportunity came along and Wave lunged an attack, he kicked out.

Wave leapt to the side, but the Lord's boot caught him a glancing blow in the side of his leading ankle. He winced and scrambled away, covering his retreat with his blade against a new series of attacks.

The injury from his battle with Beiloff nearly half a cycle earlier was coming back to haunt him.

As he continued to fend off Arcady's attacks, Wave carefully tested his leading ankle. He quickly came to the realization that the kick had exacerbated his old injury. His ankle was no longer at full strength.

"Aw, what's wrong, Gavid?" asked Arcady, feigning concern in his tone. "If I didn't know any better, I'd say you were hurt."

Wave grunted and leapt forward to press another attack, his blade a flurry of thrusts and slices that made Arcady beat a hasty retreat.

As Wave began to pursue more aggressively, Arcady caught one of his blows against his blade and spun to the side. He swung his leg wide in the process and caught Wave in the ankle with the heel of his boot.

"Gah," cried Wave. He stumbled backward and hopped back onto his good foot as the crowd gasped. Tentatively, he put weight back on his injured ankle, but he was limited by the pain that flared up his leg.

Arcady smiled smugly and wasted no time in pressing a new attack of his own. Less concerned now with his own defenses, he held nothing back in the onslaught.

Wave deftly managed to fend off the worst of the blows, but one of the thrusts caught him in the side, spilling bright red blood onto his white jacket. A second slice caught him in the triceps of his sword arm before he could repel it and he felt warm blood run down to his elbow.

The crowd erupted into yells and boos. The Sentinel Arbiter held up his hand to forestall those who would rush forward.

Wave recouped his position by luring Arcady in close with the promise of yet more openings. When Arcady overextended in a thrust, Wave used the opportunity to bind his sword with his own. In an unexpected flash, Wave reached forward to grasp his opponent's hilt and force it against Arcady's thumb.

The Lord Shore realized what was happening too late and surrendered his sword to Wave in order to grasp the mercenary's own sword hilt with both hands and pry it loose.

When both duelists stepped back, each was armed with their opponent's sword.

The spectators let out a combination of applause and gasps of surprise.

"This was wholly unanticipated," muttered Actaeon just loud enough for Trench to hear where they stood at the front of the crowd.

"This ain't good, Act," grumbled Trench.

Arcady hefted the flamberge rapier and shook his head. "Cracked Redemption knows why you use this stupid blade."

Wave smirked. "Better learn fast." The mercenary switched Arcady's sword to his left hand and began to press a series of feints and attacks to keep his opponent on the move. The switch meant his leading ankle was now the uninjured one, which allowed him to make a more aggressive push forward.

The Lord Shore was unfamiliar with how to use the wider flamberge rapier. Each time he parried one of Wave's blows, it was confusing as the straight sword impacted a different point along the wavy blade in an unpredictable fashion. It slowed him down just enough.

Wave struck true by circling his own flamberge and cutting a slice out of Arcady's right cheek.

Arcady backpedaled rapidly and maneuvered to interpose one of the Ancient stones between him and his opponent.

Wave feinted to one side of the stone and then ducked low to roll to the other side. When he alighted to his feet, he grimaced at the pain in his ankle, but his sword slash struck true.

Arcady stumbled away, gasping in disbelief at the large gash in his belly that had been torn clear through his leathers. He reached down and paled as he felt a loop of intestine protruding from the wound. "Sentinel!" he called out. "The duel should only continue with the correct weapons in hand."

Wave halted his press and turned his face so that he could see the Sentinel Arbiter from the corner of his single eye.

Mitrius sof Cignith shook his head. "Nowhere in the rules did I say you couldn't switch weapons. The duel shall continue."

Arcady cursed under his breath and Wave leapt to the attack again. The Lord Shore staggered backward as the mercenary struck again and again – a blur of motion that no person could possibly keep up with. He managed to parry many of the blows, but the flamberge was too unfamiliar, and he felt the strength leaving his body through the wound in his abdomen.

Wave smirked and continued his relentless onslaught. A careful slice cut through the Lord's calf muscle to bring him to his knees. And when

Arcady was too slow with the sword to parry, he reached up to block Wave's blow with his off hand, losing half his thumb and his pointer finger in the process.

"Mercy! Mercy!" Arcady cried as he looked up in shock at his missing digits.

"For you?" said Wave. "I'll give the same mercy you gave Olli and the rest of the Blackstone victims." That said, Wave prepared his killing blow.

And in a move of utter desperation, Arcady threw his sword.

The Lord Shore launched the flamberge rapier toward Wave's injured side, nearly passing out from the effort.

The point of the flamberge bit into Wave's wound.

The waythorn took immediate effect and the mercenary fell face first into the grassy plain.

Arcady blinked his surprise before his mouth twisted into a victorious grin. He wrapped his hand around the basket hilt of his own sword to lift it.

The Arbiter's boot upon the blade forestalled the effort and tore the blade from his grip.

Mitrius knelt to examine Wave.

After a moment he stood. "This man is dead," he announced. "The victor of this duel is the Lord Shore, Gunther Arcady."

The last thing Arcady heard were the boos and outrage of the crowd before he fell unconscious from his own blood loss.

A NEW HOLD

THE DELIBERATION WITH THE CONCLAVE was a heated one, but in the end Raedelle had another Hold.

Notably, the Lord Shore was absent from the Conclave. Rumor had it he was on bed rest, fighting off infection from the severe abdominal injury Wave had given him.

Wave, of course, had not been killed in the duel. The waythorn on his own weapon had rendered him unconscious. But with Arcady bedridden, none were too keen on making accusations about why one of the hero liberators of the Pyramid was still alive after he'd lost a duel to the death.

"Let the record show that seven stand in favor and three stand opposed, with one absence," Hamnin Dafryl intoned, twirling the end of his white mustache.

Historically, Eisandre would have served as the Overseer of the Conclave as Princess of Raedelle, but she had asked Lord Dafryl to continue to serve as the Overseer in organization alone. She vastly preferred not to run the Conclave, and she thought it would be better if the rhythm of the meeting wasn't interrupted by her Lost tendencies.

Hamnin looked at her and she nodded her approval. "Thus, a new Hold of Wither shall join Shore and Lakehold, who stood alone for seventy-three years. We, the Lords and Ladies of the Conclave, officially welcome you to Raedelle."

As hoots and hollers filled the chamber from Witherian tribals and

Raedelleans alike, Eshelle made her way up to Eisandre's stone podium and wrapped her arms tightly around her sister. "Thank you," she whispered.

Eisandre looked confused as she returned her sister's embrace. "It was not my decision."

Eshelle released her and smiled. "And yet, without your support, this never would've happened." She turned to Actaeon, who stood beside his wife just to the side of the podium. "And without your support as well, brother." She embraced Actaeon then.

"It is a logical fit for Raedelle," answered Actaeon with a grin as he returned the embrace. "At once an expansion of territory, the elimination of a western front, and a place for some of our lost 'children' to reside."

"Ever the analytical one, Actaeon Rellios Caliburn," said Eshelle before she retreated from the podium.

Eisandre nodded to the Lord Dafryl and he continued.

"Her Grace, the Princess has suggested the following division of power in Wither: Houses Nivehk, Paravik, and Tkar to represent their respective Witherian tribes. House Voitek to represent a new settlement comprised of the survivors of Czeryn. House Teki to represent a new Kainai settlement. And finally, House Arandel to represent a new joint settlement consisting of settlers from both Shore and Lakehold," concluded Dafryl. "It is this division of houses which we will now vote upon. All in favor?"

The Princess raised her fist into the air first. It was immediately followed by the fists of Lady Vanora, Lord Conmara, and Lady Fletcher. Lord Dafryl raised his fist as well, his eyes scanning the chamber as he counted. Lords Ackart and Blarth raised their hands next.

"Opposed?"

Lord Perth raised his fist and was joined by Lady Tanderly of Highwater.

Lastly, Lord Tridarch Hael of Bastion raised his fist, but not before casting a look of disdain toward his two children – Tarcy, who stood in the line of Companions before the Princess' podium, and Guybon, who stood off to one side of the Princess.

Tarcy met her father's gaze with a hard look while her younger brother dropped his eyes to inspect his boots.

"Let the record show that seven stand in favor and three stand opposed, with one absence," stated Hamnin. "We had best construct some new podiums for the next Conclave. And if there is no further business, I will hand the remainder of the Conclave over to Her Grace, Princess Eisandre Rellios Caliburn."

Lady Tanderly cleared her throat. "As you were apt to point out, Lord Dafryl, Raedelle has existed with two Holds for seventy-three years. This new addition is sure to strike disorder into the very heart of our Dominion. Let it be remembered that Highwater stood against this moment, together with Lakefeed and Bastion."

"The central Dominions continue to expand and add Holds, and yet you would have us remain as we were, Lady Tanderly? That's a foolish endeavor if I ever heard one." The Lord Ackart of Southward shook his head in disdain.

"Better than letting enemies into our very Conclave!" exclaimed Jad Perth, his voice cracking.

"Should Lakefeed ever require aid from Wither, your words today, though they cut, will not give us pause," said Eshelle. She narrowed her eyes upon the Lord Perth at his podium.

"The matter has been decided," said Eisandre sharply. "Wither will join Raedelle. Raedelle will be stronger for it."

"May we all grow, learn, and be better as a part of this union," added Lady Neryl Vanora.

"The Fist of Arandel warband will journey to oversee and aid the defense of Wither," continued Eisandre, "in order to assure that no force will break our newest Hold. Welcome, our new countrymen, we are honored to have you."

"Before this Conclave concludes, Wither has one proposal and seeks recognition from the Overseer," said Eshelle.

"The Lady Caliburn is recognized," said Lord Dafryl.

With no podium of her own, Eshelle strode to the middle of the chamber and clasped her hands behind her back.

"In the spirit of this new joining, let it become Raedelle's philosophy – nay, its battlecry – to ensure that all life in the service of our great Dominion is cherished and respected. The recognition that anyone, no matter how outlandish or strange to us, might go on to do good in this world." She looked up at her sister and brother-in-law and smiled then, before continuing. "And so, in the same way we've accepted the Witherians, the surviving Czerynians, and even the Kainai to live among us, to teach us, and to empower us, I now propose that this Conclave ratify the notion that no Lost child will ever be killed again in any Raedellean Hold."

Eisandre's jaw fell to hang open at her sister's unanticipated proposal.

Eshelle beamed up at her with pride.

"And what?" spat Lord Hael. "Poison our ranks with their broken minds? For what benefit? To burden our resources?"

Lady Vanora spoke up. "Oh, please. Don't be obdurate, Tridarch. You know as well as anyone in this chamber that those families who don't bash in the brains of their Lost children give them away to one of the Orders. The TriForge is always looking for Lost children to join their ranks."

"Just because you gave away your broken son to the Loresworn doesn't make you correct," said Lady Tanderly of Highwater. "Nothing changes the fact that he'll not amount to anything."

Neryl Vanora's gaze shot daggers across the room at the Lady Highwater.

"I think it could be a good thing," inserted Lord Conmara of Incline before things could get ugly between the two Ladies. "It fosters a connection between Raedelle and the Orders of the TriForge. It can only help us."

"And who knows?" added Lord Perth, unexpectedly. "Perhaps one of those Lost babies will go on to do some great things for us one day. We've nothing to lose."

"Nothing except food, and the time of their caretakers," said Lord Ackart. "Resources that'll not amount to anything but disappointment."

"And how do you know, Lord Ackart, that one of those 'disappointments' wasn't instrumental in the retaking of Pyramid, or the destruction of the Veiled One in the north?" came an unexpected voice. All eyes went to Gwendolyn Caliburn, the Princess' mother, who sat upon the raised dais reserved for honored guests and advisors. She unfolded her hands from her lap and adjusted her bun of gray hair before she lifted her hazel eyes to regard the Lord of Southward. "Well?" she asked when he didn't respond. "I'm waiting for your answer."

"It..." sputtered Ackart. "I know that because we won. Something that would not have happened with a bunch of shattered mind idiots leading the charge."

"Is that something you would tell our friends in the Order of Arbiters who raise many Lost children to fight and defend the neutrality in the Pyramid?" snapped the Dowager Duchess in reply. Gwendolyn stood then and spread her hands, the wide green sleeves of her dress hanging down like twin arrowheads. "Do your ears not work? Did not Neryl just explain that families who cannot raise their Lost child can give them to the Orders as she once did? They will serve Raedelle there in representing our culture and values within those organizations – something which we have not had much of before. It would take a… shattered mind idiot not to recognize the logic in that," she concluded, echoing Ackart's insult.

Ackart grew red in the face with anger at her words. "Are you…" He shook his head. "It doesn't matter. The idea's a bad one – it pollutes our population to have Lost milling about."

"It pollutes our population even more to have the murderers of babes milling about," shot back Gwendolyn. "There are unborn Lost babies right now waiting to contribute to our society. Who are you to take that opportunity from them, Aethelred Ackart?" When the Lord of Southward had nothing more to say, she lowered herself back down to her seat. She looked up at Eisandre and offered her daughter a knowing smile.

"What, may I ask, would the Lady Wither propose be the punishment for the taking of a Lost life?" asked Lord Dafryl.

"Why, the same as any other murder," said Eshelle matter-of-factly. "Death."

"You'd punish a family simply looking to survive by eliminating one useless mouth to feed?" asked Lord Blarth. "Put them to death for it?"

"Yes," said Eshelle without hesitation. "Just as we would anyone who takes the life of their non-Lost child."

"Are we so certain that these Orders – this TriForge – are not just using the Lost babies they get for experiments, or as slave-workers, like the Czeryn would?" asked Delle Fletcher of Western Rim. A murmur of discussion started in the chamber at that.

"Yes," said Eisandre with certitude. "We are. Prince Aedwyn studied with the Loresworn and never spoke of anything but the good the Lost did in Travail. I served with the Arbiters and witnessed firsthand how they taught Lost children the discipline to succeed. There are Lost Knight Arbiters guarding the Pyramid right now."

"And after all the work we just did to liberate it for them," grumbled Lord Hael.

There was a scattering of chuckles in the chamber, but they soon died out as heated discussions broke out.

Hamnin Dafryl twirled his mustache before bringing his fist down against the podium. "Order! I'll have order!" When everyone quieted down, he continued. "We will vote upon the Lady Wither's proposal. That the murder of any Lost child in Raedelle be outlawed – an offense punishable by death. All in favor?"

Eisandre raised her fist immediately along with Lady Vanora. Lords Conmara and Perth joined them.

"Opposed?"

Ladies Tanderly and Fletcher raised their fists along with Lords Hael, Blarth, and Ackart. After a moment, Lord Dafryl raised his fist as well.

"Let the record show that six stand opposed with only four in –"

"You've yet to count the votes of Wither," reminded Eshelle.

"Ah, yes," said Lord Dafryl, twirling his white mustache again. "Apologies Lady Wither. Those from Wither in favor?"

And when he looked down at Eshelle, he counted six fists in the air, including hers.

Later, in the royal suite of Caliburn Castle, Actaeon massaged Eisandre's shoulders firmly. His fingers sought to battle the tension he felt in her muscles.

"Eshelle did a great thing today," said Actaeon.

"Eshy was amazing," she agreed. "Why though, must they always disagree?"

"Dissent is a natural course of action and a beneficial one at that," said Actaeon. "Without dissenting opinions, we would lack the information we need to improve ourselves and our country. Objections should always be considered, but not always followed – not unless they are with merit. A Dominion without dissenting thoughts would be a tyrannical one at that."

"Yes," said Eisandre. She let out a sigh as Actaeon massaged the tension from her shoulders. "Your words have truth to them. Only, I wish their dissent didn't carry so much anger. I desire to do the best for Raedelle. Can't they see that?"

"We both know that, my love. But consider how few of the Conclave went forth to battle with us," explained Actaeon. "A mere four of the ten, aside from yourself, of course. The others lack the perspective needed to understand that the addition of Wither will do naught but strengthen us.

Lord Hael and Lady Tanderly have no idea. Plus, Lord Hael is angry that you made his daughter a Companion. That much is obvious."

"Why can't all of them see that so many of their warbanders failed to return from the war?" asked Eisandre. "To me that is what is obvious. And why would Hael be upset about his daughter? Tarcy's a fine addition to the Companions." She turned to face him, genuine confusion and tears in her eyes.

Actaeon reached out to wrap her in his arms and she buried her face against his shoulder.

"So many lost, Act," she said as her tears continued to run. "Balin, Davil and Matt, Caider, Varisk, Kylor, Garth..." She let out a sob. "...Largrival, the young page from Blackstone – Olli, his mother Pollia, Wayd, Aedwyn and Aedgar..." The thought of her lost brothers and sisters racked her body with sobs and she shook in his embrace. "I still see all their faces, Act. All those faces, but when I speak to them, they don't answer. Why do I still see them? I know they're dead, and yet there they are, haunting me. And... they're so disappointed in me."

Actaeon rubbed her back and pulled her in close against him. "It is a natural thing to think of those we have lost. I am preoccupied with them myself. We have lost far too many in the past cycle."

"No, Act, you don't understand." She pulled back to look into his eyes, shocked and hurt that he didn't understand her. He always understood her – her Actaeon. "I *really* see them. Where I once had visions of patterns and sounds, light and colors, now I see the dead and dying with them. They say things and they do things and they... die in front of me. I've watched Garth burn to death while he tried to save young Trello. Watched him cry out for me – cry out for his partner, and then die."

Actaeon nodded. He was silent for a long time, articulating his thoughts as he looked into Eisandre's eyes. "There are times when I find myself hiding under the shield turtle in the Underforest, or running through the darkness to evade a deathcrawler swarm, or watching the team I led out to fight the Veiled One get hacked to pieces. I think of these things – at times in my dreams and at times in my waking thoughts. In both cases it is as vivid as if I am there.

"It makes me wonder," he continued. "When I was researching my mother's condition, I stumbled across one text that described ailments of the mind. What if this – what we experienced – what if it is an injury? Not an injury to our body, but an injury to our mind. We know almost nothing of how the human mind works. Perhaps it is not designed to handle such stressors as those we experience during war and horrific death. Perhaps it malfunctions and we have waking visions and flashbacks and vivid dreams, or in the case of someone who is Lost, a modification to the visions and the labyrinth of thoughts not your own. After all, it is likely to be your mind that creates those anomalies, is it not?" He grinned and reached out to wipe the tears from her cheeks.

Eisandre smiled at him weakly. "Is it? Maybe one day you will figure out the answer to that question, my Engineer."

Actaeon blushed at the compliment and looked down briefly before returning his gaze to her face.

"Thank you, Actaeon," she continued. "Thank you for making me feel less like an oddity. It does help to know that you've experienced similar... 'malfunctions' as you call them. Do you think it will always be this way then?"

Actaeon shrugged. "I cannot say, my love. All I can do is postulate that the mind may, in time, heal, as does the body. It is for that which I hope for both of us."

Eisandre leaned forward impulsively to kiss his cheek. "I do love you so."

"And I you, Eisandre," he said with a grin.

Eisandre beamed at his grin. "Will you tell us a story?"

"Us?" Actaeon repeated, looking confused.

Eisandre laughed. "The baby and me, silly. Don't worry – there aren't really any extra people in my mind. I know that. But there is one in my belly. Matron Seraeta says the baby can hear us when we talk to them."

Actaeon laughed with her and reached down to caress her large belly through the plain gray tunic which she still wore even after being cast out from the Order of Arbiters. "Of course, love."

He guided her to a chair and helped her into it. Then he knelt down before her and laid his head gently upon her belly.

"Once upon a time, a Knight Arbiter was walking amidst the ruins when she came upon a man with a very long name," he began.

The kick stopped him.

"Did you feel that?" he asked.

"I did," said Eisandre, smiling down at him. "The baby can hear you. Keep telling the story."

Actaeon grinned and felt tears of joy well up in his eyes. "'Who goes there?' said the Knight Arbiter. But the man with a very long name would not be caught off guard and prepared to defend himself if need be..."

As the Prince Engineer told his story, their baby continued to kick and wiggle. And for that night, the signs of a new life brought them such joy that for once the fallen no longer haunted them.

The Monsoon Festival was late that cycle. Given the extensive damage to the Pyramid which needed repair and the campaign against the Veiled One, it was decided that the festival would be held on the first of Torrentfall.

Whether or not to cancel the festival had been discussed at length among the Altheans, but in the end it was decided that the people of Redemption needed joy to counter the difficulties of the cycle. Plus, there was something very important to celebrate.

Shield Dominion was selected to organize the festival and they spared no expense on the arrangements.

Inside Pyramid's Sun Chamber was a marvel. The Shieldians had set up their own monsoon inside the chamber. Rainwater from outside was funneled in through openings in the broken Northern Descent. The water then travelled down wooden channels and into barrels that hung far above amidst the Skyspiral. Each barrel was riddled with tiny holes at the bottom that let loose a steady torrent of rain.

The barrels were each positioned above one of the massive dining tables far below at the Sun Chamber floor. Each table was atop a short, constructed dais – a massive circle surrounded by chairs on the outside and filled with servers or musicians on the inside, depending upon the designated function. Some served different courses of meal and some served sweet desserts, while others provided music or theatrics for the entertainment of satiated guests.

Each of the tables had above it a grand umbrella canopy in a shimmering steel gray with blue diamonds emblazoned at intervals upon it. The falling raindrops landed upon each umbrella and ran down to fall around the outside perimeter of each table's dais, just beyond the chairs so that each guest needed to step through a gentle curtain of rain before taking their seat.

Circular, grate-covered gutters collected the water and wooden channels from each table converged in the center of the chamber. There a small waterfall had been created just before the statue of the infiltrators of Pyramid. From there, larger wooden channels funneled the water out of the Sun Chamber, through the Way of Pillars and out of the Pyramid to beyond the Avenue of Glass.

"Fascinating," said Actaeon. "With a system such as this, Pyramid could have running water for most of, if not all of the cycle. All that would be required is a storage system, distribution channels or pipes, and valves to control the flow of water." The Prince Engineer marveled up at what the Shieldians had put together.

"Pretty funny that they put all this effort into something as useless as a festival instead of coming up with that idea first," said Lauryn, amused.

"Inspiration can come from many different places, Lauryn. Do not forget that," said Actaeon. "After all, art is the most creative outlet of them all. And are we not, as engineers, just artists limited by a set of boundary conditions as defined by the physical laws of our world?"

Lauryn giggled. "That's a delightful way to look at it, Act."

Actaeon arched a brow and grinned. "Delightfully accurate, I would say."

"You should speak to the Paladin Arbiter about this," said Eisandre, who held Actaeon's arm as they approached the first table. "Such an idea could be used to help fight fires as well," she suggested, thinking about the fires that the tribal invaders had lit.

Actaeon leaned over and kissed Eisandre on the cheek. "What an excellent idea, love. I knew I married you for a reason."

"Oh?" said Eisandre with a smirk. "And here I thought it was for the sex."

Actaeon blushed brightly and offered his wife a shocked look.

Meanwhile, Wave, Lauryn, Trench, and Jezail broke into bouts of laughter. After a moment, Eisandre joined in.

Actaeon grinned and they all sat down at the first table. Eisandre beamed proudly as everyone laughed at her joke. Being with Actaeon made her feel so surprisingly comfortable.

Plates of food and cups of rice wine were put before them and they began to eat.

"Where's Companion Yanelle?" asked Wave before popping a berry into his mouth.

"She said something about meeting up with the Raja's Warrioress," said Lauryn. "What's her name? Calistra? They're becoming fast friends."

"Calisse," said Wave, the news piquing his interest. "Shouldn't she be protecting you, Act?"

"We gave the Companions the evening off tonight," said Actaeon. "Especially since we knew we would be attending with a formidable team of fighters."

"Oh," said Wave. He tried to hide the disappointment in his voice.

Trench clapped his friend heavily on the back. "Don't worry, pal. You never seem to have trouble finding a lonely lass to keep company. Chin up."

At his side, Jezail chuckled at Trench's words in between sips of rice wine.

"Well, I just owed her a kiss from the one she gave me at the duel," said Wave. He smirked at Jezail and rolled his eye at her good-naturedly.

"Aw, Wave's smitten," said Lauryn, resting her chin in her hands and gazing at the mercenary in admiration.

Trench nearly spit out the gulp of rice wine he'd just taken. The giant let out a roar of laughter.

Wave blushed and tucked a loose lock of hair back behind his ear. "Very funny, little lady. I'll have you know that it takes more than a kiss to leave me smitten."

Lauryn grinned from ear to ear. "I'm sure a pretty redhead lady like Yanelle helps get you the rest of the way."

There were scattered chuckles at the table.

Wave laughed and shrugged. "Not sure what you lot thinks is so funny that I'd think about kissing a 'pretty redhead lady', as our young Lady Engineer says it." He took a sip of his rice wine and paused in thought. "Speaking of the duel, none of you'd happen to know why I took a sudden liking to eating grass at the end of it?" He narrowed his eye and looked from Trench to Actaeon, searching their faces.

Trench averted his eyes, studying a plate of various cheeses before him.

Actaeon met Wave's gaze and grinned. "I believe you already know what happened, my friend."

Wave shook his head in dismay. "I knew it!" he exclaimed. "So you idiots put waythorn on my blade. Shattered Redemption – don't you know how stupid that was of you?"

"Admittedly, it did backfire when you decided to switch swords with Arcady," said Actaeon.

"Backfire!?" Wave nearly shouted. "I'd have ended him for good if you two nullwits hadn't interfered. Just remember next time that spineless sop Arcady schemes against you that ol' Wave would've put a stop to it had you not been so foolish."

"Ya had us worried, old friend," said Trench. "It's not been so long since Arcady's dog injured yer leading ankle."

"Not to mention your body was nearly devoured by deathcrawler larvae," added Actaeon. "I doubt that did wonders for your reaction time."

"And yet, despite that which you mention, *and* the fact that you got me piss drunk the night before – by the Fallen, ya probably drugged me too. Despite all that, I still wiped the floor with that poor excuse for a man. Only, you took that away from me," said Wave. "And now he's got the perfect reason to avoid a duel with me again – he'll say I cheated. And the Fallen know he'd be right."

"Wave's right," said Jezail, in seriousness. "You shouldn't have meddled in his duel."

"I say he shouldn't have made the challenge in the first place," growled Trench. "Whaddaya think I'd do if ya threw yer life away? After all we've fought through, ya'd just toss that all away?"

Wave gave his friend a long, hard look.

Trench stared right back down at him, the ugly scar that bisected his face turning a deep red.

After several long lifebeats passed, Wave lifted his cup of rice wine into the air. "To two true friends. Thank you for caring about me, gentlemen. Truly."

Trench roared a laugh and lifted his own cup.

When Actaeon joined them with his cup in the air, Wave led them in taking a deep draught of the liquid.

"What?" exclaimed Jezail. "You're just gonna thank them now? They screwed up your entire duel. Could've cost you your reputation. Prevented you from ending the reign of a tyrant that has long afflicted Raedelle!"

Wave nodded. "Aye, Jezail. 'Cause they're true friends. They really care about me. I ain't happy – that's for sure. But it isn't always about me, is it?"

Jezail sighed and rolled her eyes before downing the rest of her cup. "If you say so."

Lord Enrion Zar approached the table then with a retinue of Shieldian guards behind him. "Your Graces," he said, addressing Eisandre and Actaeon. "May I join you?"

"Of course, Lord Zar," said Actaeon, gesturing to the empty seat next to him. "An impressive festival your people have put together."

Enrion bowed his head in appreciation and took the indicated seat while his guards stood at attention just behind him. He accepted a cup of rice wine and took a sip before clearing his throat. "We plan on recognizing your victory over the monsoon bugs in but a moment. Would you do us the honor of saying a few words, Prince Engineer?"

Actaeon smiled at Enrion and shook his head. "I would greatly prefer if you did not, Lord Zar."

Enrion gaped at him in surprise. "But you were able to find a chemical and means of distribution to foil the plague entirely. You seriously mean you don't wish us to recognize you? The people of Redemption would do well to hear from the man who saved them from famine this cycle."

Actaeon grinned and waved away the idea. "I am Prince Engineer of Raedelle. Believe me, I need not have further recognition than I already do. The recognition I have is already too much for my liking. I would prefer to be given the privacy I need to continue my work free of distraction."

"As I recall, Prince Engineer, when we first met you sought recognition and fame," said Enrion.

"I sought funding and a purpose, both of which I now have in droves," Actaeon replied. "And you may call me Actaeon, or Act, Lord Zar. There's no need for such formalities."

"Very well, Actaeon," said Enrion. "I still think it would be beneficial for the people of Redemption to hear you speak."

"And I think it would be vastly more important for the people to hear of how the resources of the TriForge helped enable the solution and a budding Interdominional Alliance helped us to carry it out," Actaeon explained. "Indeed, an Althean herbalist named Shard helped us find the mold that was lethal to the monsoon bugs. The Arbiters aided us in the use of Pyramid's ventilation system in order to distribute the pesticide across Redemption. The Loresworn helped us with predictions as to the shift of winds to maximize the distribution across the entire city. And each of the

Dominions cooperated in the dissemination of the substance among their crops all the way down to the colonies in the south.

"That is what you should speak to the people of Redemption about," he continued. "Instill in them the value of such an alliance so that any Dominion which does not continue in such joint efforts may be frowned upon by all Redemption. That is what I think would be most beneficial for the people of Redemption to hear," concluded Actaeon.

Enrion's lips twisted into a smile. "And you say you're no politician. You know more than you think about such matters, Actaeon Rellios Caliburn of Shore."

Actaeon shrugged. "We shall see, will we not?"

Enrion raised his cup and Actaeon clanked his own against it before they both drank.

Later that evening, the Prince General of Shield himself, Indros Zar, spoke to the people of Redemption about how the TriForge helped to generate the solution for the distribution of pesticide across the city to defeat the monsoon bugs. And how the Dominions all cooperated to ensure that the pesticide was distributed across most of Redemption's crops to ensure that people would have enough to eat for the cycle.

Those gathered stood and cheered at the speech.

The rain continued to fall, and the revelry continued late into the night.

GUARDIANS

"**A**ND SO, ON THIS DAY we gather together to form an Interdominional Alliance that shall continue in perpetuity. To protect Redemption from all threats to civilization, both outside and in. To ensure the safety of all our people against that which might do them harm. To provide aid to any Dominions suffering attack, famine, or affliction," pronounced the Paladin Arbiter.

"This Council," he continued, "shall be the highest authority in Redemption and shall hold its members accountable to the mission so stated. So long as such obligations are fulfilled, the Dominions shall maintain their independent status, as they always have, and shall self-govern their people how they see fit. Each member of the Council shall comprise one vote. Those members shall include representatives from each of the Orders of Arbiters, Altheans, and Loresworn, and from each of the Dominions of Shield, Ajman, Raedelle, Niwian, and Thyr. A vote of six or more shall be considered a mandate to all parties concerned and shall warrant the intervention of the available resources of each Dominion, as needed. A vote of five shall be considered a sanction to those concerned and shall warrant the preventative measures decided on by this body. A vote of four or less shall not be recognized.

"Herein and henceforth may this governing body be known as the Guardians of Redemption. And so shall those present be designated Guardians for the duration of their tenure to this Council.

"All in favor, say 'Aye'," concluded Cignith sof Iarnus.

"Aye," said Eisandre Rellios Caliburn, the Princess of Raedelle, her hands resting upon her very pregnant belly.

"Aye," said Indros Zar, the Prince General of Shield. His beady eyes swept the others with suspicion.

"Aye," said Nadiya Ajman, the Raja of Ajman.

"Aye," echoed Seraeta, the Matron of the Altheans.

"Aye," came Amodeus Jarval, Supreme Captain of Thyr, reaching up to tip his silver helmet.

"The Loresworn are ever in assent," added Kryo, the leader of the Loresworn.

"Yes, we agree," said Faschin vor Steubick, the Lord Protector of Niwian.

"And a resounding aye on behalf of the Order of Arbiters," said Cignith. "And I find this Council to be unanimous in its creation. Let it be known that the Guardians of Redemption has been formally established on this day, the thirty-third of Torrentfall. Long may this interdominional alliance last to protect the values and security that we all hold dear."

A cheer went up inside the small meeting chamber in Arbiter Pyramid Command.

Aside from the leaders of the five remaining Dominions and the three Orders, other assorted delegates were present to bear witness, standing against the walls of the chamber. Among those on the sidelines included the Keeper Elocutor, the Raja's Portent, a newly promoted Sentinel Arbiter Corvin sof Haringar, Captain Harvand Xula, Sollemnis the Gray, and the Lady and Lord Zar.

The Prince Engineer stood among them, reflecting upon the historic moment. Aside from Eisandre, he was the sole representative for Raedelle permitted into the chamber.

Ambrosius the Wise had demanded to be present, but he'd also demanded that the Princess vote against any creation of a council or alliance. When the Princess refused to do both, he'd whipped into a cold rage, lecturing them both on how Raedelle should not give up its sovereignty to the other Dominions and that it would lead to Raedelle's downfall if she voted in favor of it. Actaeon had opened his mouth to reason with the old advisor, but Eisandre cut him short when she ordered Itarik to eject the man from her chambers.

Ambrosius had shrugged off the Companion's grasp and had left them with some ominous words. "You will regret this."

The threat had lingered in the air long after he'd left. It was something that continued to vex Actaeon since, though he couldn't place just why. There was something dangerously off about the old Raedellean Advisor. Wave's story about the old historian falling on his own sword after trying to kill old Ambrosius came to mind, and he wondered about it. It was all just fairy tales, was it not? How else could a new Ambrosius have returned all those years later? Surely, they couldn't be the same person. Or could they? If his experience with the Veiled One had shown him anything, it was that he knew so much less about this world than he'd previously known was possible. If a being like the Veiled One could control the minds of countless cross-faced raiders, then surely two Ambrosius' wouldn't be a problem for a similar entity. Was the being that controlled Ambrosius encapsulated in a similar artifact as the Veiled One then? And what were these beings that wielded so much control over the minds and bodies of people throughout Redemption?

Actaeon shook himself out of his reverie as the cheers died down.

Across the chamber, old Sol was smiling at him, a glint in his eye.

When Actaeon caught the old man's gaze he proffered his own firm glare and the shake of his head.

That didn't deter Sol though. The old Loresworn began working his way around the perimeter of the chamber until he stood beside Actaeon.

Actaeon ignored him, listening to Cignith as he spoke about the fine details of when the Council would meet, how many representatives needed to be present to constitute a quorum, and how many absences would be allowed.

After a time, old Sol spoke, his voice but a whisper. "The weakness beckons, Engineer."

"Do not start in with this again, Sol," muttered Actaeon. "You know how much this means to Redemption."

"Everything and nothing," whispered Sol. "Everything if these Guardians of yours take action now. Nothing if they do not. Travail waits for none. Every lifebeat, cataclysm draws nearer."

"Every lifebeat there is another lifebeat which draws nearer for me," whispered Actaeon, gesturing to his pregnant wife where she sat at the council table. "I shall not miss that for any of your so-called cataclysms or other tests." He drew silent after Cignith shot him a look.

"Very well, Engineer," whispered Sol. "You've been warned." The old man pulled his crimson red robes tightly about him and strode from the chambers.

"You'll take your Blackstoners and eliminate the Princess at once," said Ambrosius.

The old advisor had cornered Gunther Arcady in Pyramid's Western Tunnels.

The Lord Shore shook his head in dismay, wincing at the pain in his freshly healed gut. "As much as I'd love to come to power and lead Raedelle out of the massive hole it's been digging, I must wholeheartedly refuse. You do realize that if I did what you are requesting, it'd bring our country to civil war."

Ambrosius narrowed his lackluster eyes upon the Lord Shore. "And so you'd have Great Raedelle fall instead? You are more a coward than I'd ever have imagined."

Arcady felt the same tug he'd felt on his mind an arc of the moon prior. Only this time he was prepared, and he resisted. An anger flared up deep inside him that helped him to stave off the advisor's uncanny influence. "I'll do nothing of the sort for you. My niece is the Princess of Raedelle. You've your own self to blame for it – shattered Redemption! If you'd endorsed me instead, then we'd not have had this issue. Whatever you are, Ambrosius, you're lacking in intellect." The Lord Shore shook his head and stormed off into the Hives.

"Very well then," said Ambrosius as he watched Arcady leave. "I shall do it myself."

HISTORY REPEATS

A S THE RAIN FELL IN heaving torrents, the first rays of light broke through the night's deep gloom to reveal the line of intruders that scaled Pyramid's Northern Descent. Before the full light of day emerged, the raiders slipped into the various fissures and openings to sneak into the Pyramid.

Far below, a pair of Arbiters lay upon the cracked steps of the Northern Descent, their blood already coagulating as it ran down the fractured stair of elderstone.

The raiders made no noise, nor did they speak or even gesture to one another as, one by one, they all slipped into the Pyramid, undetected by anyone still breathing.

It would be too far late before another pair of Arbiters would find their dead brothers and sound the alarm.

"The peace we dreamed of when we first began this journey is now within our grasp," said Actaeon. He squeezed Eisandre's hand.

They lay together in bed in Actaeon's room in the Song of the Sisters, an inn located within Pyramid's very pinnacle.

Together they watched as the waters of the downpour streamed down the slanted elderglass just above their heads. What would have been a smooth stream of water running past from the zenith was broken by countless droplets. Each created a temporary crater that was wiped away an eyeblink after it had formed.

Eisandre squeezed his hand in return. "It will take more work than just this, I believe."

Actaeon nodded as he watched the droplets splash down. "Indeed it shall. But this is a beginning. The Guardians of Redemption is a foundation that we must continue to reinforce and build upon. Just a cycle ago, none could have imagined that the Dominions could come together in this way. It is a testament to the hardships we have just faced — to the friends and family we have all lost along the way. Their deaths were not in vain."

"I'm so proud of you, my Prince Engineer," said Eisandre. She rubbed his arm with her other hand and touched her temple to his own. "I know how hard you've worked to guide the leaders of Redemption to this."

"And I shall keep working hard, my Princess," said Actaeon with a grin as he turned to look at her. He placed his other hand upon her swollen belly. "So that Redemption will be a safe place for our little one to grow up in."

Eisandre turned toward him as well and smiled into his eyes. "You always —" Her thought was interrupted as her face contorted in confusion and she gasped. She reached down between her legs and felt the soaked blankets there.

"Eis, what is it?" asked Actaeon in concern. He propped himself up on one elbow.

It took her a moment to compose herself before she could reply. "It's okay, I think. Seraeta told me this would happen. It's called my water breaking."

"Yes," said Actaeon, looking excited and nervous at the same time. "I am familiar with it. I have read several books on childbirth in anticipation of this very moment."

Eisandre reached up to touch his cheek. "Would you please send for the Matron? I'd like her to be here for the baby to be born."

"Of course," said Actaeon. "I shall return right after."

In addition to having posted Itarik and Yanelle outside, they had also put up Trench and Wave in the room across the hall, a fact that Actaeon was very happy about given the current situation.

The pair of Companions started when Actaeon burst into the hallway.

He slid the door to his own room shut gently and knocked upon Trench and Wave's door.

"What is it, Your Grace?" asked Itarik.

"It is Eisandre," said Actaeon. "She is about to have the baby."

Itarik's eyes widened and before he could respond, the door slid open. Wave stood there looking groggily at them. From behind him, the resounding roar of Trench's snore could be heard.

"So much for sleeping in," said Wave, following up the words with a yawn. He noticed the looks on the Companion's faces then and arched the brow over his remaining eye. "Oh no. I don't like those looks. What's going on, Act?"

"Eisandre is going to have the baby," said Actaeon.

Wave's face went white. "Oh, that's... great news."

The snoring stopped suddenly, and the giant was behind his friend in the doorframe in an instant. "We're here, Act," said Trench, rubbing the sleep from his eyes. "Whaddaya need?"

"Someone will need to fetch the Matron," began Actaeon. "And I will need help preparing for the delivery."

"I will find the Matron, Your Grace," said Itarik. The First Companion saluted fist to chest and started off.

"I'll go with him," said Wave. "No telling where she'll be. Best we have two of us looking." The mercenary scrambled to tie his sword belt about his waist.

Trench let out a laugh. "Can't get outta here fast enough, eh Wave?"

Wave shrugged. "The Princess needs her right away. She could have that baby at any moment, ya dummy."

Trench grinned and slapped his friend on the back. "Yeah yeah. Yer happy to put a baby in a woman, but when a baby's coming out of a woman, ya run for the hills."

"It's not like that at all," protested Wave.

"Sure it ain't," said Trench, with a grin that tugged at his ugly scar. "Better hurry up and catch Itarik. Yer runnin' behind."

Wave looked over his shoulder and nodded. "You're right. Good luck, Act. Er, I mean... see you shortly." With that said, the smaller mercenary took off down the hallway after the First Companion.

Eisandre came out into the hallway then, clutching her swollen belly.

Her eyes were wide and dazed. She looked down as more amniotic fluid spilled to the ground at her feet.

Yanelle took her hands gently. "Come, Your Grace. Let's get you comfortable in your room and ready for the arrival of the new one."

Eisandre nodded and allowed herself to be led back into the room. "Act, please come. I need you."

Actaeon nodded and looked to Trench.

The giant smiled, the expression creasing the big scar that bisected his face. "Go on, lad. I'll make sure they get here with the Matron soon."

"Thank you, Trench," said Actaeon. He turned to step back into the room, but the movement he saw in his peripheral vision made him stop in his tracks.

A solitary figure rounded the bend of the hallway and rushed toward them. The pair of daggers in their hands wasn't what made Actaeon's heart stop in his chest a lifebeat. No, what did that was the black cross painted on the figure's face. The black cross that broke said face into four quadrants. The black cross which had pursued him – haunted him, for years.

"By the Fallen," said Trench. The giant yanked free his maul and held it to the ready.

A second figure emerged behind the first.

And from where the corridor curved gently away on their other side emerged another. A cross-faced raider. And then another. And another. And another.

Anger rose from the pit of his stomach and Actaeon clenched his fists. "Sol…"

Biting down the anger, Actaeon steeled his emotions and reached into the room to grab his halberd that he'd left leaning just inside the doorway.

No sooner had he lowered it, than the raiders were upon them.

Trench let out a roar and swung away with his maul, sending bodies flying in all directions.

Actaeon swept the wide blade of his halberd in a frenzy, opening a throat here, cutting through an arm there, spilling the bowels of another.

The next knocked him off balance and he fell onto one elbow, couching his weapon against the ground to impale another of the raiders.

A blade came inches from his neck but was stopped by another sword – Yanelle's.

The Companion tore into the inrushing line of attackers like a hellion, leaving a trail of bodies, spurting arterial blood, and severed limbs in her wake.

Still, some slipped past her to rush Actaeon.

The Prince Engineer struggled to pull the halberd free of the dying raider, but he knew he couldn't possibly get the weapon free in time to defend himself.

The nearest raider was upon him, eyes dead and silent as a wraith. But moments before the raider's blade could pierce his face another blade struck it aside, opening the man's throat in the same deadly arc.

The Princess stepped in between him and the raiders then – barefoot and quite pregnant. She had grabbed the nearest weapon to her: the legendary greatsword Caliburn. And now she wielded it with both hands as she protected her husband from the ambushers.

She quickly dispatched the handful of raiders who had made it past Yanelle with elegant and lethal sweeps of the sword, a shower of sparks washing over her when the point of Caliburn bit into the corridor wall.

Once the last raider had been sent from the world, she fell to one knee and cried out, clutching her belly.

Actaeon grinned nervously and wrenched his halberd free.

Trench yelled over his shoulder as he continued to obliterate raiders on his side of the hall. "Get her in the room and shut the door, Act! We'll take it from here."

Actaeon levered himself to his feet and grabbed Eisandre, yanking her into the safety of the room.

He let go of his wife and his halberd and slid the door shut against the chaos beyond.

"Oh Saints, Act," moaned Eisandre. "It hurts. What is happening to me?"

"It is normal, Eis," explained Actaeon as his mind worked for a solution to better seal the door shut. "Do you feel the contractions beginning? They should come in waves. Count the lifebeats between them. In the meantime I will find a way to better seal the door shut."

Eisandre sat down at the edge of the bed and blinked the tears from her eyes. It felt as if a hammer had struck her lower back. The blow rippled slowly through her body and down into the base of her pelvis. It made her feel light-headed and ill. After it finished, she concentrated on counting the lifebeats as Actaeon had instructed.

As she did so, Actaeon retrieved his jacket and pulled several half-through bottles out. From one he poured a viscous brown goo along the length between the door and the door jamb on the side where it opened. Next, he sprinkled from another half-through bottle some foul-smelling purple crystals so that they coated the outside of the line of brown gooey substance.

As she watched Actaeon, continuing to count the lifebeats as he'd instructed, Eisandre reached between her legs. When she lifted her hand, it was wet with warm blood. "Act, there's blood. The baby, it's bleeding. Help me."

"Lie down and get comfortable," ordered Actaeon. "Some blood is normal. It does not mean there is anything amiss with the baby. Keep counting lifebeats."

As he instructed her, the Prince Engineer retrieved a pitcher of water from their bedside and splashed it against the bottom of the doorframe.

The applied concoction sputtered and sparked to life in blue fire that quickly spread upward along the height of the door. It burned a hot and violent blue that welded the door to its frame. A haze of smoke began to fill the room, but it was swiftly evacuated into Pyramid's ventilation system.

Eisandre watched with interest before another contraction began to tear through her body, bringing fresh tears to her eyes. "Two hundred and fifty lifebeats."

Sounds of violence and death came from beyond the door. Despite them, Eisandre forced herself to lie down upon the pillows of the bed, bringing her knees up as the contraction slowly worked its way to the base of her pelvis.

Just beyond the door, Trench and Yanelle fought on, each defending one of the two hallway approaches to the room. A pile of raider corpses formed before each of the warriors. In short time, they found themselves back to back as they battled on – Trench's maul and Yanelle's blade. It was a methodical and determined action to hack and smash through the incoming stream of raiders.

It left a pile of dead that quickly clotted the corridor and impeded the progress of the assailants beyond. The more that died, the easier it was to kill more as they needed to ascend the grisly pile.

"How ya doin', lass?" Trench asked as swung his maul with impunity.

"Been better... to be honest," came Yanelle's reply between grunts as she swung her sword.

"If it makes ya feel better, there're few better who I've had the honor ta fight beside," said Trench.

"It doesn't... but... thank you," Yanelle struggled to say as she fought on.

In that moment, as if in silent agreement, the cross-faced raiders on both sides of the hallway launched themselves bodily over the pile of dead on either side.

Trench smashed the raiders on his side into the ground.

Yanelle cut the first of her flying assailants down, but the second one struck her and caused her to stumble to the side. The third hit her hard and she cracked her head hard against the open doorway of Trench and Wave's room. She felt blackness closing in. The fourth raider slammed her against the jamb again and rendered her completely down and out.

Back inside the room, Eisandre had started pushing at Actaeon's instruction. Reaching down, he could feel the top of the baby's head as it began its journey down the birth canal.

"You are doing good, Eis," he said. "Keep pushing. I can feel the baby coming. I can feel our baby." He marveled at his own words, for a moment forgetting the death and violence beyond the door, overwhelmed by the new life that was emerging in the room.

Eisandre screamed, her trim nails digging into his hands as she bore down hard upon another contraction.

Outside Trench screamed in rage as he bludgeoned the raiders who had leapt over the pile of their dead brethren to bloody pulp on the corridor floor with his maul.

The giant grabbed the collar of Yanelle's tunic and unceremoniously tossed her through the open doorway before sliding the door shut. A few well-placed strikes from his maul dented the door and effectively sealed her in.

Unbidden, Shulaya's beautiful face flashed before his eyes, the memory returning with frightening clarity. All the color drained from her face. How she smiled faintly at the lifeless form in her arms – the form she had cut from her own belly. "Is not our little one beautiful, Atrilles?"

A raider slammed into his bulk, snapping Trench out of his reverie.

The raider appeared surprised that he'd gotten past the mercenary's defenses so easily and hesitated a moment before thrusting his spear forward.

Instinctively, Trench replaced the raider's head with the head of his maul, spraying him with bloody warmth.

A dozen raiders climbed over the dead to either side of him.

But in front of Trench, the last glimmer of bright life faded from Shulaya's eyes. His kind, wise Shulaya who had seen past the exterior of the brutal hulk of a warrior to find the warmth within him and stoke a fire in it. Shulaya, who always took the time to help everyone in the village. Who always took the time to talk to each person and to really know them. Shulaya... and their baby... dead... in his arms... Again.

And then the rage was upon him. A rage which he hadn't felt since the day he got the scar that the Altheans had said broke his skull in two. A rage which only had one end to it – death.

"Not again," he muttered as he reached out and squeezed a raider's throat until it gave way inside his fist. "NOT AGAIN!" he roared.

A wide swing of his maul surrounded him in a cloud of blood, sending bodies flying in all directions.

He picked up one raider bodily – a woman – and, in one fluid motion, broke her back upon his knee before flinging the dead body into several others.

"Stop pushing," said Actaeon, inside the room.

Eisandre screamed in pure agony, the pain shooting up her spine into her skull. She saw raw, bloody colors that swirled around her. Reds and purples and oranges. Thorns pierced her skull and abdomen, and she felt her teeth bite deeply into one cheek. The taste of blood brought her back to her senses momentarily. "Stop pushing? You said to push!"

"Yes, I know I did," said Actaeon. The color had left his face as he felt the baby's neck. "Now I need you to stop pushing, Eis. Trust me."

"Something's wrong, isn't it? Something's wrong. Saints..." her words trailed off into a whimper, but she gritted her teeth and fought to resist the urge to push as the next wave of contractions hit her. The effort brought tears to her eyes.

Actaeon grinned up at her faintly. "Nothing I haven't studied, love. Do not worry." He resisted the urge to scratch the old burn on his right arm as he fumbled to find something inside the pockets of his jacket.

Eisandre screamed as he searched. "Hurry, Act! Please hurry!"

Outside the door it sounded like a wild animal had been unleashed.

Actaeon ignored the sounds and located the object he'd been looking for – a spool of thick thread. He broke off two lengths of thread from the spool.

As his wife cried out and fought against the contractions, the Prince Engineer worked with one hand to push the first piece of thread between the cord and the baby's neck. With the other hand he held gentle pressure to push the baby's head back against Eisandre to give him the extra slack he needed.

Once he'd gotten the first thread around the cord, he pulled it into a tight knot before sealing it with a second. That done, he began to work a second thread a thumb's width away from the first.

Actaeon soon had the second thread tied and he reached into his jacket one more time, still holding pressure on his baby's head with one hand to prevent the delivery. He found the strip of brightweave more quickly this time and worked it so that it was positioned between the threads and under the cord to protect the baby's neck.

That done, he pulled free his knife and began to make the most important cut of his life.

Outside of the room, Trench had yanked a sword out of one of the raider's hands by the blade. Blood ran unnoticed down his forearm as he used the blade to open the attacker's belly and lop off the head of another.

A spear entered Trench's chest on one side and he reached down to snap off the haft. He spun that around and shoved it through the bodies of two more raiders, shattering their spines in the process.

A second spear was thrust into his back, and he spun to cave in that raider's chest with a swing of his maul.

The next raider swung a club and struck him in the face.

As he fell, he could hear Wave's voice in his head: *"The bigger they are…"*

His head cracked into the door he'd sealed Yanelle behind and he crumpled to the ground.

Only a small part of Trench was aware that the raiders now ignored him. Instead they focused their efforts on the door to Actaeon and Eisandre's room.

One of the raiders passed a large ram over the pile of bodies. As a group, and without any communication, they began to ram it against the door in perfect concert.

Inside, Actaeon cast a concerned look over his shoulder as the ramming began. It produced a dent in the door that began to grow with every impact.

With a frown, he pulled a grenado from his jacket and set it before him, just in case.

There were more important things at hand though, and he turned his attention back to the baby.

He spat into his left hand and rubbed the saliva on both cut ends of the cord – a technique he'd once read would help stem the bleeding more quickly.

"Alright, Eis. It is time to push again," he instructed.

The Princess had lapsed into semi-consciousness in the massive effort to resist the contractions.

"Eis!" Actaeon shouted. He reached out to pinch the skin between her thumb and forefinger. "Listen to me and push!"

Brought back by Actaeon's voice and the sharp feeling of his pinch, Eisandre blinked through the haze and pain. Awareness returned like a sack of bricks, and she saw the dent in the door that was becoming more and more pronounced with every loud bang. She also saw the grenado that lay between her legs. She gave Actaeon a pleading look.

"Just push, my love," he insisted. "Let us deal with this first and then we shall worry about what lies without."

Eisandre nodded and began to bear down with her contractions again.

It was a relief not to resist them anymore and she began to push with all her might.

There came a sudden searing pain in her nether regions and then all of the pressure was unexpectedly gone. She laid her head back upon the pillow and looked up at the rivulets of rain that ran down the elderglass of Pyramid's pinnacle just above her head.

Actaeon cradled the baby in his arms as it slipped free. His baby. A beautiful girl!

But there was a problem – she wasn't breathing. He pulled out his luminary and shined the light into her nose and mouth. Both were plugged up with mucus.

Bending, he set to sucking the mucus free. First her nasal airway, spitting the contents to the side. Next, he pinched her nose and sucked the mucus out of her oral airway. It took several tries, but eventually he had it clear.

The baby still wasn't breathing though. He began to rub his daughter's chest briskly, alternating between that and flicking the soles of her feet.

Behind him, the makeshift weld on one side of the door failed with a resounding crack.

"Your friends need you, my beloved."

The voice came to Trench in a dream haze as the raiders continued to pound away at the door before him.

It was his Shulaya. She smiled at him. But she wasn't Shulaya anymore. Instead she was Jezail with her blazing red hair and green eyes – the skin of her face rippled and drawn above her right eye. *"Get up and save them!"* she shouted.

Trench growled and pulled himself up to his elbows.

Deep within his core he felt the familiar fire of rage relight.

The giant was up in a flash. He grabbed the rear of the ram and jerked it backward.

Caught off guard, the raiders stumbled backward and were knocked to the floor as Trench swung both his massive arms forward to strike those on either side of the ram.

The cross-faced raiders tried desperately to recover, but the giant mercenary was upon them, consumed by a blood rage.

Trench lifted up the massive ram and swung it about the corridor. Flanked by piles of bodies, he quickly added to it, smashing a chest in here, caving in a skull there.

Before long Trench realized that there was nobody left to kill.

The bodies of the raiders were piled to the ceiling on either side.

The floor was wet with blood in the few places he could see it between the corpses.

Trench sat down heavily, couching the ram in his lap as he felt the life seeping from him.

But the door before him was nearly breached. It would only take one more swing. Just one more.

The giant mustered every last reserve of energy and levered himself to his feet one last time.

With the full weight of his body, he used the ram to strike the door.

It gave way with an earth-shattering crack and fell to the floor of the room beyond.

Trench dropped the ram and stumbled to his knees just inside the room.

Inside, Actaeon stood facing the door with his halberd at the ready. Behind him lay Eisandre in the bed along with the sounds of a newborn crying.

The sound brought a stream of tears down Trench's face. "I stopped 'em, Act. They'll not take your little one."

Actaeon dropped the halberd and rushed to his friend's side. He frowned as he assessed the extent of Trench's injuries.

"You did good, Trench," said Actaeon. "You saved us. You saved our daughter."

"A daughter?" asked Trench. "Can ya help me up, Act? I'd like to meet her."

The giant's face was pale with blood loss. Even the deep scar across his face was a ghastly white.

"Of course," said Actaeon. With some difficulty, he helped his friend over to the bedside.

Trench looked down at Actaeon and Eisandre's little daughter. Tears ran from his eyes to pool in his scar.

The tiny crying baby girl squirmed and wiggled in Eisandre's arms and struggled to look around the room.

"She's beautiful, Act," said Trench, letting out a sob.

Eisandre looked up from her baby to touch Trench's hand. There were tears in her own eyes as she spoke. "Thank you for all you have given to us. We will not forget."

Trench nodded and let out one last sob. "Thanks, lass. I always keep my promises. I –"

The giant toppled to the side.

And where one life suddenly shined anew, another faded into memory.

A NEW LIFE

A VERITABLE ARMY ESCORTED THE NEW parents back down from Pyramid's pinnacle to Saint Torin's Hold.

A squad of Arbiters led by Corvin sof Haringar led the way along with several Raedellean warbands and all the available Companions.

The Southward warband and Eisandre's own Wall Breakers kept the Princess surrounded as she was pushed by Actaeon in a wheeled chair that the Altheans had brought up for her.

The Princess cradled her new baby in her arms, unsure of how to placate the infant's constant crying. She brushed her fingers through the baby's short brown hair, only recently patted dry by the arriving Matron who now walked in front of her. She had always been comforted when her sister had brushed her hair as a child, so perhaps it would help the baby to calm down. Eisandre lifted the baby and spoke into its ear, "Please stop crying. You are safe with me."

Matron Seraeta paused before her and ordered Actaeon to stop the chair. "The baby is hungry. Put her to breast, Your Grace." She knelt to rip a length of fabric from the bottom of her white robes and held it up to give Eisandre privacy. "Go ahead and take it," she ordered Actaeon, who happily complied. Without ceremony, the Matron swept up Eisandre's tunic and, placing her other hand behind the baby's neck, skillfully brought it to the new mother's nipple.

When the baby had latched to her satisfaction, the Matron nodded and tucked the sheet around Eisandre before nodding to the Sentinel Arbiter to keep the procession moving.

Arbiters ran ahead to stand guard at any vent, door, or passageway that they came to as they worked their way down into the Mirrorholds.

The warbanders maintained a tight formation around the newly expanded Raedellean royal family – a ring bristling with spears.

Within the ring were also Companions Itarik and Tarcy, who flanked the Princess on either side, their swords drawn, and Ithelie, the Voice walking along confidently beside the Althean Matron.

Companion Yanelle had been found alive but unconscious in the room where Trench had barricaded her. Arriving Altheans had carried her down to their Hall of Restoration to look after her injuries.

I just want to go rest now, thought Eisandre, using her Thoughtlink artifact to communicate just with Actaeon. *Rest and cry and hold my baby.*

I know, Actaeon thought in return. *I feel the same. Though, it is Raedellean tradition that a newborn be introduced to its community right after birth.*

Eisandre frowned and winced as the baby sucked hard upon her nipple. *Couldn't they wait awhile and we could introduce the baby after a time?*

The people are excited, thought Actaeon. *You just gave birth to the next successor to Raedellean leadership. They are also scared after what just happened and could use the assurance of seeing you both.*

I am scared after what just happened, Eisandre retorted.

Actaeon looked down at the little baby cradled in his wife's arms as it suckled at her bosom. He felt a sense of amazement and wonder that managed to shine through even the shock he felt at what they had just gone through. *As am I,* he admitted. *And that is why it is important, now more than ever, for the people to see their Princess. To see that she is not one to be stopped.*

Eisandre looked down at the strange and wondrous creature that moved against her and patted it reassuringly. *I don't suppose the Arbiters would be willing to take me back?*

Actaeon grinned, despite himself.

After a time they reached the entrance to Saint Torin's Hold.

The Arbiters lined up to either side of the Mirrorholds in a protective formation.

Corvin sof Haringar stopped just beside the entrance and as Actaeon wheeled Eisandre up to him, he lifted his sword in salute.

The other Arbiters followed suit and lifted their own swords to salute the Princess.

Eisandre looked at them in confusion.

"We'll not let you down, Princess – our sister," said Corvin.

Eisandre normally would have corrected the Arbiter, but she felt too weak and weary to argue. Instead she simply nodded, glad to have such a force protecting her after what they'd been through. "Thank you."

Actaeon wheeled her into Saint Torin's Hold.

The warbanders filed in behind her on either side and along the tapestry-laden walls where they snapped to sharp attention.

Those inside the Hold silently rose from their tables and one by one they saluted the Princess, fist to chest.

Matron Seraeta reached down and with a quick sweeping motion of her thumb, dislodged the baby's latch. She then nodded to Ithelie.

Eisandre was surprised to see that the baby didn't cry. Instead the little girl, *her* little girl just gazed up at her in wonder. She felt her head swim with emotions and colors – blues and golds. The Hold was gone then, and there was only the locked gaze between her and this new life she had created with Actaeon.

It was a moment of wonder – as the two considered one another for the first time, mother and daughter.

Ithelie's words gradually came to her awareness, though nothing could tear Eisandre's attention away from her beautiful baby.

The Voice raised her hands to the ceiling and intoned:

"Oh Ancestors we pray – attend to us this day.

"All Saints give ear unto us here, for unto thee we pray,

"A journey now begins, a story starts anew,

"With this new life, this blessed child whose care we entrust to you.

"May her path be straight and guard her heart from wrong.

"Great spirits of the Fallen shall dedicate this day to you…

With a flourish, the Voice pulled a ceremonial green cloth from one of her sleeves. She skillfully swaddled the baby in the cloth and handed her back to Eisandre.

"Your Grace, please introduce your daughter to those present and those not. To Ancestor and alive alike," intoned the Voice. "Let her name be known to all and long ring clear in this hall and many others."

Eisandre raised her baby high into the air then. "Aedwina Rellios

Caliburn, be known to the people of Raedelle and the people of Redemption." Her voice shook after what she had just been through.

"Long may the Ancestors guide you to bring change and greatness to this world," shouted Actaeon as tradition dictated for the new father.

"Ancestors guide Aedwina Rellios Caliburn," echoed all of those present in the Hold.

Up in the Song of the Sisters, Wave sat vigil over the body of his oldest and greatest friend.

When he'd first arrived back in the corridor of the Song, he'd been greeted by a river of blood that flowed along the floor to squish under his boots.

What he'd found next had been utterly horrifying.

The bodies were stacked to the ceiling, wedged and jammed into place. All dead.

It had been the most difficult to dislodge the ones at the top, but once those had been cleared, the others came more quickly.

While the Altheans he had summoned watched in horror, Wave had stacked the bodies quickly like cordwood along the sides of the corridor, noting the cross painted on each of the dead faces. Eventually there had been room for him to climb over the pile and down the other side. Dagger first, of course, in case he were to meet resistance there.

He did not.

Instead he found Actaeon and Eisandre – their newborn baby crying in the Princess' arms.

His best friend lay dead on the floor beside them.

The Prince Engineer had an arrow nocked and aimed squarely at Wave's chest when he entered. Actaeon relaxed and set aside the bow after recognition dawned on him.

Actaeon had covered Trench's head and upper body with a blanket. That hadn't stopped the blood from pooling on the floor, having leaked from the giant's many wounds.

Wave had fallen to his knees and slammed his fists against the giant's chest. It was to no avail.

His friend was dead.

And he hadn't been there to fight alongside him during the most difficult fight of his life.

So now he sat alone and in silence in a chair on one side of Actaeon's room in the Song. He stared at the giant where he lay under the extra sheets he'd placed over his body.

Wave wanted to say something, but no matter how raw the emotions were that coursed through his body, no matter how much he yearned to kill whoever was responsible for his best friend's death, no matter how much he wished he could've taken Trench's place... no words came to mind.

After a time Wave became aware that he was standing over his friend's body. He'd pulled the blanket down to look at Trench's face.

The old giant looked peaceful in death, as though impervious to all of the violence and terror of life.

"I'm sorry, old friend," said Wave at last. "Whoever did this to you," his voice choked, "I'll find them. And I'll kill them... If it's the last thing I do."

Blinking the tears away from his remaining eye, Wave pulled the blanket over his friend's face again.

He turned away to face the windows. There the heavy rain ran along in thick rivulets on its long journey toward the ground below. It was as if the gods themselves wept for Trench. The metallic smell of blood was thick inside the room.

"Guess it's just me now," he said. He wondered how Glaive would've felt about that. He shivered as he thought of how any other member of his old mercenary squad deserved better to be here now.

In his mind he could hear his old commander speaking. *Enough of that nonsense, you ass! You're here, and we're not. Now what are you going to do about it?*

Wave clenched his fist and smiled. "Oh, I'll do something about it alright."

"Excuse me, sir?"

The voice came from the open doorway where four young Arbiters stood, a litter held between them. Their faces looked white as bone after the gruesome scene they'd had to climb through. Junior Arbiters out of Redoubt, no doubt. This scene was probably a hundred times more awful than the worst thing they'd ever seen.

Wave smirked and thought about how Trench would've broken their stones. He spun to face them. "Snap to, I said," he spoke. "Get that litter in place beside him. Each of you take a limb and I'll take his head."

"Um... yessir," said the Arbiter in the lead.

They scrambled into the room and got into position to lift the giant.

"I see the looks of horror on your faces, lads," said Wave. "Not to worry. The Ancestors' tears you saw outside? All of that was this giant of a man. One of the bravest people I've ever known. Trench is his name. Tell his story. He saved the lives of the Princess and Prince Engineer of Raedelle today as the Princess gave birth to her new daughter. Can you remember that for me, lads? Can you tell of it? Don't dwell on the horror of it – instead remember what you've seen here today. That's what one man can do – that's what Trench did."

The four young Arbiters looked down at Trench in awe, several of them casting glances back at the carnage just outside. "Aye, sir," said one of them and the others echoed him.

"What're you waiting for then?" asked Wave. "Lift him onto the litter. There ya go. Now one of you has a strip of cloth, I hope? Yes, secure his hands with it. Alright, on the count of three, we lift. One on each corner and a fifth at his head."

Trench was so large that his legs hung over the end of the stretcher.

Wave grabbed one of the litter poles at his friend's head. "Alright, now lift! Aw, c'mon now. He's not that heavy. Lift! Don't let it go to his head – he wasn't that big."

And as Wave busted their stones as he and Trench would've once done in concert, they carried the giant up and over the pile of the dead and onward to Saint Torin's Hold for a morbid follow-up to Aedwina's introduction.

Jezail raced through the Mirrorholds, a mirror version of herself below her as she ran, her curly, red hair bouncing with each stride.

She'd heard that something terrible had happened. Those who had told her didn't know all the details, but they knew that something horrible had taken place near the Pinnacle of Pyramid. Many people had died, and the Princess' baby had been born.

Something had felt very off when she got the news and she'd left the Open Markets post haste. She'd find better answers in Saint Torin's Hold.

She angled across the Mirrorholds toward the Raedellean Hold and smashed right into Wave as the one-eyed mercenary stepped in front of her.

Wave caught her before she could fall and steadied her on her feet. "Jezail... we need to talk."

"Whaddaya mean? What happened? I heard the news," said Jezail hurriedly.

"Come with me," said Wave, guiding her gently by her arm. "Let's find a place to talk."

She yanked her arm out of his hand and stepped back. "I don't want to find someplace to talk. Tell me what happened, Wave."

"Jez, I really think we should –" he began.

"Cracked Redemption knows I don't care what *you* think right now," snapped the warband Captain. "Just tell me what it is I need to know."

"It's Trench, Jezail," started Wave. "He's dead."

The words were an instantaneous shock to her. It was as if something important – an essential part of her structure – had suddenly and irrevocably snapped free. Her concern and worry was gone in an instant, to be replaced with... nothing.

An emptiness opened up within her and the void of it spread until it encompassed every last bit of her body.

First Varisk and now Trench. It was as if everyone she loved was destined for death. Varisk had been young and fighting his first war. But Trench... Trench had survived not one, not two, but three wars. He'd infiltrated the Pyramid and survived. He'd journeyed north with Actaeon to fight the Veiled One and survived.

"He killed them all, Jez." Wave was speaking, but the words barely registered with her. "Every single raider. The bodies were stacked to the ceiling. They're alive thanks to him."

Alive thanks to him. And yet here she was, left alone.

Involuntarily, her legs began to carry her away from the Raedellean Hold.

She felt Wave's hand on her shoulder and it was as though it was touching someone else's body, not hers. Still, she slapped it away and increased her pace until she was moving at a full run.

She didn't stop until she was at the edge of the Avenue of Glass.

There she fell to her knees and struck the elderglass surface with her fist again and again until the red blood from her knuckles mixed with the rain.

And still, no tears came.

Trench was buried on the Windmoor less than a hundred paces from the Engineer's workshop.

The giant's body, covered in a massive green shroud, was lowered gently into an open grave as torrents of rain fell from the sky.

A massive pile of stones had been carted out and lay just to one side of the grave.

Over the head of the grave stood the fallen mercenary's closest friends. Wave and Jezail stood at the center. Jezail gazed off into the distance, an empty look in her green eyes. Wave looked away from her and down at his dead friend.

The heavy rain had created a pool of mud at the bottom of the grave. The mud soaked up into the fabric of the green shroud, darkening it with brown.

To the right stood Actaeon and Eisandre. Actaeon had little Aedwina in a sling against his chest. She was swaddled from head to toe in a leather cloth to keep off the rain. He rested his halberd against his shoulder and adjusted the beak of the swaddle above his infant daughter's head to keep the rainwater from dripping on her. The baby slept soundly despite the weather.

Behind the Princess and Prince Engineer, two Companions stood watch – Itarik Faris and Tarcy Hael.

On the left stood Lauryn and Yanelle. The young engineer's normally bright and happy face was scrunched into a despondent expression. The tears that streamed down her face were quickly washed away by the rain.

Beside her, the Companion brushed a wet lock of red hair from her eyes and gazed solemnly out over those gathered.

There was a line of mourners that stretched all the way back through the Outskirts, along the Avenue of Glass, and even back to the Pyramid's entrance. The number of people who had come to pay their respects was astonishing.

Several paces back from the grave, behind Jezail and Wave, stood other close allies of the giant. Captain Harvand Xula, who'd fought alongside Trench during the Infiltration of Pyramid. Beside him stood the Ajman's Warrioress, Calisse T'ra Coletka, who, along with Xula, had joined Trench as part of Actaeon's elite force that went north to defeat the Veiled One. The last to arrive was Lord Enrion Zar, who'd also been a part of that elite force and had worked with Trench and Actaeon during many other projects in the past.

Wave nodded to Ithelie then.

The Voice stood at the foot of the grave dressed in soaked green robes. At Wave's nod, the young woman pulled back her hood to reveal white hair that quickly matted against her face in the deluge. She spread her arms toward the sky and nodded to the first of the mourners.

The first mourner was Lord Gunther Arcady. The Lord Shore nodded back and picked up a stone. He approached the graveside with it and knelt down to gently place it upon the giant's shroud.

Wave tensed up at the sight of Arcady, but then the second mourner was placing another stone. And then a third and a fourth. He relaxed.

"Ancestors," began Ithelie. "I call upon thee to guide the soul of this brave man, Atrilles Mihr'trafa. This giant we all knew as Trench."

Aedwina began to cry as the Voice spoke. The baby's wail cut across the Windmoor as a mournful backdrop to Ithelie's words.

Actaeon rocked his baby with one arm in an effort to soothe her.

Unphased by the cries of the babe, the Voice continued.

"Open the doors of the beyond and light a fire to blaze the path for his soul to find those of his spirit family. Accept him in reunion and grace, that he may be one with you in wisdom and virtue, to be a guiding energy for our people from this day to eternity."

She drew silent then to watch over several hundred mourners as they came to lay a stone upon Trench's cairn.

There were many faces that Wave recognized as he stood watch over his friend's grave: Prince General Indros Zar of Shield, Supreme Captain Amodeus Jarval of Thyr, the Raja Ajman herself, Paladin Arbiter Cignith sof Iarnus, the artist Maerdia Bazardjan, Matron Seraeta, and even Oril from The End.

Scores of people from every Dominion had come to see his best friend laid to rest.

When the Loresworn showed up to place his stone, Actaeon unslung Aedwina and handed her to Eisandre.

The Princess held the baby with both arms, cradling her as she might one of Actaeon's grenados – uncertain and scared. Aedwina stopped crying and squirmed against her chest. *Be careful, Act,* she warned her husband.

I will, came Actaeon's thought in return.

Sol had laid his stone down and begun to walk off, but the Prince Engineer stepped in front of him.

"You have great nerve, Sol," said Actaeon. There was no humor in his tone.

The ancient Loresworn cast a disappointed look down at him with his deep gray eyes. "My poor Engineer, so deeply you have misread the situation."

"Explain it to me then, Sol," said Actaeon. "For once, strive for transparency. I know it is not your wont, but you owe it to Trench, if I have truly misread this situation."

"I've not the ability nor the will to enslave minds as the Veiled One had done before you destroyed it," explained Sol. "Thus, it must've been another of them. Perhaps one upset that you've struck down one of its brethren. None before have ever succeeded in such an undertaking. It was bound to be fraught with consequence."

Actaeon blinked, a thousand questions coming to mind. Instead of asking them, he said simply, "You expect me to believe that you would not make an attempt on my life after our last conversation?"

Sol actually laughed at that, a sound which cut into the silence and the rain. "Me? Kill the one hope Travail has left? How little you understand, Engineer. My only hope is that you might still piece together the puzzle before all is lost." The old man tugged on his gray beard thoughtfully before he turned to stride away.

Actaeon clenched his free hand into a fist as he watched the Loresworn walk off.

If Sollemnis the Gray hadn't tried to kill his family, then who had? He'd been sure that the Loresworn had been the culprit. But the old man's words carried the weight of logic with them. Why should the Loresworn try to kill him if he was indeed Travail's only hope as Sol had expressed so many times before? Which meant there was only one likely culprit left.

Biting his lip until it bled, he rejoined Eisandre and offered to take Aedwina back.

Eisandre gave him a relieved look and passed the baby to him.

Ithelie began to speak again.

"May he guide our other Fallen to their rightful place on this tragic day. I, the Voice Ithelie Faris, through the power entrusted in me by the Ancestors, do now release you from your duty to your people and to all Redemption. Go, our brother, and take your rightful place in legend among our people. May you watch over us always."

Ithelie clasped her hands before her and stood there in silence as mourners continued to pass through, each leaving a stone atop Trench's cairn.

By now it had filled the grave in and developed into a considerable pile.

Wave watched as the inevitable placement of stones hid his friend from sight. The shroud was gone, replaced by hundreds of fist-sized stones. The tears arrived, unbidden. Half of them streamed down his cheek while the others, from his missing eye, dripped down his nasal passage and made him sniffle.

The lone mercenary watched as his friend was covered. As the grave was filled. As the stones overflowed the grave and became a cairn. As they piled higher and higher until they were level with his chest.

Hundreds and hundreds of mourners continued through, each depositing a single stone from the pile, to forever confine the giant to his grave.

The last of the mourners were the Waiting Ones. The cult's flock had grown into the hundreds and each of them left a stone upon the cairn of their icon.

The last of the Waiting Ones to come was Phyrius Ricter, the First of the First of the Waiting Ones himself. The elderly man knelt and placed a stone at the foot of Trench's resting place. He leaned forward to touch his forehead to the stone before rising to his feet.

The First of the First took his place beside the Voice and began to speak to the hundreds assembled. "Today is a day of greatest tragedy. The heavens weep and the ground devours. Today we lay to rest the Visage Himself."

"The Visage Himself," echoed the Waiting Ones.

"Flawed though it may be," whispered Wave to himself with a grin. He found himself smirking at this turn of events. Trench would've absolutely hated this.

"Indeed, the Visage not only helped the Bringer of the Keeper of Light bring His light to us, but he also saved us all from annihilation. A monument to his efforts now stands in the Pyramid's great Sun Chamber. An echo of our great Keeper of Light."

"The Keeper of Light," came the gentle drone of Phyrius' followers.

"I was there, my friends," said Phyrius. "I was there when the giant, the Visage Himself, brought the Keeper of Light at the direction of the Bringer."

"The direction of the Bringer," echoed his followers.

"It is thanks to him that the Waiting Ones came to find the Keeper of Light and that the message of the Keeper of Light was once again heard by the world," said Phyrius. "Long may the message be heard, and long may the Visage Himself be remembered!"

"Long may the Visage be remembered!" cried the Waiting Ones.

Phyrius looked as though he was about to say more, but Ithelie's hand on his shoulder stopped him.

After a deep breath, Actaeon took a step forward. "Trench was a true friend. Because of his bravery in the face of certain death, my wife and I still breathe and have the blessing to be the parents of this beautiful baby. The potential of this life is thanks to our friend Trench. You shall go on to do great things, Aedwina Rellios Caliburn, but never forget that it is for Trench's courage that you may live. We shall not forget you, my friend. Rest well, Trench. We will take it from here."

Wave stepped forward then and swallowed the lump in his throat. "Well, I suppose I oughta say a few words. I've known Trench over thirty years, and I've not met a better man in all that time. I'm proud to call him my best friend. They say..." He let out a sob. "They say the bigger they are... the harder they fall. Well, when this giant fell, he shattered a piece of us all. Shattered Redemption'll not soon know someone as genuine, as brave, and as formidable as Trench. I love you, buddy."

When Wave finished, he looked over at Jezail. The Captain of the Wall Breakers just shook her head, her dead eyes staring at the pile of rock before her.

When no one else spoke up, at last the Princess of Raedelle stepped forward. With a grunt, she reached over her shoulder and drew the greatsword Caliburn. She hefted it before her and rested its blade gently against the top of the cairn. "Trench, you have steadfastly defended the Rellios Caliburns and thereby defended Raedelle. You were our stalwart defender, in life and now in death. Let it be known and spoken throughout the realm that Trench has earned his place alongside the bravest Companions of Raedelle. Let his sacrifice be spoken of for generations to come."

Wave wept openly over his friend after the Princess' annunciation.

"Go then, friends," said Ithelie. "And spread the word of our beloved Trench. Long may he watch over us."

Beside Wave, Jezail had no tears. The warband Captain stared blankly down at the cairn, a piece of her ripped away forever.

Wave placed a hand on her shoulder. "Jezail…" he began.

She shrugged his hand off and backed away. When he reached out again, she held one finger in the air between them. A warning off.

Wave opened his mouth to speak.

Jezail shook her head and spun around to storm away.

The lone mercenary watched her retreat back toward the Avenue of Glass, his heart breaking for her loss. He'd lost a best friend, but she'd lost her second love in so many years. He knew she'd never be the same.

Wave watched her walk off until she was naught but a speck in his field of vision – heading off toward the looming form of the Pyramid. There was nothing he could do for her. It wrenched his heart.

He turned back to cast one last look upon his friend's cairn and was surprised to see Yanelle and Calisse before him. The two women regarded him with concern – the Companion with her striking eyes and dark red hair and the Warrioress with her tight queue of hair and eyes framed in purple shadow that somehow resisted the rain.

Yanelle leaned forward to gently kiss the corner of his jaw. "You shouldn't be alone tonight."

Calisse reached out to caress his forearm. "I agree. You'll spend the night with us."

Wave blinked his single eye. For certain, it was a fantasy come true for him, but it didn't feel right. Not without Trench still breathing.

"I…" he began. "I'll be fine on my own."

"By the Fallen, you will," said Yanelle.

Not leaving Wave with a choice, the women led him away from his friend, each taking one of his arms.

And for at least one night, the two women helped Wave momentarily forget about his grief.

"I must needs speak with the Prince Engineer."

The Lord Shore's tone was a demand.

The two Companions who blocked his way into the Princess' private room in the Mirrorholds weren't impressed.

"Their Graces are engaged with other preoccupations at this time," said Itarik sternly. "I'm sure they'd be willing to hear from you next time they appear in Saint Torin's Hold."

"There's no time for that," said Arcady with a scowl. "I've information which I must convey to them with immediacy. Stop being daft and let me in!"

Arcady stepped forward to enter the private quarters of the Raedellean leaders.

Tarcy stepped between the Lord Shore and the doorway. When he slammed into her breast, she scowled and rebuffed him physically, shoving him to the mirrored floor.

"How dare you!" spat Arcady as he pulled himself up to his elbows.

"Try'n agin an'ill smash ye leck a bug," said Tarcy. The Companion lifted her booted foot over Arcady's face.

Arcady's face twisted in rage and his hand dropped to his dagger.

Before the Lord Shore could act on the impulse, Itarik stepped forward and forcefully pulled Tarcy back.

"Restrain yourself, Companion," said Itarik, his eyes narrowed upon the giantess.

With a growl of displeasure, the big woman looked down at her boss and stepped back.

Itarik knelt to offer Arcady a hand. "Apologies for my fellow Companion, Lord Shore."

Arcady slapped Itarik's hand aside with the back of his own. "See to it that it never happens again. An assault on any member of the Conclave is an assault on Raedelle." He drew to his feet and narrowed his burning hazel eyes at Tarcy in warning.

"What seems to be the problem, Lord Arcady?" asked Actaeon, who now stood in the open door. "It is not every day in which I find you supine upon my doorstep." The Prince Engineer grinned.

Arcady rolled his eyes. "Quite clever, Engineer. Now, may I come in?

There's something of the utmost importance I must needs share with you – and I will only share it with you or my niece."

Itarik offered Actaeon a concerned look, but the Prince Engineer waved it off and gestured for the Lord Shore to come inside.

Within, Eisandre sat rocking Aedwina in her arms. The baby was sleeping against her chest – something which the Princess found remarkably soothing, so long as she kept sleeping and didn't wake up.

"Your Grace," said Arcady. The Lord Shore dipped his head respectfully to his niece.

Eisandre blinked and stared at him for a long moment before she returned his nod.

Actaeon leaned against the wall near his wife and folded his arms. "So what is this matter of utmost importance you *must needs* share with us?"

"The person who tried to kill you –" began Arcady.

"And what would you know about that?" interrupted Actaeon. He unfolded his arms and stepped forward.

"More than I'd care to admit," said Arcady. "But it strikes me that it is high time you know."

"Who?" asked Eisandre simply. Her voice was a whisper. She didn't want to wake the baby. But still, the word carried across the room.

"Ambrosius," said Arcady simply.

Actaeon and Eisandre cast a knowing look at one another. At nearly the same time, they reached up to their ears and pulled the Thoughtlink Artifacts free.

Actaeon collected them and placed them under a bowl on a nearby tabletop.

When he was done, he looked up. "And how are you so certain?"

Arcady smirked and shook his head. "Don't give me that, Engineer. I saw your look. You've had your own suspicions about him, haven't you?"

"Answer my question," insisted Actaeon.

"Because," spat Arcady. "He's controlled the royal family for years. Duke Branwyn, Prince Aedwyn. Controlled and manipulated. The Fallen know, he must've exerted control over all the other Caliburn kids too. Every one of them but *you*." He spat the last word like an accusation, his gloved finger pointing at Eisandre.

"And you think he wanted us killed because he could not control us?" asked Actaeon.

"I *know* he wanted you killed," returned Arcady. "I know because he asked me to do it. And when I refused, he tried to put a force upon my mind somehow. Tried to force me to do it anyway. But I resisted. He has some sort of power over minds that I don't understand. He was furious that you'd killed the Veiled One and that you were bringing Raedelle into all these interdominional affairs."

"Sounds suspiciously like a protest I might have heard come from your own lips, Gunther," said Actaeon.

"I'll not lie," said Arcady. "I've worked with Ambrosius in the past and for the good of Raedelle. But I'll not take the life of one of our countrymen for him. And I'll not abide him controlling my mind. Whatever you need to destroy him, Engineer. My sword is yours."

"Well, unfortunately you alerted him through the Thoughtlink Artifacts we were wearing. Already, he is likely taking the next steps to prepare himself against us," said Actaeon.

The color left Arcady's face.

"Why can't he control me?" asked Eisandre.

"Of that I'm not certain," said Arcady. "But I think it's got something to do with your being Lost."

The look on Eisandre's face was as if someone had ripped her baby from her arms.

"Oh, don't look so surprised, girl!" Arcady smirked. "Your mother's my sister. And I've not protected Raedelle all these years by failing to keep informed."

"You..." Eisandre started. "You could have ruined me with that information."

"And I still can," said Arcady, looking at her with his hard hazel eyes. "If you don't do the right thing by Raedelle."

"You shall do nothing of the sort," snapped Actaeon. "As if anyone will believe Ambrosius' puppet when all this is through." The Prince Engineer grinned at Arcady's expression. "Do not worry, Lord Shore. If you do your part, it will not come to that." He paused and scratched his chin thoughtfully. "Fascinating that – if the condition of being Lost can protect against the mental control of these beings. Do you suppose that they are the Ancients? Or are they something else entirely?"

READY FOR ACTION

T HE TEAM ASSEMBLED IN ACTAEON'S workshop.

They didn't yet know where they were going, but, as soon as they did, they would be ready for action.

All it would take was for one of their leads to turn up something.

The last report they'd had of Ambrosius was a Raedellean cooper who had spotted the rogue counselor headed through the Pyramid's Way of Pillars enroute toward the Avenue of Glass.

"Watch your time, Varse," shouted Lauryn. "You're shutting off too late. Brewer, control your sweeps – you'll decapitate the rest of the squad. Phalto, watch Phelto – she has the perfect timing down. Good stance, Brewer – now maintain it!"

Actaeon watched proudly as Lauryn shouted commands to her light lancers while they ran through training routines at the fringes of the Outskirts. He was too distracted to pay close attention though. His mind was preoccupied with too many other things.

The Arbiters were conducting an investigation in and around the Pyramid, but they were unlikely to find much about where Ambrosius was heading.

Actaeon had sent messages out to the Raja Ajman and the Lord Protector of Niwian since the advisor was likely to pass through their territories if he was headed back to Raedelle. He'd also sent messages to Lady Eshelle in Wither, to Lord Hamnin Dafryl in Lakehold, and to Lord Cathaoir Conmara in Shore, alerting them to the situation.

If he were Ambrosius, he figured he would have gone straight to Raedelle to try and convince the people to turn against them. If he was wrong about that, then Ambrosius could be anywhere at all. He wondered if it would be worth sending another expedition to the Veiled One's sea caves, but then shook his head – there was nothing of worth left there and Ambrosius had no trouble bringing the cross-faced raiders wherever he wanted now.

They'd also posted Raedellean scouts in strategic positions all around the Pyramid and the Outskirts. If more cross-faced raiders approached, then they would at least know what direction they were coming from and be prepared for the fight.

Actaeon frowned and wished that Trench were there. The big mercenary would know the best strategic moves to make. Without the giant's steadfast confidence which he'd grown used to during the Second Invasion War, he just felt uncertain.

And Wave certainly didn't help.

"I feel like we missed something, Act. Should we send messengers to Shield too? Or maybe he went to Thyr to secure a sea passage?" Wave ran a hand through his long hair as he watched the light lancers practice. "They're damned rusty, eh? By the looks, I'd guess they've not practiced a wink since the war. I hope they can get their act together before we make a move."

"I cannot imagine that Ambrosius would flee to Shield," said Actaeon. "He has no allies there, after all."

"That we know of," said Wave.

"Correct," said Actaeon. "Talk to Itarik and have him dispatch another messenger to the Supreme Captain. Ambrosius is to be refused any sea passage and apprehended on sight."

"Aye, boss," said Wave.

"When do we leave?" rasped a voice behind them.

The two men twisted to find Jezail there.

The unburnt section of the warband Captain's face was a twisted mask of anger.

"We must first determine where Ambrosius has fled to," said Actaeon. He looked down at his old childhood friend with concern.

"And until then we just sit around, thumbs up our arses?" snapped Jezail.

Actaeon reached out to touch her shoulder. "Jez... we –"

Jezail slapped his hand aside. "Darkest Hour take your reassurances. Just tell me when we're leaving. I'm coming with you."

And with that, the warbander spun on her heel and stormed off.

"First Varisk and now Trench," said Actaeon as he watched her head back into the workshop. "She has lost too much."

"We've all lost people, Act," said Wave gravely. "It's up to all of us to make sure we don't lose ourselves as well."

"That is what worries me," said Actaeon. "That she will lose herself after all that she has endured."

"She's a tough lass," said Wave. "She'll pull through. She just has to see this through with us." Despite his words, he didn't sound convinced.

Actaeon squeezed Wave's arm. "I hope you are right, Wave. Either way, we had best keep an eye on her. Excuse me."

Wave watched as the Prince Engineer headed back into the workshop.

Yanelle stepped alongside him. "How've you been?"

The two women had been clear that their night with him had just been a one-time thing, although they'd both admitted that they cared about him as a friend. Yanelle and Calisse were committed to each other, and Wave had promised to respect that.

"Still wishing I was there to fight alongside you and Trench that day," said Wave as he stared off into the distance.

"You'll be there to fight alongside us in the next fight," said Yanelle.

"Won't bring the big guy back," said Wave.

"It won't," admitted the Companion. "But with luck it'll prevent many more from suffering at that monster's hands."

Wave nodded.

The pair shared a long moment of silence as the light lancers continued their drills behind them.

"You know there's no way your presence there would've made a difference," said Yanelle after a time. "There were just too many of them. I can't imagine anyone but Trench fending them off for so long."

"It may be so," said Wave. "But in my imagination, it will *always* make a difference."

"I should be going with you," argued Eisandre.

They were up in their little alcove in the workshop's loft. The Princess sat on the bed wincing from time to time as Aedwina suckled too hard upon her breast.

"The Matron says that you still need some time to recover," said Actaeon. "Plus Aedwina needs you."

Eisandre frowned and looked down at the little baby against her chest. It felt wrong to her – the opposite of everything her Arbiter training had taught her. To be burdened in such a way left her feeling more crippled than she had since before she'd begun her Arbiter training. She winced again, the baby's hard gums bringing tears to her eyes. And yet, she found she loved the little human that suckled against her.

"I don't want you to leave, then," said Eisandre, knowing full well the impossibility of her request.

"The next time Ambrosius attacks, Trench will not be there to protect us," said Actaeon. "If I do not put an end to this then our family will always be in peril."

"Why can't you wait until I am recovered?" asked Eisandre, her words a plea. "Or let the Companions handle it? It's their job after all."

"If Ambrosius were naught but a man, I would agree with you on this," said Actaeon. He sat down beside her on the bed and put his arm around her as he watched little Aedwina feed. "But Ambrosius is not a man. He is more likely to be whatever the Veiled One is. Perhaps an Ancient. Perhaps something else entirely. You recall the complications we had in dealing with the Veiled One. We shall need everything we can to contend with what he throws at us. I must be there to make sure this family stays safe."

His words floated past her like petals on a breeze. She didn't comprehend them at first, but after they passed her mind began to piece them back together. She winced again as the baby suckled too hard and used her thumb to break the latch as Seraeta had shown her.

Aedwina began to whimper as she searched for Eisandre's nipple with her lips.

Eisandre brought the baby to her other breast. The fresh latch brought tears to her eyes.

"We will use the Thoughtlink Artifact then," she said.

"Ambrosius will listen in on us," said Actaeon.

"Yes, he will," said Eisandre. "But what did Uncle Arcady say?"

Actaeon's eyes lit up and he grinned. "So you think by extension I will be unable to be controlled since my thoughts will be linked with your Lost thoughts? You are a genius, my love."

"I am simply your concerned partner," she said. "I don't want anything bad to happen to you. I cannot do…" she gestured down at their baby, "… this, without you."

"Then I must not fail," said Actaeon with the iron of determination in his tone.

"More," Eisandre scolded. "You must not die."

Actaeon grinned. The expression usually helped to reassure her, but it didn't this time. "I have stepped into worse situations than this and survived," he said.

"I'm not sure that's true," she ventured. "The Veiled One's mind was broken somehow, as if it were driven mad by a singular desire. Ambrosius' mind is not broken – it is sharp. He has skillfully manipulated my family for generations, if our suspicions are true. If you're right and he's the same as the Veiled One…"

"Then this will be much more dangerous," Actaeon said, completing her sentence.

She placed her hand on his knee and squeezed it, looking up into his emerald eyes. "You must come back to me, safe and sound. I cannot be there to save you this time." There were tears in her eyes.

Actaeon reached up to brush a tear from her cheek. "Yes, my Princess." He leaned down to kiss her.

The Companions raised the alarm from without and everyone rushed to the outside of the workshop to see what the commotion was.

Actaeon quickly donned his jacket and snatched his halberd from its resting spot near the workshop's big door.

The sight he saw when he stepped outside made him smirk.

The Companions of Raedelle stood between the new arrival and the workshop.

Lauryn and her squad of light lancers rushed to surround the floating silver orb that hovered before the Companions. She barked out orders, and six light lances were leveled at it.

The blue dots on the sphere's circumference flashed and a tinny voice sounded. "Not very nice to assault me with my own weapons. You've me to thank that you have them at all."

A ray of blue light projected down from the artifact and within it a figure flickered into existence.

Defocused and blurry at first, it quickly sharpened into the details of a short man.

Kryo, or rather, the projection of Kryo, stepped forward and pushed his lens frame up along his nose.

"I could fix that problem of yours with a simple strap, if you wanted me to," said Actaeon with a grin. "You would not have to waste any more time adjusting your lens frame."

The Prince Engineer stepped forward between Itarik and Tarcy.

Kryo smiled wearily and shook his head. "Why, Prince Engineer, if you're offering your services there are much more dire needs than my old lens frame."

"Yes, yes," said Actaeon, rolling his eyes. "I know. You want me to go to Travail to help repair the disturbance. You and Sollemnis are the most persistent individuals I have ever encountered." He brushed a hand impatiently through the unruly hair behind his goggles, eager to get back to his preparations inside the workshop.

"Oh, but I do believe that this time will be different," said Kryo with a thin smile.

Actaeon threw his free hand up in the air. "Sure it will. I have more important things to deal with at the moment, Kryo. Go find someone else to be a pawn in your experiments." He spun on his heel to return to the workshop.

"I suppose it wouldn't concern you then that the target of all your preparations has barricaded itself inside Travail," said Kryo. "Oh well." The projection flickered and winked away, and the silver sphere began to float off slowly.

Actaeon stopped dead in his tracks and spun on his heel.

"Give the word and we'll blast that thing out of existence, Act," said Lauryn.

The Prince Engineer shook his head and held up a hand to forestall everyone present. "No. We need to hear this. Stop being dense, Kryo. You say Ambrosius is *in* Travail?"

A ray of blue light was cast forth by the orb again and the leader of the Loresworn flickered back into reality and adjusted his lens frame once more. "He is."

"This had better not be a trick, Kryo," Actaeon warned. "We will head there at once, but if this is a deception, justice will not be kind to you."

"It's no trick, Engineer," Kryo said. "Only this time I must warn you not to go."

"Not to go?" asked Actaeon in genuine confusion.

"Not to go," repeated Kryo. "Ambrosius has set a trap for you that you will not be able to escape."

"And if I do not go?" asked Actaeon.

"Then Ambrosius will cause the weakness to expand until it envelops all of Redemption," said Kryo simply.

"Then it appears that we must go to Travail in order to stop Ambrosius *and* this weakness of yours," Actaeon asserted.

"You cannot," said Kryo. "It is too late now. The weakness has grown much too large. It has gained an incontrovertible foothold in Redemption. The time for action has passed. Only death awaits you in Travail."

Actaeon shook his head in confusion. "So what is our alternative?"

"Flee this city. Find a ship which will take you to the Great Sea in search of a new home," said Kryo. "It is the only way in which you might survive. The only way in which your newborn child might have a chance."

"There must be another option," said Actaeon.

"There's always another option," said Kryo. "Though I'd be surprised if you chose death."

VOYAGE FOR REDEMPTION

T HE *GLORIOUS REDEMPTION* SAILED ALONG the River of Arches with its precious cargo.

"Tack to port!" shouted Captain Xula over the crashing waves.

The Bosun, Lucerd, brought a horn to his lips and blew a series of notes to convey his Captain's orders.

The Thyrian sloop bucked in rhythm with the waves as it pressed on, the river swollen and rough from all the extra rain and runoff that the monsoon rains of Torrentfall brought. Despite the condition of the river, the weather had given them at least a momentary reprieve from the rains.

"Ain't this a mite risky, Cap'n?" asked Vash as she spun the ship's wheel to keep them on course down the river.

Xula traced a finger along the brim of his quadcorne hat and smiled. "What's the fun if it ain't risky, Vash? Hold course and full wind ahead."

"Aye aye, Cap'n," replied the helmsman.

Despite his comment, the Thyrian Captain arched a brow and cast it in Actaeon's direction.

"As soon as we make landfall you are to turn about and make for the Great Sea," the Prince Engineer instructed. "No matter if we succeed or fail, Eisandre will know. And you will know whether to maintain course or to turn back."

"My crew can handle that, Act," said Xula. "I'd bring my sword to fight at your side."

Actaeon placed a firm hand on Xula's shoulder. "As much as I appreciate your offer, Harvand, I would much prefer that you were aboard to make sure my wife and daughter are safe in the case that I fail."

Xula bit his lip in disappointment but nodded anyway. "You'll not fail, Act. I've seen what you can do. Just be sure to put this Ambrosius' head on the tip of your halberd."

The Captain winced and frowned as he tasted blood upon his tongue. At least Craft and her Flashbolt Marines would disembark to help the Prince Engineer. If he couldn't be there to fight, they were the next best thing.

Actaeon scratched his right arm through the thick leather of his jacket. "You have my word that I will try my best to do so. Any advice?"

Xula arched his brow again and shrugged. "Thrust the pointy end at his neck?"

Actaeon let out a nervous laugh.

Xula took a deep breath and tried again. "If anyone's got this, it's you. Don't forget that you're the one to come up with ingenious ways to solve problems. That's what'll end this, if anything. Be smart about it. You'll not defeat him with brute force alone. You'll have to be smarter than him."

"Smarter than an Ancient, or whatever he may be," said Actaeon with a grin. "Understood."

The Prince Engineer made his way down from the aftercastle and forward to climb back up to the forecastle deck. He found Wave there, leaning over the bow to look down at the river below.

"We are doing the right thing, are we not?" he asked. "Tell me we are taking the correct course of action."

The lone mercenary turned to regard him with his single eye. "There's no better course than the one leading to the demise of Trench's killer. I'm with you on this, Act. Whatever happens, we did our best. We did what we thought was right. Nobody can fault us that."

"Not even my daughter?" asked Actaeon doubtfully.

"Even if you fail in this, yer daughter'll remember how her father gave his life to protect her – to protect all Redemption," said Wave. "But I'll not let that happen, Act. Not as long as there's a breath left in my body. No," he said, letting the word hang in the air. "If I've got something to say 'bout it, I'll make sure to do what Paladin Arandel couldn't. Ambrosius can taste the cold steel of my blade."

"I hope you are right," said Actaeon. "I hope it is that simple. Though I strongly suspect it is not."

Before they had departed, Actaeon had dispatched a messenger to the Kainai to ask for help. In the message he'd explained everything – the threat of Ambrosius, the spreading weakness in Travail, the trap they expected to be waiting for them. The Kainai knew the language of the Ancients and Travail was full of it. If there were any need to discern the symbols within, the Kainai might be needed there. He hoped they would send some representation from the Underforest in response to his message.

"An old friend of Trench and mine used to say: If your intent is true, and your heart is virtuous, then the blade will strike accurately, whether it is yours or another's. Justice will not be eluded." Wave let the words hang along with the salt spray that filled the air with every wave that the ship crested.

Actaeon thought about what Wave said as he watched one of the great broken arches pass overhead. The metal and elderglass structure had once spanned the river entire. But now it was reduced to simple ruin – its missing section lost forever beneath the angry waters of the river.

"Aside from Eis, there is no one else I would rather have at my side for this," Actaeon admitted.

"I'd rather have Trench at your side," Wave said.

"Fire on the topsail!"

The shout came from high above – one of the sailors in the rigging.

In an instant, all hands were squinting up into the midday sun that hung directly overhead.

Fire on a ship was a death sentence at sea. Luckily, they were cruising down a wide river instead.

The sailors scrambled to lower buckets over the side. They hauled them up full of seawater before attaching them to a rigging pulley to be hauled upward to fight the fire.

"Jib's aflame!" cried Vash from the helm. She pointed toward the bow over her big wooden wheel.

"Something is wrong," said Actaeon.

"Nothin' gets by you," said Captain Xula with a smirk. "Fire suppression to the jib first! We'll need it more here on the river!" The Captain's voice rang out over the deck.

The Bosun ran forward to help coordinate the efforts.

It was Wave who spotted it. Everyone else was too busy squinting up at the fires in the sails or moving the buckets needed to extinguish the fires.

"To the north!" cried Wave. "They're firing arrows from the north bank!"

The Captain pulled off his quadcorne hat and pointed it to the north. "Missile crews, man your stations!"

Half of the sailors dropped their fire suppression duties in an instant. Some of them scrambled to uncover several apparatus on the main deck while the rest went belowdecks.

"Cut loose the topsail and jib!" shouted the Bosun in between blows of his horn. "Wet down the main and fore sails! Wet 'em down good, sailors!"

Actaeon watched as a volley of flaming arrows arced overhead from the north bank. Several hundred tiny figures ran along to keep pace with the Thyrian ship. Farther ahead on the bank, more archers stood in wait. It was impossible to identify their attackers at this distance.

Most of the arrows passed harmlessly over the ship to land soundlessly in the water. A handful of them caught in the fore topsail and lit it ablaze. The fore sail itself also suffered some hits and began to burn.

One extremely unlucky sailor caught an arrow in the neck and fell to the deck in a spray of blood.

"Fire at will!" ordered Xula.

The missile crews had made ready their apparatus with truly impressive speed. The deck shuddered as the massive ballista spears left the ship from belowdecks and tore into the figures on the shore. The massive projectiles sent bodies flying like tiny dolls.

A rapid series of clicks sounded as one of the boltspray apparatus on the main deck was discharged. It sent a flurry of bolts to the northern bank that caused more than a few distant figures to fall.

The Flashbolt Marines emerged from belowdecks and under the direction of Major Craft they took up position on the port side of the ship behind the rail. The northern bank was well out of their range, but they would be ready once it wasn't.

"Your Grace," came a voice. "If you'd please stay belowdecks. It isn't safe up here."

Princess Eisandre had emerged from the door of the Captain's cabin and was surveying the chaotic shipboard scene. Little Aedwina was tucked against her chest. "I want a report," she demanded of her First Companion.

Itarik sputtered and frowned. "Assailants from the north are firing pitch-soaked arrows at us to light the sails. Please, Your Grace."

Actaeon leaned over the quarterdeck at the sound of his wife's voice. "Eis, it would be best if you took Aedwina belowdecks for now. Lest she be struck by a stray arrow."

As if on cue, a flaming arrow struck the deck with a thud several paces to the right of Eisandre.

The Voice Ithelie emerged from belowdecks. She hiked up her green robes and rushed over to Eisandre. "Your Grace, your precious one needs to be taken below."

The Princess looked down at the arrow and then back at Actaeon. She gritted her teeth and nodded before returning to the Captain's cabin.

A heavy hand fell on Actaeon's shoulder.

It was Captain Xula.

"We've two sails left to us as the wind blows," said Xula. Actaeon looked up to find that the sailors in the rigging had cut away all but the big mainsail and the flying jib. "I'll have them pick up as much speed as we can, but then we must land. Where would you have me put in, Prince Engineer?"

A glance upward found plumes of black smoke forming a trail in the sky above the river behind them as the sails on the two masts burned. Sailors clung to the mainmast and its gaff pole and doused the mainsail with a steady bucket brigade to prevent it from catching fire from the blowing embers of the sails ahead. The spent buckets were tossed downward and expertly caught by a young boy below, who then tossed the emptied vessels back to the crew filling the buckets over the side rails.

Actaeon thought about the situation. If they put in on the south bank, they would be safe but nowhere near their goal. However, on the north bank they would be overrun by whoever these attackers were and that would make the landing difficult. Unless...

"Can you get us beyond Travail and put ashore just to the east of it?" he asked.

Xula grinned and nodded. "Aye aye, Your Grace. I see where you're going with this."

"Then I shall need you to get Eisandre and Aedwina away from here as quickly as possible," Actaeon explained.

Xula touched his forehead to Actaeon's and smiled. "You've my word.

We'll hug the southern bank and be away faster than you know it. Don't worry, Act, I'll keep 'em safe. You just worry about the task ahead."

Actaeon nodded and the Captain was off. He watched Xula convey the instructions to the Bosun. The rigging was quickly adjusted to maximize the wind captured by the two remaining sails.

"I want you to help me don my armor," said Eisandre.

Guybon Hael paled. "But, Your Grace... shouldn't you... shouldn't..." The young lad left the question incomplete and hanging in the air. "I... uh, I don't... think I should do that." He brushed a hand nervously through his mop of brown hair.

"I don't understand," said Eisandre, eyeing him with impatience. "You've been bothering me to put on my armor and to clean my sword since you were assigned as my attendant. Now I'm asking you to do it. Why are you now refusing?"

Guybon's older sister stepped forward. The giant Companion looked down at Eisandre and spoke. "He'un jus' wan' keep yerself safe, m'Grace," said Tarcy. "Ye shun'a go an' fight."

Eisandre looked up unflinchingly at the giantess. After a moment's deliberation, she thrust Aedwina forward into Tarcy's arms.

The big Companion accepted the baby before she had a chance to think it over. Aedwina began crying and Tarcy looked down at the infant with concern.

"If you wish to keep me safe, then what better way than for me to wear my armor?" asked Eisandre. "Get started, Attendant Hael. That's an order."

Guybon flinched away from the Princess' eyes and rushed to retrieve her armor, glad to have a lifebeat away from her critical gaze.

"Voice?" Eisandre said.

"I am here, Your Grace," said Ithelie, her tone exuding confidence.

"Will you watch over Aedwina for me?" she asked.

"Of course, my Princess. I made sure the wet nurse was aboard in case just this happened," said Ithelie with a knowing smile. "The Fallen will watch over you."

The deck beneath them shuddered as another ballista volley was fired off.

The baby continued to cry as the attendant was fastening Eisandre's cuirass in place. "You should rock her, you know," said Eisandre to Tarcy. "And she enjoys when people sing to her."

Tarcy looked horrified, but then she drew her gaze back down to the baby wailing in her arms. Her Princess' baby, whom she was sworn to protect. The giantess nodded and began to sway back and forth carefully. To everyone's surprise, she also began to sing.

The lyrics of the song that she sang were barely intelligible, but Guybon recognized them. It was a song that their mother used to sing to them when they were young – a classic called *When the Portal Opens*. He found himself reminiscing about the past when his mother would sing him to sleep in his bed back in Bastion.

"The lower straps must be fastened as well," Eisandre said, frustration evident in her tone.

"Yes, Your Grace," said the young attendant, snapping out of it. He rushed to fasten the buckles.

The *Glorious Redemption* skidded against the muddy northern bank of the River of Arches just to the east of Travail.

The six fin-like blades of the massive building jutted out from the jungle to hang over them like a looming threat. The jagged lines of luminaries set into its walls pulsed an angry purple color.

The crew quickly lowered lines from the sections of rigging that were not on fire to support a ramp from the main deck to the shore.

Once the ramp was extended, Major Ainhara Craft led the Flashbolt Marines down it. They knelt to form a defensive semi-circle once ashore.

Behind them came Jezail and her Wall Breakers and Gunther Arcady with a few of his Blackstone warbanders.

Last came Lauryn and her Light Lancers.

"Ready Act?" asked Wave.

The mercenary stood with Companions Itarik and Yanelle.

"Allow me to say goodbye first," said Actaeon. That said, he approached the door to the Captain's cabin.

Before he could reach it, the door swung open and Eisandre emerged. She didn't walk so much as waddle out, her belly still somewhat distended under her cuirass from her recent pregnancy. But she wore her full armor with her old Arbiter's sword at her side. And the legendary sword Caliburn was on her back.

"I'm coming with you," she said.

"What about Aedwina?" asked Actaeon.

"Ithelie, Tarcy, and Guybon can watch after her," said Eisandre. "I trust them."

Actaeon placed his hands on her shoulders and looked into her brilliant blue eyes. "Are you ready for this, love?"

"No," she admitted. "But I'm not ready to let you do this alone. If we're going to make this world a safe place for our little one, then we'll do so together."

Actaeon felt the tears well up in his eyes and blinked them away. "Thank you, Eis." He left it at that, not knowing what else to say.

And so, the Princess and her Prince Engineer disembarked the *Glorious Redemption* and set foot upon the northern bank of the River of Arches beside Travail.

As they watched the Thyrian sloop cast off to sail back down the river toward the Great Sea, Actaeon squeezed her hand. "No matter what happens now, Captain Xula will make sure that our little one is safe."

"I know that," said Eisandre. "But I still feel as though I belong in two places at once."

"I feel the same way," Actaeon agreed. "Here to fight the most important battle of our lives, and there to protect our most important accomplishment. If only we could split in two."

"If we split in two, we wouldn't be very effective in either location," said Eisandre in seriousness.

Actaeon grinned at that. "Then we had best stay in one piece."

Hand in hand, they watched as the Thyrian sloop receded into the distance, their daughter safely aboard it.

They didn't quite make it to the doors of Travail before they were beset upon.

"Form a wedge!" Eisandre ordered.

Jezail took position at the tip of the wedge with Major Craft just beside her. To their flanks, the Flashbolt Marines and the Wall Breakers mixed in together, moving steadily forward through knee-high ferns.

Lauryn and her squad of light lancers followed closely behind.

"Get us close and we'll cut them to pieces," said Lauryn.

"I intend to," said Jezail. She raised Varisk's sword and led the charge. "Wall Breakers, to me!"

The first volley of flaming pitch arrows decimated the wedge and stopped them in their tracks.

One of the arrows lodged itself in Jezail's clavicle and knocked her onto her back. There was a sudden heat from the flame and she hastily yanked the arrow free and threw it aside, thankful that the arrow's fire had cauterized the wound.

The rapid clicks of the Marines' triple crossbows sounded.

There was a shriek to her right that sent a chill up Jezail's spine.

One of the young twins of Lauryn's Light Lancers had taken an arrow to the eye. Her sister knelt amidst the trampled ferns holding her dead twin, Phelto her name was, and shrieking like a knife on glass.

Jezail stood and sheathed her sword before picking up the fallen twin's light lance. She reached down to grab a fistful of Phalto's tunic where it was exposed through her leather armor and yanked her. "To your feet, soldier. I need you to show me how to use this. Do you think you're any help to her on your knees?"

The surviving twin stopped her scream and offered her a shell-shocked look before climbing to her feet and nodding.

Jezail spun to rejoin the front of the wedge, a blood rage in her eyes.

But Eisandre was already there leading the renewed charge.

The Princess had Caliburn drawn and swung it effortlessly with both hands. It tore into the first arriving tribal warriors and sent them to the ground in a pile of bloody ruin.

The approaching enemy were tribal warriors, their faces covered with either blue or yellow face paint and black lines. They struck Actaeon as strangely familiar, though he couldn't recall from where, as flaming arrows rained down around him.

First Companion Itarik joined Eisandre on one side.

Jezail pulled Phalto after her and rushed to join Eisandre on her other side. "Show me how to use this," she barked.

"Watch," Phalto said. She placed her hands on both activation panels and the bright orange beam crackled to life. She swept left to right and back again in sinusoidal arcs that would have been beautiful if they hadn't torn through another group of attackers in a cloud of arterial spray and burning armor. The twin counted to twenty and then shut it off. "Now you," she said. "On twenty, off thirty. Do it exact or we're dead."

Jezail nodded and activated Phelto's light lance, the artifact metal cold in her hands.

It crackled to life, and she swept it as she'd seen Phalto do, cutting through the enemy like a hot knife through butter. Six fell, then three more, then another two. Another three were next, but Phalto wrenched her right hand away from the activation panel.

"Count the lifebeats!" the light lancer shouted. "Ya hit twenty-five. Ya'll kill us!"

"Sorry," said Jezail, looking down nervously at the deadly artifact staff in her hand.

But her words were lost in a clash of steel and wood as Eisandre and Itarik took care of the three she'd run out of time for.

They reached the outer wall of Travail and the wedge angled to hug the wall.

Just ahead were the massive blue doors that would let them inside. But the enemy forces were already there en masse – a line of bristling spears and shields with another line of archers beyond that.

"Something is quite wrong," said Actaeon.

Beside him, Wave fired his heavy crossbow and placed his foot in the stirrup to reload. "Understatement of the cycle there, Act."

"No," said Actaeon. "It is not. These tribals are from Wither." The blue and yellow face paints of the enemy suddenly made sense.

Eisandre lifted a fist and caused the whole wedge to draw to a stop some fifty paces from the enemy line.

"Wither?" Yanelle exclaimed. "How is that –"

The enemy line parted to allow someone through.

The Raedelleans present gasped as a red-haired woman stepped forward, a spear in one hand and a sword in the other. She wore the same practical leather armor as the Companions. But something was wrong – there was a familiar lifelessness in her blue Caliburn eyes.

Eisandre lowered her sword. "Eshy…" she said, her mouth hanging open in surprise.

Actaeon realized where he'd seen the look in Eshelle's eyes before.

"Eis, that's not her!" he yelled. "That's not Eshelle!"

But he was too late.

Eshelle lifted the spear. It spun in her hand as if in slow motion until it was pointed at her sister.

Eisandre lowered her sword. "Eshy, it's me... Sandre," she said, unable to conflate Actaeon's warning with the reality she saw before her.

Instead she stood immobilized at the unexpected presence of her sister. Eshelle threw the spear.

Actaeon watched the events unfold before him as if time had slowed. He tried to move forward to stop the spear, but he couldn't move anywhere near fast enough.

The empty look he'd recognized in Eshelle's blue eyes was the same as he'd seen in the cross-faced raiders. The same as he'd seen in the eyes of anyone who was under the Veiled One's control. Which meant that Eshelle was possessed.

Closest to Eisandre, Companion Itarik reflexively swung his sword and managed to catch the thrown spear with the tip of his sword. It just nicked the spear's shaft and knocked it aside ever so slightly.

Ever so slightly enough to change the course of history.

Eisandre continued to stare at Eshelle in disbelief as the spear slammed into her right shoulder exactly at the seam in her armor. Metal bent inward and it buried itself deep into the tissue there. The Princess spun about and slammed hard, face first, into the ground.

The legendary sword Caliburn swept from her fingers to tumble amidst the ferns.

"No!" Actaeon shouted. The Prince Engineer rushed forward and slid to a stop beside the Princess.

Eshelle lifted her sword high into the air and then pointed it forward.

And alongside her, the Witherian tribals charged forward.

They tore into the shocked Raedellean and Thyrian ranks and began to slaughter them.

Wave watched everything unfold from just behind the point of the wedge where he'd been with Actaeon. He shared a solemn look with Yanelle before he fired off his final crossbow bolt into the chest of an unfortunate Witherian tribal.

That done, he tossed the crossbow aside and drew his blades.

It took him a lifebeat to reach Actaeon and the fallen Eisandre. He leapt over them and swept the edge of his flamberge rapier across the throat of the closest assailant.

Wave kicked the body of that tribal aside and swept his blade to parry the strike of a second attacker. He severed the forearm tendons of the woman with his companion dagger and then thrust his main blade between her ribs and into the heart.

Before the blade could bind with the ribcage, he spun and pulled his blade free to meet the next enemy.

But what he saw next made him stop in his tracks.

On the hilltop above him stood Trench.

The giant stood watching them with his hands clasped before him as the glow of the sun radiated around his massive frame from behind.

A WORLD ASUNDER

TRENCH STOOD SMILING DOWN UPON them, the scar that had once bisected his face gone.

Next came a massive rain of stones hurled by leather slings and half of the Witherians dropped.

An ululating yell filled the air as hundreds of figures ran down from the hilltop to fall against the tribals from behind. They wielded clubs and staves with which they beat the Wither tribals until they surrendered.

"By the Fallen," said Actaeon with a grin as he looked up from Eisandre, who was cradled in his arms. He watched as an old man with wispy gray hair and blazing madness in his eyes emerged from behind the artifact statue.

It was Phyrius Ricter, the First of the First of the Waiting Ones himself.

Phyrius' followers had wheeled the glowing Trench look-alike statue to the highest point on the hilltop.

Wave's stomach sank as he realized it wasn't really his friend up there. In his mind he'd known that, but his heart had hoped.

The cult leader stood tall beside the Keeper of Light and raised his arms to the heavens. "Return them to the earth – the unbelievers! All those who seek to defile the Bringers of the Keeper of Light shall fall before us. Throw down your weapons lost heathen, for only the Keeper of Light might offer you succor! Surrender and see the truth of His Light."

More than a few of the Witherian attackers dropped their spears and fell to their knees at Phyrius' pronouncement.

The ones who still rushed forth were cut down with the orange beams of the light lancers.

Lauryn led them forward in a coordinated pattern of lethal sweeps, Jezail now among them.

When the attackers who had refused to surrender had all been cut down by the crackling beams of the lancers, only Eshelle Caliburn stood, gazing down at Actaeon and Eisandre with dead blue eyes not her own.

Itarik, Wave, and Yanelle stepped between her and the royal couple, their blades at the ready.

"That is not really Eshelle Caliburn," said Actaeon. "Do your best to keep her alive," he instructed.

In his arms, Eisandre stirred, wincing in pain at the spearhead buried deep in her shoulder. "Eshy... Don't hurt her. Don't hurt my sister."

"Don't worry, Act. I'll take care of this," said Wave, stepping forward. He risked a glance back at the two Companions behind him. "Back me up, will you?"

"My sword is with you," said Itarik.

"And mine," said Yanelle.

"I know you're not Eshelle Caliburn," spat Wave, taking another step toward the possessed Lady. "So let's see what you've got, Ambrosius."

Eshelle smiled a smile that failed to reach her eyes. "Killing the last of Glaive's Messengers will be my pleasure – especially given how many I've eliminated as the Devourer. Though it won't quite equal the thrill I got from finally felling the giant." She spoke with a strangely slurred voice that sounded almost as though she were speaking underwater.

Recognition dawned on Wave's face and his jaw fell open in shock at the mention of the Devourer. He searched for the right words but couldn't find them.

Eshelle took advantage of the moment of uncertainty and rushed forward to attack.

Wave's mouth curled into a vicious snarl, and he was ready for her. Their blades were a blur as they attacked and parried, countered and attacked.

Sparks flew in the air as their blades chipped with edge to edge impacts.

The pair weaved a deadly dance to and fro atop the trampled and bloodied ferns.

All eyes were locked on the two figures as they fought.

Phyrius Ricter continued to chant from atop the hilltop, his followers echoing his words as they watched over their Witherian captives.

Wave didn't hear any of that. He fought with a frenzy that he knew he couldn't possibly maintain. Eshelle was an excellent swordswoman – he knew that. But she wasn't anywhere near this good. Under normal circumstances, he should've been able to best her. Even with the two Companions supporting him with their swords from the sides, Eshelle was not slowing down or giving them an opening.

This wasn't Eshelle though, he reminded himself. This was something else. A possessed Eshelle had the knowledge of Ambrosius and the Devourer and who knew what else?

He was beginning to slow, and he knew it. The injury to his leading ankle from his fight with Vain began to ache.

Eshelle offered him a mocking smirk. She knew it as well. She – whatever she was – was toying with him at this point – wearing him down.

In an unorthodox move, she leaned to her off hand side all of a sudden and took a wide swing at him, throwing her weight behind the sword.

Wave used both blades to parry the blow, already seeing the fatal opening that her inadvisable move would create – his mind moving a step ahead of the battle.

But instead, there was a crack and a flash. A sudden warmth flooded down his neck to the tunic below his thick leather armor.

The fatal thrust fell short as he realized his flamberge rapier had been shattered in two by her last blow.

He had just enough time to realize that the half of his blade which had broken free had opened a gash along his lower left jaw down to his chin. That's where the warm blood was coming from.

Eshelle's fist ended the thought as it slammed into the side of his head and sent him reeling to fall amidst the red-stained and trampled ferns, his own red running in rivulets from his chin as he caught himself on his elbows.

Behind him, Itarik and Yanelle rushed forward to take on the possessed Caliburn.

Wave could hear the clash of the blades behind him and shook his head to clear his mind. The two Companions were excellent fighters, but he knew they wouldn't be able to keep up with whatever supernatural wealth of swordsmanship knowledge Eshelle was drawing from now. As he blinked his remaining eye, a solution grew apparent.

There before him among the flattened vegetation lay the most legendary Raedellean weapon – there lay Caliburn itself.

Wave smiled painfully and snatched up the great two-hander before struggling to pull himself up.

He reached his feet just in time to see Yanelle knocked onto her back. Itarik lunged forward to interject himself between Eshelle and his fallen Companion. Eshelle took the opportunity to catch the First Companion off guard and with a broad sweep of her arm took Itarik's feet out from under him.

Itarik slammed into the ground hard, all the air buffeted from his lungs. He gasped and looked up in surprise as Eshelle's blade fell upon him.

But it was stopped by another sword.

Gunther Arcady had dashed forward to parry the killing blow, saving the First Companion. The Lord Shore's swordwork was impressive as he fought against his possessed niece. "Release her at once, Ambrosius!" barked Arcady as he neatly parried Eshelle's blows and pressed his own attack.

"Foolish Gunther," replied Eshelle. "Without me you'd be nothing. You've always been nothing but my sellsword." She batted aside another series of his attacks effortlessly. "And now here you are, pretending to be the hero. Did you tell your nieces that you hacked their father and brothers to pieces? Did you tell them about how you betrayed and murdered them?"

Arcady's face went white at the accusation and he risked a glance over at Eisandre, who was gazing at him with a blank look on her face.

The tip of Eshelle's blade opened one side of his neck. Arcady blinked in surprise and clamped his maimed hand over the wound. Blood poured out and down his neck. He managed to parry several more of Eshelle' attacks before he stumbled and fell to his knees.

Eshelle laughed – a haunting sound – and lazily kicked over the Lord Shore.

Gunther Arcady landed heavily on his side, adding more blood to the flattened ferns around him as he gasped and stared at Eisandre. He appeared to be mouthing words, but they were unrecognizable.

"You've outlived your usefulness, Gunther," said Eshelle. "Now you can watch me complete the task I originally gave you as I hack your youngest niece to pieces."

Actaeon didn't have time to release Eisandre and raise his halberd as Eshelle leapt forward to cleave him in two with her sword.

But Wave stopped it. It was reflexive to swing the greatsword to block the deathblow.

The next blow came naturally too, and then the next. He forced Eshelle back and away from Actaeon and Eisandre. It was unusual to wield a single sword with two hands, but also most effective, he was finding.

The subsequent blow settled the matter as Caliburn's artifact metal shattered Eshelle's blade at the hilt.

Eshelle shrieked in rage and tried to strike out with the pommel of her broken sword.

Wave blocked the blow against her wrists using the flat of Caliburn's blade and then used the same flat to sweep her legs from beneath her.

Eshelle slammed into the ground hard and looked up at him, dazed.

Wave swept the side of Caliburn down to crack her in the temple and render her unconscious.

With blood still dripping down his chin, the mercenary flipped over Eshelle and pressed a knee into her back. He unshouldered a coil of rope and used it to tie the Lady of Wither's arms behind her back.

Once that was done, he rolled onto his side and breathed a sigh of relief.

Beside him, Arcady let out one last agonal breath and died.

"Eshy," said Eisandre, tears filling her eyes as Actaeon cradled her in his arms. "Are you okay? Eshelle, please be okay. I need you."

"She is alright, love," Actaeon assured her. "Wave captured her. I think she will recover. But first, we must stop Ambrosius."

Eisandre tried to lift her right hand, but nothing happened. She stared in horror as her hand lay unmoving upon the ground at her side.

You may enter, Actaeon Rellios Caliburn of Shore, came an unfamiliar thought through the Thoughtlink Artifact. *But none other.*

Actaeon met Eisandre's concerned expression. Silently, she shook her head no, her eyes pleading with him.

Actaeon lifted his jacket's sleeve to scratch his right arm. "I am sorry, Eis, but I must do this. There may not be another way to save Redemption – to make it a safe place for our Aedwina."

Eisandre bit her lip and nodded, tears running freely down her cheeks.

She squeezed his hand tightly with her left hand before pulling him against her to kiss him hard. "Go then, my love. Go."

Actaeon squeezed his eyes shut hard to keep his own tears at bay and nodded. He released Eisandre and rose to his feet.

Agreed, Ambrosius, he sent across the Thoughtlink. *Open the doors of Travail.*

Are you certain, Engineer? asked the disembodied voice. *Inside you will find answers beyond your wildest imaginings, but I assure you they lie in death.*

And what otherwise? thought Actaeon. *Will not all of Redemption be lost?*

Undoubtedly, returned Ambrosius. *But you might be able to flee the cataclysm. Only one way to know.*

Why? asked Actaeon. *Why would you allow this to happen? I believe you have the power to stop it.*

The answers lie inside, said Ambrosius. *As I said, the answers lie in death — if you dare.*

Actaeon carefully approached the metallic blue doors of Travail. "Open it, Ambrosius," he said out loud. "Open it, and allow me within."

This one is truly something remarkable, came Ambrosius' thought.

Open the doors, and find out how remarkable I really am, thought Actaeon.

Three clarion notes sounded from high up in Travail's ramparts, but the doors didn't budge.

None other should approach, Engineer, thought Ambrosius. *Or else instantaneous disassembly shall occur.*

Actaeon glanced over his shoulder to find his friends at his back. Wave and Yanelle, Lauryn and Jezail. All of them with weapons at the ready — Wave had given Caliburn back to Eisandre, but she'd insisted on giving him her Arbiter's arming sword. The resolve in their expressions matched the fear in their eyes in all of them except Jezail.

There was no fear in the tragic warbander Captain's eyes — only a darkness that made Actaeon shudder.

"We're with you, Act," said Lauryn. "Lead the way."

"Aye, boss," seconded Wave. "Let's end this."

Actaeon shook his head sadly. "Alas, I must walk this last path alone. Thank you, my friends, for getting me this far. I could not have gotten to this point without you all. Ambrosius has made it clear that he will only allow me inside, however. Whatever happens now, we will always know that we made the attempt to right the wrong in our world. I am proud to call you all my friends."

"Shattered Redemption take that!" shouted Jezail. "We're coming with you. I'll not leave here 'till I can shove Varisk's blade down his saints-damned throat."

Wave frowned over at Jezail.

"The Captain's right," said Companion Yanelle. "We'll not let you go this alone, Your Grace."

Webs of electricity arced up from the ground beneath them for an instant. A lifebeat later they were gone, leaving artifacts of light floating before Actaeon's eyes. His four friends all lay upon the ground, unconscious.

The powerful smell of ozone washed over Actaeon, causing him to wrinkle his nose. He stepped forward to check his friends. Thankfully, they all still appeared to be breathing. He held up a fist to stop Companion Itarik, Major Craft, and others from rushing to their aid.

"Halt," he said. "All of you. They yet live, but I will not see any others come to harm. Wait for me to enter and then have the cutters check them." He saw the argument in Itarik's eyes and continued. "That is an order, Companion. You stay and protect the Princess, is that clear?"

Itarik nodded and then snapped to attention, saluting the Prince Engineer, fist to chest.

"Don't you worry, Your Grace," said Ainhara Craft. "We'll find a way in after you. Good luck."

Actaeon grinned and returned his own salute, fist to chest.

The ground shook and a series of triangles rose from the soil just to the west, glowing blue and purple and red. Each triangle was smaller than the previous and they receded away from him, into the ground. Beneath them, the dirt appeared to vaporize, turning into a thick mist that surrounded the glowing structures. Through the mist, he could just make out a stairwell descending downward into the very earth itself, following the path of the triangles' apexes.

Keep them together, Eis, Actaeon thought over the artifact connection as he met her eyes in person. *I will return.*

The laughter that sounded through the Thoughtlink Artifact shook Actaeon to his core. But instead of shattering his resolve, it reinforced it.

"I am coming for you," said Actaeon aloud as he turned to descend the stairs, feeling each one carefully with his halberd before committing his weight to it. "Laugh while you still may."

When the Prince Engineer disappeared from everyone's view, the glowing triangles descended into the ground, and it was as though they were never there at all.

Actaeon descended the stairwell into the unknown.

When the light from behind disappeared as the entrance closed, he pulled free his luminary and secured it in the strap of his goggles. He adjusted the baffle to deliver a steady pool of light before him before continuing onward, the point of his halberd forward.

The stairs continued to descend, though they curved in toward the great structure of Travail. He knew it loomed somewhere above him and as the stairs continued to twist inward, he became certain that he was underneath the main structure. The secret exterior entrance had led him into the basement of the once home of the Loresworn.

Before Actaeon realized that there were no more stairs in front of him, he took one too many steps forward and plummeted downward into the dark void before him.

He flailed out in an attempt to grab onto some handhold, but there was none there and he continued to fall into the void until he felt a sick feeling at the pit of his stomach.

His senses all told him that he was continuing to plummet toward a certain death, but his intuition told him otherwise.

There was something incredibly wrong, and it took him several long moments of utter panic to realize what it was.

The air wasn't rushing past.

And if the air wasn't rushing past, then he wasn't falling.

As if to ascertain the truth of that thought, he performed three tests.

First, he took a deep breath. Air filled his lungs. And so, air was still present.

Second, he fanned his free hand before his face. He could feel the rush of air on his face each time his hand sped by.

Lastly, he held his halberd out before him and released it. He watched the weapon with fascination as it floated before him on a slow spin away from where he last touched it. Once he was satisfied, he snatched it back out of the air.

Which could only lead to one conclusion: he was floating in a place where gravity had no effect. Somehow the force that held everything against the ground had been negated here.

So, Actaeon Rellios of Shore, now a Caliburn, came Ambrosius' thoughts, unbidden, through the Thoughtlink Artifact. *Too foolish to realize a trap even when it was placed right under his very nose.*

"Why did you do this, Ambrosius?" Actaeon cried into the void. "You could have helped Raedelle. Could have helped all the people of Redemption. But instead you chose to destroy us in the end. As though we failed to fulfill some hidden desire of yours. So what was it?" he asked with a grin. "What goal of yours did we fail you in your manipulations and contrivances?"

Around Actaeon four points of light flickered to life. As he watched they grew into spheres. Each sphere had a black square at the center and a flowing wave of orange light around it. The outer fringe of each sphere was outlined in a blue glow.

He studied them for several long moments as they continued to grow. And he remembered. Remembered the many flames that he'd lit in various experiments over the years. They'd always been pointed upward as the hotter, lighter air had floated away from the source of combustion while it burned.

But these spheres flowed outward as they combusted. Without gravity, less dense air would no longer go upward, but would flow outward from the point of combustion.

And as he watched and pondered, it spread toward him, threatening a fiery death.

Actaeon scratched the back of his right hand through his fingerless glove as he stared at the expanding spheres of light, color, and death.

Ever it was my intent to save you, came Ambrosius' thoughts. *To save Raedelle. That was always my goal. The noblest of Redemption. A people spawned by the one Warden who would pursue her Prisoners into the dark depths of the jungle to make sure they were safe. Where all the others in Redemption were not worthy, the people of Raedelle were set apart from the rest. Proof that human life was more than just a resource. More than just a reservoir for our designs.*

"A reservoir for your designs," Actaeon repeated. "And so the truth comes to light. You always planned to use us for some means to your end. We were naught but a fuel to burn for your ambition, were we not? And now you intend to burn me."

You misunderstand, Engineer, Ambrosius thought. *It was my intention to save you from being burned. No... Raedelle was always something more, something... special. But then you came along with Eisandre Caliburn and together, you both ruined everything I had planned. You destroyed the Veiled One – one of the few Starborn left, and proved to us all that none of humanity deserved any more than our original intent for you.*

The null gravity fire spheres continued to grow. Actaeon could now feel the heat from them against his exposed skin. He strapped his halberd against the back of his jacket and pulled free his recurve bow. "So what then? You have decided that we are to die? Die with the rest of Redemption? Because you never thought the rest of Redemption was worthy. You planned on using them for something, did you not? What was it? Something to do with the artifact that made the blue spheres? Something to do with the destruction of all life in Czeryn?"

With some difficulty, he slipped his body between the bowstring and the body of his bow. He hooked the bow's limbs around his arms and flexed them forward – the body of the bow against his back. With the utmost care, he slipped the loose end of the bowstring onto the groove at the tip of the limb.

Clever Engineer, came Ambrosius' thoughts. *The devices to harvest your energy were unleashed by the Veiled One. But, of course, that was an endeavor that you utterly foiled. The gathering of the quantum lifestreams of Redemption's humans was essential to our return to the stars. And then you had to go and sabotage the effort.* Ambrosius' annoyance could be felt even through the Thoughtlink Artifact. *In one fell swoop, you proved that all humankind is worth naught but fodder for our goal. The blood of the Veiled One is on your hands, and for it you shall suffer dearly. First you, then your dear wife, then your little one. The Caliburns shall be wiped from the very face of this world along with all humankind.*

Actaeon laughed as the expanding spheres of fire grew larger. The radiant heat off of them became more intense with each lifebeat. "If you truly think that, then you know nothing about humanity." As he spoke, he pulled free the length of glass rope from his jacket and knotted it about the end of an arrow. His hair began to singe, and he could feel the skin on the back of his left hand begin to burn and blister as the expanding balls of zero gravity flame grew even closer.

I love you, Act, thought Eisandre. *And I am with you. Do not let his words give you pause.*

Ambrosius' laughter flooded the chamber he was in. *How romantic. I shall make sure that you get to feel how he burns to death, Princess. I'll see to it that it's seared into your soul.*

Actaeon grinned despite the tremendous waves of heat threatening his imminent demise. He placed the arrow to string and pulled back, waiting. *Worry not, love,* he thought to Eisandre. *I will not let this aspiring puppeteer take me.*

The expanding spheres of flame at last revealed what he was looking for – a doorframe.

He let loose the arrow, aiming for the frame.

It struck the frame and bounced clear.

With a curse, he hauled the arrow back toward him by the glass rope. The fire was nearly atop him now, and he could smell his hair burning – could feel the skin of his cheeks begin to blister as the expanding spheres of flame grew within arm's reach.

But then he had the arrow back in hand and returned it to the string for a second try.

This time the arrow sank into a part of the door's frame with a thud. Actaeon grinned and yanked the glass rope to pull himself toward the exit.

He passed through the quickly narrowing gap between two of the fireballs. The fires caught the bottoms of his trousers and he rapidly patted out the flames once he was clear.

When he reached the doorway, he shouldered his bow and withdrew his halberd once more. With the wedge at the bottom of his weapon's shaft, he pried it open and pulled himself through.

The door slammed shut behind him, and he was violently pushed headfirst against a wall. He felt one of the lenses of his goggles crack upon impact and his vision went momentarily black.

It took him a long moment to understand. It wasn't a wall he'd been pushed against. Gravity had returned, and he'd been pulled back down to the floor in whatever orientation he had been floating.

Actaeon stood and felt warm blood trickle down his face. He pulled his bandage roll from the lower right pocket of his jacket and stuffed it under the left lens of his goggles where he could feel a bloody gash.

A sudden bolt of lightning crackled a distance away. The flash of light revealed that he stood in a long, hexagonal corridor.

Another bolt crackled to life, sending a thunderous echo down the corridor, this one closer.

And then another. And another.

Each subsequent bolt grew nearer.

Impulsively, he began to run in the opposite direction.

The cracks of thunder grew faster in frequency behind him.

It was clear that there was no way he could outrun it. Plus, he had no idea what other hazards he could inadvertently run into.

The three bolts he had seen before he started running had each spanned opposite sides of the hexagonal chamber. The sides they had crossed between rotated for each subsequent burst of lightning.

One thing held true – if he was in the center of the corridor when the electrical discharges reached him, they would pass right through his body.

Instead, he threw himself into one of the corners at the floor of the hexagonal passageway.

As the rapid-fire bolts passed him by, a shock ran up his right arm from where he gripped the shaft of his halberd all the way to his shoulder. The hairs on his head and the back of his neck all stood up.

With one eye squeezed shut to conserve his vision in the dark, he watched the flashes of lightning rotate around the corridor as they rapidly receded away from him.

His right arm was numb from the shock, so he switched his halberd to his left hand and pulled himself up to continue along.

The lightning started up again behind him and the Prince Engineer resumed his run.

He leapt to the bottom corner of the hall earlier this time, also releasing the halberd's metal shaft from his grasp.

The lightning bursts passed by, followed by a rush of ozone-laden air. He could feel the hair atop his head standing straight up, and the air around him hummed with energy. Without hesitation, he stood again, snatched up the halberd, which gave him a sharp jolt, and continued running.

In this way he continued along through the corridor far below Travail, running away from lightning that couldn't be outrun. He held his breath with each pass, not knowing if it were to be his last.

As he ran, he recalled the words that Atreena once said: "Some secrets are best left buried deep down beneath the bones of the city."

REFLECTION

TENDRILS OF LIGHTNING STRUCK OUT across the sky, gone in the blink of an eye.

A deep thunder rumbled across the riverside.

The sound was a herald to the rain that arrived as the clouds opened.

It washed across the battered troops outside of Travail like an advancing waterfall. The torrent had them all instantly soaked to the bone.

The cold rain woke Wave. The mercenary sat up and snatched Eisandre's sword and his companion dagger to return them to his sword belt.

"Where's Act?" he asked in sudden remembrance. He looked around but saw no sign of his employer and friend.

Major Craft offered him a hand. "The Prince Engineer's gone inside."

Wave cursed and accepted her hand to pull himself to his feet. "Don't tell me you let him go in there alone!?"

Up the hill over Craft's shoulder, he glimpsed Companion Yanelle as she wrapped her arms around Calisse T'ra Coletka. Behind them, hundreds of Ajmani soldiers stood at crisp attention in strict formation.

Alongside, squads of Shieldians descended the hillside, led by Lord Enrion Zar. "Ah, my good man Wave. Apologies for being late. We've come to help. Tell me, where is the Prince Engineer?"

"Actaeon is inside, and he's in trouble," said Eisandre.

The Princess lay upon the ground with her sister's spear still lodged in her right shoulder. Two cutters attended to her wound carefully. First

Companion Itarik knelt beside her, his sword still in hand and his other hand on Eisandre's good shoulder.

A Niwian force arrived upon the hilltop as well, their plate armor dyed a metallic red – Colonel Wronka's old unit. With them was a small squad of Keeper Knights. Together they joined up alongside the soldiers from Ajman and Shield.

Upon hearing the Princess' words, Calisse stepped free from Yanelle's embrace. The Raja's Warrioress approached Eisandre. "We apologize for our tardiness, Your Grace. What are your orders?"

Eisandre looked from Calisse to Enrion and then from Wave to Yanelle. Everyone present was awaiting her decision for some reason. She winced as one of the cutters probed the wound around the head of the spear.

"Help Actaeon," she managed. They continued to watch her as though expecting more detailed orders. She wasn't sure what else to tell them. It wasn't clear how they could help him – just that they should. In fact, she should be helping him too, but the spear had done some serious damage to her arm. She didn't think she could get up.

Eisandre's mind raced. Actaeon needed her help, and the only ones who could help him awaited her orders. And yet she didn't know what to say. Triangles floated into her mind's eye – glowing blue and purple and red. A nauseous purple, a malevolent red, and an insidious blue. The triangles that had swallowed her love – had swallowed Actaeon. And she hadn't been there for him – hadn't been able to follow. He was all alone now. She had let him down.

As her vision returned, she saw the people there, still waiting for her to elaborate on her orders. She knew she needed to say something, but all she could think about was how those triangles had swallowed her love. What could she tell them? She didn't know.

"Purple and red and blue," she murmured.

The others leaned in to hear her words.

One of the cutters yanked the spear free while the other held her shoulder still.

Eisandre cried out, and blackness fell over her like a heavy blanket.

"You heard the Princess," said Wave, rivulets of rain pouring down his face to run into his one remaining eye and sting the fresh wound along his lower jaw. He tried to wipe the water away with the back of his hand, but the rain kept on pouring. "We go help Actaeon. Now how do we get inside?"

The ranks of the interdominional forces suddenly parted, and the Paladin Arbiter himself descended, followed by two other Arbiters. Corvin sof Haringar, the technical Sentinel Arbiter, was one of the two.

"We have mustered what forces of the Interdominional Alliance were available," said Cignith in his gravelly voice. He looked down his long, crooked nose at Wave. "The Prince Engineer is already inside, I take it?"

Wave nodded. "That's right."

"Then I gather you are now in charge of this force?" The Paladin Arbiter glanced down at the unconscious Princess where the cutters worked to clean and bandage her shoulder.

"Me?" asked Wave in surprise. "I mean, I guess. Listen, that doesn't matter right now. We've gotta get inside to help Act. Ambrosius is inside – he's gonna kill him."

"Ambrosius shall kill us all if we allow him," came a voice behind Wave.

Cignith blinked in surprise as he stared at the figure behind Wave.

Wave's hand fell and he spun on his heel. In a flash, his borrowed sword was free and raised before him.

An Ancient figure stepped forward and rolled his neck to elicit a loud crack. With one hand he stroked a dripping, gray beard that fell all the way to his waist. With the other hand, he batted Wave's sword aside with his walking stick. "Put that toy away, young man. You'll hurt someone!"

"What..." uttered Wave, at a loss for words. He sheathed the sword.

"Sollemnis the Gray," said Cignith with a smirk. "Full of surprises as always. How did you manage to appear from thin air like that?"

"Why Cignith, you hurt an old man's feelings," said Sol. "I have been here the entire time."

"Why are you here?" asked Lauryn, who had just woken up from where she lay. She retrieved her light lance and stood. "Kryo told Act –"

"Nonsense," said Sol, waving her words away with his staff. "There are things even Kryo doesn't know, young lady. Things you couldn't begin to imagine. Oh, but you'll see them soon enough I suspect. Soon enough now."

Phyrius Ricter stepped forward, his eyes ablaze with zealotry. "We must aid the Finder of the Keeper of Light," he said, using the title he had given to Actaeon. "Lead us, wise one. We are here to offer succor."

Companion Yanelle stepped forward, Calisse a step behind her. "I'm not sure about this one," she addressed Sol, gesturing with her thumb toward Phyrius. "But you must open the way inside so that we can help His Grace."

Sol offered her a sad smile that reached his eyes. "And if I told you that Kryo was right about one thing? Death awaits us in Travail. Would you still follow me within?"

Yanelle brushed a wet lock of scarlet hair from her eyes and nodded without hesitation. "Yes. I've sworn to protect that man."

"Intriguing... And your oath to him is worth more than your life?" Sol looked thoughtful at the idea.

"My oath to him *is* my life," said Yanelle. "Actaeon has risked his life many times for all of Redemption and because of it the heart our civilization still beats. Even had I not taken my oath of Companionship, I would still lay down my life for him, if need be."

Calisse reached forward to take her hand, giving it a squeeze.

An alien voice spoke that caused everyone to wince but Sol.

A small hand grasped Yanelle's other hand. "Protector."

Yanelle looked down to the person grasping her hand and was surprised to see a small boy that looked more like the appendage of a tree.

Fibrous brown lines rose from his heavily dyed skin. He wore irregularly cut clothing made from plant fibers and leaves. And the eyes that stared up at her looked completely black under the darkened sky.

"Interglot Heimgar," she said, recognizing the Kainai translator.

The alien voice spoke again from behind him. Yanelle recognized the androgynous leader of the Kainai, Saundrak. Their eyes glowed a purple that matched the glowing sphere atop their gnarled sceptre. A crown of wide leaves sat lightly atop their head, woven into reddish strands of hair.

Saundrak looked even more astounding in this place, away from the wonder of the Kainai Homeroot. All eyes fell on them as they spoke a language that, for some unknown reason, made everyone's head throb in pain.

"The Litomar expresses that the Protectors have fulfilled their promise thus far in repelling the invaders which threatened Ardianteki," translated Heimgar. "Thus, we answer the Chief Protector's summons." The Kainai tilted his head back and gasped in a way that reminded Yanelle of a snake. He backed up all the way to Saundrak and spread his arms as if to guard her.

Yanelle followed the boy's gaze to Sol and placed her hand lightly on the hilt of her sword.

Saundrak placed a reassuring hand on Heimgar's head and stepped forward to address Sol in the alien tongue.

Sol responded in kind and Saundrak nodded, bowing their head deeply before returning to Heimgar and speaking softly into his ear.

After a moment, Heimgar nodded and appeared to calm down. "The Overseer will lead the way to the Chief Protector," he said simply. "We will follow."

"Who's this Chief Protector?" asked Wave, arching the brow above his remaining eye. "Actaeon?"

"Seems like it," replied Yanelle.

"What are we waiting for then?" snapped Jezail, who had regained consciousness during the conversation. "Let's go kill this Ancient-damned bastard and save Act!"

Wave turned to Sol. "So... can you oversee our way inside, Overseer?"

Sol smirked, his eyes twinkling. "As you wish, mercenary. But heed my warning: what lies within Travail will change you all forever."

"How so?" asked Lauryn.

"Come find out, if you dare," said Sol.

The Loresworn turned to approach the jagged interface where the two main metallic blue doors came together. He slammed the base of his staff into the mud so that it stood on its own. Then he stepped forward and pressed one hand each on a section of door. A blue circle lit around each hand and Sol spoke words that once again caused Wave's head to pound when he tried to concentrate on them.

Nothing happened.

Sol stepped back and frowned. "Of course... He has merged with the central dominance. A Starborn *would* do that."

Wave stepped forward beside him. "Maybe try speaking some words we can understand here?"

Sol ignored him and replaced his hands to try the Ancient words again.

And again nothing happened.

Wave raised his arms, palms up. "Care to explain? Maybe we can help."

Sol turned and stepped past Wave to address Lauryn. "Young lady, I will need two of your light lances, if you would be so kind."

"What will you use them for?" asked Lauryn, genuinely curious.

"Why, to overload the mechanism keeping us out, of course," said Sol matter-of-factly. "It appears our Starborn friend now controls Travail. Or what is left of it, at the least."

"Show us where to cut," said Lauryn. "We can do it."

"I fear it is not so simple as you would surmise," said Sol with a gentle smile. "The doors of Travail would not be so secure if you could simply cut through them with a common artifact. No, I must use them as a conduit."

Lauryn frowned, considering. After a moment she made up her mind and pointed to Varse Perialt and another lancer, motioning for them to give their lances to the Loresworn.

Varse opened his mouth to object and closed it when Lauryn shook her head.

The two lancers reluctantly passed their weapons to Sol.

Sol tossed one to the side and carried the other over to where he'd buried his staff in the mud. He yanked the staff out and considered the door. After looking at the light lance carefully and then back at the door, he buried the base of the staff in a new location.

That done, he lifted the light lance until it was horizontal between the staff's crystal and the part of the door where he had placed his left hand. He rummaged in the pockets of his crimson robe until he found something which he attached to the light lance with a click.

When he let go of the lance, it floated in midair – held by some unseen force.

The old man then turned to hobble over to the second lance, which he'd previously discarded. His knees popped as he knelt to pick up the artifact. He brought it over to the door and placed it horizontally between the crystal and the place where his right hand had been. With another click, he secured a small artifact to the second lance, and it was also suspended in place.

The floating light lances formed a neat vee from the crystal to the spots on the door and the blue rings appeared once more and flickered before turning a sickly shade of red.

Sol stepped back several deliberate paces from the door.

"Make ready if you are foolish enough to enter," announced Sol to no one in particular. "It will only open the way momentarily before the path is again closed to us."

Wave waved everyone forward. "Get ready to rush forward. He's gonna open it."

Behind him, everyone assembled in three neat columns. Most of the interdominional force would enter if time allowed.

Sol turned his head to look at Wave from the corner of his eye.

Wave could swear that he could see amusement in the old Loresworn's expression. He scowled. "Open it up, old man." He smiled then. "Not too many people I can say that to these days."

Wave would've missed it if he'd blinked.

Sol spoke three alien words and two green bolts of energy shot from the green crystal shard of his staff to travel along the light lances and strike the door.

The rings blinked angry red and then blue and then green before blinking out completely. The jagged interface of the door opened to reveal a blue, metal corridor with a hexagonal cross-section. Where each of the corridor surface faces met was an inset strip of soft, white light – six lines that illuminated the interior and traced a path forward that disappeared around a neat curve.

"Forward!" shouted Wave and led the way past Sol at a jog.

A dozen made it through before a blade thin portcullis of translucent blue dropped down.

It cut Phalto clean in half and the back half of her body fell backward. Brewer caught the remains of the second dead twin in his arms, dropping his light lance. The warm splash of blood soaked through the tunic beneath his leather armor as he looked down in horror at the ruined half of the dead woman he now held.

Beside him, Enrion Zar turned white and screamed. But it wasn't the dead twin that caused him to yell.

The Shieldian Lord clutched at the stump of his right arm. The rest of it, sliced just above the elbow, lay in the corridor just beyond the translucent blue barrier. Bursts of arterial blood shot out from his arm to streak the barrier with purple gore and his soldiers rushed forward to drag him away. Enrion passed out in their arms.

On Brewer's other side, an entire leg and the back of a scalp lay still. The leg had the plain gray trouser leg of a Knight Arbiter.

Brewer dropped the partial corpse, fell to his knees, and vomited.

Elsewhere in Travail, Actaeon caught his breath.

It wasn't a particularly relaxing room he found himself in, but it was less dangerous than the lightning corridor.

Blobs of molten metal fell from the ceiling into tiny pools on the floor. Bursts of steam rose with every drop to fill the air with a thick haze.

A small, elevated pathway wound a circuitous path through the room. It was on this that Actaeon walked, trying to get his wits about him.

This was Travail's West Wing. It was the place which Quronos had warned him to stay away from. He recalled the mechanical man's words: *There the disturbances are turbulent and erratic. We should avoid that zone at all costs.* So much for that thought. It made sense that Ambrosius would allow him to enter this way though – it would be easy to let the weakness that Kryo and Sol had spoken of destroy him.

Ambrosius will cause the weakness to expand until it envelopes all of Redemption.

Kryo's words echoed in his mind. He wondered how quickly Ambrosius could do that. How much time did he have to stop him?

Farther along the pathway, there was a small fire burning.

Actaeon knelt to observe it and watched as another molten blob partially struck the pathway, adding to the small flame. He waited and watched the arc of the next one, and then, just to verify if he was correct, the one after that.

It hadn't been obvious, so slight was the difference, that he wouldn't have noticed it if not for the fire.

The molten blobs weren't falling straight down. Instead, they were curving ever-so-slightly to the right.

It drew his gaze to the wall on his right. The wall was the same metallic gray as the rest of the room, only something was different. It was somehow blurry and distorted all at once. The section closest to him was shorter, as though an invisible lens stood between him and the wall, pinching the rays of light before they could reach his eyes.

When he stood and continued past the fire, he noticed that the wall's distortion shifted so that the 'pinched' section of wall followed him.

"Fascinating," he said aloud. "Something is bending the light." Was it the weakness?

The Prince Engineer paused again to watch the wall. As he watched the distortion appeared to pinch the section of wall nearest him even more. His heart began to beat faster in his chest as he realized that he was watching Travail's weakness grow as he stood there.

With a frown, he began to jog along the pathway, which led him to the next room.

Inside, a swarm of tiny flying creatures created a veritable fog. Different colored light beams shone from places along the wall and were reflected hundreds of times off of the creatures. As the flies moved, so did the rays of light, which bounced and flickered in a plethora of directions and configurations.

Frequently, the light beams bounced into or near Actaeon's eyes painfully. He closed his eyes and lowered his goggles, fishing in his jacket pockets until he found the wooden frame with the darkened lenses that Lauryn had crafted for him. He clipped the frame over his goggles and opened his eyes to look out once more. A line ran diagonally through everything in the room – the result of the cracked left lens of his goggles.

The tinted lenses helped though, and he navigated carefully through the swarm, checking the black floor with the butt of his halberd to make sure he wasn't about to stumble into a hole.

Several of the creatures landed on his shoulders and he realized that they weren't creatures at all, but rather tiny machines. Their bodies were made from some kind of reflective metal and their wings looked similar to the semi-transparent half-through material that many of the artifact bottles were made from – only thinner.

With a grin, he scooped one into his hand and shoved it into the inner pocket of his jacket. It wouldn't hurt to study it later – assuming there would be a later. And if he had anything to say about it, there would be.

Once again, he noticed something strange to his right. The floor appeared to be glittering with multi-colored lights. It took him a few lifebeats to realize it was a countless number of the tiny flying machines. They all lay motionless upon the floor, scattering the beams of light that washed over them.

Actaeon gave that area a wide berth and continued along until he reached the next room.

What he found inside made him stop and stare in horror. He almost retreated back into the previous room, but for knowing that he had to continue on.

The right wall was a seething mass of fleshy limbs, each one terminating in a bony spike. Amidst the flailing appendages were humanoid heads with razor-sharp teeth that gnashed and ground together violently. Many of them were covered in blood, having bit chunks from the limbs nearest them.

Actaeon realized that they – whatever they were – were stuck to the wall on the right side of the room. Thousands of beady eyes followed him as he sprinted through the room and into the next.

There was a slight tug that tried to pull him to the right and toward the certain death of those angry teeth and thrashing spikes. He adjusted his trajectory so that he ran along the far wall, where the tugging force was much lower.

Only when he reached the far end of the wall did he start back toward the wall of scourge. And then only until he reached the door and leapt through into the next room.

When he hit the floor, the entire room canted to the side and he slid along it toward the distorted wall. There were metal spheres flying about, similar to the ones that projected Kryo. He was pelted by them as he slid along the floor.

The wall arrived before Actaeon could do anything to slow himself and he slammed into it so hard that it took his breath away.

Excruciating cold bit into his fingers and knees where he pressed against it.

With a gasp, he pushed himself to his feet and began to run along the wall, the cold biting through his boots into his feet as he ran.

When he reached the door inset into the wall, it sensed his presence and slid open like the other doors he'd encountered. Only, through this one was one of Travail's hexagonal corridors. It spiraled down and away from him, and invisible hands tried to pull him through.

Actaeon backed away from it until it closed. He then took a running leap to clear the deadly door. It slid open again as he passed over, threatening to pull him down into annihilation.

But when he hit the other side running, the door slid shut behind him. The piercing cold was beginning to hurt his feet and he hastily continued to the far side of the wall.

Far above him, or to his side, depending on what the correct orientation was, hung the door to the next chamber. He tried to climb up toward it along the floor but slid back down to the wall.

His feet were screaming in pain from the cold, and he slammed the butt of his halberd into the wall and used it to push himself up and off of the frigid surface. There he hung as he thought about how to get up to the door.

If he still had the glass rope, he might've been able to tie it around the halberd and throw the polearm through the door to the next room. Then he could pull it taught until the length of the halberd jammed and pull himself out. But he'd left the glass rope behind between the null gravity chamber and the lightning hallway.

The thread he carried wouldn't bear his weight. Nor would the bandage roll. And all his clothing tied end to end wouldn't be nearly long enough.

He felt the halberd shift beneath him as he held himself off the frigid wall/floor. A glance back showed that the wedge-shaped butt of his halberd was gouging the floor.

Could that be enough?

With a skeptical grin, he pulled his hooked dagger from his belt and lifted the blade high to stab it downward at an angle into the floor.

Sure enough, it bit several fingers deep into the material of the floor. He used it to pull himself up along the slope and away from the deadly wall adjacent to the weakness.

With his other hand, fingers tingling, he lifted his halberd and slammed its blade into the floor to then pull himself up farther.

Several of the floating spheres appeared to take interest in him and hovered about his head. As though he were shooing flies, he waved them away with his dagger. Surprisingly enough, the spheres dispersed.

The next gouge was easier and bit farther into the material of the floor at a better angle. He pulled himself upward more.

In this way, he continued to alternate blades until he had slid upward to the door. Every step of the way, the force which had pulled him down, or rather, over against the wall began to diminish.

At last, the door slid open and he pulled himself through. This time he was careful on the other side and clung to the doorframe until he could size up the new room.

He found himself inside a cylindrical passage that rotated slowly about its axis as tendrils of blue lightning coalesced along its length.

It was strangely familiar, and it took him a moment to realize that it was because he'd passed through a room just like this one when Quronos had taken him on a tour of the East Wing of Travail.

Only, and he couldn't be certain but, he strongly suspected that this room rotated in the opposite direction from the one in the East Wing.

As Actaeon watched it slowly rotate while the blue lightning danced along its walls, the final words that Quronos had spoken to him came to mind: *Remember upon your return: The halls are naught but a re – re – re –* The words that the malfunctioning mechanical man had spoken before he'd sacrificed himself and detonated at the bottom of the Pyramid's Skyspiral.

"A reflection!" announced Actaeon to no one in particular. "Of course! The West Wing is a reflection of the East. That's what he wanted to tell me."

Perhaps he could use that knowledge to help navigate around the weakness and reach Travail's main chamber.

There was only one way to find out.

It had been nearly a cycle since he'd walked the halls of Travail. Since then, he'd helped liberate Pyramid, defeated a godlike being intent on destroying the people of Redemption, unified the Dominions, saved Redemption's food supply from a plague of monsoon bugs, lost one of his best friends and nearly lost another, and had helped bring his daughter into the world.

So much had happened between now and then. And yet, despite how foggy the memories might be, he knew he had to remember the tour Quronos had given them through the East Wing of Travail.

The reflection was the key.

Thankfully, he'd been paying attention quite well. The halls of Travail had been more fascinating than any other place he'd seen in Redemption.

And so, he waited and watched the electrical arcs until he thought he could discern a pattern. Watching the ever-moving tangle of electrical bolts hurt his eyes. He was suddenly thankful that he'd forgotten to remove the tinted lenses from his goggles – they were undoubtedly helping significantly.

There was a periodicity he began to recognize as the lightning strikes progressed along the length of the revolving room. They cycled through at three different speeds, all pausing their advancement every sixteen lifebeats.

The problem was that each of the different speeds he could see applied to a different cluster of bolts that cycled back and forth through the room.

Once each deadly lightning cluster reached the end of the cylindrical room, it started back in the opposite direction. Where two clusters crossed would bring death.

But there had to be a way through – Quronos had shown them that on the tour of the East Wing.

Precious time ticked by as he continued to quietly observe, looking for a way to get through. When he finally saw it, he scratched his arm in frustration.

Since each of the three clusters moved at different speeds, they eventually reached a point in their traversals where all three were headed in the same direction. By the time he had realized it, the pattern had already changed again.

How are you, Eis? he reached out with his thoughts as he waited.

Frustrated, came her reply. *But the cutters removed the spear from my arm and bandaged it. Wave, Yanelle, Lauryn, Jezail, and others found a way inside. They'll come to help you, Act. Be careful until they can find you.*

Laughter resounded in his mind. Ambrosius.

Yes, Princess. And I thank you for that. It will be quite entertaining to see them slaughtered. And after that is finished you can stay to be a part of the Final Act.

Very clever, Ambrosius, thought Actaeon in return. *You are quite cheerful for someone that has the majority of Redemption outside your doors waiting for a chance to kill you.*

You are naught but ants to me, Engineer, replied Ambrosius. *Naught but fodder for the Starborn to facilitate the return to the great void.*

Then you should prepare yourself to be impressed with the ingenuity and determination of ants, he thought.

Actaeon pulled the Thoughtlink Artifact from his ear and stuffed it into one of his jacket pockets before rushing forward into the chaos of the electrical tunnel.

With care to keep his halberd close against his body, he wound a course between the deadly blue beams of light. The hair that rose on the back of his neck reminded him of the first long hallway he'd narrowly made it out of.

Once he passed the first cluster, he sprinted toward the second. It was essential that he pass through all three before they doubled back and began to overlap. That would be certain death.

As he stepped carefully through the bolts of the second cluster, he could see the third cluster nearing the end of the room. There was only so fast he could go as he had to wait for the coalescent pattern to cycle past him at certain points.

The third cluster reached the end of the room and began to head back toward him.

In his distraction, one bolt struck much too close to him and he felt its energy run through the right side of his body. Warmth flooded his mouth as he bit his tongue hard. He gritted his bloody teeth and continued forward deliberately until he was through the second cluster.

Almost immediately, he stepped into the third. It was the fastest of the clusters, and the most dangerous, by his estimation.

Not daring to breathe more than necessary, he wound his way through the coruscant maelstrom as fast as he could muster.

Behind him, the tearing of the bolts increased in magnitude as the two clusters began to overlap.

The hair on the back of his head began to burn from the proximity of the overlapping blasts as he carefully wound his way forward. Tears filled his eyes from the pain and pressure. He forced himself not to blink so that they wouldn't further occlude his vision.

The superposition continued to grow closer behind him until every part of his body tingled painfully.

The awareness of his own mortality was deafening as it pressed at his back.

When the door slid open before him, he was so numb and half-blinded by the bursts of light that he almost didn't realize it. Once he did though, he leapt, headfirst, through the opening to land hard on the other side.

The door slid shut at his back, but he just lay there, eyes squeezed shut and sucking in desperate gulps of air that was no longer charged or superheated.

When Actaeon finally gathered his wits about him once more, he opened his eyes and lifted his goggles to find himself in a reflected version of what Quronos had once referred to as 'the archive'. The lines of glowing characters in the language of the Ancients made his already pounding head throb even harder.

Part of him wished he could stay and study the room, but the other half just wanted to escape the place that gave him an even greater headache.

And so, Actaeon stumbled into the next room through ankle-deep water and past a plethora of mechanical creatures that swam at his feet, chirping delightedly all the while.

The room after that was familiar as well.

He was suddenly in the middle of a dense jungle under a clear blue sky. The jungle teemed with wildlife and sounds. The breeze that cooled his sore neck and head almost seemed real. Except he knew from his memories that this was naught but a simulacrum.

This he knew because it was exactly the same as the one he'd been in a cycle ago in Travail's East Wing. Naught but a reflection.

Only that wasn't entirely true.

The room that Actaeon remembered on his original tour of Travail had been a vivid simulation throughout.

This one was different.

In this room, the jungle faded at the far end to disappear against crumpled metal that appeared to have somehow imploded.

Inside the corridor Wave slid to a stop when he heard the screaming.

When he turned around the sight he saw made his stomach churn.

Everyone was walking on a different surface of the six-sided corridor.

And he was upside-down.

Jezail slid to a stop beside him, still wielding the light lance. Her body was perpendicular to his own as she stood on the upper right side of the corridor. Behind her, Companion Yanelle searched around wildly until she found her lover.

The Raja's Warrioress, Calisse, was above her, on the opposite face of the hall, looking equally bewildered. Sharing the same plane with her, Lauryn clutched at her shoulder and paled as vertigo overtook her.

Ainhara Craft gestured rudely to Wave, who'd halted before her. "Why'd you stop? Carry on!" Then she followed his gaze with her own and lowered her crossbow. "Oh..."

Paladin Arbiter Cignith stood on the lower left corridor, his sword drawn as his vigilant gray eyes rapidly swept about, assessing the situation. Just behind him was Sentinel Arbiter Corvin, who looked fascinated by the phenomenon. "It appears local gravity has been modified."

"You think?" snapped Lauryn.

On the opposite face from the Arbiters were the two Kainai. Heimgar stood before the Litomar with his hands spread wide as if to protect her. Saundrak looked over his shoulder with their glowing purple eyes. The leader of the Children actually had a faint smile upon their lips as they looked about.

Directly over Wave's head, Phyrius Ricter fell to his knees and began to chant. "Wise Keeper of the Light, guide us as we venture into the Maelstrom of the Deadlands. Lead us to the Finder, that we might save Him from the Draw of the Deadlands."

"Oh, shut up! You make us raving lunatics look bad!" said Sol.

Sollemnis the Gray was also above Wave. He was back farther toward the translucent blue door. And he was on fire.

Then he began to walk forward to reveal chaos.

Sol wasn't really on fire. On the floor at his back was a pile of burning gore. What appeared to be a body with its organs exposed lay aflame. Strangely, Wave noted, there was an arm next to it. Half of a light lance lay atop the corpse, spitting gouts of flame and spark. Through the translucent barrier, he could see the silhouettes of the people outside. They were all upside down. Which meant, he realized with a sinking feeling in the pit of his stomach, that it was really he that was upside down.

Inside, an Arbiter crawled away from the fire, his own trousers engulfed in flame. He left a blackened streak of scorched blood as he pulled himself farther from the broken light lance. With horror, Wave realized that the back of the man's head was missing.

Without hesitation, the Paladin Arbiter rushed to his Knight's side. He unclasped his red command cloak and used it to smother the flames. Corvin joined him to pull their fellow Arbiter away – in the process dragging him onto the plane they walked upon. Together they rolled him onto his back.

The Knight Arbiter's head lolled back in his commander's arms and the life left his eyes.

With a deep sigh, Cignith lowered his dead Knight back to the side of the corridor and placed a hand over his eyes to slide them closed. When the Paladin Arbiter stood, he somehow looked even more impressive without his cloak – now standing in just the spartan gray uniform of his order with the large, mirrored steel pauldrons covering his shoulders.

"His name was Delus sof Comitis, Knight Arbiter," stated Cignith as he clasped his hands before him while still holding his sword in one of them. "One of the bravest of us. Remember him, as on this day he joins the Ancestors."

Corvin sof Haringar clasped his hands as well and looked at his feet.

Cignith placed a hand on the surviving Arbiter's shoulder. "We continue on now, because we must. The future of Redemption hangs in the balance."

"Aye, sir," said Corvin. The Sentinel Arbiter straightened and took a deep breath.

"Onward then – no time to waste," said Sol as he passed beneath Wave and stepped around the kneeling cult leader. "Death awaits us all – and death waits for none!"

"Let's go then," said Jezail, starting down the passageway after the Loresworn.

Wave started forward again. He gingerly tested a foot on one of the adjacent surfaces and found that he could transition to that side of the corridor easily. He traversed the other sides similarly until he stood on the correct side.

The others followed Wave's lead until they were all on the bottom surface of the hexagonal corridor.

A crackle of energy sounded, and another translucent blue barrier slid down to seal them into that section.

"A clever one. And we thought we had them all locked out." Sol said. He lifted a hand as if to touch the blue barrier, but then thought better of it and lowered it.

"Thought you had who locked out?" asked Lauryn.

"Why, our self-proclaimed betters. Who else?" said the old Loresworn.

Saundrak said something unintelligible.

"Precisely," said Sol, his wrinkled lips curling into a smile. "It gladdens me that your memory persists."

Heimgar spoke a stream of alien words to Saundrak.

"That means nothing," snapped Lauryn, angrily. "Care to elaborate so we might understand?"

"On the contrary, my young Engineer," said Sol, his eyes twinkling. "It means everything. We should have taken better care of the place."

"So where to from here?" asked Wave.

Phyrius Ricter rushed forward then to pound against the blue barrier. The shockwave that struck him permeated through the very atmosphere of the corridor with a bang. It knocked the old man onto his back and left him unconscious.

"Travail has many ways, if you know them," said Sol enigmatically. The old man began to flicker and stepped toward the nearest wall. He passed through it as though it weren't even there.

"No!" shrieked Jezail in a rage. She ran toward the surface of the wall where old Sol had disappeared, intending to strike it with the butt of her light lance. Instead she ran up the wall and, in her disorientation, she fell to her knees. That didn't stop her though. She began to pound against the surface of the corridor beneath her until her knuckles were bleeding. "Come back here you cad! Darkest Hour take you!" She let out a bloodcurdling scream then and continued to pound against the metal wall. "Let us in! Let us in!"

"Calm yourself, woman," ordered Cignith.

Jezail's green eyes narrowed on the Paladin Arbiter and a lifebeat later she launched herself at his throat.

Wave and Lauryn caught and dragged her away.

"Easy. Easy, lass," said Wave. His words only made her angrier and she kicked and flailed in their grasp.

"Jez, listen to me!" cried Lauryn. "There's a way through. Calm down."

It was Lauryn's words that finally got through to the Captain of the Wall Breakers. Jezail stopped flailing and yanked her arm away from Wave. "How?" she asked, her eyes full of desperation as they searched Lauryn's.

"We cut our way through, of course," said Lauryn, hefting her lance.

"We cut... Yes, of course we do." Jezail stepped away from Lauryn and wasted no time. She pressed her palms against the active surfaces of her light lance and the artifact crackled to life, filling the air with the smell of ozone. A beam of orange light cut a broad arc through the wall of the corridor.

When Jezail's light lance shut off for its rest period, Lauryn activated hers and finished the remainder of the cut. Molten metal flowed into the cuts, being drawn away from the corridor by the strange gravitational effects.

When both women had nearly finished, Companion Yanelle stepped forward and kicked the section of corridor. It fell free and slammed down with a clattering bang.

Yanelle and Cignith charged into the breach, with Major Craft just behind with her triple crossbow at the ready.

"Onward then," said Wave. And he leapt forward after them.

THOUGHTLINK

ACTAEON APPROACHED THE CRUMPLED METAL that broke through the illusion of colorful jungle at the far end of the room.

As he neared it, the air grew cold and it felt as though invisible hands were pulling him toward the crushed walls. He recognized it as a gravitational shift caused by the weakness and took several steps back before it could yank him in.

Amidst the buckled surfaces of the structure, he could just make out the distorted shape of the door which he needed to go through. It was utterly inaccessible.

"Well, this is most unfortunate," he said to no one.

"Not to worry. There are always alternatives for every quandary," came an unexpected reply.

Actaeon grinned and turned to find a sphere, much like one of those he had encountered several rooms back, hovering next to him.

"Well met, sphere," said Actaeon. "I am Actaeon Rellios Caliburn of Shore. And yourself?"

"Kryo, formerly of Travail," returned the sphere.

Actaeon laughed. "Kryo. I should have guessed."

"I'd not have left you alone here, despite what you may think of me," said the sphere in Kryo's voice. "Though I stand astounded that you would come despite my last warning."

"And if I had not come?" asked Actaeon. "If I had run instead, as you advised? Would I ever have stopped running, or would this ruin follow me to the ends of the world?" He gestured with his halberd to the crumpled steel where the jungle simulation terminated.

"Too early to know," said Kryo. "Though I imagine there is a chance that it would not have."

"And had you fled, you would have been able to live with yourself afterward?" he asked, scratching the back of his right hand.

"Why yes I would," answered the sphere without hesitation. "In fact, I've already fled. I don't expect you have a great chance of success here today."

Actaeon narrowed his eyes, pushing aside the sudden urge to bat the sphere across the room with his halberd. "That is not something I could do. All those people who will be lost if we fail. I could never live knowing that I could have tried to stop it."

"Ever surprising, Engineer," Kryo said through the sphere. "In all the years that we've watched you, I never would have anticipated that you would be the self-sacrificing sort."

Actaeon arched a brow. "Then I suppose you have not watched me very closely." He gestured toward the broken portion of the room again. "Now are you going to help me around this, or do I have to decipher it on my own like one of the tests you are so fond of?"

The sphere wobbled and spun in midair. "Don't be absurd. I am here to help you. Follow me this way."

The floating artifact wound its way through the jungle, drifting easily between the foliage. Actaeon pushed the plants aside with the shaft of his halberd as he followed. The jungle was thick, and he had trouble keeping up.

"Make haste, Engineer!" prodded the sphere. "Every lifebeat you dally, Ambrosius gains more control over this facility."

"Are these not just projections of energy created by some artifact in this room?" snapped Actaeon as he inched past the thorny stalk of an orange flower the size of his head. "Why do you not simply shut them off?"

"In a different time, I might have. But I am no longer in control of anything in Travail but this rudimentary dronesphere. Continue to follow me and I may render that different." The dronesphere continued to hover along like an insect.

Actaeon followed Kryo until the small artifact hovered near the trunk of a massive tree.

"Touch here," it instructed.

Actaeon reached out toward the trunk and grinned when a green circle lit as his hand grew nearer. He touched it and a small section of the tree swung open at his knees.

"That's right," said Kryo. "Now follow me, and do hurry. He's beginning to access more of Travail. It is only a matter of time before he notices I'm here and boots me out." That said, the sphere dropped down and jetted into the opening.

Dropping to his knees, Actaeon peered inside, adjusting the baffle on his luminary to direct the light. With care, he began forward on his hands and knees into a narrow passage of the same hexagonal shape as the bigger corridors. Smaller hexagonal structures ran along the cramped byway along the sides and top. They must be used for energy or fluid passage, much like the larger cylinders in Pyramid, he thought. Perhaps this was a maintenance pathway in case any of the conduits failed.

"Faster, Engineer," snapped Kryo. "There's not much time."

"You should know as well as anyone that there are limitations to human movement and speed. And this place is putting very strict limitations upon them." Actaeon winced as his goggles bumped the conduits at the top of the duct when he raised his head to see how far ahead the dronesphere was. It was nearly out of sight. "So tell me, since you are mostly certain I shall die here – how does that dronesphere fly without wings?"

The sphere wobbled ahead and Kryo seemed to chuckle. "Oh, I'm not at all certain by any degree. Every situation has a degree of uncertainty, and you are quite the unpredictable factor in this one. All I asserted was that the chances were great that you would fail. I very much hope you do not." The sphere paused as Actaeon crawled along and caught up. "Very well. Everything in the universe is made up of small particles. When certain types of those particles are excited enough to emit what we call electromagnetic radiation there is a recoil force exerted upon the particle."

"Like the jerk of a crossbow upon the release of a bolt?" suggested Actaeon.

"Precisely. The particle emits radiant energy that is imperceptible to you and me," began Kryo.

"And the particles recoil in the opposite direction, thus propelling the dronesphere," finished Actaeon.

"That's the simplified explanation," said Kryo.

"It must take a tremendous amount of energy to accomplish such a task," said Actaeon.

"Not as much as you'd expect. Although yes, it is significant," said the sphere as it continued to bumble its way along. "Nothing that the fount cannot handle."

"The Fount? Is that the source of power that is transmitted to everything in Redemption?" asked Actaeon. "There is something wrong with it, right? Something that causes the Darkest Hour?"

"Has anyone ever told you that you ask a lot of questions?" asked Kryo.

"Everyone," said Actaeon with a grin. "But how else does one learn if not to question?"

"Indeed," said Kryo. "And here we are. If you'd be so kind as to touch this panel here, then we may carry on."

Actaeon touched the panel. It lit up momentarily and slid open. The dronesphere zipped through and he followed.

The room was a hemisphere filled with black trees that were illuminated in an eerie purple light. A hundred different trunks wound their crooked way upward to where countless limbs sprung forth and created an entangled canopy that reached forth to a height that Actaeon estimated to be higher than the peak of his workshop's roof. He examined the nearest trunk carefully and found that it consisted of tiny metal shavings. As a test, he hazarded placing the blade of his halberd near and it was drawn against the magnetic tree with a loud thunk.

"No time for that now," scolded Kryo. "Carry on."

The dronesphere floated between the metal filing tree trunks, careful to stay well between them all. Actaeon yanked his halberd free and the blade came away with a collection of black metal shavings stuck to it, magnetized.

Kryo's artifact floated across the room so quickly that Actaeon needed to sprint to keep up.

The sphere paused before another door until Actaeon approached. When the door slid open, Kryo wasted no time and sped off again.

Actaeon frowned as his attempt to catch his breath was thwarted and began to jog after the sphere again. He felt his side cramp up in a stitch as he ran. The floors, walls, and ceiling within the new room rippled with waves that distorted the surfaces and made it difficult to walk. The waves rippled their way across the room, driven by some sort of hidden resonant force.

It was easier to jog along in the places where the waves on the floor joined together. So Actaeon followed those zones of convergence as he chased Kryo.

The next room was much calmer. It was dark and featureless, with isolated pools of light in which crystalline structures stood.

Kryo's sphere flew toward the first of the structures and arm-like appendages folded open to allow the sphere within. They closed behind the dronesphere, and electricity arced across the structure.

Actaeon slid to a stop several paces from it and dropped to one knee to catch his breath. "What... what are... you doing... Kryo?" he said between gasps of air.

"Configuring this machine to work with the impulses from the dronesphere," explained Kryo. "That way I can secure you a path around the weakness. It will take some time. Do you think you can defend me until then?"

"Defend you?" inquired Actaeon, repeating the Loresworn's enigmatic words.

Before there was an answer, the crystalline structure farthest away burst into a number of pieces that flew in all directions around the room. The pieces sprouted wings and began to fly. All of them flew directly toward him.

"Unanticipated," said Actaeon with a nervous grin. He had just enough time to regain his feet and pull his goggles down to protect his eyes before the first one was upon him.

The first crystal machine came on faster than he expected. His halberd swing was too slow, knocking aside a second machine. The first one slammed into the side of his head and he felt warm blood from the razor-thin wound pour down his face and neck to soak his tunic below.

The second machine shattered into pieces which rained down at his feet.

Other machines flew at him rapidly from either side. He dropped down to a knee and swung his polearm wildly. The shaft struck two more of them and shards of broken crystal rained down atop him painfully.

The next one was easier. They weren't varying their speed at all, and he timed his swing perfectly to break it into pieces that cut into his hand and face as they struck him.

The rest of them he destroyed methodically as they threw themselves forward with abandon.

"You did well, but there will be more. We must hurry."

Actaeon turned to see a giant crystalline spider standing beside him where the structure that Kryo's sphere flew into used to be. He shrugged. "Lead the way then."

The crystalline spider dipped and then skittered its way across the room. It reached a seemingly random wall and began to use several of its legs to cut through the metal surface.

Another of the structures burst apart and this time several smaller versions of Kryo's spider rushed them.

Actaeon swept the wedged end of his halberd and knocked them aside. The act disabled two of the machines and he pierced the remaining one before it could recover.

In short order, the wall was peeled aside and the big Kryo spider stepped through. Actaeon followed him into a hexagonal corridor that ran in both directions away from the hole they had cut.

Crystal spider Kryo bent the metal wall back and methodically crimped it in two places so it would be difficult to bend back.

"Follow me. Quickly," it said, and was off skittering down the corridor.

It followed along until invisible hands threatened to pull them into the weakness once again. Suddenly forward was down and Actaeon nearly fell into it. Crystal limbs gently caught him and pushed him back to where gravity was normal, much to his relief.

Kryo began to cut through the wall to their left with his legs again. He tore the wall aside and led Actaeon through to another chamber with many wooden desks and nothing else. Then through a series of doors through small chambers that were padded on every surface by some sort of soft material. The last of the chambers was stained with dried blood, Actaeon noted with horror.

"A lovely place you have here," said Actaeon. "Is this where you keep your honored guests?"

Kryo worked at tearing through a blood-stained wall with his spider arms, not pausing as he spoke. "All of Redemption should be thankful they didn't have to face what we did in these chambers."

Once the wall was torn aside, Kryo stepped through.

"And what might that have –" began Actaeon. He was interrupted as the crystalline spider before him exploded in a blur of motion.

Instinctively, Actaeon lowered his halberd, but it was torn from his hands and a foot snapped out to catch him in the chest. It both relieved his lungs of all air and sent him to slam into the thankfully padded wall at the far end of the chamber.

As he lay there trying to suck in a breath, a figure approached more quickly than he could react to. It placed a pair of blades against his neck and leaned forward to peer into his eyes with twin abysses of jet black.

"Qur... Quronos," Actaeon coughed.

The mechanical man smiled and inclined his silver head incrementally. "You will now come with me."

Jezail tore ahead of the others to chase after Sol. "Get back here! I'm gonna kill you!"

Wave reached out to stop her, but she slapped his hand aside without slowing down.

She heard the others shouting after her as they pursued, but she ignored them and ran on. A blood rage filled her. That the Loresworn elder would leave them locked inside a corridor of Travail was insufferable. How dare he strip her of her right to vengeance? Trench's blood was still warm on Ambrosius' hands and she would not be kept from killing him.

Old Sollemnis was probably colluding with Ambrosius. After all, he'd attacked Actaeon and Yanelle on the Avenue of Glass and tried to kill them there. It was all beginning to make sense.

As she rounded the bend, she caught a glimpse of Sol's crimson red robes – appropriately the color of blood – as he disappeared up ahead.

Jezail doubled her pace and sprinted after him, rage coursing through her veins. She aimed the light lance ahead as she ran. As soon as the old man came into range, she'd obliterate him. Then it would just be a matter of finding Ambrosius and making him pay for what he did to Trench. For what he took from her.

The hexagonal corridor straightened as she ran through it. Up ahead she saw the Loresworn enter a room to the right.

She ran forward without hesitation.

The cries of the others rang out behind her as she neared the door.

Jezail ignored them and went through it.

It slid shut behind her with a slam.

In the center of a cavernous room stood Sol with a sad smile upon his face.

She growled and ran forward. Just a few paces and she could melt that smug face from its body.

Sol reached into one of the many pockets of his robe and suddenly she was frozen – her entire body tingling with invisible energy.

Jezail gasped and struggled to move, but to no avail.

Sol walked calmly forward until he was standing just before the business end of her light lance.

With every ounce of her being, she struggled to move – to touch the two panels on the artifact which would render the Loresworn lifeless. But whatever force was upon her would not allow it. No beam of energy sliced Sollemnis in two.

Instead he reached out and gently pried the light lance from her hands. Sol examined it with faint interest and then brought it down across his knee, snapping it like a twig. He tossed the sparking halves of the artifact aside.

Jezail struggled to scream, and the action broke through whatever force was holding her. "Oh!" she cried, the first part of the word abbreviated by her paralysis. "No!" She repeated the full word for emphasis, still unable to move as she yelled. "I'll kill you, you p-kin sonnuva bitch!"

Sol raised a finger in admonishment and waggled it before her eyes. "Now now, lass. None of that."

"How dare you?" she cried, ignoring his words. "It is my right to seek vengeance. How dare you stop me?"

Sol aimed the green crystal shard tipped staff at her and a concussive blast threw her across the room back toward the door.

It knocked the wind from her and she slid along the metallic floor until she came to a stop against the sealed door.

Sol offered her another sad smile. "You may be willing to risk your own life, but you'll not make that decision for the nascent one inside you." He began to walk to his right.

"The na..." Jezail trailed off, looking down at her belly.

"You surmise correctly," sail Sol, with a wink. "Keep him safe. The world needs heroes."

That said, the old Loresworn took one more step and passed through the wall of the room to disappear into whatever lay beyond.

Jezail was left alone with her thoughts and her rage. Only that rage was now tempered by something else.

Something wondrous.

Wave arrived at the door and banged against it with the hilt of Eisandre's sword.

It didn't open for him. Nor did it open for the solid kicks that Yanelle threw against it.

"Lauryn!" he yelled back along the corridor. "We need your light lance!"

"Coming!" came the young engineer's voice from around the bend.

"We'd best get her outta there before she does something stupid," said Wave.

"If she hasn't already," added Yanelle.

Several moments later, everyone else was gathered in the corridor beside the sealed doorway.

"Alright," said Lauryn. "Stand aside everyone. I've got this." She hefted the light lance to a couched position, aiming it at the door. "Hopefully nobody's right on the opposite side." She readied her hands atop the artifact's activation panels and looked to Wave for confirmation.

Wave nodded.

And then everything was Ancestors' tears.

Major Craft aimed her triple crossbow at Heimgar and pulled the trigger. The three bolts tore through the Kainai translator's body. It killed the boy instantly, one of the bolts lodging in the center of his skull. A gruesome spray of blood spattered over the Thyrian's white uniform and hair.

Without hesitation, Craft cocked the crossbow again and deftly loaded three more bolts from her quiver. She lifted the crossbow to aim it at Wave, whose jaw dropped open.

"What in shatter-" his words were interrupted as Craft's arm came off just below the shoulder and tumbled free. The crossbow clattered to the floor and launched two of the three projectiles to skitter down the corridor.

Craft lifted her stump to look at it in confusion before she fell face first to the floor, rendered unconscious from the blood loss.

Behind the fallen Major, Saundrak stood wielding their sceptre like a weapon. The purple sphere atop the sceptre glowed with a reddish tinge that quickly dimmed.

The Litomar knelt beside Heimgar and began to brush the raised brown lines that wound across the Kainai translator's face. They began to whistle a strange and mournful melody.

There was no time for everyone to reflect on the tragedy they had just witnessed.

Calisse leapt toward Yanelle to skewer her lover through the back with her falchion.

Cignith stepped between them, the Paladin Arbiter's blade knocking the Warrioress' aside a single lifebeat before the killing blow could connect. Their blades were a blur as the Paladin Arbiter fought her step by step backward and away from the others.

"Begone, foul bane of our Ancestors!" shouted the Paladin Arbiter as he fought. "Leave this one's mind at once."

There was a flash of hesitation in Calisse' eyes. Cignith recognized the opportunity and swept the flat of his blade against the side of her head with just enough speed to concuss the woman.

Her falchion clattered to the ground as Cignith caught her in one arm and gently lowered her to the floor. He spun to face Corvin. "It possesses this one. Steel yourselves, all of you! Do not let him into your minds. He will seek any opening you give."

Sentinel Arbiter Corvin winced and drew a crackling writheblade dagger from its ceramic sheath at his belt and held its pommel beside his head. He stumbled as he recovered from the attempt to possess his mind.

Cignith looked at his own hands in horror as they flipped his sword around to point at his own chest. Without his volition, his legs dropped out from under him and he fell to his knees. "No!" he said with a gurgle as the point of his arming sword punched through his armor and into his chest. The leader of the Arbiters tilted his head back and looked down his hawkish nose at Corvin. "Let him not –" The Paladin died before he could finish the sentence and rolled onto his side.

Lauryn watched on in horror and confusion before her expression went blank and she looked at the light lance in her hands as if seeing it for the first time.

It only took her a moment to locate the artifact's activation panels, but that was enough.

Wave leapt aside and tackled Corvin out of the way before the orange beam could sweep through them both.

Lauryn swept the light lance with abandon, sending showers of sparks and molten metal in all directions in the tight corridor.

Wave anticipated the beam's arc as it came back down in the other direction. He shoved Corvin in the opposite direction as he leapt backward, narrowly avoiding the beam as it tore through the corridor between them.

The floor creaked and shifted under him as he landed hard. "By the Fallen," he had a moment to say before the structure beneath him fell away and took him with it.

"Wave!" cried Yanelle, reaching out to him, but she was much too far away to do anything about it.

Lauryn considered the Companion but then found an even closer target not paying attention.

Yanelle saw the movement in Lauryn's arms first. The way her shoulders bunched. The trajectory of her forearms. Her years of experience traced the inevitable arc of the beam to Saundrak, the Kainai still kneeling beside dead Heimgar. The Heimgar whom she had failed to protect. The one who had called her Protector. It had been she and Actaeon who had promised to protect them nearly a cycle ago, deep within the chambers of Ardianteki, the massive tree that the Kainai called Homeroot.

The Companion lunged forward impulsively to sweep tiny Saundrak out of the way. The motion brought them both through the hole that Wave had fallen into. The beam of the light lance passed so close that it cropped a swath of Yanelle's striking red hair from her head just before the pair of them plunged into the void below.

Lauryn's eyes settled on the last person who remained conscious in the rapidly disintegrating corridor.

The Sentinel Arbiter had been counting his own lifebeats since the artifact had been first activated. Twenty-six. The beam swept toward him. Paralyzed, Corvin took a step back from the possessed light lancer, not knowing what else to do. Twenty-seven and the beam of the lance swept toward him.

With a start, it clicked in his mind that the person operating the artifact was not Lauryn anymore. Whomever possessed the freckled girl with the long, brownish-red hair held up by wooden combs probably didn't care whether or not the girl was lost in an explosion. He had to do something now, or they'd both be killed at thirty lifebeats.

Corvin held the writheblade horizontally to block the deadly incoming beam and ran forward straight toward Lauryn.

When the beam struck the writheblade it was neatly deflected simultaneously upward and downward, tearing through the ceiling and floor just before the Sentinel Arbiter. The beam returned to semi-coherence as it swept past the artifact blade and he felt it sear through his tunic to burn the skin of his forearm severely.

Refusing to let it stop him, Corvin dashed forward and wrapped his arms around Lauryn. He touched his forehead to her own and placed the pommel of the writheblade against both of their heads.

Lauryn gasped and dropped the light lance a fraction of an instant before it would have exploded. She went limp with relief in his arms and tears welled up in her eyes. "Oh no," she said, looking around at the devastation before her. "What did I do?"

Corvin looked into her blue eyes and shook his head. "Don't worry, Lauryn. We all managed to evade the beam of your lance. I have you now. You're safe. Keep your forehead to mine and this writheblade will prevent us from being controlled by Ambrosius."

Lauryn smiled up into the Sentinel Arbiter's eyes and leaned forward to kiss him gently upon the lips. "My hero." She found herself amused and endeared as Corvin blushed deeply. She surveyed the damage to their immediate surrounds. "So what's next?"

Corvin moved his lips unsuccessfully as he recovered from the kiss. "I'd... I'd recommend cauterizing Major Craft's arm to stop the blood loss. Then we should continue on to save Actaeon."

Lauryn couldn't resist as she leaned in to kiss him again. "Good idea, Sir Arbiter. I'll do so at once."

Her action was rewarded with another blush from the Sentinel.

In tandem with Corvin, she knelt to retrieve her lance and set to work.

The blue barrier slid open as Phyrius Ricter awoke.

A glance about told him that nobody else was left. The Maelstrom must've obliterated them all.

A sad smile formed upon his lips. "Only the faithful were protected then..."

It was surprising that even the one called Wave was annihilated. He would have thought that one who had shown such devotion as the one-eyed mercenary had – to carry the Keeper of Light out of the ruins so that the Light of His Wisdom might be shared with all. To think – a Bringer of the Keeper of Light, lost to the corruption, while he, Phyrius Ricter, was spared.

But he mustn't question the Wisdom of the Keeper of Light. If He deemed Phyrius as worthy of His protection and the one called Wave as not, then there must be a reason.

Steeling himself, Phyrius crawled over to his staff and used it to climb to his feet. He spread his arms wide and bowed his head. "Blessed Keeper of Light, thanks be to you for opening the Way before me. That I might find the Finder and return him from the Maelstrom of the Deadlands."

The old man lifted his hand up to adjust his hair, an act that only made the wispy gray matte even more unkempt. Then, shoulders straightened, he hobbled forward, leaning heavily upon the staff as a hundred new aches plagued his joints and muscles.

As he made his way along Travail's hexagonal main corridor, he rounded many turns and passed by several doorways that were sealed to him.

One such doorway opened with a hiss after he passed it and he halted abruptly. Phyrius paused to consider whether to continue on or to enter the open doorway. After a time he smiled and nodded. "Oh Keeper of Light! Even in the Deadlands you show me the Way."

With confidence, he turned and entered into the room that had opened before him. Inside, the ceiling was high and it was mostly filled with what appeared to be a gigantic artifact man three times his height.

Phyrius' jaw fell open at the sight. He fell to his knees in supplication. The staff clattered to the floor as he clasped his hands together and mouthed a silent prayer to the Keeper of Light.

As if sensing his prayer, the belly of the artifact man opened and a set of stairs unfolded from it until they reached the floor before him.

"You honor me, oh Keeper of Light," he said in awe. "I accept this holy armor you offer me. I shall not fail you."

Fighting back tears of joy that the Keeper of Light would have such faith in him, Phyrius began to ascend the stairs, crawling his way up them.

Once he was inside the belly, he found a depression that mirrored the human form. Nodding his understanding, he turned about and backed into it.

The stairs were drawn back in, and the belly slammed shut before him, trapping him inside the darkness of the artifact. Before he could object, something painful slammed into the back of his neck. Warm blood trickled down between his shoulders, but then an intense heat brought a quick stop to it.

An awareness washed over him and, suddenly, he was something more than he once was. He could feel hands that weren't his own and also legs that weren't his own, but both were somehow better. No longer was he plagued by the aches and pains of his worldly body.

No, now the Keeper of Light had blessed him truly. Phyrius Ricter was remade. He was better than he'd ever been in his life.

"That I may be a better servant to You," said Ricter and the words echoed throughout the room, the voice no longer his own, and yet somehow, more his than ever.

He flexed his new arm and brought it before his eyes – eyes that could see beyond even the colors his old eyes had known. The Keeper of Light had given him the gift to see Light which could not be seen by anyone else.

But, as he looked at his new artifact hand, he realized he could also see something else.

The knowledge of where everyone was located lay before him. He could see where everyone was within the holy site of Travail.

With relief, he found that the Bringer of the Keeper of Light was still alive and there were now several scattered groups throughout Travail.

Phyrius tried to smile and realized he no longer could.

And then he noticed him – the Finder of the Keeper of Light. The one called Actaeon. And he was in trouble. An Agent of the Deadlands had him.

"I will not fail you, oh Keeper of Light." The words tumbled forth to echo in the chamber without the same feeling or inflection they normally carried. They were strange and alien to his strange and alien ears.

"Succor comes, Finder."

Phyrius lifted his two massive artifact arms before him and tore the wall apart to open the Way to Actaeon.

Quronos dumped Actaeon to the floor of Travail's main hall like a sack of vegetables. He tossed the Engineer's halberd and bow off to the side.

The main hall was a cavernous cylindrical room whose upper end reached all the way to the top of Travail itself where it ended in a glowing dome that filled the chamber with an otherworldly emerald light. There were six levels between the dome and the floor. Each level had six hexagonal doors and was accessible by gently curving ramps which were equally spaced apart in six places. Each level had its own console – again a hexagon in form – covered in the symbols of the Ancients and each one projecting a unique scene.

In the very center of the hall was a larger version of those consoles. A plethora of Ancient characters hung in the air above it, glowing as they floated there.

Ambrosius stepped away from that console and glared over his shoulder. "What is it, machine? You've interrupted me from taking their minds."

"I bring the one you sent me to find," said Quronos. The mechanical man folded his arms across his silver, armored body, peering at Ambrosius with the twin black abysses that served as his eyes.

Ambrosius arched a brow and turned farther to regard Actaeon. "Ah... Indeed you have." He stepped away from the console and nodded his satisfaction. "And Kryo?"

"The mechanism inhabited by Kryo was destroyed," said Quronos in monotone. "The algorithm used to obtain control has been isolated."

"Superb. By the time he finds another way around the security protocols, it will be too late." Ambrosius' lips curled into a thin smile and he nudged Actaeon with the toe of one shoe. "Rouse yourself, Engineer! It is time we resolved this dilemma you've created."

Actaeon blinked and grinned up at him. "The dilemma *I* have created? That is a novel thought, Starborn. You engineered devices to steal the very consciousness from the people of Redemption, and yet *I* have created this dilemma?" He shook his head and glanced about the chamber, locating his weapons beside the door. "You have a skewed sense of responsibility there, Ambrosius – if that is even your real name."

"Find his Thoughtlink and put it on his ear," Ambrosius ordered impatiently.

Quronos knelt down and began to dig through Actaeon's pockets. The artifact man tossed the contents of the Prince Engineer's pockets to the sides, digging around until he located the device and clipped it to Actaeon's ear.

Actaeon? came Eisandre's thought.

I am here, love, Actaeon replied.

Yes, he is, Ambrosius thought. *And now you will bear witness to his death.*

"Now end him, Quronos," said Ambrosius. "Slowly, so that she may feel it."

No! Eisandre's thought came as a scream.

"Such cruelty is ill-befitting a being that considers itself to be sufficiently advanced as to harvest humankind like cattle," Actaeon said, ignoring Quronos as the machine man drew blades and advanced upon him. "At least I shall die knowing that you were truly the inferior being in this matter."

"*Cruelty?*" Ambrosius snapped out his hand to bring Quronos to a halt. The guardian returned the blades to his back and they folded into his body. "You wish to speak of cruelty to *me?* Realize you how long I knew the Veiled One? Your measly mind couldn't possibly comprehend... Eons!"

"Time is relative to one's perspective," said Actaeon with a grin. "And the Veiled One was not the best company to keep, if you ask me. I shall take the company of brave and loyal friends like Trench – a man who you murdered to get to me – over an insouciant psychopath like your buddy, the Veiled One, any day."

Ambrosius narrowed his dead gaze and turned his back on Actaeon to walk back to the console. "Kill this one, Quronos."

No! cried Eisandre again.

"You may kill me on this day," said Actaeon, aware that Quronos had drawn his twin blades in an instant yet determined to get his words out before his death. "But you shall never kill the resilience, ingenuity, and optimism that is humankind. That is where you Starborn can never be our equals. No matter how many eons go by."

Actaeon let the words hang in the air as he watched Quronos' sword flash down toward him.

MAELSTROM

T HE MECHANICAL MAN DISAPPEARED IN a maelstrom of sparks and torn metal as a tremendous section of the wall was torn asunder.

Actaeon rolled off to the side and covered his head with his arms as he was pelted with debris.

After the initial impact, Quronos rolled free of the wreckage and leapt over it toward Actaeon to complete his orders.

Actaeon spotted his halberd back near the door and realized he'd never reach it in time.

A giant metal claw snatched Quronos out of the air by one leg and flung him clear across the room.

Quronos slammed into the wall with such force that it bent with a resounding crack.

"Leave the Finder be!" The synthesized voice thundered throughout the chamber.

It took Actaeon a moment to realize that it was coming from a gigantic mechanical man three times the size of Quronos. "Phyrius?" he asked, but received no reply.

The big machine lurched across the room toward Quronos.

The silver man straightened and a shower of sparks shot out of his back. When he leapt forward again his lightning-fast movements were stuttered with minute hesitations.

Phyrius brought the two claws down to smash Quronos like an insect, but the silver guardian was faster.

Quronos deftly slipped between the claws as they shattered the floor at his feet and slid his blades through the seam along the torso of the great machine. Gouts of blood poured out along them, to drip down and pool on the floor below the massive mechanical man.

One of the blades slid into Phyrius' heart and the life quickly faded from his eyes.

Quronos pulled one of his blades free, but the other was jammed somehow in the seal of the machine. The guardian fought with it, tried adjusting the angle and pulling, but to no avail. At last, he decided to let go of the blade and leap clear of the machine.

But as life left Phyrius, an ancient backup protocol inside the machine activated. The cult leader's consciousness was downloaded to the mech's memory in sixteen billionths of a lifebeat.

Awareness returned in a way that it hadn't been before. Now there was no distraction of a body. There was only the machine – the blessed machine.

Before Quronos had leapt a hand's span from the ground, Phyrius' claws snapped out to grab him. Phyrius extended both arms, ripping Travail's guardian in two. Then, unceremoniously, he tossed the two halves clear through a hexagonal door on the second level.

That done, Phyrius, who was now an artifact, turned to face Ambrosius. "The Draw of the Deadlands corrupts you. Allow me to set you free."

Actaeon shouldered his bow and hefted his halberd once more. "Did I not warn you of the resilience of humankind?"

Ambrosius appeared unphased as his hands tapped out a series of commands upon the console before him.

The machine that was now Phyrius took one step toward the Starborn before the lights on the mechanism flickered out.

"Humankind is expendable," Ambrosius said. "Shortly, this machine will return to its original settings by my command, and you will see how easily human consciousness is erased. It is naught but a resource, after all."

"Let us see how *this* resource works out for you," said Actaeon, lowering the blade of his halberd toward the Starborn.

Before the Prince Engineer could charge forward, one of the hexagonal doors at the bottom level of the hall struggled open with a whine.

Sollemnis the Gray stepped through. The old Loresworn straightened his back, his shoulders cracking. He lifted one arm to point his walking stick at Ambrosius and his voice boomed across the hall. "Yonniker, Eater of Planets. This stops here."

"Sollemnis the Gray," came Ambrosius', or Yonniker's, reply. "And here I was, under the impression that Loresworn only run and hide."

"Witness this one before you, Actaeon Rellios Caliburn of Shore," said Sol, waving his staff in a tiny circle toward Ambrosius/Yonniker. "Born among the stars and yet stranded here on this planet because of the hubris of his people. Now reduced to a pretender called Ambrosius that preys upon the souls of the innocent – that would steal opportunity from a people eminently more worthy of the stars than his ever were." Sol let out a scornful laugh. "Yonniker, Eater of Planets. He jumps, and claps, and eats planets. He listens, and leaks, and eats planets. And today, he dies. Not the only one, but today there will be one less."

Yonniker's hands extended in a flash and both Actaeon and Sol were struck by an invisible force that slammed them against the respective wall behind each of them. He took a step toward Actaeon, and his eyes widened as he projected his thoughts into Actaeon's head.

A sudden flood of thoughts entered Actaeon's brain. Unbidden. A violation. Faster than should be possible. It was a language he didn't understand, but he vaguely recognized it as the language of the Ancients. A spike of pain shot through the back of his head and down his neck. It felt as though his brain were about to be forced from his skull. Tears rolled down his cheeks as he struggled, but could not move.

But then a shield went up and a wave of relief overcame him. The assault was still there, but it was muted. The pain was still there, but his mind began to work again, as though a fist that was crushing it had relaxed.

It was Eisandre. His Knight Arbiter. The Princess of Raedelle. She wasn't there physically, but she was there nonetheless – through the Thoughtlink Artifact. Only, her thoughts were her shield. She wrapped him with loving thoughts. With thoughts of protection. The language of the Ancients did not pierce her armor. It didn't affect her the way it caused him pain. She absorbed it instead, listened to it, and found that she understood some of it.

Yonniker took another step forward and doubled the rate of his thought attack. Actaeon concentrated on the thoughts that Eisandre sent him and managed to send his own thoughts of encouragement to Eisandre.

And outside the thick walls of Travail, beyond the weakness' maelstrom,

Eisandre felt herself grin like Actaeon. She drew her sword. And thrust it toward Yonniker.

The bombardment of thoughts made the Starborn stagger back. The assault was too much for him. The madness, the delirious visions, the waking hallucinations. They threatened to overwhelm his sanity.

Lost thoughts.

Actaeon grinned as he realized what she was doing. He was torn between fascination at the random patterns of thoughts that she was projecting and a feeling of victoriousness at the efficacy of her continued bombardment. *Yes, Eis. Give it to him. Let him see it all.*

Eisandre allowed herself to fall completely into the vortex of her thoughts. All her life she had struggled to suppress such aspects of herself. To allow herself to operate as a normal person in society. To be useful.

But this was the only way she could save Actaeon from the Starborn that had manipulated them and now threatened to kill them all.

Now her being Lost was useful.

And so, she gave herself to it and descended into the whirlpool. On her way, she encircled Yonniker and dragged him down after her.

With a start, Actaeon fell to the ground and slid down heavily to his backside.

Yonniker ripped the Thoughtlink Artifact from his own ear and threw it at Actaeon.

The artifact slid to a stop near Actaeon's boot. He reached forward to snatch it up and stuffed it into one of his pockets.

You did it, Eis. You stopped him. He could not handle your thoughts.

Only, she was no longer there.

He felt a pang of dread in the pit of his stomach.

Yonniker stormed back to the console.

"This one thinks himself special," barked Sol. "So you can manipulate quanta? There's naught that we cannot do with our own technology."

Yonniker ignored him and instead leveled his flat gaze upon Actaeon once more. "Notice how everything in Travail comes in sixes, Engineer?"

Actaeon nodded and lifted himself to his feet to lean heavily upon his halberd.

Yonniker tapped out a sequence on the console and gestured upward. "Being an engineer, you should have deciphered the power of the six by now.

The strength of hexagonality. The efficiency. But no… yet another reason why you are not worthy of anything beyond servitude to the Starborn!"

Four panels slid open on the third level. Out of them stepped four more perfect copies of Quronos.

Add to that the Quronos that sacrificed himself in the Pyramid's Sun Chamber and the Quronos that Phyrius' mech had ripped in half. That made six.

"Well, this is a most unfortunate development," said Actaeon. His mind raced as he considered how to deal with four mechanical men. He came up with nothing. Even one of the artifact men was too effective an opponent to deal with. He needed Wave now. No, he needed four Waves.

"Loathsome of you to use Travail's own guardians to aid in its destruction," said Sol. "I'd expect better of even you, Yonniker."

Yonniker smiled an empty smile. "Poetic, is it not? I wouldn't really know. Except that I was once inside a poet's head. In the moments before I forced him to run himself through with his own sword, I gleaned enough about poetry to know that this qualifies."

"Know what else'll qualify as poetic? When I run you through with my sword to avenge Paladin Arandel and Trench both, you twisted sonnuva bitch."

Actaeon grinned and looked up to the main hall's second level.

Wave stood just inside the door through which Phyrius had thrown the remnants of the broken Quronos, a blade in either hand. Behind him was Yanelle and behind her was the Kainai leader, Saundrak.

"I am certainly glad to see you, my friends," said Actaeon.

"Back atcha, Act," said Wave. He closed his single eye in what Actaeon knew was a wink. But then his eye widened in horror as his hands started moving of their own volition.

"Poetic indeed," said Yonniker.

Wave's arms twisted to aim his blades toward his belly. His legs dropped from beneath him to finish the job.

But Yanelle was quicker. She wrapped her arms around him and pulled him back atop her. Together they slammed against the ground and she held the blades away from him despite their most unnatural struggle to end their user's life.

Sol aimed the green crystal shard of his staff at Yonniker and the concussive wave sent the Starborn flying away from the console. Yonniker spread his hands out and alit gently on his feet like a bird fluttering down to a perch.

The two old men then rushed forward and began to bombard one another with a series of concussive waves. Sol cast a sphere into the air that sent tendrils of electricity at the Starborn and allowed him a window to blast Yonniker into one of the metal bulkheads.

Simultaneously, the four Quronoses each drew two blades from their backs and leapt from the third level to land effortlessly down at the first. Two of them went for Sollemnis and the other two charged Actaeon.

Actaeon bit his lip and ran toward the now vacant console at the center of the room. Yonniker had activated Travail's remaining guardians from there, so there stood to reason that he might be able to deactivate them from that same station. It was the only chance he stood against the impossibly fast artifact men. Only, he could already feel the rush of air on the back of his neck as the first guardian neared him. And he'd barely even started.

Wave's boots caught the nearest Quronos as the mercenary landed atop the machine's shoulders after leaping down from the second level. The silver swordsman slammed into the floor hard and Wave rolled to the side to attack Actaeon's second pursuer in a flurry of sword action that wouldn't have been discernible even if Actaeon had been looking. Quronos met Wave blow for blow with ease.

As the fallen Quronos lifted itself to its feet again, Yanelle's sword came down to sever its right arm. She hit the ground behind the machine hard and absorbed the impact by rolling off to the side, just in time to avoid the guardian's second blade. The Companion regained her feet and interposed herself between her combatant and the Prince Engineer.

Actaeon reached the console and saw what he recognized as a timer counting in the characters of the Ancients. As usual, it hurt his head to try and understand it, but he hit the symbols that he knew would likely cancel the countdown. It flashed several times and then went away.

But the Quronoses didn't stop.

The other two pressed Sol. The elder Loresworn directed his floating sphere off to one side to fire electric bolts to keep one of them busy. The other he kept at bay with a series of concussive blasts. Blasts that were no longer keeping Yonniker occupied.

The Starborn used the opportunity to send Sol spinning across the room. He slammed against a small console to the side of one of the hexagonal doors with such force that it tore free under him. There was a loud crack as the Loresworn's lower spine snapped and he and the broken console slid to a stop against the wall.

Sol winced as he lost complete feeling in the lower half of his body. The two Quronos, now free of his attacks, rushed at him to finish the job. He reached into the pocket of his red robes, and one of the Quronos froze mid-run. He sent a rectification command to the sphere. The artifact sped forward more quickly than the other silver guardian could move and began to harry it with a series of electrical blasts.

Yonniker laughed as he calmly made his way toward the broken, old Loresworn. "I suppose you must've expected you'd die here – at least in this incarnation. But did you ever imagine you'd die like this as I disassembled everything you worked so hard to create?"

As the Starborn talked, Actaeon desperately searched for something on the console to alter the balance of the situation. Nothing was forthcoming and he knew much better than to hit sequences at random.

"Kill this one and I shall find another," said Sol. "I'm not so easy to destroy."

"You forget, Sol." The Starborn smiled his dead smile and spread his hands. "I am Yonniker, Eater of Planets. And thus I shall devour every remaining trace of your being. There will be no others for you, Sollemnis the Gray."

At a loss for other ideas, Actaeon leaned his halberd against the console and unshouldered his bow. He put an arrow to the string and let loose, ignoring the battles that Wave and Yanelle waged with the other two Quronoses just beyond the central console.

The arrow struck home, lodging deep into Ambrosius' back. The once Raedellean advisor grunted and fell to his knees. With a gesture from the Starborn, the arrow ripped free from his back and shot in reverse along its original trajectory, now headed toward Actaeon.

It slammed into the right side of Actaeon's chest and knocked the breath from him. He staggered backward and steadied himself against the ancient console. There was a sudden warmth that bloomed within his chest that wasn't there before. With horror, he recognized it as blood beginning to fill his lung. He inhaled painfully and when he felt around the arrow at the entrance wound, he could feel a light outrush of air as he exhaled.

If he didn't seal the wound, he knew that the pressure on his lung would eventually prevent him from breathing adequately.

With a grimace, he shouldered his bow and pulled the dagger from his belt. Using the point of his blade, he began to work free the translucent, flexible material that covered the top of the console.

Meanwhile, Yonniker smiled and sat on his haunches. "A shame. This one lasted so long. But now, old Sol, the time has come for you to say goodbye." The Starborn lifted his hands for one last blast.

Sol struggled to lift his staff before him, but found that his arms no longer had the strength. "Up to you now, Engineer."

An orange beam of energy punched through the door next to the Loresworn. It swept in broad strokes and cut the door, frame and all, out of the wall. It fell forward to slam into the ground.

In the void where it used to be stood Lauryn with her light lance. Sentinel Arbiter Corvin sof Haringar stood very close beside her, holding a crackling writheblade between their heads.

Lauryn took in the scene in Travail's main hall and her jaw dropped in confusion. She looked to Actaeon for help and gasped when she saw the arrow protruding from his chest.

Actaeon cut a strip from the material covering the console and pointed with his dagger. "Destroy the mechanical men!" he yelled, which sent him into a coughing fit.

The light lancer nodded and activated the artifact's beam again to obliterate the Quronos that was frozen in mid-run. She swept the orange beam through the artifact man a half dozen times in different directions.

Sol smiled and reached a hand back into his robe. The Quronos, no longer held in stasis, fell to pieces. Instead, Yonniker froze, hands nearly raised enough before him to send one final concussive blast toward the Adept Loresworn. "Nicely done, lass. Now get the other one."

Lauryn smirked and chased after the second Quronos that had attacked Sol. The silver-skinned man dodged the broad, crackling sweeps of her beam and fled in the opposite direction. Sol's sphere floated after it, harrying it with blasts of electrical energy.

Actaeon leaned heavily against the console as he yanked the arrow free and returned it to the quiver on the back of his jacket. He leaned back and reached under his shirt to place the flexible sheet of material over his wound. It would have to be arranged and secured such that one of the corners could lift like a flap when he breathed out. That would prevent the space between his lungs and chest cavity from filling with blood or air every time he breathed in, or at least minimize it – he hoped. With a frown, he settled on how it could be managed. After running short on options, he grimaced and pulled the needle and thread from the lower right pocket of his jacket and set to work to thread the needle. It wouldn't be a pleasant solution, but without it he would die.

Worse, all of Redemption would die next.

"Engineer, listen to me," said Sol. "I need you to work the console. You must use it to grow the weakness."

"Grow the weakness?" asked Actaeon incredulously. "I thought you wanted me to come here to stop it?" The needle threaded, he tucked the front of his shirt and vest beneath his chin to hold it out of the way and began to stitch the artifact material into his skin. He cried out in pain at the first pass of the needle. The second one was even more painful, but he knew what to expect. From there he began to thread the needle along rapidly, to secure his makeshift bandage to the skin of his chest.

"Indeed I did. But you must grow it enough to swallow Yonniker. Once inside, the Starborn's massive energy can help seal it – contain it," explained Sol from where he lay dying.

The chaos of combat still raged all around them.

Wave and Yanelle fought back to back as the pair of Quronoses leapt and threw themselves against the two fighters in a flurry of attacks that they repelled in such a quick manner that Actaeon couldn't make sense of it.

Lauryn chased the remaining Quronos up the ramp to the second level. Pieces of burning wreckage tumbled down ahead of her as she cut wide swaths from Travail with broad sweeps of her light lance. That Quronos had lost a leg, but still managed to leap clear of Lauryn's attacks with its remaining leg. Sparks showered out from the machine's stump as it evaded. With a cry, Lauryn of Lakehold leapt from broken panel to chunk of fallen ceiling, giving chase.

Sentinel Arbiter Corvin slid to a stop before the console and drew his arming sword to protect Actaeon in case any of the three remaining mechanical men broke free. Beside him, Saundrak of the Kainai shouted something in the tongue of the Ancients. The leader of the Children stomped and pointed toward Sol with their sceptre of gnarled wood.

"And what if it cannot contain it?" asked Actaeon, ignoring them as he hastened to finish stitching the one-way valve into place on his chest. "What if my growing the weakness just hastens the fall of all Redemption?"

Saundrak frowned as they realized what Actaeon was doing. The Litomar stepped forward and ripped the strange material of the console from the Prince Engineer's chest. The material remained intact and the thread tore free through Actaeon's skin. He screamed in pain and surprise and was on his knees before he knew what was happening, darkness growing from the edges of his vision.

The Kainai spoke more words in the Ancient language and the purple sphere atop her sceptre glowed with a reddish tinge. They caught Actaeon with a surprisingly strong hand for such a young person and carefully pressed the sphere of their sceptre against his wound.

This time he did pass out. The last thing he felt aside from the burning sensation on his chest was the Litomar's strong hands lowering him to the floor.

"Get up! Get up!"

The words came from a distance but seemed to grow closer and closer.

"Wake up, Your Grace! We need you!" It was the Sentinel Arbiter.

The words were so close now that they reverberated in his ear and caused his head to pound.

Actaeon awoke with a start and turned on his side to vomit blood onto the floor. He retched a few times before he felt able to look around. Although his vision spun, he was able to make out the scene around him.

It didn't appear that he had been unconscious for very long. Fighting was still going on. Only Wave and Yanelle fought one Quronos instead of two. The other flopped spasmodically to the side. Yanelle was bleeding from several wounds and the Companion was having trouble remaining on her feet. A significant portion of Travail's main hall was on fire – the smoke billowing up to obscure the high ceiling. The cause of the fire, Lauryn and her light lance, were now on the third level. He could see the beam sweep out over them on occasion as she pursued one of the broken machines.

"Get him up!" barked Sol. "Time waits for none. And our time has all but passed." The elder Loresworn still lay with his broken back, holding Yonniker in stasis. But not quite. The Starborn had begun to resist whatever

Sol was using to immobilize him and was moving by fractions of an inch – enough that Actaeon could see the motion.

Corvin and Saundrak pulled Actaeon up and helped support him before the console.

Actaeon's chest felt like a piece had been torn out of it, but he leaned heavily upon the console and blinked as dizziness threatened to overwhelm him. Tentatively, he took a deep breath. He coughed again, producing more blood that ran down his chin to drip onto his tunic, but his lungs didn't feel like they were filling with more blood.

"Travail exists as a conduit of energy," explained Sol, his voice growing strained. "You must redirect that energy into the weakness until it envelops him, then bleed off the remainder."

"Again," said Actaeon, leaning heavily against the central console. "What if redirecting the energy into the weakness just hastens the fall of all Redemption?"

"It may well, Engineer," said Sol. "But if we're not to try, then the fall of Redemption is naught but a certainty."

"Very well," said Actaeon. He scrutinized the console and raised a brow. "I shall find a way to decipher this. If I can..." Some of the Ancient symbols were familiar to him. Others he had never seen before. The symbols which had been under the material he'd peeled off the top of the console were flickering unhealthily.

"Saundrak," said Sol. The Kainai turned. Sol spoke to them in the language of the Ancients.

I think he's telling the Litomar how to use the console, came Eisandre's thoughts, back once more.

Eis! Actaeon couldn't help but grin. *Are you okay?*

I am returned, she thought. And he could feel her smile.

Saundrak nodded to Sol and the Kainai's hand sped across a multitude of symbols on the console. A projection emerged and hung before them, translucent and bright. It flickered at first, but then became steady. It was a small representation of Travail in luminescent green, except that something effaced most of the west side of the building, glowing an evil red. That must be the weakness. A plethora of other structures glowed different colors inside the building, representing various energy sources, Actaeon supposed.

Each structure had a different set of symbols above it. Actaeon squinted and tried to discern them, but the attempt felt like a spike through his head. He frowned.

Look at it again, Act. Eisandre's thoughts were welcome at this point – they helped him remain focused despite the massive pain in his chest. *I think I can make sense of it.*

Actaeon forced himself to concentrate on one of the symbols, then another. He tried to project his impression of them over the Thoughtlink Artifact. The pounding in his head threatened to overwhelm him. *Anything, Eis?*

There was no response as she considered the symbols.

Wave began to break through the defenses of the mechanical man that he and Yanelle still fought. Sweat drenched the collar of his jacket and half of his hair had fallen loose from his typically neat queue. The mercenary weaved from side to side and unleashed random bursts of slashes and thrusts. While the Quronos was repelling the onslaught, Yanelle would press an attack from the opposite side.

With its concentration split, one of them would strike true and damage the machine. Then they'd back off and regroup, repulsing its attacks and keeping it centered between them. It kept trying to maneuver so that both of its opponents were on the same side, but Wave was able to keep one step ahead.

And so they kept up the pattern of assault and gradually began to wear down the mechanical man.

Finally, Wave threw his companion dagger forward to lodge itself in Quronos' eye. Both of the silver skinned man's swords spun to keep the mercenary at bay as he pressed heavily with the Princess' borrowed sword.

Yanelle shifted so that she stood in the machine's blind spot and swung her sword in a wide arc that swept its head from its body.

The mechanical man crumpled to the floor.

A moment later, another Quronos crashed to the ground beside it from four levels up. Both legs, one arm, and half of its face were missing.

High above them all, Lauryn glanced over the fourth level railing and smiled before her face disappeared once again.

Yanelle looked down at the two last disabled Quronoses and nodded before her knees buckled beneath her.

Wave was fast though. He caught her and guided her gently to the floor, cradling her head in his arms.

They're numbers, Act. I think... yes, I'm fairly sure they're numbers. Eisandre's voice was a relief to Actaeon as it flowed back into his mind through the artifact clipped to his ear.

"What sort of numbers?" he said. And then, *What sort of numbers?*

"Numbers?" asked Corvin. The Sentinel Arbiter hesitantly sheathed his sword and turned to regard Actaeon.

One is ninety-eight. Another is forty-five. Twenty-three. Six. Seventy-three. Sixteen. From left to right.

"Percentages," said Actaeon in a low voice. "They are percentages. You are a genius, Eis."

Corvin shook his head in confusion.

Actaeon was too busy to notice though. He reached out toward the character that represented the ninety-eight. His head still hurt, but it was more of a dull ache at the back of his skull now. He found a path along a series of conduits and traced it with his finger from the energy source to the weakness.

The path lit up in a glowing yellow.

And an explosion shook the entire building.

Actaeon held onto the console to prevent himself from being toppled over.

The ninety-eight percent energy source flickered and was gone along with the yellow path.

"Try another," encouraged Corvin. "That one might've been faulty."

Actaeon nodded and, with a grin, traced a path to route power from the seventy-three percent power source to the weakness. With satisfaction, he observed the weakness begin to grow. After watching it for a few lifebeats, he realized it would take much too long to get to the point where it would begin to envelop the main hall and Yonniker. With determination, he began to route the energy from several other sources into the weakness.

As he did so, he realized that his people – his friends – were still gathered and watching him perform these actions.

"You all must leave," he said.

Wave shook his head from where he knelt cradling a semi-conscious Yanelle. "We're in this to the end, Act. No way we're leaving you now."

"That's right," seconded Lauryn. "We won't leave you here alone."

Actaeon felt tears well in his eyes. His friends were willing to stay and die with him, even though the fighting was over. "Listen to me," he said, scratching the back of his right hand. "I must needs stay here to bleed the excess power after the weakness grows enough to swallow Yonniker. There exists a chance that I will make it out, but there is also a good possibility that I will not. Whatever happens now, it is important that you all go on to survive and protect Redemption. I will not allow some of the brightest and most talented people in this world to fall along with me for no reason. If circumstance allows, I will also escape. But I refuse to take you all with me. Redemption needs great people like you. My daughter needs great people like you in her life. So go. I bid you all go."

Lauryn placed a hand over Actaeon's own and smiled weakly up at him. "I can stay and do this Act. Aedwina needs her Daddy."

Actaeon lifted his hand to touch Lauryn's cheek. "Lauryn, know that you make me proud. But you also know that I am the best person to remain behind to ensure this endeavor is successful. My thoughts are linked with Eisandre's and she can help guide me in the interpretation of the language of the Ancients as needed. I have the most experience with these consoles of any of us. And so I ask you all," he said, turning his emerald gaze upon the others – Wave, Corvin, Saundrak, "to respect my orders as Prince Engineer. You are to evacuate Travail and continue to serve Redemption in whatever ways you may, for the rest of your lives."

Wave lowered Yanelle gently to the floor and stood to salute Actaeon, fist to chest, in the Raedellean manner – even though he wasn't Raedellean. "Aye aye, boss." And then, "Steady hand and level gaze, may your strikes fall true and your enemies part before you, my brother."

"My brother," Actaeon agreed with a weak smile. He returned the salute, wincing in pain as his fist touched his chest wound.

Lauryn looked to Wave and then back to Actaeon. She also placed her fist to her chest. Tears flowed down her cheeks. "Thank you, Act. For everything you've given me."

Actaeon grinned at her. "Do not be so sad, Lady Lauryn of the Light Lancers. I do not die so easily."

Wave knelt to scoop up Yanelle, who had now fallen into unconsciousness. "So, touching talk and all, but how do we get out of these Ancestors' Tears?"

Lights came on again on the surfaces of Phyrius' mech and it stepped forward. "Bringer of the Keeper of Light. Follow me. Away from the Maelstrom I shall lead."

Wave's eye widened, and he offered Actaeon an incredulous look.

Actaeon shook his head and shrugged.

"Before you leave, First of the First," started Sol. "Be sure to retrieve the young lass I left on level two, locked in laboratory two ninety-three."

The huge mech swung to face Actaeon.

Actaeon nodded. "Do what he says, Phyrius."

"It will be done, Finder," came the mechanical voice of the cult leader.

That said, the mech leapt up to the second level, ripped one of the doors aside and left the main hall.

Wave and Lauryn started up the nearest ramp, Wave carrying Yanelle. Saundrak followed them.

Actaeon nodded and turned back to the console to finish routing power sources into the weakness.

Corvin thrust Actaeon's halberd into his hands and handed him his writheblade in its ceramic case. "Good luck, Prince Engineer. I hope to see you again." Then the Sentinel Arbiter was gone, off to follow the others. Actaeon tucked the writheblade into his belt.

You forgot about one person who isn't subject to your orders, came Eisandre's thought.

I could never forget about you, my love, Actaeon thought in return as he rerouted power from another of Travail's subsystems to divert it into what Phyrius called the Maelstrom.

As your Princess, I could order you to leave, she replied.

Indeed you could, he admitted. *But we both know what is at stake here, and so you will not.*

You are correct, thought Eisandre. *But I will remain connected with you as long as I am able.*

Actaeon nodded and bit his lip until it bled. He redirected another power source.

Jezail had beaten her knuckles raw against the door of the room she'd been locked within.

She'd screamed her voice hoarse trying to get anyone's attention, but in the end nobody had come for her.

And so now she sat with legs folded and plucked a simple tune on her fiddle.

Only, whichever tune she chose to play turned into the chords of

Shulaya's Lament. As she played, she realized that she was now like Shulaya. Separated from Trench, only on the opposite side of life now. Trench was dead, and she was still among the living. And, if there was a tiny life inside her, as Sol had claimed, then it would never know its father. The thought racked her body with a sob as she continued to play her instrument, plucking the mournful melody in her isolation.

Why couldn't the giant have survived the attack in Pyramid's Pinnacle? Why couldn't he have been here to raise their child together? Was there nothing in this world that she could rely on?

The artifact mech that burst through the wall interrupted her depressed thoughts. The machine peeled aside the material of the wall as though one would the delicate petals of a flower.

In through the opening scrambled Wave carrying Yanelle, Lauryn, Corvin, and the Kainai leader.

"Jez!" cried Wave. "Get up. We've gotta get out of here!"

Jezail leapt to her feet and shouldered her fiddle. She fell in behind the others as the machine punched through the door before ripping it free to be tossed aside. It had to peel the walls around the doorframe wider to give it enough berth to step through. It paused there instead. "More allies of the Finder lie without. We must preserve them. The Maelstrom approaches!"

Jezail stepped gingerly around the massive metal tree trunks that served as the legs of the machine.

On the other side, the inset luminaries barely functioned, flickering sickly as the power was being drawn away from them. On the ground, Calisse stirred groggily and shook her head to clear her senses. Her eyes widened as she noticed the big machine, and she searched frantically for her falchion. She snatched up the blade and lifted it weakly toward the big artifact.

Jezail stepped by it and gently touched her arm to guide her to lower the sword. "It's helping us get out of here, Calisse. I don't understand it either." She shot a questioning look at Wave, who was stepping through the opening with Yanelle cradled in his arms.

Calisse slid her falchion back into its scabbard and stepped forward to take Yanelle from Wave.

Wave knelt to check Ainhara Craft – her arm freshly cauterized. The Thyrian Major didn't rouse when he shook her, but her chest still rose. That was a good sign.

An odd movement out of the corner of the mercenary's eye drew his attention. He drew his sword and batted aside the twin swords of the Quronos that snuck up on them from along the corridor. He parried another set of wild slashes from the machine. A firm kick sent it sliding along the floor down the hallway. It was only then that he realized it was only half of a Quronos he'd fended off.

"The Fallen know I tire of these damned things!" shouted Wave. He didn't take his eyes off it as he spoke over his shoulder. "I thought we killed them all?"

"Me too," seconded Lauryn.

"Truly a creature of malignance. Though I tore it in two, it cannot die," spoke the big artifact in its mechanical voice.

"Corvin, Jezail – grab Major Craft," ordered Wave. "Phyrius, if that's you inside that thing, then, by the Fallen, get us outta here. Lauryn, back him up if he needs any help from your lance. I'll guard the rear."

Nobody argued with him.

Jezail and Corvin knelt to pick up the Flashbolt Marine.

"I will not let you down, Bringer of the Keeper of Light." Phyrius' mech hunched down so that it could fit inside the smaller hallway and proceeded forward as fast as it was able.

The others followed.

The flickering lights of the corridor reflected from the twin black abysses of Quronos' eyes as the upper half of the mechanical man regarded him.

"Intruders must be terminated," it said at last.

"Not while I yet breathe," said Wave, lifting both his blades.

And he thought he saw Quronos' mouth curl into a smile as the machine dug both of its hands into the floor and launched itself toward Wave.

Metal screeched and screamed. The entire western side of Travail's main hall tore free and crumbled as it compacted and disappeared into the weakness. Maelstrom was certainly a more appropriate word. Actaeon was beginning to agree with Phyrius – the world must certainly be coming to an end, he thought with morbid amusement.

Invisible hands began to tug him toward the maelstrom, but he set the console firmly between himself and the deadly phenomenon. He found another power source deep within Travail and diverted it into the weakness.

The darkness beyond the hole in the main hall rippled and shimmered as more energy flowed into it. At its fringes, distorted and shattered sections of Travail could be seen. They were warped and stretched as though by an invisible lens.

Actaeon surmised that the maelstrom was drawing in light as well. Sucking in everything like a funnel. He wondered where that funnel led and at the same time hoped that he would never need to find out.

The remnants of the broken mechanical men began to slide along the floor toward the weakness.

Sol wrapped one arm around the console that had broken his back to anchor himself in place as the invisible hands began to tug the old Loresworn toward the deadly funnel.

"I am beginning to regret this plan of yours, Sol," said Actaeon with a grin as he rerouted another power source. "In fact, I am well past the beginning in that regard."

Sol winced as the forces began to yank the broken lower half of his body. "Never satisfied, this Engineer. And here I thought you'd have been happy now that I am telling you everything. Start planning a way to divert that power away from us. It will overcome Yonniker shortly."

"Perhaps if you had told me everything from the beginning, we would have been able to collectively decipher a solution to all this in a more timely manner," said Actaeon as he searched the arrangement for a location to which he could bleed the power off. "But do not misunderstand my criticism as a lack of appreciation for beginning to share the truth, albeit so at the cusp of the world's end."

"There was a time in my life, longer ago than you might comprehend, when I might've believed the same," said Sol. "I saw a people, my people, destroyed by it. Not all have the intellect required to manage the responsibility that knowledge demands."

"Perhaps they did not have the right teachers," suggested Actaeon, locating the paths that he needed to bring the power to a reservoir deep beneath Travail.

"Soon enough they'll be able to have new ones," said Sol. "Our end draws nigh. Millennia of vigilance come to a sudden end. I pray you are correct, Engineer."

"Given your predilection toward our doom, perhaps you would do me the honor of telling me more about your people?" asked Actaeon. He began to trace the paths from the reservoir to a single point that power had flown through to feed the maelstrom. Though he held off on completing the path. That would be last.

"It may surprise you to learn that my people were who you now refer to as the Ancients," said Sol. "Despite all our technology and understanding, despite our best teachers and our greatest efforts, my people fell. It —"

Before he could continue, one of the Quronos remnants, its body intact but missing half its face and all the limbs but one arm, reached out its remaining arm and punched a hole into the floor to use as an anchor just moments before it could be sucked into the void.

Its eerie jet-black eye turned to look at Yonniker, and its head nodded incrementally.

The ear-splitting crack that followed echoed throughout the chamber, and a wave of energy buffeted Actaeon and knocked him down onto his back. He wedged himself between the floor and the console, being tugged at by the twin forces of gravity and weakness.

Then Yonniker was moving again, and a concussive blast struck Sol.

The elder Loresworn managed to hold onto the console, but he needed to drop his staff to cling to it with both hands. The staff flew past Yonniker and into the void.

Actaeon risked a peek around the console and saw a ball of radiant energy where Quronos had been.

The outer fringe was red and blended through oranges, yellows, and blues to the center. It was quite beautiful.

It took Actaeon several lifebeats to make the connection. The Quronos that had fought with them to the interior of Pyramid had exploded before it could be killed to destroy their tribal pursuers and allow them to escape up to the Skyspiral. He guessed that Yonniker hadn't directed the mechanical guardians he'd been using to detonate until he realized that it was too late. After all, it was a suicidal move.

But Sol must've frozen Quronos in mid-explosion. Only the leading wave of the blast had caught them. The rest had been captured in a sphere of death, just waiting to be unleashed and take away all their lives.

Yonniker left Sol be to hold the explosion in stasis and turned to Actaeon with his lifeless eyes. He reached out a hand as though to command

Actaeon to halt his actions. The old Raedellean advisor and imposter leaned forward to resist the pull of the maelstrom.

Actaeon felt his thoughts begin to fog and confuse. Before the Starborn could take control of him though, he unsheathed the writheblade at his belt and stuck its hilt into the strap of his goggles so that the blade pointed up like a strange crest. The crackling and smell of ozone so close to his head was worrisome, but not so much, he supposed, as allowing his brain to be slave to the will of a millennia old being intent on the destruction of all mankind.

Yonniker narrowed his eyes and staggered forward until he grasped the other side of the console opposite Actaeon. "You'll have to destroy us both."

"What evidence have I presented you to allow you to draw the conclusion that I am not prepared to do that?" asked Actaeon, genuinely curious. He diverted another energy source.

More of Travail's main hall tore away into the weakness. The rippling shimmer of the maelstrom lapped against the fringes of Ambrosius', now Yonniker's, gray and green robes. The old man held on with inhuman strength. It wouldn't be surprising if the Starborn's capability to hold himself against the console against absurd forces tugging at him was augmented somehow with some sort of unseen artifact technology.

Actaeon lifted his finger to divert one last energy source that would grow the weakness until they were both inside it. The edge of the console bit painfully into his belly. Whatever forces pulled at him now were large enough that he no longer could tell if gravity was still present.

The world had narrowed to just Actaeon and Yonniker hanging onto the console, now sideways above the rippling maelstrom. Off to the side, the event grew to encompass Sol's legs. Inside the weakness, the explosion sphere was still visible in its eerie stasis, the colors had begun to distort and pull away toward the center of the maelstrom like a rainbow of death.

"Wait!" Yonniker shouted over the noise and intensity of the chaos around them. The old man regarded him through the translucent projection of Travail, his silver hair making him look like a ghost.

Actaeon raised a brow. "Even if I were to agree, would it really make a difference at this point?"

"Anything you want to know, I'll teach you," insisted Yonniker/ Ambrosius. "Answers to all of your questions, Engineer. All the knowledge of the Ancients could be yours."

"Right now there is only one thing I need to know about the Ancients, and that is what you did to them," said Actaeon with a grin. "Oh..."

"Yes?" asked Yonniker. For the first time, his normally lifeless eyes looked hopeful.

"And that is *Prince* Engineer to you." Actaeon's grin grew as Yonniker's eyes widened in horror. He dumped one last energy source into the weakness.

The structure around them shifted with a lurch and the base of the console snapped and tilted forward.

Yonniker lost his grip and fell backward into the maelstrom. His body twisted into a swirl, and he was gone.

A sudden cold washed over Actaeon as he realized he was now inside the weakness. He flipped over the top of the console as it fell forward but managed to keep a grip with one hand. His entire body twisted, and he swung through the projection to slam against the surface of the projector. He dropped his halberd into the void and reached up with his other hand to grasp the top of the console. There was a small ledge that had been underneath which his fingers gripped against now, holding the entire weight of his body, magnified by the violent forces beneath him.

Beside him, now upside down, the projection of Travail flickered in and out. Within its lowest point, Travail's top, was the conduit he'd configured to bleed the energy off from the maelstrom and into the reservoir beneath the building. He let go with one hand and tried to reach it, but it was still an arm's length away. He returned his grip to the console with both hands.

I beli... ...n you, Eisandre's intermittent voice spoke in his mind, and then was gone. The interference was too much for even the Thoughtlink Artifact to project through.

The forces tugging at him increased as the maelstrom grew, and the console shrieked as it began to tear away from the floor.

If he'd had his halberd still, he might've been able to use its hooked blade to lower himself down. There was another possibility though.

With one hand, he let go and drew the writheblade carefully from the strap of his goggles. Molten metal slagged past him as he used it to cut through the console near where his hand had gripped. A spray of molten metal caught him in the elbow of his jacket and on one of his knees and he could feel it burning him through his clothes. He did his best to ignore it. It was just another pain, one of many at this point. In that spot he cut two wedges of material out so that a protrusion of metal remained. Hopefully the freshly cut metal of the console would be cooled significantly by all the air rushing past into the maelstrom. He didn't have time to wait for it to cool beyond that. The job done, he let go of the writheblade and it was gone.

Next, he switched hands and pulled the recurve bow from his shoulder. He hung the bow from the metal projection from where the string was looped over the arm of the bow. And then, ever so carefully, gripping string with one hand and the wood body with the other, he transferred his weight over to the bow so that he hung from that instead. He slid down the length of the bow until he was at the bottom and wedged his left fist at the bottom between the string and the body.

The bleed off point was nearly within his reach now.

He reached out and swung his body slightly to activate it. But the projection chose that exact time to flicker off momentarily.

With a nervous grin, he tried again, swinging over to it.

He touched the activation point and the pathway lit.

The energy began to bleed off from the maelstrom and into Travail's deep reservoir.

The bowstring snapped.

And Actaeon fell into the maelstrom in a rush of freezing air.

Then another force slammed into his body.

A wave of concussive heat rolled over him.

And he was gone.

SUN RISES OVER SHATTERED REDEMPTION

PRINCESS EISANDRE RELLIOS CALIBURN KNELT in the mud on a nearby hilltop as she regarded Travail with manic blue eyes. She repeatedly clenched and unclenched her left fist as she watched the Ancient structure. A plume of virulent black smoke laced with intermittent lightning poured upward from the building to mix with the storm clouds above. The smoke had started after the explosion where Actaeon had redirected one of the first power sources. Chunks of elderstone and metal had flown so high into the air that they must have landed all the way in Raedelle.

But she'd spoken to Actaeon through the Thoughtlink Artifact after that. Actaeon had been speaking with Sol after he'd sent the others away and then suddenly, inexplicably, he was no longer there. No longer with her. She'd pulled the artifact from her lobe and replaced it. Shouted her thoughts into the void of her own mind.

There was nothing. Actaeon was no longer there.

All that remained was a sick feeling in her gut.

If he had died, would she feel it deep inside her? Would she know it? And if so, would it feel like this?

Itarik's strong hand was on her good shoulder then. "Are you alright, Your Grace?"

"How can I continue without him?" she asked aloud. "He is my final anchor."

The Companion's hand tightened upon her shoulder. "No matter what the outcome here, we shall persist. You shall persist, Your Grace."

But his words swept by her like a cold wind.

Shortly, the sky began to lighten as the sun rose in the east. The clouds dispersed as though commanded by an unseen force and the rain slowed to a drizzle.

The collective interdominional force watched helplessly as the rain fell and Travail burned.

An orange beam appeared to the left of Travail's entrance. It swept horizontally twice and then vertically twice to form a glowing rectangle.

The rectangle then flew forward to crash into the ground beyond.

Out of it stepped a tremendous machine that only rose to its full height once it was clear of the opening. It stomped forward inelegantly and touched its appendages together before it as if in prayer.

Weapons were drawn and arrows nocked.

And then Lauryn of Lakehold stepped out beside the big machine. She leaned heavily on her light lance and smiled up at the brightening sky.

Behind her came the Raja's Warrioress cradling an injured Companion Yanelle in her arms. And then Jezail and the Sentinel Arbiter, Corvin, carrying Major Craft between them. The Litomar of the Kainai came next, striding past the others as though nothing interesting were happening.

There was a collective sigh as weapons were resheathed and bowstrings eased. Others rushed forward to help the injured.

Eisandre knew she should be standing. Should be going to help the others. If only to ask them what they knew. But she already knew herself that they had no knowledge of what happened to Actaeon. He'd sent them away before she lost his thoughts. There was no way for them to know.

Wave stepped through the opening next, walking backward. Both of his blades were in his hands – her own Arbiter's sword and his companion dagger. The mercenary crouched low in a fighter's stance and was ready when half of a silver man flung itself toward him.

Eisandre stood then, ignoring the pain in her shoulder that lanced through her like a hot knife. It was Wave, who had helped her rescue Actaeon long ago. Who, along with Trench, had kept him alive through so many difficult situations. If Wave was alive, then perhaps there was still hope for Actaeon.

The silver man half had, impossibly, a sword in each hand. It thrusted one and slashed another as it flew bodily through the air. Wave sidestepped the thrust and parried the slash. The mercenary noticed the interdominional forces then and threw himself to the ground before his attacker could throw itself at him again.

Hundreds of arrows and bolts slammed into the mechanical man until it bristled like a pincushion. Its head spun on its shoulder once and it fell forward to splat into the mud. The archers and crossbowmen released another volley of arrows that obliterated the machine. The shafts of the projectiles stood out from its still form like the thorns of a barbed plant.

Wave rolled onto his back and shimmied away from the dead machine.

Soldiers from several different Dominions rushed forward to drag Wave away.

"Who has writheblades?" asked Wave, shrugging off the hands on him. "Use them to cut it to pieces. I don't need a part of that damned thing sneaking up on me again."

Shouts rang out and he heard crackling behind him as soldiers bearing the artifact blades used them to dismantle the last of the silver-skinned artifacts.

But Wave had already turned. He began to search for her, but Eisandre was already there before him.

The Princess regarded him with pleading blue eyes. She opened her mouth to say something, but couldn't decide on what, so she shut her mouth and just waited, her lower lip trembling.

Wave bowed his head before her and fell to one knee in the mud. His white jacket was streaked with blood and soot in a pattern that Eisandre found distracting. It was a long moment later before she realized that he was holding her old Arbiter's sword, presenting it to her. Reflexively, she tried to lift her right hand to take it back, but her eyes filled with stars and she gasped at the pain. Instead, she took the sword with her left hand. Arbiter training had taught her to fight with her left hand nearly as well, in case just this sort of situation were to occur. She spun the sword and awkwardly slid it back into the sheath on the same side of her body.

"I'm so sorry, Eis," said Wave. "He ordered me to go. He..."

"I know," she said simply.

Wave stood and Eisandre felt herself fall forward against the mercenary. He caught her in his strong arms and held her while she wept. A tear rolled down his own cheek from his remaining eye. Trench was gone and now

Actaeon. It felt as though his life was being stripped of meaning. There were others who still needed him though. His eyes swept the field. Calisse knelt and cradled Yanelle lovingly in her lap as cutters tended to the Companion's wounds. Lauryn spoke to her few surviving light lancers, consoling them on the loss of the twins. Jezail stood off to one side looking bewildered, one hand on her belly. And then there was Eisandre, sobbing in his arms.

But Eisandre shoved him back and ran past him toward Travail. "Act, no!" she screamed.

Before Wave could chase after her, the Darkest Hour fell. The battlefield fell into darkness as every luminary, both carried and part of Travail, winked out.

As Eisandre neared the building, she noticed a shimmering sheet between her and it. The sheet quivered with a tremulous light, reflected and diffracted from the soft rays of the day's rising sun through the clouds. She had to reach it, to help Actaeon. He needed her.

Wave's grip on her left hand was hard and unyielding. Jerked to a stop, her feet slid in the mud. Instinctively, she swung her numb right arm out to strike him, but the mercenary easily blocked it.

"Don't go near that!" he yelled.

"Let go of –"

The crack that interrupted her shook the earth itself and threw them backward, away from Travail.

Everyone on the battlefield outside the Loresworn headquarters was similarly knocked from their feet by the blast of energy.

An inrush of air followed, blowing past them all to fill the void left behind.

Wave sat up and blinked several times, not believing his eye.

The whole of Travail had cracked in two.

The center and most of the western side of the building had vanished. Two fragments of the Ancient building remained, a large chunk on the eastern side, and a thin sliver on the west, like a knife pointed at the gods above.

That knife teetered to and fro as water from the River of Arches rushed in to fill the tremendous void that was left behind between the broken portions.

The water continued to fill in the pit where Travail once stood, creating a new lake.

Eisandre fell to her knees in the mud beside him. It looked like she was murmuring something, but Wave couldn't make it out over the sound of his ringing ears and the violent inrush of water.

At a loss of what else to do, he drew his knees into his chest and watched as the water rushed in and the needle fragment of Travail wobbled as if indecisive about which way to fall.

When, at last, the ringing in his ears felt as though it had substantially diminished, he tried his voice. "He did it."

Beside him, Eisandre nodded gravely. "My Prince Engineer."

They sat in a long silence together as the sky grew brighter and the pit that was Travail eventually became the lake that was Travail as the deluge of water from the river slowed to a steady stream.

Without warning, a blue comet leapt out from the ruins of Travail and streaked in an arc across the sky before landing in the River of Arches.

Eisandre stood and began to run toward the source of the blue streak amidst the wreckage.

Wave climbed to his feet and followed.

Even as the sliver of building finally made its decision and fell to crash into the eastern section, the Princess continued to run toward it.

The cold water snapped him back into sudden consciousness.

Before he could realize he was underwater, he inadvertently took part of a breath and his lungs screamed in pain as water flowed into them. It especially hurt on the side that had been pierced by his arrow.

Determined, he held his breath and twisted, trying to establish which way was up – a difficult task in the dark, muddy water he now found himself in.

When no orientation was forthcoming, he put his hands over his mouth and, straining painfully, managed to push some air out. He could feel the bubbles of his partial forced exhalation flutter through the left side of his hand.

And so that was the way Actaeon swam. He broke the surface several lifebeats later and gasped a breath full of air that sent him into a coughing fit. Every cough felt like a blow from Trench's maul where the arrow had struck him in the chest.

Where was he? The last memory he had was of being drawn into the maelstrom. Was this the other side? Mucky water? Travail's back side had opened up to the River of Arches, so perhaps it had been sucked through the enlarged weakness before it had a chance to close?

As his vision slowly resolved, he began to make out the differences above him while he treaded water. A pair of looming shapes stood to either side of him in contrast to the cloud covered sky. The sun was behind those clouds on one side more than the other, so it was either dawn or dusk. And if there was a sun still, then could he have been sucked into the maelstrom?

With a sudden realization he laughed, which resulted in another painful coughing fit. The shapes above him were Travail – or at least two pieces of Travail.

He'd made it.

The maelstrom was gone, and with it had taken a large chunk of the Ancient structure. But why not him? It didn't make any sense why he would survive unless old Sol had some trick up his sleeve that he didn't know about.

That was it! Sol had held the Quronos that had exploded in stasis. But when Actaeon was about to reach the point of no return into the maelstrom, he'd frozen Actaeon instead. That explained the way he'd suddenly stopped. And the wave of heat that had washed past him must've been the released explosion.

Actaeon felt a wave of thankfulness toward the old Loresworn – the old Ancient. Sol had saved him that way when the old man could've saved himself instead. He'd made sure that Actaeon lived through the cataclysm.

Actaeon grinned. "Thank you, Sollemnis the Gray," he said before launching into another coughing fit. Now he just had to figure out which way to swim. It wouldn't do to squander the opportunity he'd been given by drowning in the waterlogged footprint of a building he'd always resented.

He reached back to feel for his blue fire arrow in its quiver. The arrow was still there, but he had no way to fire it. His bow had been lost.

How else could he get someone's attention?

The solution was so obvious that he chuckled again, unleashing another coughing fit. This one was less severe though. He must've been making progress in expelling the water from his lungs. Either that, or it was settling comfortably. He continued to tread water, struggling to keep his head above the churning and muddy mess.

In the lower left pocket of his jacket he found the familiar half-through bottles. He pulled the three of them free and discarded the one with water in it – he wouldn't be needing that particular ingredient today. He unstoppered one of them and with his other hand drew the boltcaster from its holster on his thigh.

With both of his hands occupied, he had trouble treading water, so he leaned back and tried to float instead. That technique was more successful, undoubtedly aided by all of the buoyant equipment in his jacket, and he used the opportunity to stick the point of the loaded bolt into the half-through bottle. Once the tip of the bolt was coated with the brown goo, he released that bottle and, using his thumb, uncorked the second bottle.

Careful to keep both bottle and boltcaster above the water, he stuck the head of the bolt into the second bottle and swept it around until a good amount of the foul-smelling purple crystals were stuck to the brown goo that coated it.

That bottle he threw far away so as to not accidentally ignite himself.

That done, Actaeon righted himself and began to tread water once more. He stuck the tip of the boltcaster into the muddy waters around him. With a sputtering hiss and a crackle, it erupted into blue flame. Without delay, he took aim toward the sky at an angle that he knew would create a nice arc between the two broken sections of Travail.

When he pulled the trigger, the bright flame became a distant blue star that flew above him and away off to the side.

After a few long moments there came shouts and several fires flickered to life in the darkness to one side of him. He grinned, returned the boltcaster to its sheath on his thigh, and began to swim.

One of the broken sections of Travail fell then. It crashed against the other segment with a crack. Waves washed over Actaeon, displaced by the movement of the massive portion of building.

While the waters churned and smashed into him, he treaded water again. Once the newly formed lake was calmer, he continued to swim once more.

The going was painful, but he swam forward despite it. This was his second chance, and, by the Fallen, he'd be taking it. It was his chance to grow old with Eisandre. His chance to see baby Aedwina grow up. His chance to continue to uncover all of Redemption's secrets – to make the world a better place.

And so he swam, kicking with his heavy boots against the muck and mud and churn. A memory came back suddenly of his father teaching him how to swim in the river. He'd been annoyed because the lesson had taken him away from his experiments, but now he felt a wave of gratitude for his father's lesson. He'd have to teach Aedwina how to swim one day.

After all, you never knew when you'd be abruptly deposited in the footprint of a millennia old building that was rapidly filling with water after you'd used the energy of a god to destroy a maelstrom that threatened to kill all of humanity. He smiled and swam onward. Yes, he'd have to teach her how to swim.

When Actaeon finally reached the mucky shore of the freshly created lake, two strong pairs of hands reached out to grab him, and he felt his energy give out as they took his weight. The pair of rescuers hauled him along through waterlogged terrain that threatened to suck them down into it like quicksand. But any time they became stuck, they crawled out of it and continued to drag Actaeon along. This went on until, at last, they were on solid ground.

One of the rescuers pressed her mud-covered body against his and kissed him gently on the lips. Surprised, Actaeon returned the kiss. He reached up to feel Eisandre's short hair and drew her hard against him. They had to pause their kiss for a moment as he rolled onto his side and coughed up what was most likely a combination of blood and river water. Hopefully the Altheans had something that would prevent an infection in his lungs, he thought.

"By the Fallen, boss," said Wave, his second rescuer, as the mercenary took stock of his injuries. "You look worse than shattered Redemption. I'll go grab a cutter." He rushed off to go find one.

And then Eisandre was kissing him again.

When she stopped kissing him, he smiled up at her. "I am returned."

"Promise me you'll stay awhile," she said.

"For the rest of our lives I hope." He reached up to touch her cheek with his muddy hand. "I thought you said you would not be there to save me this time."

"I'm making sure to keep our family together," said Eisandre. "'Keep them together,' you said. Remember?"

"You never cease to amaze me, my Princess," said Actaeon.

They both sat up to watch as the clouds opened up and the first rays of sunlight touched the wreckage before them.

"Do you ever wish that you had never encountered me in the Boneyards all that time ago?" asked Eisandre.

"Never," Actaeon replied with a laugh. "There is nowhere I would rather be than at your side, as the sun rises on this new day."

Their fingers intertwined as they sat and watched the colors bloom in the sky to herald a new day for all of Redemption. A day that, together, they made certain would come.

EPILOGUE: STARSPHERE

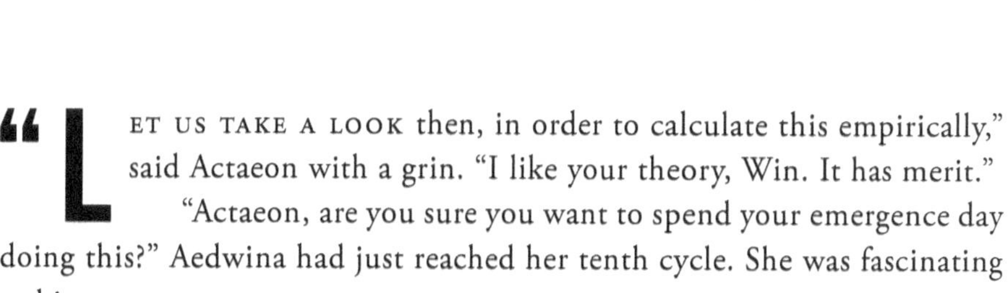

"**L**ET US TAKE A LOOK then, in order to calculate this empirically," said Actaeon with a grin. "I like your theory, Win. It has merit."

"Actaeon, are you sure you want to spend your emergence day doing this?" Aedwina had just reached her tenth cycle. She was fascinating to him.

His daughter had his wife's blue eyes and his own disheveled black hair. The way she had exact aspects of both of their minds was also astounding. Win, as they had started to call her when she was quite young, had a mind that was a combination of Actaeon's analytical ability and Eisandre's mental discipline. Both qualities were tinged with the mild characteristics of someone Lost.

Aedwina reaped the advantage of being able to learn how to read the language of the Ancients. Even at her young age, she often helped her father interpret various artifacts and consoles that they found throughout Redemption.

"Of course, Win," said Actaeon with a smile. "There is nothing I would rather be doing than deciphering mysteries with you."

They both sat some distance to the rear of the workshop. Night had fallen some hours ago, and the sky was clear of clouds and bright with stars.

"Thanks, Daddy. I love solving problems with you."

Actaeon grinned at her and set down the starsphere artifact upon the table before them. He touched it once with both hands and projected stars leaped into the air around them.

Aedwina leapt up from her chair and hopped around the table excitedly. She reached out with her finger to tap the projected stars. One and then another and on and on.

As Actaeon watched, his daughter's eyes glazed over and he saw her glancing between the actual stars in the night sky and the projections. She was looking for a pattern, one that he had never been able to pick out himself.

After a long time of her searching between the real stars and the projected ones she smiled a proud smile and hopped over to her father.

"You have something, Win?" he asked.

"Yes, Daddy." She pointed to one of the projections. "This star." Then she climbed into his lap and pointed along his line of sight. "Is this one." She pointed at another of the projections. "And this one is the same as..." she pointed to another star through his line of sight. "This one here."

Actaeon nodded and spread open the Althean almanac atop the table. In it he found the stars she had indicated. He flipped to the beginning of the book and found their initial positions. After that, he lifted his sextant and measured the difference between the actual star and the projection. In order to do that, he had to place the starsphere at the corner of the table and sight past it.

On a separate piece of vellum, he jotted down his angular findings and made some calculations. The result of the first star he compared to the second star and he nodded with satisfaction as both numbers came out the same.

"Did it work, Actaeon? Do you know the answer?" His daughter clutched his arm and looked down at the numbers and equations on the page with interest.

"Give me three more, Win," Actaeon said. "Let me check three more and we shall see whether or not your assumption is correct."

"Okay, Daddy," she said with excitement. Her eyes glazed over again as she entered deep thought once more and looked between projection and reality, calculating the likely transitions over the years. When she thought she was done, she glanced at the almanac numbers and nodded.

Actaeon recorded the next three stars she showed him and then measured the projected stars with his sextant. When he compared them to his original number, two of them matched and the third didn't.

He tapped Win on the shoulder – she had become distracted by the numbers in the almanac and was using an extra charcoal pencil to jot them down on the wooden table surface. He pointed. "See that one there? I think you got it wrong. Care to check it again?"

Aedwina shot him a look of annoyance, but then she remembered his words. It was alright to sometimes get things wrong. It was a learning experience. Without those moments, we couldn't better ourselves. She clenched her fists and set about rechecking that star.

After she rechecked it, she looked at the number in the almanac again. She hadn't considered the vector for that one. The star had the approximate position, but the measured vector in the almanac was all wrong. It had been recorded as moving in the opposite direction. Which meant...

Actaeon watched with a smile as Aedwina ran through the analysis in her head. It didn't take her very long to pick out what she thought was the correct star.

"That one, Daddy," she squeaked, pointing at it and hopping up and down eagerly.

"Be still on your feet, little one," said Actaeon. "I cannot see it with your moving."

When Aedwina was still, he checked the position of the indicated star with his sextant and noted it down on the vellum. When he finished the calculation, he nodded and smiled at her proudly. "That one matches, Win. Nice work. Now, I want you to calculate the times. Check my work." He handed her the sextant.

Aedwina took the device and turned it over in her hands to observe every little detail of it. After she was done, she put it to her eye and gazed through it.

On a fresh sheet of vellum that Actaeon gave her, she recorded her observations and then jotted down the numbers from the Althean almanac. She calculated the movement of the present star locations versus the location eighty years prior. Then she compared that to the projected star that she had matched up to each real star.

As Aedwina worked, Actaeon glanced back at the workshop and spotted Eisandre leaning against the wall, watching them. He smiled at her, and she offered him a joyful smile in return. The Princess of Raedelle folded her arms across her chest and followed her daughter's glances up to the sky full of stars.

When Aedwina finished the first calculation, the number was

astounding. She checked it against the second star. It matched. The third did too. And the fourth and the fifth.

She wrote down the number at the bottom of the sheet and looked at her father for approval.

Actaeon regarded the number and then her and nodded. He patted her gently on the back. "So what did you find, little Win? What did you learn?"

"Since this starsphere was made, five thousand one hundred and thirty-seven cycles have gone by," she said, pride in her tone. "At least the five stars we've mapped out support that."

"Over five millennia since the fall of the Ancients." Actaeon nodded with approval. "My numbers match your own. Great work, Win."

Aedwina lunged forward and hugged her father tightly about the waist.

Actaeon wrapped his arms around her and pulled her against him, tousling her hair around the matching goggles that she wore atop her head.

"Can we check more stars, Daddy?" asked Aedwina hopefully. "Make sure our 'pothesis is right?"

"Of course we can, Win."

And, as his daughter worked to find further proof of the time since the fall of the Ancients, Actaeon found that he couldn't be happier with how life had turned out.

THE END

AFTERWORD

T HANK YOU FOR READING THIS story. I hope you enjoyed the adventures of Actaeon and his friends. If you liked the book, I encourage you to please leave a review on Amazon and Goodreads. Reviews help other readers find books like this one, and, in turn, give me a reason to write more.

Writing a book is a challenge for anyone. For a writer with a full-time job in addition to writing, it is even more difficult. And for a writer with a full-time job as an engineer, a full-time volunteer position as a fire chief, and who cherishes time with his family, finishing a book feels like an impossible task. The Engineer took me three years to write. I started it in 2014 and finished in 2017. The Dark Heart of Redemption was even more ponderous a task. In 2018, I became a volunteer Assistant Fire Chief, which cut further into my already sparse time. I've risen through the ranks of my local fire department to become the Chief in 2021 and again in 2022. This has kept me quite busy with service to my community and I hope gives you, the reader, an understanding of why it took me a whopping four plus years to release this novel. I hope it was worth the wait. Thank you to my wife, Stefanie, for not only always supporting my writing efforts despite my already limited time, but also in actively editing, proofreading, and beta reading with me in order to make this a better novel.

That said, The Dark Heart of Redemption wasn't just a story about Actaeon, but about many other players who experienced some of the events described – for the world of Redemption was originally an online, text-based RPG called Redemption MUSH. This book expanded well past the events that took place in the game world, or 'on the grid' as we called it, but some parts happened while Redemption MUSH was still up and running. Thank you to Stefanie (Eisandre), Pauline (Enrion), Ben (Sol/Balin), Jodi (Mae/Jezail), Joanne (Lauryn), Joe (Indros/Allyk), and Heather (Seraeta) for allowing me to include your characters in these stories. They helped bring the tale to life. All of the other players that I've roleplayed with in Redemption MUSH also have a special place in my heart. I hope you have the chance to read this story and remember all the great times we shared together.

Thank you also to my son, Corwin, who, at four years old, randomly came up with the idea for Yonniker, Eater of Planets, and agreed to let me put him in this story. In fact, Sol's enigmatic statement on Yonniker was entirely Corwin's creation: 'Yonniker, Eater of Planets. He jumps, and claps, and eats planets. He listens, and leaks, and eats planets.' I couldn't have thought of a better and more foreboding way to describe a Starborn myself. You're gonna create some amazing things in your life, Corwin!

Thank you to all the bloggers, reviewers, and readers who have supported me over the years. I especially want to thank Nick Borrelli from Out of this World SFF, Evan the Last Librarian, Lo Potter, Joe Williams, Kevin Creedon, Ed Barkan, Christian Freed, Roe Handshaw (hi Mom!), Shane Thomas, Michele Searing, Victoria O'Connor, Lauren MacElveen, Neil Williams, Ashley from Here Be Dragons, Cassandra from the Bibliophagist, Taylor Watkins from Bitty Book Nook, Matthew Samuels, Sam from The Book in Hand, Rowena from Beneath a Thousand Skies and Raul Reads (and his Howdy, Partner! book club!) for reading my stories and giving me the encouragement to write another book in this world.

Lastly, the biggest thank you goes to Stefanie Handshaw and Simon Svensson for originally creating the world on Redemption MUSH and for encouraging and supporting me in the effort to write this story. It is an amazing world that changed my life. I only hope I have done it justice in these pages.

A BRIEF HISTORY OF REDEMPTION

AS SCRIBED BY PALADIN ARANDEL, CIRCA 64 AR

ON THE ARRIVAL:

ON THE DAY THE PORTALS opened, a new people emerged for the first time into the ruins of Redemption. Prior to that, the city had stood empty of its occupants for centuries or, perhaps, even millennia. Upon our Arrival in Redemption, the AR of which would be used to denote our passing of the cycles, there were no other people to greet us. Only the ghosts of those who we came to think of as the Ancients were left behind – the ghosts and their broken artifacts. Through the portals came both Prisoner and Warden. Bereft of all but the basic memories needed for a civilization's survival, we new arrivals only knew one thing about our identity aside from our names: whether we were a Warden or a Prisoner. Prisoners of who or for what reason we did not know. That information had been stripped somehow from our very minds – perhaps by the transit through the portals. Those groups of Wardens and Prisoners became what we now know as the Dominions. Some of them, such as Shield, were led by Wardens who declared rule over their Prisoners. Others, like Czeryn, saw their Prisoners murder the Wardens and lead themselves. Still others, like Raedelle, inspired by a Warden who would not give up on her Prisoners, banded together to work as equals.

ON THE DOMINIONS:

Raedelle, the southern gem of the Dominions, surrounds the source waters of the River of Arches like the petals of a flower in bloom. Its warbands know no equal as they spend each season keeping the mysterious, uncivilized tribals at bay. The culture there retains the better aspects of tribalism, though only on a cultural level in the local communities, and bereft of all the shortcomings of civilization that the neighboring Tribune and Wither tribes demonstrate. The people are ruled by a Conclave of Lords that gives advice and counsel to their leader, who has been anointed by them to rule from the line of the original heroic Warden from whom the Dominion bears its name. The fertile lands of Raedelle are a boon to all of Redemption and cement Raedelle's place among the other Dominions.

On the farthest reaches of the western coastlands, **Thyr** has the greatest shipwrights and sailors of the city. Thyrian sloops and carracks ply the waters, from the River of Arches to the Great Sea, bringing trade and transport alike. Much of the stone and lumber of Redemption would not find its way to the different Dominions without the buoyancy of Thyrian hulls. A Supreme Captain is elected with votes cast by the Captains of every major vessel to rule the Dominion. Thyrian nobility are known for settling their problems in the dueling ring, a practice which has since spread to many other parts of Redemption.

With Holds nestled along the northwestern coast like a pox upon the land, **Czeryn** slavers rove the ruins in search of easy prey to capture. Many an undefended and uncountried wayfarer has fallen into forced servitude for the Warlords there. The loose alliance of Warlords scattered throughout the Holds is held in check by a singular Warlord of Czeryn, who might only ascend to such a position by a rite known as the Blood Ascent, where the previous ruler is defeated in a duel to the death. The lands within their Holds are among the most ruinous in the city. Warlords frequently raise money by leasing out their slaves to other Dominions for various projects and work.

Shield is a martial Dominion, positioned like a dagger north of the depths of the Underforest. The people of Shield reside in some of the largest Ancient buildings of Redemption, including the superstructure of Rust, which is wholly deserving of its regrettable name. All of the Holds are managed by members of the Zar dynasty, which clenches its rule in an iron fist. The manufacture of weapons and the lease of its shock troops to other Dominions for the repulsion of tribal incursions are two of its top commodities.

In Redemption's center, **Ajman** stands as the polar opposite of Shield. A belief in the gods of old and the gods of new guides them in all things, and the Dominion is mired in religious rite and observance. Even the Raj of Ajman is chosen by the religious orders and, some might say, serves as more of a pawn to the orders than as a truly autonomous ruler. Ajman has a strong central military that is sworn to protect its people. With some of the best arable land in the city center, they trade well in food products and plant fibers and have a vibrant textile and dye industry. To carry these resources, Ajmani caravans travel across the interior of Redemption, bartering for goods and encouraging trade between the other Dominions. Known for their many successful traders, Ajman carries a massive presence in the Pyramid's marketplace.

Like a pluming jungle bird, **Niwian** is a Dominion concerned more with its image than its usefulness. Situated to the north of the River of Arches, its courtiers dress in all sorts of flourishing and impractical clothing in a constant effort to outdo one another. Even the soldiery is bedazzled with colored plate armor and excessive adornments. With such unrestrained embellishment, the nobility of other Dominions have even taken to competing with their looks, especially when visiting the Pyramid. The Memory Keep is one of the few completely intact buildings of the Ancients. It is a closely guarded secret that the Niwians claim holds the answers to any question. Of course, those answers come with a hefty price attached. So important is this information trade that the Lord Protector of Memory Keep is universally considered to be the leader of the Dominion.

ON THE ORDERS:

The **Arbiters** of Pyramid formed when a collection of Wardens decided that the best way to keep order in the new world was to establish a place of neutrality where the Dominions, who had begun to develop vastly different beliefs, values, and cultures, could coexist, negotiate, and trade. For this purpose, they selected the indefensible Pyramid, a massive structure of the Ancients which could be seen from nearly anywhere in Redemption. Since their inception, the Arbiters have taken in many volunteers and outcasts from the Dominions and have trained them in the Ancient fortress they call Redoubt. Once an Arbiter's training was complete, they became a Knight Arbiter and were charged with protecting the neutrality of the Pyramid. To this day, the Pyramid stands as a relatively safe place for all the citizens of Redemption.

Formed by Wardens who abandoned Raedelle in her quest to find and protect her evasive Prisoners, the **Loresworn** returned to Travail, where their portal first opened. They studied the deep wealth of technology present there in order to find the answers that would explain why they were sent to Redemption in the first place. Whether or not the leaders of the Loresworn ever found their answers is unknown. The order has become one of Redemption's most secretive. Even money cannot buy the answers that the Loresworn keep within the walls of Travail. Often when there is a new artifact uncovered, or mystery of the Ancients needing investigation, the Loresworn will find their way there.

The **Altheans** formed with similar intentions to the Arbiters, but a different approach. Where the Arbiters sought to separate themselves and provide a neutral place for gathering, the Altheans sought to infiltrate and embed themselves. Their founders decided the best way they could accomplish this goal was to make themselves as useful and unthreatening as possible. Thus, the early Altheans became experts in diplomacy, herbology, and the arts of healing. The order offered its services to the Dominions in the form of attachés who would advise the leaders and help teach their people critical skills. In the post portal society of Redemption, the Altheans became highly sought after and all the Dominions, save Raedelle, quickly adopted an Althean attaché to their service. Raedelle herself had been insulted by the Altheans upon her first excursion to the Pyramid, and so, when just three years ago Duke Macsen Caliburn was, for the first time in history, offered an Althean attaché, he rightly declined. With embedded advisors in most of the Dominions, the Altheans are in a unique position to manipulate and drive the political machinations across all of Redemption.

ON THE WARS:

Aside from minor skirmishes and border disputes, relations between the Dominions were relatively unwarlike, if not peaceful. It was not until the drought of 41 AR that the **Sustenance Wars** began. The war was long and drawn out and started as a series of battles when Niwian and Shield attempted to take Ajmani crops by force. With the displacement of Shieldian and Niwian forces, their neighbors Czeryn and Thyr decided to attack. The following period of unrest lasted for nearly two decades as the drought persisted. During that time period, alliances shifted and forces worked to pillage the resources of other Dominions. The war effort itself only served to further reduce resources, some of which were even razed during the conflict so that nobody might have them. Duke Macsen declared that Raedelle would take a position of neutrality during the conflict, a position that helped the weaker Dominion grow in power during the time period as they continued to sell food and other resources to the other Dominions.

The dire times of the Sustenance Wars were only interrupted by an even graver threat – the arrival of an invading force of tribals into Redemption proper in 59 AR and the beginning of the **Invasion War**. Raedelle promptly joined the fight and the warring Dominions were forced to work together to repel the tribal invaders, who were being coordinated by someone called the Devourer. Along with major help from a mercenary company called the Messengers, the joint forces of Redemption managed to push the invading force out of the city. Unfortunately, the Messengers perished in the conflict.

ACTAEON'S MAP OF REDEMPTION

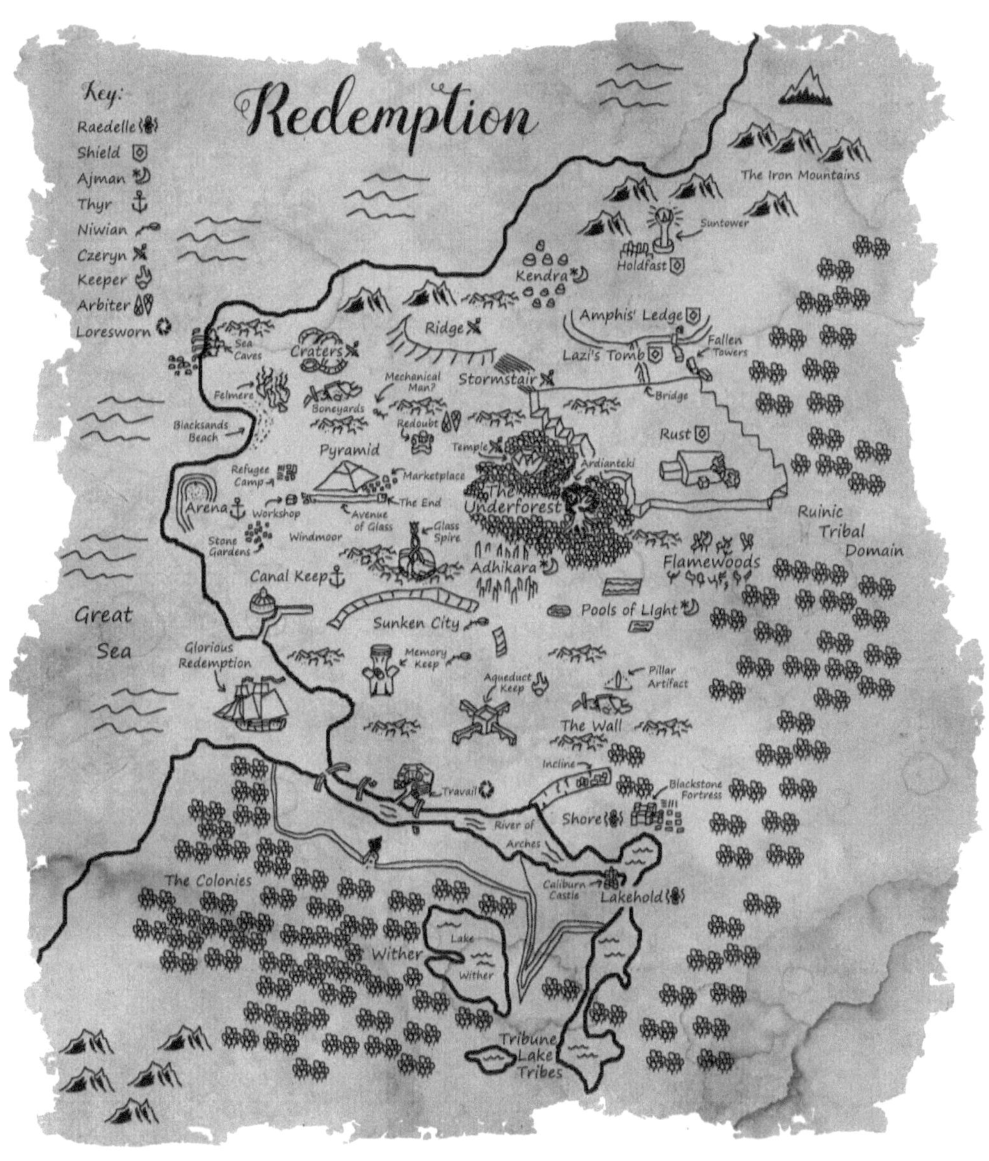

ALSO BY THE AUTHOR

The Engineer,
A Chronicles of Actaeon Story
http://getbook.at/engineer

The Machine in the Mountain,
A Chronicles of Actaeon Tale
A short story in The Quantum Soul: A Sci Fi Roundtable Anthology
http://getbook.at/quantum

ABOUT THE AUTHOR

Darran M. Handshaw is the author of The Engineer and The Dark Heart of Redemption. In addition to writing, Darran works as an R&D Engineer at a technology company. There he invents and designs new products. He holds more than 70 patents in data capture, vision systems, and emergency services. Darran also volunteers as a firefighter and EMT with his local fire department, where he serves as the Chief of Department. Darran hails from Long Island, NY, where he lives with his wife, Stefanie, and son, Corwin, who fill his life with love, wisdom, and endless adventures.

Follow Darran below:

 fb.me/ActaeonRellios/    goodreads.com/TheEngineer

 twitter.com/Engineer7601   amazon.com/author/engineer